Bitter Sweets

ROOPA FAROOKI

Bitter Sweets

ST. MARTIN'S PRESS   NEW YORK

www.stmartins.com

Library of Congress Cataloging-in-Publication Data

Farooki, Roopa.
    Bitter sweets / Roopa Farooki.—1st U.S. ed.
        p. cm.
    ISBN-13: 978-0-312-36052-8
    ISBN-10: 0-312-36052-5
    1. Family—Fiction. 2. Deception—Fiction. 3. Bengali (South Asian people)—England—London—Fiction. 4. East Indians—England—London—Fiction. 5. Bengali (South Asian people)—Social life and customs—Fiction. I. Title.

PR6106.A765 B57 2007
823'.92—dc22

                                                                      2007030569

First published in Great Britain by Macmillan,
an imprint of Pan Macmillan Ltd

First U.S. Edition: November 2007

10 9 8 7 6 5 4 3 2 1

*For my mother, my husband and my son,
because they are all funny, kind and beautiful
– although not necessarily in that order.*

Bigotry tries to keep truth safe in its hand
With a grip that kills it.

Rabindranath Tagore, *Fireflies*, 1928

The truth is rarely pure, and never simple.

Oscar Wilde, *The Importance of Being Earnest, 1895*

Nadim Rub's Most Magnificent Deception

HENNA WAS THIRTEEN when she was gleefully married off to the eldest son of one of the best families in Calcutta, and her marriage was achieved by an audacious network of lies as elaborate and brazen as the golden embroidery on her scarlet wedding sari. Henna's paternal family were liars by trade, shopkeepers from the Bengal who had made their money by secretly selling powders and pastes of suspect origin, to alleviate the boredom and fatigue of the British expats serving out their purgatory in local government in pre-Independence India. Those glory days had fled with the British some ten years previously, but Henna's father was still never one to miss a business opportunity – when he heard that the wealthy, landed and unusually fair-skinned Karim family from Calcutta would be visiting their farms around Dhaka, he wasted no time in undertaking an effective reconnaissance.

His initial modest plot had been to nurture a business alliance, but he became more ambitious when he discovered that a rather more lucrative and permanent alliance might be up for grabs. He learned that their son

Rashid, who preferred to be called Ricky, was of marriage-able age, but was so bizarre in his preferences that his frustrated family had not yet managed to find him a wife. He had been educated abroad, and insisted that his wife be someone he could 'love', an educated, literate girl with the same interests as him.

Nadim Rub looked at his wilful, precocious daughter, who constantly missed school and cheeked her tutors, who stole her aunts' film magazines to pore over the photographs of the movie stars in thrilled girlish detail. She was athletic enough to avoid him whenever he tried to beat her for these misdeeds, sometimes nimbly running away over the neighbours' rooftops where he couldn't follow. His daughter had inherited his cunning, and her dead mother's looks. She still had an adolescent slimness but had suddenly developed enough of a bosom to pass for a woman, rather than a girl. He formulated his plan.

A shopkeeper is also a salesman, and Nadim knew exactly how to persuade his daughter to go along with him. He caught her hiding at the bottom of their over-grown garden one school day, lying flat on her stomach behind the coconut palms, while she nonchalantly studied magazines instead of her books. When Henna saw her father approach, she leaped up and prepared to run, but he appeased her with an unusually jovial smile, and offered her a paper bag of dusty sweets, which she took warily.

'Henna moni, I know you hate school. And you're too good for this provincial backwater. You should be some-where better, like Calcutta, the honoured daughter of a wealthy family who could buy you all the sweets and magazines you could ever desire. It's what your mother would have wanted for you.'

Henna listened with interest – Calcutta was glamorous, the sort of place where the movie stars came from. And for once, her fat, ignorant Baba was right – she did hate school.

Enlisting the help of his sisters, Nadim made sure that Henna learned to carry herself in a sari with rather more elegance that she had hitherto shown, and with careful application of kohl, rouge and powder, managed to make her look older than her years, and almost as pale as the Karims. He had her tutors teach her to play tennis, Ricky-Rashid's favourite sport, which with her natural athleticism she picked up quickly. He found out through bribing the Karims' servants which books were to be found in Ricky-Rashid's room, and bought cheap copies for his daughter to read. He discovered she was still illiterate, and almost beat her again – all his dedicated preparation ruined because his lazy harami of a daughter had wilfully chosen to waste her expensive schooling. He stormed impotently at her while she pranced elegantly on her aunt's makeshift tennis court during one of her lessons, her precise strokes cruelly making her plump teacher race breathlessly from one side to another.

'Baba, you're being silly. Just get one of these monkeys to read out some bits to me, and I'll memorize them. It's easy,' Henna said calmly, swinging her backhand return dangerously close to his ear; 'monkeys' was the disrespectful term which she used for her long-suffering gaggle of tutors. She was enjoying the charade, the pretty new clothes, the make-up, the dissembling; she even looked forward to the prospect of learning lines from the Shake-spearean sonnets her Baba had brought. It was like she was an actress already.

Nadim pulled strings, and used bribes of his suspect poppy powder to insinuate himself into Mr Karim's presence at a club gathering. He made sure he dressed well enough to look like landowning gentry himself, and in better clothes his generous rolls of fat could be mistaken for prosperity rather than greed. He pretended that the shop was his sister-in-law's family business, and that he oversaw it out of loyalty to his dead spouse. He told them about his sorrowful burden – he had a daughter so lovely and gifted that no suitable boy would dare make an appropriate offer for her; he confessed humbly that he had been guilty of over-educating her. He was worried that she would be an old maid, as she was already seventeen years old. Intrigued, Mr Karim arranged for his own reconnaissance, and saw the beautiful Henna as she visited her aunt's house in a rickshaw, demurely holding her tennis racket and appearing to be engrossed by a volume of English poetry. He was satisfied with her paleness and her beauty, although less so by her slim hips. Deciding that the worst that could happen is that she might die in childbirth giving him a beautifully pale grandson, he arranged for a meeting.

'My friends call me Henrietta,' Henna lied charmingly, offering tea to Ricky-Rashid's parents, discreetly not looking at Ricky-Rashid at all.

'And mine call me Ricky,' Ricky-Rashid answered quickly, directly addressing her delicate, painted profile, hoping he might have fallen in love at first sight with this sonnet-reading, tennis-playing beauty. She was nothing like the moneyed nincompoops he had been introduced to before. Flouting the traditional etiquette of the meeting, he instead displayed the manners of an English gentleman, and got up to relieve Henna of her heavily laden tray. He looked defiantly at his stern parents, and for once saw them beaming back at him with approval.

The Calcutta wedding was a glorious affair, Henna's premature curves barely filling out her gold and scarlet wedding sari; her thin wrists, slender neck and dainty nose weighed down with gold. Due to the generous concession of Nadim Rub in allowing all the celebrations to take place in Calcutta, despite his fervent protested wish that it had been his life's dream to give his daughter a magnificent wedding in Dhaka, the Karims matched his generosity of spirit by offering to pay for all the festivities. Ricky-Rashid had even dismissed the idea of a dowry as barbaric, to Nadim Rub's further joy and Henna's fury – the deal she had previously brokered with her father was that she would get her dowry directly to keep for herself. Sitting graciously by Ricky-Rashid's side, her lovely eyes narrowed imperceptibly as she saw her flabby Baba working the room and accepting congratulations. Casting those eyes down demurely, she vowed to keep all the wedding jewellery that her father had borrowed from his sisters; she wasn't going to let the fat fibber cheat her as well as everyone else.

Following the wedding, Henna lay in Ricky-Rashid's quarters in her new and sprawling home, eating liquorice sweets while she waited for him. Impressed by the four-poster bed, like the ones she had seen in the films, she had dismissed the maid and jumped up and down on it in her bare feet, still wearing her elaborate sari, before stretching out and trying some poses. When Ricky-Rashid finally entered, looking sheepish and nervous, carrying a book and a flower, she tipped her head up and pouted, expecting a movie-star kiss. She naively did not know that anything further might be expected of her.

Ricky-Rashid, taken by surprise by his new bride's apparent forwardness and feeling even more nervous, kissed her quickly and, reassured by the softness of her mouth, kissed her again. Something was wrong – she tasted of liquorice, like a child. Liquorice was not what he expected his first night of married love to taste of. He felt a wave of panic that he was woefully unqualified to initiate his confident bride, who was now looking at him with a mixture of curiosity and sympathy. Deciding that faint heart never won fair maiden, and deciding further that the only way out of this sea of troubles was to take arms against it and confidently stride in, he aggressively pulled Henna to him with what he hoped was a manly, passionate gesture, crushing her breasts against his chest and circling the bare skin of her waist with his hands.

Henna, disappointed by the kiss, was wondering whether to offer some of her sweets to Ricky-Rashid, and was taken utterly by surprise when he suddenly pounced on her. She jumped as though stung when she felt his clammy hands on her bare skin beneath her sari blouse, and despite her heavy sari, nimbly slipped away from him and off the bed. Ricky-Rashid was acting like one of the villains in the movies that she'd watched, and was doubtless planning to beat her – perhaps this was how husbands behaved from their wedding night onwards. No wonder her mother was dead and all her aunts such grouchy miseries.

'I won't let you,' she said warningly. She wouldn't let her big bully of a father beat her, or anyone else who had ever tried, and she certainly wasn't going to allow this milky-faced academic to succeed where so many others had failed. Her eyes flashed scornfully at him.

Ricky-Rashid's heart wilted like the drooping rose he was still holding. His attempt at manly domination had gone horribly wrong, and from being surprisingly enthusiastic, Henna now wouldn't let him near her. And no wonder – he'd acted like a thick-booted oaf. An intelligent, spirited beauty like Henna should be wooed, not tamed. That's what he'd intended when he came in with his rose and poetry – he was going to proffer her the flower on bended knee and read her the romantic verse that he knew she loved. But her tossed-back head and invitation to a kiss had distracted him, and in the ensuing liquorice-induced confusion he had let his baser instincts take over. Intending to apologize, he walked around the bed towards her, but she simply skipped over to the other side, looking at him warily. Her scorn was dreadfully attractive, and his hand still tingled from the brush with the naked skin of her slim waist.

Defeated, and embarrassed, Ricky-Rashid sat heavily on the bed. 'I'm so sorry. I wanted this to be a wonderful, romantic night for us. And I've already ruined it.' He turned to face her and held out the flower to her. 'Look, I brought you a rose.' He sighed and put it down next to him.

Mollified, Henna sat back on the bed, a little way from

Ricky-Rashid, and continued eating her sweets. 'You are silly,' she said. 'How could trying to beat me possibly be wonderful or romantic?' She picked up the rose and sniffed it disinterestedly. 'I think it's dead,' she said, dropping it dismissively on the floor. She nudged the pink flower head experimentally with her prettily painted toes, separating out the soft wilted petals.

Ricky-Rashid looked at her in astonishment. 'Beat you? Why on earth would I try to beat you?' His surprise was so genuine that Henna realized she may have misunderstood his intentions, and perhaps given away her ignorance in some indefinable way.

Distracting him with a truce, she nodded towards the book. 'So what's that? More Shakespeare?'

Ricky-Rashid answered with even more genuine surprise. 'No, it's Byron.' The name was very clearly written on the cover; Henna must be terribly short-sighted. 'I brought it because there's a poem I wanted to read to you. It reminds me of you.' Hoping he might yet be able to salvage the evening, he opened it, and started to read,

> *She walks in beauty, like the night*
> *Of cloudless climes and starry skies;*
> *And all that's best of dark and bright*
> *Meet in her aspect and her eyes.*

He paused and looked at her expectantly.

'Hmm, that's pretty,' Henna answered, hoping he wasn't expecting her to comment any further.

'It loses something in translation,' admitted Ricky-Rashid. 'Perhaps I should read it to you in English?'

'No!' said Henna shortly. In their brief meetings before the wedding, she had only just about been able to keep up the pretence that she had a working knowledge of English, although it had proved much harder than simply pretending to be literate. Despairing of her, her English tutor had eventually given into expediency, and had given her some set phrases to learn, and developed a subtle sign language that indicated to her which phrase to use when. This had worked fine when they were in the large sitting room, with her tutor sitting at a respectful distance, within her sight, and Henna enunciating, 'I Think It's Simply Wonderful' and 'Good Gracious, No' and 'Would You Like Some More?' when prompted. However, alone with Ricky she doubted that she'd last two minutes of English conversation undetected. Aware that her response had been unnecessarily vehement, she added sweetly, 'To be honest, I'm a bit too tired to listen to poetry readings.'

Ricky-Rashid had no more weapons in his amorous armoury – his flower was discharged and in pieces on the floor, and his book of Byron's romantic poetry, which he was sure Henna had said was Simply Wonderful in a previous meeting, was being summarily dismissed. With nothing else coming to mind, he decided to try his luck by pressing on with the book. 'So why don't you read the next two lines yourself? They say everything that I think about you.'

He passed the book to Henna, who took it unwillingly. She looked at the incoherent black jumble of text for a couple of moments and knowledgeably nodded, before saying in her little-used English, 'Ricky, I Think It's Simply Wonderful.'

Roopa Farooki

'I knew you'd like it,' said Ricky-Rashid triumphantly. Perhaps tonight would work out after all; he edged closer to Henna, to take the book out of her hands. But as he saw how she had been holding it, that nagging feeling came back, the feeling that he had felt on their first uncertain kiss.

'But how could you read it upside down?' he asked. Something was very wrong, very wrong indeed. Why was she holding the book the wrong way round? Henna could surely not be as short-sighted as all that.

Aware that instant distraction was necessary, Henna smiled as meltingly as the movie stars she'd learned from and, holding out her slender hand to Ricky-Rashid, she said, 'You can kiss me again if you like.' When Ricky-Rashid didn't move, she moved towards him instead, and he couldn't stop himself kissing her and pulling her nubile body into his arms, while the urgent physical sensation fought with his racing mind. Liquorice again, the taste of liquorice, the supple too-slender too-girlish body, the comment about the beatings, the thickly accented Simply Wonderful, the upside-down book, and again, the unavoidable, intoxicating taste of liquorice sweets . . . childhood sweets.

Controlling himself and pushing her away, Ricky-Rashid held the breathless Henna at arm's length as he looked at her closely, her lipstick and powder rubbed off by their embrace, her enormous eyes ludicrously over-made up by comparison. 'How old are you, Henna?' he asked quietly.

On his wedding night, Ricky-Rashid slept alone, tormented by the discovery, coaxed from Henna with gentle words, bribes, promises and yet more sweets, that his educated seventeen-year-old bride was actually an illiterate shopkeeper's daughter, a thirteen-year-old child who had married him as a way to skip school and fulfil a schoolgirl fantasy of becoming an actress. Disturbed by the memory of her body, Ricky-Rashid was disgusted by himself for having wanted her so much – a child, she was just a child, and he had almost . . . it didn't bear thinking about. He was no English gentleman, he was practically a pervert.

It was the night that every one of Ricky-Rashid's hopes and dreams of a life lived in truth and sincerity, of an idyllic western-style marriage, was ground into a red, muddy sludge like the powder from which Henna took her name. She had stained him and blotted all his future aspirations, and he simply couldn't wash away the marks. He was forced to be complicit in the lie – she would have to remain his wife or everyone would know how he and his family had been tricked and shamed. She would have to be educated privately at his parents' house, and remain out of society until such time when she would no longer give herself away.

Ricky-Rashid had previously hoped to bring his wife with him when he returned to the varsity for his studies, but his vision of living like an English couple in his student halls had also been shattered. He would return alone, and would no longer pretend that he was the Ricky he had tried to fashion himself into, the cosmopolitan intellectual around town; from this time on, he would call himself

Just Rashid. He would not sleep with Henna until she was seventeen and had finished school, but the feelings she had innocently awoken would not go away, and in an attempt to scratch the persistent itch of desire he would spend the next few years having frustrated and unsanitary sex with kind-faced, matronly prostitutes, all the time guiltily thinking about Henna's unripe, forbidden body.

The Alchemic Conception of
Shona Kiran Karim

FROM BEING A willowy prepubescent, by seventeen Henna had developed into a rather buxom adolescent, with teenage spots and child-bearing hips that no longer had any cause to earn disapproval from her expectant father-in-law, who had patiently waited several years for a grandchild. Despite the pocked skin and the puppy fat, Henna was still very good-looking, and remained a convincing actress. From the unpromising start with her in-laws, who had exploded with anger when Rashid had nervously revealed the truth about her background the day after the wedding, she had managed to win them back with her wiles and charm and studied innocence. She was the victim in all this, after all, a child-bride sold into a marriage under the threat of violence by her vile father, treated like just another one of his grubby business deals. During Rashid's long absences at university overseas, she made herself indispensable to the Karims, and they disloyally found that they preferred her lively company to that of their stilted son, or even his spoilt younger brother. She eventually became, as her wily father had predicted, the favourite daughter, and by contrast, returning Rashid was treated as the prodigal when he came back for his vacations, with his academic affectations, funny foreign clothes and, worst of all, his funny foreign ideas.

Henna planned and hoped to get pregnant as quickly as possible once Rashid was willing to start marital relations with her. Her attempt at marriage as a way to avoid education had not succeeded; she had been unwillingly forced to continue with her lessons, and although her only interest was in the dramatic arts, she had eventually learned to read and write in both Bangla and Urdu, to converse inefficiently in English, and been given a reluctant grounding in maths and the sciences. Although privately educated by necessity, like any other schoolgirl she was made to take public examinations. She was anxious about the results, not because she might have done badly, but because she was vain enough to worry that she might have done well – although with her committed laziness such fears were ungrounded. She certainly didn't want sparkling grades, which would doubtless lead to the indefinable horror of further education that Rashid had been undertaking. Henna knew that motherhood would succeed where marriage alone could not. She knew self-interestedly that bearing Rashid's child would keep her in her cosseted position, and that once she was a mother, there would be no more forcing her to stay at the dull books. She would simply hand the child over to the nanny and then start training for her dramatic career in earnest.

Lying back on the same four-poster bed on which, years before, she had unsuccessfully faked the reading of a poem from an upside-down book, Henna surreptitiously glanced at her wristwatch from over Rashid's straining shoulders. She decided to try a different sort of faking altogether to encourage her monotonously pumping husband to climax before she died of boredom or, worse, missed her favourite radio drama. This time, at least, Henna's performance was successful, and she was rewarded with Rashid finishing the job with much greater efficiency than he had hitherto shown, for which she showed a vocal appreciation that although insincere was almost kindly meant. Rashid's pride in accomplishment, that he had finally managed to make his wife enjoy the act of physical love, was dwarfed a few weeks later by his further pride in achievement, that Henna had conceived and was pregnant with their first, and what she was later to ensure would be their only, child.

Once the pregnancy had been thus dishonestly and enthusiastically achieved, Henna was completely indifferent to both Rashid and the new life growing inside her. Only the heartbeat at Henna's occasional check-ups reminded her about the child. All she cared about was that she would now be afforded truly special treatment, and was able to loll lazily in the house or on the veranda, flicking through her film magazines, playing her imported Elvis Presley records and shouting occasional orders to the servants to bring her sweets from town, or to make her tea with condensed milk and fried pastry delicacies. In the spirit of the swinging sixties, she cut her hair daringly short, right up to her shoulders, and wore it loose in a shining bob like one of her favourite film idols. Her in-laws looked on indulgently – Henna had become their little princess and could do no wrong. Of course they didn't mind Henna's below-average grades in her examinations – she had far more important things to worry about now. Thus pampered to her heart's content, in pregnancy Henna became beautiful once more, and her skin lost its teenage imperfections and began to glow. Rashid's vain little brother, Aziz, returned from his English boarding school and developed a thumping crush on her, competing with the servants to fulfil her tiniest requests for the reward of a smile or a patronizing pat.

Rashid, mystified by the shift of power in his family household that had occurred, simply accepted it, in the same way he had always accepted his father's omnipresent disapproval. This paternal censure was magnified when he finally finished his studies, as he started training for accountancy rather than taking over the running of the family properties. He still nursed a secret hope that he and Henna would be able to move abroad one day, to the green and pleasant lands in which he had been educated, and believed that a professional qualification would pave the way. As it happened, with his father's death they were forced to move abroad faster than he thought, to a land much greener and wetter than the England of his idyllic student memories.

Everybody had wondered how Mr Karim, a Muslim in India, had managed to hold on to his grand Calcutta property during the troubles of partition in the late forties. When other Muslim families had been forced to hurriedly abandon their homes and belongings as they made for

West or East Pakistan, the Karim clan had simply re-located over the border to their property in the Bengal for a few years, with the swiftness and relative safety afforded by wealth, and had returned to Calcutta when the worst of it was over. As the new head of the family, forced to look after his father's business affairs whether he wanted to or not, Rashid discovered that the key to their dubious Calcutta comfort was a Mephistophelian pact that his father had made with a well-known local businessman. Mr Karim had signed their Calcutta property over to this Hindu acquaintance, on the understanding that the prop-erty would remain safe if already in Hindu hands, and had paid a rent for the privilege of returning. The gentleman businessman, on Mr Karim's death, proved to be more of a businessman than a gentleman – he explained regretfully to Rashid that he had kept the rent low during Mr Karim's life out of deference to their long-standing friendship, but he could no longer afford to be so generous. He raised the rent so steeply that it would barely be covered by the income from the Bengali farms over the border in East Pakistan. Although the family had the trappings of wealth, Rashid saw that they were on the verge of bankruptcy. How would they continue to manage the house, the ser-vants, or Aziz's school fees abroad? He took his first bold decision as the head of the household, and moved the entire family over to their estates near Dhaka.

Henna was furious that she was being packaged back to the Bengali backwater she had been persuaded to marry to escape – who had ever heard of an East Pakistani film star? Everyone knew that only Indians made movies. She started working on a new plan, for when things had settled down, of moving with Ricky to Bombay to one of those modern beach-front apartments she read about in her magazines, where she would socialize with the jet set and meet Bollywood directors who would be overcome by her beauty and cast her as their new romantic heroine.

Their child, tired of being ignored for so long in the womb, fought for recognition by arriving a couple of weeks prematurely, cheating Henna of her last fortnight of idleness. Henna had travelled the short distance to her father's house, not to have the child there as family tradition dictated, but with the sole intention of showing off her pregnant prosperity and sophistication to her blood relatives, most of whom she hadn't seen since her wedding. Caught short when her waters broke on her arrival, Henna found herself obliged to honour tradition despite herself. Even with the aid of child-bearing hips, Henna had a difficult birth as a result of her indolence during her pregnancy, when even the most rudimentary antenatal exercises had been ignored. Squatting on the ill-fated birthing stool on which her mother had died giving birth to a still-born brother, swearing and complaining viciously throughout the whole ordeal, Henna vowed that it was an experience that she wouldn't be repeating. Too bad for Rashid if it wasn't a boy.

When their baby girl eventually emerged, Rashid, however, was far from disappointed. He looked in awe at his tiny daughter, so delicate and perfect in snub-nosed profile, with a wide-open mouth screaming to be listened to, demanding that she finally be heard. She wasn't the milky aristocratic colour of the Karims, but nor did she have the swarthiness she might have inherited from her maternal grandfather. Instead, she was the colour of pale sand, a golden, rosy colour, with an equally golden burnish glowing across her dark-brown downy hair. The names they had discussed before, family names, now seemed prosaic and inappropriate, and insufficient to describe this magical, radiant creature. Rashid tentatively raised this with Henna, knowing that with his collective family behind her even more strongly since his father's death, Henna would be the one to have her way.

'You can call her whatever you want,' said Henna ungraciously, turning over painfully in bed. 'She's yours, isn't she?'

Grateful, despite the bad-tempered tone and Henna's obvious indifference to their daughter, Rashid suggested naming her Shona Kiran, the Golden One, the Ray of Sunshine, in deference to her colouring, and to all the new optimism in his life she now represented.

Golden Shona had been conceived with a lie, and was born in a liar's house, and into an inevitable understanding that it was always better to comfort or conceal with a lie than to hurt or expose with the truth. When older, and finding herself telling meaningless benign fibs about why she was late for work, or falsely admiring someone's new haircut, she would be unable to explain whether this need to lie was something innate, or something taught her from infancy by her mother and maternal grandfather. Whether its origin was in nature or nurture, her childhood was a battleground in which the truth never conquered, and in which she knew it was an ironic fallacy that the truth would out. Shona's lies were small, delicate, gossamer things that were woven inextricably into the fabric of her life, and were made anew each day. She spun a web so intricate and fine that only she really knew what was truth or not, and sometimes she deceived herself, so that even she no longer remembered.

Ignored by her teenage mother, Shona craved her attention and followed her around ceaselessly with tottering steps, in the hope she might be seen. One time Henna unusually conceded, and announced to the servants and to the chauffeur that she was taking Shona to the doctor's, for some imagined childhood ailment. In fact, Henna went to the clinic for herself, for what was euphemistically known as 'womb cleansing', and, leaving Shona to the clinic's nurses, returned with her womb duly cleansed of any further unborn life. Henna had two more womb cleansings, always taking Shona as her excuse, and eventually was persuaded that there might be simpler forms of birth control than abortion. Shona silently witnessed the lies her mother told, and even though she didn't understand them, she knew never to give anything away, and even nodded sweetly when the servants asked her if she was feeling better.

Until she was almost four, Shona was a silent witness to everything, as it took her that long to learn to talk. The ambivalence between what was said and what was meant was too difficult for her to unravel at first, and she knew that there were things that should be said which were not. In addition to learning the language of lying, with its complex grammar and syntax and timing, Shona was spoken to in no less than three languages: her mother's Bengali, the Urdu of the Karim household and the English that Rashid insisted on using with her, in the hope that she would learn to speak English like a native. When Shona finally did speak, so late that everyone was beginning to despair of her as retarded, she was suddenly acclaimed as a genius, a not quite four-year-old who understood three languages! Rashid had a friend who had been on a business trip to the UK, and for her birthday he requested that he order the largest, fluffiest teddy bear that he could buy from the grandest toy store in London.

'He was bought in a magical place called Hamley's, which is in England and very far away, and he flew over the sea and deserts and mountains to reach you,' Rashid explained solemnly to his daughter.

'I love him, Papa!' squealed Shona delightedly, hugging the bear somewhat awkwardly due to its ungainly, disproportionate size. She posed for a touching photo with the bear, Rashid's wise-eyed little girl soberly holding up her magnificent prize with an appropriate sense of awe, and he congratulated himself on his gift. It was some months later, when he was with Shona in the playroom, that he realized that she had almost never touched the bear again, except to carelessly pull its button eye out. She had probably found the teddy too big and cumbersome to play with, and had dragged it to the corner of the playroom, where it sat disconsolately. He realized that she hadn't loved the bear at all, and had said she loved it for his sake only. Touched on one hand, Rashid felt deeply sorrowful that Shona, at so young an age, had already been forced to learn the language of diplomacy. His golden one had lost her childhood innocence from almost before she could speak.

By the time Shona was ten years old, her uncle Aziz had taken over running the family lands from Rashid, allowing her father, now a qualified accountant, to get a job with one of the large multinationals which had opened a Dhaka office. Aziz had run the estate so successfully that he had diversified, and had also bought some lands in West Pakistan, in the Punjab where some of their distant relatives had settled. It was with these relatives that Rashid sent Henna and Shona to stay in 1971 when civil war broke out over Bangladeshi Independence. Henna had hoped that Lahore would prove another Calcutta, and was sorely disappointed at how dry, dull and provincial the town was; like it all needed a good dusting.

Shona, however, loved Lahore, with the dry heat that was so much more pleasant than the crushing, constant humidity of Dhaka. She loved the rambling old stone house in the genteel quarter of Gulberg, with its walled garden and wrought-iron swing. She was admired for her golden skin and her impeccable manners, and made all her father's relatives comfortable with her insincere compliments and admiration of everything from their clothes to their cooking. What Shona loved most about Lahore, though, was that there was a boy called Parvez staying in the Gulberg house, a distant relative of the distant relatives; he was from Karachi, and filled the house with his music, playing an eclectic mix of classical Asian and English pop records on the jumpy old gramophone, often accompanying the melodies with either his sitar or guitar, which he played with an amateur's enthusiasm. He was fourteen, and although Shona was only a few years younger than him, and only three years younger than her mother had been when she married, she felt like an awkward child around him; he was almost a man, and he had the easy grace and manliness of the film actors that her mother so admired. With his half-grown moustache, he reminded her of Omar Sharif, whom she'd seen in her mother's movie magazines. Instead of following around her mother, Shona started shamelessly following Parvez around the whole of Gulberg. He was good-natured and didn't mind her tagging along. Once she followed him up to the roof of the house with some syrupy sweets that she had asked the cook to make, knowing they were his favourite.

'Hi, Parvez,' she said shyly in English, their common language, as Shona had not yet learned Parvez's native Punjabi. She breathlessly came up through the twisting stairwell. 'I've brought you some rasgullas, and some cold pomegranate juice.'

'Thanks, Goldie,' he said affably. 'Too hot for rasgulla, but I'll take the juice.' Shona stayed in the shade of the stairwell and watched Parvez standing out in the beating heat of the full sun, only slightly relieved by a light breeze as he twisted twine around a bamboo cylinder. A gloriously coloured structure sat limply at his feet, like a shot-down bird of paradise.

'What are you doing?' she asked. 'Is that a kite over there?'

'Yes, it's a kite. Do you want to come-see?' His smile

was so magnetic and kind that Shona felt herself melting like the ice in Parvez's juice.

She stepped over willingly, while Parvez explained what he was doing. 'I'm just fixing it together. You need to wind the twine round the cylinder like this so you can release it quickly when you catch some wind; this way it can just unroll, like a yo-yo. And you can also pull it in quickly the same way, to keep the kite taut.' Remembering his juice, he politely picked it up and downed it quickly, wiping away the sweet purple drips from his mouth with the back of his hand. Shona watched this small gesture with close fascination, before forcing herself to look back at the kite.

'How will it fly?' she asked. 'There's not very much wind at the moment.' Normally there would be dozens of kites flying from the rooftops over Lahore, but Shona couldn't see any that day.

'There's enough,' said Parvez. 'Come on, Goldie, I'll show you. Come stand here.' Shona stood between Parvez's arms as he showed her how to unravel the twine, demonstrating by rolling the hollow bamboo cylinder over the rod on which it was threaded. He then took the kite and climbed to the highest point of the roof, cavalierly standing close to the edge, while Shona held on to the twine and prayed he wouldn't fall.

'Run when I say,' he called, 'and when the kite is in the air, stop and let out the twine.' Shona, desperate to impress and not fail in this challenge, gave the kite more attention than any lesson she had had in her life and ran urgently at the signal. Feeling the kite tugging in the air just above her, she released the twine and saw it soar higher. 'That's it, Goldie!' shouted Parvez encouragingly. He ran back to Shona and, standing behind her once more, his arms around her to guide the rod that she was holding, he showed her when to pull the kite in and when to let it out, to keep it swooping above their heads.

'It's working, Parvez, it's flying, it's really flying!' she said excitedly. But she wasn't truly excited about the kite, she was just grateful to the kite for giving her an outlet for her heightened emotion, for her extreme, unlimited happiness at that moment, because Parvez was standing so close to her.

As if by magic, other kites began to fly up from the neighbouring rooftops to join theirs as the boys and girls of the Gulberg district realized that there really was enough wind that day. And then across the sweeping city skyline more and more kites sailed into the bright blue sky. It was as though they had lit a beacon to announce that the skies were friendly once more. Shona saw the brightly coloured creatures shimmer and swing gracefully in the heavy air, and giddy with delight at what they had unleashed, leaned back into pomegranate-scented Parvez for support. Closing her eyes for a moment, she thought to herself, for once with unblinkered honesty and candour, 'This will be the man I marry.'

The Puppy Love of Parvez Khan
and Shona Karim

SHONA AND PARVEZ eloped when she was just twenty-
one, on the day she finished her final exams at Karachi
University. Before they met her, Parvez's family already
disapproved of her – an arriviste from Bangladesh, over-
educated, and most likely dark-skinned. What good would
she be for their son, who despite their relative poverty was
certainly handsome and engaging enough to marry a nice
Pakistani girl with a decent dowry? In turn, Shona knew
that her mother and father disapproved of 'Cousin'
Parvez, as he was loosely described, and that if they knew
her reason for going to university in Karachi was simply
to be near him, they would have forbidden her to go
altogether. He wasn't well off – a sin in Henna's eyes as
she had married brilliantly, despite a whole host of disad-
vantages, and didn't want her daughter to undo all her
good work. He wasn't university-educated, having helped
to expand the family restaurant after he had finished
school – a sin in Rashid's eyes. Rashid himself had gone
to Merton College, Oxford, but had thrown himself away
on an illiterate child; he wasn't going to let his daughter

make the same mistake in marrying a partner who wasn't her intellectual equal.

It was Shona who had instigated their love affair – she had been persistent in keeping in touch with him during her adolescence, making him an unwilling pen pal by her sheer perseverance. When she was eighteen she finally arrived in Karachi to study. He met her at the Karachi Tennis Club for drinks and was charmed to discover that his golden-skinned teenage fan club had become a golden-skinned, curvaceous woman, with her mother's good looks and her father's gentleness. She had a childish sense of mischief and humour that he shared. He was disconcerted by her foreignness at the beginning, but she would soon speak Punjabi so flawlessly she sounded like a native, her skill at putting on the appropriate accent not unrelated to her mother's acting talent. On the occasion of their first handshake, they both felt an electric shock, an instant frisson of attraction, a shiver up their spines, that warned Parvez, and confirmed for Shona, that this would be the one. Over the next few years they became the secret golden couple of the club and campus, both so attractive, and so utterly devoted to each other that they were inappropriately tactile in public, hands unconsciously knotting and intertwining, legs or shoulders brushing for that brief, sweet moment of clandestine contact. It was as though being in love was a talent they shared.

Shona was taking a break during the first week of her final exams, indiscreetly walking in the park with Parvez.

She was far from her usual merry, sweetly smiling self, and was disconsolately plucking dusty flowers from the bushes and pulling them apart. Parvez squeezed her hand comfortingly. 'What's up, Goldie? Are you worried about the French literature paper tomorrow?' he asked gently.

'You know what I'm worried about, Puppy,' she said sadly, pulling away her hand and throwing herself on to a bench.

'Shh! Don't call me that in public, people will talk,' he said in mock horror.

'What will people talk about that they haven't talked about already?' asked Shona curiously, momentarily forgetting her resolve to be dramatically melancholic that day.

'They'll say that Parvez is a puppy – a low-down-dirty-little-dog.'

'Oh, you mean a *kuttar bacha*?' giggled Shona, getting the joke and accidentally saying the swear word out loud.

'Shh!' Parvez said again, in greater mock horror. 'Now people will really talk. Parvez is a son-of-a-bitch, and his girlfriend swears like a sweet-maker.'

'You mean a sailor?' asked Shona.

'I mean a sweet-maker – you remember me telling you about my Bhai Hassan? The one who opened the sweet shop in London. He can swear for the whole Punjab. Whenever he comes back he's all Bloody this, and Bloody that. You'd think he worked in a halal butcher's, not a confectioner's.'

'You are silly, Puppy,' Shona giggled, cheered up despite herself. But then she felt her good cheer dissolve almost immediately, as she said forlornly, 'I don't know what I'm going to do without you. No one else makes me laugh like you.'

Parvez sighed. They had had this conversation many times before in the months coming up to Shona's exams. 'I keep telling you, Goldie. You won't have to do without me. When you finish, we'll go back to Dhaka together and I'll ask your father if we can please get married, and we'll live together for ever, and the gossips will have to find something else to talk about.'

'That sounds nice, but Papa will never say yes, not even for me. He'll ask why you don't have a degree.'

'A degree!' Parvez scoffed. 'Anyone can get a degree!' He saw the look on Shona's face and added quickly, 'Anyone who works hard, like you, I mean. But how many people can say that they've turned their family business around, and increased their turnover and staff by four-fold in as many years?'

'No one,' said Shona staunchly. 'Your family have been lucky to have you.' She added, a touch disloyally, giving away where her new allegiances lay, 'Papa tried hard at the family business, but he almost ran our farms into the ground before Uncle Aziz took over.'

'And I'm going to do more! Your dad is the big Anglophile, isn't he? Well, what would he think about his daughter moving to London! You know Bhai Hassan wants me to go and help him with his business over there.'

'He'd hate it,' said Shona. 'He's always wanted to move to England. For you to take me there would be like admitting he's failed. And besides, Papa isn't even the problem – he wouldn't like it, but he couldn't do anything about it. It's Amma who would never let me marry you.

She warns me against you every time I go back for the vacation, and she doesn't even know we're together. She just hears the gossip.' She sighed, 'And your family don't even know me, and they don't like me already. Puppy, I don't know what to do.'

'Shh! I told you not to say that in public,' Parvez said in a stage whisper, and Shona giggled again and reached for his hand.

A middle-aged lady in a voluminous apricot-coloured shalwar looked disapprovingly at Shona as she walked by, and stopped by the bench to address her in ringing tones.

'Daughter, do your parents know that you hold hands with Strange Boys in parks, hmm?' the lady said, looking loftily down on them.

'Auntie, this is my wife, so unless you're stopping to give us your best wishes for a long and happy life together, I suggest you buzz off,' said Parvez with all the arrogance and confidence that his entrepreneurial youthful success had brought. As the lady teetered off in her high heels in disgust, Parvez made a low buzzing sound in rhythm with her walk. And as she became aware of what he was doing, and walked away faster, he increased the pitch and frequency of his buzz until she practically ran from them. Shona, at first mortified, was soon in fits of laughter.

'Puppy! You are so naughty. Bad, bad Puppy,' she smacked him and laughed out loud again.

'You see, Goldie, we have to get married. No one else thinks I'm funny at all,' said Parvez. He looked at Shona's pretty, unmade-up face, her lips very full and pink against the gold of her skin, and said, 'I wish we were married already, so I could kiss you whenever I wanted to.'

'And if we were married already, we wouldn't have to beg all our families for permission. We could just go to London and tell them all later.'

'Well, I promised to fly over and see Bhai Hassan to discuss the job,' said Parvez flippantly. 'Pack your bags and we can go together.'

'You're teasing me, Puppy. That's not nice,' said Shona reproachfully. 'And besides, I've got my exams this week and next.'

'We can go after your exams,' said Parvez, less flippantly. Why hadn't he thought of this before? He and Shona didn't need to be stuck in the rut of tradition – it was the 1980s, for God's sake, they could get married when and where they wanted; they were grown ups, and they didn't need their parents' permission. And they didn't need their parents' money – he had already proved himself as breadwinner for his family, he could certainly look after Shona on his own.

'Puppy, are you being serious?' said Shona, noticing the change in Parvez's expression. He had the faraway look that came over him when he was planning something; it made him look like a misty-eyed dreamer but in fact was a sign that his head was ticking and turning over with ideas. Parvez looked into Shona's solemn, chocolate-brown eyes and dropped to one knee in front of her.

'Shundor Shonali Shona, my beautiful Golden Goldie, do you know that you have eyes that a man can look back centuries in, and still see his future? Of course I'm serious! Marry me after your exams. We'll fly to London the same evening. I'll organize everything – I'll get your ticket and arrange the marriage licence.'

'We can't get married just like that,' said Shona, taking refuge in being sensible to avoid being overcome by the superb honeyed sweetness of the moment. 'What about witnesses, and all that sort of thing?'

'I'll drag them off the street if I have to!' said Parvez with romantic gallantry. 'Ho!' he shouted to a couple of students cycling towards them. 'Do you want to be our witnesses? The lady has just agreed to marry me.'

'Drunk,' muttered one of the students to the other as they sailed by.

'You see,' Parvez repeated with faux dejection, getting up from the grimy path to sit beside her on the bench. 'No one thinks I'm funny apart from you.' Dusting the dirt from his knees, he added, 'Fortunately I wasn't wearing my best trousers today – it must be fate. If I'd decided to wear my good trousers this morning I might not have been able to propose at all.'

'You are the funniest puppy in the world,' said Shona, finally giving in to the moment. 'And yes, I will marry you next week, in front of witnesses dragged from the street, in my best travelling sari and with trainers on so we can run away when they come to get us.'

'Goldie, I think I might have to kiss you anyway,' said Parvez as Shona, laughing delightedly, swatted him away, her sombre mood lifted entirely.

'Buzz off, strange boy,' she said cheekily, flapping at him ineffectively.

'Bzzz,' said Parvez, avoiding her swatting hands and moving closer. 'Bzzz,' and he took her in his arms and kissed her like they did in the movies, oblivious to the curious looks and outrage of the rest of conservative Karachi parading through the park in their Sunday best.

Shona went back to her studies, and told the girls on campus that she'd be flying home straight after her last exam to explain why she wouldn't be around for any post-exam celebrations. She told the family she was staying with the same thing. Shona dissembled guiltlessly; she had lied for the past three years in order to keep seeing Parvez, so that the girls thought she spent far too much time holed up at home, and the family thought she spent far too much time socializing on campus. Before picking up her books to do some last-minute revision for her French literature paper, she picked out the sari in which she'd decided to get married. A gorgeous, orangey golden silk – like the sunrise on her new life with Parvez.

The wedding day was deliciously romantic. Ludicrously overdressed in her orange-gold sari, Shona sat her last paper and rushed out of the examination hall to see Parvez waiting, wearing his best suit and a flamboyant buttonhole, his sitar case in his hand, with a motorized rickshaw chugging black smoke over his peacock finery. Before her student friends could see, she disappeared into the rickshaw with him, and they stopped at the campus where she had stowed her bags. At the registrar's, Parvez, good as his word, called two people off the street to be their witnesses – they were workmen trying to fix the street lights, but were all too happy to take a break from the hot job for the fan-cooled registrar's office.

'Are you sure this is legal?' she asked bemusedly.

'Of course, smile for the photographer!' Parvez said. He had hired someone to take a few shots of them as they signed the papers and yet more shots as they came out of the office, with the grinning workmen behind them.

Shona was to look at one of those photos later, her sari blazing in the sun, her face looking bewildered but happy as she looked up adoringly at Parvez. And Parvez looking like he owned the world: handsome, confident, laughing at the camera, an arm protectively around her, as though he had enough strength for them both and would look after them for ever. Perhaps she and Parvez really did have a talent for being in love – in some ways, apart from their silly sense of humour, it was all they had in common. But it was incontrovertible: they were The Couple That Were In Love, and whose foolhardy, romantic elopement only substantiated the fact further. Twenty years later, she was to wonder where it all started going wrong.

The Crushed Rose Petals of a Tooting Confectioner

AFTER THE ROMANTIC high of their elopement, the sticky, crowded wait at the airport and cold, dry plane journey made for a deeply unromantic wedding night, but it didn't even occur to Shona to complain. She just snuggled up to her new husband under the Pakistan International Airlines blanket, and enjoyed the simple intimacy of being able to watch him sleep, his eyelashes fanned against his cheek, his breath deepening but his face remaining poised, and his jaw firm, as though still conscious that he was in public and under scrutiny. In the half light of the sleeping plane, Shona looked at the other husbands and fathers sitting around her, with their fat bellies, bald pates and slack-jawed, half-open mouths, and her pride in her handsome husband soared.

When the stewardesses started serving breakfast, Shona put on her headset and watched *Chariots of Fire* on the airplane TV. Her papa loved the film, and she heard his own cut-glass accent in the accents of the Oxbridge students who ran for England. She considered changing out of her sari, but the airplane loos were unpromisingly busy and there wasn't enough room in the cubicles of the Dubai stopover. Besides, it was probably best if she didn't meet Bhai Hassan in casual western dress. She wasn't sure how traditional he was, and as the first member of Parvez's close family that she'd be meeting, she wanted to make a good first impression.

As they descended towards Heathrow, Shona watched the blue sky around them dull to grey, cold-looking clouds and pulled the blanket, which she had now commandeered for her exclusive use, closer to protect her. She was glad that she had packed a shawl – she would get it out as soon as they got their bags back. As they approached for landing, Shona, who had seen desert, snow-capped mountains and wondrous oceans on their journey over, was unimpressed. So this was England, the place of her father's dreams, the location of all his happy memories and interminable university stories – this grey, patchwork quilt of a country. Even the cheerful chatter of the fellow passengers now seemed muted with the weather, and they lowered their voices to hushed whispers; or perhaps it just felt that way with the air pressure in her ears. She looked down at her sari, which seemed outrageously garish in this new gloomy and solemn world – dressed for a party, she had been taken to a wake.

'Hey, it's not that cold, it's not even raining,' said Parvez, sensing Shona's disappointment as they got off the plane. 'I want my money back – I think they took us to the wrong country.' There was a touch of concern in his bonhomie; Shona's muted reaction to this muted new country was giving him his first niggle of doubt as to whether they had done the right thing. Shona gave him a slight, tremulous smile and squeezed his hand, wondering how she was ever going to feel at home here. Perhaps the trick was not to think about it as a home, but just a long holiday, like the time Papa had taken her to the beach at Cox's Bazaar to learn to swim, or when she and Amma had gone to Lahore together, and first met Parvez. This was her honeymoon, wasn't it? How many of the tittering, giggling girls at college would have Just Died and Gone to Heaven at the idea of a honeymoon in London? Shona had got so good at lying she could even persuade herself that she was happy, which made it much easier to persuade the man standing by her side.

'Happy honeymoon, Puppy,' she said without a trace of telltale discontent, and kissed him on his slightly stubbly cheek. Parvez relaxed and banished the niggle, reassured that she was going to be all right.

Parvez, determined to be the manly, efficient one, went to the American Express office at the airport and changed some of his travellers' cheques, for what seemed a vast amount of money to Shona.

'That'll do us for a couple of days,' he said wisely, fastening the notes with the thick gold clip he had started using, which he thought looked rather natty, and which Shona thought looked rather garish.

'Just a couple of days?' said Shona faintly. London was clearly a lot more expensive than Karachi. She had no idea how much Parvez had in savings, but she knew he wasn't rich, and after paying for both their tickets it couldn't be that much. Shona's family had always been relatively wealthy, so she had never had to worry about money before. Now she wished she had some savings of her own to contribute – otherwise Parvez might have to start working straightaway, and her honeymoon might be very short indeed.

The cab journey to Tooting took up a distressing amount of Parvez's precious pinned notes. Standing at the cab rank with her glamorous sari flapping in the wind, with Parvez in his wedding blazer, with their hotchpotch of luggage littering up their feet, Shona was aware that they looked preposterously out of place. The cabbie, seeing them, was prepared to be jovially patronizing, but was stopped short by Shona reading out their address in her father's cut-glass English accent, which now had additional hints of Harold Abrahams absorbed from *Chariots of Fire*.

'Could you possibly take us to Tooting High Street in SW17, near Tooting Broadway station?' she asked, as Parvez hoisted up their bags.

'Blimey, I wasn't expecting that face to have that voice,' said the cabbie, nodding respectfully at her. 'Are you from London, dear?'

Parvez cheerfully answered for her, 'Not yet, but we soon will be, I hope.' He laughed good-humouredly, but the cabbie didn't laugh with him. Parvez's English was good, but his accent was definitely Pakistani, and the cabbie's respect disintegrated like a puff of smoke on hearing the familiar immigrant Paki accent. He looked at Shona crossly, as though she had tricked him on purpose. Parvez was unsure what he had done to cause the sudden sinking good humour, but didn't say another word in

English until they reached the grimy, litter-strewn streets
of Tooting.

Bhai Hassan was delighted to see his young cousin and
lovely new wife. He was less happy when he realized that
they were runaways, who were intending to stay in London, and who had nowhere to stay except with him. After
giving them a welcoming cup of comfortingly sweet tea,
served with rasgulla and burfi from the shop, he showed
Shona to the spare room, and made an excuse to take
Parvez into his 'office', the table at the back of the sweetshop kitchen.

Kicking off her shoes, Shona was finally able to unwind
herself out of her now crushed and rather worse-for-wear
sari and pull on a pair of trousers and a long silky shirt.
Looking out of the window through the stained yellowing
net, she was shocked to find herself wondering where she
and Parvez were going to be able to make love, and
properly begin their honeymoon. Certainly not in this
tatty spare room of Bhai Hassan's flat above the confectioner's. She lay back on the single bed and imagined
Parvez's arms around her, in a suite at the Karachi Hilton,
lying on Egyptian cotton sheets strewn with rose petals.

In the kitchen, Bhai Hassan was prosaically pounding
rose petals to a damp and fragrant sludge with sugar to
make the syrup for one of his sweets. 'Bloody hell, son,'
he said in English that was pure south London. 'She's a
nice girl but you can't keep her. You can't just roll up with

a girlfriend in a foreign country and say you're married and you're going to live here. You practically kidnapped her. Our family will be out for your blood. And her family have probably reported her missing to the flipping police by now. She'll have to go back. I'm Bleedin' amazed you got her through immigration in the first place.'

'She's not going back, Bhai. She's my wife, and I love her and she's staying with me.'

'Stop, you're making my Bloody heart bleed,' Bhai Hassan said, giving the tattered remains of the rose petals a final vicious bash. 'How are you going to afford her? You'll barely be able to keep yourself in London, let alone a wife. She don't look like she's used to earning her keep.'

'Well, you asked me here to help with the business. I'll work with you, and rent us a house. If you could just let us stay with you until then. . .'

'A house?' roared Bhai Hassan in outrage that quickly dissolved to laughter. 'Do you really think I can pay you enough to rent a house while I'm living in the Bloody flat above the shop?'

Parvez felt the niggle of doubt that he had dismissed at the airport come creeping back. He couldn't go crawling back to Pakistan with his tail between his legs; he had to make this work. He looked helplessly at his cousin for just a moment before pulling himself together and saying firmly, 'A flat, then. We'll get our own flat. I'll work with you and leave Shona free to manage our home and do whatever else she wants, continue her studies maybe.' He added with a touch of pride, 'My wife is a very intelligent woman, a college girl, you know. Just finished her final exams. She could've gone to university here in England, but she chose Karachi, just to be near me.'

'So she's not that Bloody bright,' said Bhai Hassan crushingly. 'Besides, how do you think a college girl will manage your home? I'll bet she can't even cook. I know the sort, had servants all their lives and can't make a Bloody cup of cha without someone else boiling the water and pouring the milk.'

Parvez received this disquieting insight with a nonchalant shrug; it was probably true that Shona couldn't cook, or sew, or make a cup of tea. So what? He hadn't fallen in love for her domestic skills. Besides, he knew how to cook from his time in the family restaurant; maybe he could teach her.

'So can we stay with you? Just for a bit?' he asked, with a pleading smile and the big, persuasive puppy-dog eyes that had earned him his pet name from Shona.

It was Bhai Hassan's turn to shrug. His good-looking young cousin had a lot of charm, he'd give him that. He'd be a definite front-of-house asset with the moneyed ladies of Tooting, especially with his new plans to expand the sweet shop to a tea house. Sod the bloody family – apart from Parvez, they never wrote to him anyway, except to ask for money.

'It doesn't look like I have much choice,' he said with resignation, pouring his tortured rose-petal sludge into a hot pan to melt, the sweet scent rising mournfully from the steam and hanging in the air like a mistreated spirit. Parvez bounded across the table to hug him, but Bhai Hassan smacked his hands away in an attempt to hold on to his elder cousin authority. 'Arré! Careful, this stove is hot! So when can you start work. Tomorrow?'

'In three days' time, if that's OK,' Parvez said sweetly, with the carefree innocence of someone about to spend well beyond his means. 'First, my wife and I have plans for our honeymoon.'

Shona had almost drifted off to sleep, curled up on the narrow single bed, oblivious to the honking, Tooting traffic on the streets below, when she became fuzzily aware of a naked Greek apparition in the room. Blinking swiftly, she realized that Parvez was getting changed right in front of her, and was wearing only his underwear. His caramel-coloured chest was smooth and hairless, and the muscles in his back moved like poetry as he pulled on a pair of casual trousers.

'Hey, sleepy head,' he said, noticing her stir. Clearly unembarrassed by his state of undress, he sat next to her and kissed her on the forehead. 'Sorry to do this to you, but you'll need to pack a few things for a couple of nights. We've got to head off soon.'

'Where are we heading off to? We've only just arrived,' asked Shona bemusedly, disturbed by the proximity of so much handsome flesh.

Parvez kissed her again. 'Didn't you say that you've always wanted to stay at the Hilton?'

This particular Hilton wasn't quite as plush as Shona imagined the Karachi Hilton to be, but the room had all sorts of exciting conveniences. A kettle with little sachets of tea and coffee and gingerbread. A very white, very shiny bathroom with wrapped-up soap and sachets of shampoo and shower gel. A perplexing-looking trouser press, which Shona couldn't quite work out. A TV which announced 'Welcome, Mr and Mrs Khan' across its screen. It was this last which made Shona squeal with excitement; it was the first time she'd seen her married name in writing and it made it all feel official, substantial. She was a married woman now, and had been for a whole day and a half. When she pulled the curtains open, she jumped up and down with excitement all over again. 'Puppy, look at the view! It's the park! This is Hyde Park, Papa told me about it. There's a boating lake there – can we go boating, can we?'

'If you want,' said Parvez, amused. 'Do you want a cup of tea?'

'I'll make it,' Shona said. 'We had a kettle like this in the common room on campus.' She put the water on to boil, and told Parvez seriously, 'The important thing about making English tea is to put the milk in first, so it doesn't scald. And to warm the pot first. And to wait until the water is just off the boil before you brew, and not let the tea be over-brewed when you pour. And you put in one spoon of tea per person, and one for the pot. Except we only have teabags here, so I'll just put in two.'

'I had no idea it was so complicated a business,' said Parvez, pleased that at least one of Bhai Hassan's dire predictions had been proved wrong. He sat on the bed and pulled off his shoes.

'Papa used to make tea like this at home. He never let the servants make it because they used to stew the tea and put in canned evaporated milk.'

Parvez smiled and pulled Shona on to his lap, kissing the tip of her nose. 'Goldie, can I be honest with you? I'm really not that bothered about tea right now.'

'Neither am I,' answered Shona, feeling the same tingle up her spine that she had felt the day she first learned to fly a kite, and the same electric shock she had felt the first time they had shaken hands at the Karachi Tennis Club after their long separation. She realized with slight trepidation and high anticipation that her anomalous time as a married virgin was about to come to an end. As she lay back on their plump, white pillows, Shona was aware of a gentle fragrant fluttering, raining over her. She opened her eyes to see Parvez scattering pale pink rose petals rescued from Bhai Hassan's kitchen across their bed. She sighed blissfully and pulled Parvez down towards her.

That afternoon, and evening, and night, and morning, Shona and Parvez were to discover that they had something further in common besides a silly sense of humour and a fondness for nicknames. The urgent physical attraction that they had mistaken for love was the forerunner of an intense sexual compatibility that was to keep them together for twenty years. Any arguments, disappointments and frustrations were put aside, resolved, absolved in the bedroom, crushed with the salty-sweetness of their lovemaking, and melted away in the early hours of the morning, evaporating like discharged ghosts with the sticky heat of their bodies. These bodies were instantly, instinctively comfortable with each other, hand fitting hand, mouth fitting mouth, curve fitting hollow. And as they grew older, their bodies, so finely attuned to each other, so used to sharing the same bed, were to dissolve into each other, her contours into his planes, arms and legs that knotted together like tree roots, so that even in their sleep they were in an embrace.

The Relative Cost of Gold

S HONA AND PARVEZ, during their three-day honeymoon in London, were able to act like a real couple
for the first time. None of the secretive liaisons in the
parks, waiting for a busybody to berate them or prying
eyes to report them, none of the accidental encounters at
the tennis club or campus library, no more engineering
chance meetings with mutual acquaintances, or pretending
to be somewhere other than where they really were. Shona
could bask in the openness of the new arrangement,
putting off the moment when she'd have to call home and
explain what she had done. They held hands as they
walked down Oxford Street and through Soho and kissed
more often than was decorous even in bohemian London,
where back-combed punks with metal studs looked with
pity at these unwitting new romantics with their floppy
silk shirts. They stopped for a cream tea in one of the
nicer tea shops on Piccadilly, and Parvez proudly told the
highly made-up waitress that it was their honeymoon.

'But where are your rings?' she asked, after congratu-
lating them. On hearing that they weren't an essential part

of the ceremony in Pakistan, she raised her fashionably plucked eyebrows and told them, a touch condescendingly, 'In this country, we wear rings when we're married.' She waved her hand – 'Like this, see?' – showing a diamond-studded band.

Furious for being treated like an ignorant Paki yokel for the second time in as many days, Parvez marched Shona down to the various jewellers on Old Bond Street.

'I'm not having people think that we're rednecks from the villages, and I'm not having people think that we're not really married,' he stormed, talking more to himself than Shona.

'It doesn't matter, Puppy,' said Shona appeasingly. 'I don't care whether people think we're married or not.' She was secretly thrilled; she had been wondering whether she might get a ring, and looked hopefully at the elegant display in the window at Tiffany's. However, both she and Parvez baulked at the prices they saw; gold didn't cost nearly so much at home, and Parvez was determined that Shona should have no baser metal than her own namesake.

Fortunately, Bhai Hassan, who had built up a network of useful cronies during his time in London, knew 'a-man-who-did'. Parvez resisted showing his ignorance by asking what-he-did, and was repaid by Bhai Hassan giving him the address of Dominic, a Diamond-geezer in both senses of the word, who ran a shadowy but industrious jewellery workshop above a hair salon in Hatton Garden.

'Dominic's a Diamond, I mean a Bloody Nice Bloke,' Bhai Hassan translated kindly for Parvez. 'He'll make you a couple of rings for a song if you get him the gold to work with.' Parvez pulled out his beloved gold money clip and looked thoughtfully at it. The next day he replaced it with an inexpensive wallet, and the following week he was to surprise his wife with a shining copy of the wedding rings at Tiffany's that she had admired, and a gleaming pair of delicate golden earrings that he had had made with the leftover gold.

Shona displayed an excitement for Parvez's benefit which didn't reveal how deeply it saddened her that her gift should have to be his loss, and which consequently could not show how deeply this act of unselfishness had touched her. She had lots of expensive, gem-set jewellery at home, mainly cast-offs inherited from her mother, but nothing that had been given with such love. Sitting in the squalid spare room of her husband's cousin's flat, she told herself she could do without money, without the trappings of privilege and the unthinking ease of life that she had been so used to, as long as she had Parvez.

The Beginning of the Double Life
of Ricky-Rashid

RASHID WAS PRACTICALLY middle-aged when he first fell in love. At forty-three, he had matured and filled out and become better looking than the callow, milky-faced academic of his youth. His figure was no longer skinny, and he now wore a suit rather well; the slight grey in his temples was distinguished rather than ageing, and his profile seemed fine-boned rather than weak. Although outwardly he appeared fit and well and even attractive – he was only forty-three after all – inside he felt defeated, worn and ancient. Like a ruin left abandoned to take its punishment from a brutal sun and the encroaching jungle.

The last twenty-five years of his life had been a study in apathy and disappointment. He had married a pretty child who had become a thick-waisted tyrant, who tolerated him while she took over his home, and with whom he had perplexingly proved infertile after their first child. He had given up his academic and professional dreams to mismanage his family's landed interests until his more adept younger brother was old enough to take over and undo the damage he had well-meaningly caused – his sacrifice both unappreciated and unacknowledged. He had been gifted a wonderful daughter, who until her late teens was the only good thing, the only golden ray of sunshine in his life, but from whom he had been estranged ever since she had ill-advisedly gone to university in Karachi rather than England. He had loyally ignored the gossip he had heard about her behaviour in Karachi with a certain Pakistani boy, believing her when she returned home on her vacations from campus and assured him that there was no truth to the rumours. He had been repaid for his trust by her proceeding to elope with that same boy on the day she finished her final exam.

The only thing that Rashid had managed to be consistent at was his work. After a dozen years with the same multinational he had joined in his youth, following many mergers and acquisitions, he found himself a fairly senior figure in the finance department and had to travel widely in the Middle East and Asia. He spent very little time at home, but home now meant very little to him – Henna didn't care if he was there or not, she didn't even need him as an appropriate escort to the parties she went to, or as host for her evening soirées, as the still unmarried Aziz was more than happy to oblige in his absence and she clearly preferred his company. Rashid suspected that when he was at home, his presence was an annoyance to Henna – she simply put up with him, as his mere existence enabled her a pleasant life as Mrs Karim. In the same way that she was stuck with him, he felt stuck with her. He had made a deal with her when she was thirteen; when he had accepted the marriage, he had become her guardian as much as her husband. He couldn't divorce her now, it was much too late, and besides, where would she go? Frankly, he suspected that if he ever broached the subject, he would be the one to move out, such was Henna's hold on the household, his extended family and all the retainers. They were faithful to her first and then to Aziz, not to him; his constant absenteeism did not help to engender their loyalty. And of course, Shona wasn't there any more. There was nothing of hers left but some of her old childhood toys, like that eyeless old teddy she had never loved. She had asked the servants to pack up and send on her belongings to London, where she and Parvez had moved after their elopement. She had seized for herself the English life that Rashid had wanted to give her. He hadn't seen Shona for months now – he guessed that her concerns were all with her husband and his Pakistani family, not with him or even her mother, who were now too distant to matter.

Rashid had been surprised when an appointment came up at work, and he discovered that he had been recommended for it. It was rather similar to the job he currently did and involved a similar level of travel, except the job was to be based out of the UK, in the company's regional centre in the south-east of England. After all these years, England! The place he had dreamed of living, working, raising and educating his family. Again, it was much too late. And he probably wouldn't get the job anyway; he'd need to fly to the UK for the interview. He mentioned it to Henna when he arrived home one evening at the Dhaka town house, catching her before she disappeared off for the night.

'Hold on, someone's come in . . . no, don't worry, it's

Just Rashid,' he heard Henna say to one of her cronies on the telephone as he walked in. Leisurely finishing her call, she addressed him distractedly as she attempted to fasten her earrings in front of the mirror in the long, dark hallway. 'It's just you and Ammie tonight, Rashid. Aziz is having dinner at the club, and I'm on my way to Farida's for our drama and supper evening.' Fiddling with a stubborn catch at her left ear, she added vaguely, 'I think Cook might make you some koftas or curry, or something.'

'Perhaps I could join Aziz at the club?' suggested Rashid hopefully. Eating alone again with his doleful mother didn't seem too enticing. She had once resented his frequent absences; now she seemed to positively resent his presence. Like everyone, she liked him much less than Henna and Aziz.

'If you do, you'll need to take a rickshaw there and get a lift back with Aziz – I need our driver to go to Farida's.'

Rashid sighed. Getting a rickshaw through the hot and sticky night was the last thing he wanted to do after a hard day's number-crunching.

'Henna, before you go, there's something you should know.'

'Yes, well, quickly then,' said Henna with barely concealed irritation. Her earrings now firmly in place, she was painting her mouth with a plum lipstick that matched her sari and her pretty sandals.

'There's a new opening at work. It's more senior, with more money, but it involves lots of travel in Europe and being based in the UK. They've asked me to an interview, but I'd need to go to England for it.' Rashid hesitated, before bravely admitting, 'I said I'd think about it.'

'Well, what's to think about?' she said impatiently. Rashid was so slow sometimes. 'They'll pay for your flight, yes? And your accommodation there? So you should go for the interview and see Shona and that Pakistani. Take them some presents, so they think we're not cross any more. Tell her to come home occasionally – people are beginning to talk. And you can buy me a raincoat from Burberry – Farida has one and is always showing off about it.'

'But what if I get the job?' asked Rashid, not sure that Henna had been listening.

'Well, you might get lucky, but don't get your hopes up,' said Henna, with a tone that was meant to be kind, before barking 'Cholo!' to the waiting driver. 'I really have to go now.'

Rashid followed her outside, and with natural politeness held the door open for her as she elegantly stepped into the back of the enviably air-conditioned Rover that he had so recently vacated. 'But what about the travel, and being based in the UK?'

'Rashid, you travel three days a week anyway. No one's going to notice if you travel a bit more,' Henna said with unconscious cruelty, shutting the door to signal an end to the conversation.

Rashid watched the car speed off. That had actually gone better than he thought it would – Henna had practically encouraged him to go for the job. Looking back towards the veranda, he saw his mother looking down at him with woeful, accusatory eyes. He decided that braving the sticky night was the better of the two evils. 'Hey, Ammie, I'm going to meet Aziz at the club,' he shouted to her with barely concealed cowardice, and walked swiftly out of the gate to the street before she could object, hailing his own rickshaw and letting the damp dust of the street settle in the creases of his good suit.

It was the same suit that Rashid was wearing as he sat in the BA Business Class lounge at Paris Charles de Gaulle airport. At no little inconvenience to him, his company had booked him a flight to Paris as the cheapest option, requiring him to board a separate plane to London, with a four-hour wait in between. He'd had a shower, read the papers and drunk enough spicy tomato juices to make him feel distinctly queasy, and he still had two hours left to kill. He settled near the TV, where he could watch the news for distraction. He was sorely tempted to get terribly drunk, but didn't want his first return to England for years to be clouded by alcohol – he wanted to return to his spiritual home with dignity. Yes, with dignity. The very thought made him sit up straighter, and his profile stiffen with distinction. That was how Veetie Trueman first saw him, wielding his *FT* like a shield against the grimy masses and looking like a Roman statesman, like someone who belonged.

Veetie was acutely conscious that she, by contrast to the elegant gentleman sitting in the armchair, looked like a scruffy interloper on entering the Business Class lounge, her grey suit crumpled at the back from sitting stiffly in the hot Parisian cab, and the collar of her white shirt wilting at her pale neck. She was obviously ill at ease with the supercilious reception staff, handing over her boarding card timidly as though she expected them to refuse her entry, and was struggling with two ungainly cases and a document bag that she was ill-equipped to manage along with her own substantial handbag. Rashid barely noticed her, glancing up only briefly at the noise made by her untidy, clattering entrance.

'You can't bring all those bags in under your hand-luggage allowance, dear,' said the BA representative patronizingly.

'I know,' replied Veetie tiredly, as though she'd had to give the explanation before. 'They're not all mine. They're my colleagues' – they've taken our client for a drink and asked me to look after their bags. They're joining me here later.'

The receptionist handed back Veetie's boarding card sniffily, saying, 'You can leave excess bags over there,' nodding towards a rack set in the wall, 'but at your own risk.'

Veetie tried to wheel the cases over to the rack, but one fell over, causing her to stumble awkwardly. Rashid, with natural gentility, got up politely. 'Here, let me help with those.' He lifted both cases easily and put them in the rack. 'Shall I put that bag in as well?' he offered, indicating the document bag.

'No, I'd better hold on to this one. Thanks so much,' gushed Veetie, unused to such gallantry, especially from such an attractive, distinguished-looking man. She collapsed in a seat near him, pretending to watch the TV but surreptitiously stealing long glances at him, admiring his patrician nose and creamy exotic colouring. Perhaps he was Spanish, or South American – but his English was perfect and unaccented, unless received pronunciation counted as an accent. Maybe he was Indian? Although so correct and poised, he wasn't very much older than her – maybe in his mid forties, or perhaps even younger. She noticed that he wasn't wearing a wedding ring.

Rashid would later say that it was Fate that had led him to love – Fate (and not frugality caused by squeezed corporate travel budgets) that had forced him to make this inexplicable airline interchange so close to his destination, Fate (and not rudeness on the part of her colleagues) that had Ms Trueman carrying excess hand-baggage to the Business Class lounge long before her plane was due, and Fate (not the location of the TV) that he had been sitting near enough to overhear her plight and help her.

In fact, when spinning this romantic tale, Rashid would conveniently forget that despite all this intervention from Fate, once he had helped Veetie with her bags he had not been interested enough by the timid smile on her flushed face, nor in the thin figure not set to advantage by a creased high street suit, to take any further notice of her beyond a polite nod once she took her seat. Despite all the best intentions of Fate, aided by budget restrictions in his own company, and regrettable chauvinism in Ms Trueman's, Rashid would have sat opposite the future love of his life and simply ignored her. He would have dropped his eyes back to his paper, sinking behind its peach-coloured safety and then left to get his plane. Fortunately for Rashid, Veetie no longer believed in fate and took some action for herself.

Veetie was in her late thirties, and had only recently become the sort of woman who took things into her own hands. She had spent most of her life having decisions made for her by other people, first by her Home Counties parents, and then by her controlling boyfriend, whom she unthinkingly and unwisely replaced with an exact replica when he left her. Her parents had bullishly argued against her going to university, insisting that Lucy Clayton Secretarial College would provide her with impeccable qualifications for a regular income, and invaluable training for her future career as a wife. And so Veetie spent her twenties as a secretary in the City and her early thirties as an administrator, but in fact devoted all her real energy to being a homemaker, for two successive partners who didn't appreciate her devotion enough to want to make the arrangement permanent. It was when she turned thirty-five that it became obvious to her that Pete, her boyfriend of five years, had no intention of asking her to marry him, or even remaining faithful. It became equally obvious to her that the decisions made for her by other people had not been the most helpful, and that nothing was going to happen for her unless she did something about it herself. She left Pete and enrolled in the Open University in French and Business Studies; with her degree eventually achieved, she fought for more recognition at work. It had been a major coup for her to have been taken on the business trip to Paris, even though the senior colleagues had treated her like a bag-carrier throughout the whole day, ending with the final and supreme put-down at the airport bar, when they had decided that their hand luggage was too cumbersome to keep with them and had dispatched Veetie to take their bags to the Business Class lounge, clinking their whisky glasses as she made her embarrassed, over-burdened exit.

Although Veetie was disenchanted with her love life to date, she was far from the motivated career woman she now professed to be to her personnel department during her biannual appraisals. Secretly, she remained a home-loving romantic, still deeply wanting to believe in love at first sight. In the three years that had passed since she left Pete, she had been looking for her White-Knight-Mr-Right, and hoped that the simple act of looking might be enough to help her find him. If she'd had to sum up her first impressions of Rashid in three words, she would have said, Distinguished, Kind, Gallant. Everything that she was expecting of her White-Knight-Mr-Right. She looked at Rashid hopefully, wishing that she might catch his eye and start a conversation, but Rashid was unused to being the object of any sort of attention, least of all female attention, and didn't notice. So Veetie took a deep breath and, leaning forward, asked, 'Will you let me buy you a drink? It's the least I can do, for helping me, I mean.' She'd intended to hold out her hand and introduce herself, but Rashid looked up and looked shocked. Oh God, she thought, spotting the tomato juice at his side, perhaps he didn't drink, perhaps she'd mortally offended him. Or perhaps he didn't think that women should buy drinks for strange men at airports.

After what seemed an eternity, but was really just a moment, Rashid spoke. 'That's very kind, but the drinks in the lounge are free, you know. You don't have to buy them.'

Veetie felt heat rising back to her cheeks. 'I didn't realize,' she said apologetically, before admitting, 'I don't fly Business Class very often. In fact, I don't fly Business Class at all. This is my first time.' Rashid was charmed by Veetie's candour, her refreshing honesty, and looked at her properly, noticing her hesitant smile and her pink and white complexion heated by the delicate flush. With her blonde hair untidily falling out of what had been a neat chignon earlier in the day, she seemed really quite young. Remembering her comment at the front desk, he wondered who her obnoxious colleagues were, who had left this frail, pale English rose to carry their things while they rudely excluded her from their drinks gathering.

'But thank you very much for offering, Ms. . . .?'

At the polite prompt for her name, Veetie, who said she no longer believed in fate, made a choice that was to have consequences for the rest of her life. Perhaps, deep down, she knew that this moment was the belated beginning of her grown-up life, and that her long-standing childhood nickname, along with all the disappointments it represented, was no longer good enough for her. Whatever the reason, she made a break with her entire past, and rather than introduce herself as Veetie, chose to tell him her true name, the name with which she'd been christened. 'It's Verity, Miss Verity Trueman.'

On hearing her name, Rashid's head snapped up like someone who'd been slapped awake. His wide-open eyes looked clearly and deeply into Verity's as though scales had fallen from them, and the shining road ahead was suddenly clear. He looked at Verity and saw something more than her fragility, more than her timid smile and delicate complexion – he saw a glimpse of his future, and his fate. He saw the woman with whom he could finally fall in love.

'Ricky,' he said, after some effort. 'My name is Ricky. Ricky Karim, at your service.' The saying of his real name thrilled him, an affirmation of who he really was, and who he could be again. He held out his hand to Verity and she took it, aware that something magical had happened, but not knowing what had caused it.

'Miss Trueman, or Verity, if I may call you that? Would you like to get something to eat? I have a couple of hours until my flight, and I can help you with those bags.'

'That would be lovely,' said Verity breathlessly, feeling like Cinderella. She walked out of the lounge with Ricky in her cheap shoes, with her good, but over-stuffed bag, as though walking on air, as though saved. She even smiled at the stuffy BA staff, who looked at her with poorly concealed distaste, as though to sniff, 'Well, really.'

Ricky-Rashid had an unconscious Dickensian belief that the name unveiled the soul; no man named Uriah Heep would ever be a romantic hero, no boy named Twist could expect a straightforward life. And in Ricky-Rashid's book, that by which we call a rose would certainly not smell as sweet if it were called by a less fragrant name. Which is why he had so often longed to doff 'Rashid', his Indian name, the name that bound him to his duty, and to become Ricky once more. Ricky, the English gentleman and scholar, Ricky the Lionhearted, the powerful, for whom all the limitless opportunities and giddy potential of life was waiting. But he had defaulted, for many years, to being dull, limited Just Rashid – Rashid, meaning he who followed the right and narrow course, just another Indian accountant with a plump wife and pedestrian life. In Ricky-Rashid's experience, names meant something; after all, his child-bride Henna had lived up to her name in being a beautiful flower which had seemed fragrant in fresh youth, but whose touch had left him a marked man. He had named Shona Kiran to be his golden one, his little ray of sunshine, and so she had shone for him obediently in her childhood, creating the only bright spells in his dark, wooden life.

Ricky-Rashid realized that what had defined his life with these two women was their need to lie to him – reassuringly on Shona's part, brutally on Henna's, but always to lie. Lies had penned him in, and wrapped him in tangled webs he couldn't unravel. What he had always longed for was a life lived in truth, and all that was decent and true was what Verity Trueman represented. He felt he knew everything about her just by knowing her name. Ricky-Rashid knew at that moment that Fate had decided to be kind. He saw himself leading a different sort of life with a different sort of woman – a life beautiful in its frankness and openness. He would share everything with Verity, he would tell her everything she asked. But of course, she would never ask about his other wife, or his grown-up daughter, because she would never know that they existed.

Ricky-Rashid's double life began that day – a life that he split by his name. In England, he was Ricky, Verity's husband, a leading light in the local community and keen member of the tennis and cricket clubs, an enthusiastic gentleman and scholar, successful in his work, who lived life to the full, cheerfully tolerated his stuffy in-laws and was exasperatingly happy with his wife. In Bangladesh, he was Just Rashid, Henna's absentee henna-pecked husband, a rarely missed dullard who travelled a lot on business. Ricky would believe that all his time as Rashid, his twenty-five years of married life to Henna, had been illusory, his training ground, his purgatory, lightened only by the birth of his daughter. All that time, he had simply been waiting for his real life to begin. He had been waiting for Verity as long as she had been waiting for him, and she had finally arrived.

The Triumphant Return of Ricky the Conqueror

THE DAY AFTER Ricky met Verity Trueman and took her for supper at one of the least indifferent brasseries that Paris CDG had to offer, he went to his interview and performed with an urbane brilliance that he had not realized he still possessed. He was Ricky the Conqueror once more, the College Captain of Cricket and Captain of Men, with fire in his belly and a steely glint in his eye. Ricky realized how high the stakes were – getting the job meant a future in England with his own English rose, if she would have him.

The Global Head of Finance was impressed, and although he did not offer Ricky the job on the spot, made it clear that he thought Ricky was a very serious contender. He asked Ricky, off the record, whether his potential relocation might cause any problems, suggesting that he might need to discuss it with his family and would need a certain amount of time to organize the move.

'I can move here as quickly as you need me,' Ricky said without a flicker of doubt. 'My daughter already lives in England, she'd be delighted if I were to move here.'

'And your wife?' asked the Global Head of Finance, a touch indiscreetly.

'My wife and I are separated,' said Ricky firmly. 'I have no ties in Bangladesh.'

Satisfied, the Global Head of Finance suggested that Ricky meet the team of people he'd be working with, should he be successful. The next week, Ricky would receive a call in the Dhaka office; the job was his.

Ricky the Conqueror's next task, which he was to take on the very same day, was that of wooing his English rose, although he didn't think of her as a rose at all; roses were showy, bumptious, over-ripe and blowsy, and like sirens they tempted you with their scents towards a bed of thorns. No, Verity was more like a violet; pale and shy, as delicate as whimsy. You needed to tread around violets at your feet as carefully as you trod around the dreams you had laid out on your narrow path – Ricky knew from experience that the slightest false step could crush them.

Ricky had already started putting his old life aside for his new life, beginning by cutting short his afternoon reunion with his errant daughter in order to be free to take Verity to dinner. He had arranged to meet Shona after his interview, at the tea-shop-cum-sweet-shop in Tooting, where Parvez was still working. Ricky hadn't seen Shona in months, not since her unexpected elopement, but while they had their tea (made on Shona's specific instruction the way she knew her Papa liked it), instead of deploring her ill-advised marriage to a Pakistani pauper, instead of drinking in the sight of her and revelling in her warm and happy glow, instead of passing on all of Henna's instructions, he found himself looking at his watch. It was almost 5 p.m. In an hour, Verity was due to leave her office, but he hadn't yet called her to arrange where to meet. He had intended to call her earlier, but his interview had overrun and he had been coaxed into pressing flesh with his new colleagues.

'Is there something wrong, Papa?' asked Shona, disconcerted that for the last hour, her father hadn't shown even the slightest sign of telling her off or commenting on her betrayal, as though it was already swept under the carpet and forgotten. He had hugged her with an unnatural bonhomie on his arrival, congratulated her on her Finals result (a respectable 2.1), told her enthusiastically about his interview and completely failed to mention either her marriage or her husband, or even comment on Parvez's infuriating absence. Now he just seemed distracted. Perhaps it was all too much for him to take in after his long flight: her new life in England, coupled with her new conspicuous poverty, given away too easily by the downtrodden area in which they lived, and by the confusing subcontinental familiarity and tackiness of the Tooting tea shop in which her husband worked. And this despite her well-pressed English clothes with the trendy shoulder pads and her gleaming golden wedding ring. Perhaps he had arrived intending to tell her off, but now felt too sorry for her to say I Told You So. Was that why he was hiding behind this odd and uncharacteristic bravado? Shona wished she could have met him in town, perhaps at the

Ritz, but she would not have been able to afford the bill. She surreptitiously glanced at the clock on the wall behind the tea-shop counter; Parvez had better come back from that damn Cash & Carry soon – tardiness was no way to give a good impression to a father-in-law. Her father was fidgeting with his watch strap distractedly, and showed no signs of having heard her. She hoped he would relax over dinner, berate her and Parvez, and get it over and done with. Shona sipped her tea, and cleared her throat noisily to ensure her father's attention.

'Of course, you'll stay for dinner, Papa? You must meet Parvez, and you can see our flat, it's just round the corner, we redecorated it ourselves.' She was pleased that they had at least managed to move out of Bhai Hassan's spare room in time for her father's visit.

Ricky, who had been thinking about where he could take Verity for their date, looked up at his daughter's wide eyes and lied with a merciless readiness that surprised even him.

'Jaan, I was just thinking that I should head off soon. I have an early flight in the morning and I'm still jetlagged from yesterday. And the interview took a lot out of me. I'm sorry, I know it's been a long time.'

Shona nodded. This was the Papa she knew, tired, anxious and apologetic. He probably didn't want to see how she lived; it would upset him to see his daughter in a one-bedroom flat in this grimy part of London, however content and independent she professed herself to be. 'I suppose that I'll see you lots more in the UK if you get this job. Amma says you'll be travelling to and from here all the time. You can see the flat when you're next in town. Parvez will be sorry to have missed you.'

As Ricky went to leave, still looking at his watch, barely looking back at his daughter, Shona again misread his distraction for sorrow. She ran up to him and hugged him tightly at the doorway, protesting furiously, 'I'm very happy, Papa. Please don't think that I'm not. Parvez looks after me, I don't want for anything. I really couldn't be happier.'

Surprised by her vehemence, wondering what had brought it on, Ricky answered, 'I believe you, Jaan. I believe you are.' It made it easier for him to believe his daughter was happy and no longer needed anything from him, as it made it easier for him to ease himself away from her embrace and towards the phone box a safe distance away, knowing that on the other side of London, Verity was sitting listlessly in her office, waiting for his call.

Ricky eventually decided to take Verity for dinner at Rules off the Strand and, on seeing her discomfort, wished he'd chosen somewhere a little less stuffy. But once ensconced in a cosy booth, her boxy navy-blue jacket removed to reveal a pretty dress, the generous helpings and good wine helped her unwind. Verity found Ricky a disarmingly good listener, he seemed to hang on her every word, and she found herself opening like a flower, telling him about her past, about Pete and the one before who was just like Pete.

'I just wish I'd been less naive and stupid about it all. I'm almost thirty-eight, and I've wasted most of my life with people who didn't really care.' She looked at Ricky, who was nodding sympathetically, and apologized, 'Goodness, listen to me. You shouldn't let me go on so much. You haven't told me anything about you yet.'

'There's not much to tell,' said Ricky honestly, refilling her glass courteously. 'I had an arranged marriage when I was very young, which didn't work out. And I've been alone for a very long time. Too long, really. I'm forty-three, and I feel like I've wasted most of my life by not being with someone who cared, or whom I could care for.' Ricky smiled ruefully. 'I guess that's something we have in common.'

Verity's pale blue eyes widened, and she instinctively held her hand out across the table towards Ricky. He took it with great care, as though it was a fragile gift he'd been offered, before laying it back on the table underneath his own warm palm.

'Would you like coffee, Verity?' Ricky asked, seeing their officious waiter approach, and intercepting the request before the haughty tones of the waiter could put Verity back on her guard.

'No, thank you,' she answered, smiling nervously towards the waiter, withdrawing her hand discreetly to dab at her mouth with her napkin. Ricky nodded and asked for the bill, trying not to show his disappointment that Verity didn't want to extend their evening. Once the waiter had left, Verity, showing yet again that she had become the sort of woman who took things into her own hands, asked Ricky with a nervousness that even a gin and tonic and half a bottle of wine could not disguise, whether he might prefer to have that coffee back at her place.

'I know you've got an early flight tomorrow, so it's all right to say no. I was just thinking that we might not see each other for an awfully long time . . . that is, if you want to see me again. I can see how it might be difficult . . . with the distance, I mean.'

Ricky was seduced once more by her candour, by her laying herself on the line, awaiting his verdict, her wide-open eyes so used to being let down. It was like looking in a mirror. 'There is nothing I'd like better than to have a coffee with you at your place,' he said simply. He had only just found Verity, there was no way he was letting her go.

They took a cab to her little flat in Clapham, immaculately kept but with a cheerful splash of clutter in the spare room that reminded him of his own untidy study, and which made him feel instantly at home. He walked around the flat, looking at her books – romantic novels and Jane Austen – and her degree proudly displayed on the wall. He saw the photographs of her with her stern, horsey-looking parents, and of her on her horse, Brontë, that she kept at home. They had coffee and talked until the early hours, and this time Ricky did not need to present a flower, or to quote from a book of poetry, or to pounce manfully, to be able to hold his true love. He merely had to sit and wait, enjoying the rare pleasure of being himself. And when he finally had to leave, it was

Verity who kissed him, shyly turning up her head as she walked him to the door, and she tasted of bitter coffee, sweetened with brown sugar. A grown-up taste that he came to cherish above English tea.

Of Sunflowers and Sunny Side Ups

SHONA AND PARVEZ had been married for some time, and were perplexed as to why all their frequent and enjoyable lovemaking had not yet succeeded in bearing fruit. For the first few months, they had been philosophical, thinking perhaps they simply needed to be patient. The few months after that, while Parvez remained genial and relaxed, Shona became paranoid and tetchy. She had intended to put off continuing her studies for motherhood, and yet motherhood was stubbornly eluding her.

Convinced that it was their fault for being too naive and easy-going about the whole thing, she adopted a more businesslike approach to the matter of conception. She stood on her head after making love, and read voraciously on the best diets for them to follow. Parvez found the loving inedible messes that Shona used to produce in her attempts at home-cooking were replaced with unsalted, barely heated green leafy vegetables and steamed fish. His usual morning tea was switched for unappealing herbal alternatives, and his whisky bottle inexplicably banished. But Shona's enthusiastic efforts out of the bedroom were unfortunately not much more effective than their joint efforts within it. Every time her irregular menstruation began, she locked herself in the bathroom and cried secretly.

On one such occasion, Parvez had returned to the flat unexpectedly in the middle of the day to surprise Shona with some flowers, and heard muffled sobs through the bathroom door. He tried the door, but it was locked. 'Goldie, are you in there?' he asked unnecessarily, before asking the more pertinent question, 'Are you OK?'

He heard Shona blow her nose noisily, and answer in a tremulous voice that was intended to be stern, 'I'm fine. I'm just going to the loo. What are you doing back here?'

'I brought you a present, come out and see.'

'Just leave it somewhere, I'm going to be here a while. It's a woman thing.'

Parvez, nonplussed by this odd behaviour, stayed at the door. 'Are you sure you're OK – you don't sound it.'

'I said I'm fine – can't I get some damn privacy in my own bathroom?'

'I'm not leaving until I see that you're OK for myself. I'll be waiting in the living room.' Parvez tossed his flowers on the well-scrubbed kitchen table, annoyed that his gallant gesture had been circumvented, and, stalking to the sofa in the living room, sat down heavily.

Shona remained stubbornly in the bathroom and Parvez, watching the seconds and minutes tick by, eventually gave up. He went back to the bathroom, which opened off the back of the kitchen and, sighing, leaned his forehead against the door, the palm of his hand touching it. 'Goldie, I need to get back to work. Will you be all right?'

Shona had composed herself, and her voice sounded firm and almost cheerful, in an uncanny imitation of her father's false bonhomie the day he had visited, as she said, 'Of course, darling. There's no need to worry. It's just a stupid girl thing – sorry I'm taking so long.'

On the other side of the door, as she spoke to Parvez, Shona was mirroring him, her forehead leaning against the door, the palm of her hand flat against it, as though she could feel the heat of him through the white painted wood, trying to draw some solace from his closeness without having to let him near. She turned her face and looked at herself in the mirror above the sink, her eyes red, her face puffy and disfigured with tears, all its cheerful definition dissolved by her unhappiness. She was such a pitiful sight that her resolve almost weakened, and her fingers traced the door with yearning, willing herself to tell him the truth. It was too hard. Hearing Parvez finally walk away, she called out with the same firm, cheerful voice, 'I'll see you when you get back, thank you for the present, Puppy.'

When she was sure that Parvez was gone, Shona opened the door carefully and saw the golden sunflowers that he had left on the table. She picked them up and unaccountably held them to her nose even though she knew there would be no scent. She collapsed to the floor clutching them, letting the raw sobs tear wantonly through her body.

That evening Parvez came home to a smiling Stepford wife, wearing her pinny with pride as she cooked up a fish stew with yet more inedible vegetables, the flowers sunnily smiling from a vase at the centre of the table. She ran to the door and kissed him as he came in and Parvez, relieved that the mood was over, kissed her all the way back to the kitchen.

After dinner, Shona mentioned casually that she had picked up some leaflets from the local GP. She suggested they make an appointment. The surprise sunflower day was thus to mark the beginning of months and months of tests, in which Parvez's sperm was analysed and criticized, as were the contents of Shona's barren, non-ovulating womb.

'It's me,' Shona said to Parvez, over breakfast some months later. Having been persuaded by the gynaecologist to relax the restrictive diet she had previously forced Parvez to adopt, she had made his favourite dish the night before, lamb koftas, only slightly burnt this time, and maybe with just a bit too much garlic. Shona's cooking had not greatly improved, although Parvez was always uncomplaining and even complimentary at her efforts in the kitchen. As a result she had begun to think that her cooking was now quite acceptable, and for a special treat she gave him a couple of the less burnt koftas on the side of his fried eggs, with plenty of the juices from the pan to moisten his toast.

'Mmm, smells great, Goldie,' said Parvez insincerely, looking sorrowfully down at his quite acceptable sunny side ups ruined by the addition of burnt meatballs and black charcoal bits swimming in oily juice. 'I really don't think it's you, it's probably me.'

'It's me,' Shona disagreed stoutly, 'Look at my parents – they couldn't have any kids after me. I remember Mamma used to drag me off secretly to a clinic sometimes, but whatever they did, it didn't help. I must have inherited their infertility.'

'Well, if they were infertile, how did they have you?' Parvez asked.

'They were both very young, Mamma was only eighteen. Maybe they just got lucky.'

'Well, I was the one who got lucky, wasn't I,' said Parvez, reaching out to stroke Shona's forearm, so gently that the little hairs shivered under his palm. 'Really, Goldie, it's much more likely to be me. You're doing everything right. You eat like a Saint of Good Nourishment and they think you're responding to the medication. I'm the one with the lazy swimmers.'

'And I'm the one with the lazy ovaries.'

'If we're both that lazy, we should be spending a lot more time in bed. We could start after breakfast . . .' He traced an equally lazy line up Shona's arm to her bare shoulder, and back down again to her fingertips.

'It's not the right day yet – we have to hold off until

the day after tomorrow,' Shona said matter-of-factly, pouring herself another cup of decaffeinated tea.

'Arré, when did you get so businesslike . . .' Parvez said regretfully, returning his attention to breakfast. Realizing that there was no way he could avoid eating the koftas in front of Shona's watchful gaze, he made a manly attempt to spear some with his fried eggs.

'Puppy, if it doesn't work this time, what are we going to do about the next stage?' Shona asked delicately. She didn't need to say any more; if simply stimulating Shona's hitherto unproductive ovaries to ovulate didn't succeed, the next stage of assisted conception had a long waiting list, and after that there were only procedures which would most likely have to be done privately.

Parvez sighed and pushed his eggs away. 'I'll sort out something for us. I might be able to get a loan.' Shona didn't say anything in reply. There was no way he would get a loan; he had already taken one out to buy a share in the restaurant business across the road from the sweet shop, and it was all he could manage to pay the interest and the rent and their meagre housekeeping. Seeing her face, Parvez got up and walked round to her side of the table, kneeling at her side, and stroked the wedding ring on her hand. 'I promise, my Shundor Shona, that I'll work something out. I'd sell my soul to make you happy.'

Shona smiled a small hard smile, unconvinced by his expansive offer. Parvez squeezed her hand and, to lighten the mood, started one of their little in-jokes, delivering a corny chat-up line that usually made her laugh.

'Hey there, gorgeous, how do you like your eggs in the morning? Scrambled or Fried?'

'Unfertilized,' answered Shona automatically, although with little joy. She was already thinking how they might raise the money for private treatment and, not for the first time, she felt some resentment of their impoverished circumstances. She could perhaps sell her jewellery that had safely arrived from Bangladesh, but she didn't know how much it was worth, and it was all she had to pass on to her children, if they ever had any. If she was still at home her father would have been able to pay for all her treatment – but he was no longer responsible for her, and that had been her choice, not his. Perhaps she could remake that choice and ask him to take care of her once more in this one sensitive matter.

Shona thought about alternatives, but all roads and possibilities led back to one incontrovertible truth – her father was the only one who both could and would lend her the money for treatment; he was the only one who could help. She decided to visit her father's London apartment; she would go that very day.

A Glorious Spring Wedding for Verity Trueman

R ICKY AND VERITY accelerated their relationship in a manner that was viewed as positively unseemly and inappropriate by Verity's parents and friends. They advised her against getting involved too quickly with this foreign divorcé who, apart from being Asian, seemed too good to be true. Secretly they were jealous; Verity's poor life choices and unluckiness in love had always provided a secret, unworthy comfort to her nearest and dearest. Her parents had privately believed that their dowdy daughter would never get married, and although they had outwardly complained about still having her on their hands, they knew that this meant she would always need them. And her friends knew that whatever they did in life, they would never be as badly off as poor little Veetie, what with her horrible, feckless Pete, and the one before who was just like Pete; she made them all seem quite successful by comparison. So it was unthinkable that Verity, when she was quite beyond the age that anyone should reasonably expect to marry, was now in the throes of true love with an almost handsome, moderately successful, jet-setting businessman, who seemed to harbour only honourable intentions towards her.

The question that everyone asked, although no one asked out loud, was why would such a man choose Verity? Why would such a man, who could surely choose from many better-appointed contenders, choose a nervous, ageing administrator with a tremulous smile, whose youthful bloom had so clearly faded, leaving nothing to recommend her excepting a thinness of figure which was currently quite fashionable, and her English rose colouring? Perhaps it was because she was blonde – didn't Asian men always like blondes? They didn't understand the secret of Verity's innocent seduction, because they had never seen Ricky for the man he was before he met her; a man who had been unhappy for almost all his life. The secret was simple; with Verity, he saw the hope of happiness. That was all. That was enough.

Verity's family and friends actively made it their business to try and expose Ricky and find out the ulterior motive he might have for seeing their Veetie, persuading themselves they had only her best interests at heart. Ricky, aware of their suspicion, was acutely aware that they had good reason to be suspicious; he was still a married man, after all. He therefore went on an extraordinary charm offensive, wooing Verity's inner circle with the same enthusiasm with which he had wooed and won Verity's heart.

Invited to dinner back at Rules off the Strand, Gerry and Babs, Verity's horsey parents, found to their disappointment that their barbed comments that Ricky might be seeking a British passport failed to offend him or put him off. Instead he agreed with them that it was the first question he would ask any foreign adventurer intent on such a fair prize as their precious daughter, and reassured them that his corporation provided him with a flexible working visa for the UK and the markets with which he had to work, so that a British passport would prove neither necessary nor convenient. Looking across the table at their embarrassed daughter, whose earnest eyes silently pleaded, please like him, please don't chase him away, they found their stiffness melting, and even more so by the time they had got to the brandies that Ricky generously ordered. The third time Ricky asked them to dinner, it was to ask the permission of Gerry for his daughter's hand, and Gerry, touched despite himself at such old-fashioned good form, found he had neither the reason nor will to refuse. Shaking Ricky's hand, he surprised himself by hoping that Veetie didn't make a balls-up of this relationship like she had all the others.

Ricky's proposal to Verity, just a few months after they met, took her by surprise, as she had first taken him by surprise. Despite now having his own company flat in London, near the commuter station for his office in Slough, he often stayed at Verity's Clapham flat, sharing the bitter coffee that she brewed first thing in the morning before he left for his office or the airport, and last thing at night when he returned, taking her face between his hands to kiss her gently, as though she might break at his touch. One such evening he returned from a week's absence in Bangladesh and found Verity more nervous than usual, with no welcoming coffee brewed. She turned her face when he went to kiss her, and so he brushed his lips against her cheek and sat in the armchair opposite her, removing his tie. Ricky already understood Verity too well to be annoyed with her, or to suspect that this odd behaviour had anything to do with him.

'Is something wrong, Verity? Has something happened at work?' he asked gently, leaning forward. He often listened sympathetically to Verity's stories of mistreatment at the hands of her colleagues, and guessed that something had upset her. The sooner she found another job, the better. He had even started looking for openings in his own company that might interest her.

'Something's happened, Ricky. I've been dying to tell you for days, but I just couldn't tell you on the phone. To be honest, I've no idea how you'll take it. I hope you'll be OK with it.'

Ricky felt his heart sink; it was like his wedding night all over again, a sudden revelation that was about to break his happy idyll. Was his Verity ill? Or had she found someone else? He said nothing, and just looked at Verity, waiting dumbly for her to pronounce the sentence that would dash all his dreams. Verity took a deep breath, trying to control the quiver in her voice.

'I'm pregnant. I know you thought that you couldn't have children, and I thought it was too late for me. But there it is, I'm pregnant.' Looking at Ricky, whose mouth was wide open in shock, Verity lost the battle to stay calm and firm, and quickly pleaded, 'Ricky, please say something. Please tell me you're pleased.'

Ricky closed and opened his mouth, struggling to master himself, before managing to say, 'Verity, are you sure, are you absolutely sure?' Verity nodded dumbly, waiting for him to pronounce the sentence that would dash all her dreams. What if he didn't want the baby, what if he thought they were too old for children, what if he just wasn't ready to make this sort of commitment so early in their relationship? Five years ago, Pete had made her abort their child, saying he wasn't ready for children. She couldn't lose this one, she just couldn't. This was her last chance to have a child with someone she loved, maybe her last chance to have a child at all.

Ricky stood up, walked heavily over to the armchair where Verity was sitting and, kneeling down, put his arms around her waist and buried his head in her lap. Realizing he was crying, Verity started crying too, for herself, for him, for the baby. Imagine letting herself get knocked up at her age, like some stupid teenager. Everything had been going so well, and somehow she had managed to ruin things for them all. 'Oh, Ricky,' she said helplessly. Ricky looked up at her, his face wet with his tears.

'How can you ask me if I'm pleased? Verity, my darling Verity, we're going to have a baby, we're going to be a family.'

Having started to cry when she had feared the worst, now the worst was over, Verity found she simply couldn't stop. Ricky lifted himself onto one knee before her and, taking her hand, surprised them both by saying, 'Verity Felicity Trueman, I think you'd better marry me as soon as possible, and make me the happiest man on earth.'

Fighting to smile through her tears, Verity just sobbed and nodded, holding tightly on to Ricky's hand.

The engagement thus confirmed, Ricky truly was the happiest man on earth. Barely six months before, his daughter had eloped with a Pakistani, leaving him bereft and abandoned in his dark Dhaka house, with no one to love him and nothing to reflect upon except how his life had passed him by and how it was too late, much too late, to do anything about it. Now he had a job and a home in England, and a woman who both loved and needed him, who had agreed to marry him, and was about to bear his child. His real life had begun, and taken over the old life that he had doffed as quickly as he had doffed his old name. He was looking forward to his first English Christmas with Verity, and the only dark clouds on the horizon were the fortnightly trips back to Bangladesh, to keep up appearances with Henna.

Given the circumstances, Ricky did not think Verity would want a big wedding; it was his second marriage, there was an obvious reason to marry in haste and they were hardly of an age for meringue lace and orange blossom to be appropriate. He was thinking of a simple civil service at the Chelsea Registry Office, with confetti thrown on the steps outside, and then a champagne lunch for ten at the Ritz, just with Verity's immediate family, their witnesses, bridesmaids and best man, whoever that might be. He would wear his best suit, or perhaps hire a morning suit, and Verity would look charming in a pill-box hat and Chanel suit, beautifully tailored to hide the signs of a telltale bulge.

However, on meeting some of Verity's female friends, whom she had kept away from Ricky until the engage-ment in the sure knowledge that they would flirt with him and show him what he was missing by tying himself down to her, Ricky realized how much this wedding meant to Verity. Her friends, with their shiny lipsticked mouths, fashionably sprayed hair and talon nails, had all been married already, and said how pleased they were that it was finally little Veetie's turn. She had been a bridesmaid several times, and they had all but given up hope of her becoming a bride. As Verity smiled and nodded to her friends' questions, comments and suggestions for their wedding, Ricky saw that his quiet Verity had always dreamed of the day when she could walk up the aisle in a gleaming white dress and have her moment in the sun, for once the centre of attention. The day where she could prove to all her friends and family that she was quite as good as the rest of them, as she too had finally found someone to love her.

Ricky regretfully abandoned all thoughts of the pleas-ant little lunch for ten, and enthusiastically helped Verity plan their glorious spring wedding at her parents' village, with a cream satin dress embroidered with false pearls on the bodice, an organist to accompany her up the aisle of the pretty local church and a wedding breakfast for a hundred in a marquee on her parents' land. The hardest part for him was finding enough guests to fill his side of the church; he invited a good deal of his work colleagues, and his local cricket club and tennis partners. He surprised his boss by asking him to be his best man. He explained the lack of immediate family apologetically to Verity – his mother was too unwell to make the journey from Bangladesh, his brother Aziz was needed to look after her, and besides, they had never approved of him moving to England, so much so that they were all but estranged. 'So you see, Verity, you are my family; you're really all the family I have. And you're all the family I need,' he told her sincerely, and Verity was touched that she was enough to replace his mother and brother for him.

The wedding itself passed in a vivid blur for Ricky. Satisfied by how truly happy Verity looked and acted, his only regret was that his daughter wasn't there to participate. She was only thirty miles away in a poky flat in Tooting while he was sipping champagne in a flower-filled tent, with his new in-laws laughing at his jokes. He wished he could have invited her and then cast a magic spell so that she would forget all about it; in a funny way, he thought Shona would have been happy for him, on this day of all days. In a funny way, he thought she would have understood.

The Importance of Not Forgetting to Check Under the Bed

RICKY WAS BARELY back from his honeymoon in Florence when Shona called, quite out of the blue, to say that she needed to see him.

'Papa? Good, I'm glad you're in. I need to see you about something urgent, I'll be over in an hour.'

Ricky, who had only popped to the company flat to pick up some of his books, looked nervously around. It seemed to him to have every telltale sign of his double life on its neutral, uninhabited walls. 'No need to rush all the way here, Jaan. I'll come over to you. Did you want me to take something to Bangladesh for you? I can pick it up from your place.'

Shona didn't want to see her father in Tooting in case word got back to Parvez. She didn't want him to know anything about the meeting. 'No,' she said firmly, 'it's really best if I come over to you. I know where it is, I've looked it up in the *A–Z*. I'll see you soon, Papa. I'll bring you some food from here, some samosas and things . . .'

Ricky, reverting back to Just Rashid, lost the will to argue and let Shona have her way. Looking round the flat more closely, he decided he really didn't have too much to worry about. It was fortunate that he and Verity stayed here so little, he mainly used it as storage for his non-essential items, as Verity's flat was so tiny it could only just about fit his clothes, toiletries and work things. He then remembered with a cold shudder that Verity had offered to come over with him that morning to keep him company, not wishing to lose the easy intimacy of their honeymoon. Thank goodness he had urged her to stay in bed and relax. Imagine how it would have been to answer the phone to Shona with his pregnant wife in the room, his two worlds colliding down the wire. He would have had no idea how to have dealt with it; perhaps if it were to happen, he could simply speak to Shona in Bangla, so Verity wouldn't understand or suspect anything. But he never spoke Bangla to anyone, so that would seem suspicious in itself.

Shaking his head at the narrow escape, Ricky began methodically tidying away anything in the flat that he thought looked suspicious. The framed picture of Verity was taken down, wrapped lovingly in a tea towel and hidden in the bedroom drawer which held the spare bed linen. He replaced it with a shot of Henna and Shona which he had kept for just such an occasion. He inspected the bathroom for any feminine pots and potions and put them away; Verity kept a towelling robe hanging on the back of the bathroom door, which he removed and hung up in the wardrobe. The bedroom looked tidy and sterile, like a hotel room. The kitchen had very little in it, just some tea and coffee. It all seemed quite harmless. Satisfied, he popped out to buy some milk to make tea with.

He might take his daughter out for lunch somewhere, if she had the time. That would give her less time to inspect the flat. He wondered what the urgent matter was that she had to discuss, and why she wanted to come halfway across London to discuss it. Of course! She was doubtless having trouble with the Pakistani; that's why she didn't want to see him in Tooting. Well, he'd be as supportive as possible, and not tell her I Told You So; he knew from experience that life was too short to spend it tied to the wrong person.

Shortly after Shona was due to arrive, the phone rang again. She must have got lost and needed directions. Ricky picked up the phone. 'Hello, Jaan,' he said automatically.

'Darling it's me. Who's Jaan?' asked Verity with surprise.

'I knew it was you,' said Ricky, cursing himself for his stupid assumption. What was it he'd told his junior colleagues during a training seminar the other day? 'Never assume, ladies and gentlemen. A lesson as vital in business as it is in life. Remember what assume spells – "ass-u-me" – when you assume, you're making an ass out of both you and me.' They had all laughed respectfully at his little witticism – he was their boss after all. 'It just sort of means "Darling" in Urdu, I thought I'd surprise you.'

'Well, Caro Ricky, you certainly did,' laughed Verity with relief, pleased to have a chance to use the smattering of Italian she had picked up from the honeymoon. 'Are you going to be long? I thought I might make us some lunch.'

'I'm sorry, I am. My books are in a mess and I need to

sort them out to find the ones I'm looking for. I'll be back in a few hours.'

'Well, I can come to you and cook over there, if you like,' Verity offered sweetly. 'I said I didn't mind keeping you company.'

'No, I want you to stay home and rest,' said Ricky firmly, before adding jokily, 'We can't have you gadding about town in your condition.' Verity giggled and was about to say something, when the doorbell rang, followed by a sharp rap on the door. Shona had arrived.

Ricky stood stock-still, aware that his nightmare had occurred. His two spinning worlds on a collision course in this apartment, Verity on the phone, listening and wondering who was visiting, and Shona's knuckles descending to rap once more on the door, signalling the fatal impact. She had only to open her mouth, and call out, 'Papa,' and that would be the end of everything.

'Well, aren't you going to get that?' asked Verity.

'It's just a delivery for the man in the flat next door. He had to pop out, so I said I didn't mind getting it for him,' said Ricky with extraordinary presence of mind, skipping speedily as far out of the room as the phone cord would allow, so Shona wouldn't be able to hear him through the door. 'I'd better go and sign for it. I'll see you later, Verity darling.' Just as he hung up the phone, Shona's voice called out, ringing clearly through the whole flat, 'Papa? Papa! Are you there?'

Ricky took a deep breath, composing himself before opening the door. 'Sorry Jaan, I was on the phone,' he apologized.

'Was it Amma?' asked Shona, kissing him on his cheek and walking in to survey the apartment with daughterly interest. 'This is a nice place. Lots of space just for you, though. You must rattle around in here.' Oh God, thought Ricky. She's left the Pakistani and wants to move in with me. Attempting to change the subject from that of his apartment's spaciousness, he just said, 'No, it wasn't your Amma. She never calls me when I'm away on business.'

'Well, London isn't exactly away on business, is it?' pointed out Shona. 'Amma says you practically live here five days a week.' Ricky shrugged in acknowledgement; in fact, he only went back to Bangladesh every fortnight, and then just for a couple of days. However, it didn't surprise him that Henna had not remarked upon his lengthy absences; she probably hadn't even noticed, as she was just concerned with the keeping up of appearances, too. He had become vaguely aware, on his last visit, that Henna and his little brother appeared to have widened the personal interests that they were pursuing beyond Henna's amateur dramatics, and were now spending an unseemly amount of time with each other. The revelation had filled him with nothing so much as relief – if they were busy flirting they would have less time to suspect him of any untoward behaviour.

Shona inspected the untidy boxes of books in the middle of the living room. She recognized some of her father's favourite volumes and cherished first editions. 'Goodness, Papa! What are all these doing here? Won't you miss having them at home?' When she lived at home, she remembered how her father would shut himself away in the cheerful untidiness of his office, his little haven to which her mother, Nanu, uncle and the servants never sought entry; and away from the disconcerting hubbub of the household, he would sit with just his books for company. His books were his comfort in Dhaka – they were his best friends, his companions.

Ricky wished his daughter was as unobservant as her mother. He shrugged his shoulders casually. 'Well, you know what your Nanu is like. I asked for a few books, and she had Musharaf bundle up the whole lot of them and send them over. I was just sorting them out.'

'Are you going to send them back, then?' asked Shona, nodding with understanding. Her grandmother had no interest in her son's books, and would be very likely to ask her old retainer to send them all, rather than go to the trouble of picking out a selected few.

'Well, I thought about it, but it's such a needless expense. I may as well keep them here and take them back as I need them. And besides, it's nice to have them here in the evenings. And I read a lot on the plane,' Ricky added uncomfortably, before again attempting to distract Shona from his discomfort. 'Would you like some tea, Jaan?'

'I'd love some, thank you,' replied Shona, wondering why her father seemed so ill at ease. Seating herself on the sofa, she picked up his favourite leather-bound collection of Shakespeare's tragedies, and looked searchingly towards Ricky who was busying himself in the kitchen, with dawning comprehension. If her father had decided to keep his books here, he must really have started to think of London as home. But if this was where he was living, where did that leave his relationship with her mother? She wondered if her father had heard what some gossips were saying about her mother and uncle, and had decided to stay away on purpose. Her poor father. Chased away from his own family home by the unkind, unfounded words of busybodies; no wonder he had sought refuge in England, the place of his happy bachelor days. But this flat was no refuge, it was certainly no home from home; grand though it was in dimensions, it was severely lacking in character and comforts – the only personal feature was the photo of her and Amma on the mantelpiece, and even this had a somewhat wistful air, as though harking back to a past life.

She followed Ricky into the kitchen, marvelling at its gleaming state of disuse – the enamel hob looked like it had never been cooked on. Opening the fridge to deposit her gift of samosas and bhajis, she noticed that it was empty, apart from a pint of milk. Of course, her father couldn't cook for himself. She guessed he ate out most nights, or perhaps ate at work.

'This place needs a woman's touch, Papa. It's like a hotel room, it's so impersonal. Do you want me to come round and decorate it for you?'

Ricky smiled at the genuine concern in his daughter's voice. 'It's company property, so I can't do too much to it. It's fine, I like it.'

'Still, it's no way to live. I could make it cosier for you. Bring some flowers, some nice cushions and candles. Help you put out your books. I could even come round and cook for you the odd night. I've become quite a good cook now – Parvez loves my koftas.'

Ricky remembered why his daughter was here in the

first place and sighed. She clearly wanted to stay with him. 'That's very kind of you, Jaan, but really, there's no need.' Picking up the tea tray on which he had carefully laid a pot of tea, the sugar bowl and the milk jug, he walked through to the sitting room. There seemed little point in putting off the inevitable, so as he sat down, he raised the subject of the Pakistani with fatherly concern. 'So how is young Parvez? I'm glad you're feeding him well.'

Instead of responding with the anticipated barrage of complaints about her husband, Shona surprised her father with her warm and effusive reply. 'Parvez is wonderful. He's got a great business head; he's already bought part of a restaurant across the street. He's managing that as well as the tea shop now – he works so hard he hardly has a spare minute. He barely plays his music any more – you remember how he used to love his music? All he does is think about us and our future.'

Ricky was confused. This didn't seem to add up at all. If Shona was happy with the Pakistani, then why was she here? Had she heard rumours about her mother's insensitive flirtation with hapless Aziz? Pouring the tea with a delicate splash of milk, he passed a teacup to his daughter. 'Thanks, Papa,' she said and, reaching for the sugar, noticed something odd. 'Papa, the sugar's brown.'

'Sorry, Jaan, I know. It's all I have.'

'But why brown?' Shona asked. Her father had never had brown sugar in his life, as far as she was aware.

'I have it with coffee, in the mornings sometimes.' Coffee? Shona raised her eyebrows, and Ricky felt obliged to explain himself. 'I've discovered that coffee is better at keeping me awake if I've had a long flight, or have a long day ahead. They drink a lot of coffee at work here in England. Sometimes you can't even get tea. I guess I've just got used to it now. Coffee, I mean.'

At this uncharacteristic gabble Shona realized that her father was lying to her, but she had no idea why he would lie about something as inconsequential as coffee and brown sugar. Deciding not to let herself get distracted by her papa's strange behaviour, she bravely plunged into the reason for her visit. 'Papa, I need to ask you for something. Parvez would be furious if he knew that I was asking this, that's why I had to come here.' Ricky waited, on tenterhooks, saying nothing. 'I'm going to need you to lend me some money. In fact, give me some money. It's very important.'

Ricky tried to stop himself sighing with relief. How obvious it was, and how dense he'd been. His daughter, living in poverty in south London after her ill-advised love marriage, had something urgent to ask him – of course, it was just to ask for some cash. It was so simple, and so easily resolved. He could wave his pen like a magic wand over his cheque book, and make all his and her troubles go away with one magnanimous gesture.

'Of course, Jaan. How much do you need, say about £500?' Doubtless she needed the money for some unexpected repair, or to replace one of the old appliances in her kitchen.

Shona took a deep breath. 'No, Papa, I think more like £15,000. Maybe even more.'

Ricky almost dropped his teacup. 'Shona, are you in trouble? Is Parvez in trouble with his loan?' He'd heard stories about these south London loan sharks, getting people into debt and charging outrageous interest. But how could they be so much in debt so soon? They'd not even been in England for a year. Shona realized instantly what her father was thinking, and reassured him quickly.

'No, Papa, no. It's nothing like that. It's for something private, something medical.'

'But are you ill, Jaan?' asked Ricky with concern, looking at Shona critically. She had never looked healthier, but these women's things sometimes didn't show.

'No, Papa, I'm not ill. Neither is Parvez. But I do need the money. Please don't ask me to explain why.'

'Jaan, that's a lot of money, I'll have to talk to your mother about it.' Ricky was thinking about the wedding and honeymoon that he had already paid for, and the plans that he had to buy a house with Verity. He had done a great deal of creative accounting so that Henna would not suspect the enormous sums he was siphoning off his salary each month; fortunately, an increase in his salary had ensured he could continue sending an acceptable sum back to Bangladesh.

'Papa, please. I don't want Amma to know. I don't want anyone to know. It's cost me a lot to even come and ask you, but I have no one else to go to.' Shona put down her teacup, looking almost tearful. 'Please think about it, Papa. You're my last hope.' Dabbing at her eyes, she got up and asked where the bathroom was.

'The bathroom's ensuite, through the bedroom,' said Ricky distractedly.

Shona walked swiftly through to the bathroom where, after locking the door, she put down the toilet seat and sat on top of it. If she gave her father a little time by himself, thinking that she was crying in the bathroom, he would hopefully be more likely to capitulate to her outrageous request.

Looking around, she saw that there was toothpaste in the bathroom, but no toothbrush. Doubtless her father was keeping it in his toiletry bag, as though he was living in a hotel and was expected to pack up at a moment's notice. All his clothes were probably still neatly folded in his suitcase. Wandering back through the very neat, bare bedroom, she wondered where his suitcase was; it wasn't on top of the wardrobe or anywhere obvious. Opening the wardrobe, she saw no luggage there, either, just a solitary cream towelling robe hanging up, looking rather lonely. Something was wrong, very wrong indeed. If her father was no longer living in Bangladesh, he must be living here. But where were all his clothes? Feeling a touch guilty, she gently pulled open one of the drawers. It was empty apart from bed linen. The rest of the drawers were empty altogether. There must be some explanation. Of course, the suitcase was under the bed! Dropping to her knees, she looked underneath and saw no suitcase at all. Instead, she saw a pair of cream bedroom slippers, with pretty stitching on them. She realized that they matched the towelling robe in the wardrobe. Shona's mind ticked over rapidly. Coffee and brown sugar. The bare, uninhabited flat. The unexplained absence of both toothbrush and suitcase. The inexplicable presence of both towelling robe and pretty cream slippers. Ladies' slippers. Her father wasn't living here, after all. He was, very possibly, living with a lady who wore size 6 shoes, who liked coffee and brown sugar.

Going back to the living room, after rubbing at her eyes to make them red and tender-looking, Shona sat down silently opposite her father. Ricky asked gently, 'Shona, Jaan. This is clearly very important to you. But how do you think I'm going to be able to hide spending £15,000 from your mother?'

Shona looked straight at him. 'Papa, you're an accountant. And you're a very good accountant. I know you can hide spending £15,000 from Amma.' She glanced downwards, before giving an almost imperceptible nod towards the bedroom. 'You can hide all sorts of things, if you want to.' She added significantly, reassuringly, 'We both can.'

Ricky realized instantly that Shona knew. He didn't know how she knew, but she did. He also knew that she wouldn't tell. Her eyes made a promise to him, Keep My Secret, and I'll Keep Yours. The fatal impact he feared would never happen and their family would remain safe in ignorance, held together by the close-knit embrace of their lies. Shona reached for his hand and squeezed it. 'Papa?' she said questioningly. Ricky nodded slowly, and squeezed her hand back. They had made a deal, and shaken on it.

'Can I take you out for lunch, Jaan?' Ricky said, with a rueful smile. His clever, observant daughter. She was wasted on her mother, wasted on that Pakistani. Wasted on him, even.

'That would be lovely, Papa. But just a quick one. I need to get back before Parvez misses me.'

Ricky picked up Shona's coat and helped her into it

with instinctive courtesy, the natural gentleman. The phone started ringing as they left the flat, and they glanced at each other only for a moment before tacitly agreeing to ignore it.

The Middle-Naming of the Sons of
Parvez and Shona Khan

AFTER THE INVASIVENESS and discomfort of the fertility treatment, when Shona's pregnancy was finally confirmed, she was too overjoyed to believe it. Although constantly sick right from the beginning, and gaining weight at an alarming rate, she superstitiously insisted that she and Parvez not celebrate, or even tell anyone, until she had her first scan. The scan showed the pregnancy was well established, and revealed the reason for Shona's unseemly size and unusual level of sickness – there were two heartbeats instead of one. They were having twins.

After they left the hospital, Parvez picked Shona up and gleefully swung her around. 'Goldie – we've hit the jackpot! It's like these bloody London buses. You wait years for a baby and then two come along at once! Instant families!'

'Parvez, put me down!' protested Shona firmly. 'Think about the babies.'

Surprised by the unexpected solemnness in her tone that replaced her usual flirtatious banter, and even more so by the alien sound of his real name from her lips, Parvez put her down immediately. 'What are you first-naming me for?' he asked reproachfully. 'You only call me Parvez when you're upset with me. Aren't you excited, Goldie?'

'I'm sorry, Puppy,' Shona said appeasingly. 'Of course I'm excited. They're my children, too. It's just that we have to be careful now – we're so lucky that we conceived, I don't want anything to harm them.' Parvez was pouting, and she added, to mollify him, 'Besides, I'll need to get used to calling you Parvez when the babies come along. We can't have them thinking that your name is Puppy. They should learn to call you Baba.'

'Why Baba?' complained Parvez peevishly. 'It sounds like a cartoon elephant. Baba indeed! You don't even call your own father Baba. And it's not as if I'm even Bangla-deshi,' Parvez said.

'Well, Abbu then,' said Shona. 'They can call you Abbu like good little Pakistani boys.'

'I don't want good little boys,' retorted Parvez, his voice softening as he added, 'I want good little golden girls who'll look just like their Amma.' He traced Shona's jawline. 'The prettiest Amma in the world,' he whispered, kissing her.

'I'm pretty sure that they'll look more like you,' Shona said after their kiss. 'You have stronger genes.'

However, when the boys were born, tiny and perfect, in a south London hospital, Parvez couldn't see himself in them at all. Sitting quietly with Shona some hours after the terror and excitement of the birth, he found himself inspecting them critically. They were so pale, paler even than Shona, with the milky whiteness that the Karim clan had. They looked like milky-faced Karims through and through. Shona, holding the little aliens, looked up at Parvez's handsome, confused face, willing him to keep hold of the thrilled reaction he had when the first bloody baby had emerged, willing him to feel the paternal pride in their shared achievement. 'This one has your eyes, I think,' she said, passing their first-born to him.

'But his eyes are blue, Goldie,' replied Parvez, holding his child gingerly. He instantly regretted his prosaic comment; out loud it sounded almost petulant.

'All babies' eyes are blue, Puppy. But he will have your eyes, I can tell,' Shona said firmly. 'And this one has your nose,' she added, brushing her lips against the tiny forehead of the child that lay in her arms.

Parvez saw this tiny, delicate gesture and realized what was wrong, and why his reaction to these tiny longed-for miracles was now so muted. Since Shona had first come to Pakistan for her studies, he had suffered no other competition for her affections; no one else had ever come close. Her father seemed to love her, but despite living near her in London, had kept a distance that was so respectful of their privacy that it bordered on the disinterested. And as for her mother – Parvez had no time for Shona's self-seeking, self-interested mother. She had deigned to visit them just once during the whole of Shona's difficult, uncomfortable pregnancy, during which she had sniffed at their surroundings, criticized their home and put the fear of God in Shona about the actual birth by telling her how her maternal grandmother had bled to death. Henna had proceeded to spend the rest of her trip shopping in town, buying the Burberry raincoat that absent-minded Just Rashid had so far forgotten to get her, despite her repeated requests. No, Shona had no one apart from Parvez, and Parvez had no one apart from Shona, his Bhai Hassan notwithstanding. It was just the two of them, Shona and Parvez, Goldie and Puppy, against the world.

But suddenly, in the last six hours, the children had stopped being part of Shona and had become their own independent, crying, breathing persons; two little people that Shona would love just as much as him – in fact, more than him, as they were two, and he was only one. And they were her creation – she had made them with almost no help from him; he had simply accompanied her to the fertility clinic a few times, and masturbated into a tube. Every other visit and painful medical procedure, Shona had handled alone, while he went to work and continued building up the business. He was no longer the only man in Shona's life – now he had competition. He was already jealous of Shona's children.

Grateful that Shona hadn't realized the unworthy thoughts muddling his head, Parvez squeezed himself a bit closer to Shona on her hospital bed. The baby in his arms squirmed a little, and then settled with a yawn. 'What shall we call them?' he asked Shona. She smiled benignly; they had discussed lots of names, some family ones, some silly ones, but had agreed to make no decisions until they were born.

'I think we should name them both after you.'

'Parvez 1 and Parvez 2? Like Thing 1 and Thing 2 in Dr Seuss? I like that.'

'No, I think we should call them Omar and Sharif. After their daddy with the movie-star looks,' she said sweetly, without any hint of sarcasm.

'They'll never forgive us, Goldie,' laughed Parvez, pleased despite himself. 'Ouf!' he said, as, disturbed from his brief slumber, Sharif grabbed his finger with a healthy grip. 'This one's strong, let's call him Samson instead.'

'I think that's Jewish,' Shona said vaguely. 'Let's stick with Omar Sharif.'

'Those can be their middle names,' suggested Parvez. 'Why don't we call one after your Baba, and the other after my Abbu?'

'I think Papa would like that,' Shona agreed. 'Rashid Omar Khan and Khalid Sharif Khan,' she tried musingly. 'Those seem such big names for such little boys.'

'They'll grow into them,' Parvez said.

But they never did grow into them. They were called by their middle names throughout infancy by unthinking habit, one of Parvez and Shona's silly, long-running jokes, like their own pseudonyms of Puppy and Goldie. Once they got older, whenever their father or mother called them by their formal first names, on rare occasions when propriety or sternness demanded, the boys replied reproachfully, with the woeful puppy-dog look copied from their father, 'What are you first-naming me for?' As though they were being unfairly told off for something they hadn't done.

The Married Life of Ricky Karim and Verity Trueman

RICKY AND VERITY had their first argument shortly after their wedding and, predictably enough, it was about names. Ricky came back late one evening from the airport and, on drowsily entering the tiny Clapham flat, was surprised to see that Verity was not only still awake, but sitting at the table, surrounded by forms and paperwork.

'Hello, darling,' she said brightly, on seeing him hesitating at the door. 'Would you like some coffee? I've just put on a new pot. It's decaffeinated.'

'Verity, darling,' said Ricky, crossing the room to kiss her. 'You must make sure you get enough rest, it's not good for the baby. What on earth are you doing up at this ungodly hour? It must be close to midnight.' He checked his watch, 'In fact it's one in the morning; that cab must have taken me round the houses.'

'I couldn't sleep. I was lying awake waiting for you to come back, when I realized that I've been married for over four weeks, and no one would even guess it. I went into a shop yesterday and I paid for some groceries with a cheque, and they called me "Miss", not "Madam". Here I am, practically forty, married and pregnant, and I'm still getting called Miss! And you want to know why?'

Ricky sat down and took off his tie and jacket. 'Well, you're not forty yet, and you certainly look nothing near it. And they might not have seen your wedding ring. And you're not really showing very much yet. You're so slim normally that the extra weight looks like nothing. You could hardly see a thing even in your wedding dress; all the guests who didn't know you were pregnant kept saying how lovely you looked now that you'd gained a few curves.'

Verity acknowledged the compliment and patted Ricky's hand, but said almost sternly, 'It's not because of any of those things, darling. It's because my cheque book said Miss Verity Trueman. What else are people going to think?' So I've decided to write to everyone: the passport office, the driving licence people, the banks, everyone, and get them to change my name to Mrs Verity Karim. I really should have done it weeks ago, but we were so busy with the wedding, and the honeymoon and . . .'

Ricky surprised them both by interrupting Verity vehemently. 'No! Verity, I'm putting my foot down. I absolutely forbid it!'

'But forbid what, darling?' asked Verity, confused.

'You changing your name. You have a perfect name. You should absolutely never change it. Your name is beautiful and wonderful, and it's staying the same.'

'But Ricky, darling. Everyone I know changes their name when they get married, it's practically odd not to.'

'Well, then, let's be odd. Your name is important to me – it stands for everything I love about you.'

'But Ricky, I want to change it. Don't you understand? I want to be Mrs Verity Karim. I want the world to know. Don't you?'

'Verity,' Ricky said heatedly, 'I don't want you changing your name. I wouldn't have married you if I thought that you'd be changing it.'

'Ricky, that's just cruel!' said Verity, her lip trembling. 'How can you say you wouldn't have married me . . . It's only my name I want to change, it's not me . . .' Blinking back tears, she ran to the kitchen.

Ricky realized he had gone too far, and went after her. 'Verity, I'm sorry, I'm tired. I didn't mean to upset you. You just took me by surprise. We'd never even discussed you changing your name.'

Verity had been dabbing her eyes ineffectively with coarse kitchen towel, which she put down quickly when Ricky came in, busying herself instead with the coffee percolator. 'I'm not upset,' she said bravely, her eyes still wet with the tears she hadn't managed to wipe away. 'I just came in to get the coffee.'

'Here, let me do that,' said Ricky appeasingly, and taking the steaming pot of coffee off the plate, poured out two cups, stirring in the brown sugar; he brought them through to the sitting room.

Verity sat down heavily beside him on the sofa, her face messy with sudden unhappiness. She nursed her hot coffee for a moment, and then said quietly, with a gentle hiccup, 'Don't you want people to know I'm your wife?'

'Darling, of course I do!' said Ricky. 'We haven't done anything in secret – we had an enormous wedding in your parents' village and announced it to the world.' Lightening the mood had never been his strong point, but he joked feebly, 'We'll get the wedding shots back from the photographer soon, in case you don't remember.'

Verity hiccupped sadly again, 'I don't mean the people at the wedding. I mean your people. Your family. Why haven't I met your brother, or your sister-in-law, or your mum? Or any of the people from Bangladesh that you see when you're here? Don't you want them to know that you married an English girl?'

Ricky paused for a moment, wondering what sister-in-law she could be talking about. Then he remembered that he had once let slip to Verity about Henna's presence in the house back in Bangladesh, and had passed her off as Aziz's wife, which didn't seem quite like lying. Buying a bit of time, he reached over to his jacket and pulled out some of the dark bitter mints that Verity liked; he had bought them at the airport while waiting for his plane home. Setting them on the table between their coffee cups, he took Verity's hand firmly. 'Darling, I meant what I said before. You're my family. Those other people mean very little to me, and I mean very little to them. Even my own Ammie makes it very clear that she prefers not to have me around, she would rather have Aziz and her daughter-in-law, and so that's what she's got.' So far, so true. He took a surreptitious breath and, looking frankly into Verity's eyes, prepared to lie to reassure her. 'And of course they all know about you. It's me they disapprove of, not you. They didn't like me before, for not managing the farms and being a dutiful son and heir. And now I've gone and married an English girl in an English church, hardly the act of a good Muslim.'

Verity sniffed, not quite appeased, and said, 'I just don't want to be excluded from your world. I've been left out enough in my life as it is.'

Ricky answered, sincerely, 'I don't want you to feel that you're excluded from my world. You can't be, you and the baby are my world.' Seeing Verity's eyes lift towards him, shining with hope and happiness, he made a decision, and committed to it so quickly that he surprised himself with his resolve. 'If it'll make you happier, I'll only go back to Bangladesh every month, or less if I can manage it, and only for an overnight stay at most, just to check on the lands and that Ammie's still kicking and complaining. And I'll stop seeing the people who turn up from Bangladesh – I only meet up with them out of politeness anyway.' He thought with a fleeting, genuine sorrow about Shona – the imaginary visitors from Bangladesh were almost always an excuse which would allow him to see her occasionally; he would have to try and see her during working hours now. Besides, Shona didn't need him; she had his money for whatever secret she had planned; she had her husband and her life in Tooting. She was more of an exile from the family than even he was.

Verity nodded, her tears almost dried up, and was even able to give Ricky a tremulous smile. 'That would make me happier. But I still don't understand. You'll share your life with me, but not your name.'

Ricky had an idea. 'Why don't we share our names, Verity? If it means so much to you to take my name, I'll take yours, too. What do you think? Mr and Mrs True-man-Karim?'

Verity was astounded. 'You'll take my name, too? I mean, you don't mind? On your passport and everything?'

'What?' said Ricky, this time his attempt at humour judged a bit more accurately. 'Don't you like the idea? You mean you'll share your life with me, but not your name?'

'Oh, Ricky,' said Verity, hugging him with sudden delight. 'You do love me! You do want the world to know about us.'

In the congenial coffee-scented embrace that followed, in those early hours of the morning, while Ricky fed Verity her favourite bitter-mint chocolates, he reflected that spinning a lie was like spinning smooth threads of chocolate; it melted in the mouth sweetly, and made everything so much more palatable. He had no intention of changing all his paperwork – he would keep a separate set for his different lives; his Bangladeshi passport would remain the same, but the British passport which he could apply for now that he and Verity were married would carry his new, married name.

The second disagreement that Ricky and Verity had was also about names. This time it was about the name of their child – a wonderful long-limbed little girl with pale, creamy skin and lustrous chestnut hair. Ricky, predictably, wanted to name her Verity, but this time Verity put her foot down with a new confidence that motherhood had imposed, and quashed the argument before it could begin. 'Really, darling. Nothing could be sillier. Neither of us will know who you're talking to when you call us. And Verity doesn't have a nice short version. Everyone called me Veetie for years; they're still doing it now. You don't want to wish that on our child, do you?'

Ricky thought of Verity's unprepossessing parents bellowing 'Veetie' at his little girl, as though her fate would already be sealed to emulate the unhappy early adulthood of her mother and, shuddering at the idea, capitulated. 'No, I wouldn't, darling. You're right, as always.' He paused a moment. He had another suggestion that had come from seeing Verity's French books while they were being unpacked in their new home counties house near his Slough office. A slim volume by Voltaire had caught his attention and given him an idea. 'Had you ever thought about Candida? Like Candide, only for a girl. I think it's a lovely name – it means truthful, honest, sincere, forthright. Lots of good things, a bit like Verity, only different.'

'Candida . . .' mused Verity, trying it out. 'Candida, Candy, Dida, Didi . . .' Holding their little daughter in her arms, she spoke softly to her, 'Candida? Are you a Candida, little one?' She looked up at Ricky. 'I think it's a lovely name, darling. And it shortens so nicely, doesn't it? Who could ever be cruel to a little girl called Candy or Didi?'

Ricky took Verity's face between his hands, looking at her wide-open blue eyes and the faint blush on her cheek. He kissed her carefully on her forehead, on the bridge of her nose and on her thin, soft lips. 'I don't think we'll need to abbreviate. No one will ever be cruel to our little girl,' he promised Verity.

He wasn't to know that, in twenty years or so, their little girl would meet a notorious heartbreaker, the lead singer of a band with a cult following, who paid his rent by occasionally waiting tables in his father's restaurant.

The Musical Memories of Sharif Khan

MUSIC IS MY memory. If I were to tell you when my life began, when our story began, I wouldn't start with our birth in a south London hospital, or my mother's birth on a Bengali birthing stool at her maternal grand-father's house. I would tell you when I first had the sensation of being alive; the first time I heard the cha-cha-cha, the ay-yi-yi, the wails, grunts, groans and mournful sighs of discharged love – the first time I heard song.

And if I were to tell you when I first started living, it would be when we started to control that cha-cha-cha for ourselves – with the beat-beat-beats and the explosion of words and melodies in our mouths. It was when we started the band, in the flat above my dad's restaurant.

Our parents were a local success story. My father had gambled on getting a loan to buy a share in a restaurant, and eventually took it over, moving us to the two-bed flat above it when we were toddlers. By the time we were teenagers he had opened a second restaurant, further up the Northern Line at Balham, cunningly buying it with a long lease before the first signs of gentrification appeared in the area. We abandoned the honking, tooting traffic of the flat on the Broadway, as my dad did well enough to buy Amma and us a nice family house on the Heaver Estate in Tooting Bec, one of the most respectable addresses in Tooting. Again, he bought it before the prices rocketed.

While my father was the business success of his family, my mother was the academic success of hers. Once we were at school, she followed us, returning to school herself. She took an MA in modern languages, and then a teaching qualification. She didn't teach in our school, but in a private girls' school in Wandsworth. She spoke to us in English as pure as that of the chilled angels frozen on any dreaming spire; she chose not to speak to us in any other language as we were growing up, and insisted sweetly that our father didn't either. Her intention was to avoid us having foreign accents that might set us below our fellow pupils – she wanted us to have accents that would set us apart, English accents as crisp and stiff as architecture, that would carve the way for us in our future endeavours. When we eventually learned our father's native language, we spoke it like the firangis we had become. We were never taught our mother's Bangladeshi; we only heard her speak it on the phone to her own mother. On the occasional family trips to Dhaka, never more frequent than every other year, we were like deaf and dumb aliens, trapped in our bubble of well-spoken English.

But everyone believed that our parents were successful for another reason, a deeper reason than their business and academic prowess, than their fight from an unprepossessing start as penniless immigrants back into the middle classes from which they had originally hailed in their native lands. They were successful, because they were The Couple That Were In Love. Everyone saw it, everyone knew it. From the moment of their romantic elopement to London, to their walking down the Tooting streets with our double buggy, hands instinctively intertwined, only letting go when Omar or I started to cry.

We don't know when it started to go wrong. Maybe, just as our early toddler tears forced their hands apart, as we grew up, we forced their hearts apart, too. Perhaps we drained the love from them, taking it for ourselves so they no longer had enough for each other. Drawing love out of them, as poison from a wound, taking away the dizzy giddiness of love, and leaving them clear-headed, empty and cold.

They used to sit together in companionable silence, in a loose embrace on the sofa, her legs sprawled across his lap while Abbu listened to his music or fiddled with his sitar, and Amma marked her papers or read her French novels. Sometimes they would delight us with their silliness, a childish silliness that could have been put on for us as a show, but more likely was simply for themselves alone and we just the fortunate spectators. A new Indian pop song would come on the radio, and Abbu, who had never lost his Punjabi accent, would leap up and swing Amma around, oblivious to the customers eating below our flock-carpeted feet, dancing and singing along. '*Ilu*,

Ilu!' he'd bellow tunefully, and with a comic waggle of his head, and pressing his heart, would finish the chorus, '*Ilu, Ilu!* means I love you, I lah-uv yo-ou!' As we clapped along, Amma would only mock protest and giggle with pleasure, her papers and books forgotten. They were just in their early thirties and, despite being parents, could at times still look like the young lovers they had been when they first met.

But as the years went by, those incidents became more and more rare and the loose embrace on the couch less and less common. They still held hands when they walked, but it was now a gesture of habit rather than affection. They only seemed to hold each other in their sleep, and for this reason more than any other, Omar and I used to get up out of our beds in the mornings and join them in theirs, clinging to either side of them while they clung to each other, to share that moment of instinctive intimacy before it dissolved with the consciousness that came with the morning light. 'My men,' Amma would say, as she woke sleepily and looked at us; but somehow we already knew that Abbu was being excluded from that seemingly inclusive term. Abbu spent more and more time with his business colleagues, with his music; Amma came back later and later from work, and spent more time with her books. They stopped spending so much time in the same room – Abbu would continue to listen to his records in the living room, but Amma would often disappear to the kitchen or her bedroom and listen to French stations on the radio, saying she needed to keep abreast of things for school.

Alone, Abbu would cover the cracks by sharing his

music collection with us – his vinyl and tapes and CDs, like sympathetic comrades, providing wise words and comfort, and sometimes a searing insight so sharp that it hurt him like a physical pain. At those moments, his sorrow was tangible, palpable.

Our parents' new unhappiness polluted the very air we breathed. We began to look nostalgically at old photos, with smiling faces and turned-up eyes, and wondered how we had managed to live through and yet simply miss the time they had been happy. Before the cold war that followed with our adolescence, we had been embarrassed by their outrageous, demonstrative affection. Had someone told us what would happen, wouldn't we have savoured every moment, every loving word, every unthinking embrace in between?

If an unhappy marriage was my father's lasting failing, his last failure, and the one that offered another type of poignancy, a new kind of pain, was demonstrated by his increasing dependence on music. My father had always appreciated music, but now he began to cherish it, pouring his emotion and energy into it and using it to fill the vacuum left by love. When he listened to 'O Mio Babbino Caro' in our living room, his handsome face became equal to the most beautifully crafted cinematographic shot of weeping Mafiosi in La Scala. But he didn't simply weep – he was transported. He became more democratic in his tastes, now treating jazz and opera, pop and soul, and classical Indian melodies as equal in his own United

Nations of Music. It was a bittersweet gift as, despite all his efforts, his gift was simply that of knowing and appreciating great music – he played a little, but he was acceptable rather than good. He could strum a sitar, a guitar, and he even learned to play something recognizable on keyboards, but he could never play a tune as he would want it heard. He could never write a melody that would transport him. His displaced yearning for the love he had lost made him a musical dilettante – a jack of all instruments but a master of none.

My father didn't lose his love for music, but his resentment about his mediocrity added to the unhappiness he already felt. His wife was withdrawing, remaining close to him only in her sleep, and his musical mistress had only held up another mirror to his shortcomings. He played up a very slight deafness in one ear, hoping this might suffice as the excuse for this lack of talent, and listened to Beethoven like a martyr. But the bitter truth was, he could not pretend to have any cultured skill or aesthetic gift that might win our mother back; he could not claim to be an unfulfilled artist who had just played at business for her sake, to give her back the material comfort she had given up when she chose him. The unfortunate truth was that he was a businessman who played at art.

When we began the band, he was at first irritated and then appalled to hear the type of music we were playing – Indie punk rock was not yet invited across the iron curtain of his living room to join his private United Nations. Perhaps he was even a little bit afraid – afraid that his children would succeed where he had failed, that they would not only become accentless English gentlemen, with pale faces that barely hinted at their ethnicity, but that they would become musicians too. When I became more serious about music, at the expense of my schooling, he urged me into the restaurant business instead, and to give up my musical ambitions. Sometimes, I think he might have unconsciously done this so I might have the opportunity to fail where he had proved he could succeed.

The Balti Ballads of Tooting Broadway

S HARIF WAS FIFTEEN when he decided to start the band. He was already quite handsome, although not in the same way his father was, less swarthy and finer boned. He had puppy-dog eyes that were chocolate-brown and appealing – Shona still insisted that they were his father's eyes. By his teens he had become conscious of the fact that you couldn't tell his ethnicity immediately by looking at him, which slightly embarrassed him – he didn't want people to think he was a wannabe white; he thought 'coconut Bounty Bar' was one of the worst insults bandied around his school, worse than Paddy or Paki. To counter any such accusations, he grew his black hair long and straight, defiantly let his teenage bum fluff grow on his chin and adopted an Asian sarf London accent, which he used comfortably to win the respect of his cronies, and which he dropped effortlessly when he loped back home to the gentrified Heaver Estate, his school tie hanging so loosely that it looked like a noose. Sharif was not only handsome, but with his new, vaguely rebellious look and his air of studied insouciance, he was now quite cool.

Better than cool, he was street. Girls began to pay attention to him, and he began to notice them back.

He started the band for four reasons, in this order:

1) It would be cool to be the lead singer in a band
2) Girls liked people in bands, especially the lead singers
3) Being in a band would irritate his dad
4) Oh, and he truly believed that Music was to be his Great, All-Fulfilling Destiny

He held the auditions in the flat above the restaurant in Tooting Broadway, where he had once lived as a child. His dad rented the flat to one of the cooks and two of the waiters. Sharif was a charmer, and often cadged fags off them in the alley behind the kitchen door, making them feel at home with his modified, expedient accent. They were fond enough of him to let him use the flat – it was Monday night, anyway; they would all be downstairs at work, and there wouldn't be anyone eating in, at least not until the pubs closed.

Sharif, armed with Pringles and a mixed nut collection stolen from his mum's larder, and Kingfisher beers filched from the restaurant fridge, set up the living room with his guitar artlessly draped across the ancient sofa, and some sheet music for decorative effect. After a couple of unpromising turns from a couple of lads in his class, one of whom inexpertly played the fiddle, and the other who had uselessly demonstrated his proficiency with the clarinet, Sharif broke into one of the beers himself. He was surprised that the third person who turned up was Micky

O'Shea, a stocky Irish lad from the year below him, who was known for being a bit of a scrapper and had the broken nose to prove it.

'It's a fourth-year band, Micky. Sorry, mate,' Sharif said with the unquestionable superiority that the automatic hierarchy of school bestowed.

'Fock off, man,' said Micky respectfully. 'Y've not even heard me play yet.'

Sharif considered this and nodded magnanimously. No one further had turned up. He might as well get some entertainment from the carrot-topped runt.

Micky pulled his guitar strap over his head and played a stunning riff. Sharif was annoyed and impressed; he was no mean guitarist himself, and could recognize talent in others. He maintained a stoical face and, giving nothing away, passed a sheet of paper to Micky. 'Can you read music, too?' he asked.

Micky nodded. He squinted at the hand-written squiggles for a few moments, humming in his head, and began to play. After a few bars he stopped and, shaking his head at the shaky writing, began again. Sharif listened, enraptured, trying hard not to let his pleasure show at the fluid harmony of the chords. 'This is good,' said Micky, when he reached the end of the page, 'but your notation's crap – did you just copy it down by ear? Y'know y'can buy sheet music for lots of bands – I've got Oasis and The Smiths.'

'I didn't copy it down, Micky, I wrote it,' Sharif said haughtily, secretly thrilled at the company in which Micky had unconsciously placed him – Oasis, The Smiths and Sharif Khan. 'We're not going to be some shite tribute band, we have to write our own stuff. It's about credibility.' He got up to take back his sheet, when his own credibility was marred unavoidably by his geeky little brother bursting into the flat.

'Sharif, what are you doing here? Abbu's going to kill you!' said Omar, breathless from racing up the stairs, blood dripping from his nose. He paused, seeing Micky, and although surprised, nodded politely towards him. 'All right, Micky,' he said, looking questioningly towards Sharif.

'All right, Omar. What the fock's happened to y'face, man? Were you in a fight?' Micky asked with interest. Sharif held his breath – please, he pleaded wordlessly towards Omar, please say you were in a fight, please say someone hit you. Say anything that might preserve an iota of our dignity, just please don't embarrass me in front of a carrot-topped third year, by saying . . .

'No, I just get nosebleeds sometimes. The doctor thinks they're stress-induced, although sometimes I get them when I run too fast or something,' said Omar apologetic-ally, taking a seat next to Sharif on the couch and wiping his nose. Sharif exhaled heavily and shifted himself imper-ceptibly away from Omar, disassociating himself without even realizing what he was doing.

'Oh,' said Micky with disappointment, while every-thing else in his demeanour said, 'Wimp.'

'I'll speak to you later, Micky,' said Sharif, masterfully taking control of the situation. 'I'll let you know. I've got lots of other people to see. Fourth years, you know. It's meant to be a fourth-year band. But I'll keep an open mind about you.'

'Thanks a million, Sharif,' Micky grinned, revealing his

train-track brace and crooked incisors. 'I'll see youse both later.'

Sharif looked at Omar, still pitifully sniffing and dripping blood, and, sighing with resignation, went to get some Kleenex and held them to his brother's nose, applying the pressure with a practised hand. 'Hold your head back a bit,' he commanded. Omar obeyed, and the bleeding began to abate almost immediately. 'So why is Dad going to kill me?'

'It's Monday, remember? Nana's come over for dinner, and you're half an hour late. Amma's fretting because she's made some massive effort to cook an English meal for him, but now the roast is drying out, the veg are getting soggy and the crisps and nuts she bought for pre-dinner nibbles have mysteriously disappeared. Abbu's furious with you. I said I'd come and get you.'

'Shit,' said Sharif. 'Of course, Grandad! I completely forgot that the old man was coming round. Where did you say I was?'

Omar gave him a small conspiratorial smile. 'I said you had to stay back for extra after-school maths, after your lousy results in that last test.'

Sharif grinned. 'You excellent little liar!' he said with admiration, 'Utterly believable and blameless. I owe you one, kid.' He nudged Omar gratefully with his shoulder, lifting off the blood-soaked tissues experimentally. 'So how did you know where I really was?'

Omar pulled out Sharif's flyer, announcing the auditions,

from his trouser pocket. He put it on the table, gently smoothing it out. 'I saw it on the notice board outside the music room,' he explained, before adding a touch reproachfully, 'Why didn't you tell me? I can play. I can play keyboards *and* guitar. And I'm a grade above everyone in our year, apart from you on the guitar.'

Sharif felt caught out, and said a touch shiftily, 'Well, I didn't think you'd be interested, and Indie rock bands don't really need pianists, and we've already got two guitar players . . .' he trailed off, as Omar was looking at him frankly and unconvinced, with dried blood sticking like rust to his nose and upper lip. 'And the thing is, it's not just about playing, you've got to be, well, a bit cool to be in a band.'

'Like you and Micky?' asked Omar.

'Like me and Micky,' agreed Sharif. 'Micky might be a third year, but he's almost the same age as us, and he's bloody hard. When he gets a bloody nose, it's not from a friggin' stress-induced nosebleed.'

'I can be hard,' said Omar crossly. 'I hit Tariq back when he punched me at football practice. I punched him so hard I broke my thumb and had to go to Casualty.' He pounded his fist lightly into his palm at the memory.

Sharif looked at this innocent gesture and said pityingly, almost kindly, 'You didn't go to Casualty because you hit him hard, kid. You broke your thumb because you don't even know how to make a bloody fist.' He took hold of Omar's still clenched right hand, and said, 'For a bright boy sometimes you bloody baffle me. Look, kid. Look at what you're doing. Your thumb is meant to go on the outside, Omar. Put it on the outside!'

Omar splayed his hand and looked thoughtful as he flexed his fingers and put them back into a fist, this time with the thumb on the outside, instead of neatly tucked in as he had it before. 'It doesn't feel right,' he confessed humbly. 'God, I'm rubbish. Why didn't you tell me before?'

'I didn't want to hurt your feelings,' Sharif shrugged. 'Sorry, I should have told you.' Seeing how bereft Omar looked, Sharif got up and pulled him to his feet, and said jokily, 'Well, kid. At least you got the brains in the family. All I got was the looks.' Omar shrugged. Too upset to play along or attempt a smile, he hung his head, looking down at his stupid weak hands. Sharif softened, and found himself saying something that he was sure he'd regret. 'Well, I said I owe you something for covering for me tonight. Why don't you come to our first practice session and see how it goes?'

Omar looked up, and when he finally smiled, it was like a soft white cloud drifting across a pale sky. 'You mean that, man? That would be so cool.'

''Course I do,' said Sharif insincerely, already cursing himself. He had wanted an über-cool Indie band, and now he was stuck with his geeky brother, a ginger third year, and he had already agreed that spotty Stevo Morgan would be on drums, as he was the only boy in his class who had access to a full drum kit.

While they walked down the narrow stairs past the takeaway, Sharif flicked some gum out of his pocket to cover up the beer smell and companionably passed one to Omar. As Omar took it, he asked Sharif, a touch nervously, 'Sharif, when we start rehearsing and that, could you please not call me "kid", not in front of the others. You're only fifteen minutes older than me.'

'Even if it was the other way round, I still think I'd call you "kid". But don't worry, man, I won't embarrass you,' Sharif said reassuringly. You do that to yourself, he sighed silently to himself. And such was the inauspicious birth of the Balti Ballads of Tooting Broadway, in the flat above the restaurant–takeaway.

Deciding the band's name was no easy process. Sharif, as founder member (after all, he had held the auditions, he had the flyer to prove it), thought that he had the right to name the band, and had already decided upon Balti Boys. He made the announcement at the inaugural meeting of the fledgling band, which found them once again in the flat above the restaurant. Sharif was confident of Omar's support, and was surprised when, on this occasion, Omar chose to differ. Nibbling on the peanuts that they had once again filched from Shona's larder, Omar asked, 'I get the Boys bit, but why Balti? We've got nothing to do with Balti. Abbu doesn't even have Balti dishes on the menu. Where's the logic in that?'

'What, so you think we should have a name that matches something on Dad's menu?' said Sharif scornfully, annoyed that Omar was questioning his authority in front of Micky and Stevo. 'The Prawn Dhansak Boys of Tooting Bloody Broadway?'

'I agree with Omar,' piped up Stevo. 'What the fuck's Balti got to do with me and Micky? How about Broadway Boys?'

'Yes, why don't we call ourselves the Broadway Boys?' agreed Sharif sarcastically. 'And while we're at it, why don't we wear bloody stockings and heels and audition for Forty-Fucking-Second Street.'

'Why don't we just call ourselves "Tooting"?' offered Micky. 'Or SW17? Stevo's right, we've got fock all to do with Balti, and everyone can see we're bloody boys.'

'But I don't mind the Boys bit,' Stevo objected. 'How about Tooting Boys, we're all boys from Tooting, apart from Micky here.'

'I am focking so from Tooting,' Micky countered furiously.

'Well, you don't *fucking* sound like it, Paddy,' said Stevo with the infuriating superiority of a fourth year talking down to a third year. Stevo could get away with saying things like Paddy, as his dad was Irish.

Micky turned white with fury and stormed to the other side of the room, sitting down heavily on an over-padded armchair. 'Zitface,' he muttered under his breath.

'Listen, I want Balti Boys,' insisted Sharif stubbornly. 'We need people to know there's some bloody Asian influence in the band.'

'There's only you and Omar,' pointed out Stevo, scratching his spotty chin and sprawling his long, lanky legs out in front of the sofa. 'You're only half the band.'

'Well, we'll be playing my bloody songs until one of you gets off your arse and writes some of your own stuff, so I'd say my influence was quite bloody significant,' retorted Sharif heatedly. Bloody insubordinates. He'd half a mind to go it alone.

'So if you and Omar are the Balti part of the band, what are Stevo and I?' asked Micky, having calmed down a bit.

'You're the Boys,' said Sharif patiently.

'But we're all Boys,' Omar added. He was a touch embarrassed by the storm his first comment had unleashed, but again his intellectual pride would not allow him to ignore the flaw in Sharif's argument.

'Well, what else do Micky and Stevo have in common?' Sharif muttered. 'He's ginger, he's not, he's a third year, he's not, he moved here five years ago, he's lived in Tooting all his bloody life, his dad runs the Crown, his dad works in a garage . . .'

'Well, we're both Irish,' suggested Micky.

Sharif snorted, 'And what have the Irish given to music? Bloody Eurovision winners, The Corrs and Daniel O'Donnell. Bloody soppy balladeers. We may as well call the band Bloody Balti Ballads . . .'

Sharif took a breath to continue his scornful rant, when Micky and Stevo surprised him by looking at each other, and roaring 'Yeah!' in unison.

'Bloody Balti Ballads, that's a rocking name!' said Stevo, 'That's got to be the one.'

'It's wicked, man, that's focking inspirational,' agreed Micky, stepping across the room to shake Sharif's hand.

Flattered by the sudden effusiveness that had suddenly materialized out of so much bad humour, Sharif decided that the name he had unintentionally come up with wasn't half bad – it was definitely more subversive and rock than Balti Boys.

'Omar?' he asked, unnecessarily, as he already had a majority vote, but didn't want his brother to feel left out.

Omar shrugged. 'I don't mind it. I still don't think we've got a lot to do with Balti, but whatever, man, I'm easy. D'you think they'll let us put "Bloody" on the posters, though?'

Sharif smiled indulgently. Sometimes his brother didn't have a clue. 'Don't worry about the bloody posters, man. We've got to become a bloody band first.' He stood up authoritatively. 'Now that we've got our name, let's work out when we're going to rehearse. We've already got our first gig – Mr Crowe is giving us a slot at the end of term concert if we can get our act together.'

Of course, Omar was right. Mr Crowe, their music teacher, was fond of both Sharif and Omar for their musical ability, but he wasn't having 'Bloody Balti Ballads' emblazoned on his posters across the school hall or on his concert programme. He curtailed the name to 'Balti Ballads' and, just to prove a point to the local governors about his ability to nurture local talent in the community, added 'of Tooting Broadway' in brackets.

After the first concert, everyone was talking about Sharif's band, and his unembarrassed, bravura performance during which he lurched across the school stage and abused his guitar like a latter-day Hendrix. The girls, who had been curious about Sharif before, now looked longingly at him as he passed by them in the school corridors, with his floppy, straight hair and his noose of a tie.

Overnight he became the sort of boy who literally had heads turning. And somehow, the band's new name stuck.

'Tell me about it,' Omar asked urgently, sitting on Sharif's bed in his checked M&S pyjamas. Now seventeen, going on eighteen, he had grown a lot taller, but had barely filled out. Despite taking up some martial arts classes, he was still scrawny and lanky, and his emerging fluff only accentuated his weak chin.

He had been waiting for Sharif ever since he sneaked out of the back window at 11 p.m., keeping himself awake by reading his revision notes for the end of term exams. It was the early hours of the morning before Sharif had climbed back up the drainpipe. He was now stripping off his clothes, his body much more developed and photogenic than Omar's, and wearing only his boxers, climbed into bed, nudging Omar off to the end.

'I'm fucking knackered, kid. What are you still doing up?'

'Come on, Sharif, tell me about it!' pleaded Omar. 'Who was it?'

'A gentleman doesn't tell,' Sharif said smugly, readjusting his balls in his boxers at the memory.

'You're not a gentleman. Come on, man. Who was she?'

Sharif sighed with mock annoyance. 'Well, man, if you insist. You know Cassie Rantell?'

Omar frowned. He knew Cassie; she was from the neighbouring girls' school. Short, sporty and busty, with a wild mane of golden curls and a reputation for shagging the more athletic boys from school on the Common. Although a nice enough girl, and good-natured enough not to bear any grudges when her conquests failed to call her again, she herself was hardly a conquest for Sharif to boast about. She'd even shagged Stevo Morgan last term (who'd become admittedly better-looking since antibiotic treatment had dealt with his teenage acne).

'I didn't think she'd be your type,' Omar said. 'A bit young, and a bit, well, she gets about a bit, doesn't she?'

'Of course she's not my type, shitwit,' said Sharif derisively. 'But she has a very hot big sister, almost nineteen.'

'Omigod,' said Omar. 'Ali Rantell? Hasn't she left school already? She's really fit – how did you get to meet her?'

'I met her last week – she came up to me after that gig we did in that crummy pub in King's Cross. She's a bit of a gig groupie – she was really drunk, and put her hand on my crotch while we were talking, so I took her number and asked her out.'

'Where did you go?' asked Omar, trying to keep the slight jealousy from his voice. He had been at the same gig, and while he and the others had been diligently packing up their gear, it seemed Sharif had been chatted up by a gorgeous older girl. He'd been in the band for two years and had never received the sort of attention that Sharif got. Sharif had been getting lucky with the 'gig groupies', as he called them, from the very beginning; but the only girls who ever talked to Omar just looked over his shoulder to where Sharif was standing and waited for him to disengage himself from whoever he was with, waiting for him to notice them.

'I didn't think she'd be a cheap date, so I took her out to the Ministry, out over at Elephant. Took a couple of tabs, saw some of the guys out there. Took her home and that was it.'

'Oh, right then,' said Omar, disappointed. Normally when Sharif went out like this, he had wild tales of sexual prowess to report, everything from blow jobs in club toilets to knee-tremblers in back alleyways, always clandestine, and always outside. Omar felt that listening to the stories, participating vicariously, somehow took the edge off his own virginity.

'She had a fantastic arse, though . . .' continued Sharif wistfully. 'Even you'd have got the horn for her, man. She had a butt like a ten-year-old boy.'

'What's that meant to mean?' asked Omar, sitting up, offended.

'It's an American expression,' Sharif explained patiently. 'It just means she had a great, tight, little butt. I heard it once in an Arnie movie, a real classic one.' Omar sat back down again. A classic Arnie movie was a virile enough reference for him not to take further offence. Sharif continued dreamily, 'You know, man, when you've got a girl like that bending over in front of you, you feel like a bloody king. I felt like shouting "I'm King of the World."'

'You watch too many movies, man,' Omar said critically. 'No wonder you plough all your exams. Besides, I thought you just took her home.'

'I did,' said Sharif smugly. 'I took her back to her front

door, halfway up a block of flats. And I knew she was well up for it because when we were making out, she rubbed herself against me, and didn't say a word when I got hold of her butt under her skirt . . .'

'You didn't do it outside her front door!' said Omar, gasping at the audacity. Her parents could have come outside at any moment.

'Don't be daft. She told me we could get up to the roof of the building on the fire exit. She's a bit more experienced and sophisticated than the girls from around here; she wanted me to do her from behind while she held on to the railing, which I thought might be weird 'coz I couldn't see her face. But I had a great view of her tight little ass, and the rooftops across Tooting, and she was bloody loving it. I'm telling you, man, when I was coming I felt like a king.' Sharif was silent, in reverence at the act, at the memory, already anticipating the next time.

'Are you going to see her again?' asked Omar quietly.

'Yeah, I think so, if she calls me I'll see her. I might even call her myself. For a good-looking girl she was really dirty. She was a bit too keen, though – afterwards, she kept asking me if I liked her. She kept saying, "You like me, don't you?" and kept kissing me needily when I didn't answer.'

'Why didn't you answer?' asked Omar.

'Well, it's a stupid question, isn't it? I say yes, she'll think she's my fucking girlfriend. If I say no, I'm a bastard. She must have known that I liked her a bit – I paid a mint to take her out and get her loaded. I don't have to do all that just to get laid. Girls only ask that because they want reassurance.'

Omar was silent at this. It was a question he asked in his head all the time, to his parents, to his schoolmates, to the girls who looked past him at the gigs, to his brother even. 'You like me, don't you? Please say you like me.' Sharif was so lucky never to need reassurance – to be so confident that he would be loved and desired just for being himself.

'I'll get off to bed, man. I've got a test tomorrow,' Omar said, heading back to his room. Lying alone in his bed, staring at the moonlight reflected on his ceiling, he tried to imagine making love to a faceless body; someone who took pleasure in him touching them in the most intimate way possible, and who made him feel like a king, and wanted nothing more from him for all of this than the simple reassurance of being liked

Parvez Khan Mourns the Loss of Love

FAILURE SHOULDN'T BE surprising – it's just a part of life, like breathing and eating and singing. We fail at something at every stage in our development, every small success preceded by failure after failure. And sometimes followed by it, too. Each first faltering infant step preceded by flump after flumpy fall chest-first on the floor or, if you're lucky, into someone's arms. We fail at exams at school, which seems terrible, until we leave school and then we fail in all sorts of new ways that we hadn't even known about before. At our driving tests, at having children, at understanding those children, in our financial decisions, in our workplaces . . . and then we fail to keep our tempers about our failures, and let our bad humour affect those unfortunate enough to be close to us.

So we shouldn't be surprised when we fail at love. But we are. Of course, everyone expects the odd hiccup at the start – kiss a few frogs until you find your true love, and all that. That's different – that's the search, the thrill of the hunt, the seeking of the One to make your life complete. But when you've found the woman of your dreams, when you look at her longingly and find out to your absolute surprise and delight that she's looking right back at you and seems to think that you are the man of her dreams too; and you make a relationship, a home, a life of shared love and shared ideals and infinite happiness – how could that possibly fail?

Of course, you are astounded when it starts to go wrong. You absolutely deny it. How could that small errand she refused to run for you mark the beginning of the end? Don't be stupid, she just didn't want to go out of her way to the post office, there's not really one on her school run, and you could pop it in on the way to work anyway. Of course she wasn't being difficult, of course you're not cross about it. It's nothing, just a letter you had to post to the bank.

But then, how could you suddenly feel such intense, dramatic anger with her for simply scraping her fork on her plate at dinner? The dinner is still as abysmal as it used to be when she first attempted to cook, but after all this time you no longer compliment or reassure her, and she no longer expects you to. There's no school run any more; there's just the two of you at home, sitting across the yawning chasm of the dining table into which all conversation sinks. She used to follow your progress in doing little jobs around the house with loving, appreciative eyes – so why does she now follow you around the house with resentful eyes simply because you came back from the garden twenty minutes later than you said you would? And why does she complain about your muddy boots? You were weeding the back borders, the very borders she had insisted on having and you had fondly agreed to, even though you'd have preferred lawn to the end, so you and the boys could have had a bigger space for a kickabout or cricket, or maybe even a vegetable patch. You were weeding around the buddleia, the rosemary bushes, the pink roses that you'd bought together – you'd bought them when you first moved into the house, your first home together with the luxury of a garden. She used to love you coming into the house after looking after her plants, with the scent of rosemary on your fingers. You used to bring in a sprig of rosemary for her, too.

You'd forgotten to bring one in for her this time; in fact you'd forgotten that you used to do it at all, but surely that's no crime. You've had other things on your mind – the worrying dip in profits at the second restaurant in the summer, the competition of the new Italian, and the latest hire who hasn't been pulling his weight. Sitting alone in the kitchen with your muddy boots, your empty wine glass still on the table, your muddy footprints jigging cheerfully on the tiled floor, you can smell the scent of rosemary on your fingers yourself. Didn't someone say that rosemary was for remembrance?

And why does she clunk everything about so much when wiping up the mud, and why do you clunk everything about so when you are cleaning yourself up? And why do you take your drink to one room to listen to music, whilst she goes to the other to watch the TV? When did talking become so difficult, so alien? You've been together for ten, fifteen, twenty years. You've had children who have grown up in a loving home. Everyone says you're so lucky, everyone thinks you're the perfect couple – The Couple That Are In Love. You don't know when you started losing love. You can't explain when the window of your heart opened up to show that you were falling apart, day by day, hour by hour, minute by thudding minute, just waiting for the relief of the night, when you can escape into your happy dreams and wind yourselves around each other like you used to do, and at least be at peace in your sleep. You wish you knew when you started failing at the one thing that was the shining success of your life.

You don't believe it, and so you ignore it and hope that the disappointment and dread that comes with every waking morning will go away. And yet every waking morning it remains – you know it when your sleeping embrace loosens, and your legs and arms unwind and stiffen, and the curves and hollows that fit each other so well move callously apart to the cold, uninhabited far reaches of the bed. Let it leave, let the disappointment and dread leave – haven't we suffered enough? Isn't the losing of love bad enough, without watching the sorry corpse of it decay in our lives, in our lips? Let our unhappiness expiate our bad temper, our shortcomings, our failures and failings, and let us love again.

You think you'll never love again. You just want her to stop being a nagging shrew, and you want to stop being the interminable old bore who makes inappropriate gags and tells pointless long-winded stories about your blessed business, stories that she needs to cut across in company with her own truncated versions, so she can get on and serve the pudding. You show more regard for the dog than you do for her; and now so does she.

And all the time, in those moments when you remember your romantic youth, and the blush of the first and only real love you ever had, whom you miss even though she is lying thin-lipped and silent, just a foot away from you in your bed, all you want to say is, For God's Sake Please Stop This And Let Us Love.

Shona Khan Discovers Photos
from the Past

S HONA WAS IN her early forties when, much like her
father before her, she found herself having something
of a mid-life crisis. She looked around at her comfortable
three-bedroom house in the gentrified Heaver Estate, at
her pretty garden with rosemary and sweet-scented pink
rose bushes planted at the end, at her days spent teaching
in a convivial, middle-class school. She looked at her own
middle-class, middle-of-the-road life that was punctuated
by stilted, suburban dinner parties in which she attempted
to make up for her mediocre cooking with expensive raw
ingredients and lavish puddings; that was made bearable
by her occasional art courses, her newly acquired Labrador puppy, and . . . what else, exactly? Her children had
left home, and it was just her and Parvez again; only this
time they had all the material comforts that they had done
without before. They should have been happy – they had
it all: time, space and companionship. And yet Shona felt
bereft, perhaps unreasonably bereft. She felt that she had
somehow grown into the wrong person, and was living
the wrong life, and had only just begun to notice it.

It was a sad truth that as the children grew up, Shona and Parvez began to grow apart, as though the very fact of their growing was driving a wedge between the couple who had been such hopeless, dreaming romantics. They had been united in the struggle against their disapproving families, united in their struggle against their new-found poverty in the UK, united in their struggle to have the children they so desperately wanted and united in their front towards their children, to bring them up the best way they knew. But the more their children grew, the less they needed them, until eventually they had nothing against which to unite.

Omar was his family's pride and joy – his entire extended family participated in the credit for his fantastic success in his Oxford entrance exams, earning him a practically guaranteed place in illustrious, ancient New College with a two 'E' offer. When he got straight Bs in his A levels, everyone excused the quite average results for nerves and his rambunctious brother keeping him up with their band at all hours throughout the summer of the exams. His grandad, Nana Rashid, practically wept when he heard that his English grandson was going to his alma mater, as though his own life was being relived the way it should have been.

Sharif, meanwhile, had failed in all his exams, apart from music, quite spectacularly. He was uninterested in going to college, and took up his father's offer of working in the restaurant. Again, his family found something to be proud about – their eldest son taking up the reins of the family business. What could be more fitting than that? True, his childhood musical hobby seemed to continue to distract him, but it was something he'd grow out of as he began his real working life. Now he had responsibilities beyond messing around in sound-proofed basements with his old schoolfriends.

Both boys left home the same week, not very long after their eighteenth birthdays, Omar to go to college, and Sharif to move in with friends in Collier's Wood. Parvez, seeing how much this affected Shona, surprised her with one of his romantic gestures, which had become so rare that she had practically forgotten he ever did them. She came back from school, and in a tall, brown box on her doorstep, tied with a pink ribbon, was an adorable Labrador puppy, with melting brown eyes and a dark chocolate coat, like an Andrex puppy in negative. Still in her sensible teacher's coat and court shoes, standing on the doorstep, she pulled him out, and giggled delightedly as he scrabbled affectionately at her and licked her face.

'Do you like him?' asked Parvez, opening their front door.

'Oh, Puppy, I love him!' exclaimed Shona, stepping forward to put her arm around Parvez in an embrace that was awkward as it was unusual. Parvez, surprised and pleased by their sudden renewed intimacy, put his own arm around her and kissed her on the top of her neatly bobbed hair. She hadn't called him Puppy for years; once the children were old enough to speak, she had stopped calling him Puppy in front of them and had switched to Abbu or Dad. And whenever they were in company, she had made sure to call him Parvez, until eventually it had seemed that they were always in company, whether with the boys or someone else, so it had been a natural transition to call him Parvez on the rare occasions when it was just the two of them. And he himself had stopped calling her Goldie, although sometimes he satisfied himself with 'Shonali', the affectionate form of her name, which was quite appropriate enough for company.

'I thought about getting two of them, to keep each other company,' said Parvez, 'but then I thought we had enough trouble with the last two, so perhaps it was time to give us a break, and just look after single figures.'

Shona smiled, but this time, the smile didn't reach her eyes. She had mistaken the gift as a romantic gesture, but now saw it for what it was – an attempt to replace the boys and paper over the cracks with another shared endeavour. Still, the puppy was undeniably gorgeous. She stepped back from Parvez and, closing the front door behind her, asked, 'What shall we call him?'

'You name him, Shona. Your names are the ones that stick,' said Parvez, without rancour. 'Maybe I'll give him his middle name.'

'Well, he's Irish,' said Shona, inspecting his collar. 'Perhaps we should give him an Irish name, like Patrick.'

'Pat the puppy?' laughed Parvez. 'Are you sure that's wise? The poor thing will get enough attention without his name being an instruction.' He took the puppy and patted him lightly and enthusiastically. 'Pat the puppy, Pat the puppy.' Watching the puppy squirm with pleasure at the attention, Shona started laughing and Parvez, grinning that his joke had worked, added, 'Why don't we call him Bob for his middle name?' He bobbed up and down with the scrabbling, excited puppy in his arms. 'Bob the dog, Bob the dog.'

'OK, Patrick-Bob. That's his name. Is that all right with you, sweetie?' she cooed, but she was talking to the puppy, not to Parvez, and chucked the puppy under his chin. As she walked through to the kitchen, Parvez put down the puppy and joined her. 'Are you checking that we've got enough chitlins and vittles for when the rest of the Waltons come to visit Patrick-Bob for supper?'

The fun of the moment had already passed, and Shona took a deep breath, fighting the urge to snap at Parvez for his silliness. 'Yes, Parvez,' she said patiently, 'That's exactly what I'm doing. I'm also making a cup of tea if you want one.'

A month later, Shona was sitting at home during the mercilessly damp autumn half-term break. She had too much time on her hands, which she had begun to find was a Bad Thing. Too much time meant that she started thinking, and when she started thinking, she found she wasn't thinking particularly happy thoughts. Thoughts like – This isn't the real me; maybe once it was, but it's not any more. This isn't my real life; maybe once it was, but it's not any more. Maybe I'm just waiting for my real life to begin . . . Consequently, Shona started to find herself chasing away time as urgently as most people chase away boredom. She cleaned her already clean house, making their Ugandan cleaning lady's job deeply unfulfilling. She baked chocolate-chip cookies from a packet recipe, and, realizing she had no one to share them with, ate half of them miserably herself in front of daytime TV until she remembered that cookies were the sort of food you could send by post and packed up the remainder to go to Omar and Sharif. She listened distractedly to French radio, and flipped listlessly through the Ikea catalogue. She considered visiting her father, whom she hadn't seen in months, but didn't know how she would answer his first and most obvious question: 'So, how are you, Jaan?'

She remembered that she had a chore to do, something that she had been saving for just such a rainy, listless day. She went up to the attic, pulled out a large cardboard box of photos, collected in their little packets from the developers, and the smart grey albums that she had recently bought to arrange them into, and brought them down with her to the sitting room. It wouldn't take too long to stick the photos in – what would take the time was organizing them into some kind of order.

The photos went back years, from when she had first married Parvez; they were all the pictures they had taken together before they had become a family. Once the children had come, all the family photos had been pasted proudly into a set of golden lacquer albums that Parvez had bought her as a present, ready to show to guests, and for the children to fumble through when they were bored. She also kept a few photos on display in the living room in sturdy wooden frames, which she would occasionally update as new shots took her fancy. Rather than going to the trouble of putting the replaced photos back with their original set, she simply popped them in a manila envelope that lived at the top of the box, telling herself she would sort them out later. It was this envelope that Shona came across first, and she spread the photos across the carpet.

These were the most poignant photos, as they were the ones which had once had pride of place in her living room, and which had eventually become so familiar that they had lost the power to move or delight, becoming mere wallpaper before being decisively rejected for new, more recent developments.

The first picture that caught her attention was the photo she always thought of as her wedding picture. Her orange silk sari blazed in the sun as she looked up with bewildered adoration at her laughing, handsome husband, as though she couldn't quite believe what they had just done, and that he would now be hers for ever. They were so happy, so foolish in their happiness; they both had the myopic look of people who couldn't see further than each other, as though they were all that existed in the world, The Couple That Were In Love. The photo reminded her of secret assignations in the Karachi Tennis Club, of pink rose petals in a Hilton bedroom, of making love surreptitiously in the syrup-sweet-smelling flat above the confectioner's when Bhai Hassan went out; it was like facing a ghost of her past. Handsome Parvez, looking straight through the camera lens and into her eyes seemed to be saying, 'See, you can't deny it. We've changed. Look at what we once were, Goldie. And look at what we've become.'

When did it go wrong? Shona asked herself. Perhaps it went wrong the moment she took this photo off their mantelpiece and replaced it with ... with what? She couldn't imagine what she could have possibly replaced this picture with. Then she remembered; it had been the first picture of Parvez and herself holding their scrunch-faced newborn boys, taken in the hospital after they had given them their names. She looked for the photo and, finding it, was surprised to see that this time she was looking adoringly at her children instead of at Parvez, her myopic blind adulation reassigned instantly, whilst Parvez looked directly at the camera again, a studied beam on his face instead of a spontaneous laugh. 'See what happened, Goldie? I didn't change, you did. You cared more for them than you did for us.'

So what? she argued back to him. So what if I cared more for them? I went through hell for them. I black-mailed my own father for the money to have them, I went through the most painful, invasive treatments you can imagine again and again until it worked, I carried them with fear every day until they were born, afraid that we'd lose them and have to start again, I spun them from my flesh and knitted them from my own blood and bones. They were my blood, my boys. I poured everything I was into them. You just masturbated into a tube, and were too busy with the business to come to the clinic with me all those times; you thought it happened like magic, with the effortlessness of the gods. Of course I changed! And you should have changed too, but you didn't. You stayed the happy-go-lucky twenty-something I married; you left all the changing, all the coping and the managing to me, while you kept cracking your silly jokes and doing your silly work to keep us in not quite the manner we'd been accustomed to back home.

'So that's it!' said another photo of Parvez triumphantly, standing with his hand on Shona's shoulder, while she posed with her mortar board and her MA diploma. 'You resent me. You've resented me for not suffering like you did, for not being as rich and successful as the family I took you from. Don't you think I'd have taken every little bit of pain from you, if I could have, every bitter disappointment month after month when you cried and mourned every time you bled? I loved you, Shona. It wouldn't have mattered to me if we'd never had kids, as long as we had each other. Everything I did here – starting the restaurant business, expanding it, buying the house – I did for you.'

Don't be stupid, replied Shona. I don't resent you. Why would you say that? How could you feel how I felt? And I know everything you've done for us; we have a good life, a beautiful house, a nice car that I still haven't learned to drive. I don't resent you for not suffering like me; but why couldn't you have changed with me, Parvez? Why couldn't you have grown up, too? I can't explain what happened to us; all I know is that slowly, gradually, every single little thing you said or did just felt wrong, as though you could never do anything right again. And so I snap and criticize and nag, until you throw accusations at me, saying things like, 'You resent me,' and then you begin to resent me yourself, for being what I've become. So maybe it is all my fault; I didn't just make the boys, you know. I made us, too. I sought you out in Pakistan, I looked for you and made you mine. I was responsible for our beginning; maybe it only makes sense that I should be responsible for our end.

Sitting on the floor, surrounded by photos of her past, betrayed and exposed by the images of her legion former selves, Shona hugged her knees and began to cry quietly to herself. Patrick-Bob, who had turned out to be a she rather than a he on closer inspection, scuffled into the living room and nuzzled against her. Pulling herself together, Shona gathered all the photos before the dog could put muddy paw prints on them, and put them back in the envelope, back in the box, and put the box back in the attic.

As she walked into the kitchen to get Patrick-Bob's water, she saw that she had left the french windows to the garden open, and that tiny paw prints had made a merry, muddy dance all over the kitchen tiles. Sighing, but at once relieved for this new diversion, Shona cleaned the kitchen floor until it sparkled, and made dinner for Parvez. When he came back, she was unreasonably cross with him for the accurate charges that his photographically captured self had made in her imagination, and answered all his attempts at conversation with monosyllables, scraping her plate clean because she knew the sound annoyed him.

'I picked up that book you said you needed, Shona,' Parvez said, when he had finished eating.

'Right, thanks,' said Shona disinterestedly, continuing to scrape her plate, even though she didn't know which book he was talking about.

Parvez sighed, and battled on, '*The Iliad*. Don't you remember? You said you needed a copy of *The Iliad*, you said you needed it for school.'

'Yes, I did. Thanks,' Shona repeated, finally putting down her jarring cutlery.

Parvez got up from the table and pulled the book out from his briefcase. 'They didn't have the Penguin Classic version you wanted, so I got this one instead. It cost quite a bit more, but it's beautifully illustrated; I thought you might prefer it.' He put it in front of her, and waited expectantly for her approval.

Shona looked at it cursorily and, instantly appalled, flicked from the inside front cover to the back pages in disbelief. A glossy coffee table version of *The Iliad* was the last thing she needed. What on earth had Parvez been thinking? Did he really think that pretty pictures were all that mattered in a book? She resisted the urge to snap, and said matter-of-factly, 'It's a bit too heavy for me to take into school; and I really wanted the foreword and notes in the other version. Just leave me the receipt and I'll return it when I go into town tomorrow.' She got up and took their plates to the sink to rinse.

Parvez looked at her stiff back and said quietly, unable to keep the reproach from his voice, 'You could at least say thank you, Shona. I was trying to do something nice for you.'

Shona didn't turn around, and carefully put the plates in the dishwasher. She knew she should apologize for being so offhand, but she couldn't stop herself saying instead, in the same matter-of-fact tone, 'But I did say thanks, Parvez; I said it twice.'

Chased outside by the icy climate within, Parvez disappeared to the garden to do some useless task out there, and the rice pudding Shona had put on for dessert burnt dry as he stayed out twenty minutes longer than he said he would. Shona binned it without telling him, and when he came back in, his muddy boots messing up her newly cleaned kitchen floor, she said nothing in criticism, and clanked the mop and bucket round with an eloquent noisiness that said it all. It was funny, she thought, that she hadn't minded cleaning up after the puppy, but cleaning up after Parvez filled her with an anger that she couldn't even express. Parvez courteously poured her another glass of wine, and himself a whisky, and disappeared to lose himself in his music in the lounge. She took the wine without comment, and went upstairs to their bedroom to watch a comedy on the television.

Much later, when Parvez came up for bed, she pretended to be asleep, but he knew that she was awake as she didn't automatically turn into him, resting her head in the hollow between his head and shoulder, as she did in her sleep. He whispered to her, 'I just want you to be happy, Shona. You want me to be happy too, don't you?'

It was the simplest question, and she suddenly realized it was the most profound. It was far easier to answer than the hackneyed, 'Do you still love me?' Because how, Shona thought, could you talk about love after twenty years, when the relentless tank of habit is all it's become, from the wedding bands you still wear, to the golden earrings you put on every morning that were his first present to you, to the united front you present to both your families and to your friends? It would be stupid, infantile, to still talk of love. But did she still care if he was happy? That would answer it all. Did she still care if he was happy? Because she knew that if the answer was no, she could start to withdraw, to disengage, to break apart and mourn the loss.

The saddest thing for Shona, on that still, chill night, were the silent tears that she began to shed on realizing the brutal answer to his question; not the tears themselves, but her realization that her tears weren't even for him, but for the coldness of her own unhappy heart.

The Octopus in the Garage

SHONA WAS UNDERSTANDABLY annoyed when she wasn't considered the automatic replacement for the post of head of languages at her school when old Monsieur Matthieu retired. She had already given thirteen years of service to the school, and was certain she merited to be first in line. She wasn't sure if the perplexing decision against her had been made because she was a woman, or because she was Asian, or because she didn't have any overseas working experience, or simply because she wasn't considered good enough. When the newly appointed head of languages turned up, male, Caucasian, barely older than her and scrubbed up well enough to charm the head teacher, she was even more annoyed. And his language experience was in Spanish, of all things. Spanish! Who learned Spanish in England? Everyone learned French, and maybe a bit of German or Italian if they were arty or romantically inclined. No one learned the language of the Costas here; Shona privately believed that the sort of Brits who went to Spain were the sort of people who thought that speaking English louder and more slowly would

miraculously make them understood to the pesky foreign-
ers. She and Parvez had taken most of their family holidays in different parts of France, when they weren't
dutifully visiting Pakistan or Bangladesh.

Jane, the head teacher, organized a little drinks gathering on Friday after school to welcome the new arrival and
to say goodbye to Monsieur Matthieu, who had already
turned sixty-five and had been kindly caretaking the post
until his replacement was able to begin. Shona had already
decided to dislike Mr O'Connor on sight and was irritated
when Monsieur Matthieu introduced them to find the
arriviste Irishman attempting to charm her in the same
way as he had charmed the head. 'Well, Mrs Khan, or
Shona, if I can call you that, you've certainly received a
glowing press from your old boss. I hope I live up to your
exacting standards.'

'I think you may have been misled, Mr O'Connor,'
Shona said frostily, with just the barest veneer of politeness. She was holding her glass of white wine stiffly, and
not sipping from it at all. 'I've heard my standards are
nowhere near as exacting as yours.'

Monsieur Matthieu, who knew that Shona was still
smarting about being passed over, thought about saying
something to defuse the situation before remembering that
he was now retired and didn't have to care any more. 'Oh
look, nibbles!' he said. 'How marvellous. I'll see you in a
minute, my dears. Must get to them before Jonty wolfs
the lot.'

Left to themselves, with Shona looking mutinous and
determined not to break the embarrassing silence, Mr
O'Connor sipped his soft drink calmly and eventually

said, 'Shona, first of all, please call me Dermot. We'll be working together, and there's really no excuse for not being on first-name terms. Secondly, I know it's no secret that my appointment was something of a . . . disappointment for you. But there it is, and we both have to get on with it. In my experience it's the only thing you can do.' He attempted a slight laugh, which he cut short when he saw that Shona showed no sign of defrosting.

Shona thought such frankness was verging on the ill-bred. Why did he have to say out loud what they both already knew? It hardly helped her save face for him to brag openly that he had got the job instead of her. Some things, most things, in fact, were better left unsaid.

'So what is your experience, exactly?' Shona said. 'Jane was rather vague when I asked.' Seeing as she was stuck with him and couldn't politely get away until someone joined them, she might as well find out what had made him such a good find and worth waiting over half a term for.

'Well, I'm from Ireland, originally. I went to university in Dublin, and then went back to teach near my home town. Do you know County Kerry?'

'No,' said Shona, and then deciding that her curtness could be mistaken for out and out rudeness, which she was well mannered enough to avoid, added, 'I'm afraid I don't. Is it nice?'

'Not so nice that I wanted to stay. I spent four years in Spain teaching in international schools, in Madrid and Barcelona. And then I went to the States and taught in New York, and then I came to London. I'll have been teaching nineteen years come January. I'll bet that makes me sound ancient to a young lady like yourself.'

Shona wasn't sure whether to bristle with annoyance at the 'young lady', or to take it as a compliment. She grudgingly accepted that Dermot was both more qualified and experienced for the job than she was, with her thirteen years trudging the beat in the same school, and found her resentment abating. Perhaps it was just as well. It was enough to have cold war at home, without having confrontations at work to boot. 'That's kind, but I'm hardly a young lady. I've got two grown-up boys, one is at college already.' She said college, rather than university, deliberately, as she always did, as she hoped that those in the know would automatically infer that Omar was at Oxbridge without her having to boast.

'I'd never have believed it. You look far too young to have grown-up boys!' Dermot said with what sounded like genuine astonishment. He's trying to charm me again, thought Shona. 'You must have married terribly young.'

'Are you married?' asked Shona, changing the subject.

'No, not any more. I was, sort of, but not now,' answered Dermot, looking uncomfortable for the first time, ironically as now Shona was actually trying to make an effort.

'So, any children?' Shona asked automatically, wondering what 'sort of' married meant.

'No,' Dermot said curtly. It could almost have been described as rude, but he added no softening sentence as Shona had done.

Shona regarded Dermot with a mixture of curiosity

and sympathy. She remembered, before she had the boys, how she too had snapped curtly at anyone who asked whether she had any children, or enquired when she and Parvez were going to start trying. She still recalled her silent fury at Parvez's father, who had droned on and on about how they were wasting their lives by not allowing themselves to bring the pleasure of children into them. 'You can't imagine the joy that children bring,' he had said smugly, as he sat fatly and fatuously on their sofa during what felt like an interminable visit from Pakistan. Shona had honestly wanted to kill him.

Jane bustled up to them with a tray of her precious nibbles. 'So how are we getting on? Grilling the new boss, Shona? Have you found out that Dermot here speaks five languages! What are they now, Dermot? Let me try to remember. English, Castilian, Catalan, German . . . and what was the other one, Dermot dear?' She fluttered her pale blonde eyelashes at him.

'Italian, but really not as fluently as the others,' Dermot replied with a smile, his composure regained.

'I speak five languages, too,' Shona said, but in a gentle tone and with a smile, so it didn't sound like an assertion or a challenge, but an expression of kinship. She made her excuses and went over to the buffet table to join Jonty, the corpulent English master, who was eagerly hoovering up the prawn thingies without any concern for niceties or mingling.

A couple of weeks after Mr O'Connor's arrival, Shona would have hoped that everything might settle back into the normal, comforting routine. However, it still wasn't quite normal. Although you couldn't exactly call Dermot good-looking, his natural charm and the ease with which he talked to the women in the staffroom had many of them, regardless of age or marital status, almost fighting for his attention, offering to make him cups of tea and asking solicitously after his classes. Young Ms Adams in particular, an attractive singleton in her early thirties, had developed a thumping crush on him, which she was convinced he reciprocated. 'He always asks how I am, every time he comes into the staffroom. What do you think that means?' she confided in Shona, with a mixture of triumph and uncertainty, reapplying her lipstick before Mr O'Connor came back after his class.

Shona replied reassuringly, 'I think it means he wants to know how you are.' She didn't add that he was the friendly type who made sure to ask everyone how they were, sometimes to the point of silliness.

'Exactly!' said Pam Adams, 'That's exactly what I think.' She looked expectantly at the clock, as she had memorized Dermot's schedule and knew exactly when he would walk back through the heavy oak door.

The other thing that wasn't yet quite normal, and this was not specific to Mr O'Connor but seemed to happen any time a new teacher joined, was that everyone appeared to have pulled up their socks, and be working much harder. Instead of the usual banal chatter and flicking through Ceefax that used to accompany tea breaks in the staffroom, now everyone began to stride purposely about with their papers, or bury themselves in their books and marking as soon as Mr O'Connor walked in. It was a natural group instinct of self-preservation, no one wanted to get shown up by fresher, keener new blood, and so everyone pretended to have an über-enthusiasm that tended to wear off as soon as the new teacher had been broken in and broken down by the relentless turn of the clock. Even Jonty, for whom Chaucer could hold no more secrets after a decade of ploughing through Canterbury Tale after Tale with his A level classes, was seen marking up his battered copies and muttering to himself audibly in Middle Englyshe any time anyone was close enough to hear.

Right on cue, Dermot walked in after taking lunch duty and greeted the teachers in the room collectively and individually – a lunch duty in itself, as it took him almost five minutes out of his precious remaining break. Shona, reading Voltaire's *Candide* on the small window seat, stifled a smile as a flurry of feminine activity broke out concurrently with heightened energized working. 'Pam, there's really no need, I'll make it myself this time ... Well, if you insist, that's really very kind of you, again.' Dermot looked around the staffroom and made a beeline for the only person who wasn't really looking at him.

'Could I join you, Shona?' he asked politely. Shona looked around wistfully at the many empty chairs that he could have picked, instead of squeezing himself next to her on the narrow window seat. Parvez had a customer in the Balham restaurant who did something similar – always taking the same seat at the small corner table and, even if the rest of the restaurant was empty, and the large table next to the corner table was full and blocking his way, making the other customers stand up so he could get to his usual seat.

'Sure, Dermot, if you don't mind holding your breath. It's a bit narrow, I'm not sure it's even made for two.'

'Ah, but you're just a scrap of a girl,' said Dermot. 'There's plenty of room for my skinny Irish backside.' Shona giggled, despite herself. She couldn't help noticing that Dermot was a lot less formal with her than with the others; perhaps that little confrontation at their first meeting had broken the ice.

Dermot coughed, and then asked, 'Is it my imagination, Shona, or does everyone seem to work harder when I'm around? It might sound odd, but it seems as though everyone seems to leap into action when I walk in.'

'It's not your imagination,' Shona said. She added wryly, 'You must have great motivational skills.'

Pam approached the window seat, fluttering prettily, 'Here you are, Dermot. Just the way you like it, strong with two sugars.' She handed it to him, and as Dermot thanked her again, she looked for somewhere to sit down and join them. The window seat, however, was unavoidably contained, and there were no other seats next to it. She hovered for a moment, saying coyly, 'You really should look after yourself and cut down on all that sugar. You can get great substitutes now. I don't have any sugar any more, haven't done for years. Neither does Shona,' she added, generously including Shona in her conversation.

'Ah, but unlike yourself and Shona, I'm certainly not sweet enough already,' said Dermot charmingly.

'Would you like my seat, Pam?' offered Shona, keen not to be gooseberrying in on a flirtatious encounter.

'Shona, if you don't mind, I wanted to ask you something about one of your classes. Could you stay a moment?' Dermot interjected hurriedly, before Pam could accept.

'Well, I'll leave you to it, if you're talking shop,' said Pam, bravely hiding her disappointment. 'I have the most horrendous stack of assignments to sort out myself. Better get on with it, eh?' She walked off quickly and sat down with her papers, her back to the window seat so they wouldn't see her pouting.

'Well?' asked Shona, looking at Pam's too straight back, and feeling a little sorry for her. It wasn't nice of Dermot to flirt and then pass her over immediately afterwards.

'Could I sit in on a couple of your A level French lit classes next week? I have some free periods, and I've not yet had a chance to acquaint myself with your teaching methods. Just to see how you do things here.'

'Of course,' said Shona. 'You don't have to ask. I'm surprised you haven't sat in on my classes as yet. You've been to Mrs Cellotti's Italian class, and Miss Taggart's German class. I was beginning to feel rather left out that the evil eye of the new broom had managed to evade me.'

'Evil eye?' laughed Dermot. 'Very good, I like that.' He lowered his voice, and said a touch conspiratorially, 'The truth is, Shona, I've been a little embarrassed to attend . . .'

'Oh,' Shona said, nodding with understanding. It was because she had gone for his job. It might feel a bit awkward for him to throw his weight around where she was concerned.

'Yes,' nodded Dermot in reply. 'I thought you'd have worked it out. It's just that French is the only language we teach here that I don't really have a working knowledge of, and I was worried I wouldn't be able to follow the class without interrupting you and being a bit of an octopus in a garage.'

'An octopus in a garage?' asked Shona, looking at him for clarification. She was a bit annoyed that the only one who still seemed sensitive to the awkward situation of being passed over for the job was her; at least his odd choice of phrase gave her an easy way to hide her discomfiture.

'Yes, it's a Spanish phrase, *como un pulpo en un garaje*. It means, like a fish out of water,' explained Dermot.

Shona frowned just for a second. What a silly language Spanish seemed to be. Whoever heard of a phrase like 'an octopus in a garage'? She looked at Dermot, who had broken into a laugh. She breathed with comprehension. 'Oh, I get it, you're taking the mickey. I should have known.'

'No, I swear, it's a real phrase!' said Dermot, still laughing. 'It's just your look of utter disdain, it was priceless.'

Shona pursed her lips and said sweetly, 'Well, you'll get on fine in the French lit class. We read the work in French, but mainly discuss it in English. We're doing *Andromaque*, by Racine. Do you know it?'

'Vaguely, do you have a copy?' asked Dermot.

'Sure, it's in French, though,' Shona said, enjoying the look of exasperation on Dermot's face, before adding, 'But there's a very useful foreword and critique in English. I'll pop it in your pigeonhole before I head out today.' The five-minute warning bell signalling the end of lunch rang, and Shona shifted herself off the window seat. 'I'll see you later, then,' she said affably. She popped her bookmark into her slim volume of *Candide* and, dusting her skirt, started to walk off.

'So, Voltaire's not on the syllabus?' Dermot called after her.

'No, Voltaire is just for fun,' Shona replied, over her shoulder.

'Because this is the best of all possible worlds, and couldn't possibly be better?' he asked her retreating back. Shona turned round quickly, smiling with surprise, but saw that Pam had taken her place on the seat and already engaged Dermot in some cheerful banter. She surreptitiously checked whether the quote was printed obviously on the back of her volume. It wasn't. He didn't speak French, but he knew Voltaire. She was oddly touched that he had read the book that she was re-reading; it was an unexpected, not unpleasant, expression of empathy. It had not occurred to her before how much Dermot and she might have in common. Perhaps it wasn't such a bad thing that Dermot had joined the school. Perhaps they might even become friends.

'Dans ce meilleur des mondes possibles . . . tout est au mieux,' she said to herself. In this, the best of all possible worlds, all is for the best.

The Academic Pursuits of Omar Khan

WHEN OMAR STARTED university, he was swept into his turret room in the Holywell Quad of New College on the crest of a wave of familial happiness that was so powerful it practically carried him up the winding stairs. His manly, capable father brought up the heavy cases that Omar would never have been able to manage himself, and his mother plugged in the kettle and looked tearfully out of his window at the grey-green quad, the elegant chapel at odds with the substantial stones of the thirteenth-century walls. While Omar unpacked and his parents sat on the bed and drank tea, a couple of second year students wandered up to his room to give him the invitation to PPE drinks that evening.

'Well, that's nice, darling, isn't it?' said Shona. 'You'll meet everyone on your course tonight. You make new friends so quickly at college,' she added wistfully. Omar nodded cheerfully, giving away nothing but enthusiasm for this new adventure.

It was only afterwards, once his parents had gone, that he locked the door to his turret room and lay face down on his bed, ignoring the knocks of further enthusiastic students from his staircase, calling to introduce themselves. He had arrived at New College, Oxford University; he had arrived in this venerable centre of learning under the pretext of being academically gifted, and he was terrified that he would be found out for what he really was. A mediocrity. A run-of-the-mill, middling Mr Average, as his three Bs at A level testified. Whenever he had been asked about his disappointing grades, he had asserted with much bravado that after he had got his unconditional offer from Oxford, he had let his studies slip, and been too busy with the band over the summer to concentrate on his exams. He lied so fluently that he could almost believe it himself; almost, but not quite. The truth was that he had worked like a demon towards his exams. It was true that the monotony of constant revision had been relieved by playing a few gigs, but they were nothing terribly strenuous. In fact, after he had spent fourteen hours studying with nothing but strong brewed tea to sustain him, a forty-minute set in a local pub or club was a walk in the park. The terrifying truth was, he had worked as hard as he possibly could, and still got three Bs; the terrifying truth was that they were the grades he deserved.

If he had to explain how, despite his obvious mediocrity, he had managed to get an unconditional offer in the first place, he would have described it as a combination of dumb luck and plagiarism. During the Oxford entrance exams, he was lucky enough to get papers with questions that matched those he had already prepared over the previous summer as part of his revision. For the actual interview, he had crammed a year's worth of *Economist* and *FT* articles, and found that he was able to expound other peoples' words and opinions with much more confidence than his own when it came to meeting the politics and economics tutors. He had not done so well in his philosophy interview, as he was expected to think for himself rather than quote knowledgeably. But he had the good luck that this particular philosophy tutor was also involved in a scheme which supported black and Asian candidates, and so he suspected that he had probably benefited from positive discrimination.

Omar wished, not for the first time, that he was someone else. Someone like Sharif, who was confident enough to be himself, and was loved and liked for being who he was. Omar felt he, by comparison, was a faker, a dissembler. He had carved out a niche for himself, created an identity for himself in reaction to Sharif. If Sharif cared nothing for books or academia, then Omar could care for nothing else. If Sharif was to be the rebel, then Omar could be the model student. Omar found it relatively easy to be a model student, in that he found it easy to be quiet, clean, attentive, punctual and rigorous in handing in well-prepared work. He discovered that being a model student meant that everybody, including his teachers, mistook him for a bright student. And yet Omar sincerely believed that he was blessed with neither superior intelligence nor original thought; he had only two abilities, the ability to read quickly, and an excellent memory that allowed him to memorize and repeat all he read.

Omar sat up on his bed, scratching his stomach disconsolately. He splashed some water on his face at the sink in the corner of his room and looked at this face reflected back at him, blank, expressionless, pale. Even his colour was indistinct; he was neither brown nor white. It could be anyone's face, he thought to himself. It was a blank canvas. He looked at the family photos on his shelf, and imitated his mother's articulate, thoughtful expression, and then his father's handsome laugh, and then his brother's sexy smoulder. He blinked and looked at himself again. If it could be anyone's face, that meant he could become anyone, he could mould it into the face he wanted. The face of a someone, rather than an anyone; someone who was intelligent and academic. He had played the part of a model school student, so why couldn't he play the part of a model Oxford student? It was just a question of theatre – he had to say the right lines, wear the right clothes, attend the right classes and lectures, so that no one would be able to tell him apart from the real students here, the clever ones who got their places on merit. As long as he read everything he was told to, as long as he learned it and repeated it in an appropriate order, who would notice the difference between assiduous research and straightforward plagiarism? No one had so far. 'And no one will now,' said Omar to himself, leaning his forehead against the glass. He had to make a choice – to hide in his room forever, or to let himself out and play his part.

At that moment there was another knock on the door. This time Omar opened it, hanging his towel over his shoulder. There were three students in the hall, a handsome boy in a checked shirt, with a flush of high colour across his cheeks, accompanied by a pretty red-headed girl, and a bespectacled boy who looked even more skinny

than he did. 'Hello Rashid!' said the handsome boy cheerfully. 'I'm Jim Oakley, I've got the room at the bottom of
the staircase. I thought you'd died in there. We hadn't
heard a peep from you since your parents left.'

'Yeah, sorry,' answered Omar sleepily, stifling a fake
yawn, and dabbing at his face with his towel. 'I must have
fallen asleep. Had a late one last night, you know what
it's like.' He shrugged sheepishly as Jim and his companions nodded sympathetically, and perhaps even with
approval. 'It's Omar, by the way,' he said, stretching out
his hand. 'Pleased to meet you all.'

'Omar? You know it says "Rashid Khan" on the
staircase list downstairs,' said Jim.

'Oh, that's my middle name. Well, Omar's my middle
name really. But it's what everyone calls me. I'll ask them
to change it when I get a chance,' Omar explained with a
smile.

'Yeah, tell me about it,' said the other boy. 'I'm Ted,
and they've put Edward on my sign. Edward, I ask you!'

'We thought you might want to come to the JCR with
us,' said the pretty girl. 'There's a tea for all the new
students.'

'Sure,' said Omar and, putting his key in his pocket,
shut the door behind him on his old life, and his old
mediocre self, and walked down the winding spiral staircase to his new one. 'So, what are you reading?' he asked
companionably as they made their way downstairs. 'I'm
reading PPE.'

After the flurry of the Freshers week, with the drinks parties and the long evenings in the bar, Omar found his natural place in the college community. Unlike school, where he was without doubt at the bottom of the pecking order, at college he found he was accepted quickly. Part of this was to do with Jim, who was clearly the most popular boy in his college year. After the first day, when Jim had taken it on himself to knock on every door in the staircase and take command of the introductions, Jim never had to knock on a door again. He was lucky enough to have an enormous room at the bottom of the staircase, with a view to the street rather than the college. Despite the size, his room was always full of visitors, and the notepad that hung on his door was constantly covered in scribbled messages.

Against the odds, given the competition, Omar found that he and Jim became friends quite early on, from the first time he had helped Jim back to their staircase after too many drinks at one of the welcome parties. He was glad he didn't have to drag him up too many stairs, as Jim was quite a bit bigger than he was. He put him on his bed and as he turned to go, he heard Jim lurch. He raced over with the waste-paper bin, into which Jim threw up messily and copiously. 'Thanks, Omar, you're a bloody good mate,' mumbled Jim. 'Come round for tea tomorrow.'

Omar remembered the invitation, although he doubted that Jim did. Returning up the street to college at teatime, he heard music from Jim's room and thought he may as well pop in. He hovered nervously outside the door for a moment and, hearing voices inside, debated whether to knock; when he finally did, it was so lightly that he thought it might not be noticed. However, Jim opened the door immediately. 'Omar, you're late, come on in. I've started cutting cake already.' Omar wandered in, and felt he'd walked into a tardis. Jim's room seemed to have expanded with the volume of people that filled it; some he didn't even recognize. He sat next to pretty red-headed Karen, from the staircase, and chatted about the hangover he didn't have. Jim, the perfect host, brandished an enormous purple-spotted teapot and poured Omar a cup of tea, before popping over to have a few words with him. 'Are you going to the Union thing next Thursday?' Jim asked, slurping ostentatiously from his own cup of tea.

'I can't, I have to nip back down to London for the night,' Omar said regretfully, as everyone else seemed to be going.

'Parents giving you grief already? Or is it your girlfriend?' asked Jim.

'Neither, I've just got a gig,' Omar said modestly. 'I'm in a band.'

'That's fantastic!' said Jim. 'Listen, everyone, did you know that Omar here is in a band in London!' He turned back to Omar. 'So what do you play?'

'Oh, just guitar, and I do some backing vocals. I don't really sing.'

After that, Jim insisted that Omar fetch his guitar and play for them and, sheepishly, Omar agreed. At Jim's tea party, he was suddenly the star turn, while the students listened and whooped. His reputation as one of Jim's crowd in college was thus established, and in the following weeks he was surprised to find that so many likeable people seemed to like him. Even more surprising, no one thought that he was particularly unusual or geeky for spending eight hours a day in the Bodleian or college library, when not attending lectures or tutorials, emerging only for social events, meals and evening drinks. He really wasn't that odd at all, he realized; he was like almost everyone else.

One evening, after Hall, Omar was cramming on the Cold War and détente for a politics tutorial, when there was an urgent knock on his door. 'Omar, mate, you've got to let me in NOW,' Jim whispered. Omar opened the door.

'What's up, Oakley?' he asked, honoured that Jim had come up to his room. Jim hardly ever had to visit other people's rooms for company, people came to him.

'Bloody Boring Benjy saw I was in from the street, and he's coming round to visit with that appalling girlfriend of his from Christchurch. I had to escape or I'd be stuck with them for hours.'

'Won't they think it a bit odd that you've suddenly disappeared?' asked Omar, a bit disappointed that Jim hadn't come for a chat.

'Nope, I didn't let them see that I'd seen them, I had my head over my desk. They'll just think I nipped out, and hopefully get bored and go away,' said Jim cheerfully, sitting on Omar's armchair and reaching for one of his biscuits without waiting to be asked. 'Cool, I love Hob-Nobs,' he said, his mouth full.

'Your table manners are appalling,' chided Omar. 'Would you like a tea, or coffee, or hot chocolate?'

'I know, my mother keeps telling me,' Jim said, before adding dramatically, 'Tea, please. I'm positively *dying* for a cup of tea.' Looking critically at Omar's drinks selection, he asked, 'Why do you have so much hot chocolate? You don't even drink the stuff, do you?'

'I keep it for the girls, it's all they ever ask for,' admitted Omar.

'God, I know. Bloody girls are costing me a fortune in Baileys, hot chocolate and biscuits; maybe if I go cold turkey and stop supplying refreshments, people will stop coming,' Jim said, with only half a smile. He looked out of Omar's window. 'God, you've got the best view. I wish I had a room like this. You've got the sunset and the spires. You're out of the way, so no one can see if you're in, and it's small enough to have no one crowding you like you're the bloody JCR. It's an utter curse having a big room . . .'

'Do you really think people come to you just because you've got Baileys and a big room?' asked Omar, interested.

'No, they come for my sparkling wit and repartee,' said Jim, this time with a proper smile, as he accepted his tea graciously. 'You know what? I'm glad Bloody Boring Benj turned up. I've been working for hours, and I didn't realize how much I needed a tea break.'

'Having an essay crisis?' asked Omar sympathetically, trying out this new snippet of college lingo that he had learned.

'Yeah, but I've had enough. I think I'll go to the bar after this and scrounge the papers off the second years to copy out.'

'Won't the tutors notice?' asked Omar, perturbed by the openness of Jim's subversive intentions.

'I've thought about it – the trick is to borrow lots of papers, not just one. After all, it's only plagiarism if you borrow from one person. Borrow from lots, and it's research,' Jim said innocently. He saw a brief flash of frozen horror on Omar's face, and stopped mid-munch. 'Are you all right, mate? You look like you've seen a ghost.'

'No, I'm fine,' said Omar, realizing that he hadn't been found out, and that Jim hadn't come upstairs to expose him. He was just making conversation. 'You just reminded me of my own essay crisis. It's hard keeping up and playing with the band. I'm down in town again tomorrow.'

'Another gig? You guys must be doing well,' said Jim. 'Do you have lots of groupies following you around?'

'My brother has a few,' said Omar. 'He's the lead singer, and . . . well . . . girls seem to like him.' He nodded towards a family photo sitting on top of the cupboard, in one of Shona's chunky wood frames. It was a half-posed picture from that summer, with all of them at the sunny garden table. Shona and Parvez were standing behind the boys with poised smiles to the camera, waiting for the timer to go off, while Sharif and Omar were sitting at the table with part-finished beers in front of them, looking at each other and laughing at some private joke. Omar liked the picture, as there weren't many photos of him laughing and he thought it made him look less like himself. Although there was the telltale give-away of the beer, whichever way Omar looked at the photo, whether with eyes wide or with a squint, it always seemed to him that Sharif's beer glass was half-full, and his own was half-empty. He wondered if that's what other people thought, too. He looked expectantly at Jim, waiting for the inevitable comment, the one that tended to follow in just a few seconds. One . . . two . . . three . . .

'Christ, your brother's good-looking!' said Jim, right on cue. Omar gave a disappointed smile at being proved right again; even his brother's two-dimensional image in a four by six inch frame was more influential than him, when he was sitting here, real, living and breathing and offering tea and biscuits and sanctuary. Jim saw what he had done instantly, and added diplomatically, 'I mean, your whole family's bloody good-looking. Your dad looks like James Bond. And is that really your mum? She looks about thirty.'

'Yeah, well, add ten and you'd get it about right,' said Omar, unoffended. 'So, like I said, Sharif gets all the girls.'

'And what about you? No little band bitch waiting for you back in London?' Jim said affably.

Omar shrugged, and smiled despite himself. 'Nope, no band bitch. No bitch at all. Unless you count the new puppy that's at home. What about you? Have you got a girlfriend back in Cornwall?'

'Nope, no girlfriend, and no boyfriend either; just a pitifully large circle of close acquaintances to make up for the gaping hole in my sex life.' Jim sighed comically, and took another slurp of his tea. When he saw Omar's jaw drop, Jim asked, 'You knew I was bi, didn't you? It's hardly a secret; one look at my record collection gives it away.'

'Well, I like Abba and Erasure too,' argued Omar. 'Sorry, I didn't realize. I'm a bit dense about noticing things.' They sat in silence for a moment, Omar worried that he'd embarrassed Jim. He opened his mouth to say something, but had barely muttered, 'Um, I guess . . .' when Jim sprang up and put his hand over Omar's mouth, indicating towards the door in mime. Omar was too shocked by the physical contact to do anything. Jim's hand was very warm from holding his cup of tea, and smelled of soap and cookies – it smelled like his mother's hand. Then Omar understood, and crept towards the door, where voices could be clearly heard coming up the staircase, the unmistakable braying of Bloody Boring Benj and his horsey girlfriend. Omar gently clicked the lock on the door and scribbled quickly on the back of his notes, 'Benj in same Philosophy class as me; he's probably come up 2 wait here until U get back.' Jim nodded, rolling his eyes as the voices got closer and louder and, mouthing, 'Sorry about this,' he flicked off the light. They sat conspiratorially in the shadows, lit only by the flickering gas fire, until Benj and his girlfriend got to the door, the girlfriend complaining shrewishly about the number of stairs she'd had to climb in her new high-heeled boots.

Benj rapped sharply on the door, and then waited a moment and rapped again. 'Omar, you there?' he called.

'He's not there, Benjy. You can see his light's not on,' the girl said. 'Anyway, I only wanted to see Jimmy, he's so sweet. Not his hangers-on.'

'I just thought his light was on outside. Maybe it was the next window along,' mused Benj. 'Let's go and see Abigail, she's just a couple of staircases down.'

'Just as long as she's on the ground floor,' grumbled the girl, tip-tapping down the stairs.

Omar waited a moment, and flicked the light back on. Jim let out a great sigh of relief. 'Sorry about that, you can see why I had to escape. They're such tossers. "Jimmy's so sweet." Makes you want to puke.'

'Maybe you're too nice to them. My mum's a bit like that. Nice to everyone, sometimes insincerely. If you're always nice to them, how would they know you don't like them?'

'How could they honestly think that anyone *would* like them?' said Jim bitchily, but with such apparent wide-eyed sincerity that Omar had to laugh.

'I was going to say, before they came up, that I guess it must be hard, being bisexual. Like you don't quite belong to one thing or another, or that you can't quite be yourself,' Omar asked, hoping it didn't sound too personal.

'Well, maybe back in Cornwall it was hard. I wasn't terribly open about it there; I was the head boy at my school. I kissed girls in public and boys in private. But here, in Oxford, it's different,' Jim said thoughtfully. 'Haven't you noticed, Omar? Here, no one quite belongs, and no one is quite themselves. They're all big fish from little ponds and they don't know what to do now they're not special any more. They're all playing a part – pretending to be clever, pretending to be best friends with people they met a few weeks ago, pretending to care about all the twee Oxfordy stuff like the Union and rowing and stripy scarves and crap like that, just to fit in.'

Omar felt chastened, and relieved at the same time;

he'd been wallowing in his complexes and melancholy, and yet here was Jim blithely saying that everyone shared the same disease as him. 'I guess we're all guilty of doing that a bit,' agreed Omar. He felt a great weight lifted from him.

Although the threat of Benj had also been lifted, Jim stayed for another cup of tea and finished the rest of Omar's HobNobs, inspecting his record collection with a mixture of glee and groans. 'Are you sure you won't come down to the bar?' he asked when he finally made to leave.

'No, I'll try and finish this essay off the old-fashioned way,' said Omar, 'but good luck with sharking the second years.'

As Jim got up, Omar couldn't resist asking him, out of pure self-interest, 'So what do you think you do, if you don't want to play a part, if you just want to be yourself?'

Jim smiled naughtily. 'You do the only honest, sincere thing that an Oxford student can do,' he said, gesturing towards the moonlit buildings beyond Omar's turret window. 'You admire the bloody architecture.'

Between Greek Tragedy and
Courtly Romance

THE DAY THAT Dermot was due to sit in on her lesson, Shona walked into her classroom a good five minutes early, to see that he had already installed himself at the far end of the long, oval table at which she took her class. He was being accosted by the anally keen Imogen, a bespectacled, frazzle-haired student who must have raced straight up to the room after her lunch to get a head start on her classmates.

'Of course, Racine's not a patch on Euripides,' Imogen was saying pompously. She was taking Greek and Latin A levels, and planned to read Classics at university. She was turned towards Dermot, away from the door, and wasn't aware of Shona's entrance. 'He tries to write ancient Greek tragedy, but what he actually writes is seventeenth-century French courtly romance. I mean, look at this from the second act – "Je l'ai trop aimé pour ne le point haïr" – it's just pure romantic cliché, isn't it, sir?' Dermot looked confused, and seemed visibly relieved at Shona's entrance, his eyes eloquently asking for help.

Shona coughed to alert Imogen to her presence, before

translating kindly for Dermot. 'I have loved him too much not to hate him now,' she said. 'It may also be considered a universal truth.'

'Miss, you should have said you were there,' Imogen said reproachfully, putting down her book.

Shona was going to ask Dermot if he wouldn't mind taking a seat by the window, away from the table, so that he would be more of an observer than part of the class, but at that moment, two of the other girls rushed in. 'I told you we were late, Harriet,' said a worried-looking, pretty girl, with thick, dark hair cut squarely at shoulder-length.

'We're not, we're two minutes early, aren't we, Miss?' said a confident, crop-haired blonde, with a pointy nose and a too-short skirt.

'You are indeed,' said Shona, checking her watch. 'As you can see, we've got Mr O'Connor joining us for this class. He's not here to check up on you, he's just observing how we do things here, so do just be yourselves.' The other girls joined the class, the last one still in her lacrosse kit and apologizing for being late, and they all squashed themselves up at the centre of the oval table, rather than take a seat next to either Shona at the head of the table, or Dermot at the other end.

'Très bien. Bonjour tout le monde, on va commencer,' said Shona. 'Imogen here was just telling us how she felt that Racine was romantic rather than tragic. There are certainly complex relationships in *Andromaque*, and if you're not already familiar with the characters from Greek texts, mapping them out can be useful. Who wants to start us off?' Predictably, Imogen raised her hand quickly and keenly. 'Thank you, Imogen, let's start with Oreste . . .'

Later in the class, Shona had Becky, the pretty, dark-haired girl, reading Oreste and Charlie, the lacrosse player, reading the part of his friend, Pylade.

'Vous me trompiez, Seigneur,' Charlie said, attempting to sound righteous and to roll her r's at the same time.

'Je me trompais moi-même,' Becky said mournfully.

'Thank you,' Shona said. 'So what exactly does this exchange mean, in the dynamic of the play? Harriet?'

'It's where Oreste is forced to come clean about his feelings for Hermione,' said Harriet casually, as though she were talking about a daytime soap. 'Oreste admits why he's really come to see Pyrrhus; it's not because of ambassadorial duty, but because he's still in love with Hermione and wants her back. He wasn't just fooling his best friend, he was fooling himself. And now they both know the truth, their mission has to change.'

'Very good,' Shona said, pleased that Harriet could give such a simple explanation of a complex moment. 'But let's dig a little deeper. Is this really just about fooling oneself? What does Pylade mean when he says "Vous me trompiez"? Is he just saying, "You tricked me, sir," as though it was a gag between friends? Pylade is indignant, he's upset, this is something more than a joke gone wrong. What do you think "Vous me trompiez" could mean in this context?'

'You misled me?' asked Charlie.

'You disappointed me?' suggested Becky.

'You deceived me,' stated Dermot.

'Exactly!' said Shona triumphantly, before she registered who had said it. 'Umm, thank you, Mr O'Connor.' A touch flustered, she continued, 'It's about deception, and self-deception, a very powerful crime against a friend, and against oneself. Their honour and integrity is bound in the truth. For Oreste to self-deceive, he has been lying to himself, and so he's been divided.'

After the double lesson had finished, Dermot helped Shona rearrange the chairs neatly around the table. 'That was fascinating, Shona,' he said sincerely. 'Your enthusiasm for the text is really infectious. I think even our little cynic Imogen might have re-appraised her views about it just being a love story.'

'She's entitled to her opinions,' shrugged Shona. 'I'm not against love stories, but they're rarely as simple as she might think.' She began wiping the board clean with deep, efficient strokes.

'But you think it's a universal truth that deep hate follows deep love? Isn't that a simplification? It sort of implies that you never really loved someone unless you hate them afterwards, that can't be right.'

'I don't think I really believe that. I was probably just putting Imogen in her place. I don't think true love turns to hate, when it goes away, I mean. I think it just . . .' Shona paused in mid wipe and shook her head. 'What am I saying? You didn't come to my class to hear my opinions on true love . . .'

'I'm sorry,' said Dermot, his chair-arranging complete. He went to the door, and held it open for her.

'What for?' Shona asked sharply, turning to face him, wishing she hadn't said so much.

'For interrupting in the class. I got carried away, I couldn't resist.'

'Oh, that,' Shona said, smiling. 'You're quite forgiven. I'm glad you felt able to participate.'

As they walked down the corridor, Dermot said, 'You know, I might get *The Iliad* out of the library and read it again. I want to know more about Hector; he's the missing hero in *Andromaque*, isn't he? He's already dead at the start of the play, but his heroic presence infiltrates everything – the unseen husband. Pyrrhus is nothing by comparison, he just can't compete for Andromaque's affections. She'd rather be unhappy with the memory of true love, than happy with a real, breathing love.'

'The library copy's missing. I ended up buying my own. I'll lend it to you if you want,' offered Shona generously, trying not to think of her own unseen husband, and the memory of true love. 'It's the Penguin Classic version,' she added.

The Balti Ballads Play Brick Lane

WHEN OMAR REACHED the gig venue in Brick Lane, he was suitably impressed. 'This place is fantastic!' he said in awe to Sharif and Stevo, looking at the high ceilings and the raised stage of the warehouse. 'How did we get a gig like this?'

'Through contacts,' said Sharif wisely. 'I've been busy while you've been pissing about at uni with pretty buildings and plain girls.'

'Through fucking stupidity,' contradicted Stevo, who was noisily setting up his drum kit. 'We're doing this gig for free again, thanks to your brother's negotiation skills; they're taking five quid on the door, of which we get fuck all. Business brain of the century, our Sharif.'

'Have I told you what a wanker of a banker you've become since you've started that business degree at South Bank?' replied Sharif cheerfully, unoffended. 'Besides, we're not doing it for free – we get free drinks and we get five per cent of the bar.'

Slightly mollified, Stevo said, 'Well, you better give it all to me. I'm owed for the set-up costs of our website.'

'We've got a website?' Omar asked.

'It'll go live next month,' Sharif explained. 'You were away, so Stevo, Micky and I sorted out all the content. Just gig dates and photos and shit.'

Micky, who was in his final year of school, slouched in looking shattered. 'Football practice,' he said grimly. 'Focking Tariq almost broke my foot with a dodgy tackle from behind. He'll be a focking liability in the inter-school play-offs next week.'

Balti Ballads were the first band on when the bar opened at nine p.m., and there were just a few dozen people for their first set. Omar was relieved, as despite the rehearsal session they'd had beforehand, he hadn't really got the hang of Sharif's new songs which were so aggressive and high energy that he could hardly hear the words as he shouted them, or keep up with the relentless rhythms. He'd practised them in college, but with nothing like this pace. He hid behind Micky's virtuoso playing and Stevo's now more than competent drumming, and noticed how they were drawing in more and more people from the neighbouring bars, until the place was packed with leaping, sweaty bodies thrusting their fists in the air in unison with Sharif. Omar was relieved and embarrassed when they finally had a break between the sets – he was expecting the rest of the band to bollock him, but they were so pleased with the response that they just downed their pints. Sharif lit a fag and wandered over to Omar.

'I've got a favour to ask you, kid.'

'Sure,' said Omar, feeling that he owed Sharif something for doing so little justice to his new material.

'You remember Ali Rantell? Well, I'm still seeing her,

on and off. And tonight she's brought her little sister along with her – she's just been dumped, or something. Do you mind taking her for a drink or something afterwards so Ali and I can get off on our own?'

'You don't mean Cassie?' Omar said, appalled. 'Why can't Stevo take her out, or Micky?'

'Micky's seeing someone, and Stevo dumped her once already, so she's not going to go anywhere with him. Go on, mate. She's always liked you – she told me she thinks you're sweet. You might even get lucky. Cassie gets off with everyone.'

'Yeah, well that's the point,' muttered Omar. Although he privately thought Cassie was rather nice, she had an appalling reputation. He looked out into the audience and saw the beautiful Ali sitting gracefully at the bar, radiating huge confidence in a tiny skirt. He could just about see her short, curly-haired sister – she had cropped her hair and looked small and vulnerable. He suddenly felt a bit sorry for her; it wouldn't be much fun for her to be stuck alone at the bar while Sharif and Ali shagged backstage. 'OK, I'll have a drink with her or something,' he said grudgingly.

After their set, Omar wandered over to the bar with what he hoped was a nonchalant air, and raised a hand in greeting to Ali and Cassie. Ali, whom Omar didn't really know, exchanged a few words with Cassie and slid her long legs off the bar stool. 'Good set, kid,' she said, patting Omar's cheek in an annoying imitation of his brother, and strutted over to where Sharif was waiting by the stage.

'Hi, Omar. That was a great set,' Cassie said apologetically, looking reproachfully after her sister.

'Hi, Cassie. Nice to see you. Long time, no . . . see,' Omar said hesitantly, realizing halfway through the sentence that there was no way of avoiding repeating the word 'see', but deciding the bar was loud enough for it not to matter. He kissed her on the cheek, and took Ali's seat at the bar. He had never kissed Cassie on the cheek before, but it had become second nature to do it with the girls in college, and so it was almost automatic. It immediately made him feel better, as though Cassie was a friend, rather than a vague acquaintance whom he knew mainly by reputation.

'Would you like a drink?' Cassie asked. 'You must be parched after all that.'

'Yeah, um, a pint of Stella, please, if that's all right.' Watching Cassie struggle in her purse for change, Omar remembered his manners. 'In fact, let me. What would you like?'

'Diet Coke, please,' said Cassie gratefully.

While they sipped their drinks, Omar looked properly at Cassie, who looked much more appealing than he remembered. Her cropped hair suited her, and she had either lost weight or discovered more flattering clothes, as she looked less busty, and rather svelte in her dark jeans and black, shiny vest. After Omar had run through asking after all the mutual friends he could rack his brains for, wisely omitting Stevo, he had to resort to asking how she was herself.

'Oh, I'm OK,' said Cassie, with a studied nonchalance that Omar recognized from his own experience to be put on.

'Well, how's college, and life and stuff? Are you seeing anyone nice?' Omar asked this before he remembered that she had just been dumped. Shit, shit, shit.

'No college, yet. I'm retaking my A levels. I kind of screwed up,' Cassie said, dropping the nonchalant air as she looked deep into the dregs of her Diet Coke and pulled out the lemon slice. She starting chewing on the sour skin. 'No someone nice in my life, I got kind of screwed over. Screwed Up, and Screwed Over.' She gave a feeble laugh at herself. 'Hey, I should give that to you guys for a song, it sounds like one of yours.'

Omar looked back out to the stage, wondering how long Ali was going to be. 'Would you like a proper drink?' he asked kindly. He didn't mind listening to Cassie's problems, he was quite good at listening.

Cassie turned to him with a sigh. 'You're sweet, Omar, but all I really want is to go home and eat something. I didn't want to get dragged out by Ali, and she made me drink all these vodka shots to cheer me up, and I don't think it helped.'

'Do you want me to help you get a cab, then?' Omar offered.

Cassie shook her head. 'No, I promised I'd wait for Ali. I can't just leave her in Brick Lane, she'd be furious.'

'Well, would you like to pop out and get some food then? Some dinner? No point you starving while you're waiting.'

Cassie looked up gratefully again and nodded, with a

slight smile. He went with her to get her coat, before they walked out into the chilly bright lights of Brick Lane, and realized, as someone tried to sell him a rose out of a plastic bucket at the exit, that he had asked someone to dinner, and they had said yes. To all intents and purposes, he was on a date, with a girl.

In the curry house, Cassie politely ordered a veggie biryani, which was one of the cheapest things on the menu, and fell on the poppadums with indecent haste. Omar felt comfortable enough with Cassie to order a Coke for himself, something he would never have dared to do with Sharif and the boys, and listened sympathetically while she told him about the demise of her last relationship. It seemed that the boy, not a local one, had also been seeing a friend of hers; and when she had found out and confronted him, he had pointed out that she was just too much of a slut to go out with properly; he had just been using her for sex. And to make it worse, her hardly virginal friend had continued to see him, without any apologies, and had in fact cut Cassie out of her life instead. It was an unpalatable story that she seemed to find a lot easier to tell on a full stomach.

'Thanks, for this,' Cassie said. 'I feel so much better now. I think all that vodka was just making me maudlin.' She mopped up her remaining curry with a bit of the naan bread that Omar had insisted on ordering. 'The thing that hurts is that I really thought that Nico liked me. I didn't think he loved me or anything like that, but I really thought he liked me. It's all I wanted. It didn't seem so much to ask for.'

'It's not so much, it's all you deserve,' Omar said,

covering her hand with his in a comradely gesture. Cassie was a nice girl. He had always thought that she seemed sweet, and could never understand why she slept with so many people. Didn't she realize what people would think of her, what it did for her reputation? 'Did you like him?' Omar asked.

Cassie looked at him thoughtfully. 'I did like him; but then, I think I started to like him just because I thought he liked me. I'm always doing that.' She dipped her head and ran her hand over the back of her bare neck in an unconscious gesture, smoothing back her boyish crop. 'What about you, Omar? Are you seeing anyone at college?'

Taken aback at the perfectly normal question, Omar stuttered, 'No, not really.' Bizarrely, he thought about Jim and his legions of fans, not so unlike Sharif really. 'Not at all, in fact. I've made some really good friends, with other guys and girls. It's been really good so far.'

'I'm sure you're a really good friend,' Cassie said, looking straight at him.

After Omar paid the bill, with Cassie insisting on taking his address to post him what she owed, they stumbled out into the night and back towards the club, high on curry and spices. In a dark part of the street, Cassie stumbled against Omar on purpose, pushing him a little way down a shallow alleyway.

She stood in front of him for a moment, and then started kissing him. Omar was too shocked at first to react, and then thought, She really is a sweet girl, she's quite pretty . . . what would it matter if I kissed her back?

It's just a kiss. And so he started kissing her back, hesitantly, and as he did so, found himself drawn closer and closer to Cassie's body, his hands slipping down over her bottom, which was really quite nicely firm and tight under her jeans. Cassie put her hands over his, unembarrassed, making his grip on her bottom tighter. With this gesture, something snapped in Omar, and he started kissing her fiercely, almost aggressively. In a cruel, dark moment on the dark street, while Cassie pressed her body against his and reached down for the buttons below his waist, Omar was appalled to find himself wanting to shag her, then and there, to turn her round and push her roughly against the wall, to prove himself with her, to use her. He didn't feel passion or excitement towards her, he simply felt cold and in control. The emotion he felt was like violence. 'You like me, don't you, Omar?' she said, with innocent appeal. And Omar began to understand why she had ended up being mistreated quite so often.

'I do, Cassie, I do really like you. You're a nice girl,' Omar said firmly, pushing her away gently. He removed her hands, and held them kindly. 'You're a nice girl, and you don't need to do this just because I bought you dinner, or because I listened to you.'

'Don't you think I'm attractive?' asked Cassie, in a small voice, turning away.

Omar squeezed her hands reassuringly. 'I do. I think your new hair really suits you, and you have a fantastic arse. A butt like a ten-year-old boy, as Sharif would say.' He was rewarded with a slight puff of a giggle from Cassie, as she turned back towards him, eyes shining hopefully. 'I'm sorry I kissed you back and misled you – you are pretty and you are very nice. But I just don't feel that way for you.'

Still holding her hands, Omar pulled her out of the alleyway and started walking her back towards the club. 'Well, this is new. I normally get rejected afterwards, not before,' Cassie said, but not quite disconsolately.

'Maybe you should wait a little while, then you might not get rejected at all.' Omar knew he had no experience in these matters, but continued regardless. 'I think that blokes, especially blokes our age, are basically selfish. If you offer them something, they take it, and ask themselves whether they want it afterwards.'

Cassie walked on for a bit in silence, and said, 'You know, the first time I did it, I was only fifteen. It was on the green outside school. It was dark, and I thought he really liked me, and I didn't enjoy it at all but I thought he would like me even more afterwards. But he only said he liked me to my face, and told everyone else that I was a bloody good ride. And the next person I went out with expected it, and said I couldn't really like him if I wouldn't, after I'd already done it with someone else. And I did it, just to wipe away the last time. And it was better, but not much. I'd had sex with four people before I was sixteen.' She scuffed her toe against the curb. 'Maybe I am just a slapper.'

'You're really not,' said Omar fiercely. 'Men are just bastards,' he added without thinking. He had to stop and laugh. 'God, that made me sound like a girl, didn't it . . .?'

Cassie squeezed his hand, and stopped to kiss him on the cheek. 'I think you really are a sweet man, Omar.'

When they got back to the bar, Ali and Sharif were waiting for them. Ali looked thunderous, and Sharif was casually leaning against the wall, with a fag dripping out of his mouth. 'About bloody time. I've been waiting fucking forever for you,' Ali said crossly to Cassie. 'Come on, we're going.' She didn't say goodbye to Sharif, and made off down the street with Cassie in tow towards the minicabs, with strides as long as her miniskirt would allow.

Omar looked at Sharif, waiting for an explanation. 'So, nice date with Cassie?' was all Sharif said, after a long pause. 'Snog her, did you? Or just shag her against the wall?'

Omar pursed his lips, and thrust his hands deep into his pockets to stop himself shaking Sharif. 'That's bang out of order, mate. She's a sweet girl, you've no right to talk about her like that. And yes, we had a nice dinner, thank you.'

'Oh, put your handbag away before I get scared . . .' retorted Sharif in a bored voice. 'Is it your time of the month or something?'

Omar ignored the jibe, and nodded towards Ali and Cassie, who were getting in a cab. 'Did you and the lovely Ali have a fight, then?'

'Not exactly. I just said that I thought we might stop seeing each other so much, start seeing other people,' Sharif said casually.

Men really are bastards, thought Omar. He'd bet that Sharif waited until after they'd had sex before he said it. 'What brought that on?' he asked diplomatically.

Sharif shrugged. 'She was just getting a bit territorial.

Complaining that we never meet at our flats, that we're always outside somewhere when we, you know . . . But that's how I like it. What does she want me to do – stay over and have breakfast with her bloody family?' Sharif stubbed out his cigarette. 'I'll miss her a bit – for a pretty girl she was pure filth.' He looked at Omar. 'Are you coming back to mine tonight, or staying at home?'

Omar felt his stomach churn with loathing for his brother, and looked at his watch. 'I'll do what I did last time, I'll get the coach back to college. They run through the night, and I've got lectures in the morning.' Sharif's behaviour had helped him find the little bit of indignation and bravery to say what he'd been thinking about for a while. He swallowed nervously and said, 'Sharif, I need to talk to you. You know how hard it's been coming down for gigs with me being at college. I just don't think I can do it any more.'

'Don't be soft. What are you saying? You're going to leave our band? Just because you're fannying about in college somewhere hardly an hour from here – give me a break,' Sharif scoffed.

'Yes, I am. I can't be part of the band any more,' Omar said. 'I'm sorry.'

Sharif heard the seriousness in Omar's voice, and looked at him with a sudden cold fury, as though he'd been betrayed. 'You know what, kid. You can't stop being a part of the band, as that would mean that you actually belonged in the first place,' he said cruelly. 'I'm not sorry you're buggering off. I only let you in because I was sorry for you. You were always the weakest link.' Nodding at the doorman, he walked back into the club.

Omar walked down towards Liverpool Street. He would get a bus to Marble Arch to get the Oxford Tube back to college. He realized how much he was looking forward to seeing Jim over tea and biscuits, and telling him about his last gig.

The Trouble with December Evenings

JONTY AND SHONA were sitting in the staffroom, long after the end of school, and were both avoiding going home for similar reasons. Jonty had argued with his wife, and was flicking through the Ceefax pages, going through a packet of bourbons all by himself. Shona was doing some marking, which she could just as well do at home, but didn't really want to. Things would be better at home when Omar came back for the Christmas holidays; she hoped he hadn't made any plans with his new friends from college. She wondered what he'd think of Patrick-Bob. And Sharif would come back for Christmas Day, maybe she could persuade him to stay until New Year. It would all be back to normal then; they could go back to being a happy family for a few days.

Jonty and Shona were both surprised by Dermot walking into the staffroom. Jonty had stopped trying to look busy around Dermot, and raised his hand in a silent greeting. 'Hello, both,' Dermot said affably. 'Still burning the midnight oil?'

'It feels like midnight,' Jonty said despondently,

looking at the pitch-black gloom outside. 'Where've you been?'

'I was setting some stuff up in the language lab,' Dermot said vaguely. 'It's hard to get some time in that room without someone else hogging it.' He looked at his watch. 'Well, it's six-thirty, so I think that it would be permissible to have a drink. Anyone care to join me?' He looked expectantly at both of them. 'Jonty, are you game?'

A text beeped on Jonty's mobile. He looked at it and sighed. 'From the Trouble and Strife. Sorry, Dermot. I think I had really better get home. Maybe Shona will go with you?' He finished off his last bourbon biscuit wearily.

Dermot looked at Shona. 'Well, Shona, how about it? Will you join me for a drink? A very quick one, I promise.'

'No thanks,' said Shona. 'I'd better be getting home, too. My husband will be wondering who's going to burn his dinner tonight . . .' Privately, she would have rather liked a drink, but didn't like being the second choice. Dermot had clearly wanted a laddish drink with Jonty and was only asking her to be polite.

Shona was waiting at the damp bus stop, and opened her umbrella as she felt the first spots of rain. Bloody miserable December evenings, she thought to herself, as though it was all December's fault that her evenings had become so miserable. A dark blue car pulled up next to the bus stop. Hope he gets a fine, parking in the bloody bus lane, she continued to gripe. She was surprised when Dermot wound down the window and said, 'Do you want a lift home, Shona? It's a grim evening. You're just in Tooting, aren't you?'

'Hi, Dermot. No thanks, really, I'm fine,' Shona demurred, but looking down the icy road, she saw no cheerful red bus in sight. 'Well, OK then, if it doesn't take you too far out of your way. It's just near Tooting Bec tube.' She hopped in, and pulled the seat belt on. 'So, I guess you didn't get your drink?' she said politely.

'Well, I didn't really want to sit in the pub by myself on a Friday night. I'd probably bump into half the students littering up the local, anyway.'

Shona laughed. 'Did Pam ever tell you about the time we bumped into some of our girls in the Admiral's Arms one afternoon? We both had a double free period as it was GCSE exam week, so we skived off to the pub, and saw a group of our girls from the lower sixth on the other side of the bar.'

'What did you do? Report them?' asked Dermot, amused.

'Oh God, no. They shouldn't have been there, and neither should we. So we all did the decent thing, we pretended we hadn't seen each other, drank up quickly, left, and didn't mention it once we got back to class.'

'Outrageous!' laughed Dermot. 'Jane would not be pleased!'

'You're not to tell tales about Pam and me to the head,' Shona said firmly. 'We'll flatly deny it,' she added with a twinkle.

'So, any plans for the evening?' asked Dermot. 'What are you going to burn for your poor husband tonight?'

'Oh, the usual,' Shona answered airily. 'What about you?'

'I've got a hot date with Tamarind, my local Indian. I can never bear to cook for one on a Friday. I always get a takeaway.'

'Is that Tamarind Khan, in Balham?' Shona asked with interest.

'Might be. It's up on Balham High Street, near the Boots.'

'That's one of my husband's restaurants,' Shona said delightedly. 'You might have seen my son in there from time to time, he's started working there. Answers to the name of Sharif. Very handsome lad, always has the girls after him.'

'Must take after his mum,' Dermot said, 'but I can't say I've seen him. Maybe he doesn't work on Friday nights.'

'Oh, maybe not,' said Shona, although she was sure that Sharif was meant to work five days a week. 'Well, I'm glad I'm not taking you out of your way. Balham's just a few minutes from me.'

'We're almost at Tooting Bec now,' Dermot commented. 'Have you never thought about driving to work? It's only a few minutes in a car, but that bus must take forever.'

'Haven't learned to drive yet,' Shona said lightly. 'I started some lessons after I had the boys, but it didn't quite agree with me. And the lessons were so expensive, it seemed a bit wasteful. Parvez took me out a few times but I never felt comfortable with him as my teacher. It was the only thing we ever argued about, back then.' She looked out. 'Could you just drop me off here, near the station? I need to get something from the corner shop,' she lied. She didn't want Dermot driving her all the way home. She didn't want him to meet Parvez, who would probably offer him a drink for his gallantry. She wanted to keep her school and home life separate.

'I could teach you, if you want,' suggested Dermot, pulling over and parking. 'I taught my ex-wife to drive, and she'd failed four times before she met me. I'm a good teacher – it's what I do, after all.'

'I'm sure you are,' said Shona as she stepped out onto the pavement, noticing that it was the first time he had mentioned his 'sort' of marriage since their first stilted meeting. 'Thanks for the offer, but I think my driving days are over. And thanks very much for the ride.' She waved enthusiastically as he drove off, and then turned down the street to walk home.

The school play that Christmas was Noël Coward's *Private Lives*, directed by the sixth-formers under Jonty's watchful, jaundiced eye. Two performances took place on Tuesday and Wednesday of the last week of term, and most of the teachers turned out for the closing party, some with their partners. Parvez had begged off; he normally turned up just to show a united front with Shona, but he really didn't like plays, or theatre, and it clashed with a concert that he wanted to listen to on the radio. After some deeply diluted mulled wine, with so much orange juice added that it was verging on the pink rather than red, most of the teachers headed off to the Admiral's Arms, led by a triumphant Jonty with his embarrassed, sober wife. Shona and Dermot were hemmed into a banquette by the merrymakers, and sat squashed together.

'I knew you'd come out for that drink with me eventually,' Dermot said, clinking his pint glass with Shona's white wine.

'I didn't know you drank Guinness,' Shona said a little stupidly, feeling a bit tired and drunk after the long day.

'I'm Irish, of course I do. I also play the fiddle and dance with my arms glued to my sides,' he answered seriously.

'Do you?' Shona asked, before seeing the twitch in Dermot's mouth. 'Oh, you are taking the mickey. This time, I mean.'

'Am I? I admit I don't play the fiddle, but you've not seen me dance,' laughed Dermot. Shona noticed what white, straight teeth he had. Very un-English teeth. But of course, he wasn't English. Dermot cleared his throat. 'I meant to ask you something, Shona, something about Racine.'

'Sure, what is it?' Shona said amicably. She knew she was on very safe ground with Racine.

'What were you going to say, that day, when you said true hate doesn't follow true love, but something else does? What were you going to say takes the place of true love, once it's gone?'

'I'm not sure that's a question about Racine,' Shona said quietly.

'Maybe it's just a question, then,' Dermot answered.

'Fairytale of New York' struck up on the pub jukebox. Pam, looking very pretty and flushed, with a lot of make-up and a slinky black top, staggered over to join them. 'Where's your handsome husband tonight?' she asked Shona.

'Oh, just busy,' Shona said lightly.

'Shame. Tell him that I missed him,' Pam hiccupped, adding to Dermot, 'Have you met Shona's handsome hubby?'

Dermot shook his head. 'I've not had the pleasure, but I take it that he's quite a catch.'

'Ding and double-dong,' confirmed Pam, 'and he's sooo funny. And he can really dance, too. Tell him, Shona.'

'Oh, I don't like to brag,' said Shona, unable to keep a straight face. She'd not seen Pam this tipsy in ages. Pam downed her drink and pulled Dermot by the hand. 'Come on, Dermot. Dance with me to this one. It's Irish, you know.'

'That I know, Pam,' said Dermot, rising to the occasion with a smile. He let Pam pull him off his seat, and went to dance with her. 'You'll see if I was lying about those arms, now,' he said in an aside to Shona as he got up.

Much later, Shona left the pub, swaying just a tiny bit. As she tip-tapped up the street in her smart heels, she heard someone shouting her name behind her. 'Shona!' Dermot called. 'Hold up!' He ran up to her. 'Isn't your husband picking you up?'

'No, there's a concert he wanted to listen to this evening, and I didn't want to bother him. I thought I'd just get the bus. I don't think you or anyone else is in a fit state to give me a lift tonight,' Shona said. 'Are you heading back to the pub?'

'No, I think I'll call it a night, too. I'll walk you to the bus stop. It's on my way to the station.'

'Sure,' said Shona, although she had already kissed him goodbye that night, on the cheek. She had kissed everyone on the cheek before she left the pub. It was unusually affectionate for her, and proof that she was a little tipsy, but then it was Christmas.

They walked together wordlessly, until Dermot broke the silence by saying, 'I should apologize to you, Shona. I lied to you when we first met.'

'Oh, don't worry about it. I'm sure I've lied to you thousands of times. Everytime I've said Nice day, Nice haircut, Nice assembly, Nice class. Thousands of times,' she said lightly, wondering why she was suddenly being so frank.

'No, really, this is important. I never lie, and I really don't want to have lied to you.'

'What was it?' Shona said, amused at the passion in his tone.

'When I said I didn't really have any children. That was a lie. I did have a child once. She was premature. She died the same day she was born. That was eight years ago.' He said it matter-of-factly. 'I know I was only a father for a day, but I was a father once, and I shouldn't have lied.'

'Oh my God, Dermot, I'm so sorry,' Shona said, woken out of her pleasantly woozy stupor with shock. The fear of losing her children had been her worst nightmare, and one that haunted her throughout her pregnancy. She went to touch his arm with sympathy, but he kept walking, and so she hurried to keep up with him. They were silent until they reached Shona's bus stop.

'Well, here we are,' said Dermot, but he didn't make to go. He just stood there.

Shona had made a decision while they were walking, and said to him bravely, 'You wanted to know what follows when true love goes away? It isn't hate. It's just a nothing, like a void or a vacuum. It's nothing but emptiness.' She looked up at him to kiss him goodbye again; she wished she was brave enough to kiss him on the lips, she could excuse it on the drink, on Christmas; she could deceive herself and him that she hadn't really meant to; she could apologize and say that she was aiming for his cheek but had just missed.

But she didn't have a chance to see how brave or foolish she was, as Dermot said, 'Goodbye, Shona,' and took her by surprise by kissing her quickly, but deliberately, on the lips. There was no mistake, and no apology.

As he walked off, Shona leaned back on the bus stop for support, her knees suddenly weak. She didn't look after him, but stared fixedly ahead at the lights of her approaching bus. When the bus arrived, she sat on it in such a daze that she went two stops past her house and had to get another bus back.

Châteauneuf du Pape in a Clapham Common Flat

THE NEXT DAY, Dermot was conspicuous in his absence from the staffroom. 'Maybe he's in the language lab?' said Jane.

'No, I saw him in the library,' said Jonty.

'I think he's avoiding me,' whispered Pam conspiratorially to Shona, joining her on the window seat. 'I'm sure he wanted to kiss me when we were dancing last night, I could tell. And when he left, he didn't say goodbye to everyone like you did, he just got up and belted off.'

'You might be right,' answered Shona neutrally.

Pam noticed the lack of enthusiasm in Shona's voice, and asked, 'Are you a bit hungover or something? You look dreadful.'

'I'm fine, just a bit tired. And this is how I look without make-up,' Shona said flatly. She had not put any make-up on deliberately, and had worn a dreadful sack of a dress that her mother had sent her, which she normally wore to clean the house in. It was her equivalent of a hair shirt. She thought she was making amends.

Looking at herself in the mirror in the ladies' loo,

Shona saw herself clearly, and realized how ridiculous she was being. It was just a drunken kiss that she hadn't even instigated, and it was probably Pam who had got Dermot all wound up, not her. She combed her hair and applied a bit of lipstick. She looked vastly improved, and felt immediately better. However, as she went to her pigeonhole, her spirits sank. Along with the prep that her students had left for her was a small folded-up note, in Dermot's tiny, precise hand. 'Shona, if you are available, please meet me at Clapham Common tube station tonight at 6 p.m. I have some questions on Racine I'd like to clear up with you before next term. No need to RSVP. Yours, D.'

So what now? Shona thought to herself. She owed him a meeting, didn't she? Just to clear the air before the next term, as he said. Otherwise it could be very awkward working together. And if she didn't go, what did that mean? He had told her not to RSVP, so would he just wait for her, and get the message when she didn't turn up? What message would that be exactly? That she didn't want to be friends, that she didn't forgive him for kissing her when she was tipsy? Well, that wasn't true. She did want to be friends with Dermot; she valued his friendship, even. She could talk to him about books, and language, and literature, and art exhibitions. He had gone with her when she had taken her class to see the performance of *Andromaque* at the Riverside Studios, and talked with enthusiasm about the staging. Sometimes he made her laugh, but most often he made her think. She thought he was probably the most intelligent person she knew. She didn't want to lose him as a friend and colleague over a silly misunderstanding, caused by too much unnecessary truth-telling after too much unnecessary drinking.

She folded up the note, and put it in the pocket of her grey sack dress. Then she called Parvez and told him she'd be late home as she had an off-site meeting with her department head.

Shona was at the tube station fifteen minutes early. She stood nervously by the gates, checking her reflection in the Photo-Me machine. She reapplied her lipstick and then wiped it off, thinking it looked too obvious. She reapplied it, and then wiped it off again, definitely. She was meeting a colleague, she told herself. She really didn't need to look or feel pretty. She pulled out her copy of *Andromaque*, and looked at the pages, not really reading them. When Dermot arrived, she would give him a bright smile and a firm kiss on the cheek. Then he would know that they were friends again, and everything would be back to normal. He'd know that she wasn't cross, and that she knew that he hadn't meant anything by what had happened last night.

At ten minutes before six, Dermot arrived at the station. He didn't come up the escalator from the tube, as Shona had expected. He came down the stairs from the street. When he saw her, he broke into a smile so genuine, of such unadulterated relief and hope, that her firm intentions withered – he practically shone with happiness. He walked quickly towards her, and she reached her arms around his neck and kissed him passionately, breathlessly. Her knees felt weak again. When he pulled away, it was to hold the length of her slight frame against him, and kiss her reverently on her forehead.

Shona pressed her face against his chest, and said disconsolately into his jacket, 'Vous me trompiez, Seigneur.'

'Je me trompais moi-même,' he answered. Shona looked up at him. He was still smiling, but she was practically tearful.

'I'm so glad you came,' he said, unnecessarily, as Shona could read it on his face with more eloquence than his clumsy words could express.

'I think I had to,' Shona answered. He held her close to him as they walked upstairs and out of the tube station, on to the wet, icy street.

'You look beautiful today,' he said sincerely, smoothing a strand of her hair back in place, and brushing his thumb against her full, un-made up, lower lip.

As Shona and Dermot walked along the muddy paths of the Common, his arm protectively around her in the security of the darkness, Shona asked, 'Why here? Why Clapham Common tube?'

'It's where I live,' answered Dermot.

'But I thought you said you lived in Balham?' Shona asked with a frown.

Dermot stopped walking, and kissed her where her brow had furrowed. 'You said I lived in Balham, and I let you assume it because I didn't want you to think I was going out of my way when I drove you home. I thought you might not let me take you any more.'

They walked a little further and sat on a bench, hidden

from the road by the trees, and started kissing again, Shona's small hands reaching inside his jacket to feel his warmth. As they clung to each other like teenagers, Sharif and his new girlfriend approached the bench from across the Common.

'Shit, someone's already there,' he said with disappointment, stopping short a hundred feet from the bench. It was one of his many preferred venues for making love, if you could call it that. He peered through the dark and distance, trying to make out the shadowy forms that were holding each other. 'I think they'll be there for a while. Look at them, they're practically shagging.'

The pretty girl he was with squeezed his waist, and turning to face him, slipped her hand inside his back pocket. 'Don't worry, babe. I know somewhere else we can go.'

As they walked on, Sharif turned and looked back at the embracing couple, sure that there was something disconcertingly familiar about the shape of the woman's hair, but the girl's insistent pull on his hand distracted him, and he didn't think anything more about it.

Oblivious to her passing son, Shona was aware of nothing but Dermot and the cold air separating them. 'Where do you want to go, Shona?' Dermot asked between kisses. 'There's a little bar near here, or we could go to a quiet pub or café, somewhere we can talk.'

Shona didn't answer. Only passion, she felt, would take her through this; if she stopped and talked, she would realize what she was doing and stop altogether. 'Let's go to your place,' she said finally.

'Shona, are you sure?' Dermot said with concern. 'I don't want to rush you into anything.'

'I'm sure,' she said.

As they entered Dermot's bijou bachelor pad, they were still kissing, even as they tumbled through the door. 'Would you like some wine?' asked Dermot.

'No, thank you,' Shona answered. Whatever she was going to say or do, she wanted to say or do it with a clear head so she would have nothing to blame it on apart from herself. She didn't even look at the apartment, she simply pulled off her coat and started undoing Dermot's jacket.

'Shona, we need to talk, about all of this, about us,' Dermot said gently.

'Afterwards. Let's talk afterwards,' she said, not realizing until she said it what she had just proposed. Dermot understood; instead of embarrassing her by asking, 'After what?' he simply took her hand and led her through to his bedroom.

'Only because I have to get you out of this God-awful dress,' Dermot said, pulling the long zip down the length of her back.

'It's my hair-shirt dress. I was doing penance for having impure thoughts,' Shona explained, pulling it down her shoulders.

'And I thought it was just us Catholics who felt guilty for impure thoughts,' Dermot said.

Shona had said that they would talk afterwards, but was surprised at how much Dermot talked to her as they made love. With Parvez, their lovemaking was animal, instinctive and silent, there was no need for words. With Dermot, he admired her, reassured her, asked if she liked this, or liked that, and asked how this or that felt; he was exploring her, learning about her, and in a strange way this vocal, intellectualized lovemaking felt much more intimate, almost uncomfortably so, as he asked her to admit all her likes and feelings and thoughts, so nothing was left hidden or secret. As they moved together, he asked her to look at him, and she opened her eyes to find herself looking straight into his, and their eyes remained locked, connected until the end; she had never noticed the colour of his eyes before they were grey-blue. Afterwards, Shona lay back, her arms behind her head, and reflected that it was either the best or worst sex she'd had in her life; she was unable to decide which.

Despite the cold of the evening outside, the flat was warm, and Dermot, naked above the duvet, stroked the insides of her arms. 'Would you like that wine, now?' he asked.

'Yes, please,' Shona answered politely, as though nothing at all had happened, and he had offered her a cup of tea in the staffroom. He got up unselfconsciously and still naked, walked through to the kitchen. Parvez would have put his shorts on before he left the bedroom. Shona noticed how pale his skin was compared to Parvez's. It glowed in the low light of the flat. She looked around at his room for the first time. It was filled with books. Huge numbers of books. There were books on literature, books of literary criticism, books on language and grammar, huge coffee table tomes on Dalí and Catalonia, books on Spanish regions, books on philosophy. She saw Voltaire, Rimbaud, Molière, Hugo, and a new copy of Racine, all in translation. She felt instantly comforted. It was the sort of bedroom she would have liked, if only she had the shelf space. It was like her father's study in Dhaka before he repatriated all his books to London.

Dermot walked in with two glasses of dusky red liquid. 'Oh, I'm sorry,' said Shona, 'I thought you knew, I never drink red wine.'

'You said you never drink red wine unless it's a really, really good one,' answered Dermot. 'This is a Château-neuf du Pape.' He passed her a glass. 'Cheers,' he said, clinking lightly.

'Gosh,' said Shona, sipping it appreciatively. 'This is wonderful. Do you normally keep fine red wines at home to drink by yourself?'

'No,' said Dermot, with a touch of embarrassment. 'I bought this one after you said you only liked really good red wines, with the vague hope that you'd share it with me one day.'

Sitting up, pulling the covers up over her breasts, Shona put down her glass and said reproachfully, 'You never told me. All this time, this last term. You never told me, you never even gave me a hint.'

'You never gave me the slightest impression that you'd be interested if I did tell you,' Dermot replied frankly. 'I asked you for a drink once, and you said no, you had to go back to your husband. I went out of my way to find time with you. I waited for you so I could offer you rides home, but you never waited for me, you never asked me to give you a lift.'

'When?' asked Shona. 'When did you start to . . .' She didn't know how to finish the sentence, it felt juvenile to say 'like me', as though they were in the school yard themselves, but nothing else seemed appropriate. '. . . like me?' she finished feebly.

Dermot sighed. 'I liked you almost from the moment we met – not the day we met, when you were a frosty witch, but almost straight away afterwards. You're funny, and you're so kind to everyone, and I think . . . you might be the most intelligent woman I know.' He kissed her on the forehead again, holding her temples gently on either side. 'This is what I like about you, right here, in your head. You have a wonderful mind, Shona. It's like the British Museum, with hidden gifts in hidden rooms. I want to wander in it with you and roam around.'

Shona was speechless. He thought she was funny; everyone knew that Parvez was the funny one, not her. He saw her well-meaning dissembling for kindness. And unlike Parvez, he liked her for her intelligence, not despite it. It all brought her back to the chivalrous ghost in the room, the unseen husband of the happy, dead memories. 'Don't you want to ask me about Parvez?' she asked.

Dermot exhaled deeply. 'To be honest, Shona, I don't. I know that he's a nice guy, Pam's told me all about him. I know he's good-looking and successful, and that you've been with him for twenty years and raised a family with him. I also know there's something wrong with you and him, or you wouldn't be here with me. I don't want to know any more.'

'You don't think it's your concern?' asked Shona.

'No, you're my concern. I told myself that I could be happy just being your friend, but I was fooling myself; when you kissed everyone in the pub yesterday and left, I couldn't stand it. I've waited a long time to meet someone like you, and I'm not going to give up on you just because you're tied to someone who you don't love any more. I turned forty-one in October, Shona, I'm forty-one years old, and I have nothing to show for my life, absolutely nothing, apart from a moderately successful career.'

He's younger than me, she thought, but she felt the young, foolish one. She had no idea what she was doing here, in this flat, in this bed. It had come from nowhere.

Dermot stroked her hair. 'When did you know that . . . you felt something for me?' he asked.

Shona hugged her knees. 'I didn't know, I didn't even let myself know until I saw you tonight. I wasn't jealous when I saw you flirting with Pam, I didn't mind that you didn't flirt with me, I didn't notice that you were waiting for me to give me a lift home, I didn't even think you had wanted to ask me out for a drink that time, I thought you were just being polite. All the time I was telling myself that I just wanted us to be friends. I just like your company so much, I just like you so much . . .' she trailed off. 'I deceived myself,' she said humbly. 'It's something I've got good at doing, in one way or another.' She finished her glass of wine. 'I'm sorry, Dermot. I really think I had better go now.'

'Shona, please stay. Let me take you out, or cook for you. I promise that I never burn dinner,' Dermot said appealingly.

'I'm sorry, Parvez will be waiting for me. I said I had a meeting with you.'

'Oh, Shona,' he breathed with disappointment, closing his eyes. 'Let me drive you home, at least.'

'No, I don't think that's a good idea. But could you walk me to the tube? I don't think I'd know how to get there. I wasn't really paying attention on the way over.'

Dermot watched Shona dress for a moment before pulling on his jeans, and stepping behind her to help her with the zip. 'You must burn this dress,' he said. 'On the other hand, maybe you should wear it every day. Then no one apart from me will be able to see how heavenly you are.' He pushed aside her hair from the back of her neck as he pulled the zip up to the top, and kissed the skin there, between her hairline and her collar. Shona felt her knees go weak again and she turned round, leaning on his chest of drawers, and kissed him again, as though she really couldn't stop.

They walked back to the station slowly, with a sense of finality. As they approached the steps down to the underground, Dermot pulled her round gently to face him. 'Shona, this wasn't just tonight, was it? I don't want to embarrass you by getting all dramatic, but please don't tell me that this is all it'll be.'

Shona felt seen clearly, and seen through, all at once. She felt like a character in one of the novels she taught, like Anne in *Moderato Cantabile*, letting her almost-affair of a few days last her for her lifetime of monotonous marriage. She stepped back from his arms, and asked, 'You tell me, Dermot. How it can be anything more? All we can have is more nights like this, stolen time when I'll be watching the clock, wondering what excuse to come up with next. And you'll get tired of it, and who can blame you, and you'll go find some lovely unmarried girl, like Pam, whom you can have a proper relationship with, and have children, and have something to show for your life.'

'I don't want a girl like Pam. I don't want children with someone I don't care for. I want you. Don't worry about me getting hurt; I'm a big boy, and I can look out for myself.'

'Well, maybe I'm the one who'll get hurt,' Shona said quietly, her face turned away from him even while he pulled her into his arms.

'Look at me, Shona,' Dermot commanded. And she looked into his grey-blue eyes and felt that connection, that overbearing complicated intimacy she had felt while they were making love. She and Dermot shared neither a silly sense of humour, nor a natural physical compatibility. She realized they shared something quite different, something less accessible and more insidious, something innate; it wasn't a feeling she'd had before, and she didn't know how to put a name to it. Dermot continued, 'You said you liked me before. How do you say that in French?'

'I like you is just "Tu me plais", you please me,' Shona explained, taken aback by the question. 'You don't really translate "I like you" directly, as that's "Je t'aime", which means something . . . quite different.'

'Which "I like you" did you mean?' asked Dermot. At Shona's silence, he said, 'You don't have to answer that, it wasn't a fair question. But I need you to know something. I like you; I mean, I think I'm falling in like with you. And I meant what I said, about not giving up on you.'

Shona blinked back silent tears. She didn't think she was funny, kind or intelligent; she thought she was dull, deceitful, and downright stupid to have got herself into this situation. And yet, despite all her faults, she had somehow become loved once more; somehow, in the course of her deceit and dissembling, she had become lovable.

Burnt Cookies and Driving Lessons

ON THE LAST day of winter term Dermot arrived in school earlier than usual, hoping that Shona would have had the same idea and that they might have some time to spend together before the rest of the staff blundered in with Christmas goodwill. In fact, she arrived late, like all the others, barely before the nine a.m. bell, and distributed a batch of home-baked cookies before rushing off to her middle-fourth class. There were no more lessons after the mid-morning break, as the grand hall was turned into a Christmas fête, with stalls manned by parent, teacher and student volunteers. During the noisy and bustling set-up, accompanied by the school Barber Shop Quartet rehearsing Christmas standards, Dermot sought refuge in the staffroom, and for once got his own tea as his usual fan club were engrossed in comparing the presents they had been given by their various classes. He munched on one of Shona's chocolate-chunk cookies, which really weren't that bad as they had probably twice the number of chocolate chunks that were required, which disguised the rather thin and burnt biscuit they nestled in.

He was slightly perturbed by the realization that Shona's first act on having gone home, after they had confessed their feelings and made love, must have been to bake a batch of cookies.

On cue, Shona walked into the staffroom, struggling with the heavy door as she balanced some little presents in her arms. On seeing Dermot eating her cookies, she gave him a bright, artificial smile, before joining Pam at her spot on the window seat. Shona didn't give him a second glance, and let Pam chat animatedly to her while she smiled and laughed occasionally. She was wearing make-up and her hair was perfect; she had neither dressed up nor dressed down. When Pam left the seat, Dermot swallowed his tea anxiously and approached. Shona smiled brightly again and asked casually, 'So, Dermot, are you going to the fête later?' She had none of Dermot's nervous dryness, and she cast him no meaningful glance. She was acting perfectly normally – it was as though he had imagined the night before.

'I thought I might,' he almost stammered. 'Just to give, you know, a show of support.' When Shona looked like she was going to turn her attention back to her tea, he asked, 'And you?'

'Oh, I'll stick around until they call the raffle. You never know, I might get lucky and win the stash of home-made wine that Jonty's donated,' Shona said cheerfully.

'Well, I was after that little stash myself,' Dermot said, his nervousness abating with annoyance at Shona's insouciance. How could she not feel a little bit of what he was feeling? 'You can't have Châteauneuf du Pape every day, after all.' After dropping that hint, he looked deeply in her eyes for longer than was discreet, and saw that she was giving absolutely nothing away. She was the picture of serene normality. So this is how she thinks it's going to be, he thought. She's going to pretend that nothing happened, and wipe it away like a third-year pupil's bad conjugation on the whiteboard. He turned his attention to Pam, who was furiously pretending not to be interested. 'Pam, are you doing anything for the fête?' he asked with a charming smile that crinkled the edges of his eyes.

When Shona left the staffroom, Dermot made an excuse and followed her swiftly; she went into the little cubby where the staff pigeonholes were, which led through to their cloakroom.

'Shona,' he said urgently, shutting the door firmly behind him.

'Oh, hi Dermot, you surprised me,' said Shona pleasantly, taking out the little Christmas cards and tardy prep that littered her pigeonhole, shuffling through them. Even alone, she didn't show a sign of dropping the act. He had no idea how she could dissemble so fluently after what had happened between them. He remembered something she had said to him, about lying to him thousands of times about little things.

'It's not going to be like this,' he said calmly, taking a step towards her.

'Like what?' she replied innocently, still looking at her papers. 'Did you have some questions about next term's syllabus?'

Dermot walked up to Shona, took her in his arms and kissed her fiercely, pinning her against the wall. She just stood there for a moment, not reacting at all, her arms hanging limply by her sides and still holding her papers; but then Dermot felt her almost lose her footing as her knees went weak, and he held her more tightly, almost picking up her slight frame as her lips softened against his.

'Dermot, please,' Shona said quietly. 'Someone might walk in any moment.'

Dermot let her go, and reached forward and smoothed a strand of her hair back. 'I know you feel something for me,' he said. 'I can't go through the holidays not seeing you.'

'Maybe it's better just to leave it,' Shona said, leaning back against the wall, as though her treacherous legs still couldn't quite support her, looking down at the scuffed wooden floorboards. 'I don't know how we'd manage it.'

'I do,' said Dermot. 'I've been thinking about it.' He put his palm to Shona's cheek, and was gratified to see that she turned her face towards it. 'Shona, please look at me,' he asked. Shona looked into his eyes, and he looked back into hers, chocolate-brown with flecks of gold, dark liquid eyes sparkling with depth. 'I could give you driving lessons over the holidays, and you could repay me by giving me some French instruction. No one would think anything of it – it would just be two colleagues helping each other out.'

'Let me think about it,' Shona said after a long pause. Dermot looked into her eyes again, and unthinkingly leaned in towards her. 'You're getting too close,' she said, half holding her breath.

'You've got too close already,' Dermot answered, his lips almost brushing hers. The turn of the squeaky brass knob made them both jump, and Shona dashed sideways into the cloakroom, leaving Dermot leaning awkwardly against the wall.

'Dermot, are you all right, dear?' Jane asked with concern, wondering what her head of languages was doing.

'Not quite,' Dermot answered truthfully. 'I think I've got a bit of a funny head. I'll be fine in a bit.'

Dermot went back to the staffroom, and was persuaded to join Jonty roving around the fête, chatting to the parents and students he knew from the stalls. He saw Shona doing the same, and when he accidentally caught her eye, her face again gave nothing away. Watching her slim figure in the crowd, Dermot felt a knot in his stomach. Shona was offering him nothing more than the cheap, shining hope of a tawdry affair – to be with him in secret. He almost wished that was all he wanted; it would make things so much less complicated. But he knew that he would never have started anything with Shona if he didn't secretly hope and believe that she could eventually leave her husband and be with him properly, honestly, out in the daylight where everyone could see.

He realized bitterly that he was no different from any mistress of a married man. He didn't just want to sleep with Shona, he wanted to wake up with her and read the Sunday papers with her, and listen to her quiet, clever comments and funny asides. He didn't just want to sleep with Shona; he wanted to do everything with her.

But driving lessons might just be a start.

Becoming Accustomed to a Face

OMAR WAS WORKING in the elegant arched library of the Radcliffe Camera. He didn't need to refer to anything at the Rad Cam itself; he'd brought his own notes and his own books borrowed from the faculty libraries. He'd just fancied a change of scene from the Bod and the college library; the Rad Cam was one of the few buildings as pretty on the inside as it was on the outside. He put down his biro and looked dreamily at the delicate stonework on the pillars. Suddenly, he felt warm, dry hands over his eyes, a familiar smell of soap and biscuits. 'Penny for them,' whispered an amused voice in hushed tones.

'They're not that cheap,' he whispered back.

Jim removed his hands, and crouched grinning by the side of Omar's desk. 'I know how cheap mine are, but then I'm an old tart,' he said with deliberate campness. Looking at his watch, he said in his normal voice, at an inappropriate volume, 'Sod this for a lark. Let's go for a drink.'

The students on the desks around Omar looked at Jim

with distaste, and one of them even shushed him. Jim looked at her rudely and shushed her back, rolling his eyes with unjustified indignation. Stifling a laugh, Omar got up, leaving his books and papers, and ushered Jim out. As they left the building, both Omar and Jim burst out laughing with the easy familiarity of friends who found everything funny as long as they were together. 'That was rude,' he chided Jim, when they calmed down.

'Well, silly old bitch, if she's that concerned about her work she should go somewhere less picturesque,' Jim said unrepentantly. 'What were you doing there? I thought the Bod was your usual poison.'

'Oh, you know me. I was just admiring the architecture,' replied Omar with a shrug. 'And you?'

'Ditto. King's Arms or the Turf?' asked Jim.

'I guess the King's Arms, it's nearer,' said Omar.

'Turf it is,' said Jim, putting his hands deep in his pockets and striding off.

'I really don't know why you bother even asking me,' muttered Omar, without any real annoyance, walking quickly to catch up with him.

The Turf Tavern was filled with a heady scent of mulled wine and was quieter than Omar had seen it, but it was quite early in the afternoon. If he hadn't been working on his last essay of the term, he wouldn't have let Jim persuade him to stay for a second pint. Jim insisted on ordering a new brew on the blackboard, Fuggles Chocolate Ale. 'Come on, with a name like that it's criminal not to try it,' he burped. Despite dedicated practice, the nice Cornish lad still wasn't very good at holding his drink.

'It doesn't taste like chocolate,' said Omar, who was still extremely sober as his time with the band had hardened him up. He started humming a tune he had recently begun working on.

'Is that one of your brother's?' asked Jim, his handsome face flushed with the heat of the pub and the drink.

'Nope, one of mine,' said Omar, a little proudly. 'It's called "Screwed Up and Over". A friend of mine from Tooting gave me the idea.'

'Are you going to give it to the band? Belated parting gift?' asked Jim.

'Well, I thought about it. But I know Sharif wouldn't think it was right for the band. A bit too bluesy, and the lyric is really for a girl. I guess I just wrote it for me.'

'You should go solo. You're the one with the bloody talent. Sod the rest of them,' said Jim a little drunkenly.

'Thanks, Oakley, you're a mate,' grinned Omar.

After the third pint, Omar thought he really had better get back to the library, if only to pick up his papers. He walked Jim back the short distance to his room out of habit. 'How come I'm always the one who has to look out for the college drunks?' he said as he opened Jim's door for him with the key that Jim kept strung round his neck on a slim leather string, trying not to choke him in the process.

'I don't think you really drink,' said Jim, staggering into the room and collapsing in his chair. 'I think you've got a little tube that collects all the beer in a plastic bag hidden under your jumper.' By the time Omar had made him a coffee, still humming 'Screwed Up and Over', Jim had sobered up a bit. 'Fuggles Chocolate Ale? What a bloody rip-off. I think they just gave it a Christmassy name to sell the stuff off. I bet you at Easter it's called Fuggles Eggnog Bunny Ale.' He rifled through his CDs and, bizarrely, put on the soundtrack of *My Fair Lady*. 'I've grown accustomed to the tune that she whistles night and noon . . . accustomed to her face . . .,' he sang along with a tuneless bellow.

'Mate, you're the one who should be going solo,' Omar said dryly. 'Are you heading back to Cornwall at the weekend, then?' Michaelmas term officially ended on the Friday, and most people were heading home, as the college ground to a halt.

'Yep, lucky old me,' said Jim. 'My parents are picking me up on Saturday morning.'

'Mine are coming Saturday afternoon,' nodded Omar. 'It'll be weird being back home for Christmas; I haven't made any plans for New Year's yet. Sharif and I normally go to the same place, but he's not really forgiven me for leaving the band yet. He's got bloody righteous about it all.'

'I meant to ask you,' Jim said suddenly. 'Do you want to spend New Year in Scotland with me? My cousin has a flat up in Edinburgh and he's throwing a bash for Hogmanay or whatever the heck they do up there. It should be great.'

'Wow, that would be fantastic!' said Omar, deeply flattered, although he and Jim were clearly best friends now, and no one described him as a hanger-on any more.

'I'd love to, but I'll need to see how my folks are.' Seeing Jim raise his eyebrow, Omar quickly qualified, 'Not to ask permission or anything, but I just think that things have been a bit funny at home. My mum called me last night and said she really missed me, and she sounded sort of upset. I don't think they've been getting on.'

'Sure. Well, why don't you see?' said Jim reasonably. 'It would be nice to see you in Scotland – I think I might miss your ugly mug over the hols.' He let out a slight, embarrassed laugh. 'I guess I've got accustomed to your face.'

'Aw, thanks mate,' said Omar, a bit embarrassed, too. He downed his mug of coffee quickly. 'I'm going back to the library. Do you want me to pick up your stuff from the Rad Cam for you?'

'Cheers, that would be great,' Jim said. 'See you in Hall?'

'Yeah, see you later,' Omar said. As he left he saw Karen from his staircase, who looked like she had been waiting for him to leave, nip out of her room and walk up to Jim's door with a box of his favourite biscuits.

'Hey, Jimmy,' she said cheerfully, opening the door. 'Knock, knock!'

'Darling, how did you know I had the most hideous munchies!' he heard Jim cry with delight. Omar shook his head ruefully. All the girls had a crush on Jim.

Back in the Radcliffe Camera, Omar decided not to bother to try and finish his essay on international politics. His head was too fuggled by the chocolate ale. He started on some reading for the following term for philosophy of mind, on self-deception. One of the books compared it to Orwellian doublespeak – the ability to hold two contradictory beliefs in one's mind at the same time. He read about the divided self – one person with two parts, one of which must be necessarily lying to the other in order to deceive himself; whilst at the same time, the part that is deceived knows that he is being deceived, as he is the same self. The trouble with philosophy, Omar thought, was that he found himself thinking about what he was reading, rather than simply committing it to memory; it took up a lot more mental energy. He found the idea of self-deception hard to get his head round, as he was sure that it was practised so often as to lose all its cachet. 'I didn't drink very much just now,' he thought to himself, testing the idea. He didn't believe it. 'My parents are happy,' he tried, but again he didn't believe it, he wasn't even slightly deceived. 'My brother loves me,' he thought. Aah, that was interesting. He felt a conflict, a tug in his head; he wanted to believe it, but he didn't quite; but he didn't quite not believe it, either. 'I'm still a virgin because I haven't met the right girl yet and because I'm not a git like Sharif, who would take advantage of girls just because they're willing.' Well, that gave him a satisfying moral high ground. Did he really believe that was why he was a virgin? It was true that he hadn't had much opportunity, but then he thought of the dark thoughts he had briefly entertained towards Cassie – a violent, cold-blooded itch that needed scratching. Perhaps he was no better than Sharif, just less honest.

He looked at Jim's papers that he had collected up, along with the pair of glasses that Jim vainly almost never wore as he didn't think they suited him. 'He's just a friend,' he tried, daringly, 'that's all he is.' Yes, thought Omar, that was right, he believed that. There was no deception in that at all. And yet why, insisted an annoying little voice in his head, when he formulated this belief statement, did he refer to his friend just as a 'He'? Why did he dare not speak his name? Hadn't he got accustomed to his best friend's face, too?

'I'm fuggled,' thought Omar, finally, to himself. 'I'm fuggled and I'm thinking a load of crap.' He was glad when the bell signalled that the library was shutting. He gathered all of his and Jim's papers, and left.

Ricky-Rashid Makes a Damning Discovery

IT WAS JUST a few days before Easter, and Ricky was
still jet-lagged after a duty trip back to Bangladesh,
where his mother was cussedly clinging on to ill-health
and ill-humour, and Henna and Aziz barely attempted to
share a single meal with him. He'd just chaired an all-day
meeting at the company offices in London Bridge, and
was shattered to the point of illness. Verity and Candida
were right, he should have taken early retirement at sixty.
He had only stayed on to improve his share options,
because he was worried about the sort of income they'd
have once he retired. They'd need to rent out the Clapham
flat, or let it go. Despite his tiredness, he asked the cab to
drop him off at Clapham, rather than going straight home;
he knew that he had better check on the flat while he was
in town. At the flat, he had trouble opening the door due
to the small mountain of junk mail that had gathered
there. All else was well, although the place was a little
dusty – he'd call Ana, the local cleaning lady, to give it a
once over. He decided to walk to the main road to hail
a cab, rather than call his corporate cab company – it was

a bright, crisp day, and the air might do him some good. He passed the local florist on the corner of his street, and on a whim, bought some flowers for Verity. The only decent blooms were the roses, and even those were a bit blowsy, but he picked some pale pink ones and had them tied in brown paper with a pink ribbon.

As he walked down a little terraced street towards the main road, the sort where the houses had all been converted into flats, he was distracted by a car with conspicuous L-plates turning too quickly into the road and screeching to a halt a touch too wide of the kerb. The couple in the car, a slim woman and a tall man, got out swiftly and banged the doors, and Ricky, sure that they had been arguing, hung back under a plane tree, not wanting to be the unwilling witness to a scene. Instead, he was embarrassed to find a very different kind of scene taking place, with the couple colliding into a passionate embrace on the pavement, kissing ardently and unreservedly on the apparently empty street. The woman's back was to him, but there was something disconcertingly familiar about the cut of her hair. 'I'm so late, I've really got to go,' said the woman regretfully.

'Not right now, just stay a little bit. We've only just got back,' said the man, looking at her adoringly, smoothing her hair back from her face.

'Yes, right now,' said the woman firmly, unhappily. 'I'm sorry, I'll be missed.'

'You're right, you will be. Tu me manques déjà,' said the man. 'See, my French really is improving.' He still hadn't let her go.

'More than could be said for my driving,' said the

woman. She turned and walked swiftly away, and then turned and walked back just as decisively to kiss him again. The man held her face between his hands, and brushed his lips tenderly to her forehead.

'Go on with you,' he said gently. 'You're right, you'll be missed.' He watched her retreating back, and then shaking his head with a rueful smile, took the L-plates off the car and let himself into his flat.

Ricky stood paralysed with pain as he watched Shona take leave of her lover. His daughter was having an affair with a man who lived in Clapham. His daughter was in her forties now, with quite grown-up children, and she was having an affair, with a man who lived in a flat in Clapham. The last time he had seen Parvez and Shona together, they hadn't seemed that cheerful, but that was twenty years of marriage to a Pakistani for you. But this, this was different – he recognized tenderness, he recognized a look of love. Shona loved this man, and yet she was forcing herself to continue living with the Pakistani, the uneducated man she had ill-advisedly eloped with when she was barely older than Candida was now. How long had it been going on? Oh God – Ricky thought of Shona's pale, pale children, who he was convinced took after his side of the family. Were they even Parvez's? Gossips had joked that the twins looked practically half-caste, but that was just a joke in bad taste, wasn't it?

It was a nightmare he could never have dreamed of

having: his daughter reliving his life, his lies, his long-running deceit. He thought he had escaped blame and censure for living his double life – apart from some minor administrative inconveniences and more long-haul travel than he would have liked, he had been guiltlessly and wholeheartedly happy. But now, here was his punishment. He had let his daughter down – he was responsible for this. Ricky felt an icy hand close around his heart – it was too much, it felt like his heart was breaking. A dull heavy ache in his chest and shooting pains up his arm made him clench his fist, and the blowsy roses fell to the ground, scattering their petals like pale confetti. The light and shadow of the plane tree swam into nothingness ahead of him, and he walked a few faltering steps, before passing out cold, hitting the pavement with a heavy thud.

Dermot, looking out of his window after Shona, saw an elderly man tottering by the trees. Another neighbourhood drunk, he thought prosaically; Clapham hadn't become half as gentrified as most people thought. He saw the man sway down the street briefly, before falling over. He'll get up in a moment, thought Dermot, but the man didn't get up. Sighing, he went to get his phone, but a sudden burst of rowdy noise got him running back to the window. Some kids came cycling with irresponsible speed round the bend of the pavement, and almost hit the prone body. They were white, black and Asian, a politically correct union of criminal adolescence. One of them stopped his bike and ran back to the old man. Well, that's shown me, thought Dermot, feeling slightly ashamed for his cynical judgement of the kids. However, the apparent good Samaritan simply took out the old man's wallet and disappeared back on his bike up the street. 'I think it's dead,' he called to his mates.

'Oi! You little bastards, get back here,' shouted Dermot, heaving open his window. He ran down his stairs, his phone still in his hand, to where the old man – who was really dressed well enough to be an old gentleman, with smartly cut hair and highly polished shoes – was still definitely alive. And had not a whiff of drink about him. Loosening the man's collar, Dermot called 999 and put him tentatively in the recovery position.

Dermot was in the ambulance when Ricky came round. 'It looks like you've had a heart attack, sir,' a young, fresh-faced paramedic said, efficiently ministering to Ricky.

Ricky ignored him, and looked with confusion towards the concerned face of Dermot. 'What are you doing here?' he asked.

'I found you, sir. You collapsed outside my building. I thought I'd better come with you until we could get hold of your family. Some kids stole your wallet before I could get to you, I'm afraid.'

Ricky nodded, struggling with the tightness in his chest. What a nice fellow he seemed. He sounded educated. 'What do you do, young man?' he asked recklessly.

'I'm a teacher, sir,' Dermot answered, surprised by the question.

Ricky closed his eyes and lay his head back down,

capitulating to the paramedic, who was urging him to keep still and relax. 'My daughter's a teacher,' he said, more to himself than anyone else.

When Verity and Candida arrived at the hospital, Dermot was surprised to see that the daughter looked little more than nineteen or twenty. Much too young to be a teacher. The old gentleman must have been thinking about a different daughter. 'I can't thank you enough for finding my husband,' his wife said tearfully, wringing his hand with gratitude. 'When I think of what might have happened . . .'

'Mummy, it's OK,' said the daughter. She had a confident accent of pure Home Counties privilege. 'They think Daddy's going to be fine.' She shook Dermot's hand. 'You've been very kind, but we mustn't keep you.'

'Well, if you're sure. You've got my number if you need me to make a statement about the stolen wallet,' Dermot said. The young girl was refreshingly capable and there was something about her he couldn't place, something familiar. As he left the hospital by the side exit, he narrowly missed Shona racing in from the hospital car park.

Shona Khan Makes a Damning Discovery

WHEN SHONA HAD returned home to Tooting, there had been two messages blinking on the answering machine. One was from Parvez, saying that he was extending his golf afternoon with dinner in Wimbledon – he was being taken out by a supplier. Shona cursed herself for not checking her messages at Dermot's – she hadn't needed to rush home at all. The second message was almost indecipherable with background noise and bleeping, but it sounded like Mr Crackle-Beep-Buzz Karim was at St George's Hospital following a heart attack, and was she a relative? Numbed with shock, Shona sat down on the chair, with Pat-Bob delightedly jumping on her, and played the message again. She called Parvez on his mobile, and heard the handset merrily ring in the kitchen. Parvez was always forgetting his phone. She called Sharif, who was meant to be at work. He answered his mobile. 'I'll be there in ten minutes, Ma. I'm just up the road in Collier's Wood.' He drove them to the hospital in Parvez's car, which he was no longer insured on.

Ricky-Rashid had been moved to a private room by the time Shona arrived. She almost didn't find him, as they had managed to get his name completely muddled up with someone else and he had been registered under Trueman-Karim. She was advised that his condition was stable and, too relieved to argue over administrative failings in the NHS, Shona left Sharif to park the car and went up to the waiting room. There were just a few other people there. A thin, blonde woman in an oyster-coloured twinset that didn't suit her pale colouring was dabbing at her red, puffy eyes. Sitting opposite her was a young, dark-haired woman, talking to her in a muted, soothing voice and holding her hand. In the corner, a tearful young couple were embracing fulsomely. Shona looked at them grimly – they looked as though they were enjoying their grief a bit too much. Go get a bloody room and leave the rest of us in peace, she thought uncharitably.

The young, dark woman got up. 'I'll get you a coffee, Mummy, and then we should go. Daddy just needs some rest. We'll come back tomorrow.' The girl was maybe nineteen, or perhaps twenty, given her self-assured manner. She was wearing a flowing skirt in silver silk that was so light it billowed about her ankles when she walked, with tennis shoes and a fitted white T-shirt. Shona thought ruefully that only youth could carry off an outfit like that. The girl walked so lightly herself that she could have been a dancer. Shona looked after her as she left the room, reminded of what it was like to have been young and graceful, an age when you still believed that you could control your own destiny. 'She walks in beauty, like the night ... Of cloudless climes and starry skies...' she thought, remembering the dusty volume of Byron's poetry that used to live in her father's Dhaka study.

A pitiful sniff reminded Shona of the wretched-looking mother, whose face was a red splodge of unhappiness. Her handkerchief looked crushed and sodden. Shona felt a surge of sympathy – here was real grief, not like that irritating couple who were using it as an excuse to neck inappropriately in public. She went over to the woman and offered her a clean tissue from her pocket pack. 'Excuse me, would you like one?'

Verity looked up in shock. The kindness of strangers was a phrase which had meant very little to her until she had met Ricky, and she was surprised to encounter it twice in one day, once with that nice teacher, and now with this pleasant-looking woman. 'So very kind,' she choked out. And accepting the tissue, she blew her nose hard and felt a little better. Aware that she was making something of an exhibition of herself, she explained to the nice young lady. 'It's my husband, you see. He's everything to me. I couldn't bear to think of something happening to him, and then it just did.' She blew her nose again, and carried on, 'The silly thing is that he's fine now. But I still feel awful just thinking about what might have happened . . .' She trailed off as her face collapsed into another messy heap of tears. Despite the fact that the woman was several years Shona's senior, Shona calmly took the used tissue from her and passed her another, as though she was a student crying in the playground.

'Of course you're upset,' she said gently, 'and it's best to let it out.'

Verity attempted a quivering smile. 'Are you visiting, too?' she asked.

Shona nodded. 'My father. I've just heard that he'd had a heart attack, but they think he'll be fine.'

'My Ricky had a heart attack,' Verity replied, composing herself a little. 'I kept telling him to slow down, but he keeps working so hard, and travelling all over the place. He's only just back from Bangladesh – it's no good for someone his age.'

'My family's from Bangladesh,' said Shona slowly, finding herself looking at the poor woman assessingly instead of sympathetically. Her father had just been in Dhaka visiting her Nanu; until the phone call she hadn't even known that he had come back. The woman looked up and, seeing Shona's suddenly hard expression, misinterpreted it as criticism.

'I'm sorry, I shouldn't blather on so . . .' she said miserably, looking down at her feet. Shona, ashamed at herself for her suspicions, looked down too. Her own guilty affair had made her paranoid. But then she couldn't help noticing the woman's feet, which were just a few inches away from her own. They were a couple of sizes bigger than Shona's feet – probably size 6. Shona reminded herself that size 6 feet were perfectly ordinary and in themselves indicated nothing of significance; but then the woman's pretty, dark-haired daughter returned, without the promised coffee.

'Sorry, Mummy, the machine coffee doesn't look up to much. The black coffee button isn't working, and there wasn't any sugar at all, much less brown. Let's go down to the hospital café.'

'If you think so, dear,' replied Verity, gathering herself together. She hesitated shyly before turning to Shona. 'Thank you so much for the hankies.'

'Really, don't think anything of it,' said Shona, who could no longer deny the significance of size 6 shoes, especially combined with coffee and brown sugar. But that had been years ago, before the boys had even been born. She was distracted from drawing any disturbing conclusions by Sharif swanning in, looking very pleased with himself and even more handsome than usual, so much so that one part of the kissing couple stopped in mid-embrace to admire him.

'I have just met the most gorgeously amazing girl,' he said, sitting down on the seat that Verity had vacated. 'Here you go,' he added, giving her a cup of machine tea.

'I didn't ask you to get me tea, I asked you to park and come straight up,' Shona said pointedly, looking at him crossly.

'Ah, but the Amazing Girl was by the drinks machine. She had a walk like pure poetry, and the most amazing name, like something from a song: Candida Trueman-Karim.' Sharif pronounced the name reverently, giving attention to every syllable. 'Can-dee-da,' he sighed blissfully.

Shona's tea-holding hand shook so much that the tea spilled and squelched wetly over her. Fortunately it was only lukewarm. She looked at her son, who showed no signs of noticing her reaction to the name. He probably didn't even remember that Karim was her maiden name; it was such a common name, after all.

When the nurse came over and said that they could see the patient, Shona asked Sharif if she could see him alone.

Ricky-Rashid was lying wired to a heart monitor, and with a drip standing to attention by his side. Now he knew that he was unlikely to die he was slightly embarrassed to have Shona called to his bedside. What did he think he would do – confess his sins and ask her for absolution? Expect her to confess her own? Tell her to look after her mother? To look out for Verity and Candida? It all seemed stupidly melodramatic now that he was placid and rather bored and simply waiting to get better. Still, when she walked in, he couldn't help feeling cheered to see her, especially without the Pakistani. She was wearing the same clothes from earlier that afternoon.

'Papa, you had us all so worried,' she said, going to him and kissing him on the cheek. She sat down beside him and held his hand. 'I was so relieved when they said you were stable. There was a name mix-up, so it took a little while to find you.'

'I'm so pleased you could come, Jaan,' Ricky-Rashid said, a little insincerely, squeezing her hand with the modest amount of energy he could muster. 'I'm sorry about the mix-up – there's someone else here with a similar name, and I think they've put me under that instead. Trueman-Karim or some such.'

Shona nodded, and cleared her throat before saying, 'Yes, I met Mrs Trueman-Karim outside, and her daughter.' Ricky-Rashid looked up quickly, and Shona held his gaze for a little too long to be discreet. 'She seemed very upset about her husband; he's Bengali, too.'

Ricky breathed deeply, and looked down at their loosely intertwined hands – his own hand seemed so feeble next to Shona's golden, glowing skin, with her long fingers and unvarnished, oval nails. He had little doubt that Shona knew; perhaps she was expecting him to confess, after all. For a moment it was tempting. It would be so easy, it would just take a few seconds of weakness, of unblinkered honesty. Naked under his gown, he would become as clean and fresh as a newborn baby, reborn in his new life. Ricky let go of his daughter's hand and smoothed down the sheet; yes, the confession would be easy, but it was the aftermath that would be unthinkable. He would lose everything he had built – his false life in Bangladesh that kept Henna in such respectable comfort, that kept his mother at such disapproving distance; his new life with his wonderful wife and daughter. He could imagine the hurt in Verity's eyes, even more painful than the tears she had bravely tried to hide as she had visited him that day; betrayed yet again, by the one man who had promised he never would. To be told that their marriage was an illegal sham. She would never understand. Ricky made a decision: she would never need to.

'Jaan,' he said gently to Shona. 'There's something I need to tell you.'

'Yes, Papa,' Shona said encouragingly, leaning forward, reaching for his hand once more.

'I'm afraid I've misled you about something. I know that you thought I would still be in Dhaka today, but as you can see I decided to return a little bit earlier. I had something to do.' Shona nodded, wondering where this was going. Ricky put his hand on Shona's cheek, picking his words carefully. 'You remember the flat in Clapham, the one that I used to stay in when I was in town . . . ?' Shona's eyes widened as she realized what he was going to say. Ricky confirmed, 'I went there this afternoon, I thought I had better check on it, I hadn't been there in a long time, as you know.'

Shona swallowed uncomfortably, before asking, 'And was everything OK, Papa?'

Ricky replied, as gently as he could, 'Jaan, everything wasn't OK. I saw something that I wasn't meant to see, and it almost broke my heart.'

Shona looked at the bleeping heart monitor, and back to her pale father, and understood. 'Is that what gave you the heart attack, Papa?'

Ricky avoided her direct question deliberately. He was aware that his heart rate was rising incrementally, and breathed slowly, so that they wouldn't be interrupted by the nursing staff. 'Shona, there's something I've learned, and which I think you know, too. There are some things that we're not meant to see, that we're better off not seeing. We might look at each other, but we don't always need to see each other, if you know what I mean. All I want, and all I've ever wanted, is for you to be happy.'

Shona said nothing. She wasn't sure whether this was blackmail on the part of her father, or pure kindness. She remembered the first tacit deal they had made in his Paddington apartment all that time ago: you keep my secret, and I'll keep yours. Before, her silence had been easily bought – what was the harm in his having an inconsequential dalliance when away from home, while her mother had been flirting outrageously in Dhaka? But there had been consequences, dire consequences of her silence, because this was no affair to be hushed up. There seemed to be a marriage, a wife, a daughter who was presumably his. A sister that she had never even known. Could he really expect her to pretend that she had seen nothing? But then, the consequences of her own adultery were unwittingly as bad, if not worse. She had almost killed her own father. She owed her father something; she had seen how unhappy he had always been in Dhaka, and how the years in England had transformed his life. She knew that her father was watching her now, awaiting her verdict. She opened her mouth to speak, but was interrupted by Sharif barging in.

'Sorry, Ma. Visiting hours are almost over, so I thought I better pop in and see how you're both doing. Nana, do you feel as bad as you look?'

Ricky smiled weakly. Sharif wasn't his favourite grandson; so brash and handsome, he reminded him too much of the Pakistani. He had only the paleness of his Karim genes to recommend him.

'Quite as bad, son, thank you for asking. They say I shouldn't be in here too long though . . .' Firm steps at the door heralded the appearance of a nurse, who told them that visiting hours were over. Shona drew herself up resignedly.

'Well, considering how long it took them to get us up here, they seem pretty efficient about kicking us out.' She got out of her chair by Ricky's bedside and kissed him. 'I'll come back tomorrow. Is there anything you want?'

'No, thank you, Jaan. I'm sure I'll be well looked after. Company health plan and all that,' Ricky replied. He paused, before asking hopefully, 'It would be better if you came in the afternoon though, rather than the morning, if that would be OK.'

Shona understood. He would have other visitors in the morning, visitors who would probably provide for him better than she could. He had been well looked after for the past twenty years, but she just hadn't seen it. Or rather, she had looked, but she hadn't seen, just as her father had said. As she went to leave, she turned and said to him in Bangla, so Sharif wouldn't understand, 'Papa, I think we both deserve to be happy. I just want you to be happy too.'

Ricky felt the tightening around his chest that had begun in the last few moments start to subside. 'Thank you, Shona,' he said gently. There would be nothing else to say.

At home, Shona sat in the dark of the kitchen and watched the moon in the french windows. She had poured a glass of wine, which she sipped too quickly. She had never felt so alone, and so tortured by secrets and silence. She was half waiting for Parvez to come home, and half hoping that he would call and say he wasn't. At another time, she would have clung to him for support and told him everything that her suddenly tender heart had to say – told him about her father's betrayal and secret life, and her complicity so that she would never know the man her father had become, never know the woman who had made him happy, or the sister that she never knew she had. But that time was gone – she could no longer tell Parvez everything. In fact, she could no longer tell him anything. The only person she could tell the truth to was sitting alone, like her, in a flat a few miles away. She glanced at the phone, and shook her head. She couldn't call Dermot now; it was far too risky. Parvez was due home any minute. She checked her watch; it was almost midnight – still too early to call her mother in Dhaka and tell her about the heart attack. Draining her wine, she decided to call anyway.

The phone rang at the other end with a distant echo and crackle, and gave way to Uncle Aziz's crisp accent announcing that she had reached the Karim residence, and to leave a short message after the tone. 'Amma,' Shona said softly, 'I guess you're not up yet. I thought someone might be up. I just need to tell you something . . . it's Papa, he's had a heart attack. He's stable, and they think he won't be in too long. I don't think you need to worry or fly over or anything, we're taking care of him here. I'm going to bed now, but I'll call again when I'm up.' Putting the phone down, she felt emptier than she had before. She had just lied to her mother by everything she hadn't said.

It was almost one in the morning when Parvez came home, smelling of brandy and contrition. He entered the bedroom quietly, undressing in silence. He knew Shona was still awake, as she was lying on the far side of the bed, very straight and still. 'Shona, I didn't mean to be so late,' he whispered as he got into bed. 'Jay wanted to make a night of it, and I didn't think you'd mind. I stopped by the restaurant on the way home. Sharif told me what happened. I'm so sorry about your father, I'm sorry I wasn't here for you. I know how much he means to you.'

At his words, Shona turned away from him and curled up into herself. He saw she had begun to shiver and shudder, and suddenly she let out great, choking sobs that welled up from deep inside and shook her whole body. Parvez tentatively touched her shoulder, and as she kept sobbing, oblivious to him, he put his arms around her and held her while she sobbed, burying his face between her neck and shoulder. 'Shona,' he whispered, 'Goldie, don't upset yourself so. He's going to be fine.' He kissed her hair reassuringly, but Shona couldn't stop her tears.

'You don't understand, it's never going to be fine,' Shona choked out, 'I can't do this any more. I can't keep pretending it's fine.'

Parvez misunderstood what she said, and didn't let her finish. 'Shh,' he said soothingly, 'I'll look after us. It will be fine, I promise. We'll see him tomorrow, we'll go together.' He stroked Shona's hair and bare arms, and curled himself against her, comforting her with his warmth and physical intimacy, the only way he knew how to comfort her after their long years of marriage. As her sobbing calmed down to deep, ragged breathing, without being quite aware of what he was doing, he began making love to her, and she, half asleep and tearful, found herself responding to him as she always had before, as though simply being next to his skin would replace the closeness they had lost.

Afterwards, Shona went to the kitchen to get a glass of water, and looked back at the silver light of the moon streaking into the kitchen. She had managed to make things worse, if that were possible. She still had the burden of her father's great secret to carry, unabsolved, in addition to her own clandestine affair. And now she had not only been unfaithful to Parvez, but she had compounded her sin by being unfaithful to Dermot, too. If she had to keep any more secrets, tell any more lies, she felt as if she would break.

Shona resolved to see Dermot the next day, and tell him everything. She realized how much she needed Dermot now, as she needed someone to whom she could tell the truth, someone who could hold every secret about her. She needed to know that if she was struck down like her father had been, or knocked over by a bus in the morning, the truth wouldn't die with her – she needed to know that at least one person in the world knew who she really was.

Sharif Khan Meets an Angel in Tennis Shoes

S HARIF FIRST SAW her across a crowded, scruffy hospital corridor, walking so lightly it was as though the
bottoms of her feet didn't quite touch the sticky, laminate
floor. She was dressed like no other girl he knew, in a
flowing silver skirt that swept voluminously in glistening
ripples around her legs, with white tennis shoes and a
snug, shining white T-shirt that moulded to her slim waist.
She looked like an angel, so clean and fresh that she
glowed in the unflattering hospital lighting. The other girls
he knew seemed like grubby, painted hussies by comparison, with their tight skirts and tight jeans and low-cut
tops.

She stopped at the drinks machine, and Sharif stopped
and stared. She was soon stabbing buttons in annoyance,
rejecting each murky cup of liquid as it appeared. Sharif
watched her, fascinated, until she became aware of his
gaze, and turned to look at him. She had a heart-shaped
face, with creamy pale skin that didn't have a trace of
pink, and thick, dark hair. It was the sort of fresh, sweet
face that he might have imagined his mother having when

she was young. A song started in Sharif's heart instinctively, and he almost said the words out loud, as they were beating so strongly in his head:

And you saw the girl who'd make your dreams come true
She looked like no other, she looked straight back at you.

'I'm sorry, can I help you?' asked the Amazing Girl. Her voice was pure Home Counties, Sharif realized. She certainly wasn't from Tooting. He dropped his usual working-class hero accent and spoke with the voice he used at home.

'It's just that I needed to use the drinks machine, but I'll wait. My mum wants a cup of tea,' he said charmingly.

'Funny,' she said, 'I'm trying to get a drink for my mummy, too. She only drinks black coffee, and this bloody stupid machine is putting out white coffee no matter which button I press.' She tried again, and the machine produced yet another cup of milky sludge. 'See what I mean? Maybe you should go ahead of me, I might try to find another machine.'

Sharif replied quickly, 'No, really, it's OK. I'll wait. I can't stand queue-jumpers.' The last thing he wanted was to have her wander off while he got an unwanted cup of tea. 'I guess you're visiting, you don't look sick,' he hazarded, realizing too late how ungracious that sounded. It wasn't like him to make daft comments when faced with a pretty girl. Normally he was the coolest customer around.

'Thank you, I think,' laughed the Amazing Girl. 'Yes, we're here for Daddy. He had a heart attack from nowhere, but he's all right, thank God.'

'My grandad has just had a heart attack. He's stable, too. Mum literally just found out. We got here in a blind panic,' Sharif answered. He realized how close he was leaning in towards the Girl, as though her sheer magnetism was drawing him closer; he had to force himself back.

'Well, I'm giving up,' she said, after yet another attempt at getting a black coffee. 'I'll see if Mummy wants to go to the cafeteria instead. We should be leaving Daddy to rest, anyway. Good luck with your grandad, and the tea,' she said kindly.

'Do you like music?' Sharif asked, just as she was walking away.

The Girl turned back, looking adorably perplexed by the question. 'Yes, I do. Well, it depends on the music, I guess. Why?'

'It's just that I'm giving a concert this week, not too far from here, in Clapham.' He dug into his pocket and handed her a professional-looking flyer that had been knocked out on Micky's home PC. 'If you're in the area, it would be great to see you there. You might like it.'

'Oh, well, thanks,' said the Girl, looking surprised, but not displeased.

'If you tell me your name, I could put you and a guest on the list at the door, so you won't have to pay,' Sharif persisted, turning to press the button for tea in an attempt to appear rather more nonchalant than he sounded.

'That's very kind of you . . .' She hesitated as she realized she didn't know his name.

'It's Sharif, Sharif Khan. It's sort of my band,' Sharif said modestly, pointing to his name on the flyer.

'That's very kind of you, Sharif,' the Girl said. 'I'm

Candida, Candida Trueman-Karim.' She turned to leave, but then turned back. 'It was nice to have met you,' she said politely, as though she had just remembered a child-hood lesson in manners.

Sharif stood by the drinks machine, watching her move away in time to the music in his head. 'Candida,' breathed Sharif, 'Can-dee-da'. He tried it out, and felt the melodic syllables dance across his palate, tongue and teeth. It was a name that was almost impossible to say without a smile; it was a name that left you open-mouthed with longing as you finished it. Can-dee-da.

Candida didn't come to the concert, but called the venue to apologize. Undeterred, Sharif pursued her, hanging around the hospital at visiting hours until he saw her and bumped into her accidentally on purpose. This time, they went for a coffee, and started to go on dates. Sharif was so careful with Candida that he didn't even try to kiss her, until the miraculous day when she leaned in towards him while they were waiting for her train home. He even introduced her to his mother, who must have known that this one was special, as she took an unprecedented interest in Candida above all his other girlfriends, asking her to supper, and asking after her mum, and asking what she did at her art college.

'Your mummy's lovely,' Candida said one evening on the way to one of Sharif's gigs. 'I feel like I've known her forever.'

'Well, she shouldn't monopolize you so much,' Sharif

answered, kissing the top of her head. 'I hardly got to say a word to you during dinner. Sorry about the burnt chicken, by the way.'

'I'm not much of a cook, so I'd never criticize someone else's food,' Candida shrugged. 'Speaking of food, why did you tell your mum that you were working at the restaurant tonight? Doesn't she approve of you playing?'

Sharif shrugged. 'I find it better not to tell Mum when I've got a gig, or she might tell Dad, and as he's my boss he wouldn't be too pleased about me playing hooky from the restaurant. I'm meant to have given up music and be doing real work now.'

'But why play hooky?' persisted Candida. 'Why not just tell them you're taking a night off?'

'Babe, it's much easier not to tell them, and for them to think that I'm working. Otherwise Dad might stop paying me for the nights I'm not there,' Sharif answered guilelessly.

'You're appalling,' chided Candida, not without a grin. 'I think you're one of those bad boys that my daddy keeps warning me against.'

'Do you like bad boys?' Sharif asked, squeezing her waist.

'I do now,' Candida answered coquettishly, and stopped to kiss him full on the lips.

After the gig, Sharif was walking Candida back through Clapham Common when she surprised him by stopping by his usual make-out bench. Pulling him down, she began to kiss him urgently, and against his nobler instincts they were soon passionately making out. 'I'm feeling very bad myself, Sharif,' Candida said breathily. 'I think you're a bad influence.'

Some moments later, Sharif realized with a start that Candida, as she slid his hands underneath her thighs, was giving him an unprecedented licence, and that she was intent on going much further than they had before. As her own hands reached for his shirt buttons, Sharif stopped her. 'Candida, no, I don't want to do this.'

'What?' she said, in genuine surprise, and seeming more than a little hurt. She saw the concern in his eyes in the poor light and relaxed. 'Sharif, really, I want to. Don't worry about me.'

'I mean, I don't want you here. I don't want you outside, on a bench in a park. I want to take you home. I like you. I really, really like you. I want to take you home, and wake up with you.' He gestured hopelessly towards the bench. 'I don't want to do this sort of thing any more.'

'Sharif,' Candida answered gently, 'I've never done this sort of thing before – out in the open, I mean. I just thought it might be fun. And you know I can't go home with you tonight. I've got my own home to get back to, before Mummy gets worried.'

'Maybe you could stay over at the weekend?' Sharif asked hopefully. 'There's a market near me in Merton Abbey Mills. It's got lots of girly, arty-farty stuff that you'd love – scented candles, old mirrors, sequined cush-ion covers, carved bits of tat . . .'

'Sounds lovely,' said Candida, sitting back upright and

smoothing down her skirt, another pale floaty number, this time with bonbon-coloured stripes. 'It would be nice to spend a proper amount of time together.' She hesitated a moment, and then said, 'The thing is, I'd be happy to stay over, but I really wouldn't feel comfortable about, well, you know, with your flatmates around. The walls in your place are really thin, and . . . well, it's hardly romantic with Beavis and Butthead banging around next door with their PlayStations and girly mags.'

'Point taken,' Sharif said. 'I'm sure I can get rid of them.' He looked around the damp, musty park. 'Did you think that this was romantic, then?' he asked. 'I've never thought this was a particularly romantic location. Convenient, maybe, but definitely not romantic.'

'Of course it's romantic,' Candida said. 'You've got the trees, the stars, the moonlight, and the chance of being arrested for an indecent act in public.'

'You're a funny girl,' said Sharif.

'Funny ha ha or funny peculiar?' asked Candida pertly.

'Funny peculiar,' answered Sharif. 'Utterly perfect in every way, of course, but undeniably, just a little bit . . . mad.'

'Come on,' said Candida, getting up and pulling up Sharif by the arm. 'Your mad girlfriend has a train to catch, and given that you're disinclined to shag me senseless on a park bench, I've got no reason to miss it.'

'When you put it that way, I'm the one who sounds mad,' said Sharif.

Sharif had never planned a romantic weekend before, and was looking forward to it. It seemed so much more clean and natural than what he had done before, furtive fumbling in the shadows of the parks and the streets and the rooftops. He imagined bringing Candida breakfast in bed, and scenting his room with fresh flowers for her.

He was crushed when she called and tearfully told him that she wouldn't be able to come. She said that her mum had been fine about her spending the weekend with her new boyfriend, but that her dad had gone absolutely uncharacteristically ballistic when he found out who she was seeing, and had forbidden her to see him again.

'It was scary, I've never seen Daddy like that. He's the most tolerant, easy-going person I know. He never gets cross or upset about anything,' Candida told him. 'I mean, maybe I should have mentioned to him sooner that I was seeing someone, but I normally don't bother him about who I'm dating until it gets serious. Mummy knew about you, and she was shocked at how Daddy reacted too. He was perfectly cheerful about it until I mentioned your name, then he just blew up.'

'Is he racist or something?' Sharif asked, completely confused as to why a stranger would take such exception to him on mere mention of his name.

'Well, he can't be. He's Bangladeshi himself, and you're half-Bangladeshi, just like me. But he was going on about how he knew all about boys like you, and that you were no good, and that I shouldn't date you, and all sorts of rubbish.'

'He must be racist,' said Sharif. 'There are lots of Asians around who want to forget where they came from.

He doesn't want his perfect little girl dating an Asian boy; he wants you to go out with white boys and breed out all his brown genes and have nice white grandchildren . . .'

'Oh, shut up, you're as bad as him. You don't know him at all, so there's no need to generalize,' said Candida crossly. Sharif stopped in mid-tirade, realizing that Candida would brook no criticism of her father. 'I mean, I went out with Greg last year, and he was black, and Daddy didn't have a word to say against him.'

'Well, I don't see how he could say all those things about me if he doesn't even know me,' said Sharif stubbornly.

'Babe, I know. I asked him exactly that – I asked him to give me one solid reason why I shouldn't go out with you,' said Candida.

'And what did he say?' asked Sharif, holding his breath.

'This is the scariest part. He burst into tears and collapsed into his chair, clutching his chest. Mummy and I were terrified that he might be having another heart attack. He said that if I loved him, I would just trust him and promise not to see you any more.'

'Great – he can't give you a reason, so he resorts to emotional blackmail by asking you to make a ridiculous promise,' Sharif said unsympathetically. 'What did he say when you said you weren't falling for it?' He waited for her response, but Candida didn't say a word. 'Candida, you did tell him that you weren't falling for it, didn't you?' He was aware of his voice rising with slight panic. 'You didn't actually promise, did you? You couldn't have done.'

Candida paused for far too long, and said, 'Sharif, I'm

so sorry. I felt I had to. You know how ill Daddy's been; I couldn't be responsible for his heart giving out again. He needs to stay unstressed, and I know it was totally unreasonable of him, but maybe he's not quite himself at the moment.'

Sharif felt his whole body go cold. 'I see,' he said curtly. It had finally happened; he had fallen for someone, only to find that he felt more for her than she did for him. Perhaps she had only wanted him for arm candy, for street cred, for the sex they hadn't quite had. The irony was awful; he could imagine his cohorts of ex-conquests and his faggy twin cheering Candida in the wings.

'No, you don't see,' Candida said, 'so don't go all cold and distant on me. It's only for a little while, and I've made a decision. I've never lied to my parents before, but when my daddy's health is at stake it seems as good a time as any to start.'

'So you didn't mean it,' said Sharif, feeling waves of relief wash over him. 'You'll find a way to come this weekend?'

'No, not this weekend, and not to London. I don't think that would be very wise,' said Candida. 'But you know, next weekend I might visit a friend who lives down on the Kent coast, in a little seaside town called Broad-stairs.'

'I don't think I know it,' said Sharif.

'You'd like it, I think. It's between Margate and Rams-gate, and prettier than both, with lovely beaches perfect for painting. Wouldn't it be a funny coincidence if I bumped into you down there next Saturday, say at the station at midday?'

'That would be a funny coincidence,' agreed Sharif.

Candida laughed. 'Oh, and before I forget, better let your mum think we've broken up, too. Daddy still has to go back to St George's for his follow-up appointment, so Mummy might bump into your mum there, like they did before.' She paused, and said huskily down the line, 'This is quite sexy, isn't it? Forbidden lovers meeting in secret.'

'You have a funny idea of sexy,' Sharif said. 'And this is the funniest break-up I've ever had.'

'Funny ha ha or funny peculiar?' asked Candida.

'Funny peculiar,' said Sharif.

The Romantic Memories of Sharif Khan

I HAVE ALWAYS believed that I wasn't really alive until I first heard music. What I didn't know before, and I only realize now, was that I had never really heard music until the day I met Candida. She put a song in my heart from the moment I saw her, a relentless, haunting melody that wouldn't go away, with an underlying beat that would drum heavily in my chest whenever she wasn't there, just waiting for her to return.

We arranged to meet one weekend by the seaside, and I waited for her at the station, sitting on a bench, lighting cigarette after cigarette. I watched as trains came in and carriages emptied, and I realized that I wasn't angry with her for being late. Much worse than that, I was frightened. I was frightened that she might not have been able to get away, and that I might not see her at all. When she finally arrived, having decided to drive down rather than take the train, she kissed me warmly and complained about the traffic. But I didn't care about the traffic; all I could say was that I had missed her, because it was true.

She drove us to a curving beach lined with enormous

chalk cliffs. There were a couple of families at the entrance
to the beach, but once we strolled around the cliffs, it was
utterly deserted, nothing but the waves, the flint scattered
on the sand, and us. Candida collected chalk that had
fallen from the cliffs. She took a piece and asked me to
pose for her, while she drew my portrait on the side of a
flat, grey rock that rested under the tide line. Then she
drew her own portrait next to mine. We sat back on our
blanket and watched the sea come in, and the foaming
waves dissolve our chalked images as the salt water licked
over the rock. 'We're mer-people now,' said Candida.
'We've turned into sea foam and become immortal.'

We held hands and walked down the empty beach. For
the first time, I really understood what my parents must
have felt to have lost love, as to have found it was so
precious that I could not bear to ever let it go. My heart
had been collected like chalk from the beach.

'Where are you staying tonight?' I asked. 'Are you
staying with your friend in town?'

'No,' replied Candida. 'I'm staying with you.'

In the morning, I left her sleeping in the hotel, and
returned with croissants and coffee in paper cups, and
pink roses from the newsagents. I'd dreamed of waking
her with breakfast in bed and the scent of roses, but in
fact she woke when the clumsy door banged behind me.
When I climbed back into bed, Candida lay resting against
me, her head on my shoulder, her light frame still heavy
with the remains of sleep.

'What did you think of me, when you first saw me?' I asked her.

'I thought you were one of the prettiest men I'd ever seen,' said Candida. 'Look, you've got longer eyelashes than me.' She reached forward and gently brushed the tips of my eyelashes with her fingertips. 'Now I have to ask you, don't I? What did you think of me?'

'I thought of music when I first saw you. I saw your back, that swishing silver skirt, and I thought you were a dancer. Your head was held so straight. I followed you to the drinks machine, and willed you to turn around.'

Candida got up and, wrapping a towel around her, went to the window, looking out over the bay. 'I used to come here as a child, on day trips. We'd go to the amusement park in Margate, and then come here for the beach. Daddy and I played a sort of tennis on the beach, with big plastic rackets and enormous spongy balls.' She turned back to face me. 'We had such a perfect day yesterday; it seems crazy that Daddy thinks you wouldn't be good for me.'

I went up to her and put my arms around her, watching the waves roll in over the beach. 'If you ever give me the chance to meet your dad, I'll tell him, I'll promise him, that I would never hurt you, and never leave you, and never let you go. I'd rather hurt myself first.' Candida's face was suddenly very solemn in the morning light, so solemn that I felt forced to ask, 'You do believe me, don't you?'

'Yes, I do believe you,' Candida said. 'That's the scary thing.'

Omar Khan Celebrates May Day in Oxford

O MAR WAS QUITE excited about the approach of mythical May Day in Oxford; the night of all night parties, of dancing until dawn, when everyone would crowd to Magdalen Bridge to hear the choir sing in the sunrise, and then leap off into the water in their black tie and ballgowns.

'I read two people had permanent spinal injuries doing that last year,' said Karen disapprovingly. She was sitting on one of Omar's chairs with a massive cup of hot chocolate. Omar had noticed with some irritation that she now limited her visits to when 'Jimmy' was in residence. He wished she wouldn't come; she was getting more and more territorial about Jim, so much so that Omar felt a bit like a gooseberry in his own college room.

'Bollocks – how would you get a spinal injury by jumping into water?' scoffed Jim, who had spread out a map of Oxford on Omar's coffee table, and was scribbling over it with thick, coloured marker pens.

'The water's not very deep at some points under the bridge,' explained Omar, wondering why he was bothering to back up Karen. 'I think you have to jump from the middle, or not at all.'

'Well, if you say so, mate,' said Jim non-commitally.

'Typical, you always listen to Omar over me,' pouted Karen flirtatiously. Jim grinned cheekily at her, before pouting back at her, causing her to giggle delightedly. Omar almost had to hide a sigh; Karen's single-minded pursuit of Jim was beginning to pay off. They were edging closer and closer to becoming a couple, and there was nothing he could do about it; Jim was far too lazy to avoid being pursued for too long, and far too vain not to enjoy the attention. Omar knew that it shouldn't really bother him – they were both his friends. It was just that Jim was his best friend, and he didn't really want to share him, that was all. To distract himself from the disturbing niggles of jealousy, Omar asked Jim how he was getting on with his party-planning.

'It's all worked out, mate. These flag pins are us three,' Jim started poking them into the map where the college was.

'You're poking holes in my coffee table,' muttered Omar in exasperation.

'Mate, I poke where, when and whom I want,' retorted Jim. 'So, we're here in the college at the start of the night, and we go to the bar for the first party of the night and get tanked up.' He picked up the flag pins and began dancing them along the thick red line he had marked up earlier. 'We then head over to Balliol, to pick up Giles and Lydia from their bar, have a few drinks there just to be polite, and then Giles drives us all over to the big bash in the Parks.'

'Isn't Giles drinking, then?' Karen asked

'God, you and your bloody health and safety obses-sions. No, he's not drinking,' Jim said tersely.

'Antibiotics,' Omar clarified kindly for Karen. 'So we're going to stay out in the Parks all night? What if it rains?'

'Good question. If it rains, and all the bars are shut, I reckon we just head over to NCL. They're having a house-party,' Jim said, bouncing the flag pins along to the undergraduate house that sprawled across two buildings at New College Lane. 'Look, did you see? I've marked up wet weather plans with the blue broken line,' he added, with a touch too much pride.

'So you have,' Omar said. 'I think we've finally found a practical use for your new-found interest in military history.'

'Don't mock what you can never understand,' said Jim, who had amassed an impressive collection of children's books on the subject.

'So are we going to the bridge for dawn, then?' asked Karen, looking casually over at the map.

'Duh, it's marked right here – we get to the bridge for dawn, five a.m. or whenever it is, listen to the angelic voices, jump off the bridge, run back and get dried off, and then it's off to the King's Arms for the champagne and croissant breakfast.'

'I think you need to book that,' Karen said.

'I think that the Pantry might be giving champagne and croissants for free to all first years who've signed up for it,' Omar added.

Jim rolled his eyes at the insubordination in his ranks.

'Fine, I'll book the King's Arms for all of us, including Giles and Lydia. And we'll go to the Pantry first to get our free froggy pastry and champers; no point in letting our share go to waste.' He uncapped his red marker and added a line with a little arrow that stopped at the Pantry.

'And that, men, is our plan of attack. Any questions that do not involve wussy health and safety considerations?' Jim asked, in a pastiche of a WWII general.

'You might want to ask Giles if he actually wants you to book the King's Arms breakfast – he probably won't want to pay a tenner for champagne and croissant if he's not drinking . . .' Omar started to say, but was interrupted by his mobile, which played one of his favourite Balti Ballads songs as the ringtone. He went to flick it off, but seeing it was from Sharif, answered it immediately. 'All right, mate?' he asked. Sharif never rang him. He had to want something. He opened his door and stood outside in the echoing stairwell so he wouldn't have to speak in front of Karen and Jim; God, he hoped they didn't start snogging in his room, that would be horrible.

'Kid, I need a favour,' Sharif said urgently, and depressingly predictably.

'I'm not lending you any more, you're the one with the job,' Omar said.

'Not that kind of favour. It's just that me and my girlfriend want to get away for the May Day bank holiday. She's going to tell her parents she's meeting a friend in Oxford; could we take over your gaff?'

'Why the cloak and dagger?' Omar asked.

'Stupid story – her dad's got the impression I'm no good, and has forbidden her to see me,' Sharif said.

Omar choked back a laugh. 'Forbidden her to see you? God, how funny. So does he lock her up at night with a chastity belt?'

'Not funny, mate. I really like this girl. She's . . . well, she's special. You'll know what I mean when you meet her. Even Mum loved her. And we hardly ever get to see each other.'

'You introduced her to Amma?' Omar asked in bemusement; Sharif seemed to have changed overnight. 'Who are you and what have you done with my obnoxious slut of a brother?'

'Very funny. Funny ha ha, I mean,' said Sharif. 'So is that OK? We'll just stay a night.'

'Luckily for you, I'm actually planning to be out all night, so I guess it is OK. Make sure you arrive before formal Hall so I can let you in, about seven-ish.'

'Cheers, kid, I owe you. See you then.' Sharif was about to ring off, when Omar stopped him.

'What's her name? This special girl who's made such a changed man of you?'

'Candida,' said Sharif, surprised by the question.

'Candida? Is she Candy for short?' asked Omar. Candy seemed a more suitable name for one of Sharif's girl-friends.

'Nope, Candida doesn't abbreviate,' Sharif said proudly, before hanging up.

On the big day, Omar was fretting as Sharif was late, and he was in danger of missing his much needed dinner before the long night ahead. Karen and Jim had already gone to Hall, and Omar was sure that Karen was secretly pleased that he'd had to stay behind. Fiddling with his scruffy black gown, Omar tried Sharif's phone again. It went straight through to voicemail. Bastard, he was sure that his brother's Romeo and Juliet sob story was some elaborate ploy to humiliate him in some undecipherable way, or at the very least to ruin his first Oxford May Day. Sod him. Omar decided to go to Hall anyway; he left a scrawled message on his door, and was racing down the stairs when he heard a familiar voice on the landing. 'Where's the fire, kid?'

'Where the hell were you?' said Omar crossly, doubling back and seeing Sharif standing outside the bathroom on the second floor. 'Look, here's my key, you know where the room is. Top floor, turret. See you tomorrow.'

'Hold on, Candida's just in the loo. Don't be so bloody rude. Wait to say hello at least,' Sharif said.

'Well, God forbid I embarrass you with my bad manners . . .' Omar stopped in his tracks as a vision stepped out of the bathroom, smoothing down her hair.

'Oh, you must be Omar. I'm sorry we're late, traffic was murder. I'm delighted to meet you, Sharif's told me so much about you.' She smiled sincerely, and held out her hand.

'No, I'm the one who's sorry,' said Omar regretfully, taking her hand. 'I'm afraid I have to dash off. Make yourself at home upstairs. Hopefully we can meet properly in the morning. Come and have breakfast with us, in the King's Arms.'

Walking down, he paused and looked back up the

winding staircase, where Sharif was talking in a low voice to Candida, his arm placed protectively around her shoulders as they climbed the steps together. Surely Sharif must have seen how much like their Amma she looked? A younger, arguably slimmer version, with skin that was creamy-ivory rather than rose-gold, but the resemblance was incontrovertible. They might have been sisters. Omar shook his head in shock; it was a Freudian minefield. He would have loved to talk to Jim about it, but there'd be too many people about tonight, and Jim would get drunk too fast. Remembering himself, he jumped down the last few stairs and raced across the quad to Hall; he hoped that the lovebirds had saved him a seat.

When Omar arrived at the Hall, they had already started serving up. He looked vainly for Jim and Karen at the front of Hall, where they'd promised they'd be, and couldn't see them anywhere. He felt bereft; I've already become a spare wheel, he thought miserably to himself. Jim and Karen had each other now, and Sharif had just hooked up with an angel; no one needed him. Perhaps they never did. Perhaps he was just a way of treading water, buying time.

He was ludicrously relieved when a voice shouted, 'Hey, Omar, spare seat here!' He recognized the voice. It was Dieter, his occasional tutorial partner in philosophy, an unashamed geek who wore jumpers knitted by his mum, unnecessarily thick glasses, and who frequently forgot to remove his cycle clips. He was sitting with his own usual group, a couple of other PPE-ists, and a mixed bag of mathematicians, biologists and chemists. Like Dieter, they were all deeply uncool. Jim would have refused to sit within a foot of them, and usually only tolerated Dieter because Omar was obliged to share lessons and notes with him.

Omar had no such reservation about associating with the uncool, and sat down gratefully next to Dieter. He liked Dieter. When they did the long and winding walk down to their rotund tutor's house, they had lots of interesting conversations about everything from the Middle East crisis to Chomskian linguistics. Dieter was about a hundred times cleverer than Omar, but he never made him feel small or stupid. In the beginning of the Michaelmas term, before Omar had become firm friends with Jim and been pulled into his starry circle of the college great and good, he had socialized quite a lot with Dieter and the less pretty, less fashionable people that Dieter had been drawn towards. He had found them warm, friendly and always inclusive. It had been with some regret that he had drifted gently away from their comforting circle towards Jim's people, with whom he secretly felt that he was a mere pretender just waiting to be found out and discarded, to be chewed up and spat out like so much gum when he stopped being flavour of the month. His natural place was probably with the geeks, and he always suspected that he would return to their welcoming fold one day, the prodigal son blinded by the light of popularity. Perhaps his time had come.

Omar smiled broadly at Dieter and his group. 'Cheers, guys. Why's formal Hall so packed tonight?' he asked. 'I only waited for late Hall because I thought it would be quieter.'

'Dear, did you not hear the rumours?' said Dieter.

'Did you just call me "Dear"?' Omar asked with confusion. It wasn't like Dieter to be camp.

'No, I said "Deer". Cute dappled things with antlers. Apparently there was a cull at Magdalen, and some of the surplus has gone to us. The rumours are that deer might be on the menu tonight. Change from curry, eh,' said Dieter cheerfully.

'I've never had deer,' Omar said. 'Do you have to watch out for shot or something?'

'No,' said Ledley, a horsey biologist, 'that's more of a problem with birds. I broke a tooth on some shot in a partridge once.'

After the wet vegetable soup, there were groans of disappointment up and down the hall as the familiar platters of rice and poppadums and chutney were laid out on the table, and the ghostly smell of curry invaded the Hall.

'Well, so much for the rumours,' said Dieter. He asked one of the serving ladies politely, 'So, when are we due to have the deer? Is it still hanging?'

'No, dear,' said the lady, 'it's on your plate. Chef didn't know how to cook deer, so he curried it.'

'Bloody hell,' said Ledley, looking despondently at the steaming platters of venison curry. 'What a bloody awful waste of good game. I don't think I can bring myself to eat this.'

'What's it like?' Omar asked Dieter, who was tucking cheerfully in.

'Oh, the usual really. Tastes just like a regular curry,' he said.

Reassured, Omar tried it and agreed. 'It does, doesn't it? Like a chicken curry mixed with a beef one.'

After a while, Ledley shrugged, and, pulling only a slight face, started eating.

After dinner, Omar still couldn't see Jim and Karen any-where. He was dragged slightly unwillingly by Dieter's little group to the bar, where they cheerfully warmed up with beers, and moved on to tequila shots. After the third round of lick, down and bite, Ledley fell into Dieter, who fell into the table, which caused everyone else to fall onto the floor in a hiccuping hysterical heap, with Omar in the midst of them. This is where I really belong, he thought fuzzily, laughing hysterically with the rest of them; life with the geeks didn't seem so bad. Here he would be accepted for what he was, not who he was friends with; here he could be a king, rather than a pretender.

The sound of the crash was heard throughout the bar, and welcomed with an enormous cheer by those standing around. Jim saw Omar and went up to him. 'Where've you been, mate? Been looking all over for you. Didn't you go to Hall?'

'Yeah, I couldn't see you guys anywhere,' Omar said to one of the three Jims that stood above him, trying not to sound reproachful. 'Thought you might want some privacy.'

'You can't have looked very hard,' said Jim. 'We were at the front, like we said, near the High Table.' Omar realized through the fug of tequila what had happened. Of course, to Jim, the front of the Hall meant the end of the Hall where the High Table was set up. To Omar, the front of the Hall was naturally the entrance. Jim, looking impatiently at Omar, and for once less drunk than him, said, 'Anyway, get up. We're heading off to Balliol now to pick up Giles and Lydia.'

'I think I might be stuck,' Omar said apologetically, as Finola, a not too slim mathematician, was lying across his legs.

Jim did his trademark eyeroll, before pushing up his shirtsleeves, 'Up you come, sweetie,' he said, pulling Finola roughly to her feet in a businesslike way. He called her sweetie as he didn't know her name, or the names of any of Dieter's group, nor did he ever have any intention to waste his time learning them; he filed them all under 'R' in his head, for 'Random People I never need to know'. He yanked up Omar too, only slightly less roughly.

As Omar left he waved to Dieter's group cheerfully, and shouted back to them the running joke that they'd started with their first tequila shot. 'Bye, guys, see you later. Why did the Mexican throw his wife out of the window?'

'Tequila!' Dieter's group shouted back, waving their empty shot glasses.

'Thanks for coming to find me,' Omar said later, leaning on Jim a little drunkenly.

'Well, I couldn't leave you slumming with that lot for May morning,' said Jim. 'They might have brainwashed you to join their Geek Gang by the end of the evening and you'd have been stuck with them forever, like some moonie in a cult.'

'I like them,' protested Omar. 'I like Dieter, Ledley and Finola, and the rest of them.'

'You see,' said Jim. 'They'd started already. I came just in time.'

'They're sweet,' insisted Omar.

'Nope, dogs are sweet. They're just wallpaper,' Jim said meanly, waving to Karen who was waiting for them at the porter's lodge.

By the time they got to Balliol, the stroll in the cool, damp air had begun to sober Omar up. In the bar, Jim insisted that he and Karen do some shots together: 'We've got some catching up to do, Omar's well ahead of us.' Omar tried not to feel left out as they licked salt from each other's hands, and bit the same piece of lemon. He was relieved when Giles and Lydia turned up.

'Hey, Giles,' said Jim, thumping him on his broad back. 'And hello, Chlamydia. You look deliciously dirty tonight. Will I catch something if I snog you?' He caught Lydia in his arms in a sweeping gesture.

Instead of being offended, Lydia giggled with so much delight that Karen looked almost cross. 'Oh Jimmy, you're so naughty.'

'Oi, keep your faggot hands off my bitch,' said Giles good-humouredly, heading to the bar; he often used appalling language in an attempt to cover up his old Etonian roots. 'It's going to be a long, long night,' he said to Omar as he passed him, 'and I've got to get through it on sodding alcohol-free lager.'

As they made for the Parks, the light, damp mist became a light but persistent shower, which didn't get much heavier but showed no signs of abating. Normality had returned, as Jim was now the most drunk one in the group by far, and insisted on getting a stinking kebab, which he danced with while bellowing 'Singin' in the Rain' tunelessly along Broad Street. The rest of them decided to follow Jim's military planning, and dragged him along to New College Lane, where the party was still going strong. At some point in the early hours, fuelled by vodka and orange squash as the wine and beer had run out, bottles started spinning, in combination with Truth or Dare.

Omar, who'd been listening sympathetically to a girl crying about her love life in the chill-out room upstairs, walked in just as the bottle landed on Jim.

'Dare,' Jim said.

Omar felt reckless. He had no idea why he instinctively said what he said next, except that he was drunk, and suddenly wanted to get all the doubt out in the open, to let that sword of Damocles finally fall. If it was going to happen, why not make it happen now?

'Kiss Karen,' he said loudly, collapsing onto a cushion at the edge of the circle.

Karen, who was flushed prettily with the heat and the drink, looked at Omar with a combination of outright surprise and gratitude.

'Easy,' Jim said, and bounding up to her, took her in his arms and kissed her chastely on the lips. Karen tried to smile and giggle, but only Omar could see that she was disappointed that he hadn't done anything more daring.

'That was rubbish,' said Giles, who had smoked enough dope to get over the fact that he wasn't allowed to drink. 'You're not eight years old. Open your mouths.'

'OK, but no tongues,' said Jim, and kissed her more fulsomely, a soap opera kiss.

The bottle span again, and landed on Jim once more. 'This is bloody rigged,' Jim said, picking up the bottle and inspecting it, before draining the dregs of warm liquid still clinging to the bottom. 'Dare,' he said again.

'Kiss Omar – with tongues,' said Lydia, getting into the spirit of it, and was gratified to hear squeaks of excitement from the others.

Jim looked at Omar and raised a quizzical eyebrow towards him. Omar, who had been staring at his feet since the Karen kiss that he had stupidly been responsible for, looked up. 'What? No way, man. That would be gross! It would be like incest, or something,' he protested vigorously.

Lydia shrugged. 'You know the rules – if either party backs out on a truth or dare, they have to run round the cloisters naked three times.'

'Cool, we win either way,' burped Jim.

'When did those rules come into play?' said Omar. 'I don't remember agreeing to that.'

'We must have made them while you were upstairs,' said Lydia.

'Come on, mate,' said Jim. 'I'm not running round without pants in this weather. Stick your tongue down my throat and we're done.'

'Why tongues?' protested Omar again. 'Karen didn't have to do tongues.'

'That's because Karen's a lady, and it's bad enough that you made her snog Jimmy in the first place with his kebab breath,' said Giles, blowing out smoke in a deeply mellow manner.

'Oh, let them off, you guys,' said Karen. 'It's not fair if Omar wasn't here when we did the rules.'

While Omar opened his mouth to protest again, Jim strode over to him and, pinning him down by the shoulders, kissed him even more fulsomely than he had Karen, with lots of tongue, to the cheers of the room.

Omar managed to push him off, blurting out, 'Jim!' in shock and outrage. He looked at Jim, and Karen, and Giles, and Lydia, and the whole room staring at him. 'Man, I've got to gargle. That extra chilli on the 'bab was too much,' he said, racing out.

'You idiots,' he heard Karen shout out to the room after he left. 'He's Muslim, you know. I think you've really upset him.'

The bathroom was miraculously free, and Omar locked the door and sank on the edge of the bath. He felt like he was the only still point in the spinning world; he'd been exposed, he knew it. He didn't gargle, even though he felt nauseous. And now his nose was starting to bleed; he hadn't had a stress-induced nose bleed for months; he held a tissue to it with mechanical despondency. After a few minutes, there was a gentle knocking on the door. 'Mate, are you in there?' Jim said quietly. Omar sighed, and wetting his hands, ran his fingers through his hair to cool him down. 'Omar?' Jim called out, a bit louder. Omar opened the door and let him in. Jim shut the door, and joined him on the side of the bath. 'Sorry if I embarrassed you, mate. I just thought a quick kiss would be easier than a naked run round the cloisters, is all. I might have got a bit carried away with the snog. You know me – utter drama queen. Love an audience.'

'You don't need to apologize; I probably embarrassed myself more than you did by running off like that.'

'What happened to your face?' asked Jim, just noticing the bloody stain on Omar's upper lip.

Omar checked his reflection in the mirror and washed away the blood at the sink. 'Nothing, just a nosebleed,' he said.

Jim nodded and got up to go, but then sat back down again. 'We're friends, right? We'll always be friends. Nothing's going to change that.'

'Of course not,' said Omar, surprised.

'So I can tell you anything, and you won't get weird. Because we're friends,' persisted Jim. Omar nodded, realizing with a sinking heart that perhaps Jim was going to tell him that he and Karen were finally an item.

'The thing is, the real reason I kissed you wasn't to avoid a naked run around the cloisters. It was because I thought that the opportunity would never present itself again. That's all.' For a moment, Jim sounded totally sincere, and looked almost sheepish, before adding with his usual bravado, 'Mate, I am so wasted. Do me a favour and ignore everything I say and do tonight. Look, I'm heading back to the party. Are you still up for the bridge at five a.m.?'

Omar looked at Jim, the numb shock he felt replaced

by another, undefinable feeling. A little like the reckless-
ness he had felt when he dared Jim to kiss Karen, again
he suddenly wanted to get all his doubt out in the open,
to let that sword of Damocles finally fall. But this feeling
was an affirmative one, one of near hope rather than
dread. 'Wait,' he said to Jim, and standing up, stood
opposite him and kissed him quickly and softly on the
cheek. 'I thought that might have been my only opportunity, too,' he explained. Jim looked at him in amaze-
ment, and hesitated just briefly before smoothing back
Omar's wet hair from his forehead, taking Omar's face in
both hands, and kissing him back.

Mrs Henna Karim Extends a
Cordial Invitation

SHONA HAD MANAGED to avoid thinking about her mother for several weeks following her father's heart attack, until Henna inconsiderately barged back into her life. 'Shona moni,' Henna brayed loudly, into the answering machine at an ungodly hour, 'Shona moni, it's Amma, pick up!' Pausing for a moment, Henna started a sing-song chant that would test the patience of the most charitably disposed acquaintance, 'Pick up, pick up, pick up . . . Pick up! Pick up!'

Shona, bleary-eyed, wrapped a dressing gown around her and obediently picked up the bedroom phone, taking it on to the landing to avoid waking Parvez, who was sleeping heavily with slow and deliberate breaths. Just as she reverted to her cut-glass patrician accent when speaking to her papa or to her colleagues at school, with her Amma, she automatically fell into Bangladeshi vernacular, perhaps to make her feel closer to her, she wasn't sure.

'Ouf, why are you shouting so much? Don't you know what time it is here, Amma?'

'Tch! Why did you take so long to answer?' said Henna

unrepentantly. 'This is long distance, you know. Does the fat Pakistani keep you chained up so that you can't answer your old mother when she calls?'

'Amma, Parvez isn't fat,' said Shona, getting drawn in despite herself.

'Of course not. Parvez is perfect in every way, Rashid is perfect in every way. Everyone is perfect apart from your stupid old mother whom you never call, and who you ignore when she calls you for help.'

'Amma, what's wrong? What do you need help with?' Shona asked, suddenly concerned; she had been thinking that it was unlike her mother to use the endearment 'moni' when calling, and it was also not very like her to become belligerent so quickly; insulting Shona's loved ones and life choices was one of her favourite themes, but normally she warmed up to these with much greater calculation and finesse.

'I can't tell you over the phone. You have to come over here. I need your help, Shona moni. I need you here,' Henna entreated, now sounding almost distressed. 'Please come next week, as soon as you can.'

'Amma, summer term doesn't break up until the middle of next month. I can't just up and leave,' Shona started to explain.

'The middle of next month?' Henna mused, considering the proposal. 'Say on the fifteenth? Yes, that will just about do. Well, come in the middle of next month, then,' she said, suddenly not sounding distressed at all, but businesslike. 'So it's all settled.' Shona pursed her lips, realizing how her mother had just manipulated her, using her lifetime experience of amateur dramatics for that very purpose.

'Amma,' Shona protested, 'you have to tell me why you want me to come. Are you quite well? Is it Nanu? You can't just expect me to pay for a ticket to Dhaka with no reason.'

'Well, get the money from your prosperous father,' Henna snapped at her, 'if your great Pakistani husband is so poor that he can't afford to send his wife to visit her poor old mother.' Realizing from the silence at Shona's end that this tactic was proving less than persuasive, she added, 'Shona, I'm sorry for being cross. But this is important, I wouldn't ask you if it wasn't. Why are you making me give you reasons, when I've told you I can't? Do you want me to beg you to come? My own, my only daughter, my own flesh and blood, wants me to beg? All right then, I'll beg, I am begging you now. Come to Dhaka, Shona moni. I need you here.' By the end of her little speech, Henna's tones had shifted from bridling in cross words to wheedling in honeyed, humble tones.

Feeling instantly ashamed, even while she knew she was being played like putty by a seasoned expert at getting her own way, Shona said, 'Amma, don't speak like that. All right, I'll come.'

Having achieved what she wanted, Henna ended the call instantly, with barely a veneer of civility. 'Good, well I have to go now, Shona. Let me know which flight you'll be on.'

Shona looked at the clock in the passageway; it was four in the morning, and she felt too tired to be angry at her mother. She put the phone down, and went back to bed.

Parvez was in the same position, but his breathing was

lighter and shallow – he had, not surprisingly, woken up. Shona lay down at her end of the bed, and wished she had the comfort of someone's arms around her. She went back to sleep with difficulty, counting the hours and minutes until she would see Dermot again.

'So why exactly are you going to Dhaka?' asked Dermot, as Shona drove them to his flat during her after-school driving lesson.

'I wish I knew. Amma was very persuasive, but managed to avoid giving me a reason altogether. And she went on so much that it just seemed easier to say yes.' She turned briefly to look at Dermot's set profile. 'Go on, tell me I'm a sucker. That's what you're thinking.'

'I wouldn't presume to tell you that you're a sucker; besides, it would be pointless, seeing as you've already worked it out for yourself,' Dermot said with a smile. 'But seriously, you're over forty years old. You really don't need to do everything your mother says, especially without question. Don't go if you don't want to.' He hesitated before adding, 'Besides, I'd miss you.'

Shona looked at Dermot gratefully for much too long, before his warning look reminded her that she was still driving, and she turned her attention back to the mercifully quiet road in a flustered panic. 'Darling, the car's struggling a bit up the hill,' Dermot said quietly. Shona, who hadn't even noticed the fraught engine, pushed the car back into third gear.

'Sorry,' she muttered. She'd never stop her mother

from controlling her, and she was never going to pass her bloody driving test either.

In the haven of Dermot's flat, away from prying eyes and accidental encounters, Shona lay on the sofa with her feet raised onto Dermot's lap. 'Tell me about your mother,' Dermot said. 'You never talk about her.'

Shona hesitated. Ever since she had told Dermot about her father's secret life, she had avoided speaking about her family altogether. She had felt comforted telling him at the time, in the same perverse way that she had felt comforted when she had made love to Parvez; it was the comfort of laying oneself bare, of giving someone else her disquiet and her troubles, expelling her demons from her flesh. But in both cases, she had felt guilty afterwards; in the first instance, she had betrayed her father for her own comfort, in the second, she had betrayed her lover.

She had confessed to Dermot about that night with Parvez, and Dermot had said he understood; he even made excuses for her, saying that she had been confused and upset after finding out about her father's heart attack and then discovering his bigamy. Although he claimed to have appreciated her honesty, she could tell that the truth had upset him, as she had known it would. She had selfishly put her own conscience above his feelings, and she now felt little pride in this deed, which had seemed so noble at the time; how could you say someone deserved to hear the bitter truth, unless they also deserved to be hurt? She had decided to put an end to this new and damaging instinct to confess. The truth was overrated; it was rarely pure and never simple, that was the real truth that she had known since she was a child.

Given this, she wasn't sure if she should, or even if she could, expose her other demon; her ambivalence and resentment towards her mother. Besides, why did she dislike her mother so much? She barely knew her. Of course, she had worshipped her as a little girl, this fragrant, beautiful creature who was constantly flitting out dressed in sparkling, butterfly brightness. While other mothers wore their hair in long, undistinguished plaits, or pulled back into chaste buns, Shona's mother wore her glossy hair cut fashionably at her shoulders like a movie star, where it swung provocatively. But Henna had never paid her daughter the slightest bit of attention, passing her over indiscriminately to servants and nannies when her father wasn't available, except on a few precious outings, when it had just been her mother and her. She couldn't remember why her mother had relented, and taken her out on those visits to the clinic. She had only vague memories of kind-faced nurses, of lollipops and white coats. And after she had left with Parvez, her mother needed nothing else to do with her; it was as though the idea of her daughter was enough and she didn't need a flesh and blood one littering up her pleasant, indulgent life. Shona imagined that she was just a character in her mother's stories, something she used to boast to her friends: My Daughter, she lives in London, you know; My Daughter is an MA; My Daughter's son goes to Oxford. So where does your daughter live, Roshan, the one with the BA in English? Connecticut? Where's that? Oh-well-never-mind, I'm sure it must be nice. And Mina, where does your grandson attend college? Oh, really? Right here at Dhaka University. Well, it must be a comfort to have him so close . . .

Shona had visited her mother once every other year, when the boys were old enough, just so they would be able to say they knew their grandmother. She spoke to her about once a month, during which times her mother was always unfailingly critical. Of her parents, perhaps her father was the one who had misbehaved most profoundly, but despite this her father was the one she understood, and the one who had her love, because he had loved her first.

Aware of Dermot's eyes on her, and the overbearing silence in the room, Shona finally replied. 'There's not a lot to tell. I don't have much of a mother, really,' she said, sidestepping the question with obvious intent. She withdrew her legs from his lap, indicating unconsciously that she would not be receptive to any further questions on the matter.

'Do you not think that's something to tell, in itself?' said Dermot, pulling her legs back, running his hand over her instep. 'I didn't have much of a wife, but the one thing she did provide was conversational subject matter forever and a day.'

'Ah, but you're Irish, you love the chance to talk,' said Shona, seizing the chance to change the subject. 'What did you say your ex was doing these days?'

Back at home, Shona was surprised to find that the deadlock on the front door was already open. Turning the top key, she called out, 'Parvez, did you come back early?' while she considered several plausible reasons why she wouldn't have been back home at her normal time.

'Amma!' shouted a delighted voice. It was Omar. He ran in from the living room, closely followed by Pat-Bob, and hugged her.

'Darling, it's so lovely to see you!' exclaimed Shona, in genuine delight tinged with just the slightest bit of relief. 'I thought you were coming back tomorrow. Abbu and I were going to pick you up.'

'A friend of mine gave me a lift down, I thought I'd surprise you,' said Omar, cheerfully not mentioning that he and Jim had spent the last two days clubbing in London after their Prelims, and had stayed with a friend in Mile End. 'My friend Jim, I think I mentioned him? He hung around for a bit to say hello to you, but had to leave about an hour ago.'

'Yes, sorry darling, I had to . . . stay a bit later than usual. Staff meeting thing,' Shona said artlessly. 'What a shame I missed him.'

As they sat down to tea, Omar spoke brightly about the latest family gossip. 'What's the scoop on that angelic new girlfriend of Sharif's?' he asked carelessly, less good at keeping other people's secrets than his own.

Shona's brow furrowed. 'They broke up ages ago,

darling, not long after Easter, unless he has a new girl-friend he's not mentioned to me.'

Omar shrugged, covering up his careless mistake. 'Oh, right then. You know me, always behind on the news.'

'Well, here's some up-to-the-minute news for you,' Shona said. 'I'm going to see your Nanu in Bangladesh after we break up for the summer, around the fifteenth.' She asked entreatingly, although without much hope, 'I don't suppose you might like to come with me? Just for a couple of weeks? I'll get your ticket, it wouldn't cost you anything.'

Omar paused for a moment. He had a few weeks to kill before August, when Jim would be back from his family holiday. He had thought he would just lounge about in Tooting and catch up with friends, but he had lots of time to do that before the fifteenth. And once his mum was away it would be pretty dull at home, what with his dad working, and Sharif doubtless spending every spare moment with Candida, when he wasn't gigging or pretending to work. 'Sure,' he said eventually. 'Why not? I've not seen Nanu and old Ammie for ages.'

Shona hugged Omar from across the table. 'That's wonderful, darling. We'll have so much fun.' She breathed with relief that she wouldn't have to face her mother on her own. She would have her clever son as her protection; her mother was much more likely to behave herself if her Oxonian undergraduate grandson was there. Perhaps then she might choose to play the role of gracious matriarch rather than wicked, scheming witch.

The Dhaka Tea Party

TYPICALLY, WHEN SHONA and Omar arrived at the Dhaka townhouse, sweaty and tired after the long flight and the hectic drive, there was no one there to greet them. 'Your Amma must be out visiting,' said the young chauffeur, far more louche and familiar than the respectable, elderly driver of past years. They settled themselves in their usual guest quarters, and while Omar fell asleep, Shona sat in the dining room and waited for her mother. A sweet-faced village girl, whom Henna must have taken on since her last visit, brought Shona a glass of cold lemon sherbet with just a bit too much sugar. 'Has school finished already today?' Shona asked kindly, just to make conversation. The girl looked very young, barely older than ten, and giggled, delighted at such a funny question.

'School is finished. Now I am twelve, I work instead,' she said proudly, adding unnecessarily, 'I work here.' She went back into the kitchen with a light, cheerful step.

Shona frowned. Of course her mother would not have seen the value in sending the girl back to school; her own claims to have almost avoided school by a prepubescent marriage were well documented.

Henna eventually bustled in, looking very glamorous despite her age, in a cool-blue silk sari and enormous Gucci sunglasses. 'Oh, there you are, Shona,' she said a touch reproachfully, for all the world as though Shona was the one who had been late.

'Hello, Amma,' Shona said, getting up dutifully and pecking her on the cheek. 'Omar's asleep, he was shattered after the flight. Where is everyone? Where's Uncle Aziz and Ammie? Are they over at the farms?'

Henna had seemed momentarily nonplussed by this perfectly normal question, but then seized on Shona's suggestion too quickly for her answer to seem completely credible. 'Yes, yes, they are at the farms. Let's wake Omar; why must he sleep the moment he gets here? He must get that from the lazy Pakistani. We'll have tea on the veranda now it's a little cooler.' She shouted out for the village girl in the kitchen, 'É, Banu-Bibi!' but this time, not one, but two, appeared, with similar gentle demeanour but not quite similar enough to be sisters. 'Banu and Bibi, this is my daughter. We'll have some more lemonade, and tea, with pooris and sweets.' She said in an aside to Shona, 'Omar likes sweets, I remember.'

'I think it's you that likes sweets, Amma,' Shona said matter-of-factly, but lightly enough not to cause offence. 'Why do you have two new girls? Where's Osama, the cook?'

Henna deliberately pretended to misunderstand the question. 'Well, you must always have two girls rather than just one, otherwise they get lonely and want to go back to their village, and you have to start all over again.' She looked over Shona critically. 'You had better get changed. You look like a crushed piece of old linen, and Shameela from my am dram group is coming for tea soon. We're doing a Gilbert and Sullivan season. We all laughed when she suggested *Trial by Jury* – she's married to a rich attorney, and is bringing her elderly, ugly daughter.' She winked cheekily at Shona, as though to say, They're not as good as us. We'll have some fun with them.

Shona sighed as she capitulated and went to leave the room. As usual with her mother, so many things were left unanswered, unaddressed and hung in a thick, conspiratorial fog in the room. She was deeply unsatisfied with this first encounter; there had been no explanation for the sudden rush to come to Bangladesh, or the puzzling absence of Uncle Aziz and her grandmother, and no reason given for the ancient cook's replacement. Osama had often let her sit in the kitchen as a child, while he gave her tasty tit-bits of the sweet halwa and toasted almonds that he sometimes prepared for special occasions, like Eid or birthdays. There was probably a very simple explanation behind Osama's departure. This, at least, her mother could tell her. She deserved to know if he had passed away, or retired. Pausing at the door, Shona turned back and asked again, 'But Osama? Where is he?'

Henna shrugged. 'He's not Osama any more, you know. He changed his name in protest against that bearded Saudi cave-dweller who was hiding in Afghanistan; he's Osman now. I told him it was a stupid name. It doesn't sound Bangladeshi at all, it sounds like the name of a Turkish carpet-seller. Imagine, an old man like that doing such silly things, as though he has anything to do with world politics.'

'But where is he?' Shona persisted.

Henna looked at her as though she was a touch retarded. 'I told you, Shona. At the farms with the rest of them.'

Shona looked mutinously between two outfits. One was a gleaming shalwar kameez that she had bought in Tooting. It was in a shade of sophisticated green that she loved, and looked unmistakably Pakistani in design; it would certainly irritate her mother. Or, after having been compared to crushed linen, it was very tempting to dress in it; she picked up a linen trouser suit and shook it out. Why not? She deserved to have a little fun at her mother, after the way she'd behaved this afternoon.

Omar was already on the veranda, still dressed in his jeans and Sex Pistols T-shirt. He was speaking earnestly to Henna about his course, and Shona was pleased to see that Henna was looking both bored and lost, while nodding sagely, and pretending to know what he was talking about. 'Hey Ma,' he said as she seated herself in the wicker chair facing her mother, 'did you know that Nanu is doing a rep performance of *Trial by Jury* and *The Mikado* this week? They're performing at the college. Lucky we got here, or we'd have missed it; and Nanu wouldn't have had any other fans in the audience with everyone else being away.'

Shona looked at her mother in surprise. So was that all

it had been? She had wanted her family to support her from the audience for her latest event, as Aziz and Ammie wouldn't be available. Why hadn't she just said? Shona realized quickly that of course her mother wouldn't have told her over the phone; she had played it just right by making it sound like it was something urgent with dire consequences. With the price of the airfare, the play was the most expensive evening out Shona had ever bought. Henna had the grace to look a little sheepish, and said brightly, 'I think that's Shameela coming through with her daughter,' as she bustled to the door.

Shameela was an elegant woman who was about Henna's age, but looked much older – her greyhound thinness did not complement her, and her face looked especially haggard, with the skin pulled tautly across her high cheekbones and jutting forehead. Her daughter, Parvine, was neither elderly nor ugly; she was only a few years older than Shona, and simply a little bit plain. Her worthy, nun-like looks were not helped by the frazzled grey hair scraped back and held with a plastic clasp, nor by her thick, heavily framed glasses. Despite the unprepossessing appearances, both mother and daughter seemed very friendly, and had thoughtfully brought a gift, a large box of multicoloured burfis from one of the city's most celebrated sweet-makers.

During the gossipy conversation that followed between Henna and Shameela, mainly in English for Omar's benefit, Shona found herself staring a little too much at Parvine – she was thinking that this was what she could look like in a few years, if she decided to wear glasses rather than contact lenses, and let her hair go grey and long rather than colouring and styling it. She wondered what Dermot would think of her then, if she lost her looks before he did.

'These are great sweets,' said Omar politely, biting into a peach-coloured burfi. 'As good as Uncle Hassan's.'

'My husband's cousin,' Shona explained to Shameela and Parvine. 'He owns a confectionery shop in Tooting.' Seeing the warning look from her mother, that clearly told her not to make further reference to her husband's Pakistani, plebeian, shopkeeping relatives, she recklessly added, 'We used to live above his shop when we first moved to London.'

Henna looked thunderous, but regained composure instantly. 'Yes, my daughter was such a free spirit. We always supported her in her whims: going to London, living above a sweet shop. A kid in a candy shop, like the Americans say; I think she inherited my sweet tooth!' She laughed at her own joke, pleased at having turned Shona's embarrassing early poverty into a sugary anecdote.

'I love London,' sighed Shameela. 'I would love my granddaughter to live there so I had an excuse to visit. I would go to the theatre every night.'

Shona asked after Shameela's role in Henna's amateur theatre production, and was surprised to hear the older lady giggle in delight. 'Me? An actress? At my age? We are not all blessed with your mother's looks. I think she keeps a picture in an attic that does her ageing for her. No, I used to be a dancer, many years ago, and I am the choreographer of the dance routines. Your mother puts the others to shame. She should have been a dancer.'

'You dance, Nanu?' Omar said, impressed. 'Wow, that's amazing.'

'And I'm very good,' said Henna proudly. 'You'll see me tomorrow, during the production. You can come to the dress rehearsal too, if you want. It's in the morning.' She threw a significant look at Shameela and Parvine.

Up until this point, Parvine had been rather quiet, sitting very straight in her chair during tea, making polite comments about the pooris and lemonade, but otherwise contenting herself with following the others' conversations. Despite her glasses, she had been myopically observing Omar quite a bit, perhaps trying to make out the slogan on his T-shirt. However, at the mention of the dress rehearsal, as though jabbed into action on cue, she leaned forward earnestly, and in the breathy, quick voice of someone who might expect rejection, said to Omar, 'Yes, my daughter will be at the dress rehearsal. She has been helping me with the costumes. She said she could show you around town later, she knows Dhaka very well, and she's about the same age as you.'

'Sure,' said Omar distractedly, trying to prevent his burfi crumbling into his tea, 'that's really nice of her to offer. If Amma doesn't mind.' He turned towards Shona with an obvious lack of suspicion. 'Amma, did we have plans for tomorrow?'

Before Shona could prevent the obvious set-up and claim they did already have plans, Henna smiled and said, 'How nice, that's all settled then.' Shameela and Parvine smiled just as broadly, and Parvine visibly relaxed back into her wicker seat. Despite her nervousness, her mission had been accomplished, and she glanced to her mother for approval.

After all the tea and refreshments had been exhausted, Shameela and Parvine made their excuses to leave. Omar remained on the veranda, while Henna and Shona led them out. 'Such a wonderful afternoon,' Shameela said in Bangla to Henna. 'And such a pretty daughter, Shundor Shona,' she added, moistening her finger delicately with the inside of her lower lip, before touching Shona's cheek for good luck, 'and clever grandson. A philosopher, no less! You must be very proud.' Henna smiled graciously, and inclined her head like the lady of the manor she had become. Shameela continued as she reached the door, 'And please pass my best wishes to Bhai Aziz and his mother. I'm sorry to have missed them again, but they must have so much to plan for with his wedding coming up so soon.' She smiled conspiratorially at Shona. 'Imagine, a confirmed bachelor like your uncle finally getting wed. If someone like him can change his ways, there's hope for all the unmarried girls out there.'

Shona took this revelation with outward calm, while she finally made the connection between her mother's uncharacteristic cry for help last month, and the inexplicable absences from the household. Gilbert and Sullivan had less to do with this visit than she had thought; she realized now that there were more serious changes afoot. Her mind was ticking over so rapidly with this new information and the possible consequences, that she didn't notice Shameela asking her a question, and had to ask her to repeat it.

'I just asked if your father will have recovered from his

heart attack sufficiently to fly back for the wedding,' Shameela asked. 'We see him so rarely in Dhaka these days.'

'I really don't know,' Shona said honestly. 'Perhaps he won't be well enough . . .'

Henna interrupted impatiently, 'Of course Rashid will be back for his younger brother's wedding.' She added guilelessly, 'And as I've already told you all, you will be seeing much more of him in Dhaka before too long. With his retirement coming up, he won't need to spend so much time in England. I'll soon have my dear Rashid home.' Shona looked at her mother in barely concealed astonishment; what things had she been telling the cream of Dhaka society? For all intents and purposes, her parents had separated years ago; she couldn't possibly expect him to return for good.

'Such a hard worker, putting his family's comfort before his own for so long,' Shameela said with approval, while Parvine nodded. 'He must be looking forward to his retirement immensely.' They finally took their leave.

At the door, in the long dark hallway, Shona and Henna faced each other silently. Shona looked pleadingly at her mother: Please speak to me, please explain it all, please don't make me have to drag it all out of you, don't let it all be unsaid again and again. Henna took a deep breath, and then smiled brightly as she skitted off girlishly to her quarters. 'I've got a visit to make before dinner,' she said cheerfully, over her shoulder.

Shona caught up with her, keeping ruthlessly in step with her. 'Amma, we need to talk, now.' Henna kept walking, trying to shake her off by looking straight ahead and ignoring her, as she had so often when Shona was a tottering infant trailing persistently after her pretty mamma.

'Besides, you must be very tired, Shona,' added Henna, as she reached her door. 'I'll be back for dinner.' She went to shut the door smilingly in Shona's face, but Shona wedged her foot in the heavy door. She was fortunately still wearing her heavy airport loafers rather than sandals better suited to the climate. I can't believe she's making me do this, Shona thought to herself, as she found herself forced to fight with the door in a manner that was hardly dignified. She managed to push the door back open, and stood purposefully with her back against it.

'Mamma,' she said pleadingly. 'We must talk. We really must.'

Henna, having lost the battle of the door, was already at her dressing table smoothing out her glossy hair with an expensive bristle brush. 'What about, dear?' she said artlessly. 'Are you and the Pakistani having problems? Is that why he didn't come with you?'

Shona wasn't going to be thrown so easily this time. 'Amma, you know that Parvez is working. Why aren't Uncle Aziz and Ammie here? Why have the old chauffeur and Osama left? You've fallen out over this wedding, haven't you?'

Henna's back was to Shona, and her shoulders started shaking as though she had a deep laugh rumbling upwards from her stomach. 'You stupid, stupid child,' choked out

Henna through the laugh when it finally erupted. For a moment Shona thought that all was well, and that she had simply misunderstood everything. But then she saw that Henna's laugh was so strong it was bringing her to tears. 'You've fallen out? You've fallen out?' she mocked Shona, imitating her voice cruelly. 'As though we were children squabbling over a ten-taka note in the gutter. Don't you realize what this bloody marriage means?' Shona remained silent, having no idea what had upset her mother so deeply, and not wanting to risk displaying any further ignorance. Her mother had the ability to make her feel very small and simple indeed. Henna took a deep breath. 'No, of course you don't. You only think of yourself and your fat Pakistani and your darling father.' She turned fully to face Shona, who was still standing at the door. 'Sit down, dear,' she said, indicating the divan seat. When Shona remained standing, preferring the support of the door, Henna shrugged and explained in a more composed voice, just slightly trembling with anger, 'It means that I have given that man and his mother the last twenty years of my life, and he repays me by replacing me with another model, and barely a younger model at that!' Shona held her breath, thinking that Henna must have found out about Verity, but then Henna continued, 'An ugly spin-ster, a doctor who thinks she is so special just because she has worked for a living. Hah! She calls that work? That woman has spent her life looking down people's throats and down her thin nose at real wives and mothers like me.' She looked earnestly at Shona. 'You see? He is bringing another woman to this house, usurping my place in our household, and in our society.'

Shona did not understand why her mother was talking like a jealous wife. Uncle Aziz was free to marry whoever he wanted, although now that he was in his late fifties, most of Dhaka society would have no longer expected it. People joked that he was married to his farms, and to his family. She was about to say something calming to her mother, when she noticed the photo of her mother on the dresser. It was taken maybe ten years ago at a charity event in Dhaka, and her mother looked radiant and beautiful, and very happy. She had seen the photo many times before, but had never registered who her mother was dancing with, as his back was to the camera and the face couldn't quite be seen. Of course, it was Uncle Aziz; her father never danced, and would certainly not have gone willingly to one of those events during his flying visits back, even if Henna had deigned to ask him. Realization finally dawned on her, as she remembered the unkind, unfounded words of gossips all those years ago, and she sat down heavily on the divan.

'Uncle Aziz?' she asked. 'All this time, you and Uncle Aziz? Here in this house?'

Henna looked pitifully at Shona. 'Oh, for God's sake, don't be so naive, child,' she spat impatiently. 'Did you think I would sit here like a grieving widow while your father played with his Air Miles? Playing the English gentleman over in the UK, playing house with some insipid, weak-chinned, crooked-toothed Lady Limey?'

Shona had to admit that she was indeed, a stupid, stupid girl. 'You knew? About Papa and Verity? You know?' Everyone, it seemed, knew about the family skeletons, secrets and hidden liaisons apart from her. She struggled to find a firm place for her confused thoughts to settle. 'So Papa knew about you, too? He must have.'

Henna looked impatiently at Shona. 'Arré, what did I do to have such a slow daughter!' she muttered, practically rolling her eyes. 'If your darling father knew, do you think he would be flying back here with such guilty regularity, do you think he would be keeping up appearances over here with such efficiency, do you think he would be sending back such a big chunk of his salary to us every month? Of course your father does not know; he suspects, as he has suspected us for years because of the bloody gossiping servants, like your precious Osama, but he was too guilty himself to ever confront us. If your father found out, I would have had to divorce him and marry Aziz; and I would have lost my position in society here with the scandal.'

'Would that have been so bad?' Shona asked quietly, almost afraid to speak up amid this whirlwind of revelation, in case it whipped round her and pulled her away with it. 'Then Uncle Aziz wouldn't be marrying someone else now, and Papa wouldn't be riddled with guilt and making himself ill with long-distance travel.'

Henna shook her head. 'Well, your papa won't be weakening himself any more with travel or guilt. He can make up for this sorry mess by coming home and taking up his place as head of the house, so Aziz and his ugly old doctor-didi can be put back in their place, or move out if they don't like it.' She moved swiftly over to Shona, who flinched as though half expecting a blow or more sharp words, but Henna simply knelt by her entreatingly, her hands on either side of her face. 'This is why I needed you to come. I need you, Shona moni. I need you to persuade your father to come back to Dhaka and take up his place here, or my position will be lost forever. Everyone will realize what has happened, and I'll be a laughing stock. Everything I've built here will be gone; I'll just be another pathetic old woman abandoned by her husband.' Getting up, to sit companionably by Shona on the divan, taking her daughter's hand, Henna continued, in a soft, reasonable voice, 'Besides, I've let your father play long enough in England; it's time to come home. He's had twenty years with that wife, which is long enough for any love match to last, and his English daughter is grown up now, so he can't say she needs him. His real family needs him now; his real wife, his old Ammie, his daughter and grandchildren . . .' She looked wide-eyed at Shona, teary with emotion.

Shona wrenched her hand away. 'Ammie prefers Uncle Aziz, and always did. And you clearly did, too. And my family aren't in Dhaka, they're in England, where Papa is now. You'll be taking him away from us, and from everything he loves.' Her voice was getting higher but, unable to stop it, she practically shrieked, 'How long have you known about Papa? About his other family? How long?'

Henna looked calmly at the hand that Shona had rejected, polishing a brilliant sapphire and diamond ring with the edge of her silk sari. 'Well, from the beginning, Shona. I am not as slow as you and your father; I did some snooping and read his correspondence when he came over. At the time I was pleased that he had something to distract him.' Looking up at Shona, she asked, 'Why are you so upset? Didn't you know? If I knew all the way here in Dhaka, how could you not have known right there in London? Didn't you wonder why your father spent so little time in that London flat, and why he got a new place in the country? Didn't you ever visit and work it out for yourself?'

Shona looked down, not wanting to meet her mother's pitying look. Perhaps her mother was right. Perhaps she was just small and simple, hiding her ignorance behind her degrees and her book-learning. 'The boys were born after Papa bought his new house; it was too difficult to visit with the twins, so he used to come to us. I think we went a few times, but he always took us out for lunch or dinner, we never stayed . . .' She added, quietly, as though to justify herself, 'I did think he might have met someone in England. I suspected a long time ago when I went to his first flat, the company one he had in Paddington, but I never thought he was married, with another daughter, another life. I only found out when he had his heart attack at Easter. I saw Verity at the hospital.' She said bitterly to her mother, 'How could you have known, all these years, and not told me? You knew that Papa had a wife, and that I had a sister, all these years, and you kept it hidden. You made Papa keep this stupid lie going on and on, while you must have been bleeding him and Uncle Aziz dry.'

Henna was already getting impatient with Shona. She went back to the dresser, pulled out a lipstick in a golden case and started painting her lips. 'Tch!' she tutted in disgust. 'Your father marries some wilting English flower, raises another daughter and you still manage to make *me* the criminal? Always taking your precious father's side.'

Shona felt like crying, but didn't dare to in front of Henna. It would just confirm her mother's poor opinion of her. 'Mamma, why does it have to be like this? We all know the truth now, so who would you be protecting? We shouldn't have to keep up this pretence.'

Henna, satisfied with her reflection, picked up her handbag and went to the door. 'We won't have to soon. Just make sure your father comes back; he'll listen to you. The sooner he leaves his silly fairy-tale idyll in England and comes back to Dhaka, the sooner everything will be back to normal.' She walked out of the door, saying crossly, 'You've made me late for my appointment now. I'll be back for dinner.' She marched off purposefully, leaving Shona in a crumpled heap of linen on the divan.

I can't do this, Shona thought, exhausted. I was telling myself that the truth was overrated, but the real truth is this: I can't pretend any more, for someone else's sake, that things are the way they should have been rather than the way they are. She stood up unsteadily, and went to pick up the photo of her mother and Uncle Aziz on the dresser. Her unanswered question echoed insistently through her mind: who would they be protecting by bringing Papa back to play-act at happy families twenty years too late? Not herself or Amma, who both knew the truth about Papa's double life already. Not Uncle Aziz or Ammie, who couldn't care less about Papa and would prefer, as Amma knew well, that Papa remain where he was and the status quo remain unchanged. Not Verity or

Candida, who would lose their husband and father, just so that Henna could gain back her trophy husband for appearance's sake, and so Shona could maintain the cheap, flimsy pretence that her parents were happy. And this was worthless now that she could no longer deceive herself that they had a satisfactory, if unusual, arrangement.

Omar knocked softly on the door. 'Hey, Amma, are you OK in there?' he asked.

'I'm fine, darling,' replied Shona, replacing the photo and smoothing her hands over her face before opening the door.

'You don't look fine,' commented Omar. 'Have you and Nanu been arguing again?'

Shona shrugged, and nodded.

'Something of a record, I guess. You managed to hold off for four hours,' Omar teased gently. 'Do you want to go for a walk before dinner? Head out to the bazaar or something.'

Shona nodded again, and managed a weak smile. She remembered something from the teatime, and said apologetically to her son, 'I'm sorry about the set-up, I had no idea they had that planned. You don't have to go, just to be polite.' Shona paused, and then picked her words carefully. 'What I mean is, I don't want you to have to pretend to go along with things that Nanu might have planned, just for appearance's sake.'

Omar looked surprised. 'What set-up?' he asked, before he realized, 'Oh, you mean Parvine's daughter? I didn't think that was a set-up.' He added, 'Really, Amma, there was no need to argue with Nanu about that. I honestly don't mind hanging around Dhaka with someone my own age for a day. If she's anything like her mum and Shameela, I'm sure she'll be very nice. Besides, I'm sure I can protect myself from her; I'm sort of off the market, anyway.'

Shona felt her sober mood lightening. Here at least was some good news. 'I thought you looked particularly happy since you've come back from college. Who is she?'

Omar held his finger to his lips. 'Shh, it's a secret,' he said conspiratorially. He took her arm as they left the house. 'You know, I'm luckier than you, I think.'

Shona looked at him suspiciously. 'Why's that?' She wondered if he was going to compare his new relationship with the state of her own less than happy partnership with his father.

'Because I've got a much nicer mum than you have,' he explained, kissing her on the cheek.

Shona felt much, much better, and squeezed her son's arm.

A Performance, a Bookmark and a
Drastic Decision

S HONA AND OMAR dutifully went to the performances
of *Trial by Jury* and *The Mikado* that Henna performed on consecutive nights with her drama group.
Although the audience numbered at least a hundred, they
were without exception family and friends of the cast and
backstage crew. They used the hall in Dhaka University,
and Shona was reminded of her school production at
Christmas, which had been slightly better attended. When
they sang, 'She may very well pass for forty-three, in the
dusk with a light behind her,' Omar nudged his mum.
'When was your birthday again, Amma?' he asked.

'Shut up,' she said good-naturedly, feeling a little bit
old and worn-down compared to her glowing, all-singing,
all-dancing mother, who with heavy make-up and under
the stage lights, could have easily passed for her sister.

The next night, at *The Mikado*, Shona was amused to
notice that her Amma, who despite her age must have had
a secret yen to play the starring role of Yum-Yum, had to
make do with Katisha. She had deliberately resisted making herself plain enough to carry off the role, apparently

allowing the make-up team to do no more than put a high, dramatic flush on her cheeks, and to make her brows heavier. Nor did she deliver the line about not having a beautiful face with much sincerity, although she made up for it with her comic timing and wide-eyed candour when she added, 'But I have a left shoulder blade that is a miracle of loveliness. People come miles to see it.'

'Now that, you can see she really meant,' commented Omar, and Shona choked back a snigger in response. However, when she saw her mother sing back to her bandy-legged suitor, 'Willow, titwillow, titwillow,' so gently and softly, and when she saw her dance with the chorus in bare feet, her toenails gleaming like polished pearls, her face transported, Shona wasn't sniggering any more. This was what her mother had lived for, to perform; perhaps if she'd been able to become an actress or a dancer in her youth, she would have been less of an actress at home with her family. She felt a little sad that this was what Henna was trying so hard to protect – her place in Dhaka society, her place in a well-regarded little amateur dramatic group, which performed to friends and family, coerced spectators who made jokes at her expense while they watched the performance. It seemed so little to show for her mother's life.

In one of the lazy afternoons that followed, Shona was guiltily awaiting a call from Dermot that she planned to take in her father's old, abandoned study. She checked her watch; almost ten minutes. She thought she might seem a bit suspicious hovering so closely to the phone, so she wandered out to the dining room, where Omar had books and papers out, writing notes for his next year's work. 'I didn't realize you were studying linguistics,' Shona said in surprise, seeing a tome by Chomsky open at his elbow.

'I'm not,' said Omar, drinking some pomegranate juice that Bibi had sweetly whizzed for him in the blender. 'It's for a philosophy paper that I'm taking on innatism. You know, nature versus nurture, what's naturally in us, like natural morality, versus what we're taught.'

'Oh right,' said Shona nodding. 'So I guess language is an example of something we're taught.'

Omar shook his head. 'You know, that's what I would have thought too. In fact, according to this, language is an example of something that's innate. I think the idea is that you can't really teach someone their first language, as they'd have to understand the language in the first place to be taught it. So children must already have this innate structure that's ready to accept any language they're first exposed to, and they sort of discover it, or invent it for themselves.' Omar frowned with frustration. 'Well, at least that's what I've copied out. I'm writing it all down, but I don't quite understand it. That's the trouble with me and philosophy – you can't just learn it, you have to . . . get it, too.' He smiled disingenuously. 'I guess I'm just a bear of little brain.'

Shona ruffled his hair affectionately. 'It's enough to be clever, darling. You don't have to be modest, too.' The phone rang, and they both jumped. 'I'll get it,' said Shona quickly; Dermot was uncharacteristically early. But Omar was too quick for her. 'Hello, Karim residence,' he said.

'Oh, all right, mate!' he answered in delight on recognizing the voice. 'Thought it might be you. Hold on, I'm taking it in the other room.'

'Is it Sharif?' asked Shona, as he put the phone down and headed to Rashid's office.

'Nope, Jim from college. Calling from Portugal,' Omar answered briefly over his shoulder.

Shona sighed. While they were gossiping about girls and suchlike, Dermot would call and not get through. Oh well, she'd text him and arrange another time. Glancing at Omar's notes, she thought about what he'd said. Perhaps she had never learned to dissemble, to pretend, to play-act, as she knew she did so effectively; perhaps it had always been with her, part of her heritage from her duplicitous mother and bigamous father, and she had just needed to be exposed to the right stimuli to discover it for herself. She couldn't claim to have been taught to behave this way; it was the way she had always been. Or was deception just another language she'd been taught, along with Urdu, Bangla and English? Was it something that could be unlearned, or was it part of her? Maybe I could learn something new, to replace it, thought Shona; I'm a language teacher, so why can't I teach Amma, and Papa, and me to learn a new language, a new way of speaking, of behaving. She sighed again; how vain she was, as though she believed she really could intellectualize away adultery; it was one of the oldest sins, and one that they were all three guilty of, and it was what had caused this convoluted turn of events. And yet, she was still trying to keep her secret hidden. Because it would be better for the boys, she told herself. Her throat suddenly felt very dry.

Shona reached for Omar's pomegranate juice and, taking a sip, an underlined phrase in his notes caught her eye. 'Shklovskij: People living at the seashore grow so accustomed to the murmur of the waves that they never hear them.' Intrigued, Shona sat down and read on, the lines copied out by Omar's neat, precise hand. 'By the same token, we scarcely ever hear the words which we utter . . .' That was all, it was the last thing he had written; she must have interrupted him before he finished writing out the rest. She picked up the book Omar had been reading to see if there was any more, and his bookmark fell out. A slim copper bookmark, engraved with an etching of New College and 'Omar R Khan'. On the back, also engraved, was 'Yours, JO'. So that was the name of Omar's new girlfriend. Jo. She replaced the bookmark, and found the rest of the phrase in the book: '. . . we scarcely ever hear the words which we utter . . . we look at each other, but we do not see each other any more'. Her father's words in the hospital echoed back to her; she had agreed not to see his double life, if he had not seen hers.

When Omar came back, he was flushed with excitement. 'Jim's been having a miserable time in Portugal, he's already planning his next holiday. He's organizing some trip to go clubbing in Ibiza. I thought I might go, too.'

'Sure, if you can afford it,' Shona said. 'You don't have to ask. Will your girlfriend be going, too?'

'I wasn't asking, Ma,' Omar said with slight reproach. 'I'm a grown-up, and I'll find some work when I get back to pay for it all. And don't worry about girls, Oakley's insisting that this is a lads-only trip.'

'I'm not sure that sounds like any less to worry about,' said Shona dryly. 'And who's Oakley?'

'Oakley is Jim's surname, I call him Oakley some-times,' said Omar, sitting back at the desk and getting out his mobile. 'I'm going to text Sharif and tell him, he'll be sooo jealous; he always wanted to go clubbing in Ibiza, but can't, what with all his . . . um,' Omar hesitated for no apparent reason, before saying, '*work* commitments.' He got back up again. 'In fact, I'm going to email him so I can gloat properly . . .'

'Well, it's about time he started to take his work seriously,' Shona said. 'I don't know what else he's doing with his time. Your Abbu says his constant absenteeism is getting beyond a joke. And send him my love.'

She looked again at the line in Omar's book: '. . . we look at each other, but we do not see each other any more'. She sighed. How true it was; how often had she missed what was right before her eyes, waiting to be remarked upon, to be noticed, to be discovered. With Amma, with Papa, with Dermot. She looked at the book-mark again; it was very elegant, with a slight ripple to the metal above the etching of the college. It was a thoughtful present; what a nice girl this Jo must be. Shona looked again. Of course, it wasn't Jo, it was JO. Jim Oakley; it was from Omar's friend, his best friend at college. He didn't talk about him much at all. In fact, he hardly mentioned him, but he always seemed so happy to hear from him. His face was an utter picture of joy just now, she couldn't remember when she had last seen someone so happy. But then she suddenly did; an image flashed back to her, of Dermot walking swiftly down the stairs at

Clapham Common tube station, and on seeing her, his face breaking into an expression of pure happiness and relief, as he walked straight into her arms.

Oh my God, thought Shona. Putting the book down, she walked swiftly into the garden for some fresh air, taking deep gulps on the humid terrace. She sat down on the swing, moving herself gently to and fro with her feet. I've been deceiving myself, she thought: 'Je me trompais moi-même.'

This revelation made everything suddenly very clear to Shona. She saw that the intricate web her family had designed to keep them together, had actually entangled them, and pulled them further and further apart. Her Amma and Papa's pretence had benefited neither of their children, neither Shona nor Candida, in the end; they should have divorced twenty years ago, when Papa must have met Verity, and Amma had started her affair with Aziz. She thought about what she was doing with Parvez and Dermot, and suddenly felt very cold and very guilty. She'd been judging her parents and, yet again, she was following their lead, their unhealthy pattern of lies and subterfuge. She could no longer argue that it was better for the boys if she and Parvez remained together, unhappily, for appearance's sake, and she could no longer pretend that it was better for either Parvez or Dermot.

I didn't hear the waves; I've looked but I haven't seen, thought Shona. I thought that I was lying to protect the children, and all I've done is push them down the same path as me, the same path as my parents. So Omar feels he has to hide the truth, to protect us, and I'm losing my own son to his secret. And I might have already lost Sharif; he may never forgive me for holding back the truth about Candida during those few weeks when he was seeing her. I made him live with a guilty secret that he didn't even know.

Shona made a decision. This is where it would end. She would tear through that intricate web, and damn the consequences. With a sinking heart, she realized she would have to start with herself; Parvez deserved to be the first to know.

Sharif Khan and the Terrifying Truth

'Y OU KNOW, I still can't believe it,' Sharif said to Candida, pulling off another slice of the take-out pizza they were having for lunch. 'Mum is barely home from Bangladesh, and then she and Dad tell us that they're separating.'

'It's such a shame. Your mummy's lovely,' said Candida. 'Your dad's mad to let her go.'

'It's not his choice, poor sod. Mum didn't say in so many words, but she's basically met someone.' He chewed on his pizza. 'And then a week later, Omar finally tells us about his new college squeeze, and it's not a she, it's a he! I mean, I know I always called him a bloody big poofter, but I didn't expect him to go and prove me right. And Mum was right there sticking up for him, like she knew all along. Dad was furious with them both – I think that's the only reason he's let Mum go with so little fight. He's become insanely parochial, and started talking about sending Omar to Pakistan to get fixed up with some poor chick.' He glanced towards the fridge. 'Is my beer cold yet?'

In Sharif's tiny Collier's Wood kitchen, Candida could reach out and open the freezer compartment on top of the fridge without even getting up from her place at the table. As she inspected the contents of the freezer, she said, 'I'm glad Omar's happy, that's all that's important, isn't it? He was clever to run off to Spain so quickly, to leave the fallout behind . . . OK, your beer is sort of cold, my wine still isn't.'

'You can share some of my beer, if you want,' Sharif offered gallantly.

'My hero,' said Candida wryly. 'It starts off with breakfast in bed and roses, and ends up like this. You know, when you said you'd be making lunch for us today, this isn't quite what I expected.'

'I have so little time with you, I just didn't want to waste it cooking,' Sharif said, using a cheeky grin to mask his sincerity.

Candida looked at him coyly. 'Well, we're alone in the flat for once. Aren't we wasting time right now?' Sharif raised a quizzical eyebrow, and then leaped out of his chair and picked her up, carrying her screaming with delight to his bedroom.

Afterwards, with wine so cold it was almost frozen, and picking at the cold, chewy pizza in bed, Sharif explained, 'I think the funny thing about my parents breaking up is that I always thought of them as one person. Like lying here in bed, we're two people, Candida and Sharif, who are choosing to share the same space. But with my parents, it was like one person, one creature in the bed, an Amma-Abbu-Amma beast, so you couldn't tell where one began and the other ended, like they were physically joined together. When we were little, Omar and I would come into bed with them some mornings, and I swear you couldn't get between them, they were so moulded together in their sleep. We always had to go on either side.'

'I think that's so sweet,' said Candida. 'They must have been very much in love. Don't forget they had you when they were very young.'

'The thing is, I don't think they were in love for so very long,' said Sharif. 'But they were still joined together in this thing called a marriage – joined isn't even a strong enough word, it's like they were conjoined, like Siamese twins; they were still tightly wound together in the mornings when they slept, like they didn't have a choice. Like that thing in Dr Dolittle, a push-me-pull-you, the same creature but with two heads that wanted to pull in different directions. I could see that they were falling apart, I saw it more and more, but I didn't think they'd ever break up, because they were just . . . stuck together.'

'Marriage is like that,' said Candida wisely. 'It provides an odd kind of glue that sticks you together when you should have split up ages ago. My daddy was married once before he met Mummy, an arranged marriage. He never talks about it much, but he said that once you're stuck in an arrangement like that, you feel bound to it; even though it never had anything to do with love.'

'Why don't you ever talk about love?' Sharif asked curiously.

'What do you mean?' Candida asked, widening her eyes.

'I guess I mean, why don't you ever say that you . . .'

He paused with embarrassment. 'Oh, you know, don't make me say it . . .'

'Say what?' asked Candida, looking at him in genuine confusion.

Sharif took a deep breath, and tried to think of a way he didn't have to say the words; it would be way too humiliating to have to ask outright. 'Do you remember that Indian pop song that I told you we used to dance to when we were children in the flat above the restaurant?' he asked.

'Yes,' Candida nodded. '*Ilu, Ilu!* means I love . . .'

Sharif interrupted her. 'That. Why don't you ever say that. *Ilu*, I mean. You know how I feel about you.'

'Oh, is that all you meant? Well, you know how I feel about you, too,' Candida said, smiling warmly. 'It just seems such a big word, and we're maybe too young to use words like that unless we're really sure we know what they mean, and besides, it wouldn't be fair, to you, I mean. How could I talk about things like that, when I still can't even tell my family about us, until I'm sure that Daddy is better.'

'He might never get better,' Sharif said petulantly. 'He's getting on a bit, isn't he? I think my old grandad could give him a run for his money.'

Candida leaned over to his furrowed brow and kissed him between his eyebrows where the flesh had gathered in a frown. 'You look so cute when you do that,' she said, getting out of bed and stretching her arms.

After Candida had left, Sharif threw away the pizza box and beer cans with a flourish; he took a lazy man's satisfaction in that the only washing up he had to show for his romantic lunch was Candida's wine glass, and the knife and fork she had insisted on using. He left these on the draining board, in the hope that one of his flatmates might wash them up for him. Micky had moved in after he had finished his A levels, and had proved to be surprisingly well house-trained.

Sharif decided to pop by the Tooting house on a whim. He knew his mother was moving some of her stuff out that afternoon with his grandad, who was helping her move to his barely used Clapham flat. Omar was still in Spain, and she had deliberately not asked Sharif to help, as she didn't want it to look like she was asking him to take sides against his dad. As he got to the front door, he heard raised voices. Perhaps Dad had come back, and they were having an argument. But then his parents never really had arguments. When they were angry at each other, there were just lots of long, painful silences, punctuated by unnecessarily loud clattering in the kitchen or bathroom. He went to walk away, but then curiosity got the better of him, and he quietly let himself in the back door, and went into the kitchen.

He heard his mum speaking crossly upstairs, and realized with a shock that she wasn't arguing with his father at all, she was arguing with Nana, his grandad. He'd have thought that she would be a bit gentler with him, given his dicky ticker.

'How dare you speak about my boys that way,' Shona seethed with uncontrolled fury. 'They have absolutely bloody nothing to do with you, or Amma, for that matter. You know, as far as I'm concerned, you're not even related to them. It was me, I made them, I made them happen without any help from either of you.'

'As far as you're concerned? Shona, you're speaking like a madwoman. They're my grandchildren, whether you like it or not. Just because you've had this insane need to confess to the world and break up your marriage for the sake of some Irish teacher you've just met, you can't expect us all to accept these things. I love Omar, but he's not gay, he's just a perfectly normal boy who needs help. Maybe we could send him to a psychiatrist, to get him over this funny phase. And Sharif, how could you ever have let him date Candida? Were you mad? Didn't you think about the consequences?'

'I wanted to meet her,' Shona admitted, a little stubbornly, 'and I knew you would never introduce me, but at least Sharif did. I know now that I was very wrong not to tell Sharif about her. But I really didn't see the harm in them dating for a bit. It was only for a little while, anyway.' Sharif's ears had pricked up. How did his grandad know about Candida? Perhaps he knew her dad? Sharif suddenly realized the reason for Candida's father's irrational hatred of him – it all became clear. His grandad must have told Candida's father that his grandson was disreputable, and caused the whole bizarre vendetta. To think that his own Nana was the back-stabbing old dog that had caused him so much heartache. Sharif went to march up the stairs to have it out with him, when his Nana's next words stopped him in his tracks.

'I don't believe I'm hearing this! Didn't see the harm!

Shona, you really are mad. She's my daughter, for God's sake. They're not children any more. What if they had slept together, or, God forbid, he had got her pregnant? It's illegal, I'm sure it is. She's his aunt!'

Sharif's heart felt like it had actually stopped beating, and just begun to swell and swell until it filled his whole chest. He walked out of the kitchen, out through the garden, and out to the street in a daze, where he had barely managed to round the corner onto Tooting High Street before he retched violently into the gutter, throwing up everything he'd had for lunch, and kept retching until nothing but painful hot gas and sour drips of stomach acid came up. Straightening up, and wiping his mouth on his jacket sleeve, oblivious to the outraged looks about him, he didn't stop walking until he reached his flat, where he practically ran up the steps and shut the door behind him. He went to the kitchen to get some water for his dry and burnt mouth, and on seeing Candida's wine glass and cutlery in the kitchen sink, he did something he hadn't done since he was a small child. He burst into tears. He picked up Candida's wine glass, cradled it against his face, and sank to the floor, sobbing against the grubby yellow-painted wall.

Won't Let Us Have a Breakdown

CANDIDA HADN'T HEARD from Sharif for over two weeks; not since he'd given her cold pizza for lunch. He didn't reply to her flirtatious text messages, or return her phone calls. For the first few days, she thought he'd decided to be cross over her stubbornness for refusing to say 'I love you', and didn't think too much of it. For the next few days, she thought that he really must care to be so stubborn about not calling back, and felt a sneaking admiration for his tenacity. She began to wonder what harm there might be in giving him the three little words he wanted; they were just words after all, just spoken puffs of air. '*Ilu, Ilu!* means I love you,' she hummed to herself at home, testing out the words with the pop song that Sharif had told her he used to sing along to when he was little.

By the second week she stopped thinking that it was about their not-quite-tiff about *Ilu, Ilu!* but something much more serious. Perhaps he was ill, perhaps he was so cross with her he'd run off to join Omar in Ibiza. But if he was ill, he'd let her know, wouldn't he? Unless he was in hospital with something terrible. But then Omar would tell her if something had happened; he was the only member of Sharif's family who knew that they were still together. She decided to text Omar, and was appalled and embarrassed by his delicate, walking-on-eggshells reply. Sharif was definitely still in London, Omar texted back, and was definitely fine. He was working on some new material for the band, for some big concert in the autumn. The subtext to the text was unmistakable: Omar obviously thought she'd been dumped, probably in the same abrupt way as Sharif's legion of previous girlfriends, and that she was too vain, or not quite bright enough, to have worked it out yet. Candida couldn't believe it. Sharif loved her, didn't he? She began to doubt herself – perhaps she was too vain, and had tested his patience too much by keeping their relationship a secret for so long. She decided, like her father before her some four decades previously, that the only way out of this sea of troubles was to take arms against it, and confidently stride in.

She went to Sharif's flat the next morning, arriving early to avoid the chance that he might not be in. Sharif never got up, much less left the house, before ten a.m. if he could possibly help it. Confident that she was looking her fragrant, glowing best, her newly washed hair shining lustrously in the morning sunshine, Candida pressed the bell. Micky from the band answered, his voice crackling on the ancient intercom. 'Who is it?' he asked suspiciously.

Candida, who almost never lied about anything, paused for a moment, before saying, 'Postman.'

She heard some muttered expletives, before he said, 'OK, I'll come down. Is it a package or something?'

'Mmm-hmm,' she assented, feeling a bit foolish.

When Micky opened the door to see Candida, looking both radiant and nervous, the only words he could spontaneously muster were, 'Focking hell.'

Candida walked past him and up the stairs, ignoring him as he ran up behind her, whispering urgently, 'Candida, he doesn't want to see you. He'll be furious that I let you in.'

'Well, I want to see him,' she said resolutely, her lips very tight to avoid them trembling. She got to the door of the flat, and pushed it wide open before Micky could get to it, or any other fellow conspirators hiding in the flat could shut it in her face. She stood in the narrow hallway. 'Sharif?' she called.

Sharif came loping out of his bedroom, unshaven, hair sticking up, wearing nothing but a pair of fashionably baggy sports shorts. His stomach looked very concave, and the muscles on his torso sharper and stringier, like he hadn't eaten properly in days. His eyes widened slightly at seeing her, but otherwise he gave away nothing. 'Hello, Candida, you're looking well,' he said with infuriating calm.

'Well, you're not. You look awful. What's going on?' she said shortly. She wanted to run up to him and comfort away whatever it was that had made him avoid her, but his indifferent demeanour made the few feet between them too great a distance to negotiate.

'Mate, I'm so sorry, she tricked me, she told me she was the postman,' Micky started to explain. Sharif's lip twitched, almost as though he was trying to suppress a smile. 'Yes, I can see how you thought she might be the postman,' he said drily.

'Please go away, Micky, Sharif and I need to talk,' Candida said firmly. Micky was younger than her, and she found that he tended to listen to her deferentially as a result.

'Please go away, Candida. Micky and I need to work,' Sharif said, imitating her. 'We're working on some material for the band, you're interrupting us.'

Micky looked indecisively between the two of them, Candida pale with concern, and Sharif pale with what might prove to be unexploded fury. He decided he'd rather not be alone with Sharif after he had just expressly disobeyed his orders to keep Candida out of his way; Sharif had a filthy temper when provoked. 'I need to pop out to get . . . something, anyways,' he said weakly, and walked out of the door and back down the stairs.

Candida looked back to Sharif. 'What's going on, Sharif?' she asked softly, entreatingly, her lower lip now trembling just slightly despite herself.

Sharif looked at her, an angel in his hallway, her hair shining like a halo around her face, and her summer dress of pure sky blue. He faltered for a moment, before recovering himself. 'I'm . . . going back to bed, Candida. I'm working. You can make yourself a cup of tea if you want, before you go. You know your way around the kitchen, don't you?' He wandered back into his room, and Candida stood still and stunned, until she heard the taunting sound of chords being strummed casually from his guitar. Furious, she strode into his room. 'This isn't funny, Sharif. Is this your sick way of telling me that we're over, just like that?'

'Funny ha ha or funny peculiar?' said Sharif, without

humour. 'You know, you're right, I am a little bit sick,' he added. 'And yes, we are over, just like that.'

'Sharif!' Candida exploded. 'What the bloody hell are you talking about! Why are you doing this? I deserve to know why!'

Sharif looked at her sadly from his bed, and started strumming a melancholy tune. He loved Candida too much to tell her that they'd been having an incestuous relationship for months; he didn't want to destroy her as he'd been destroyed. She didn't deserve to be hurt that way.

'No, sweetheart, you don't deserve to know why,' he said softly, regretfully, dropping his bravado for a moment.

Calmed slightly by his change of tone, Candida sat down next to him on his bed, and reached out to touch his stubbly cheek. 'Sharif, darling,' she entreated gently, 'I do not accept this. I do not accept this break-up. I simply won't, and that's all there is to it. I'm going to stay here all day until you speak to me about what's happened, so you may as well start speaking to me now.'

Sharif stopped strumming, then started picking out the thread of a haunting melody. 'I guess I wouldn't accept it either, if I were you. But that's all there is to it. You kept telling me that it takes two to make a relationship work. Well, I know that it only takes one to break it up. So it doesn't really matter whether you accept it or not. That's just the way it is.'

Candida looked at him blankly for a minute, and then her smooth, lovely face crumpled into a wet, soggy mess of angry sobbing. 'You bastard!' she spat through her tears. 'Why are you trying to hurt me so much? You promised that you would never hurt me, never leave me, never let me go. That's what you said. You promised!'

Sharif watched her break down, with her head in her hands, and tears started running down his face, too. 'I know I promised,' he said miserably. 'I'm sorry. Candida, please stop crying. I can't do anything about it. I really can't.'

'Is this because I didn't say "I love you?"' Candida said suddenly, seizing at the cheap, forlorn hope that all their hurt could be whisked away with the three puffs of inconsequential air that she had so far withheld from him. 'Because I do, you know I do. I love you, Sharif. I love you.' She held her breath after saying the three little words, as though she really believed that they might have made everything better, as if by magic.

'I know you do,' Sharif said, shaking his head. The long-awaited words made no difference at all now. If anything, they probably made everything worse. Candida started sobbing again, with deep, guttural, choking tears, and Sharif just sat there, watching her, powerless to do anything about it. He had just broken the heart of the woman he loved and he couldn't even tell her why; he couldn't even let her know that his heart had been broken first.

When Candida started to quieten down, Sharif leaned over and handed her a piece of paper with musical notation – a song was written on it. 'I wrote this for you, I guess to say goodbye. I was going to send it to you, but you're here now. You can take it with you, if you want.'

Candida looked at the scrawled notation and scribbles. So this was it, then. This was all the explanation that she was going to get for the end of their relationship, some unintelligible code that she was expected to decipher. 'You know I can't read music,' she said, not bothering to add that he also knew she had never been able to read his chaotic handwriting. She held the song back out to him, and when he didn't take it she put it down on the bed between them. 'You'd better play it to me.'

Sharif hesitated. 'I don't think so; I don't think I can . . .'

'Sharif, please!' Candida insisted. 'It's the least you can do. You can't just give me something you know I can't understand and expect me to trot off happily with it.'

Sharif sighed, and nodded. 'If I play it to you, will you just leave?'

Candida nodded, crossing her toes in her sandals while she wiped the tears from her red and swollen eyes.

Sharif started playing the same set of melancholy chords that he had picked out just a few moments before, and began to sing very softly, deliberately looking down at the neck of his guitar, and not anywhere near Candida at all.

> 'Dark clouds of depression, they leak from every pore
> Our loved ones' lies and repression, can't protect us
>   any more
> I promised to stay with you
> And to keep away the pain
> But we didn't know what we were doing
> And so we hurt ourselves again.'

Sharif glanced up at Candida briefly, to see her staring at her feet, and biting her lip furiously. He looked down swiftly before she could catch him and began to sing the chorus:

'There were dark clouds of desire, when we lay so
   close in bed
Now the dark clouds of depression, have left our
   memories for dead
And when we breathed,
We infected the air,
And I could cry,
We didn't know enough to care
I knew you loved me, though it wasn't what you said,
But I won't let us have a breakdown
I'll let it have me instead
I'll let it have me instead.'

Sharif was going to begin the second verse, when Candida spoke. 'Stop,' she said, 'please stop.'

'There's another verse,' Sharif mumbled, both disappointed and relieved that she didn't want him to finish. He picked up the piece of paper to hand it to her. He didn't know what reaction he'd expected from her, when she didn't even know what the song meant. He had sort of hoped that despite everything, she'd somehow understand without him having to tell her. That the song would be enough to absolve him from responsibility, to ease the pain of what he knew he had to do.

'Sharif, darling,' Candida said, suddenly very calm and purposeful. 'It's a beautiful song, but it's not about us. It's about you. I've understood it all now, and I'm sorry that I didn't before. You're not breaking us up because there's something wrong with us, you're breaking us up because you're depressed. You're talking about us having done some terrible thing, and we haven't, we really haven't. Irrational guilt is a classic sign of depression.'

Sharif sighed. 'I'm not breaking us up because I'm depressed, I'm depressed because I'm breaking us up. Look, you promised to go.'

'Don't preach to me about promises,' Candida said sharply, before reaching out for his hand appeasingly. 'Sharif, don't you understand? Depression is an illness. It's a disease. We can go to the doctor's and get counselling, get a prescription. We can cure it. I'll help you; I promise I'll be here for you, I won't make us hide any more.' Her eyes shone with hope.

Sharif shook off her hand. 'You were right to make us hide. Get out Candida, please. Don't make me force you.'

'I'm staying right here,' she said stubbornly.

Sharif couldn't take it any more. He'd sung his swansong, and he had no emotional energy left. He couldn't be calm, or nonchalant, or kind, or rational any more. He simply snapped. 'Fuck off!' he screamed at her. 'Just fuck off! You shouldn't be here. We should never have been together. I wish I'd never fucking met you.'

Candida backed off as though she'd been hit, and all her composed demeanour evaporated, as she couldn't stop herself crying again. 'You don't mean it,' she said through her tears. 'You're ill.'

'Get out! I said get the fuck out!' Sharif screamed and, grabbing her arms, he dragged her out of his room and out of the hallway, pushing her brutally out of the door. He slammed it behind her, and heard Candida slump to the floor on the other side. Petrified by his bewildering, unbidden violence, she got up and raced down the stairs and out into the street, to sob in the safety of her car.

Sharif watched her leave from the window. So that was it. He had not only broken the heart of the woman he loved, he had made her hate him, too. He had made her afraid of him. He reflected that she was the lucky one; she would never miss him now, the way that he would miss her. She would never long for him the way he longed for her. He would become a footnote in her life, the boyfriend who went crazy and violent and dumped her for no reason, who she was well rid of. He wished she could become a footnote in his life, like Ali, and the girl after Ali, and the many girls before. But he knew that nothing but utter oblivion could take away the pain he felt in the deep pit of his stomach, in the throbbing chambers of his heart which was thumping so loudly he thought the treacherous organ might explode out of his chest and fly after Candida, falling in a bloody, irresolute heap at her terrified feet.

Oblivion. Sharif knew exactly where he could find it. He went to the kitchen cupboard, and pulled out the bottle of vodka that he had asked Micky to buy the other day. He poured it down his throat like medicine, letting it splash over his face in his haste. Sitting back on his bed, with a third of the bottle drained, he quickly realized that alcohol alone wouldn't work. He went to the bathroom cabinet, and pulled out every bitter pill it contained, both medicinal and recreational. Popping them out of their foil containers, he thought how pretty they looked, like sweets. As he downed them with vodka, he started singing the counting nursery rhyme that Shona had taught him and Omar as children, to the tune of the Inch Worm song; 'Two and two are four, four and four are eight . . .' he sang to himself, swallowing the pills as he went along, 'eight and eight are sixteen, sixteen and sixteen are thirty-two . . .' Having taken all the pills, he walked unsteadily back to his bedroom, finishing off the vodka with deep swigs that made him almost spit it back up again. 'Two and two are four . . .' he continued. 'I knew you loved me, though it wasn't what you said. But I won't let us have a breakdown, I'll let it have me instead . . .' He felt nothing any more. In fact, he felt much better. He slumped on the bed, and as he passed out his stomach and guts spasmed involuntarily, so he lay comatose in a blissful stupor, in a puddle of his own vomit.

Micky came back to the flat. 'Sharif, is the coast clear, mate?' he called out, letting himself back in. He went to Sharif's bedroom, and took in the scene from the door. 'Aww, mate,' he said helplessly. He would later remember, with no little shame, that he stood there in shock for a full minute before he ran to the phone to call an ambulance.

Confessions Across a Hospital Bed

PARVEZ AND SHONA faced each other across Sharif's bed in St George's hospital. His stomach had been pumped, and he looked bruised and horrible, with a drip trailing out of him. 'He's so still. Why is he so still, if they say he's not in a coma?' Shona asked, holding her son's hand carefully, so as not to displace the needle which was taped into his veins.

'He's just passed out, they said he'll come round soon,' Parvez said soothingly. He added, 'It will probably hurt too much for him not to come round. The anaesthetic will wear off soon.'

'We were so lucky he threw up some of it first, we were so lucky that Micky was there,' Shona said. 'I can't believe I let this happen, it's all my fault.'

'This isn't your fault, Shona,' Parvez said wearily.

'You're a saint not to blame me, but I still blame myself. Sharif will blame me when he wakes up, and he'll be right to. I should have told him the truth.'

'It wasn't your secret to tell,' Parvez said simply. They sat in silence for a few minutes, with nothing but the flimsy pale curtains hanging around the bed of their frail, pale son to separate them from the rest of the bustling hospital ward. Parvez broke the silence. 'How's the flat? Rashid's flat in Clapham, I mean. Are you quite comfortable there?'

Shona sighed at this polite attempt at small talk. 'Yes, thank you. It's quite comfortable. How's the house?'

Parvez shrugged. 'Quiet. Big. I'm rattling around in there. At least I've got the dog, although she's become a bit quiet recently, too. I guess she misses you.'

Shona nodded. 'I miss her too, but it wouldn't be fair to take her to the flat, she needs a garden to run around in.'

'Is that all you miss?' Parvez asked curiously, without bitterness. 'Just the dog?' He cleared his throat, and then spoke quickly. 'Shona, I want to say something. I know this isn't the right time or place, but I really don't know when the right time or place would be. Do you remember how I said that I didn't want you leaving, and that I'd forgive you, and we should stay together and try and work it out . . .'

'Parvez, please . . .' Shona started.

'No, please let me finish,' Parvez said. 'That's what I said a few weeks ago. But I just want you to know that now I think there was one thing you were right about. We weren't happy. We hadn't been happy for a long time. I do forgive you, and I do miss you, of course I miss you, but I don't miss being unhappy. There. That's all. I've said it.'

Shona looked at him with surprise. She hadn't expected this accord, this capitulation from him so soon. How ironic, that the first thing they had managed to agree on in years, was the merits of their separation. 'You're not in love with me any more,' she said with comprehension. 'I'm glad.'

Parvez shook his head, with a rueful half smile. 'Goldie, you don't understand. I will probably love you until the day I die. I always have loved you, not for your degrees or cleverness, and not for your perfectionism or your criticism, and definitely not for your cooking. I loved you despite all those things. I loved you for your heart, your good, kind heart.' He reached over and touched her lightly on her chest, the flat of his palm resting gently above her left breast, without passion, but with tenderness. 'The thing is, Goldie, the way I see it, I've been a very lucky man. For over twenty years I got to live with the woman I loved, the woman who sacrificed everything she had to be with me.' He paused, and withdrew his hand from her with a touch of embarrassment at his emotion. 'But I think I deserve to spend the next twenty years with someone who loves me, with someone who doesn't feel that being with me is a sacrifice.'

'You're letting me off,' Shona said, her eyes bright with tears at his generosity. 'You deserved so much better than me.'

'Maybe I am letting you off. But you must know that I didn't want better than you,' Parvez said. 'And you gave me our beautiful boys.' He stroked Sharif's hair gently back from his face. 'As I'm in the confessing mood, can I tell you a secret? Deep down, I always thought that the boys weren't really mine. I thought about all those secretive clinic visits you went on, where you didn't want or need me to go at all, and then the boys came, and they were so pale, practically white, just like your father's family, and they were so much their Amma's boys, and not like me at all. I thought that the clinic had given you another man's sperm to conceive.' Parvez shook his head ruefully again, 'I thought that for years, and kept it hidden so far down that nobody would ever guess. Who would ever guess that I doubted my own children? And then Omar suddenly claimed to be gay, and I was so bloody furious at him, and more than anything, terrified for him, for what the future might hold for him if he didn't snap out of it. And then I got the call that Sharif was in hospital, and I felt like the ground had been taken away from under my feet . . . and I realized how much I care about them, and I knew that they were my sons after all. That they always were and always will be. Whatever happened all those years ago, they're my sons.' He looked questioningly at Shona, and held his breath. He had told her his secret, now he was waiting to see if she had one, too.

'Of course they're your sons,' Shona said, in answer to his unspoken question, her voice trembling with emotion. 'Did you really not see that Sharif had his daddy's eyes, right from when he was a baby?' She paused, and then continued falteringly, 'But you're right about one thing, I have kept something from you, all these years.' Parvez looked up quickly, and held Sharif's unconscious hand for support, awaiting the verdict he'd been dreading. 'The truth is . . . the truth is, that the boys are yours, but they weren't mine. Genetically, I mean. I didn't produce enough eggs when I went to the clinic. I signed up for a scheme where we got eggs from a donor; it was a Caucasian donor, there weren't any Asian donors in the scheme. That's why the boys were so pale.' Shona stumbled over the words, unwilling to stop. Here, at Sharif's hospital bed, she too felt the need to confess, to unburden herself from a deceit that she had held so long it had become part of her, a parasite woven into her body. 'You spent years worrying about whether they were yours, and I spent years worrying that they'd realize they weren't mine. My boys, I went through hell to conceive them, and grew them out my own flesh and blood, and yet they weren't my flesh and blood, not like they were yours. I didn't want them to ever find out that I wasn't their mother.'

Parvez took a deep breath and leaned back in his chair, rubbing his face with his hands in disbelief. 'My God, Goldie, how could you have kept that secret? For all this time. Of course you're their mother – nothing could ever change that.' He looked at Sharif's still, pale face, and said with confusion, 'So does that mean that Sharif and Candida aren't related at all? That's why you didn't stop them dating?'

Shona nodded. 'You see, it really is all my fault. I almost killed my own son for the sake of keeping my own selfish secret, like some stupid Greek tragic heroine. Candida's not his aunt; the boys have got nothing to do with my Amma or papa.' She stopped herself running on in self-loathing, as both Parvez and she became aware of their son shifting, and his lips beginning to move.

'Mum?' said Sharif, through dry, rasping lips. 'What did you say?'

'Darling!' Shona cried, and pulled his hand to her lips.

'Oh, thank God. Candida's not related to you, darling. Your Nana didn't realize. He's coming over now, he's bringing Candida. I'll explain it all to them, I'll explain to everyone. Just get better, darling, and it'll all be all right. I promise.'

Sharif could hear his mother talking, but it sounded like she was underwater; he could see her and his father's relieved faces, overhanging him like twin moons swimming over the clouds of his sheets. Amma-Abbu-Amma; the push-me-pull-you of his childhood, but this time they were facing the same direction. This time, for the first time, he was lying in the bed between them. He heard a soft pattering, the step of someone running so lightly it was like dancing. The white curtains around his bed were pushed back with a decisive gesture, and there, standing at the foot of his bed, was an angel in a sky-blue dress, a radiant halo of lustrous hair around her head, and a hand stretched out to him, in forgiveness, and understanding. 'You saw the girl who'd make your dreams come true,' he thought, his own weak hand stretching out to meet hers.

The Mother and Child Reunion

IN THE EARLY hours of the morning, the phone began
ringing in Shona's Clapham flat. She swore to herself, and put her head under her pillow to drown out
the din. 'Shona, are you there?' the familiar, insistent
voice of her mother called out. '*Arré*, so pick up!' She
began the sing-song chant that grated on Shona more
than nails across an old-fashioned blackboard: 'Pick
up, pick up, pick up . . . Pick up! pick up!!' Shona
groaned, and reaching across to the bedside table,
obeyed.

'Ouf, Amma, please stop calling at this time. You
know it's three in the morning here. Why can't you wait
like a normal person?'

'Tch, always so slow, Shona,' her mother said, before
adding coyly, and rather bitchily, 'Why so slow? Do you
have *company*?'

'Why are you calling, Amma?'

'Why do you think I'm calling, you stupid girl. It's
your uncle's wedding next week. When are you bringing
your father back to Dhaka?'

'I didn't know the wedding was next week,' said Shona, surprised. 'I guess I haven't been invited.'

Henna sighed. Why was she cursed with a daughter as slow as her father? 'Of course you haven't been invited, dear. I don't want to offend you, but adulterous little harlots who leave their Pakistani husbands and then shout about it to the world don't get invited to respectable people's weddings. If you had half a brain in your head, you'd have done whatever you wanted, but just kept quiet about it. People don't mind other people misbehaving, they just prefer not to know about it. Do you remember, when you were little, Shona? For New Year's Eve we always went to the respectable parties that didn't serve alcohol, but that didn't mean we didn't drink, we just brought our own in secretly and spiked our punch.' Henna giggled slyly at the memory of tiny little whisky bottles tied to the underside of her arms beneath her voluminous long-sleeved shalwars.

'Well, I don't care if I haven't been invited. Uncle Aziz is an old hypocrite, anyway. And I'm not bringing Papa back to Dhaka; I told you already, he's not going back. He's going to spend his retirement here, with Verity, if she forgives him. If he goes back at all, it'll be to finalize your separation. You'll finally be a free woman,' she added, hoping her mother might have come round to this idea as being a good thing. 'You'll get your own settlement, your own income, you could do whatever you want, go travelling, anything . . .'

Henna exploded at Shona. 'You *shorer bacha kuttar bacha harami*,' she shrieked, the expletives falling freely from her lips. 'I ask you to do one thing for me in your sorry little life, and you refuse! You've ruined your life, and now you want to ruin mine. You ran out on your husband for some Irish tramp you met last week, and you've raised a faggot and an overdosing drug-abuser. You were a bad wife, a bad mother, and now you're a bad daughter, too. I disown you Shona! I have no family any more!'

'You haven't had a family for years,' Shona screamed back. 'Don't you DARE tell me what it is to be a bad mother. You never even knew I was there. You just used me like some commodity, some bauble to brandish, someone to boast about to your friends. You were never there for me, you were never there for my boys. I had twin sons in a foreign country and I had no one to turn to for help, but you didn't care. You didn't even come to see them until they were at school. They love you, you know – they think you're bloody fantastic. But you don't even know the first thing about them – you don't know their first names, do you? Or their birthday, do you? Do you, Amma?' She paused for air, breathing heavily. 'So, you're disowning me? That's a bloody joke – you disowned us all years ago, long, long before I married Parvez and Papa came to England. And you know what? You can't have us back now. Enjoy what you've got, Mamma, it's all you'll get.' Shona hung up, slamming the phone down violently. She pulled up her knees and held them tight, rocking on the bed and shaking with fury.

Dermot, who had gone to the kitchen when the phone rang, came back through, and put his arms around her, holding her warmly against him. 'It's OK, sweetheart,' he soothed comfortingly, and although he had no idea what

Shona had said, as she had spoken in Bangla, he added, 'Bravo for standing up to her.' The phone began to ring again, and he felt Shona's heart thumping faster and faster, anticipating her mother's shrieking rebuttal on the answering machine. He got up, and eased the phone cord out of the socket gently. 'Give yourself a break, eh? We don't want you getting upset, not in your condition. I'll make you some camomile tea, and then we'll try and get back to sleep. What do you think?'

Shona nodded dumbly. She wondered when she was going to summon up the courage to tell her mother that on top of all her other sins, this adulterous harlot, this bad wife and bad mother who had raised a faggot and an overdosing drug-abuser, had also managed, miraculously, after years of sterility, to get pregnant.

Shona still didn't quite believe it herself. Her periods were never completely reliable, and after three months without one, her natural thought had been that she was prematurely menopausal. When the doctor suggested a pregnancy test, she had almost refused out of sheer embarrassment, and was shocked to see an incontrovertibly positive result. She had told Dermot straight away, unsure of his reaction, and his excitement had worried her even more. Shona was sure it was a false alarm but she was sent for a dating scan immediately, as the doctors thought she might already be quite far along. They were right; she was fourteen weeks pregnant.

She saw the baby moving in the ultrasound picture,

whilst Dermot held her hand tightly, and she still didn't quite believe it. All the dedicated preparation she'd done for her twins – the special diets, the folic acid, the not-drinking, the exercise, the medication – it had taken years of work to conceive. And yet now, with no preparation or warning at all, this child had come from nowhere. It was tempting to romanticize and say that the child had come from love alone. She was forty-three, and she was having a baby. She had to look at the scan picture every once in a while, just to prove to herself that it wasn't some phantom daydream.

It was in the rosy glow of her unexpected achievement that Shona finally managed to succeed in that other test she had expected to fail. Despite what seemed an appalling drive on her long-awaited driving test, her examiner had passed her, chiding her indulgently to check her mirrors more often while he wrote out her certificate.

A week later Shona was preparing for her first day of school for the autumn term. There would be no students there for the first two days; she was more worried about the reactions from her colleagues about the changed state of her relationship. Most of them would know by now that she had left Parvez, but few would realize that she had taken up with Dermot. No one knew that she was precariously carrying his child. She was putting all her administration in order when the bell rang insistently. She wasn't expecting anyone; Omar had taken a summer job in the local adult education college above Sainsbury's, to pay for his Ibiza holiday; Sharif – who had stopped pretending to work at the restaurant – was working flat out for a big concert that his band had been booked for at the end of September; and Dermot was at the school already, attending a meeting for all department heads. Perhaps it was Papa – maybe things were not going well with Verity, after she had finally found out the truth, and he needed his flat back. She went downstairs to open the door, and stopped short in shock. Standing on the steps, resplendent with her enormous Gucci sunglasses and a small mountain of matching leather luggage, was her mother, while a black cab with a ticking meter waited patiently behind her.

'This is my daughter that I was telling you about,' Henna said indulgently to the cab driver, in her still heavily accented English. 'She's a teacher, you know.' She leaned over to Shona to peck her on her astounded cheek, whispering in her ear, 'Shona moni, you had better pay the cab. I forgot to change my travellers' cheques at the airport. And give him a tip so he can carry my things upstairs.'

Sitting decorously on the sofa, with a cup of tea in hand, and chewing on some shortbread she'd bought herself at the airport, Henna chatted amiably to Shona, as though their last conversation hadn't happened, and as though her visit was completely expected.

'It's not a bad apartment, this,' she said, looking around. 'Your father always kept it very well. Too small, though. Much smaller than the place in Paddington that his company paid for. This used to be Verity's flat, you know.'

'No, I didn't know,' Shona said warily, sitting on the chair opposite her mother, waiting for Henna to explode at her. She decided to get it over with: 'So, how ... was the wedding?'

'How is the wedding, you mean – it's happening today. I'm sure it's all very dull and tedious, and that the guests have just turned up for the food. They're having the reception in a hotel. No imagination, those two. I left them a card, though; I said I hoped that Aziz would be very happy with his pointy-nosed elderly, ugly bride, and that she'd be very happy with her baldy-headed elderly, ugly groom.' Henna smiled smugly with pride at her parting gesture, and looked to her daughter for approval. 'I only said the truth, that's what you're so fond of these days, isn't it? I thought it would take lots of practice, like learning English, but I found it very easy. Wonderfully easy. And quite refreshing, I don't know why I don't do it more often.' She stretched out her arms in a cat-like, satisfied gesture.

'Why are you here, Amma?' Shona asked quietly.

'Well, I'm doing what you said, dear. I'm giving tired old Dhaka a break, and I thought I'd travel. Spend some time in the UK, with my daughter and my grandsons. Get to know my new son-in-law; I hope I like him more than the first one. And I thought I'd give you a hand, what with you being a working woman now,' she added disingenuously, as though Shona hadn't been a working woman for years already.

'A hand with what?' Shona asked. Her mother was hardly equipped for helping with housework or cooking, or anything else, for that matter. Her skills lay solely in acting, singing and dancing.

Henna looked at her indulgently. 'With the baby, of course. You're not a young woman any more. I was already a grandmother when I was your age. You'll need help with the baby. Omar told me all about it, although he thought I already knew; he and I are becoming great pals on email.'

Shona said nothing, looking very hard at her mother in shock, and then she threw herself into her mother's arms, squeezing her fiercely and knocking the breath out of both of them. 'Oh Mamma, thank you,' she said, trying hard not to cry, not quite sure what exactly it was that she was so grateful for.

Embarrassed at such a display of extraordinary affection, Henna patted Shona's back tentatively. 'Tch, you'll injure yourself diving around like that,' she said. 'Jau, Shona, go make your old mother some more tea.' When Shona went to the kitchen, Henna took out her compact and checked that her daughter's embrace hadn't shifted her exquisitely applied maquillage. Motherhood wasn't really a role she had willingly chosen, she acknowledged to herself, satisfied that her lipstick was in place and her eyeshadow remained smoky and elegant; she had only been a starry-eyed teenager when Shona was born, barely more than a child herself. Motherhood had been expedient, that was all; it was her get-out-of-school-free card. But perhaps now she had reached her sixties, now she was almost a grown-up, perhaps she could choose to be a mother, and a glamorous grandmother, too. After all, Omar and Sharif were adults now, and quite interesting young men, too; they didn't bore her like Shona had when she was a teenager. Maybe she might even like the baby when it came along – the benefit of being a grandmother was that you could coo and spoil but not have any of the tiresome responsibility that went with parenting, and when you'd had enough, you could just hand the baby back.

Shona popped her head back around the kitchen door, and caught her mother patting her powder back into place. 'Mamma, you told everyone in Dhaka that you were coming to the UK to join your husband, didn't you? You told them that you'd agreed to join him in his retirement here, rather than have him join you in Dhaka. You covered up why he wasn't going back.'

Henna winked at her conspiratorially. 'I might have . . . given that impression, Shona moni. Truth-telling is all very well, but it doesn't do to tell everyone everything, you know. One messy public separation in the family is quite enough to be getting on with for a while.'

Party in the Park

THE END OF September didn't seem like the ideal time for an outdoor concert, Parvez thought; it was bright, but it just wasn't warm enough any more to hang around outside for hours. And Victoria Park in Hackney didn't seem like the most prestigious location – miles from anywhere, and not even near a tube line. He didn't think there'd be much of a turnout. So he was surprised, when he approached the park with Omar, at how busy it was. There were flyers promoting the concert all over the gates and trees and lamp posts, and there were fast food vans and drinks stalls – an almost carnival atmosphere. He heard the music thudding in the distance. 'They haven't started already, have they?' he asked, checking his watch. He'd treated himself to a satisfyingly chunky Rolex for his birthday. It was in steel and gold, and reminded him of the substantial gold money clip he'd had melted down all those years before. He'd wanted the watch for years, but he had never dared get one before as Shona had disapproved of extravagance.

'I'd keep that hidden if I were you, Abbu,' Omar said.

'No, Sharif's set was due to start in twenty minutes, but he's texted me: they're already running a bit late. Balti Ballads is just one of the bands on the playlist; they've got an early shift.'

As they approached the enormous stage, Parvez looked at it in disbelief. The figure on the stage was a skinny, dark speck, but screens all around showed him to be a dissolute-looking youth droning into a mike. There were hundreds of people around, maybe even over a thousand. He hadn't realized what a big thing this was; he had been persuaded by Omar to come along to see Sharif play in a show of support, but he had thought it wouldn't be very different from when Sharif used to play in his school concerts, or down the local pub.

Omar saw his father's surprise, and grinned. 'They've done brilliantly to get this gig. They're one of just two unsigned bands who were asked to play – everyone else has a deal already. There'll be scouts here from the music labels, and most of the fan club too, hopefully.'

Parvez nodded authoritatively, as though he knew what this jargon of unsigned, deals and scouts meant. Had Omar really said that Sharif's little school band had a fan club? 'Do you want a drink?' he asked his son. He could do with one himself.

In the same part of the park, but closer to the stage, Ricky laid out a blanket for Verity and Candida. 'Thank you, darling,' Verity said, unpacking a little picnic basket. She pulled out a couple of large thermos flasks, looking apologetically at Candida. 'I know you prefer white wine, darling, but I thought it might be a bit too nippy for that. I've done us some coffee and hot chocolate.'

'That's lovely, Mummy, thank you,' said Candida distractedly, looking at her phone. 'Sharif says they're a bit delayed. I'm going to go and see if I can go backstage to wish them luck.' She did up the laces on her tennis shoes, and ran down towards the stage.

Verity and Ricky were left alone on the blanket. 'When are we meeting the others?' she asked Ricky.

'They should all be here now, but we'd never find them. Omar gave me directions to some pub on the edge of the park, we're to meet there after Sharif's band have played their piece,' Ricky said, pouring out two cups of coffee and crumbling brown sugar into them.

'I'm really looking forward to seeing Shona again; she's such a lovely woman. Such a credit to you,' Verity said, a little hesitantly.

Ricky looked at her in wonder and, taking her hand, reverently kissed it and then turned it over to kiss the palm. 'What did I ever do to deserve you?' he said humbly. 'All that time I wasted away from you, running back for weekends in Bangladesh, just to keep up a stupid pretence.'

'It's all in the past, Ricky,' Verity said, 'and it didn't matter that you went to Bangladesh occasionally; you did have to see your mum, after all. What mattered most, is that you came back.'

'That girl at the drinks stall liked you, son,' said Parvez with some of his old bonhomie, sipping his not quite cold beer. 'I could tell.'

'Abbu, please stop doing this,' said Omar, embarrassed, before riposting shrewdly, 'besides, I think it was you she liked – she must have a thing for stylish older men.' He was only half joking; his father looked rather dashing that day, in his dark jeans and expensive blue sweater. Omar suspected that his Abbu was unconsciously reverting to the dandy he'd been before he'd married his mother.

'OK, enough,' winced Parvez with discomfort at the compliment, marring his good looks with a frown. 'I'll stop going on. But you know I only do it because I worry about you; you've chosen a hard path. You were already an ethnic minority, now you're a sexual minority in an ethnic minority.'

'Abbu, I didn't choose anything. It's just what I am. And there's nothing so hard or difficult about it any more – it's not like it was when you came to England.'

Parvez sat for a moment, remembering when he had got off the plane with woefully insufficient funds, still in his wedding suit, with no plans beyond getting to his cousin's sweet shop in Tooting. Back then, he had been dismayed into silence by a cab driver's reaction to his accent. And yet here they were, Omar in college, and Sharif at this big event, a thousand people waiting to hear him play. Perhaps things were different. 'Did you want me to give you a lift to college next week, son?'

Omar smiled gratefully. 'That would be great, Abbu. I'll take you out for tea or something. My treat.' Omar hesitated for a moment, before adding lightly, 'Maybe you could stay and meet some of my . . . friends.'

Parvez understood what he meant, and shook his head. 'I'm trying, Omar. I promise I'll keep trying. But I'm not ready for that, not yet.'

Omar smiled to hide his disappointment. 'It's OK, Abbu. I understand.'

Shona and Dermot were sitting a little way away from the stage, where they had a good view of the screens. 'He should have been on by now,' she said impatiently.

'He'll be on soon enough,' Dermot said soothingly, 'Stop fretting, it'll be fine.'

'They've just never done anything like this before, this could be their big break . . .' she said, and then paused as Dermot raised an eyebrow at her. 'OK, I'll stop fretting about the concert, and start fretting about afterwards, when we have to meet everyone in the pub.'

'That'll be fine, too,' Dermot said. 'Parvez has never been anything but civil to me; maybe he knows how puny and pale I feel standing next to him. And don't forget that I practically saved your dad's life, so he won't be demanding pistols at dawn for breaching your honour.' He pulled Shona towards him for a hug. 'So how's the baby bump?' he said, patting her tummy.

'Still barely bump,' said Shona. 'There's nothing there at all. If I hadn't had the scan I still wouldn't have believed it. I was enormous with the boys at this stage. And with the boys, I was really sick, not just in the morning, almost all the time. But with this one I haven't felt even the slightest bit ill,' she complained.

'Isn't not being ill meant to be a good thing?' said Dermot affectionately. 'I think they're coming on.'

Shona watched as Sharif and the band loped onto the stage and her handsome son's face appeared in close-up on the big screen. He looked so much like his father. They erupted into one of their most popular songs, to tumultuous cheers and screaming from the front. Young kids, who had sat down while the dirgeful youth was on stage, jumped up and began to dance in the cool September air. During the first chorus, an insatiably catchy, jingly Indian riff came up, and then Shona saw her.

Henna made her entrance, resplendent in a flowing silk dancer's outfit, with loose trousers and sleeves and a glittering embroidered bodice, bracelets at her ankles and wrists, and her hair elegantly swept up. She led a trio of Bangladeshi dancers who stamped and swayed to the music. Shona watched her mother on one of the screens; she looked beautiful, she looked twenty years younger, her face transported with happiness as she performed to hundreds of admiring strangers in the park, her life's ambition fulfilled. It had been Henna's idea to create a dance to go with this song, and although Sharif had his doubts initially, it worked wonderfully. Shona was bursting with pride for both of them, and almost wept at the sight.

Dermot was watching her curiously. 'You're glad, aren't you, Shona, that you told them all the truth?'

Shona smiled and nodded reassuringly at him, her eyes shining with tears. She knew that she was still learning how to tell the truth, or rather unlearning how to deceive; gradually unspinning the silken webs she had woven into her conscious and unconscious life, that had become so much a part of her they were like something innate. It was just like learning to speak a new language, Shona thought to herself: the more she practised, the more fluent she would become.

Acknowledgements

The following people helped me enormously with this novel, which was written in a succession of rented apartments during a French winter, while I was pregnant and we were renovating our ruined farmhouse. My husband, Phil Richards, gave me tireless, unselfish support and a room of my own. My mother, Niluffer Farooki, told me inspirational stories and cooked untold delicacies whenever I returned to visit her in London. My sisters, Preeti Farooki and Kiron Farooki, gave me confidence whenever I had a dark night of the soul, with their cheerful and unfounded assumption that I could write. And my beautiful niece, Raman Newton, helped me to remember what it was like to be a little girl.

I'd also like to thank Geeta Nargund of St George's Hospital in Tooting, for her advice on fertility treatment, and not least for the treatment she gave my husband and me, which enabled us to have our wonderful little boy, Jaan.

And finally, I must thank my editor, Sarah Turner, for her infectious enthusiasm in championing my work; the team at Pan Macmillan for the tender care with which they have treated my manuscript; and my agent, Ayesha Karim at Gillon Aitken, for her support and advice.

Bitter Sweets *is about the impact of deception on family relationships. What drew you to this story?*

I've always been fascinated by the dynamics of truth-telling within families, a fascination which began from observing how my own extended Pakistani/Bangladeshi family behaved. Like my character Shona, I noticed at an early age that certain things were left unsaid and unexpressed by tacit agreement for the sake of maintaining familial harmony, as though not discussing them somehow made them acceptable.

I quickly learned that this moral fog used to cover up awkward or uncomfortable realities was something shared by most families; whether motivated by kindness or convenience, the immediate instinct for many of us is to comfort and conceal with a lie rather than to hurt and expose with the truth. With *Bitter Sweets,* I wanted to tell a story about a family that uses deceit to hold their fragile family structure together across emotional, cultural, and geographical divides, to the extent that deception and double lives become something of a family tradition, inherited from one generation and passed to the next. Their journey is how they learn that the lies that are supposedly binding them are in fact keeping them apart.

Does deception play a prevalent role in the Pakistani and Bangladeshi immigrant cultures?

I think that many Pakistani and Bangladeshi immigrant families still struggle with the disparity between their traditional Eastern and Islamic values and those of the Western society in which they have chosen to live, to the extent that traditionally "unacceptable" behaviour such as homosexuality, dating, drinking, or gambling are not openly acknowledged by the first generation, forcing the younger and more Westernised family members into secrecy. That said, in *Bitter Sweets* the moral conflicts of the characters which lead them to deceive are not a result of religious dilemmas or culture clashes, but rather due to their very personal and ambiguous emotions.

Are your characters representative of the Pakistani and Bangladeshi immigrant communities?

I lived in three areas of London with high proportions of immigrants—in Tooting, Bethnal Green, and Southwark, and drew inspiration from the locals that I met there, as well as from my own experience. Bhai Hassan's sweetshop and Parvez's successful restaurant business have many real-life equivalents in Tooting. However, my characters are middle class, which doesn't yet represent the majority of immigrants; it was recently reported in the UK (April 2007) that as many as two-thirds of Bengali immigrants still live in poverty.

The novel opens with an arranged marriage in the 1950s—do arranged marriages still take place? How successful are they in your opinion?

Henna's arranged marriage to Ricky-Rashid was rather enlightened for the 1950s as they had the opportunity to meet each other on a few occasions before the day itself; back then, it wouldn't have been unusual for all arrangements to have been made between the heads of the families, and for the bride and groom to have met for the first time on their wedding day.

Arranged marriages were the norm for my grandparents' generation, and still very common for my parents' generation—my own parents were considered unconventional at the time, as they met at work, married for love, and organised their own wedding without parental involvement or approval. Arranged marriages still take place today, in the UK as well as in the Indian subcontinent; those that I know of have been approached in a more modern way, allowing for much greater consultation with the potential bride and groom from the outset, and involving several meetings before they agree to the marriage. In some cases, it's more about "introduction" rather than "arrangement," as it is left up to the couple whether or not they want to proceed and get to know each other better with a view to marrying. It's hard for me to give an opinion on whether marriages like this are successful per se—as with any marriage, it depends on the willingness of both parties to work at it.

How autobiographical is your book?

I think it is tempting for many first-time authors to stick to what they know best and write semiautobiographical accounts—in my case, I got that out of my system with the first full-length manuscript I wrote, which was completed a year before I wrote *Bitter Sweets,* but wasn't published. *Bitter Sweets* is a work of fiction, but I've used my personal experience for the locations; I lived for several years in southwest London's Tooting, an immigrant melting pot where Asian, West Indian, and Irish cultures meet; like Omar, I read PPE [Politics, Philosophy, and Economics] at New College, Oxford University, and remember all the Oxford locations fondly from my student days. I hadn't been to Bangladesh or Pakistan for many years when I was writing *Bitter Sweets*, but fortunately my mother was able to reawaken my childhood memories of these places through the stories she told. With regard to my characters, there is no single one whom I identify with, as the characters represent different aspects of myself, or the self that I would be if I were a scheming extrovert like Henna, or an unfulfilled romantic like Ricky-Rashid; like most authors, I have drawn heavily upon my own experiences of love and desire, despair and guilt, awkwardness and aspiration in creating them.

How has the Asian community reacted to Bitter Sweets?

I've had very positive reactions to the book; some have said that it was refreshing to come across a novel that portrayed modern Bangladeshis in such a positive light, rather than the more traditional depiction of them as poor victims dragged from their villages into urban squalor. Henna is a very different sort of Bengali housewife than we are used to seeing in the West, in that she is extroverted, unrepentantly manipulative, cosmopolitan, and stylish. However, I have also been criticised in some quarters for not being "political" enough, and not representing the clash of East/West cultures as a driving force in the novel. This was a deliberate choice—I'm fortunate enough to be of a generation that doesn't have to wear one's ethnicity as a chip on the shoulder or a soapbox to stand on; it's simply what I am. In the same way, although my characters are Asian, my concern isn't to explore issues to do with their "Asian-ness" but rather their deeper emotional and psychological motivations that are unrelated to their race—in this sense, my characters are universal, as I'm far more interested in what lies beneath the skin.

What is your own Asian background?

Like the twin boys in my novel, my father was Pakistani, and my mother is Bangladeshi. I was born in Pakistan in 1974, but my family moved to London when I was seven months old; by the time I was sixteen I had taken dual British/Pakistani citizenship. My family was always rather international and relaxed with regard to our Muslim faith; when my parents separated, my father married a Chinese-American Catholic, and my mother's long-term partner (who gave me away at my wedding) is English-Iraqi of Jewish origin. My sisters and I were brought up in a liberal environment where we were free to date or drink without censure, but still retained our Muslim identity. No eyebrows were raised in the extended family when I married my Anglo-Irish husband in a civil ceremony (I wore a sari, he wore a suit), although my aunt did express astonishment some years later when I explained that I'd left him at home that day to look after our baby by himself: "But he's a man! Are you sure he's capable?"

When did you first realize that you wanted to be a writer?

I've always wanted to be a writer, and wrote short stories and poems for myself when I was very young; I even wrote a science fiction novella when I was fifteen, which I hopefully sent out to every publisher in town. I didn't think that I could make a career of writing, and so instead went into accountancy, and then into advertising. It was only when my first full-length manuscript attracted some interest from a well-known publisher back in 2003 that I decided to take some time off work in order to write full time. I left my job as an Advertising Account Director in 2004, and was lucky enough to sign a two-book contract a year later on completion of *Bitter Sweets*. This has been my dream job, as writing is something I do for pleasure; despite having had two children since 2005, I have already written my second novel, and am now starting to research themes for my third.

Mark Billingham has twice won the Theakston's Old Peculier Award for Crime Novel of the Year, and has also won a Sherlock Award for the Best Detective created by a British writer. Each of the novels featuring Detective Inspector Tom Thorne has been a *Sunday Times* bestseller. *Sleepyhead* and *Scaredy Cat* were made into a hit TV series on Sky 1 starring David Morrissey as Thorne, and a series based on the novels *In the Dark* and *Time of Death* was broadcast on BBC1. Mark lives in north London with his wife and two children.

Also by Mark Billingham

The DI Tom Thorne series
Sleepyhead
Scaredy Cat
Lazybones
The Burning Girl
Lifeless
Buried
Death Message
Bloodline
From the Dead
Good as Dead
The Dying Hours
The Bones Beneath
Time of Death
Love Like Blood
The Killing Habit
Their Little Secret
Cry Baby

Other fiction
In The Dark
Rush of Blood
Cut Off
Die of Shame

MARK BILLINGHAM
Rabbit Hole

sphere

SPHERE

First published in Great Britain in 2021 by Sphere

1 3 5 7 9 10 8 6 4 2

A CIP catalogue record for this book
is available from the British Library.

Hardback ISBN 978-1-4087-1243-6
Trade Paperback ISBN 978-1-4087-1244-3

Typeset in Plantin by M Rules
Printed and bound in Great Britain by Clays Ltd, Elcograf S.p.A.

Papers used by Sphere are from well-managed forests
and other responsible sources.

MIX
Paper from
responsible sources
FSC® C104740
FSC
www.fsc.org

Sphere
An imprint of
Little, Brown Book Group
Carmelite House
50 Victoria Embankment
London EC4Y 0DZ

An Hachette UK Company
www.hachette.co.uk

www.littlebrown.co.uk

Dedicated, with gratitude and respect, to the memory of the great many doctors, mental health nurses and health-care assistants who lost their lives to Covid-19.

You only tell the truth when you're
wearing a mask.

BOB DYLAN

I was on my way to scrounge some tobacco from Lucy, who I sometimes call L-Plate, and is probably the poshest person I've ever met – who doesn't like anyone touching her and thinks the world is flat – when I heard it all kicking off in the little room next to the canteen. The room with the yellow wallpaper and the settee. The 'music' room, because there's some dusty bongos on a shelf and a guitar with four strings.

I could still smell that watery curry Eileen had done for lunch.

I'd eaten it all, don't get me wrong. Two plates full, because I've always had a big appetite and you eat what's put in front of you, but the whiff of it an hour or so afterwards was making me feel slightly sick. Yeah, I remember that. Mind you, lots of things make me feel a bit green around the gills these days and it's not like this place ever smells particularly lovely, let's be honest.

So ... I was bowling down the corridor, trying not to think about the smell and gasping for a fag, when I heard all the shouting.

Swearing and screaming, stuff being chucked about, all that.

This was a Wednesday afternoon, two days before they found the body.

The sound really echoes in here, so I didn't think too much about it to begin with. It's not like I haven't seen people lose it before, so I thought it might just be a row that sounded a lot worse than it was and it wasn't until I actually got to the doorway and saw how full-on things were that I knew I was going to have to do something about it. That I needed to step in.

I'm an idiot. *Three* days before they found the body. Three . . .

It was a proper scrum in there. A couple of people were watching – one bloke I don't know very well was actually clapping, like he thought it was some kind of special entertainment that had been laid on – but everyone else was grabbing and grunting, lurching around the room and knocking furniture over. Watching from the doorway, I couldn't really tell who was doing the fighting and who was trying to stop the people who were doing the fighting. It was too late to work out what had started it, but I guessed it didn't really matter by then and had probably never mattered much to begin with.

It doesn't take much round here.

Half a dozen of them tangled up, scratching or pulling hair and calling each other all sorts. A *mêlée*, that's the word, right? French, for a bunch of bad-tempered twats making idiots of themselves.

Wrestling and cursing, spitting threats.

The Waiter, he was there, and the Somali woman who likes touching people's feet was getting properly stuck in, which was amazing as she's about five foot nothing and skinny as a stick. Ilias was throwing his considerable weight about as was Lauren, while Donna and Big Gay Bob wriggled and squealed. And The Thing was there, obviously . . . he was right in the thick of it, kicking a chair over then trying to swing a punch at Kevin, who was backed up against a wall, while somebody else whose face I couldn't see beneath their hoodie was hanging on to The Thing's arm for dear life.

I mean, Christ on a bike.

I wasn't remotely surprised that none of the people who get paid to sort out stuff like this were in much of a hurry. They've seen it all before, that's the truth. What I'm saying is, I couldn't just hang about waiting for one of that lot to get their arse in gear and put a stop to it. Besides, I'd broken up plenty of rucks in my time, so it wasn't a big deal. I've been trained for it, haven't I?

Bloody hell, Al . . . get a grip. Getting the facts straight is important, right? Something else I've been trained for.

The *first* body. The first of the bodies.

It was obvious pretty quickly after I'd steamed in that I wasn't really making a lot of difference, that I wasn't going to be able to do much physically. To be fair though, I didn't have my equipment – baton, pepper spray, taser, what have you – so I wasn't going to give myself a hard time about it. In the end, the only thing I could do was climb on to one of the few chairs that was still the right way up, take a breath and scream louder than anyone else until I had their attention.

Well, most of them at least, though a few were still muttering.

'I'm going to give you one chance to break this up before things get serious, all right?' I left a little pause then, for what I'd said to sink in, because I've always thought that's effective. Makes them think a bit. 'So, do yourselves a favour and stop playing silly buggers.' A good hard look after that, at each and every one of them. 'Do you understand what I'm saying? I'm not messing around, here. This is a public order offence and I am a police officer . . .'

And I have to say, that did the trick, though watching some of them put the furniture back where it belonged while the others drifted back out into the corridor, I can't say I felt particularly proud of myself. Like, I wasn't exactly happy about it. I knew even then that, later on, crying myself to sleep, I'd be thinking about why they'd done what I wanted.

Not because I'd made anyone see sense or frightened them.

Not because I had any kind of authority.

Truth was, they just couldn't be bothered fighting any more because they were all too busy laughing.

PART ONE

SUDDEN OR SUSPICIOUS

ONE

In the interests of getting the key information across as efficiently as possible, as well as jazzing the story up a tad, I've decided to pretend this is a job interview. I think I can still remember what one of those is like. So, imagine that I'm dressed up to the nines, selling myself to you in pursuit of some once-in-a-lifetime career opportunity, and not just mooching about in a nuthouse, wearing tracksuit bottoms and slippers, like some saddo. Right, *nuthouse*. Probably not the most politically correct terminology, I accept that, even though it's what the people in here call it.

So . . .

Acute. Psychiatric. Ward.

That better? Can we crack on? Last thing I want to do is offend anyone's delicate sensibilities.

My name is Alice Frances Armitage. Al, sometimes. I am thirty-one years old. Average height, average weight – though I'm a bit skinnier than usual right this minute – average . . .

everything. I'm a dirty-blonde, curly-haired northerner – Huddersfield, if you're interested – something of a gobshite if my mother is to be believed, and up until several months ago I was a detective constable in north London with one of the Metropolitan Police's homicide units.

To all intents and purposes, I still am.

By which I mean it's something of a moot point.

By which I mean it's . . . complicated.

The Met were very understanding about the PTSD. I mean, they have to be, considering it's more or less an occupational hazard, but they were a little less sympathetic once the drink and drugs kicked in, despite the fact that they only kicked in at all because of the aforementioned trauma. See how tricky this is? The so-called 'psychosis' is a little harder to pin down in terms of the chronology. It's all a bit . . . chicken and egg. No, I'm not daft enough to think the wine and the weed did a lot to help matters, but I'm positive that most of the strange stuff in my head was/is trauma-related and it's far too easy to put what happened down to external and self-inflicted influences.

In a nutshell, you can't blame it all on Merlot and skunk.

Very easy for the Met though, obviously, because that was when the sympathy and understanding went out of the window and a period of paid compassionate leave became something very different. I'm fighting it, of course, and my Federation rep thinks I've got an excellent chance of re-instatement once I'm out of here. Not to mention a strong case for unfair dismissal and a claim for loss of earnings that he's bang up for chasing.

So, let The Thing and the rest of them take the piss all they like. I might not have my warrant card to hand at the moment, but, as far as I'm concerned, I am still a police officer.

I think I'll knock the job-interview angle on the head now. I can't really be bothered keeping it up, besides which I'm not sure the drink and drugs stuff would be going down too well in an interview anyway and the work experience does come to something of an abrupt halt.

So, Miss Armitage, what happened in January? You don't appear to have worked at all after that . . .

Yeah, there are some things I would definitely be leaving out, like the whole assault thing, and, to be fair, *Detained under Sections 2 and 3 of the Mental Health Act, 1983* doesn't tend to look awfully good on a CV.

Actually, limited job opportunities aside, there's all sorts of stuff that gets a bit more complicated once you've been sectioned, certainly after a 'three'. Everything changes, basically. You can choose not to tell people and I mean most people do, for obvious reasons, but it's all there on your records. Your time in the bin, every nasty little detail laid bare at the click of a mouse. Insurance for a start: that's a bloody nightmare afterwards and travelling anywhere is a whole lot more hassle. There are some places that really don't want you popping over for a holiday, America for one, which is pretty bloody ironic really, considering who they used to have running the place.

It's the way things work, I get that, but still.

You're struggling with shit, so you get help – whether you asked for it or not – you recover, to one degree or another, then you have loads more shit to deal with once you're back in the real world. It's no wonder so many people end up in places like this time and time again.

9

There's no stigma when you're all in the same boat.

Anyway, that's probably as much as you need to know for now. That's the what-do-you-call-it, the *context*. There's plenty more to come, obviously, and even though I've mentioned a few characters already, there's loads you still need to know about each of them and about everything that happened. I'll try not to leave anything important out, but a lot of it will depend on how I'm doing on a particular day and whether the most recent meds have kicked in or are just starting to wear off.

You'll have to bear with me, is what I'm saying.

Difficult to believe, some of it, I can promise you that, but not once you know what it's like in here. Certainly not when you're dealing with it every minute. When you know the people and what they're capable of on a bad day, it's really not surprising at all. To be honest, what's surprising is that stuff like this doesn't happen more often.

I remember talking to The Thing about it one morning at the meds hatch and that's pretty much what we were saying. You take a bunch of people who are all going through the worst time in their life, who are prone to mood swings like you wouldn't believe and are all capable of kicking off at a moment's notice. Who see and hear things that aren't real. Who are paranoid or delusional or more often both, and are seriously unpredictable even when they're drugged off their tits. Who are *angry* or *jumpy* or *nervy* or any of the other seven dwarves of lunacy that knock around in here twenty-four hours a day. You take those people and lock them all up together and it's like you're asking for trouble, wouldn't you say?

A good day is when something awful *doesn't* happen.

A murder isn't really anything to write home about in a place like this, not when you think about it. It's almost inevitable, I reckon, like the noise and the smell. You ask me, a murder's par for the course.

Even two of them.

TWO

I know they found Kevin's body on the Saturday because it was the day after my tribunal and that was definitely the day before. Official stuff like that never happens on a weekend, because the doctors and therapists aren't around then and certainly not any solicitors. They're strictly Monday to Friday, nine to five, which is a bit odd, considering that the weekends are probably the most difficult time around here and you'd think a few *more* staff might be a good idea. Saturdays and Sundays are when reality – or as close to it as some people in here ever get – tends to hit home. When the patients realise what they're missing, when they get even more bored than usual, which often means trouble.

The Weekend Wobble, that's what Marcus calls it.

Again, in the interests of accuracy, I should say it was actually my second tribunal. I'd already been through one when I was first brought into the unit on a Section Two. That's when they can keep you for up to twenty-eight days, when theoretically you're there to be assessed, and obviously I wasn't remotely happy about the situation, so I applied for a tribunal as soon as I could. Why wouldn't you, right? No joy that time, though, and a fortnight later, after a couple of unsavoury incidents which aren't really relevant, my Section Two became a Section Three.

A 'three' is a treatment order that means they can keep you for up to six months, because they think you're a risk to yourself or others, so you won't be very surprised to hear I got another tribunal application in before you could say 'anti-psychotic'. Trust me, I was knocking on the door of the nurses' office before they'd finished the admission paperwork.

Whatever else happens in here, you should never forget you have *rights*.

My mum and dad wanted to come down for this one, to support me, they said, but I knocked that idea on the head straight away because they'd made no secret of the fact they thought this was where I should be. That it was *all for the best*. To be honest, apart from the solicitor – who I'd spoken to for all of ten minutes – I didn't really have *anyone* fighting my corner, but you certainly don't want your own nearest and dearest agreeing with the people who are trying to keep you locked up.

I might not be well, I'll grant you that, but I'm not mental.

So, it was the usual suspects: a table and two rows of plastic chairs in the MDR (Multi-Discipline Room) at the end of the main corridor.

Marcus the ward manager and one of the other nurses.

Dr Bakshi, the consultant psych, and one of her juniors, whose name I forgot straight away.

13

A so-called lay person – a middle-aged bloke who smiled a lot, but was probably just some busybody with nothing better to do – and a judge who looked like she'd sucked a lemon or had the rough end of a pineapple shoved up her arse. Or both.

Me and my solicitor, Simon.

To begin with, I thought it was going pretty well. There was a lot of positive-looking nodding when I made my statement, at any rate. I told them I'd been there six weeks already, which was longer than anyone else except Lauren. Actually, I think Ilias *might* have been there a bit longer than me . . . I've got a vague memory of him being around the night I was admitted, but those first few days are a bit of a blur.

It doesn't matter . . .

I told them I thought I was doing well, that the meds were really working and that I wasn't thinking any of the ridiculous things I'd been thinking when I first arrived. I told them I felt like I was *me* again. Marcus and the other nurse said that was very encouraging to hear and told the judge I was responding well to treatment. That sounded good at the time, but looking back of course, what it really meant was: so *more* treatment is definitely a good idea.

You live and learn, right?

Even then, I still felt like I was in with a chance, until they read out an email from Andy. I'll have a lot more to say about him later on, but all you need to know for the moment is that Andy's the bloke I'd been in a relationship with until six weeks earlier, when I'd smashed him over the head with a wine bottle.

He was worried about me, that was the gist of his email. He wanted the doctors and the judge to know how very concerned he was, following a phone conversation with me a few nights before, when I had allegedly told him I still suspected he was not who he said he was. When I got hysterical and said that I wouldn't hesitate to hurt him if I needed to defend myself against him or any of the others.

She still believes all that rubbish, he said, the conspiracy stuff.

She threatened me.

There was a bit of shouting after that was read out, I can tell you. Crying and shouting and I might have kicked my chair over. While the judge was telling me to calm down, I was telling *her* that Andy was full of it, that I'd never said any such thing and that he was gaslighting me like he always did. Making it all up because of what had happened the last time I'd seen him.

The bottle, all that.

Anyway, to cut a long tribunal short, I walked out after that and it wasn't until about twenty minutes later that Simon found me and told me the decision. They would send it in writing within a few days, he said, along with information about when I could apply again, but I'd already decided that I wouldn't bother. Nobody enjoys repeatedly banging their head against a wall, do they? Well, except Graham, who likes it so much that he has a permanent dent in his forehead and they have to keep repainting his favourite bit of wall to get the blood off.

That afternoon, after the tribunal, when I'd calmed down a bit and had some lunch, I was sitting with Ilias in the music room. I was wearing my headphones even though I wasn't actually listening to anything. Sometimes I am, but if I'm honest, most of the time the cable just runs into my pocket. It's a good way to avoid having to talk to people.

Ilias waved because he had something to say so I sighed and took the headphones off. Waited.

'I'm glad you're staying,' he said.

'*I'm* fucking not,' I said.

Someone started shouting a few rooms down, something about money they'd had stolen. Ilias and I listened for a minute, then lost interest.

'Do you want to play chess?'

I told him I didn't, same as I always do. I've never seen Ilias play chess and I'm not convinced he knows how. I've never even seen a chess set in here, although there are some jigsaws in a cupboard.

'What day is it?' Ilias asked.

'Friday,' I said.

'It's Saturday tomorrow.' No flies on Ilias. 'Saturday, then Sunday.' Just a nasty rash on his neck. 'Saturdays are rubbish, aren't they?'

I couldn't disagree with him, though the truth is I was never a big fan of the weekend in any case. All that pressure to relax and enjoy yourself. That was if you *had* a weekend. Criminals don't tend to take the weekend off, the opposite if anything, so working as a copper never really gave me much time to go to car-boot sales or pop to the garden centre anyway. One of the things I liked about the job.

'Boring. Saturdays are so *boring.*'

Like I said before . . .

'They last so much longer than all the other days and nothing interesting ever happens.' Ilias looked sad. 'I don't mean like fights or whatever, because they're boring, too. I mean, something really interesting.'

Remember what I said about memory? What I might and

might not have done? I can't swear to it, but I really hope that, just before Ilias broke wind as noisily as ever before wandering away to see if anyone else fancied playing chess, I said, 'Careful what you wish for.'

THREE

The alarm goes off in this place a couple of times a week, more if it's a full moon, so it's not like it's that big a deal. Yeah, the nurses snap to it fast enough, but the patients don't rush around panicking or anything like that. Mostly you just carry on chatting shit – albeit a bit louder – or eating your tea or whatever until it stops. But this time there was a scream first, so it was pretty obvious something bad had happened.

Debbie, the nurse who found the body, has got quite a gob on her.

This was the Saturday night, just before eleven o'clock, and most people were already in bed. I was sitting with Shaun and The Thing in the canteen – which in a pointless attempt to sound a bit more upmarket is officially called the *dining room* – just letting the last meal of the day go down a bit and talking about nothing.

Music probably, or telly. Bitching about the fact that Lauren never lets anyone else get hold of the TV remote.

When we walked out into the hall, we could see Debbie running from the corridor where the men's bedrooms are, so that's when I knew it was her who had done the screaming and most likely her that had sounded the alarm. All the staff have personal alarms attached to their belts and, if they press them, it makes the big alarm go off all over the unit. I remember a patient getting hold of one once and hiding it, then pressing it when he was bored and causing mayhem for days.

Anyway, Debbie looked seriously upset.

The three of us stood and watched as George and Femi came tearing out of the nurses' station, and even though Debbie was trying to be professional and keeping her voice down when she spoke to them, once the alarm had stopped we all heard her say Kevin's name and the look on the other nurses' faces told us everything we needed to know.

'Fuck,' Shaun said. 'Oh, Christ, oh fuck.' He started scratching hard at his neck and chest, so I took hold of his arm and told him it was going to be all right.

'Maybe the Thing got him,' The Thing said.

I stepped away from them and moved as close as I could to where the nurses were huddled so as to try and hear a bit more, but George looked at me and shook his head. Then they all hurried back down the men's corridor, presumably heading for Kevin's room to take a look at what Debbie had found. A few minutes later, Debbie and Femi came back, grim-faced, and shortly after that George began herding those who had been in the other rooms on the men's corridor towards the lobby. Most of them stumbled along peacefully enough, bleary-eyed, one or two clutching their duvets around them. A few were shouting about being woken up and demanding to know what was going on.

'You can't make me leave my room.'

'I'm sorry, but—'

'It's my room.'

'There's been an incident—'

'I don't care.'

Once the bedrooms had been emptied – well, apart from Kevin's, because that poor soul wasn't going anywhere for the time being – George stood guard at the entrance to the corridor to make sure that nobody went back. He just stared and raised one of his big hands whenever anyone looked like they were about to. Under normal circumstances, that would probably have been Marcus's job as ward manager, but he doesn't work nights. I wondered if anyone had called him, if he was on his way in, but I don't remember seeing him until the next day.

'Where are we going to sleep?' Ilias asked. 'I'm tired.'

'We will get it all sorted out,' Femi said.

It was easier said than done, of course. With eight or nine blokes to find rooms for and no spare places on the female corridor – even as a temporary measure – it took some doing. Drugged up and sleepy as most of them were, nobody was very happy about the situation. Ilias and The Thing immediately volunteered to take the two 'seclusion' rooms and planted themselves outside the doors to make damn sure they got them. There happened to be a couple of empty rooms on the ward directly opposite this one and a few more on the floor below, though nobody was particularly keen on that, because by all accounts there's some hardcore head-cases down there. There wasn't much choice in the end and, except for a couple of the Informals who were collected by ambulance and taken to a nearby hospital, all the male patients were bedded down again by the time the police arrived.

That was the worst bit for me, the real kick in the teeth.

Shunted out of the way, like I was useless.

Like I was the same as the rest of them.

Even though it was the men's corridor where the 'incident' had taken place, the nurses made it clear straight away that they wanted all the female patients who weren't in bed already to return to their rooms.

I was wide awake, buzzing with it, but not being anything like ready for bed wasn't the most annoying thing. I marched straight up to Femi like she didn't know the rules. 'We don't have to be in bed until midnight.'

'I know,' she said. 'But this is not ... normal. We need every-one in their rooms so that the police can do their job when they get here.'

'That's the point,' I said. 'I can help.' My fingers were itching to wrap themselves around a warrant card that wasn't there. 'I know how this works.'

Femi just nodded, flashed a thin smile, then placed a hand in the small of my back and pushed. I pushed back, but only because I was pissed off. I knew it was a waste of time, because I could already see Lauren and Donna and a few of the others who had been woken up by all the commotion drifting back towards their rooms.

'It's not fair,' I said.

'We have a protocol,' Femi said.

'When someone dies, you mean?'

Femi said nothing, just made sure I was moving in the right direction.

'Kevin is dead, isn't he?'

For obvious reasons, women are not allowed on the men's corridor and vice versa. For some of the same reasons they're

21

not awfully keen on anyone going into anyone else's bed-room. I mean, privacy is important to everyone, I get that. That doesn't mean certain stuff doesn't happen between patients, because trust me, it certainly does. In plain sight, quite often, because I've seen them at it.

A quick hand-job in the corner of the music room.

A fumble in the bushes when patients are allowed outside.

Still, isn't it nice to know they have rules that are meant to prevent such terrible things?

I reckoned, though, that with everything that was hap-pening on the ward that evening, and with coppers causing chaos all over the show, the staff would probably be way too busy to worry about an innocent spot of bedroom-hopping. So, half an hour after I'd been safely tucked up, I knocked quietly on a couple of doors and brought L-Plate and Donna back to my room to see what they made of it all.

'He killed himself, didn't he.' Donna wasn't asking a question.

'Most obvious explanation,' L-Plate said. She was sitting on the end of my bed brushing her hair, wearing expensive pyjamas with embroidered stars on them that her parents had brought her from home. 'I don't think he's been awfully happy lately.'

L-Plate's lovely, but even if you discount the heroin and the flat-Earth stuff, she's not the sharpest tool in the box. 'How many people in here are happy?' I asked.

'Well, yeah . . . but even less happy than usual.'

'Topped himself,' Donna said. 'Course he has.'

'How's he done that, then?' I stared around my room, a replica of the other nineteen on the ward. A single bed and a grimy window behind a rip-proof curtain. A chair made

22

deliberately heavy so nobody can throw it. A wardrobe with three shelves and nothing you can hang anything from.

Least of all yourself.

'You want to do it bad enough, you find a way,' Donna said.

Donna, the Walker, who was here because she's threatened to do it countless times, who *has* been doing it for several years in one of the slowest and cruellest ways possible. I looked at her, perched on the chair that probably weighed three times what she did. Wrists that a baby could wrap its hands around and a collarbone knitting-needle-thin beneath her ratty pink dressing gown. 'Not sure I buy it,' I said.

Killing yourself in here is actually incredibly difficult and you won't be surprised to hear that's because it's supposed to be. If you're deemed to be at risk, then they tend to keep an eye on you, like *all the time*. Plus, you're permanently denied anything you might be able to hurt yourself with, and even when you first come in, when you're getting the measure of the place and the staff are getting the measure of *you*, they take away anything they class as risky.

That first night, once I'd stopped wailing and trying to kick whichever nurse was daft enough to get close, they took away all sorts.

My trainers (laces, right?).

My belt (OK).

Nail scissors (fair enough).

Tweezers (annoying).

A bra with under-wiring (taking the piss).

They confiscate your phone, too, and God knows how anyone is supposed to kill themselves with a Samsung. Maybe they're worried you might choke yourself with it, or call a hitman to come and do the job for you, but to be fair, unless there's some specific reason not to, they do give it back within a couple of days.

I mean, thank Christ, right?

If I wasn't allowed my phone, I think I might actually *want* to kill myself.

'So, what do you think happened, Al?' L-Plate asked.

I didn't tell her what I thought because, to be honest, I was scared as much as anything. I was excited, don't get me wrong, all those professional instincts starting to kick in, but I was ... wary. Right then, with a body cooling just yards away, it was no more than a feeling and I try to steer clear of those, with good reason. Eighteen months before, I'd had a feeling that the crack-head who'd invited us in to his flat on the Mile End Road was harmless. If it hadn't been for that, there wouldn't have been any PTSD or any need for the variety of things I poured and snorted and popped into my body to numb that pain. I would not have ended up thinking that the people I loved most in the world were trying to kill me or that strangers could read my mind. I would not have hurt anyone.

Looking at L-Plate, I could feel myself starting to shake a little. I tried to smile and shoved my hands beneath my thighs so she wouldn't see.

I said, 'I really don't know.'

It was a feeling that put me in here.

FOUR

Fleet Ward (home to yours truly for the time being) is located directly opposite Effra Ward, one of four acute psychiatric wards in the notably knackered and unattractive Shackleton Unit – the dedicated Mental Health Facility at Hendon Community Hospital. Fleet – don't ask me, the names are something to do with lost rivers of London – is a mixed ward that can take up to twenty-one patients at a push, but usually holds somewhere between fifteen to eighteen. Normally, there's more or less a fifty-fifty split between men and women, and around the same when it comes to the voluntary patients – the 'Informals' – and those who had no say-so in the matter.

Those of us who were dragged here, kicking and screaming.

Or were tricked into it.

Or don't even remember.

I don't tend to hang around much with the voluntary lot,

because there doesn't seem any point trying to get to know them. Most of the time, they're only in for a few days and some of them are only here at all because they're homeless and fancy a bed for a couple of nights and four meals a day. 'Revolving door' patients, that's what the nurses call them. In, out, then back in again, when they get fed up with cardboard mattresses and getting pissed on by arseholes in the middle of the night. When it all gets too much or there's a cold snap.

Fair play to them, they're probably every bit as messed up as the rest of us, but as far as the business with Kevin and everything that happened afterwards goes, they're not that important.

So, for now I'll stick to talking about those who were around at the time and, in most cases, still are. The strangest of the strangers who, ironically, stop me going mad. My fellow Fleet Ward Fuck-Ups. My best friends and, every now and again, worst enemies. My tribe . . . my family.

This wild and wet-brained gang of giddy kippers I knock about with.

The *sectioned* . . .

So, to coin a poncey phrase . . . allow me to introduce the ladies and gentlemen of the chorus.

Blokes to begin with, I think, because there's a fair few to remember.

KEVIN. Well . . . dead, obviously, but it doesn't seem right or kind that's *all* he is, or all you ever know about him. He was ten years younger than me and he supported West Ham, which was a shame, but there you go. He had 'issues', of course, and you can take it as read that everyone I'm going to describe has plenty, so I won't use that stupid word again. Kevin's were all about his parents, I think, but he never went into details. He was one of the friendliest in here. Too friendly sometimes, if I'm honest, meaning that certain people took advantage and he didn't really stand up for himself enough, which you've got to in this place. I think he was a skinhead before he came in and I remember how much he smiled when he showed me his tattoos. He had a lovely smile. I never found out how he ended up on Fleet Ward, what went on before he was sectioned, but I do know there'd been a lot of drugs, probably still were . . . well, you'll see.

He was fit, too, I don't mind telling you that.

GRAHAM, aka The Waiter. I should point out that nearly all these nicknames are ones I've come up with myself and most of the people concerned don't even know about them. I've always been rubbish at putting names with faces, so they helped me remember who was who early on, and now sometimes I use real names and sometimes the ones I've made up, depending on my mood or my memory, or how drugged up I am, which tends to affect both those things. This one isn't the most inspired nickname, I'm well aware of that, but it works. Graham doesn't bring people meals or carry drinks or anything like that. He's the *waiter* because he waits, simple as that. All the bloody time, *waiting*. You always know where Graham is, because once he's had his breakfast he'll be standing at the meds hatch, waiting for it to open. As soon as he's taken his meds, he'll be outside the dining room waiting for them to start dishing up lunch. Then back to the meds hatch, then the dining room, then the meds hatch again, same daft routine every day. You get

27

used to seeing him, just standing there staring into space, always the first in line even if it's half an hour early. Once, when it had started to get on my tits a bit, I marched up to the meds hatch (which wasn't due to open for like an *hour*) and asked him what the hell he was standing there for, what the point was. He looked at me like I was an idiot and said, 'I don't like queuing.'

Graham is probably pushing fifty and always wears Fleet Ward's limited edition and stylish pale-blue pyjamas. He is very tall and very thin; a bit ... spidery. His face never changes much and he's not exactly chatty. In fact, that might have been one of the longest conversations I've ever had with him.

ILIAS, aka The Grand Master. The chess thing, right? Greek, I think, or maybe Turkish. Ilias is early thirties, I'm guessing ... dark and squat and properly hairy. I know that, because he's fond of walking about with his shirt off, and sometimes his pants, no matter how often the staff tell him it's not really appropriate. He can lose his temper at the slightest thing and when that happens it's like he really hates you, but ten minutes later he's crying and hugging you and, frankly, that can wind you up a bit. I'm talking about *massive* mood-swings, when you don't know whether you're coming or going. I'm no expert, but my guess is that he's a proper schizo; I mean like bipolar to the max. He certainly comes out with the weirdest shit of anyone here, just out of nowhere. Stuff that can make you fall about one minute, then something else that makes you feel like you need to stand under a hot shower for a while. I say that, but basically he's a big, stupid puppy most of the time and, if anyone was to ask, I'd still tell them Ilias was my mate and that I think he's probably harmless. Obviously, nobody in here is completely harmless, I mean tell that to Kevin, but you know what I'm saying, right?

He's harmless *enough*.

ROBERT, aka Big Gay Bob. Robert, who's, I don't know . . . forty? . . . isn't particularly big – he's actually a bit on the short side, and a lot on the bald side – and I have no evidence whatsoever that he is even remotely gay, but sometimes it's how things go. What everyone around here does know is that Bob talks about the women he's slept with constantly. I promise you, he's got shagging on the brain, and if you find yourself in a conversation with him – and he does like a chat – it'll end up on your brain, too. I swear, you could be talking to him about anything – football, steam engines, the fucking Holocaust – and he'd find some way to crowbar in a story about the things he once got up to with some 'pneumatic blonde' in a hotel room in Brighton or the 'foxy redhead' he got seriously fruity with in a pub car park in Leeds. I don't want you to think he's sleazy though, because he's really not. It's more comical than anything, actually, a bit . . . *Carry-On*. All that happened was that one of the women – maybe it was Lauren – pointed out that constantly banging on about your success with the opposite sex is a clear sign that you're actually preoccupied with your own. A closet-case or whatever. So, that was when the nickname first got thrown about for a laugh and it stuck. It's all a bit of fun and the truth is that Bob seems to like it, plays up to it even, as if he's secretly thrilled to have an . . . identity, you know?

And the truth is that, actually, he *is* rather camp.

*

SHAUN, aka The Sheep. Yeah, he's Welsh, so shoot me for being predictable, but it's actually a boss nickname because he's a . . . follower, you know? Shaun's one of the younger ones and he's just a bit lost, I think, but the fact is he'll do pretty much anything anyone tells him to and believes whatever you say to him. Literally, anything. I'm secretly a multi-millionaire. I was on *Love Island.* You name it. Who knows if he was that gullible before whatever happened to him happened, but something's got messed up in his head and now it's like he's a blank page or just something that other people can twist and mould into whatever suits them.

The other thing you should know is that Shaun can be a bit needy. Almost every day, he'll come up to you more than once and point to some tiny blemish on his chin – a spot or whatever – and ask, 'Am I going to die, am I going to die, am I going to die?' Once he's been reassured that he's not likely to pop off any time soon he's right as ninepence, but half an hour later, he'll be panic-stricken and asking you again. I mean, my mum's a bit of a hypochondriac, but that's ridiculous.

He's not daft though, I really don't mean that, and he's probably the person I've had the nicest conversations with . . . the most *normal* conversations. He's pretty bloody lovely as a matter of fact, but he was very angry for a while after what happened to Kevin. They were close, those two, I might as well tell you that. I'd thought they were just mates, until one lunchtime when I saw Shaun with his hand on Kevin's cock under the table in the dining room, so I suppose it's understandable that he was a bit upset. He hasn't stopped being upset, actually. He still cries, a lot.

*

TONY, aka The Thing. Now, the thing you need to remember about The Thing is that *he* isn't actually the Thing. He's just *called* The Thing because the Thing is the thing he's obsessed with. The Thing is what scares him to death twenty-four hours a day. The Thing is . . . his thing. You also need to bear in mind that Tony is what a lot of people would think of as seriously scary himself. He's a massive bloke from Croydon who looks like Anthony Joshua, if Anthony let himself go a bit. I'm telling you, he's built like a brick shithouse, but just the mention of the Thing . . . seriously, just one malicious whisper of the name . . . is enough to reduce him to a gibbering wreck. Screaming, trying to climb out of the nearest window, the full works. So . . . the Thing – according to the World of Tony – is an evil entity of some sort that, for reasons none of us can or particularly want to understand, is trying to kill him and – here's the crucial bit – has the special power to transform itself into anything it wants. Anything or anyone. The Thing could be me, then the next day it might be one of the staff. Or a dog, or a daddy-long-legs, or a pair of shoes. The Thing is a hugely powerful and endlessly cunning shape-shifter.

My ex-flatmate Sophie came in to visit me one day and found herself alone with Tony in the music room for a few minutes. To this day, I don't know what he said to upset her so much, but a few days later she sent him a postcard which read: *Dear Tony, it was lovely to meet you. Oh, and by the way, I have transformed myself into this postcard. Have a nice day. Lots of love, the Thing x*

Tony did not leave his room for almost a week afterwards.

FIVE

I can't say it was the most restful night's sleep I've ever had. I was far too excited by what was likely to be happening on the other side of the ward, though to be fair it probably had more to do with the fact that I'd set an alarm on my phone to wake me up every half an hour. I wanted to see what was going on.

Why wouldn't I?

I didn't want to miss anything.

The first time I crept out, Femi ushered me back to bed as soon as she saw me. I didn't make a fuss, just told her I needed the toilet on the way and, after lurking in the bog until I thought she'd probably got bored, I managed to sneak another few minutes before she collared me again.

Eyes like a hawk and ears like a bat, that one.

The corridor that Kevin's room was on had been cordoned off with crime-scene tape. Just seeing that familiar ribbon of blue and white plastic was a proper buzz. Made the butter-flies start to flutter a little, you know? Kevin's room was at the

32

far end, so I couldn't hear anything that was actually being said or see much beyond the odd figure wandering in and out of the bedroom in question, but that didn't matter. I knew what was going on, obviously. I knew what stage they were at.

A Homicide Assessment Team. Just a couple of officers, probably, there to examine the scene and try to establish whether or not a sudden death was actually a suspicious one. There to decide if they needed to bring in detectives, CSIs, all the rest of it.

There was a local uniform standing just in front of the cordon and I picked my moment to try and grab a few words. Femi had gone back to the nurses' station and from where I was standing I could see her and George drinking tea and talking to Debbie. Femi laid a hand on Debbie's shoulder as she was still clearly upset at finding the body. When I was sure they wouldn't see me, I darted across to see what I could get out of the uniform. Like a bloody ninja, I was.

'Oh,' he said. The poor lad had obviously been told that all the patients were safely tucked up out of the way and clearly hadn't got the foggiest what to do, confronted with me. He actually jumped a little and began looking around for help.

'What do you reckon?' I asked. 'The HAT team going to call it?'

'Sorry?'

'It's OK,' I said. 'I'm Job.'

He looked at me: nodding up at him, all business, in a ratty dressing gown and slippers. He said, 'Yeah, course you are,' then began waving over my head to try and attract the attention of someone in the nurses' station.

I could happily have slapped him, but I knew I wouldn't be doing myself any favours and I guessed I didn't have long.

I saw an officer stepping out of Kevin's room, so I raised a hand and shouted past the uniform.

'Tell Brian Holloway that Al says hello.'

My DCI. One of the decent ones. A good mate, as well.

The officer at the far end of the corridor glanced my way, ignored me, then stepped back into Kevin's bedroom. I don't really know what I was expecting, because Hendon isn't my team's area anyway, so I wasn't likely to know any of this lot and there was next to no chance they would know any of mine. It was annoying, all the same.

I turned back to the uniform. 'Holloway's my guvnor,' I said. 'We've worked a lot of cases together.'

Now, the bloke had his arms spread and his size tens firmly planted, like he was expecting me to bolt past him at any moment. He still hadn't got a clue what to do with me, that much was obvious, but before I could make things any harder for him Femi and George arrived to save his bacon, giving it 'Come on, Alice' and 'Back to bed, there's a good girl . . .'

I couldn't help but smile at the look of relief on the wood-entop's face as I trotted back towards my bedroom like a *very* good girl. I wasn't that bothered, because I already knew how things were going to pan out. The next steps on the investigation's *critical path*.

I'd taken those steps myself plenty of times.

They'd be bringing in the big guns soon enough, and I'd be there when they did.

Maybe being stuck in here's thrown my timing off a little, because an hour or so later – I'd decided to leave it a bit longer, in case Femi and the rest were keeping an eye out – when I snuck out of my bedroom again, things had moved a lot faster than I'd reckoned on. The most irritating thing was that I'd missed them taking Kevin's body away and that's not because I'm ghoulish or anything, but because that's a moment that counts for something as a copper. Should do, anyway. It's about paying the proper respect, besides which, as someone who'd cared about the victim – and I'd already decided that's what Kevin was – I had no way of knowing when or if any of us would get the chance to say a proper goodbye.

I'd wanted to be there when they carried that body bag out.

By now, the forensic bods were busy doing their thing, coming and going with toolkits and evidence bags, decked out in their plastic bodysuits and bootees, same as the detectives. It was easy to tell who was who though, because, as usual, the detectives were mostly standing around and nattering, looking uneasy, waiting for the CSIs to finish. I'd found a spot just inside the doorway of the dining room where I knew I couldn't be seen directly by anyone in the nurses' station and I watched one of the CSIs on their way out. I guessed all the emergency vehicles were parked outside the main entrance. I watched him – I think it was a him – signal to the nurses' station, then wait at the airlock for one of the staff to open up. A minute later, Malaika – one of the healthcare assistants – came running towards him brandishing the keys.

'Sorry,' she said.

'No rush,' the CSI said.

Not for poor bloody Kevin, at any rate.

For the half a minute or so the CSI was standing inside the airlock waiting to be let out the other side, it was like something out of a science-fiction film. I imagined he was an astronaut about to step into the blackness of space or on to the platform of an orbiting station, and not just that grim brown lobby and the stinky lift down to the car park. I remember thinking it would be fun to tell people that, wondering who would get the biggest kick out of it. I could probably convince Shaun that I *had* seen an astronaut, of course.

I was also wondering exactly what that CSI was carrying away in his Styrofoam evidence box; what they'd found in Kevin's bedroom. A weapon, maybe? Was there a lot of blood? Debbie had certainly screamed like she'd stumbled across something horrific, and, trust me, it takes a lot to give a mental-health nurse the heebie-jeebies.

A knife would have made sense, I decided. Easy enough to pinch one from the kitchen or even bring one in from the outside. Yes, they're supposed to search you if you've been out, but on the rare occasions they bother to pat anyone down, it's always a bit . . . sloppy.

They're more hands-on at the average airport.

When I looked away from the airlock, I could see that one of the detectives was standing near the men's toilet staring at me, so even though I knew I wouldn't be given very long I wandered out into plain view, shoved my hands into the pockets of my dressing gown and stepped across to have a word.

'Who's the SIO?' I asked.

'Excuse me?' He had his hood down, so I could see the confusion. He was forty-something, with a shaved head and glasses. Like a football hooligan trying to look clever.

'Only, you can tell whoever's running the show that I'm around if they want a word.'

'I'll pass it on,' he said.

It was hard to tell if he was taking the piss or not, but I decided to give him the benefit of the doubt. 'I've got intel, make sure you tell them that.'

'Good to know.'

'*Inside* intel.'

'Right.'

I nodded and he nodded back. I said, 'You know where I am, yeah?'

Sadly, it quickly became clear that Femi and George knew where I was, too. They loomed behind the detective who immediately stood aside when he clocked what was going on.

'Alice,' Femi said. 'What do you think you're doing?'

I shook my head and pressed my wrists together, like I was waiting to be cuffed. I glanced at the cop to see if he appreciated the joke, but he didn't seem to find it any funnier than Femi and George did.

George began guiding me back towards my own corridor. He said, 'This is getting silly, now, pet. You do know we are dealing with a very serious situation.'

'Of course I know. Why do you think I'm out here?' I looked back at the cop who was watching them lead me away. I shook my head, like, *Isn't this ridiculous?* Like, *They just don't get it.*

When we were outside my bedroom door, George said, 'If we catch you out of your room again, we're going to have a problem. You understand?'

I knew he was talking about changing the status of my obs. At that time I was on hourly observation, like most of the others, but he could easily change it to fifteen-minute intermittent obs if he thought I was playing up, or *within eyesight observation*, or even the dreaded *within arm's length*, which would mean someone being in my bedroom with me. Nobody in their right mind wanted to be on WAL.

I told him I understood perfectly and leaned across to give Femi a hug.

'She'll be good,' Femi said. 'Won't you?'

Half an hour later, when I opened my bedroom door again, Femi was sitting outside, smiling at me. Half an hour after that, she was still there and, this time, she didn't even bother looking up from her magazine. I told her she was an ugly bitch and slammed my door and shouted for a while, but I knew she wasn't going anywhere.

I didn't sleep much for the rest of the night, but I didn't try and leave my room again.

It wasn't a big deal, because I'd seen what I needed to. I'd put a word in where it mattered, I'd made myself known. I kicked off the duvet and lay awake thinking about Kevin and my ex-partner Johnno and about knives twisting in bellies. I closed my eyes and tried to imagine what it would feel like to *be* the knife. Sliding and turning, hard and sharp and wet.

I knew that, by the morning, Kevin's bedroom would be sealed off and that the staff would be doing their best to get things back to normal. Ilias, Lauren and the rest of the gang would be mooching around, curious, but none the wiser. I knew that the crime-scene tape would have been taken down and any crucial evidence logged and locked away. I knew that the homicide team would be gone.

It was cool, though. It was all good.

Because I knew they'd be back.

SIX

Say what you like about Fleet Ward – and trust me, I've got plenty to say on the subject – but it puts most other places to shame when it comes to the variety of its breakfast menu. Just a picturesque fifteen-second totter from dining room to meds hatch gives all customers the option to start their day with a cheeky benzodiazepine after tucking into their Frosties. Or, you might prefer an artisanal Selective Serotonin Reuptake Inhibitor – which perfectly complements lighter 'fayre' such as fruit or pastries (currently unavailable) – or even, for those with a somewhat more unusual perspective, a custom-crafted anti-psychotic, designed to follow a full English that's guaranteed to put hair on your chest and take ten years off your life-expectancy.

There's even a mixture of 'desserts' for a few select occupants with more complicated demands. Uppers, downers, mood-stabilisers . . . whatever the customer requires or their consultant prescribes. Take it from someone who knows, if you're not overly bothered about décor or service, this is the place to be. Reservations are not required, but it's always busy, and if happy pills and botulism are what you're into, the Fleet caters for all tastes and conditions.

It helps if you're bonkers, obvs.

That Sunday morning, the day after they'd found Kevin's body, I breakfasted like a champion on scrambled eggs, which would soon be followed by olanzapine and some tasty sodium valproate. While Eileen and one of her less than chatty assistants cleared the dirty cups and plates away, I sat in the dining room with Ilias (bacon sandwich and risperidone), Lauren (sausage, egg, beans, lorazepam and clozapine), Shaun (toast and sertraline) and Donna (Greek yoghurt brought in by a visitor – unopened – and lamotrigine).

'That was gorgeous.' Lauren dropped a meaty hand on to Eileen's arm as she passed. 'Best ever.'

Eileen smiled and said, 'Glad to hear it.'

Lauren took this as a cue and began to sing a song in praise of her breakfast, but it was mercifully short and then she just sat looking grumpy, because she hadn't been able to come up with anything that rhymed with sausage.

'Where's Kevin?' Ilias asked.

Everyone stared at him.

'Oh, yeah,' Ilias said.

Donna pushed her uneaten yoghurt away. 'It feels weird, doesn't it?'

'Takes a while to sink in,' I said.

'I still think he killed himself.' Donna was stretching in her chair, getting ready for a few hours' walking. 'It's so sad.'

'You're wrong,' I said.

'You don't know any better than the rest of us,' Lauren said.

'Oh, I think I do. I've already talked to one of the detectives.'

'Bollocks,' Lauren said.

Shaun had begun to cry. He put his hands over his face.

'It's OK to be upset,' I said. 'You need to get it out.'

Lauren grinned. 'He's always getting it out. Under the table, usually. Or was that Kevin?'

I shook my head and nodded towards Shaun. 'Seriously? You reckon it's all right to make stupid jokes like that when his friend's been murdered?'

'Who's been murdered?' Ilias said.

'You're full of shit,' Lauren said. 'Piss off.'

When Shaun stopped sobbing and took his hands away, he left one finger pressed to his chin. He leaned towards me, wide-eyed.

'Am I going to die? Am I going to die? Am I going to die . . . ?'

I assured him that he was going to be fine and he nodded, grateful. He plastered on a smile and I watched him get up and walk slowly towards the door where Malaika was standing ready to wrap an arm around his shoulder.

'Come on, darling,' she said.

People were getting up from the other tables, lurking. We watched Graham dabbing gently at the corners of his mouth with a paper napkin before standing up and heading out, ready to take his place at the meds hatch. The Thing walked across and stood by our table for a minute or so swishing his kilt around.

Did I mention that Tony wears a kilt?

I probably should have done, considering that he's about as

41

Scottish as I am, but I suppose it's just not one of the things I find remotely strange any more.

I've got used to all sorts of weirdness.

'I need to go and pack,' Tony said.

'Course you do,' Lauren said.

Something else I forgot. Tony spends at least a couple of hours every day standing by the airlock with his coat on and his bags packed, waiting for his relatives from America to come and collect him. I'd been there several days before one of the nurses told me that Tony doesn't have any relatives in America. I'm not convinced he has any relatives anywhere, because nobody comes to visit. That may be his choice, of course, because he can never be sure he isn't sitting there passing the time of day with the Thing.

When Tony had gone, Ilias said, 'Does anyone want to play chess?'

'Oh for fuck's sake,' Lauren said.

I shook my head.

'Come on,' Ilias said. 'Sundays are so boring.'

'Not boring any more.' Lauren sat back and sniffed. Jerked a thumb in my direction. 'Not now Juliet Bravo over here reckons there's been a . . . murder.'

She rolled the Rs, showing off, and Donna laughed, which was annoying. I resisted the temptation to point out she was doing *Taggart* and not *Juliet Bravo*. 'I don't reckon anything,' I said. 'There were homicide detectives here all night. A full forensic team. I told you, I've talked to them. I'm actually going to be helping with the investigation.'

Lauren began to sing again, changing the words to that old song by Sophie Ellis-Something-or-other. 'It's murder on the Fleet Ward . . . like to burn this fucking place right down . . .'

'Is that true?' Donna asked, when Lauren had finished. 'You helping?'

'It makes sense, when you think about it,' I said. 'To make use of a professional on the inside.'

'Can I be your what-do-you-call-it?' Ilias asked. 'Sidekick.'

Lauren laughed, hissing through her manky teeth like someone had let the bad air out of her. I looked at one of the egg-streaked forks that Eileen hadn't taken away yet and thought about pushing it into Lauren's fat face.

'I'll see how it goes,' I said. 'I'll have a word with the DCI.'

Lauren was still laughing when Marcus came over to sit with us. He's not normally here on a Sunday, but obviously this was no ordinary weekend. He asked how everyone was feeling and said he hoped that we weren't too shaken up by what had happened the night before.

'I'm used to it,' I said. 'I was just telling this lot that the Murder Squad were all over this place while they were all asleep.'

'Now, hang on, Alice—'

'There were detectives here though, weren't there?'

'Please don't talk about murder. It's not helpful.'

'Tell them.'

'Yes, there were detectives here. And by all accounts, you were being very naughty.'

'Just doing my job,' I said.

Marcus shook his head, then said what he'd come across to say. 'I wanted to let you know that unfortunately there won't be any classes tomorrow, because the occupational therapist won't be coming in.'

'That's not on,' Lauren said.

'Doesn't bother me,' Ilias said.

'What about doing my drawing?' Donna's pale-blue eyes filled immediately with tears. They're probably no bigger than anyone else's, but because the rest of her face is so thin they always seem enormous, like she's E.T., or one of those sad-looking kids in the paintings. 'When's she coming back?'

Marcus shrugged. 'I can't say. You know how it goes.'

We knew well enough, even if most of them didn't actually understand the reasons. The ward psychologist had gone on maternity leave before I arrived and had never come back. There were two fewer beds than when I first came in, one less nurse and more agency staff.

All about money, same as usual. The allocation of resources.

'Same bullshit in the Met,' I said.

'It's less than satisfactory, but what can we do?' Marcus stood up. 'As it happens, we would have needed to suspend tomorrow's classes anyway, because the police have said they will be coming back. They will need to talk to everyone. Staff and patients.'

It was an effort not to punch the air or shout something.

I *was* thinking about Kevin, of course I was – about that body bag being unzipped on a slab somewhere and what those who loved him would be going through – but there's no point pretending that I wasn't as stupidly excited as I'd been since the night they frogmarched me in here. That morning dose of olanzapine was already starting to kick in and take some of the edges off, but even so, I suddenly felt as alive, as much like myself, as I could remember feeling in a long time.

'Statements, right?' I was trying not to shout. 'They need to take our statements.'

'I believe so,' Marcus said.

'Find out where everyone was, what they were doing when the body was discovered. *Before* it was discovered.' I was nodding and looking round the table, at Ilias and Donna, then finally at Lauren. I let my eyes settle on hers: piggy and puffed-up. I let what I'd said hang for just long enough.

'So we'd better get our stories straight.'

SEVEN

'Hello, ladies!'

It's what major-league tossers say, isn't it? Blokes out on the sniff, stinking of Paco Rabanne and coming on to any group of women in a bar or wherever, on the off-chance there might just be one who's thirsty/short-sighted/desperate enough to let some stubbly bellend buy her a drink. It might well be the kind of thing Andy's taken to saying, now he's single again. To be honest, it might be the kind of cheesy crap my ex always trotted out. We weren't really together long enough for me to get to know him all that well. Oh, I certainly found out enough, though, and before you say anything, I don't need reminding that he probably thinks exactly the same thing. That he's well shot of a mentalist like me, that he had a narrow escape and was lucky he discovered what I was really like when he did.

Fractured skull notwithstanding.

What *am* I really like, though? Well, that's the $64,000 question . . .

Was I me when I was making an honest living, doing my best to catch rapists and killers? Or was I only the real me once I became 'unwell' and started to see just how evil so-called innocent people can be? What the ordinary punters we think of as *good* and *kind* are actually capable of? The dark desires and the secret schemes and the deals they make with the devil (figuratively speaking; I was never that far gone) . . .

It's a tricky one, you can't deny that, surely.

Are you . . . *you* when you're stone cold sober or does the real you only come out to play after you've had a few? Maybe you should think about that for a while before you judge me, or anyone else who's sitting where I am for that matter. All I'm saying.

Talking of which . . . hello, ladies!

To be fair, I think most of this lot would let you buy them a drink, and I dare say one or two would happily shag you if there was a bag of crisps thrown in, but you need to bear in mind that a lack of self-esteem is a major issue in here.

So, take a bow, my bitches.

LUCY, aka L-Plate. I reckon her parents probably own most of Sussex or something, because she talks like she's one of the royal family and they're always bringing her in fancy food and gorgeous clothes, but for all that, she's actually dead nice. We have a real laugh, me and L-Plate, though she can lose it a bit if you stand too close to her and she does *not* like being touched. Gets properly freaked out about it. I saw her spit at George once, when he tried to put his arm round her. Same as a lot of people, I don't know if L was messed up

47

before the drugs, or if the drugs messed her up, but either way … I know why kids from *my* neck of the woods end up on the hard stuff, but I've never really understood posh people and heroin. Like, I've got a polo pony and a house that has a maze in the garden, so what am I missing? Oh yeah, a decent smack habit.

Only the finest China White though, and needles from Cartier, natch.

I already mentioned the flat-Earth thing, but that's pretty tame compared with some of the theories L-Plate trots out. The coronavirus 5G thing and 9/11 was an inside job and the moon isn't real and the Beatles never existed and do not get her started on the vapour trails that planes leave. Depending on what mood she's in, either the government's trying to control the weather or they're spraying us all with something that's going to turn us into zombies. Look, I know I've come out with some strange stuff in my time, but this is proper nutter level, and it's even funnier when she's doing it in this cut-glass accent and looks like something out of *Vogue*. From a distance, I should add, because when you get close (as close as she'll let anyone) you can see that she's got iffy skin and teeth like that bloke out of the Pogues. She's not got a bad bone in her, though, that's the most important thing, and you'll never hear her slagging anyone off. When L-Plate's not ranting like some loopy duchess, she'd give you the shirt off her back, and believe me, any one of her cast-offs would be well worth having, because if you stuck it on eBay you could probably pay your mortgage for a few months.

DONNA, aka The Walker. The fact that Donna makes L-Plate (who's got a figure I would kill for) look a bit on the chunky side tells you all you need to know, really. Well, it doesn't, of course. It doesn't tell you *why*. If I knew what was actually going on in anyone's head, I'd be the one with the Mercedes and the office at the end of the corridor. The truth is, I can only tell you about the oddballs I'm holed up with based on what they do and which meds they're on. What they come out with.

Donna doesn't actually come out with anything that you wouldn't hear at the average bus stop or post-office queue, but you only need to look at her to see what's wrong. What the wrongness has done to her, at any rate. You only need to watch her taking an eternity to cut a carrot into twenty pieces, push it around her plate for a while, then spend the next couple of hours walking furiously up and down the corridor to burn off the calories she hasn't taken in. She wears a tracksuit all the time, like she's in training for something.

She's not the only patient who says she shouldn't actually be here, but (not counting yours truly) Donna's probably the only one who really shouldn't. By rights, she should be in a proper eating-disorder clinic, but apparently they can't find anywhere that's got room for her. Ilias says it's ridiculous, because it's not like she takes up a lot of space.

She told me once she was from the south-west somewhere, but I can't remember the name of the place. She's got an accent, but it's very soft like the rest of her. Her personality, I'm talking about. Her body's all angles and pointy bits. She's a gentle soul, wouldn't say boo to a goose and never raises her voice, but it's like she's on the verge of tears all the time, so you have to tread a bit carefully with her. First time my dad saw her, he said she was like a ghost and I know what he was on about. She floats around the place like she's haunting

49

it, though I think he just meant that you could virtually see through her.

So, yeah, Donna walks. Morning, noon and night, wearing out the lino, and she won't stop, even when she's having a conversation. If you want to talk to her about anything, then you'd best be prepared for a half-marathon, which is ironic really, as I've never met anyone in more need of half a Marathon ... and several Mars bars. Yeah, I know they're called Snickers now, but the joke wouldn't work, would it?

JAMILAH, aka The Foot Woman. Fifty-something, if I had to hazard a guess. A petite Somali woman, with the most beautiful grey hair which – when she takes her headscarf off – comes down to her waist. Jammy (I'm not sure she loves it when I call her that) is another one who doesn't have much to say for herself, though there is one topic about which she's unusually vocal. She probably doesn't suggest it quite as often as Ilias suggests playing chess or Shaun asks if he's going to die, but there isn't a day goes by without her offering to give me – or anyone else in the same room – a pedicure. There's nothing threatening or creepy about it, I don't want you to think that, because the truth is she's always extremely polite.

'Would you like a pedicure, Alice?' Softly-spoken, a thick accent. 'No? OK, then ...'

First thing in the morning, she's all set to go to work, keen as mustard to get at your trotters. Same if you're eating, or, even stranger, after a tap-tap on your bedroom door in the middle of the night.

Now, I've no idea if this is something she's done professionally, if it's part of a past life she's clinging on to, but I doubt it, somehow. I know I'm a fine one to talk about clinging to anything, but my relationship with the Job is very different, all right? There's some serious unfinished business. So, with Jamilah, I can only presume it's something . . . sexual. I mean some people have a thing about feet, don't they? Granted, she doesn't look like she'd find anything sexually arousing, not even sex, but this is probably the last place you should judge any book by its cover, so I'm keeping an open mind.

I do know that I'm not queuing up for her services any time soon.

I don't know exactly what a pedicure involves, but I've had mates who've done it and I know there's a certain amount of . . . shaping involved and trimming. I know things get removed. I mean, I'm guessing she had as much gear taken off her when she came in as the rest of us, but some people are sneakier than others, so is it really worth taking the risk?

I'm not letting anyone in here come at my feet with tools.

LAUREN, aka The Singer. From Kent or Essex . . . that neck of the woods, and I almost went with another nickname entirely, because a couple of nights after I got here she marched into my room, asked if she could use my bathroom and proceeded to piss all over the floor. I mean *everywhere*, and not just in my bathroom, either. Everybody else's too as it turned out, like she was marking her territory. So I nearly went with Cat-Woman, but even though the piss-spraying is marginally more unpleasant than her tuneless wailing it happens a bit less often, and trust me, she's nothing like those sexy women in the Batman films, so The Singer it is.

Lauren could be anywhere between thirty and fifty, and actually looks a bit like Adele (before she started living on fresh air and kale and lost all that weight) but sadly labours

51

under the tragic misapprehension that she also sounds like her. I must say, though, sometimes the singing can be quite funny. This is her third time on section, and I have to admit that I did laugh a few days after I came in, when I found her in the toilets, serenading herself in the mirror.

'I'm once, twice . . . three times a loony . . .'

But . . .

You know how prisons have a 'Daddy' or whatever? Someone who everyone's a bit wary of and who more or less runs the place? Well, Lauren's the Daddy on Fleet Ward. Nobody messes with Lauren, not Ilias, not Tony . . . nobody. Even George and Marcus give her a wide berth when she's got one on her and she's on a WAL more often than she isn't.

She's just . . . bad.

Some people are, right? I met plenty of them when I was working, nicked my fair share, so there was something about her I clocked straight away that I definitely did not like the look of. It's not drugs, I'm fairly sure of that, so I can only think it's some kind of bog-standard disorder. Serious ADHD or a skewed personality thing. Who knows, maybe she can't help herself. Maybe she skulks back to her bedroom every night and weeps into her pillow, hugs a teddy bear or whatever, but the fact is that, out here during the day, she can be a dreadful cow. Like all bullies she wants a reaction and she usually gets one from most people. Tears or fawning, a daily shouting match.

I try not to get involved and steer clear of her, but it's hard.

We're living on top of each other, so sometimes you haven't got a choice.

One day, me and Lauren are going to kick off and it won't be pretty.

EIGHT

They held the interviews first thing Monday morning in the MDR, calling us in from the dining room one at a time. I think it was probably alphabetical, but I couldn't swear to it, because I don't know everyone's surname. Ilias was in first, I remember that, then a couple of the Informals and then Jamilah. The rest of us sat there, twiddling our thumbs in the dining room, waiting our turn.

I had my headphones on, listening to nothing.

I can't lie, I was like a cat on hot bricks.

There was a copper in there with us – a woman who smiled a bit too much – and she'd made it clear that they didn't want us talking to each other about what had happened two nights earlier, and definitely not talking to anybody who'd already been questioned before we went in. Didn't stop some people talking about other things, obviously. Didn't stop Ilias asking the copper if she wanted to play chess or Jamilah offering to sort her feet out.

It was properly frustrating, though.

I just had to hold it in, tell myself that I'd have plenty of time to find out what the others had said later on.

I understood why, course I did. You don't want information to be tainted or untrustworthy so it can be easily discounted down the line. You'd be amazed how careful you need to be about that … about everything. We once had a six-month murder inquiry fall apart at the last minute because nobody had thought to offer a suspect – who had been brought in the night before his interview – something to eat. Can you believe that? His solicitor argued that his client had not been in a fit state to be questioned, so the entire statement got thrown out and the case fell apart. That's the way it is, these days.

It got me wondering, sitting there waiting to be called down to the MDR, just how reliable any of our statements might prove to be. I wasn't including myself, obviously, but surely these coppers knew the kind of people they were talking to. Easy enough for a brief with five minutes on the job to pick holes in anything L-Plate had to say, or The Thing. Not very hard to convince a jury these were not what you'd call solid witnesses.

Ladies and gentlemen, you have been told that Witness A can clearly identify the accused, but you should also know that she believes the moon to be a hologram …

I know, I was probably getting ahead of myself just a little back then, but in the early days of an investigation it always pays to think about what might be down the road, because nothing is ever that easy. You need to prepare for all eventualities.

When the copper told me it was my turn, I was out of my seat and away down that corridor like shit off a shiny shovel.

Marcus and Femi were standing outside the nurses' station and Femi said, 'Nothing to be scared of,' as I walked past them, which was ridiculous because I was the last person who had anything to be frightened about. I smiled, so they could see that. Behind me, Ilias was shouting, 'Don't tell them anything,' and Lauren was singing her Murder on the Fleet Ward song again.

Before I'd reached the MDR, a female officer directed me into one of the treatment rooms and asked very nicely if I would be willing to provide DNA and fingerprint samples for elimination purposes. She explained that she was asking everyone on the ward.

'Some of them will almost certainly say no,' I told her. 'The patients, I mean. Don't waste your time reading anything into it, though. A few of them won't tell you their names or else get off on giving you false ones. One or two of them might well bite you if you go anywhere near them with one of ... those.' I nodded, watching her as she snapped the seal and removed a swab from its container. 'You need to know who you're dealing with.'

Her smile showed plenty of perfect teeth but was dead as mutton.

'Oh, don't worry, we do,' she said. She began talking me through the process as if I was slightly simple, told me that it was painless and explained how she would need to swab both sides of my mouth.

I held up a hand to stop her. 'I've done this,' I said.

'You've had your DNA taken before?'

'No.' My turn to smile. 'I've done what you're doing.' The look on her face was priceless and, just for once, I didn't give a toss if she believed me or not. 'So you don't need to worry

55

too much. I mean yeah, I'm chock full of drugs right now so I'm a bit all over the place, but I probably won't bite you.'

It was the same detective I'd spoken to outside the men's toilet on the night it happened. Well, the early hours of the following day if you want to be accurate about it. The thug in glasses. He was sitting behind a desk in a suit and tie. The same desk the judge had sat behind when I was in there for my last tribunal.

'I'm Detective Constable Steve Seddon.'

I leaned forward to check out the lanyard around his neck. 'I'm Alice Armitage. Al.'

'I know.' He turned a fresh page on the notepad in front of him and began writing.

He'd been given a list of all the patients, of course, and it was probably just that, but sitting there, I preferred to think that someone had told him about me. A colleague of a colleague. Word gets around and there's always some gobshite in the Met you can count on to beat the jungle drums.

'I'm a DC, too,' I said. I leaned back and turned to look at the rain running down the small window. 'Homicide Command East.'

He didn't look up from his notepad. 'Right.'

You can imagine how much DC Seddon's reaction – his lack of it – pissed me off. It was like I'd told him I was Britney Spears. I might just as well have been L-Plate, wittering about chemtrails. He looked up finally and took a deep breath, the hint of a smile to let me know that he understood, and I could see straight away that he didn't really want to be there. That he thought interviewing a bunch of mentals was a colossal waste of time.

Hard to blame him for that, mind you.

'Miss Armitage ... you understand we're here this morning to gather as much information as we can about what might have happened on the evening of Mr Connolly's death. That's Saturday evening, yes? Two evenings ago.'

So Connolly was Kevin's second name.

'You could start by telling me anything you think might be important, anything you might have seen or heard that you think could help?'

I said nothing and turned towards the window again. I was going to make *Steve* work for it a bit, see what he was made of.

'OK, so let me ask you if you saw anyone going towards Mr Connolly's room—'

'I saw loads of people, obviously,' I said. 'Members of staff, other patients. All sorts of comings and goings.'

'Let me be more specific then. What about after eight-thirty? We know Mr Connolly went to bed early, just after dinner, so ... '

I thought about it, but not about his question. It was blindingly obvious that they had not yet managed to establish the time of death. 'I didn't see anything suspicious,' I said.

'Nobody hanging around near Mr Connolly's room?'

'No.'

He scribbled something, but I couldn't make it out. 'So, can you recall what *you* were doing that evening?'

'I was watching TV until about ten o'clock,' I said. 'Plenty of others in there with me, so easy enough to corroborate. *Casualty* and some rubbish with Ant and Dec. After that, I sat nattering in the dining room with Shaun and Tony. We were still in there when the body was discovered.'

He wrote some more. 'Thank you.'

'Was it a stabbing?' He looked up, put his pen down. 'Easiest way, I would have thought. Nice and quiet.'

He took off his glasses. 'I'm afraid I'm not at liberty to reveal details at this stage—'

I raised my hands to let him know I got it, although, one copper to another, he shouldn't have been quite so Job-pissed. In his shoes I'd have been happy to bring a colleague up to speed. I sat back and told him why a blade was the obvious weapon and let him know how easy it was to smuggle anything smaller than a baby elephant on to the ward. I told him that if they were looking for the murder weapon – and why wouldn't they be – they should widen the search to include the hospital grounds, because there were several patients on unescorted leave who pretty much had the run of the place.

I waited.

I was wearing a T-shirt and I could see he was looking at the scars on my arms.

'Like I said.' He put his glasses back on and turned a fresh page, ready for the next customer.

'There was a fight,' I said. 'Did anyone tell you that? A big one and Kevin was right in the middle of it. It was me that broke it up, actually.'

'When was this?'

'On the Wednesday. Three days before Kevin was killed.'

He didn't like me putting it like that, I could tell, but he was obviously interested. 'Who was the fight between?'

'Well, there were lots of people involved, but mainly it was Kevin and Tony. I don't know if you've talked to Tony yet.'

Seddon looked at a list. 'Anthony Lewis?'

'Yeah. He can be a bit . . . volatile, you know?'

'So, what was the fight about?'

I'd heard several conflicting stories and I wasn't convinced that Lauren didn't have quite a lot to do with what happened, but at least one version of events involved Kevin saying something to upset Tony. Something about the Thing, most likely. So that's what I told Seddon, because I thought he should know.

He thanked me, which was nice. Told me I'd been very helpful.

'Least I can do,' I said. 'I mean, I do know how this goes. Waiting for the PM results, whatever the forensic boys come back with . . . and obviously you've got the cameras.'

'Yes, of course.' He was done with me, I could tell. 'We'll certainly be reviewing the ward's CCTV footage. So . . .'

Bingo. The lack of enthusiasm wasn't just down to the fact that he was having to waste his time questioning a bunch of fruitcakes. There are cameras almost everywhere on the ward and yeah, there's a couple of blind spots, but there's certainly one that gives a perfect view of the men's corridor. So he was sitting there, cocky as you like, thinking he'd have the whole thing wrapped up by the end of the day.

Remember what I said about nothing being easy? About thinking ahead?

'Good luck with that,' I said.

He looked at me. 'What?'

'Well, I'm guessing that nobody's told you about Graham.' I saw him glance at his list again. 'About Graham's . . . issues with being watched all the time.' Another look towards the window, because I was in no rush. I was proper buzzed up and loving it. 'What Graham likes to do with leftovers.'

NINE

With one or two exceptions, the staff on Fleet Ward are pretty decent.

Don't get me wrong, I've had run-ins with all of them at one time or another, but by and large they're not a bad lot. Most of the time they're just doing their jobs, right? It's meds and meetings. It's all about your various tests and whether you're behaving in your classes and if your observation status needs reviewing. Thing is, I've had cracking chats with several of them. We've shared a few secrets, talked about partners and kids or whatever, but I still wouldn't say that any of them are . . . friends. End of the day, they can't ever really be mates, doesn't matter how well you get on with them. It's not easy to form that kind of relationship, however nice they might be, because you never know when one of them is going to be holding you down while another one's jabbing a needle in your arse.

If you might be swinging a punch at one of them.

I think it's high time you were properly introduced to the men and women responsible for my care, but I've decided to mix things up a bit. Nobody needs another list, do they? After the excitement of my interview with DC Seddon, the rest of that Monday was predictably uneventful, so, as I mooched around, I decided to entertain myself by casting the members of staff in rather ... different roles. Dealing with them at the meds hatch or in the dining room or nattering with them in the hallways, it struck me that, compared to what goes through the heads of some people in here every day, imagining the doctors and nurses in a series of no-holds-barred, to-the-death UFC bouts wasn't actually that weird. You do need to understand that when people aren't getting murdered, this place can be seriously boring.

On top of which, I've definitely imagined things a whole lot weirder.

So, picture a crowd baying for blood, a microphone descending from the heavens as the fighters are introduced and me in a sparkly bikini prowling the ring between rounds. On second thoughts, best not imagine that if you want to keep your dinner down ...

FYI, I haven't bothered giving any of this lot nicknames because they have their names on their badges, like I used to have mine on my stab vest. Oh, and as far as job titles go ... well, the doctors are obviously the doctors, but I still don't really know the difference between a nurse and a healthcare assistant. I mean, in theory an assistant would be assisting a nurse, because they're probably a bit less qualified, but most of the time that doesn't seem to matter and everyone just mucks in. I suppose that, when the only thing there's no shortage of is patients, it's all hands to the pump.

OK ... let's get ready to *rumble*!

Dr Bakshi is the consultant psychiatrist, so she's the big cheese around here. Her first name's Asma, or maybe Asha, and I'm guessing she's Indian. She's always been nice to me; reassuring, you know? Says that there's no reason I shouldn't get well again, but that I do need to be careful with the psychosis, because any further drug use could bring it on again. It's like breaking the seal on a bottle, she said, or once the genie's out of the bottle ... something along those lines. All scary stuff, but only if you believe that you were properly *un*well to begin with. I'm not saying I was behaving what you'd call normally through the whole thing, but there are shades of grey, you know? Shades of crackers.

She doesn't use too much medical gobbledegook and she listens a lot – I guess that's just being good at her job – but I certainly wouldn't want to mess with her, because she's the one with the power to send me home, or, if not, to make my life in here a lot harder than it is. She's also the one member of staff I try not to be too much of a smartarse with – even if I can't help myself, sometimes – because she's the only one I know is cleverer than me.

Bakshi's a bit older than the others and she doesn't strike me as much of a scrapper, so to make things a bit fairer when the fighting starts I'm pairing her with someone, two against one. I need to partner her up with one of the nurses and it's a fairly obvious choice.

Debbie's very Scottish and *very* ginger, but more important ... she's big. Not big like Lauren's big, but like she could easily bench-press Bakshi if she had to. Or me, come to that. If something kicks off between any of the female patients, it's likely to be Debbie who'll come steaming in to sort it out. Actually, most of the blokes in here are more scared of Debbie than any of the male members of staff, even Tony, who's still not convinced she isn't the Thing and always gives her a wide berth. She's loud and rude and she's ridiculously sweary.

It's one of the reasons I thought that Kevin's room, after the murder, must have been a proper horror-show. Debbie's scared of bugger all and she was the one that found him, remember. She came bombing out of that corridor like she'd stumbled into the Texas chainsaw massacre.

I mean, I know better now, obviously.

I'm teaming Debbie and Bakshi up to take on George, who's another one of the nurses. He's the ward's gentle giant, and yeah, I'm being just a bit sarcastic. I'm not saying he's rough when he doesn't need to be, but let's just say he's well aware that he's a big lad. Holding himself back, like he'd love nothing more than for Ilias or Tony to have a pop at him. He's got a proper Geordie accent and of course he's a Newcastle fan, which I take every chance to wind him up about. Telling him that clearly means he's madder than anyone in here.

He told me once he always wanted to be a copper, but they wouldn't let him join, and that made me wonder just what George might have got up to when he was younger. I mean, these days they'll let any nutcase in.

So, first up then, it's Bakshi and Debbie versus George. *Result*: even with two against one, and despite the fact that Debbie would probably fight dirty, George is the only winner here, taking the pair of them out inside the first thirty seconds. Quick and ugly.

I reckon a match-up between the ward's two healthcare

assistants would give the crowd a better spectacle and certainly a longer one. Malaika's Indian, same as Dr Bakshi, only with a really thick Brummie accent. Pure *Peaky Blinders*, Malaika is, but with a better haircut (red streaks which look cool) and without the hidden razor blades. Trust me, none of the people who work in here are a soft touch, but she's definitely not the strictest. If you're watching something on TV, she'll maybe let you have another ten minutes after you're supposed to be in bed, and if you were on escorted leave and she took you outside for a cigarette, she wouldn't rush you back in the second you'd stubbed it out. She's a smoker herself, so she's always happy enough to go with you.

Malaika's pretty tight with George, always whispering in corners, and for a while, I thought there was something going on between them. Then I found out she was gay – it was actually George that told me – so I let my overly fertile imagination run riot in other ways. It's fun to make things up about the staff, invent weird and wonderful private lives for them. Like Malaika probably had quite a strict upbringing, maybe an arranged marriage she got herself out of, so now, when she's not at work, she's wild and into all sorts. Death-metal and coke and stuff. I know she's got a temper on her, too, because I heard her arguing about something with Debbie the other day.

I wonder how she'll fare, toe to toe in the arena with the Polish Punisher.

Mia would probably be popular with the crowd. She's got spiky blonde hair and a cute accent and she's pretty, but if I'm honest she's a bit of a black hole, personality-wise. She doesn't socialise much, by which I mean she never 'hangs out' or tells you anything about her life outside Fleet Ward.

She probably thinks she's being smart, because some of her colleagues who have let things slip have paid for it later on. Thing is, that just means we make it up, like I did with Malaika. So, Mia . . . definitely some kind of dominatrix on the side, and that's not as much of a leap as you might think. Sometimes I catch her staring at some of the other patients, when she doesn't know she's being watched, and once or twice I've seen that pretty face looking seriously cruel.

Malaika versus Mia. *Result*: a much trickier one to call, and Mia's a bit of a dark horse, but my gut says Malaika would probably come out on top.

The final bout is another one that's going to be close, even if it's a man against a woman. Marcus is the ward manager, because he's the senior nurse, I suppose. Very tall and wiry, Nigerian, I think, because he told me he was born in Lugos. That's in Nigeria, right? I reckon 'even-tempered' would be the best way to describe him. I've only seen Marcus really lose it once – with Lauren, no surprise there – but he doesn't really smile a lot either. In fact thinking about it, he doesn't seem to have much of a sense of humour at all. I would have thought that was pretty bloody important working in a place like this, some of the stuff that goes on, but he's obviously good at his job or he probably wouldn't be ward manager. The rest of the staff all seem to like him, anyway.

He talks very slowly like he's choosing his words carefully, and in perfect English, like someone reading the news, but every now and again there's a slight stammer which gives certain patients a golden opportunity to take the piss. Some people just enjoy being cruel – naming no names – but a few of the others seem to genuinely find it funny because they don't understand boundaries. You know, 'Look out, here comes M-M-Marcus', all that. Lauren always manages to dig out an appropriate song to try and wind him up. Elton John or David Bowie are particular favourites.

Ch-ch-ch-ch-changes ...

B-B-B-B-B-B-B-Bennie and the Jets ...

Ha, ha, ha. Stupid b-b-b-bitch.

I'm not too sure what part of Africa Femi's from, but she's got a thicker accent than Marcus. Small, but stronger than she looks (I think all the nurses are), and she's really good at bringing certain patients out of their shells. The ones who just withdraw in here, you know. She talks about her kids with them or tells terrible jokes and sometimes she even joins in when Lauren's singing, which is probably taking the cheery thing too far.

She's another one who's definitely got a short fuse, though, but I've only ever seen it with other members of the staff. Saying that, I don't think she likes confrontations because one time I caught her crying in the toilets after a bust-up with someone. She doesn't take any shit, I mean she's not a pushover or anything, but Femi's one of those the patients will go to if they need a favour or a word putting in with Dr Bakshi or something.

I said there's nothing of her, right? She's properly tiny, like her clothes would fit a ten-year-old, so I do wonder if maybe she had her own issues with food once upon a time, because she's always picking at something grainy-looking in a Tupperware container. I mean, apparently a lot of people working in mental health used to be patients, so I wouldn't be surprised. Poacher turned gamekeeper sort of thing. It's funny, because the only person she's ever remotely spiky with is Donna, so maybe she's a bit freaked out dealing with someone who's got the same problems she had. Once, she gave Donna a major telling-off about something and ever since then Donna's called her Femi-Nazi, which would be a pretty nifty UFC nickname now I think about it.

Marcus versus Femi. *Result*: controversial, but I'm going with Femi for this one. I'm not sure Marcus has got a lot of fight in him and I think Femi could take care of herself if she had to.

So, a few fight-night facts about the men and women who take care of us and perhaps a bit of creative 'embroidery', but you get the picture. Full disclosure, I should probably mention that one of the members of staff stepping into my imaginary UFC ring almost certainly sexually assaulted me. Right, 'almost certainly' . . . makes it sound a bit vague, but I'm as sure as I can be, taking into account the issues with memory and medication. I'm not going to say who it was because I really don't like to think about it very much, but if they did it to me, you can bet they've done it to others.

L-Plate told me the same thing had happened to her once, at a different hospital. She told me that she'd made a complaint, but that she'd just been called a drama queen.

'Best to keep your head down,' she'd said. Crying in my arms she was at the time. 'Don't make waves.'

Obviously, as a copper, I want to see people who do this kind of thing get what's coming to them, because that's my job, but I also know that, things being the way they are – me being where I am – I need to steer clear of trouble. Believe me, it goes against the grain, but it's a little easier to come to terms with now I'm smack in the middle of a murder case.

TEN

Visiting hours in here are pretty relaxed, but there isn't any sort of official visits area. You just have to grab a bit of privacy wherever you can, so just before dinner time on the Tuesday, me and Tim Banks found a couple of chairs in the music room. Jamilah was already in there reading a magazine and she was clearly earwigging, so I just gave her evils for a few minutes until she pissed off. As soon as *she'd* left us alone, Lauren stuck her head round the door and asked Banksy if he wanted to hear her song.

He said that he was busy.

She told him it was a really good one.

He said maybe another time.

She told him he was a cunt and then closed the door.

'Nice.' He looked at me. 'So, how you doing, Al?'

Tim's probably the most regular visitor I've had. Mum and Dad have been down a couple of times, but it usually means a night for them in some hotel and it's never pleasant because they get so upset. Sophie came in once, which was nice, but she was a bit freaked out by Tony (the postcard incident) so I don't think she's in a hurry to come back. We text and talk on WhatsApp, so it's all good. She tells me how boring her new flatmate Camilla is, even though she's apparently a lot tidier than I was.

I was never boring to live with, nobody could ever say that.

Banksy's been great, though. He understands. Yeah, it pisses me off that nobody else from work has been in, all those people I'd thought were mates, but I get it. I'm damaged goods, aren't I?

I told Banksy I was fine. He said I was looking well.

'Relative though, isn't it?' I smiled. I knew I looked like death warmed up.

'Better than last time, anyway,' he said. 'Colour in your cheeks.'

'So, come on then.'

'Give me a bloody chance.' He dug into his pocket and brought out a notebook. He'd made notes, God bless him. Like I said, he's someone I know I can count on.

A bloody good copper, Banksy is.

On top of which, he was Johnno's best mate.

I'd called him two days before, on the Sunday night, after I'd talked to Seddon. I'd brought him up to speed, told him to do some digging and asked him how soon he could get in to see me. Like I said, it wasn't our team working this, but I knew he'd be able to ask around and call in a few favours. I knew he could find out *something*.

'What's the story, then?'

He was flipping through the pages of his notebook. 'Can't remember the last time I saw you this fired up,' he said.

'A murder tends to do that,' I said. 'Plus, I've been a good girl, so they've cut the dose of my mood stabiliser.'

Banksy found the page he was looking for. 'Well, you were right about that much, at any rate. It *is* now a murder investigation.'

'*Yes!*' It was just me and him, so I didn't bother trying to hide my excitement. 'I fucking knew it.'

'Not a stabbing, though. You jumped the gun a bit there.'

I waited.

'Cause of death was asphyxia. Victim was suffocated, basically. Pillow's their best guess.'

I thought about that. Kevin wasn't a weakling, but he wasn't a big lad either and he'd have been half asleep, zonked out on whatever meds he'd been given last thing. Pressing a pillow over his face wouldn't have been difficult and it wouldn't have taken very long. 'What about time of death?'

'That's a bit trickier,' Banksy said. 'The pathologist reckons some time between nine o'clock and ten-thirty.'

'Which pathologist?'

'That weirdo at Hornsey. The one with all the tattoos and piercings.'

'Right.' I'd never met the bloke, but he had a reputation.

'Now, they think they can narrow that down because they already know the victim went to bed early, just after eight-thirty, and they know the nurse who was doing the rounds—'

'Debbie.'

'Yeah ... she checked on him at nine-thirty and he was sleeping, not a problem. They've got her observation charts or whatever, got her on camera going in and out, right? So, now they're thinking, OK ... we're obviously looking at whoever killed him sneaking into his room sometime between then and when Debbie makes her next round just after ten-thirty and discovers the body.'

'Screams the place down.'

'All nice and straightforward, so they reckon, because they'll have their killer on tape, but apparently there's some kind of technical issue with the cameras. So . . .' He stopped when he saw me grinning.

'Not exactly technical,' I said.

I told him the same thing I told Seddon yesterday.

Aside from his pathological fear of being second in line for anything, I explained, Graham – the Waiter – is more than a little twitchy when it comes to being watched. 'He usually does it straight after mealtimes,' I said. 'With whatever food's left over. He stands on a chair and uses anything he's not eaten to screw with the cameras. Porridge or pudding or whatever. Mashed potato is his favourite; he's deadly with that. A nice handful of leftover mash . . . *splat* . . . camera knackered.'

Banksy looked horrified. 'Can't they stop him?'

'Oh yeah, they try to. He always gets a major bollocking and they put him on Within Eyesight or Within Arm's Length or something, but they can only keep it up for so long. After that, they do what they can to keep an eye on him, but he's pretty sneaky about it. Eventually he finds a way to clamber on to a trolley or get on somebody's shoulders and smear something gloppy over as many cameras as he can get to before they catch him. At first it was a big deal, I mean they took it dead seriously and they'd be cleaning the cameras up straight away. Then it just became something they got used to and nobody could really be arsed to get it fixed that quickly. Marcus says it's a health and safety issue, nurses with buckets and cloths climbing up on stuff or whatever, so these days they tend to wait for one of the hospital janitors to come along with a ladder and sort it out. Pain in the arse for them, obviously, but pretty funny.'

'Not if you're running this investigation,' Banksy said. 'According to the log, the camera covering the men's corridor went out just after half-past nine and wasn't . . . cleaned up until just before the body was discovered. So, yeah, they're looking at the murder taking place during that same hour, but it's also an hour when the camera was out.'

'Fucking Graham.' I shook my head.

'Fucking Graham.'

'Just when dinner's finishing,' I said. 'Staff cleaning up, people milling about all over the shop. Always a bit full-on, that time.'

'Something else.' Banksy was looking at his notepad again. It was hard to contain myself. 'They found drugs in the victim's bedroom. Quite a lot of drugs.'

'What kind of drugs?'

'I don't have the details, but . . . pills. Prescription stuff, sound of it.'

'Jesus.'

'That's it.' He closed his notebook. 'Trust me, I had to twist a few arms to get *that* much.'

I told him I appreciated it, said I'd try not to bother him again. 'I can't promise, obviously.'

'Obviously,' he said. Then, when he'd stood up and was hanging about looking awkward: 'Listen, Al, don't bite my head off, but I'm not convinced this is the kind of thing you need right now. That it's good for you.'

'Are you joking me? It's exactly what I need.'

'I mean, shouldn't you just be . . . ?'

'What? Chillin'? Putting my feet up? Catching up on all those good books I should have read?'

'You know what I mean, Al. Come on, I don't want to debate this with you again, but you know you've not been well. I mean, you do admit that much, right?'

'You're a top bloke, Banksy.' I walked to the door, waited for him to follow. 'But you're not my dad.'

A minute later, while we were standing at the airlock waiting for someone to let him out, he said, 'I saw Mags the other night.' Like it had just popped into his head.

'OK.' I could feel something jumping inside and was trying not to let it show in my voice. 'How's she doing?'

Maggie was Johnno's girlfriend.

Five months pregnant when he died.

As pregnant as she was ever going to get, as it turned out.

'Yeah, she's all right,' Banksy said. 'She was asking after you.'

That didn't help things and I was grateful when I saw Mia coming with the keys. 'You all done?' she asked, a little more chipper than usual.

'Yeah, we're done,' I said.

Banksy gave me a big hug before he stepped into the airlock, and when he was inside with Mia, signing out and waiting to go through the second door, I pressed my palm against the window, then kissed the glass, pretending to cry like we were lovers saying a final goodbye or something.

It made him laugh and he stuck two fingers up.

As soon as he was gone, I checked my watch then went back to my room to make a call. That calmed me down a bit, knowing I'd be sorted before very long. Then I went to get my dinner.

ELEVEN

It was just a regular house call, that's all. An everyday ACTION as part of an ongoing sexual assault case that involved talking to everyone on the local sex-offenders register. Run-of-the-mill stuff. Obviously, though, no story like this – no once-in-a-career tragedy – ever starts with 'we were on the trail of a vicious, chainsaw-wielding serial killer', does it, because then you'd know how it was going to turn out.

There'd be no surprise.

You look ahead. I said that earlier, didn't I? You try to prepare for all eventualities, but no amount of preparation or due diligence or just bog-standard keeping your wits about you is going to help when life just turns round, says 'bad luck, mate' and gobs in your face.

Turns the world upside down.

Turns you into somebody else.

The somebody Johnno and I were looking for that morning was not at home, but his flatmate seemed happy enough to let us in and answer a few questions. It was a flat above an electrical shop in Mile End and, from the doorway, it looked nice enough. Nicer than we were expecting, anyway.

Not too much of a shithole and we'd visited plenty of them the previous few days.

Yeah, I could see that the bloke was wired, you learn to recognise it, so straight away Johnno and I exchanged a look. *We good with this?* I seem to remember that I rolled my eyes or raised my eyebrows or something and he knew what that meant. Just a doper or a crackhead who probably won't be able to string a sentence together anyway, so let's get this over with and head to that greasy spoon a few doors up for an early lunch.

I've already said I had a feeling we had nothing to worry about and that everything was going to be fine, but if I'm honest it wasn't quite that. It was more like I didn't have a feeling that it *wasn't*.

I should have had and I didn't.

I asked the bloke, nice and polite, if he'd mind me taking a quick look around, while Johnno sat down with him on the settee to ask a few questions about his absent flatmate. The bloke – stick-thin, a bit weaselly, par for the course – said he didn't have a problem with that, but we'd need to get a shift on because he had to go and meet somebody.

Johnno and I looked at each other again. A dealer, most likely.

I went into the bedroom of the man we were actually looking for and started poking around. I put on some nitrile gloves and opened drawers and looked in the wardrobe and under the bed. Standard stuff, but you never know what you might stumble across, so I was cautious, like I always was.

75

I could hear Johnno in the front room.

Do you know where your flatmate is now? Do you know when he'll be back? Have you any idea where he was four nights ago . . . ?

It didn't sound hugely productive.

As soon as I'd lifted the mattress I could see the DVDs gaffer-taped to the bed frame, and I was just reaching in to take one out when I heard the bloke shout. I can't remember what he said, and thinking about it, it was probably just a noise. Hoarse and high-pitched, like he was in pain.

When I came back in, I could see the pair of them struggling on the settee, and when Johnno turned his head and shouted at me to call for back-up as I was on my way across to help him, that's when the bloke threw the punch.

What I thought was a punch.

It wasn't until the bloke staggered to his feet and dropped the Stanley knife that I saw what had happened.

The blood on the blade.

The blood that was starting to pulse between Johnno's fingers and splash on the carpet.

That pattern – those hideous blue-green swirls – is still there sometimes when I close my eyes.

The rest of it's all a bit scrambled in my head, if I'm honest, like it was just a few seconds and like it took for ever. The bloke mumbling and strolling out of there like it was nothing and he was pissed off that we'd held him up. Me trying to key the radio and still keep my hands pressed against Johnno's neck. Those stupid gloves, slippery with all the blood, and his shirt changing colour.

Shouting about an ambulance and whispering to Johnno.

Telling him to keep still, to hold on.

Feeling his boots kicking against the carpet underneath us and knowing I was wasting my time.

Knowing that both of us were gone.

There. Not to excuse the fact that I did some stupid things, that I *still* do them now and again, but just so you know . . .

As we've already established, Within Arms' Length is at the shitty end of the obs stats ladder. A status that really means you've got no status at all. But for those privileged few, for the *chosen*, the Holy Grail of stats awaits them in the 1983 Mental Health Act's very own VIP enclosure. I'm talking about the five-star, business-class status that is . . . Unescorted Leave.

Be still my beating heart.

Actually racing most of the time, thanks to the anti psych meds.

To put it more simply: Fuck yeah!

Fifteen minutes might not sound like much, but trust me, you savour every sodding second of it, because you're *outside*. On. Your. Own. Free to smell air that actually smells like air – as much as it ever does in north-west London – and to enjoy the relatively dogshit-free green space available within the hospital grounds. It's something you have to earn, naturally, and you must demonstrate a clear understanding that, if you leave the hospital grounds, the police will be sent to bring you back pronto, and you can kiss goodbye to unescorted anything for a good while.

Yeah, of course I understand. Police, totally . . . got it.

Like I'd said to Banksy a couple of hours before, I'd been a very well-behaved patient of late. A damn sight better than the few weeks previously, that's for sure. I'd earned a degree of trust, Dr Bakshi had said, and I should do my very best to maintain it.

'I promise,' I said. 'It means a lot.'

George let me out of the airlock just before nine o'clock. He looked at his watch and told me I needed to be back by quarter past.

'To the second,' I said.

'I'll be waiting,' he said.

I smoked a cigarette by the main entrance to the unit, just in case George or anyone else was of a mind to pop down and check, or was watching me from one of the windows.

I thought about the drugs they'd found in Kevin's room.

Had one of his visitors smuggled them in for him? *Quite a lot*, Banksy had said. OK, sneaking in the odd bottle wasn't out of the question, but more than that was hard to imagine. Kevin must have been trying to sell them to someone on the outside, though, however he got hold of them. There'd definitely be a market for it and I had a feeling he'd been involved in stuff like that before he came in.

I couldn't think of any obvious way he'd got hold of the drugs in here, though.

Nicking a pack or two of aripiprazole from an unguarded trolley was not beyond the bounds of possibility, but there's some proper locks on the medical supplies rooms, so a large quantity would definitely have been trickier. No, some things on the ward might not be as shipshape as they should be – the mash-on-the-cameras thing for a kick-off – but they do tend to be quite careful about the meds.

The whole suicide thing.

So, where was Kevin getting the drugs and why was he stockpiling them in his bedroom?

I was still thinking about it while I strolled down to a spot just inside one of the hospital gates. Billy was waiting by the wheelie bins, playing some stupid game on his phone.

'Been a while,' he said.

I handed over the twenty pound note and he handed me the baggie. It would be more than enough. He'd pre-rolled a freebie for me, which was thoughtful.

'Things got a bit messy,' I said.

Billy folded the note into his well-stuffed wallet and began scrolling through his messages. 'Got messy again, have they?'

'In a different way,' I said, as he walked away towards the main road.

At exactly nine-fifteen I rang the bell and watched George sauntering towards the airlock. He nodded, reaching for his keys, so I leaned against the window and said, 'Bang on time, mate,' and hoped I wasn't shouting or grinning like an idiot without knowing it.

I told George I was going to get an early night and winked at Donna as I marched straight down to my room.

'Sleep well, pet,' George shouted.

He'd smelled it on me, though, course he had.

Ten minutes later, him and Marcus were knocking on my bedroom door and there wasn't a fat lot I could do. While they turned my room upside down, I stood outside in the corridor and cried for a few minutes, holding Malaika's hand and listening to her telling me I was 'daft'. I knew they'd find the weed – it was tucked into the toe of one my trainers – but I'd rolled a couple before coming back in and stashed them, so at least there was that.

Think ahead and keep your fingers crossed, right?

Later, after I'd shouted for a while and kicked the door

until my foot hurt, I lay down and tried to sleep. I thought the weed would help, because it usually did, but there was too much rattling around inside my head. Mine would be the first name mentioned at the following morning's staff meeting and my next assessment wasn't likely to go well, but I decided it had been worth it.

A short-term fix, I'm well aware of that, but it was what I needed.

TWELVE

There aren't too many secrets in this place — there are plenty of patients and staff members with big mouths — so I wasn't the least bit surprised that several of my fellow sectionees were keen to join me for breakfast and get the skinny on my escapade the previous evening. They all chipped in or had questions. I told them it was just a bit of weed, that it was no big deal and it's not like I'm the only person in here that's ever tried to smuggle drugs in, but I suppose anything that breaks up the monotony is exciting.

You'd have thought I was Pablo Escobar or whoever.

Lauren was smirking, like I'd made her day. 'Should have come to me and we could have sorted something out together.'

'Sorry.' I raised my arms and mock-bowed like I wasn't worthy. 'I'll know next time.'

'Fuck you,' she said.

'Should have used the old "prison wallet",' Ilias suggested.

'Stuck it up your arse. I don't reckon they'd have looked up there.'

I thanked him and said I'd bear that in mind as well.

'You reckon somebody snitched on you?' L-Plate asked.

'I didn't tell anyone,' I said. 'Because I'm not stupid.' If I had then someone would almost certainly have had a quiet word with Marcus or one of the others. Donna, because she was trying to help me. Ilias, because he thought it was funny. Lauren, because she's a bitch.

'They bump you back to Within Eyesight obs?' The Thing asked.

'If you're lucky,' L-Plate said.

'They haven't told me yet.' But they would, as soon as the morning staff meeting had finished. I wasn't massively worried, because even if they wouldn't be letting me outside again in a hurry, I knew I could be on basic hourly obs again quickly enough. I knew how to behave to get back into Dr Bakshi's good books, besides which there simply weren't enough staff around to keep an eye on everyone all the time.

'Careful who you talk to,' Tony said. 'I still reckon one of the nurses is the Thing. The Scottish one.'

Graham, who hadn't spoken up as yet, patted me on the shoulder. He whispered, 'Nice try, though,' then grabbed a plateful of porridge before setting off to mess with some cameras.

Lauren started singing 'Back on the Chain Gang.'

L-Plate and Ilias both asked if I could let them have my dealer's number.

Ten minutes later at the meds hatch, once Femi had handed my paper cup of pills across, I leaned close to her and asked, 'Have any drugs gone missing lately?'

'I don't understand.'

'From in there.' I nodded behind her. 'Any stuff unaccounted for?'

'Not as far as I know.' She was holding out the cup of water and smiling at the voluntary patient who was waiting in line behind me, but I didn't move.

'So, you would know?' I waited. 'All the staff would be told about it, right?'

'Why are you so interested in this?' Femi was starting to look concerned or uncomfortable, I couldn't be sure which.

'It's part of my investigation into Kevin's death,' I said.

She shook her head, still brandishing the water, then raised a hand, inviting the Informal behind me to step forward.

I turned and smiled at him. 'Almost done.'

'The police have already asked us these questions,' Femi said.

'So, what did you tell them?'

'I'm afraid we are not allowed to discuss such things with patients.'

'Maybe not normally.' I leaned closer. 'But somebody killed Kevin and drugs had something to do with it—'

'You need to step away now, Alice—'

'—and I'm going to find out how he got them.'

Behind me, the Informal muttered something as he stepped back to let Donna walk past. I turned and winked at him as she marched away down the corridor. I said, 'She's working off breakfast.'

'Take your pills and fuck off,' he said.

'There are other patients waiting.' Femi had raised her voice a little. 'Are you going to move?'

I turned back to her. 'That depends.'

'Do you want me to bring Marcus over here?'

For a moment I thought about asking her to do exactly that. I'd wondered all along if Marcus should be the one to question about the drugs in Kevin's room, before deciding I'd be more likely to get a straight answer out of Femi. Now I reckoned there was no point in getting the ward manager involved until I needed to.

I smiled and took the cup of water.

I swallowed my olanzapine then my sodium valproate, watched her tick my chart and said, 'Thanks for your help.'

That afternoon, I was in the music room with Big Gay Bob, chatting about this, that and – as always – the *other*, when it all kicked off in the 136 Suite.

'I shagged a policewoman once,' Bob said.

'Yeah?'

'In the back of a police car.'

'Nice. Did she put the blue light on?'

'I swear, I always thought women in uniform batted for the other team. No offence, but you know what I'm saying. Bang up for it she was though, the dirty mare.'

'Did she take down your particulars?'

As usual, Bob hadn't a clue that I was taking the mickey and he was grinning and saying something about his 'helmet' when our uplifting conversation was interrupted by the row out in the hall.

Screams and shouts from a voice we didn't recognise.

The 136 Suite is where all those brought in by the police (under Section 136 of the Mental Health Act, hence the imaginative name) are taken to be assessed. It's a 'place of safety' to which the police, having removed them from street/

pub/wherever, are obliged to take any individual deemed to be in immediate need of care and control.

Right then, it didn't seem like a particularly safe place for anyone.

I found out later on that the kid – he couldn't have been more than seventeen – had been picked up after a member of the public dialled 999, having spotted him dodging cars on the North Circular. God only knows what he was on or what had happened to make him so agitated, but nurses were running around, grim-faced or barking at one another, while the poor bastard was locked inside the suite, shouting and smashing his head against the glass.

Some shit about spiders . . .

For obvious reasons, the staff don't really appreciate having an audience when there's business like this going on, so Big Gay Bob and I had the good grace to hang back a bit. As did Ilias, L-Plate and everyone else who'd come out to have a nosy. Donna even stopped walking for a few minutes, which I'd never seen happen before.

Seriously, 'restrictive intervention' is not a part of the job that any of the staff enjoy, even if some of them are better suited to it than others. Nobody likes doing it, least of all completing the paperwork and taking part in the compulsory 'incident debrief' afterwards, but when the immediate safety of staff or the service-user is threatened and a de-escalation of the situation is required quickly, swift tranquillisation is usually the only option.

Basically, hold the bugger down and jack them full of sedatives.

I watched as Malaika tried to calm the kid down verbally, while George and Marcus discussed how best to approach and restrain him, Femi did the necessary on the computer and Debbie and Mia ran off to prepare the drugs they would need. A poky lorazepam and aripiprazole cocktail.

The rapid-tranq.

It was dead impressive.

They were a seriously well-organised team and, if it hadn't been for the screaming – I had to cover my ears – and the look of terror on that poor lad's face, it would almost have been a pleasure to watch.

It made me start to think, though.

'Come in handy,' Bob said. 'A couple of bottles of that tranquilliser stuff. You know, if you didn't want ladies to put up a fight.'

'What?'

He said something else after that, probably equally revolting, but I wasn't really listening to him. I was listening to the new arrival yelling and watching him smear drool on the glass and thinking that if, just for the sake of argument, it had been some kind of . . . performance, it was as good as I'd ever seen. I was putting it all together and – then, at least – it made perfect sense.

I began walking away just as George and Marcus steamed into the 136 like a two-man Tactical Support Unit, so I didn't see what happened after that. Must have gone OK though, because apparently the kid settled down and was discharged the following morning. I've no idea what happened to him after that. He might be getting therapy somewhere or he might be playing chicken with himself on a motorway somewhere else, but either way, he was the one that put the idea into my head.

Right then, though, while they were pumping a syringe full of benzos into his backside, I needed to get to my room as quickly as possible and make a call while it was still fresh in my mind.

'So, any news?'

'Bloody hell, Al, give me a chance.' Banksy's voice was low, like he didn't want to be overheard. 'I only saw you yesterday.'

'Quick and the dead, mate.'

'Far as I know they're still waiting for forensics.'

'Yeah, I mean there's no rush. It's only one less nutter, after all.'

'To be fair, I think there's a bit of a backlog, all right? Besides which I don't think they're hopeful it's going to be a lot of help.'

I knew what he meant. Like forensicating a hotel room. More prints and DNA than you can shake a swab at. In the case of Kevin's room that would certainly include all the staff and most of the patients.

I started to tell him the real reason for the call, told him what I'd just seen.

'The Informals come in and go out,' I said.

'Right.'

'Same with anyone who gets brought in on a 136.'

'So . . . ?' Banksy did not sound convinced.

'So, let's say Kevin had got himself involved with some nasty drug dealers.'

'They're all nasty,' Banksy said.

'Properly nasty, yeah? Say Kevin's in over his head. Say he's been paid up front for something he doesn't deliver, or maybe he decides he wants to get out of it but he knows too much. It's the perfect way to get rid of him.'

There was silence for a bit. I could hear squad-room noises in the background, phones and chit-chat. I felt like someone who'd lost a child and then seen a woman out with her new baby. OK, that's putting it a bit strong, maybe, but you know what I'm saying.

'Go on then,' Banksy said.

'Someone comes in, pretending to be a voluntary patient, an Informal, yeah? It wouldn't take them long to figure out the situation with the cameras in here, so they wait until Graham shuts the right one down, do what they've come for, then discharge themselves as soon as.'

'That simple?'

'Yeah, that simple. Listen, I bet I could easily find out who left the day Kevin was killed, or the morning after.'

Another silence. Then, 'It's a bit far-fetched, Al.'

'You haven't even thought about it.'

'I *am* thinking about it. You're telling me that some gangsters hired a hit-man to pretend to be mad. They don't normally go for anything that complicated. They'd just threaten his family or burn his house down.'

'Yeah, but doing it this way wouldn't draw attention, would it?'

'Also, aren't the staff in there trained to know if someone's putting it on?'

'They get things wrong sometimes.'

'Did they get it wrong with you?'

Now I was the one saying nothing for a bit. 'They get things wrong.'

I listened to that gorgeous office chatter for another few seconds. I pressed the phone hard to my ear, but I couldn't make out what was being said or hear any voices I recognised.

'It's a bit of a stretch,' Banksy said. 'You must see that, and, like I said the other day, I'm really not sure this is doing you any good, so—'

'If Kevin was getting the drugs from in here, he had to be getting them out somehow. You've got to admit that much, right?'

Banksy sighed. 'Makes sense, I suppose.'

'So I think you should talk to Seddon,' I said. 'Tell him he needs to check out all Kevin's visitors.'

'I'm sure they're already doing that, Al.'

'We should make sure.'

'They're all good officers.'

'*I* was a good officer.'

Banksy said nothing.

'I was *really* good,' I said. 'Point is, everyone thinks they're a good officer until they're washing the blood off.'

THIRTEEN

This Is What I Believed.

Part One ... because frankly there's quite a lot to get through and I can't really bring myself to think about it for too long. I should tell you that some of it might seem a bit all over the place, but that's only because *I* was all over the place, and I can't swear that I've got what happened when exactly right. I've talked to the various witnesses (Mum and Dad, Sophie, Andy, etc.) to corroborate statements where I could and tried to put together a timeline.

Like every case I ever worked on the Job, except that I was the major suspect.

The PTSD didn't kick in straight away. I mean, I didn't walk out of that flat in Mile End barking like a dog. I got cleaned up and gave my statement. I went home and just curled up, then cried on Sophie's shoulder for a couple of days. But I couldn't sleep and then I started having panic attacks. I swear, these days, it's like every Tom, Dick or

Harry has them, needs a nice cup of tea and a biscuit now and again, but I knew pretty bloody quickly that no amount of breathing into a paper bag was going to sort me out.

Chills or nausea or thinking I was going to shit myself.

Pins and needles, *everywhere*.

Sweating like a rapist and feeling like I was going to choke.

My doctor put me on Prozac fast enough (popping my SSRI cherry), and my boss and his boss were both great about it. *You've been through a terrible ordeal, Al. Take some time* – paid sick-leave, yay! – *and let's see if you're ready to come back to work in a few weeks.*

A few weeks became a few more, but I don't think they really understood how bad things had become until I was actually needed again, when the arsehole who'd carved up Johnno was about to go on trial.

See, I didn't *mind* taking the tablets, but it wasn't particularly enjoyable, and pretty quickly I discovered that a bottle of red wine and a few spliffs every night could do the job equally well. So, on top of some prodigious pill-popping, I started bulk-buying at Oddbins and filling daily prescriptions with Billy. Twice-daily, sometimes. And I felt absolutely great, to be honest; no point pretending I didn't. The panic and the piss-myself terror were all but gone, and I was calm for a while, at least. Until I found out what getting out of your head really means.

So, the trial . . .

I was the prosecution's star witness, of course, but that soon changed when a couple of the DCs working the case came round to go through my forthcoming appearance in court. All very straightforward, and not even official because they weren't allowed to 'coach' any witnesses and were just there to talk about a couple of the questions the defence might throw at me. Sod's law – I was midway through a bit of a bender when they turned up, so it only took a few minutes with them before 'forthcoming' became 'not-a-cat-in-hell's-chance'. Never mind take the stand, I was hardly in a fit state *to* stand, so it was quickly decided I would not be giving evidence at all.

I was gutted, because I'd wanted to be there for Johnno.

I knew both those DCs, but the way they stared while I ranted at them, it was like they didn't know *me* at all.

It didn't much matter in the end, which is the only good part, because the toe-rag got was what coming to him anyway. They had my original statement, a Stanley knife with his prints on, and the bloodstained clothes which the moron had not thought to get rid of.

Next thing, there's a lot of official coming and going with Police Federation reps and the like. Everyone was 'shocked and disappointed' but it was not the behaviour expected of a Met officer – whatever said officer had been through – and, being permanently unfit to return to duty, I hadn't left the powers that be with much choice. The extended paid leave became 'medical retirement', and even though they were nice enough not to nick me for possession they made it clear they were actually doing me a favour and maybe I could do them one by not making a fuss about it.

Handing over my warrant card nice and quietly.

Fair enough back then, I suppose, and being 'medically retired' means I get a small pension which comes in useful, but it still pisses me off looking back at it now. The lack of sympathy or understanding. Yeah, I had a problem with drink and was doing way too much skunk on top of all the pills. As if all that wasn't enough – and it was more than enough for most of my so-called friends – it was around this time that I started to believe some of the things that led me, eventually, to the tender mercies of the Fleet Ward, by way of the less-than-tender process of being sectioned.

Maybe we should leave all that fun stuff until next time.

I should mention, though, that I'd also turned into a bit of a slapper. Up to that point – before Johnno died, I mean – I'd had a couple of longish relationships and even been engaged at one time, but afterwards, once the booze and the weed had begun to work their magic, I decided to really let rip and throw casual sex into the mix.

Why not, right?

There were a lot of wild nights spent in clubs and bars and a lot of miserable mornings spent telling myself I would never do it again after waking up with one loser or another. You know what Coyote Syndrome is, right? When you wake up curled around some stranger and you'd rather chew your own arm off than move it and risk waking them up. I was very familiar with that. I think I fell for the 'Hello ladies' line more than once myself back then, though I was usually the one looking for a quick bunk-up.

Worst part is, I can't remember any of the sex.

Not a single moment.

It was probably all terrible, but still . . .

All very sordid and, believe it or not, it's the aspect of my somewhat chequered past I'm least proud of. That's probably because of where one such encounter led. Because of who it led to.

I can't even remember where I met Andy, but the morning after wasn't quite as terrible as usual and he stuck around until the afternoon. I told him a bit about myself, but not all of it. He told me about his boring job in an office and I remember feeling quite jealous. We saw each other a few times after that and suddenly we were going out. Restaurants and the pictures and stupid cards on Valentine's Day.

All fine and dandy.

It's how things are supposed to be, isn't it?

He knew exactly what he was getting into, I want to stress that right now. He knew. How could he not, for God's sake, the state of me back then?

When he suggested that I move into his flat, I wasn't convinced it was a good idea, but Sophie certainly was. I must have been a total nightmare to live with, so I don't blame her for encouraging me.

'New start,' she said.

Looking back now, it's quite funny, because I can see how desperate she was.

'Could be just what you need, Al . . .'

It wasn't, and you already know that things with not-as-nice-as-I-thought-he-was Andy went tits-up very quickly – before I'd taken all my stuff out of the boxes, more or less – but there's all manner of fun and games you don't know about yet, and I think I'll save the more lurid details for the next instalment.

The cutting and the masks and the hospital.

The plot to murder me.

You really don't want to miss that. Watch this space.

FOURTEEN

Half an hour or so after I'd talked to Banksy, Marcus knocked on my door. I shouted 'fuck off', which is my standard reaction, to be fair, but I was angry that Banksy had rubbished my take voluntary idea. I still thought it was something worth following up.

Marcus knocked again and this time he didn't wait for an answer. The bedroom doors can be locked and we've all got our own keys, but most people don't bother because we're in and out all day and the staff have to come in so often for checks. We've each got a small cupboard inside our room with a padlock. That's useful for any valuables, because sometimes phones or iPods can go walkabout, but the doors themselves tend to stay unlocked.

Marcus walked in and sat down on the end of the bed, like we were best mates. 'Back to WEO,' he said.

Within Eyesight Observation. No big surprise, but it didn't do much for my mood. It's exactly like it sounds and would mean a nurse keeping an eye on me twenty-four hours a day. Watching me eat and following me into the toilet. Even at night, there'd be someone sitting outside my half-open bedroom door.

'Fine,' I said. 'Whatever.'

He didn't seem in any hurry to leave, just sat there fiddling with his ID, dangling from its ever-so-cheerful rainbow-coloured lanyard. 'It's a shame, that's all,' he said, eventually. 'You'd been doing really well.'

'Not well enough to be sent home.'

'*Well*, all the same. Better.'

He was trying to be kind, I can see that now. His voice, as always, was low and dripping with concern. That didn't stop me wanting to upset him and make the rest of his day as awful as mine was going to be. 'Maybe I'm just messing you all about and behaving the way you want me to,' I said. 'Saying all the right things.' I tapped the side of my head. 'Maybe in here I'm still massively fucked.'

'If that is the case, the only one you're making a fool of is you,' he said. 'It's your weekly assessment the day after tomorrow, so let's see what happens.'

'I know exactly what's going to happen,' I said. 'Well, I know what's not going to happen.'

'Do you not think we *want* you to go home?'

He looked like he genuinely meant it but, staring at him, I found myself thinking about what Tony had said about a member of staff being the Thing, and even though the whole idea is just about the maddest thing I've ever heard I sat there for half a minute trying to imagine what it would be like if it was actually true.

'We want all the patients to go home,' he said.

96

I tried to manufacture a smile. 'Well, whether I'm massively fucked or not, and I'm not saying one way or the other, I mean it's your job to work that out—'

'Not true,' he said quickly. 'Perhaps that is Dr Bakshi's job, or part of it anyway, but the rest of us are here to keep you safe.'

'Either way . . . I might be massively fucked, but you're the one that *looks* like you are.' I leaned close and studied his face. 'You look knackered.'

He laughed, gently. 'Yes, I am very tired. We all are.'

'You need to pace yourself, mate. It's not even Wednesday lunchtime yet.'

'We don't have the luxury of pacing ourselves,' he said. 'On top of which Malaika is off sick today.'

I hadn't noticed she wasn't around.

'The agency have not sent a replacement.'

'Never enough dosh,' I said.

He nodded. 'Governments have short memories.'

'Yeah, I hear what you're saying.' It wasn't very long ago that Marcus and the hundreds of thousands like him were heroes. The saviours of a nation. I'd been one of those standing outside my flat, clapping in the street.

'It was never applause we needed.' Marcus stood up. 'It was money and the proper equipment. Four nurses died on this unit.'

'Yeah,' I said. 'Public funding is one thing that's always been massively fucked. Same in the Met.'

He stopped at the door. 'That's another thing.'

'What?'

'This is what tells me that you still have a fair way to go before you *are* well. You talking about the police.' He was

97

playing with his stupid ID card again. 'Like you are still working for them.'

'OK, now you really *can* fuck off,' I said.

He didn't. 'Why were you asking Femi those questions?'

'I don't know what you're on about.'

'Missing drugs.'

'You've got no idea how crime is actually solved, have you?' I was kneeling up on the bed now, my voice a good deal louder than his and both fists clutching the duvet. 'You probably think it's all about CCTV and mobile phones and all that technical crap, don't you? The truth is, doesn't matter how much of that stuff you've got, crime actually gets solved because human beings like me ask questions.' I took a few deep breaths. 'One of your patients was murdered, I'm not sure if you're aware of that.'

'What happened to Mr Connolly was truly horrible,' he said. 'But I still have patients like you to take care of and keep safe.' He took hold of his badge again, held it up like I'd never seen it before. 'That is my job.'

'Right, and I don't need you to tell me how to do *my* job, fair enough?'

'It's not your job, Alice.'

I was still screaming when he closed the door.

After that I tossed my duvet and pillows around for a while, heaved the mattress on to the floor exactly as George and Marcus had done the night before and turned the bed over. Then once I was out of breath and had put everything back together again, I lay down until I was feeling a little less like putting my fist through a window.

I needed to get my act together, because there was lots to do.

I would start getting into this properly the next day.

There were plenty of people to talk to and I had no short-age of questions to ask.

FIFTEEN

I woke up Thursday feeling jumpy and knowing that if anyone so much as said good morning there was every chance I would do them serious damage. All I wanted was to scratch and kick at something or someone. I don't know if they'd upped my dosages without telling me, but half an hour after I'd taken my morning meds – fighting the urge to fly across the counter at Femi – things had swung much too far the other way and just walking to the toilet and back felt like wading through treacle.

When Donna walked past it was like she was sprinting.

I knew that the morning was a washout. I was no use to anyone, up and down like a yo-yo, so I went back to bed.

All being well, I'd get stuck into the interviews come the afternoon.

That's just the way it goes sometimes.

A bit later, before I had a chance to talk to anyone, Jamilah left.

It's not like there's a fanfare when it happens or anyone

makes an official announcement, so most of the time people just go home or get sent somewhere else without you even knowing. They're just ... not there any more. But a few people were talking about it when I got up again so, when the woman of the moment finally appeared in the corridor with her wheelie suitcase, me and a couple of the others were standing around to watch her go.

It wouldn't be doing my investigation any favours, of course. It was one less person to talk to, one less witness who'd been on the ward when Kevin was killed, but the Foot Woman had never been high up on my list of suspects. I just couldn't see her sneaking into Kevin's room, giving his feet a quick rub then popping a pillow over his face. Like I said, it wouldn't have taken much, but she was just too ... wispy. I doubt she'd have been able to strangle a mouse.

When she was at the airlock, shaking hands with the nurses, we all took our shoes off and waggled our feet at her. It was Lucy's idea. Jamilah smiled and nodded, but I don't think she got the joke.

'I give it two weeks,' Ilias said. 'Two weeks and she'll be back.'

I went to the toilet and had a little cry after Jamilah left.

For me though, not for her.

Yeah, it would have been nice to commandeer the empty MDR and use that as a makeshift interview room like Seddon had done, but with nowhere else even remotely suitable, I had to think on my feet a bit. Use whatever opportunities presented themselves. Also, now the staff were starting to get on my case, I didn't want to make too much of a song and dance about it anyway.

I needed to do things quietly, to be subtle.

Neither of which I'm good at.

After lunch, I saw that The Thing, the Walker and Big Gay Bob were still sitting in the dining room, so I joined them. Obviously one of the nurses – Mia, as it happened – joined me.

I sat and listened for a few minutes. Subtle . . .

'How long's that corridor out there?' Tony asked Donna.

Donna shook her head.

'Whatever it is, I reckon you must walk miles every day, right? You must be dead fit.'

Donna lifted her T-shirt and pinched at her belly, struggling to squeeze as much as a millimetre of fat between her fingers and thumbs. 'Need to get this off,' she said, looking away. 'It's disgusting.'

Tony grabbed a handful of his considerably larger belly. 'Maybe I should join you. I need to start getting in shape. The Thing's coming for me soon, I can feel it.'

While Tony started telling Donna all about his shadowy nemesis for the umpteenth time, I slid across to Bob and leaned close.

'How did it go with the police the other day?' I glanced across, but happily Mia, who was sitting a few tables away, wasn't paying the slightest attention.

Bob nodded slowly. 'The one taking the samples was a little cracker, I know that much. I gave her my phone number.'

'What did you tell them?'

'What do you mean?'

'Like, where were you when it happened?'

'When what happened?'

'When Kevin was killed.' I punched him on the arm. It was meant to be playful, but I saw him wince.

'I can't remember.' He winked at me. 'That's what I told them.'

'Right . . .'

'Because I was having a bad day and I really couldn't.'

'Meaning you can remember now?'

Now the nodding was a little more enthusiastic. 'Yeah, I was watching the telly.'

'OK.' He'd certainly been in there when I'd left to go the dining room. Several of them were – Donna, Lucy and Ilias for starters – and I already knew that's what they were likely to tell me.

'I wanted to change the channel,' Bob said, 'but Lauren wasn't having any of it. There was a film on the other side with Gwyneth Paltrow in it and she's the one who talks about her fanny all the time so I really wanted to watch it. Lauren said I couldn't, though. I remember sitting there, staring at the back of her stupid head and thinking how badly I wanted to punch it.'

'Did you hear anyone saying anything about Kevin? Anything bad, I mean . . . before it happened?'

Bob shrugged. 'There's always somebody falling out with someone, isn't there? I know Lauren didn't like him very much.'

'Did she say why?'

'He just got on her nerves, I think.' He lowered his voice. 'They were arguing by the airlock one time and I heard her call him a two-faced little ponce . . . something like that. Mind you, everyone gets on Lauren's nerves, don't they?'

I saw Tony get up to fetch a glass of water from the jug at the serving hatch. I stood up and went across to get one myself.

'Funny sort of time, isn't it? A strange atmosphere, don't you reckon?'

'Same old, same old,' Tony said.

'Yeah, but now, I mean. After what happened to Kevin.'

He downed half a glassful, then stared at me. 'I suppose.'

'You must be feeling a bit bad, though.'

'Must I?'

'After that fight and everything. I mean, did you and him get the chance to make up before . . . '

'That ruck wasn't my fault,' he said. 'The police were giving me grief about this the other day and I told them, it was nothing to do with me.'

'Certainly looked like it from where I was standing.'

'That's bollocks. It had already kicked off when I got there. I was trying to break it up and someone threw a punch . . . can't even remember who it was, now . . . I was just defending myself.'

He was starting to get a bit worked up, so I checked to see if Mia was watching, but she was deep in some conversation with George.

'I'm not going to stand there and let myself get smacked, am I?'

'Right,' I said. It's hard to take anything seriously, coming from a bloke who believes a demonic entity can disguise itself as a postcard, but it certainly seemed as though Tony was telling the truth. I felt a twinge of guilt because of what I'd told Seddon a few days before. 'So, who did start it?'

'Not really sure.' Tony finished his water and examined the empty glass as though there might be something lurking at the bottom of it. 'Lucy told me she thought maybe Kevin and Shaun were having a row and it got out of hand.'

'Yeah?'

'Lovers' tiff or something.'

I'd check with Lucy. I'd never seen Kevin and Shaun exchange a cross word, so if that was what had started the big fight a few days before the murder it would be interesting to find out what the two of them had been arguing about.

'It was well funny, though.'

'What was?'

He jabbed a finger into my shoulder. '*You*. Standing on that chair and making a big speech.'

Suddenly I didn't feel quite so guilty any more. I had half a mind to get on the phone to Seddon, tell him I had more information and drop Tony even further in it. Tell Seddon he'd confessed or something.

'Laying down the law,' Tony said.

Because I could, couldn't I?

If I felt like it, I could say anything about any of them.

They'd deny it, but that didn't matter. Most people in here are too drugged up to remember what they've told anyone half the time, never mind what they might have done. Most of them don't even think they should *be* here, for Christ's sake.

Now Tony was laughing, a deep *hurr hurr* that was annoying at the best of times, and right then made me want to smash my water glass into his face. He pointed and started to shout, so that everyone else in the room could share the joke. Bob started to laugh, too.

'I am a police officer . . . remember?' Tony was bellowing and trying to do my voice, high-pitched and stupid. 'I am a *police* officer!'

Now I could see that Mia, along with everyone else, *was* looking. I decided that I'd got about as much information out

105

of Tony as I was likely to get and headed quickly to the door. Donna was already on her way out, keen to put in some hard yards, so I followed her out into the corridor, fell into step next to her and began to walk.

SIXTEEN

'What was all that about?' Donna asked.

I still felt angry about it and the speed-walking wasn't helping to ease the tension. 'Just Tony taking the piss,' I said.

'Want me to mess with him a bit? Tell him I'm the Thing?'

'No, you're all right,' I said.

We had already walked the length of the corridor three times as far as the MDR, turned and walked back again.

'I think it's good that you're trying to find out what happened,' Donna said.

'It's important,' I said.

'Police are obviously doing sod all.'

I don't know why I suddenly felt the need to defend a service that had seen fit to kick me out on my arse. Something deep-seated that hadn't gone away in spite of everything, I suppose. I couldn't think of a time when I hadn't wanted to be a police officer. I still can't.

I said, 'I'm sure they're doing everything they can. It takes time to build a case, to put a list of likely suspects together and interview them, to process forensic evidence.'

'Like on *CSI*?'

I bit my tongue. That stupid show is the bane of a detective's life, making shit up and presenting it as gospel. I'd seen any number of trials go down the toilet because jurors thought they knew things once they'd seen them on the TV. Because they were too stupid to know the difference between forensic fact and fiction.

'They'll be able to find out exactly who'd been in Kevin's room, won't they?' Donna nodded.

'Not necessarily.'

'Because these days you just need a sample of the air.'

Like I said . . .

We walked past the examination rooms again, the occupational therapy room and the meds hatch. Again. Mia, who was clearly taking her WEO duties seriously but had drawn the line at following the pair of us up and down like an idiot, had staked out an observation post in the doorway of the nurses' station. We walked past the music room and the 136 Suite, turned right at the dining room and headed for the airlock.

Lauren stuck two fingers up from the toilet doorway.

Ilias said, 'Idiots,' as we marched past him.

'Did you hear anything about Kevin and Shaun having an argument?'

Donna shook her head.

'You know, the big fight?'

She shook her head again, eyes wide and fixed. With these athletes it's all about focus. 'What about drugs?' I asked. 'You know anything about drugs going missing?' She nodded as we turned at the airlock and began another lap. I quickened my pace to keep up with her. 'What?'

'*My* drugs,' she said. 'They go missing all the time.'

'That's not what I—'

'Well, they get taken at any rate. Soon as I get them brought in, they confiscate them. My Hydroxycut and my caffeine pills. That bitch Debbie even took my laxatives, for pity's sake. They take everything I really need off me, then give me anti-depressants and Kwells to stop me drooling, like they know what's best. *I* know what I need, Al, because it's my body.' She glanced at me and shook her head, tears in her eyes. 'My *laxatives* . . .'

As we walked past the nurses' station again, I saw Mia writing something down. Behind her, Marcus pointed at me and something snapped. I felt it, you know? Like a tiny bomb going off inside.

I turned to Donna. 'Why do you *do* this?'

Donna swallowed and began walking even faster.

'Seriously, what is the point? Marching up and down this corridor like a clockwork lunatic, trying to lose the weight you haven't put on because you don't eat anything. Literally, nothing. Staring at yourself in the mirror all the time and thinking you look fat, which is what ordinary idiots like me do because most of us probably are . . . while you actually look like a jogger in fucking Auschwitz or something. I mean, seriously. All that rubbish you were coming out with the other night about Kevin killing himself. You don't even see the irony of that, do you . . . ?'

I stopped to get my breath back. Donna had moved ahead of me anyway now and I could hear her crying. Ilias was watching me, sitting backwards on a chair outside the 136. He said, 'You tell her. Skinny bitch.'

Suddenly I felt terrible for upsetting Donna and I knew I needed to knock it on the head for a bit.

Have some time to think.

My meds were beginning to wear off. I'd become well used to the sensation, like bathwater draining away, and to tell you the truth I didn't know if that was a good thing or not. Was I better at all this, at doing my job, with or without the anti-psychotics and the Selective Serotonin Reuptake Inhibitors, whatever the hell they are? I wasn't sure what 'clear-headed' even meant any more. I stood in the corridor staring at the sickly-yellow wall, panting like some knackered old dog and wondering what Johnno would think about it.

Knowing exactly what he would say.

Take a fucking break . . .

I could see that, as per usual, Tony was standing at the exit with his bags packed, as I walked across to the meds hatch. There was, equally predictably, one person ahead of me, waiting for his mid-afternoon prescription. That was fine though, because the Waiter was exactly the person I was looking for.

'Sounds like you had fun with those cameras,' I said. 'Last Saturday, after dinner.'

Graham spoke without turning round because he did not want to miss that hatch opening. He was staring at it all the way through our conversation. 'I always have fun.'

'Just random, is it?'

'What's that mean . . . random?'

'Which camera you shut down. Just an accident, was it, that on Saturday night it happened to be the camera covering the men's corridor? Kevin's room.'

'Yeah, an accident,' Graham said.

'You sure nobody suggested it? Nobody asked you if . . . maybe you fancied doing what you do to that particular camera?'

'I just picked that one.' He shuddered and shook his head. 'I didn't like the look of it.'

'Do people ever ask you?'

He took so long to answer that I wasn't sure he'd heard me. 'Sometimes.'

'Like when?'

Another long pause. Graham looked at his watch. He thrust his hands into his pockets, took them out again. 'Once someone asked me to put food on the camera in the music room because someone else had been playing the guitar and she didn't like it, so she wanted to go in there and smash it. Smash the guitar. Don't ask me who it was, though, because I'm never going to tell you her name.'

I didn't bother, because it wasn't important. Lauren, obviously . . .

'Did you tell the police about that?'

'Yes, I had to, didn't I?' He tapped at the hatch window. 'Someone obviously told them that sometimes I mess about with the cameras, because they asked me all sorts of questions about it. It wasn't very nice, actually. It was like they were accusing me of something.'

'That must have been upsetting,' I said.

'Are *you* accusing me of something?'

'Absolutely not,' I said.

He tapped at the hatch again. 'Good, because I wouldn't like that.'

The window opened to reveal George, who said, 'Hello, Graham. Fancy seeing you here.'

Graham laughed and leaned on the counter, so I knew the interview was finished. He took his meds like a child collecting a prize. He said, 'Thank you, George,' and marched away without looking at me.

I stepped forward to take mine, then moved quickly away.

'No, thank *you*,' George said.

L-Plate was next in line, so I lingered while she picked up her pills. Just your basic anti-depressants and stuff to combat the withdrawal. Methadone or whatever. I knew that, because she had an injection once a month for the heebie-jeebies.

I can't stand needles, so I've always opted for the tablets. Sometimes, if I'm lucky, I'll get oral dispersibles, which are basically just these wafer-thin squares that melt on your tongue. Yum!

I collared her as soon as she stepped away from the hatch.

She raised her hands. 'Too close . . .'

'Sorry, L.' I raised my own hands in apology and moved back a little. 'I just wanted to ask you . . . I heard that you know what started the big fight a couple of days before Kevin was killed.'

'Heard from who?'

'It doesn't matter, honestly. Something about a row between Kevin and Shaun?'

'Oh, that, yeah.' Lucy leaned back against a wall and began doing weird stretches, like she was practising some kind of psych-ward t'ai chi. She was wearing a Calvin Klein T-shirt and tracksuit bottoms same as me, only I was damn sure she hadn't bought her trackies at JD Sports. 'Well, to be honest I didn't hear very much, babe. They were shouting at each other after the last occupational therapy session. I was only in there because I wasn't very happy with what I'd painted that day and I was trying to tidy it up a bit.'

'What were they arguing about?'

'I wasn't trying to eavesdrop or anything. I mean I really wasn't, so I just caught snippets of it. There was something Shaun wanted Kevin to do and Kevin wasn't keen. Shaun was telling him he had to, that he was being stupid . . . that was about it.'

'So that was what the fight was all about?'

'Who knows what started *that*,' Lucy said. She stopped the stupid stretching and leaned as close to me as I ever saw her get to anyone. 'You think it had something to do with why Kevin was murdered? A grudge or whatever?'

'I'm trying to piece it together,' I said.

She put her arms up, stretching her fingers towards the ceiling tiles, then cocked her head to whisper, '*I'd* heard it was a drugs thing, and I have to say that wouldn't surprise me. Obviously, you know my history, right? Well, the fact is, one does learn to recognise it in other people.'

I knew what she meant. Like coppers knowing when someone was iffy.

'I suppose it's kind of a junkie gaydar.' Lucy laughed, a silly, high giggle. 'I'm just saying, I always thought drugs were a part of Kevin's life in one way or another.'

I didn't tell her that she was bang on the money. As far as I knew, I was still the only person on the ward – the only patient, at any rate – who knew about the drugs discovered in Kevin's room, and I certainly wasn't going to tell her about it. A detective learns early on that it's not clever to furnish a witness with any information that may prejudice the statement they're about to give you.

Lucy resumed her exercises, tossing back her head and rolling her hips around. 'Is that any help to you, babe?'

I hadn't got the first idea, besides which I'd noticed Mia wandering across from the nurses' station. She stopped a few feet away from us and smiled, just to let me know that she knew exactly what I was up to, had been up to most of the day.

As it happened, at that moment I was perfectly happy to stop for a while.

I'm still not sure if it was some kind of early comedown, but I felt like a sodden blanket had been thrown across me. It wasn't even two o'clock, but I was wiped out suddenly; bone-tired, as though, when I'd been talking to Donna, I'd walked a hundred times further than I did.

I can see *now* that it was mental – isn't everything? – because I was doing it all. Normally, on a job like this one, I'd have been working as part of a good-sized team. Maybe talking to a single witness, collating statements or putting together a report on suspicious mobile activity, while Johnno, Banksy and the rest of the squad were busy doing other stuff. I'd have one thing to concentrate on, one area of the investigation to put all my energy into, but now everything was down to me and I was finding it all a bit stressful to say the least.

I trudged back towards the women's corridor thinking about the three people I still wanted to talk to.

The Grand Master, the Sheep, the Singer.

It would have to wait, though, because right then I was finding it hard enough to put one foot in front of the other.

I all but fell into my room and slept for the best part of eight hours.

SEVENTEEN

You probably won't be amazed to discover that, once dinner and after-dinner meds are out of the way, the most popular recreational activity in this place of an evening is settling down in front of the idiot box, and not just because of the appropriate nickname. Actually, I don't think that anyone in here is an idiot, but you know what I mean. A lot of people are probably quite smart, unlike the TV itself, but even though that's not got the biggest screen in the world or the widest selection of channels, it's where most of the patients end up in the hours before bedtime.

Watching what's on, or arguing about what's on, or ignoring what's on but still there anyway.

Make no mistake, there *is* a variety of other pastimes and pursuits catered for on Fleet Ward. Aside from looking out of the window at the breathtaking views of the A41 there are newspapers every day and, for readers, a decent selection of books in the OT room (if you like thrillers or chick-lit, which I do). There's a few jigsaws (pieces gone missing or been eaten). There's Jenga and Cluedo and Scrabble and of course, if you prefer a solo hobby, there's always frantic masturbation, which, judging by the faces of the housekeeping team when they're changing the beds every day, remains a perennial favourite. Now I think about it, leisure-wise, there's often a degree of multi-tasking, and I say that with confidence, because I once saw someone masturbating *while* they were playing Scrabble.

But it's the telly that tends to unite everyone in here, even if they rarely get a say in what they get to watch, and it strikes me that the makers of *Gogglebox* are seriously missing a trick.

. . . and in a hospital in north London, Ilias, Donna and Bob have settled down to watch Bake Off. *It's pastry week and the contestants are . . . oh God, no . . . Donna is running round and round the sofa and Ilias appears to be taking his pants off . . .*

I woke feeling a damn sight better, but also annoyed at having slept through dinner. I made short work of some crisps and a box of Jaffa Cakes that Banksy had brought in because, aside from being properly ravenous, I didn't fancy taking my last lot of meds on an empty stomach. Having sweet-talked Femi – who had just shut up shop – into handing them over after hours, I wandered into the TV room, well up for it.

Aside from Donna, who someone told me later had gone to bed early because she was upset about something, pretty much everyone was in there, which was helpful.

Most important, Ilias, Lauren and Shaun were in there.

There are two fake leather sofas at the front and a variety of chairs scattered around behind. A few armchairs that almost certainly have things living in them and plenty of the hard blue ones that are knocking around all over the ward. They're usually lined up around the walls in here, but as soon as the TV gets switched on people drag them into the middle of the room to get a better view. There's even a few low tables dotted about so people can keep their tea or nuts or Fanta within easy reach.

It's nice enough, as it goes, long as you don't mind the farting.

Everyone has their spot, of course, and I've seen it kick off more than once if a favourite perching position is snaffled. Ilias likes to sit at the back, from where he can provide a foul-mouthed commentary if he's in the mood, or occasionally throw things. Shaun prefers a chair near the door and Lauren, as always, was in prime position on a sofa at the front, her fat fist wrapped around the remote control as though it were a sceptre. Or a sock full of snooker balls.

I pulled one of the empty chairs across and sat down next to Ilias.

'What's on?'

'It's all shit,' Ilias said. He stared at me, suspicious. 'You weren't there for dinner.'

'I was asleep.'

He grunted, then cupped his hands round his mouth, like nobody would hear him shouting otherwise. 'Turn it over!'

Lauren stuck up a finger.

'Why do you care, if it's all shit?'

'It's the what-do-you-call-it ... the principle,' Ilias said. 'Why should that cow decide which shit we have to watch?'

We sat and watched for a couple of minutes. Some chefs on a road trip. It wasn't unenjoyable, as it happens.

'You've been here about as long as me,' I said.

'Longer.' He sounded proud of the fact, and said it again, keen to make sure I knew. 'I was here the night they brought you in.' He let out a low, phlegmy chuckle. 'Shouting about lights in the garden and funny music and all that.'

I ignored that, took a few seconds, and nodded. 'Makes sense, because you always know what's going on around this place. Who's getting off with who, who's got the hump about something, all that. You keep your ear to the ground.' I looked at his ear as I said it. Huge, and sprouting long black hairs like he was a hobbit.

Ilias sat back, smiling and humming with pleasure, delighted that someone had finally noticed his contribution. I took the chance to glance over at Malaika, who was running WEO/WAL interference for the evening. She was sitting in a corner, next to one of the less-than-realistic plastic ferns that are dotted around all over the place so that we don't lose our connection with the natural world.

She looked content enough, slowly turning the pages of *Take A Break*.

'So, bearing all that in mind, what's your take on what happened to Kevin?'

He folded his arms and thought about it. 'Kevin wasn't very happy.'

As insights went, considering where we were, it was hardly Hercule Poirot. I said, 'I don't think anyone's exactly thrilled, stuck in here.'

'I'm perfectly happy,' Ilias said. 'You have to have a positive attitude.'

'So why wasn't Kevin happy?'

'I think he felt trapped.'

119

'Did he say that?'

'He said . . . something. He couldn't get out because people would be upset. I can't really remember.'

'Was this anything to do with Shaun?' I was thinking about the argument the two of them were supposed to have had. Was Shaun the one Kevin felt trapped by?

'Shaun is also unhappy. Now, because of what happened to Kevin, but he was not happy before.'

'Why not?'

Ilias looked at me like I was an idiot. 'You need to ask Shaun.'

I intended to, but I was saving him until last. I told Ilias that maybe the two of us should play chess some time, then stood up and walked to the front of the room.

'Turn it over!' he shouted again.

There was an Informal I'd never spoken to sitting on the sofa next to Lauren, so I turned on the menace and told him to move, told him he was in my *fucking* spot. He swore at me a bit – ignoring the angry shushing from Lauren – then stood up, and from the corner of my eye I saw Malaika doing the same thing. 'It's fine.' I turned and smiled innocently at her. 'Thing is, I can't really see from back there . . .'

Malaika sat down and so did I.

Without taking her eyes off the screen, Lauren moved the remote control to the hand that was furthest away from me. She said, 'Don't even think about it.'

Getting anything at all out of Lauren was going to be a tough one, I'd always known that, but I'd thought about it. About the best way to come at her. I leaned across and started singing, quietly.

'It's so funny . . . that we don't talk any more.' I smiled, but she didn't react. 'Cliff Richard,' I said. 'His best one, if you ask me.'

She turned to me. 'Are you serious? What about "Congratulations"? What about "Wired for Sound"?' She shook her head, disgusted. 'You're a moron.'

'It's true though.' I turned back to the screen, like I didn't care one way or the other. 'We did use to talk.' It was certainly the case that, once upon a time, me and Lauren had exchanged words rather more often than we did now, even if most of the words had four letters in them.

I waited. The three chefs – one of them was Gordon Ramsay – were somewhere in the American south, arguing about the best way to roast a pig.

'What do you want to talk about?' Lauren asked.

I didn't see a lot of point in going round the houses. 'Why didn't you like Kevin?'

'Who says I didn't?'

'A "two-faced little ponce". That's what I heard you called him.'

'So?' She shrugged. 'Doesn't mean I killed him, does it?' She looked at me. 'That's what you're going round trying to find out, isn't it? Miss fucking Marple.'

Ugly as it was, Lauren had a decent head on her shoulders. She was the only one who'd really sussed out what I was up to. Or who let me know she'd sussed it, at any rate. It was my turn to shrug.

'Got any suspects, have you?'

'Bit early for that,' I said. 'It's just a question of gathering information at this stage.'

She said, 'Ooh,' like she was impressed. It might have been at one of the chefs, but I'm pretty sure she was taking the piss.

'So, why was he a two-faced ponce?'

'Because he always tried to come across as such an inno-cent . . . like he was a victim. Him and his boyfriend.' She flicked her head towards the door, where Shaun was sitting on his own. 'Love's young dream, over there. Well, we're all victims of something or other, mate, that's why we're here. So I for one wasn't having any of it.' She sniffed, hacked some-thing into her mouth and swallowed it. 'He was into all sorts.'

'Like what?'

She smiled and it wasn't a good look. 'They found stuff in his room.'

'What stuff?'

She smiled again. 'You think you're the only one in here that knows anything?'

'Who told you?'

'One of the nurses told me. I've been in here a while and they know I don't go around shooting my gob off like some. Can't say I was surprised, mind you. About the drugs, I mean.'

I said nothing.

'Dangerous game to get into, that one.'

I had every right to be annoyed that I wasn't the only one who knew about the drugs, who had inside information, but I'm still angry at myself for letting it show. Clenching my teeth, I said, 'Where were *you* when it happened, then? Did you go into the men's corridor that night?'

'Jesus, love, you're getting a bit desperate now, aren't you?'

'You're not going to answer, then?'

'No comment.' She was enjoying herself now. Like she was the one in the box seat. 'How's that suit you?'

I couldn't think of any other way to get the upper hand again, and before I knew it I was on my feet and moving to stand – very deliberately – between her and the TV screen. There were one or two jeers and the odd shout of complaint from fans of the three chefs, but I could see straight away that I'd got the reaction I wanted from Lauren.

'Move,' she said.

'Make me,' I said.

Malaika laid her magazine to one side and stood up. Debbie appeared in the doorway.

Lauren didn't hesitate. She heaved herself to her feet, and as soon as she'd begun lumbering towards me I ducked quickly past her, grabbed the remote that she'd left behind on the sofa and changed the channel.

'You're dead,' she said.

I made full use of the few seconds I had before Malaika or Lauren could get to me, acknowledging the cheers and the standing ovation from Ilias. It was lovely. I raised both my arms like I'd won something, then lobbed the remote at Lauren before pushing my way through the chairs and settling down nice and quietly next to Shaun.

I waited ten minutes or so, until it had all died down.

Until Debbie had gone back to the nurses' station and Malaika was sure things were calm again. Until the programme with the chefs had finished and Lauren had made a show of changing the channel, so that we could all enjoy *Celebrity Botched-up Bodies*.

'How you doing, mate?' I asked.

'OK, I suppose.' Shaun looked at the floor and began scratching furiously at his head, as though his hair was full of ants. He grunted with the effort. He was never the easiest person to talk to, but he'd gone even further into himself in the days since Kevin had died.

Grief, I presumed, but it could easily have been something else. I was still thinking about what Ilias had told me about a big argument, about Kevin feeling trapped. 'Come on, I know how you must be feeling. It's better if you let some of it out though, mate. What Dr Bakshi always says, right?'

Shaun nodded and scratched.

A woman on TV was showing off her horrendous pair of fake tits.

'The thing is, Shaun, the police have asked me to help them with their investigation. Like, an extra person on the inside kind of thing.'

'Yeah?' He gave me a thumbs-up. 'That's pretty cool, Al.'

'Yes, but it means I do need to ask you a few questions, if that's OK.'

He mumbled something that sounded to me like it was.

'Was everything good with you and Kevin?'

'Good?'

'Before what happened to him, I mean?'

'It was OK.' He was mumbling and the looking at the floor wasn't helping, so I had to lean in to hear what he was saying.

'Only I heard you'd had a row . . .'

Now he looked up, like he'd been tasered or something.

'It's fine,' I said. 'Nobody ever gets to say the things to someone who's died that they wish they'd said. Sometimes the last things you say to a loved one aren't . . . kind, but that's how it goes. Don't beat yourself up about it.' I blinked, remembering a voluntary who'd been here for a couple of days and had spent most of the time doing exactly that. Daft bastard had knocked himself unconscious several times.

Shaun was nodding again and his eyes were all over the place.

'Take your time,' I said.

'We were arguing about the drugs,' he said eventually. It was still quiet, but suddenly he was talking nineteen to the dozen. 'Fighting all the time. He was getting these drugs, a lot of them, and I told him it was stupid. I begged him and begged him ... I told him that he'd end up going to prison and he wouldn't be able to get well and I'd be stuck in here and we wouldn't see each other again—' He stopped suddenly and the hand that wasn't scratching went to his mouth.

'Where did he get the drugs from, Shaun?' I waited then leaned across to lay a hand on his arm and began to rub. 'Come on, you're doing ever so well. You're being dead brave, mate.' Rub, rub, rub. 'Where did he get them, Shaun?' Keep saying the subject's name to get their confidence. 'Was there someone bringing them in for him?'

Then I saw his eyes widen suddenly, shift and fix, and I turned to see what he was looking at.

'No, not Malaika ... it's not ... are you saying he got them from someone in here? Is that what you mean, Shaun? Did someone in here—'

I stopped because I saw what was coming. He looked terrified and that bloody finger was pressed to his chin.

'Am I going to die? Am I going to die? Am I going to die?'

I tried to shush him, but the volume just built and built until he knocked the chair over as he scrambled upright.

'Am I going to die? *Am* I?'

Malaika was on her way across and I was trying to hold on to him.

'No, of course you're not going—'

'AmIgoingtodieAmIgoingtodieAmIgoingtodie*AmIGoingToDie*?'

He was screaming it by now and other people in the room

were already on their feet, some of them getting visibly upset and moving away, pressing themselves back against the wall.

Above the cacophony I could hear Lauren yelling, 'Will someone shut that little twat up?'

Having asked me to step away, Malaika was already doing her best, but for once her soft words of reassurance seemed only to be making it worse. I could see the genuine fear on her face, then the relief as Debbie came steaming in to take over.

'What's the matter, Shaun?' Debbie stood there, the spittle flying on to her face and neck as he asked and asked, screeched and pleaded. She closed her eyes and sighed. 'Yes,' she said, finally. 'Yes, I think you are. In fact I very much doubt you'll make it to bedtime.'

Shaun stopped immediately, froze as though he'd been slapped.

Then he dropped to the floor like he'd taken a bullet to the back of the head and began to convulse, thrashing and squealing as Malaika pressed her alarm and Marcus and George rushed in to clear the room.

EIGHTEEN

This Is What I Believed.

Part Two . . . and I'm not going to waste my time or yours, so I can tell you straight off that it began with the lights at the end of the garden. Dim lights I could see pulsing through the trees from my bedroom window. I'd spotted them a few times when I was living with Sophie and she said it was just passing cars or lamps in the houses opposite us. She laughed and said maybe I should think about how much money I was putting in Billy's pocket every week but I wasn't convinced. I could sense it was something more than that, something bigger. I heard music, too, but not anything I could ever place; never a song I recognised or an instrument I could really identify. Just a funny kind of music I hadn't heard before.

I knew I was meant to hear it.

It felt like someone was watching me.

At Andy's place it got worse very quickly, late at night usually, and he said much the same thing as Sophie had said.

So, in the end, I stopped telling him and he probably thought I'd forgotten all about it, besides which everything got sort of taken over by the cutting for a while.

I'd come across it on the job a time or two before. Young girls, usually, with scars on their arms and legs like rungs on a ladder and because I didn't know any better then, I'd always asked myself why.

Stupid fucking question.

It was a . . . numbness, I suppose, an inability to feel much of anything. It was the agony of being ignored. I could always feel that blade against my arm, though (a Stanley knife quite often, oh the irony), and there was no way that even a dolt like Andy could ignore the bloodstained tissues on the bathroom floor. So, yeah, we spent a ton of time in A&E and there were lots of tears and plenty of shouting, but I thought my scars looked pretty cool, and however many days went by when I would say nothing or not leave the house, I never stopped being vigilant. I was always aware that there were people waiting out there in the dark that I couldn't see, keeping an eye on me.

Then I *did* start seeing them and that's when the whole business with the masks started.

In a nutshell (I might as well say it before you do – nut*case* more like), I'd see these people in the back of shot on television shows. In crowds or walking through a scene. They were all people I'd helped put away at one time or another. A bloke who'd killed his wife with a hammer, a woman who drowned both her kids in the bath, a rapist who attacked women outside underground stations. I'd just be sitting there on the sofa with Andy eating crisps and I'd spot them in the background, pretending to be extras or whatever they're called. Thing is,

I knew it wasn't actually *them*. It was people I didn't know wearing masks – people connected to the lights and the music and the watching – *disguised* as these criminals from my past.

Standing at the end of the bar in the Queen Vic.

Or in a restaurant in *MasterChef*.

Or on *Made in Chelsea*, sitting at a table in some coffee shop.

I spent a lot of time on the Internet, back then – OK, I still spend a lot of time on the Internet – but it was exactly what I needed, because I realised I was not alone and believe me, that was massive. There were plenty of other people in plenty of chat rooms, plenty of people in YouTube videos all saying *this is some scary shit* and talking about the anonymous organisations that orchestrated this kind of stuff. They were speaking out about ruthless and powerful groups that were capable of anything and were seriously well connected. Secret societies that watched and waited, then moved against anyone they perceived to be a threat.

That was the only thing I never really understood. The thing I spent every day trying to crack. I couldn't figure out *how* I was a threat to anyone, but I knew as surely as I've ever known anything that I *was*, and that one day soon they would come for me.

I could feel them getting closer.

The people behind those masks were looking straight at me, not remotely concerned that I saw them for what they were. Enjoying it, like: *This is a warning you can do nothing about.*

I was not going to be a pushover, though. I was not going to let myself become anyone's victim, because that was not what I'd been trained to do.

But . . . you have to know your enemy, right?

I suppose I should say that this is when things got . . . cranked up a bit.

One day I just got out of bed and had a smoke and realised that there had to be people in my life who were part of this. It became blindingly obvious and I felt very stupid that I hadn't worked it out before. How could these people who wanted to hurt me do it without recruiting those I was close to?

The ones who always looked so worried and told me to cut down on *this* and stop smoking *that* and, you know, maybe I should think about upping my meds.

Them.

I'd been such an idiot.

A few people laughed when I finally confronted them, which only made me angry and confirmed my suspicions. Sophie looked really sad, but I knew that was simply because I'd rumbled her. Because I'd seen through all of them. My mum just refused to engage however much I told her that I knew who she really was, and I remember the sound of my dad crying down the phone when I asked him how he could betray his child and how it had felt to sell his soul.

I was on it. I was one step ahead of the game.

I can still remember the look on Andy's face, the night it all kicked off. He was just sitting there watching football when I walked in and told him that we had to leave. He wasn't in a great mood anyway because Arsenal were a goal down, but he paused the TV and followed me into the kitchen, stood staring at me like an idiot as I gathered up all the knives.

Asked me what I was doing.

Told me to put the knives back and calm down.

'They're coming,' I told him. Why didn't he look bothered?

130

Why was he still standing there? 'They're coming to kill us right now and we have to get out.'

It only got physical when he tried to take the knives off me and the next thing we were scrabbling about on the kitchen floor with him talking about the police and me shouting that he was being stupid because we needed to protect ourselves.

I was trying to protect *him*, which was exceedingly fucking noble of me because I knew that he was involved in it, too.

I think I'm stronger than Andy is anyway and I was certainly feeling stronger than normal right then. The whole fight or flight thing, I suppose, and I was determined to do both. It was easy enough to push him away, and when he tried to take the knives off me again – pretty bloody carefully, mind you – I just reached for the half-empty wine bottle on the worktop because he hadn't left me a lot of choice.

I wasn't trying to hurt him.

But if I'd needed to, I wouldn't have thought twice.

There was a lot of red wine everywhere and a fair deal of blood, but I couldn't really think about it too much because obviously I had to search the rest of the house to try and find more weapons. I'd wrapped the knives in a tea towel so I could carry them, but while I was still rooting through the toolbox, Andy had managed to crawl back into the lounge, pick up his phone and ring for an ambulance. The ambulance came with a police car in tow, and after Andy had told the police that he didn't want to press charges – I should be grateful to him for that much, I suppose – we both got taken to the hospital.

One of the nurses in A&E recognised us.

Made some joke about a loyalty card.

So anyway, while Andy was being X-rayed and stitched

up, I was in another room being assessed by a couple of psychiatrists and junior something-or-others from the mental health team. I wasn't remotely taken in by them, of course, because I'd learned to recognise people who were part of the plot to kill me. I told them that all that business with the knives was just because I hadn't slept for two days, but of course they didn't listen, because they didn't want to. They just looked shifty and refused to answer my questions about the organisation I knew damn well they were involved with, but either way, several tedious hours later – with my dad on the phone crying (again) as next of kin – forms were being filled in, calls were being made, and several hours after that, I was in the back of another ambulance and I was on my way.

Here.

Home Fleet home.

As I've tried to explain, a few things may have got jumbled up, the odd detail or whatever, but no names have been changed to protect those who may or may not have been innocent. That's a fair account of how it all went down, and even if I can't always remember exactly *what* happened and when, I will never forget the way I was feeling at the time.

This is what I believed.

Believed. Past tense.

For the most part.

NINETEEN

There aren't too many reasons why I would ever be looking forward to my weekly assessment. I've sat through half a dozen of the bloody things already and the chat never changes much and the outcome's always the same. Basically, I shouldn't start packing just yet. That Friday though, after the conversations I'd been having over the previous couple of days, I was moderately excited by the prospect of sitting in a room with several people who could at least string a sentence together, none of whom was as mad as a box of frogs.

Whom. Listen to *me.*

All I'm saying, sometimes you miss just talking.

It was the usual suspects gathered in the MDR, though they'd moved aside the big desk that was used for staff meetings and tribunals. Or police interviews. Assessments were a bit more informal, a chat as much as anything, so that meant the tried-and-trusted circle of chairs, so beloved of junkies, alcoholics and other group therapy lovers everywhere.

Of people who need to *share*.

As always, once I'd sat down, they wasted a few minutes by formally introducing themselves for the record. There's a camera mounted up in the corner, of course – it's not one Graham's been able to get at yet, far as I know – so I'm guessing the sessions are actually filmed. Maybe, when I finally get out, they'll send me away with a copy of my greatest freakout moments as a souvenir, like leaving Chessington World of Adventures with a picture of yourself screaming on a rollercoaster. A memory of a happy time you can treasure for ever. Anyway . . . Bakshi was present and correct, obviously, and Marcus and Debbie, and a trainee psychiatrist who said her name was Sasha, then didn't speak again for the rest of the time I was in there. As always, I'd been told that I could have a friend or family member with me, but I decided against it. Aside from the fact that Mum and Dad were coming to visit later that day anyway, the last time they'd been there for an assessment, it hadn't gone well.

I'd told Marcus that I didn't need any help fucking things up.

When the staff had finished saying their names and telling people who already knew what they did . . . *what they did* . . . Bakshi looked at me expectantly.

'Oh, I'm Alice,' I said. 'I'm the basket case.'

Nobody who knew me reacted at all, but I did get a smile from *Sasha*.

Marcus kicked things off by running through the current dosages of the assorted medications I was on and confirming that said medications had been taken and appeared to be effective.

'That's all very good,' Bakshi said. She wrote something

down then looked at me across the top of some rather snazzy glasses. 'So, how are you feeling, Alice?'

'Tip-top,' I said. 'Ticking along nicely, ta.'

'I'm glad to hear it. I have to say I'm not quite so pleased at hearing about some of the things you've been discussing with the other patients.' She glanced at Marcus. 'With some of the staff, too.' She waited, but I just stared at her. 'Asking questions about this and that ... the tragic events of last Saturday evening ... as though you were still working for the police.'

I was getting seriously cheesed off with hearing the same thing and I really didn't want to talk about it. I told Bakshi as much. 'I will say this, though.' I sat forward. 'Aren't we always being encouraged to hang on to who we are? Stuff like that. How important it is to remember the people we were before we became ill? Just seems like you're saying one thing one day and then you're moving the goalposts or whatever.'

I noticed Sasha making a note, which pleased me enormously.

'Normally, that would be the case,' Bakshi said. 'But it can be dangerous if the thing you were doing before was what led to your illness in the first place. One of the earliest things you said to me was that it was what happened when you were working with the Met that started all this. The death of Detective Constable Johnston.' She was looking down at her notes. *My* notes. 'The PTSD and so on.'

I had no smart comeback.

I was thinking about Johnno and all that blood coming through my fingers.

It was time for Marcus to chime up. 'Alice, what Dr Bakshi is saying is that it's fine to think like someone who works with the police ... that's understandable, because you did so for many years ... but you need to stop acting like you still are.'

Bakshi nodded. Debbie nodded. Sasha nodded.

'People who retire from the Job are used for all sorts these days,' I said. 'Cold cases, all that.'

'Not when they have been *medically* retired.' Bakshi looked at her notes again. 'Not when they are deemed unfit to ever return to work.'

I was just about ready to smash something, but I didn't want them to know that. I wrapped my fingers around the edge of the chair and took a few long breaths until I felt calmer.

'Then there's the unfortunate incident with the cannabis.'

I smiled, because I couldn't help myself.

Cannabis, like she was saying *phonograph* or *wireless*.

'If we're going to move forward at all, I need your assurance that you will not try to use again. It's my professional opinion that the use of these drugs has been negatively impacting your mental health for a long time and will continue to do so.'

I tried to look shamefaced. I'm good at it, because I've had plenty of practice.

'Obviously while you're denied unescorted leave that can't happen, but if such restrictions were to be lifted ...'

'I won't do it again,' I said. *You won't* catch *me doing it again*. 'I promise.'

'Well, I'm going to have to take you at your word,' Bakshi said.

'I'm sure she means it,' Marcus said.

'But what is more problematic is yet another email from

Andrew Flanagan.' She raised a printed sheet. 'Another message left on his voicemail two nights ago.'

'Not by me it wasn't.'

She began to read the email out, but I had no intention of listening, so I closed my eyes and tried to think of something else. A happy place, or a babbling brook or whatever it is that shrinks and therapists are always wanking on about. I couldn't think of anything suitable quickly, so I just made the loudest noise I could inside my head and thought about Andy being on fire.

'Well?' Bakshi said, when she'd finished.

I kept my eyes closed. 'It's not true, obviously. It's . . . *fake news*. He's gaslighting me again, same as the last time. He hates me because I "attacked" him.' I used my fingers to put quotes around the word. 'Talking about *me* being violent when you should hear some of the things *he* liked to get up to in the bedroom. I can tell you all about it if you want. He's obviously still angry and he's vindictive and he's obsessed with doing anything he can to make sure I don't get out of here.' I thought about hitting him with that bottle; the *clunk* of it and the lovely vibration that ran up my arm. 'He's probably got brain damage.'

'His email is very reasonable,' Debbie said. 'He sounds concerned.'

Now I opened my eyes and stared hard at her. 'How's Shaun today?'

Debbie smiled, like she'd been expecting the question.

'Only I heard he's still not speaking.'

'You know very well that we're not allowed to discuss the health and welfare of other patients.'

'Alice . . .' Bakshi waited until she had my attention again.

'I'm sure you understand that in light of this, and the incident with the cannabis, I won't be approving any lifting of your section today.'

'Oh, really?' I stood up. 'I'm all packed and everything.'

'But I think we can put you back on to basic fifteen-minute observation and we'll see how things go from there.'

I said, 'Cheers,' but I was already on my way to the door. I opened it then turned to look at Sasha, the trainee. 'What does any of this actually train you for? No, really, I'd love to know.'

She opened her mouth and closed it again, looked to Bakshi for help.

I walked out, slamming the door behind me and shouting as I walked away down the corridor.

'Sitting in on a water-boarding session next week, are you?'

TWENTY

I was still in a fairly arsey mood after lunch and post-lunch meds. Trudging towards the music room, I noticed Tony sitting patiently by the airlock with his bags, as likely to be leaving any time soon – courtesy of his non-existent American relatives – as I was. He waved but I couldn't be bothered waving back.

Ilias was already in there playing Connect Four with himself and ignored me when I took off my headphones and asked if he wouldn't mind buggering off. I tried asking a bit more politely, but that didn't work either. Even five minutes of me bashing the living shit out of the bongos didn't shift him, but at least he wasn't showing too much inclination to chat, so I gave up and sat there.

Alone, thankfully, or as good as.

It was all stupidly unfair, because so much of what I'd told Bakshi and the rest of them about Andy was true. He *was* still angry, I knew he was, and he *is* obsessed with me. Oh, and I certainly wasn't making it up when I said he sometimes liked to get a bit rough in bed; the fact that I didn't actually mind is neither here nor there.

The sad truth is that, right then – six and a bit weeks without so much as a snog – I'd have settled for action of any sort. Rough or smooth, kinky or vanilla. There probably wasn't a bloke *in* there I hadn't thought about that way at some point. Tony, Marcus . . . even the hairy little bastard who was playing games with himself in the corner, God help me.

A cuddle would have been nicest of all, though.

Andy had been good at that, once upon a time.

There was a knock, and when I looked up my dad was standing with Femi outside the door. He smiled and started waving at me through the glass like I hadn't seen him (which I obviously had) or might not remember who he was (which had happened the first time he'd visited).

Femi opened the door and my dad came in.

I stood up when he was halfway to me, that big lolloping walk, and he pulled me into his chest as soon as I was within range.

Yeah, a cuddle was good.

'Hello, you,' he said.

As he was taking off his coat, I saw him clock Ilias in the corner before he looked at me and grimaced. I shook my head to let him know it wasn't a problem, that this was as private as we were likely to get.

'So, how you feeling, love?' He sat down.

He asked the question with a little more sincerity than Dr Bakshi had done a few hours earlier, which was nice.

'Where's Mum?'

'Oh . . . she's back at the hotel,' he said. 'She wasn't feeling too clever.'

'You don't need to make things up,' I said.

He nodded. 'Yeah, well she gets upset coming in here, that's all.' He looked at his feet for a few seconds, smiled when he looked up again. 'You sleeping OK?'

I told him that I was probably sleeping too much. The drugs I was on.

'Well, that might be a good thing,' he said.

'I suppose.'

He looked around and pulled a face. 'Bloody Nora, do you ever get used to the smell in here?'

I think I've mentioned Fleet Ward's distinctive aroma already, but in case I'm misremembering, just assume that it's there all the time, and even though I didn't bother answering my old man's question, *no*, you never get used to it.

There's that . . . bleachy hospital smell, obviously, but that's just what's always around, lurking underneath. On top of that, you've also got – in various pungent combinations, depending on the time of day and the 'condition' of certain patients – all manner of other special stinks.

What do wine ponces call it? Top notes . . .

Blood, shit, sick, sweat, piss, jism.

Sometimes you just catch a niff, if a *niff* feels like you've been punched in the face, and other times it's something that lingers and you can't shift, that you can smell on your-self in bed at night however hard you've scrubbed in the shower. Oh, and you smell fresh paint quite a lot, because even though bedclothes and curtains get cleaned regularly, removing any of the above from the walls is going to involve a fair bit of redecoration. There's usually someone in here slapping emulsion around once a week, and even though too much of that can make you feel like throwing up, given the choice I'd take the smell of paint any day.

Dulux Lemon Zest, if you want to be accurate about it.

'Oh ...' Dad grinned and held aloft the plastic bag he'd brought in with him. He set it down on his lap and rummaged inside, to remind himself of the things my mum had put in there so he could list them correctly. 'There's some of those biscuits you like ... a bit of fruit and a few little boxes of juice.' He leaned forward and winked. 'And several *Twixes*, obviously.' He said it like he'd smuggled in a kilo of heroin, or a cake with a file inside, even though the bag might have been checked while he was signing the visitors' book in the airlock. The truth was that, unless you were visiting someone whose diet needed to be carefully monitored, you could bring in more or less whatever you fancied.

I'd actually gone off Twixes a bit, but I didn't say anything.

'So.' He sat back. 'How did it go this morning?' My dad knew what Friday morning meant as well as I did.

I held out my arms. 'Good news,' I said. 'Well, good news for you at least, because the section is still in place.'

'Listen, love—'

'I'm not going anywhere ... and don't tell me you're planning to sit there looking like a wet weekend, as if you're disappointed for me. Can you honestly tell me that isn't what you want?'

'You're not being very fair.'

'Best place for me, right?' I nodded towards Ilias. 'Stuck in here with the likes of him.'

Dad puffed out his cheeks and shook his head. 'Come on, Alice. Even if I do think that now ... how does that mean your mum and me don't want you home and don't want you better?'

I looked away and stared at the wall for a bit, done with a conversation we had in some form or another every time he or my mother visited. It was never going to go anywhere.

'Oh ... Jeff and Diane from next door. They wanted me to say hello. Pass on their best.'

I turned back to him. 'You told them I was in here?'

'No, but they were over and they asked how you were doing and your mum was getting a bit flustered. I told them you were having your appendix out.'

I laughed a little bit and so did he.

'So, come on then.' He leaned forward and he actually rubbed his hands together, silly old sod. 'What's been happening, then? That funny woman still trying to do things to your feet?'

'She's gone.'

'What about the one who's always waiting? Or that woman who sings?'

I just stared at him. I suddenly realised that my dad hadn't got any idea what had happened since the last time he was here. About Kevin's death and my investigation. It seemed amazing to me because it was so massive, but he didn't know a thing about the murder, the drugs, any of it.

So I told him.

He looked appropriately shocked to begin with and he was nodding like he was interested, but slowly I saw his face change, saw it ... crease a little, like it always did when he was worried. So even before I'd finished I knew what was coming and knew exactly what that tone of voice would be. I'd heard it when I was fifteen and started going out with a

143

lad who was three years older. I'd heard it the first time I told him I was thinking of joining the police.

'Listen, love . . .'

I tuned out straight away. Some variation on the same tedious *is this* really *a good idea?* toss they'd trotted out in the MDR. Same warnings I'd had from Marcus and Bakshi and even from sodding Banksy.

How come I was the one least qualified to know what was good for me?

I was vaguely aware of Ilias grunting on the other side of the room, so I turned my head still further to see what he was doing. I watched him drop a counter into the Connect Four board, then stand up and move to sit in the chair opposite to plan an opposing move. He clapped a hand to either side of his head, evidently stumped by his own brilliance.

'Alice? Are you listening?'

I slowly turned back to look at my dad. 'I'm really tired,' I said.

He looked like I'd punched him. 'You want me to go?'

'Might be best,' I said. 'Thanks for the Twixes, though.'

'Right then.'

It was only when my dad got slowly to his feet that Ilias decided it was high time he joined in. I watched him march purposefully across to my father and stand close to him. My dad didn't look thrilled about it.

Ilias jerked his head in my direction. 'You her dad, then?'

'That's right.'

Ilias nodded and stepped even closer to my father. 'Listen, if you *procreate* with your daughter . . .' He stopped, seeing the look of disgust on my dad's face. 'Yeah, I know, horrible word, right? But if you *do* . . . you can live for ever.'

144

I had no idea what to say and could only watch as Ilias, having passed on his pearl of wisdom, strolled from the room. Struggling a bit, I turned back to look up at my dad.

'This place,' he said. He picked up his coat and started to cry.

TWENTY-ONE

Saturday morning, after a fried breakfast and the usual assortment of meds, I prowled about looking for Shaun, but every member of staff I asked was a bit cagey and none of the patients I spoke to knew where he was. Nobody could remember seeing him since he'd lost it in the TV room on Thursday night. There was no shortage of expert opinions, of course.

'I don't think he's been around all day,' Lucy told me. 'Like they spirited him away or something. I heard that he's not speaking to anybody.'

'They're feeding him in his room,' Donna said, as we walked.

'They've moved him to another ward.' Ilias whispered and nodded, the fount of all knowledge. 'Downstairs with the real head cases.'

'The Thing got him,' Tony said.

Shaun finally appeared at lunchtime. Mia led him into the

dining room, fetched his meal, then sat with him at a table well apart from the rest of us. It didn't feel like she was sticking that close because Shaun was on Within Arm's Length obs – though that might well have been the case after such a major wobble – but more that she was there to keep the rest of us away and make sure he had space.

It seemed to me she was being . . . protective, you know?

Like he was vulnerable as opposed to dangerous.

We all stared, obviously, didn't even pretend not to and why would we? Shaun didn't look at anything except the plate in front of him. He didn't say a dicky bird, not to Mia even, and once he'd finished she escorted him out; her hand hovering a few inches away from his back, like she was afraid to touch him.

After he'd gone – back to his room, I guessed – a few people hung around and drifted across to congregate at the same table. They slurped tea or pushed apple crumble around their dishes, many of them only too keen to share their freshly revised opinions of the situation.

'He looks bad,' Donna said.

Ilias grinned at her. 'You think *you* look so fantastic?'

'I reckon it's some kind of post-trauma thing.' Bob looked at me. 'Isn't that what you had?'

I ignored Lauren's bark of laughter and stared at him.

'It's what we've all had.' Lucy laid a hand on my arm. 'We've all been through something, to one degree or other. There's trauma and there's trauma, that's all.'

'Has he spoken at all?' Graham asked. 'Since the other night, I mean.'

Heads were shaken. Ilias let out a loud burp then shook his.

'That's fairly serious, then.'

147

'It wasn't like he said much before,' Donna said. 'I mean, he was always quiet.'

'If he's actually . . . silent, though.' Graham let out a whistle. 'Just saying, that's not nothing, is it?'

'Yeah, it's bollocks,' Lauren said.

Graham turned to look at her and pointed. 'You were the one shouting at him the other night.'

Bob nodded enthusiastically. 'Yeah, you *shouted*.'

'Shouting because he was being too loud.' Graham was suddenly getting as worked up as I'd ever seen him. 'Because you couldn't hear your precious programme.'

Lauren jabbed a spoon hard towards Graham's face and smirked when he recoiled like it was something a bit sharper. 'Shouldn't you be standing by the meds hatch already like a tit in a trance?' She looked at the watch she wasn't wearing. 'Best hurry up, mate, it'll be open in twenty minutes.' She watched as Graham scuttled from the room, panic-stricken, then went back to her pudding and quickly shovelled a spoonful into her mouth. 'Shaun's putting it on if you ask me. Poor baby's looking for attention.'

I tried not to sound too sarcastic. 'You think?'

'Course he is.'

'It's possible,' Ilias said. 'Maybe he's playing a game or something.'

Lauren nodded, chewing. 'I did something like that myself once. What I did though was just keep repeating the same word over and over, to mess with the nurses a bit. That's all I said, that one word, whatever anyone asked me. Kept it up for two weeks.'

'That's really clever,' I said.

'I know,' she said.

'Shaun's probably feeling bad enough as it is, today. It's been a week since Kevin was killed, remember?'

'So?'

'So you should think about that, and maybe doing all that shouting the other night, when he was already so upset, might not have been the most sensitive thing you could have done.'

Lucy nudged me. 'You're wasting your breath, babe.'

Like I didn't know.

'I couldn't give a toss,' Lauren said.

I turned away, remembering, feeling like it was important. That freaky woman on the TV, showing off her messed-up fake tits. Shaun with his finger glued to some invisible scab or pimple on his chin, asking the same question as he always did, only this time looking like he was genuinely terrified it was really going to happen. Malaika doing her best to calm him down, but getting nowhere. Then Lauren up on her feet, outraged and shouting her big mouth off, demanding that somebody shut him up.

Well, somebody certainly had.

'What was the word?' Bob leaned towards Lauren. 'The word you said over and over again.'

Lauren licked her spoon clean then dropped it into the bowl.

'Cunt,' she said.

Later on I was mooching around, while those who weren't already in bed or otherwise too zombified to watch claimed their pitches in the TV room, when I spotted Malaika heading into the toilets. I stood outside and waited for her to emerge, turned on the tears when I heard the hand-dryer going.

'Hey, Alice. What's the matter?'

I shook my head as though I was far too upset to speak

and let her lead me into an empty treatment room next to the 136. She handed me tissues and gave me some water until I'd calmed down. She shuffled her chair closer until our knees were kissing and asked what was upsetting me.

'I . . . saw . . . *Shaun.*' One word at a time, breathy and ragged like it was being dragged out of me. I swallowed some more water. 'It's horrible.'

'I know, my love.'

'What's happened to him?'

'I shouldn't really discuss other patients, Alice. I can't—'

'He's my *friend.*' Verging on the hysterical now. 'It's *important.*'

Malaika shook her head. 'I didn't know the two of you were that close.'

'After what happened to Kevin, you know?' I glanced up and saw Ilias peering in through the window. He stuck his tongue out, then, thankfully, moved on. 'We bonded.'

Malaika sighed and took the empty water glass from me. 'You're right, of course,' she said. 'This latest episode *is* horrible.'

'What kind of episode is it, though? What's going on?'

'Well, the good news is that Dr Bakshi is fairly certain that it's only temporary.'

'Oh, that's great,' I said.

'Something has clearly traumatised him.'

'Not what happened to Kevin, though. I mean, this happened after Kevin was killed, so . . .'

'Yes. We can only assume it's a direct result of what happened in the television room the night before last.'

'Really?' Fucking . . . *really*? Like that wasn't blindingly obvious.

'When a patient becomes extremely disturbed, something ... shuts down and they just switch off. They retreat into themselves, into their shells. It's a defence mechanism.'

'Defence against what?'

'Everything,' Malaika said.

I nodded, as if I was thinking it all through, which I was. Shaun had been trying to tell me something, but had been so scared that the whole dying thing had kicked in. That's what had started it and I remembered only too well what it was that had finished him off.

'I suppose you had some sort of meeting afterwards,' I said. 'You always do, right? After an alarm or whatever.'

'A debrief, yes.'

'So, what did everyone think had happened?'

'Well ...' Malaika seemed a little uncomfortable and looked back over her shoulder. To check that nobody was watching through the window? To make sure the door was shut? 'It's always very difficult to diagnose these things on the spot. What's important is that we follow correct clinical procedure, which, of course, we did.'

'What did Debbie think? She was right there when it happened.'

'Debbie was extremely upset.'

'Yeah, I bet. I mean, she'd obviously been trying to help.'

'Of course. When someone is as manic as Shaun was ... stuck in a loop almost ... often the best option is to shock them. To do whatever you can to snap them out of it.'

'Snap' was the right word for it.

'Dr Bakshi assured Debbie that it had certainly been something worth trying.'

'You heard Dr Bakshi say that?'

'That's what Debbie told me she'd said.' She shifted her chair back. 'I shouldn't really be telling you any of this, Alice. It's a bit naughty of me, and it's only because I can see how distressed you are.'

'I won't tell anyone,' I said.

Malaika stood up. 'So, are you feeling a little better, now?'

'Yeah, yeah . . . I'm good.' I got to my feet and wandered out through the door she was holding open for me. I didn't look at her or even say thank you, but that's only because I was suddenly struck as dumb as poor old Shaun had been.

There were so many things rattling around in my head. Kevin and the cameras and Seddon and the drugs and the nurses and Shaun. I was struggling to process the information or make sense of any of it. I knew the answer was in there, fighting to get out, but it was all so jumbled.

The drugs, maybe. *My* drugs, I mean.

When it came to seeing the wood for the trees, which was always going to be important if I wanted to break the case, I was seriously starting to wonder if the meds were doing me any favours. If these 'inhibitors' they fed me three times a day weren't inhibiting the very bits of my brain I needed to be working at full tilt.

Names and faces, bits of things people had said.

All racing around my brain and I couldn't put the brakes on.

Stuck in a loop.

TWENTY-TWO

I've worked a couple of murders where attending the victim's funeral was as much about hoping the murderer might show up as it was paying respects to the victim. Sounds a bit far-fetched, I know, and yeah you see it on cop shows, sometimes – *Keep your eye on the mourners, Lewis ... our killer's in this church somewhere* – but I'm telling you from experience that once in a blue moon it pays off. Maybe it's one of those where the murderer might not be able to resist showing up to gloat or they're a bit weird and need to make doubly sure the person they've done in is actually dead. Sometimes it's a bit simpler than that and you just suspect that the killer is one of the victim's family or friends.

Either way, all I'm saying is that, every now and again, it's worth a detective's while to dig out their black suit and dip into the petty cash for some flowers.

I wish I could say that when I'd woken up Sunday things were any clearer. I was still all over the shop, I'm not pretending I wasn't, but at least I'd woken with an idea. A pretty decent one too, I reckoned, despite all the things I didn't know or couldn't work out. Because I knew my killer *was* in the church somewhere.

In the church, on the ward, you get the point.

I talked to Marcus about it after breakfast – not about the killers going to funerals thing, obviously – and he wasn't against the idea.

'It might be nice.' He didn't seem in the least bit suspicious. 'It's very thoughtful, Alice . . . let me know if we can help.'

'Least we can do,' I said.

It wouldn't really *be* a funeral, of course.

I did briefly consider a kind of *mock*-funeral, knocking up a cardboard coffin or whatever, but in the end it got way too complicated – I couldn't figure out how to replicate the burial or cremation and I didn't even know which of those Kevin would have preferred – so I ditched that plan. Decided to stick with something simpler. The actual funeral might already have happened for all we knew, and even if it hadn't, I didn't think any of us were likely to get invitations, so I spent the rest of the day making arrangements for what I had told Marcus would be a memorial.

First off, I told everyone, including the Informals, what I was planning and did my best to persuade them that they ought to be there.

'He was one of us,' I said. 'It'll be good for everyone to . . . let their feelings out, to express themselves a bit.' And, 'It'll be fun.'

Some were predictably keener than others, but by mid-morning I was pretty sure a fair few would rock up when it came to it. It was something to do, after all, something different. A welcome change of routine.

L-Plate helped me out a bit – Donna couldn't take time off from her packed walking schedule and Ilias said he had a chess match – but putting it all together still took most of the day. Once I'd blagged a suitable space, there was a ton of stuff to move and set up. We had to get the chairs arranged in rows and we needed to get everything looking nice. I wanted pictures, if we could get them, and some suitable decorations, and I wanted music.

I wanted it to be proper.

It would probably end up detracting a little from the dignity of the proceedings, I was well aware of that, but I decided to do it while afternoon meds were wearing off as opposed to when the evening ones were kicking in. It would make things a bit more interesting, I thought, and, with luck, more *useful*. So at six o'clock I was ready and waiting and, half an hour later, I watched – trying my best not to look too excited – as they trooped into the occupational therapy room in dribs and drabs.

All the sectionees, which was perfect.

A few of the Informals, which couldn't hurt.

Most of the nurses.

I guided people to their seats and did my best to calm them down where it was necessary. The music was helping, I think. I'd connected my phone up to a portable speaker Lucy had lent me. I'd wanted something to suit the occasion, maybe a bit of classical, but I don't have a lot to choose from, so in the end I'd settled for Michael Bublé. You can't go far wrong with a bit of Bublé and I have to admit it seemed to be doing the trick.

I wouldn't say the atmosphere was ideal because frankly it was like trying to herd cats, but when things were as settled as they were ever going to get, I turned the music off and walked slowly back to my spot at the front of the room to say my piece.

I'd spent half an hour writing it that afternoon.

'Thanks to everyone for coming.' Ilias shouted 'Get off' but I ignored him. 'I really appreciate you all making the effort and I know Kevin would have appreciated it, if he wasn't dead.'

I nodded towards the picture of Kevin that Marcus had been kind enough to print out for me, which I'd taped to a clipboard and propped up on a table against a plant pot. Not to brag, but I reckon I'd done a tip-top job with the whole room, considering. Me and L-Plate had carted in a bunch of the plastic ferns from other rooms and arranged them on either side at the front, and I'd laid out a bunch of candles on a tray. Smelly ones, like people use in toilets or whatever, but they were all I could lay my hands on.

'This doesn't have to be sad,' I said. 'Because it's all about remembering Kevin when he was still with us. The laughs we had with him, the stupid things that happened. All the same, we should not forget why he isn't with us any more.' A pause for maximum effect. 'Nobody in this room should ever forget that a crime was committed. The very worst crime of all.'

I stopped for a couple of seconds and I have to admit I was a bit flustered because I'd heard a couple more arseholes shouting things from the back. I could guess who they were and what kind of comments they were making, but I needed to press on. I certainly didn't want to look up and risk catching the eye of one of the nurses. Marcus, having sussed what I was up to, glaring at me from the doorway.

'Someone took Kevin from us, and if anyone has anything

they'd like to say about that, I'm sure we'd all like to hear it.' Now I looked up. 'So if any of you has something they'd like to contribute . . . maybe something they remember and would like to share, now's the time.' I pointed to Kevin's picture again. 'Come to the front and maybe light a candle for him, and please say whatever's on your mind.'

I stepped to one side and waited. I wasn't sure whether to turn Michael Bublé back on or not, how long I should give it, so I just stood there shifting from one foot to another, and I probably looked a bit awkward, thinking back.

Ilias – why did it have to be Ilias? – saved my bacon.

'He was a cocky little wanker sometimes.' Ilias sniffed and jabbed a finger towards the picture, in case anyone wasn't clear who he was talking about. 'Still out of order, though. What happened to him.' He picked up one of the candles and started walking back to his seat. When I stepped across and tried to take it off him, he got a bit stroppy and said, 'I thought they were free,' so I decided to let him keep it.

Donna came up next, a bit trembly. She said, 'Kevin was really sweet and he never said anything nasty to me, so God bless him.' She took the lighter that I'd set on the tray, lit a candle and went back to her seat.

Several others followed in quick and remarkably orderly succession.

'I didn't know him very well,' Bob said.

'Kevin was good at Scrabble.' Graham nodded sadly. 'Good at doing the rude words.'

L-Plate had written a poem, bless her, and read it very loudly, like a princess in a school play. Something about a seagull flying home that went on too long, then some other bit where 'sadness' rhymed with 'madness'. A couple of the

Informals came forward after that. While they were lighting their vanilla cupcake candles and saying nothing, I looked over to where Shaun was sitting with Femi at the back of the room. He hadn't stopped weeping since he came in.

Then it was the Singer's turn.

I'd been dreading madam's contribution, of course, but even though nothing so far had told me anything I didn't already know, *she* at least genuinely surprised me. She stood there staring at everyone for half a minute or more and there was genuine tension in that room, like she might rip all her clothes off, or just run screaming at someone. Instead, she took a deep breath and started to sing a half-decent version of that 'Hallelujah' song off *X-Factor*, and I swear it was nearly in tune. When she'd finished, almost everyone clapped, and it's the only time I've ever seen Lauren look genuinely happy about anything that didn't involve upsetting someone.

I almost forgot what I was doing this for.

Just when it looked like nobody else was going to do anything and I was getting ready to put the music back on, the nurses and the healthcare assistants started coming forward one at a time. They weren't all in the room at one time, of course, a couple had to be manning the nurses' station, but three or four of them took a turn.

Marcus lit a candle, then George and Malaika.

I looked across at Shaun again, hoping against hope, but his head was on Femi's shoulder and his eyes were closed. Stupid of me really, because what was I actually expecting? I knew what I *wanted*. I wanted him to miraculously recover the power of speech, to stand up and run to the front. I wanted him to say, 'Kevin was being held to ransom by such and such a drug gang and he did ... something they didn't like and in the end he had to die, so he was killed by ...'

I wanted that witness who blows the case wide open.

I wanted him to tell everyone what he'd been so afraid to tell me.

Debbie was the last nurse to come up. I saw that she had tears in her eyes as she lit the final candle. I swear I heard a sob before she gently touched a finger to Kevin's picture, then crossed herself.

Quite touching, I suppose, if you give a stuff about any of that.

Everyone drifted away pretty quickly after that. Places to go, people to see. I offered to tidy the room up, but Marcus said the staff would do it later on.

'So, were you pleased with how that went?' he asked.

I told him I was, that I thought it had all gone really well.

'Pleased to hear it,' he said, as I walked past him. He wasn't really trying to hide the sarcasm and it was obvious he was pissed off because I'd shafted him, but I was beyond caring.

My brain was still racing when I got back to my room and more than ever I felt the urgent need to talk everything through with someone. I couldn't get hold of Banksy, so I called Sophie. Maybe I was gabbling or just not making any sense, but either way she didn't seem very interested, so in the end I gave up and let her ramble on about her job for a while.

Her fantastic new flatmate, again.

Her new boyfriend.

After that I decided to just chill in my room for a while until dinner. I'd been working on the memorial all the way through lunch, so I was bloody starving. More important, I was keen to know what people had made of it all and to find out if grief – or what passed for it in a place like this – had shaken anything loose.

TWENTY-THREE

Johnno and I worked this fatal stabbing in Dollis Hill one time.

It was a bad one; not like any of them are ever good, but this one was really nasty. A teacher named Gordon Evans, carved up in his front room in the middle of the day. Point is, we knew very well who'd done it and why – were talking about making an arrest within twenty-four hours of catching the case – but the problem was we were struggling to prove it.

Even with (almost) all the evidence anybody could want.

It was a dispute between neighbours, something simple and stupid. A lawnmower that never got returned or someone complaining about a noisy party. I can't remember the details of why they fell out, but several other neighbours told us they were aware of tensions, so we knew damn well they had. Our only suspect – a charmer of a long-distance lorry driver named Ralph Cox – lived in a house with a garden that backed on to the teacher's. After one conversation with Mr

161

Cox, despite him claiming that he'd been indoors all day, we were convinced that he'd marched round to Evans's place to have it out and things had got out of hand.

Forty-two separate stab wounds out of hand.

Yeah, so this evidence . . .

Cell-site data meant we were able to place Cox's mobile at the scene, but it was quickly pointed out that living within fifty yards of the victim's property meant his phone would have been pinging off the same mast if he was at home. Marvellous. We had our suspect's prints inside Evans's house, but Cox's claim that he had been there before to discuss the dispute – which to be fair he'd never denied – could not be disproved. We never found the murder weapon, but we had a knife-block from Cox's kitchen that just happened to be missing a knife whose blade was the size and shape of the one that had sliced up Gordon Evans.

We had an eye witness, another neighbour, who said he saw Cox leaving Evans's house on the afternoon in question. By the time we came to take a statement, though, that had become *thought he saw*, then *I'm not actually sure it was him* and eventually he made it clear that whatever he might or might not have seen, he wasn't willing to talk about it in court. Yeah, Cox was a scary-looking sod and this witness only lived a few doors away, but still it was a pain in the arse.

Then there was the camera.

There was no CCTV on the street, but the neighbour opposite had a security camera that happened to cover Evans's front door. You can see where this is going, right? A DVR that was full, so nothing recorded.

That just about put the tin lid on it.

All this, on top of which, Johnno and me were getting it in

the neck from a useless DI who was desperate for a result and couldn't understand why we weren't delivering one.

So one night I went round to Johnno and Maggie's place to talk about this case that was doing our heads in. We got Chinese and ate off our laps, the three of us just sitting round moaning about it.

What were we doing wrong? What *weren't* we doing?

'Sometimes you're just going to get jobs like this,' Maggie said. 'Doesn't matter how much you know you've got the right person, it won't go your way.' She leaned against her boyfriend. 'Maybe you should just chalk it up and let it go.'

I was starting to agree with her, but Johnno wasn't having it.

'We're making it too complicated,' he said. 'Coming at it from too many angles and getting . . . bogged down.'

'Bogged down and buggered up,' I said.

'Letting all this evidence we've got get in the way.'

'Not to mention the evidence we haven't got.' I remember I had a gobful of spring roll or ribs or whatever. 'That bastard camera.'

'Sod the camera.' Johnno tossed his fork down and sat forward. 'We don't need the camera . . . we go after *him*. The cocky prick thinks he's laughing, because he knows very well he can dance round everything we've got. So we forget all that and start again. We find something else. We do what we do and we come up with a way to nail him.'

I remember how worked up Johnno was that night, and I'll never forget how excited he was five months later. That was the day we walked out of court having seen Ralph Cox get sent down. Life, with a minimum tariff of twenty-one years.

Six months for every one of those stab wounds.

Long story short, we started digging and found a report filed nine months previously, when Cox had lived south of the river. A woman who lived upstairs from him whose complaint of violent harassment had never been passed on. We brought Cox in for a friendly chat and Johnno broke the scumbag in the interview room.

Wood for the trees, right?

I woke up in the middle of the night and someone was having a shouting match with themselves a few doors along. A proper ding-dong. It sounded like Lucy, but it wasn't a big deal because I was well used to it, and anyway I didn't think that was what had woken me.

I was wide awake and sitting up because I *knew*.

The police had got it all arse about face. I mean, up to that point so had I to a degree, but now I knew exactly where I'd been going wrong. Why I'd been bogged down and buggered up.

You're a star, Johnno.

I'd been wasting valuable time trying to get to the bottom of this or that argument, wondering how drugs had got in and pissing about with daft ideas about hitmen. Newbie mistakes, so bloody stupid. Most important of all, me and DC Seddon both had been casting the net too wide, thanks to Graham and the fun he liked having with mashed potato and the like.

Screw the camera . . .

It was no great surprise that the official investigation had stalled – and it certainly felt that way – because they were still looking for a motive and, biggest mistake of all, they were focusing on a time-frame that left them with two dozen suspects.

Well, for once I was ahead of the game.

Now, I had just the one.

See, it didn't make the slightest bit of difference when that camera had gone off, because Kevin Connolly had been murdered in plain sight.

TWENTY-FOUR

I'd thought it was definitely worth a punt, because they could only say no, but I can't say I was overly confident that Banksy would be able to pull it off. That man is a marvel though, I'm telling you. A right hard bastard if he needs to be, but he can charm the pants off someone when he wants to.

As soon as we'd both lit cigarettes, I pulled him into a hug.

'Thanks for sorting this,' I said.

Banksy said that I was welcome, but I'm not sure I really was, and bear in mind this was before I'd told him what I'd actually brought him in to hear. We sat down on a bench opposite the main entrance and I said nothing for a while. I wanted to spend just a couple of minutes enjoying my fag and feeling sunshine on my pale face before I got into it.

The break in the case . . .

Even before Banksy had turned up – he'd told me on the phone he'd be in sometime late afternoon – I'd decided we should at least give it a bash. The obs stats are the obs stats for good reason, but I knew that every now and again, if such and such a nurse was in a good mood, they might do someone a favour or look the other way. Ilias goes out for a smoke with Malaika sometimes and I'm damn sure he's not supposed to. A month or so before, Donna's sister had been allowed to take her outside for an hour because it was her birthday. Outside as in *away from the hospital and down to the shops*. Obviously with the usual provisos about trust and not absconding and sending the police after her and all that.

So, I definitely thought me and Banksy should at least ask. I mean, we *were* the police.

Banksy said that Marcus was a bit dubious to begin with – yeah, I thought, I bet he bloody was – but apparently, once Banksy had flashed a pukka warrant card and explained that we really needed privacy because there was a sensitive police matter to discuss, he'd softened a bit.

Bansky had thanked him for his cooperation, he told me, and promised that we wouldn't go far.

I stubbed out my fag and turned to look at him.

'Let's hear it then,' he said.

I won't lie, I've seen him look keener. So I tried to stay calm as I laid it all out and not let on how fired up I was. I told him about the drugs that had been smuggled out of the ward after being given to Kevin by an insider (with a healthy percentage presumably coming back to that same insider once they'd been sold). I told him about the irrelevance of the camera on Kevin's corridor, the time when it was on and when it wasn't. Finally, I told him what had happened to Shaun – or, to be accurate, what had been done to him to ensure that he couldn't tell anyone what he knew.

I asked Banksy for another cigarette when I'd finished.

I lit up and waited.

'So, why kill Kevin?' he asked, finally. 'You know, if there's this cushy little drug thing going which presumably everyone's doing very nicely out of. Why scupper it?'

'I don't think Kevin wanted to do it any more.'

'You're just guessing though, right?'

'Look, I know him and Shaun had been arguing and I think that's because Shaun wanted him to stop. In the end Shaun got his way, so Kevin told everyone involved that he wanted out. That's why all those drugs were found in his room, because he wasn't passing them on to his connections any more. He'd had enough.'

'So they decided to kill him, that's what you're saying?'

'Yeah, maybe they did . . . his connections on the outside.' I held up a finger. 'Or maybe it was just one person's decision.' Banksy nodded. He already knew who I was talking about of course, because I hadn't wasted any time in telling him who had killed Kevin. 'What about if Kevin had been stockpiling those drugs? Holding on to them as some kind of insurance policy or something?' Then another idea struck me which suddenly made perfect sense. 'Maybe he was using those drugs to blackmail her.'

'Seriously?'

'Why not? Or at least planning to down the road.' I was a bit annoyed with myself for not working this out before, but I wasn't going to blame myself for not being match-fit after everything that had happened. 'Sounds like a pretty decent motive to me.'

'How come she didn't take the drugs, then? When she killed him?'

I shrugged. 'Couldn't find them.' I still didn't know exactly where in Kevin's room the drugs had been hidden. 'She certainly wouldn't have had much time to go looking for them, turn his room over, whatever. A couple of minutes, that's all she would have been in there for. In, pillow over his face, and out again.'

Bitch, I thought. Stone cold bitch.

I flicked my fag-end away and watched Banksy nodding like he was thinking about it. Course, he was actually trying to decide the best way to tell me what he really thought, but I didn't know that at the time, did I? Right then, I was still buzzing because I'd broken the case wide open, sitting there like a twat waiting for him to tell me how we should work it.

'I still don't quite get this business with Kevin's boyfriend.'

'Shaun,' I said. 'I've said his name like a hundred times.'

'Yeah, with Shaun.'

I told him again what had happened that night in the TV room when Shaun had gone up the pole, what had been said to him and how he'd been ever since.

'So, she knew that's what would happen, did she?'

I nodded, remembering her exact words. Stone cold . . .

'She knew he wouldn't be able to speak afterwards?'

'That's her *job*, isn't it?' I chose not to tell him what Malaika had said to me on Saturday. All that bull about an attempt to 'shock' Shaun out of his mania and Dr Bakshi *allegedly* saying it had been something worth trying. I didn't bother telling him because it was blindingly obvious that Malaika had been every bit as alarmed by what had happened in the TV room as me. That she only said what she did afterwards because the nurses look after one another and she was trying

169

to stick up for her colleague. As a copper I'd done similar things myself and so had Banksy.

So it wasn't relevant.

I said, 'Look, Shaun had been trying to tell me everything that night. He was desperate to let me know it was one of the staff ... right? That was what set him off, because he was terrified. Because he knew what the woman who'd killed Kevin was capable of.' I didn't want to talk to Tim like he was daft or wet behind the ears, but I couldn't understand why he wasn't *getting* it. 'She needed to shut him up.'

'Yeah, I hear what you're saying,' he said.

We watched a well-dressed, middle-aged couple walking hand in hand towards the entrance. Lucy's parents. I waved and Lucy's father conjured a frosty smile.

'I tell you something else,' I said. 'The woman who killed Shaun also sexually assaulted me.'

'*What?*'

'When I first came in.'

Banksy looked properly confused. 'Why are you only telling me this now?'

'I just want you to know the kind of person we're dealing with.'

'What did she do?'

'I don't want to talk about it.'

'Fair enough, but you know ... make a complaint, Al. I mean that's something we *can* arrest her for.'

I shook my head.

He sighed and sat back. Muttered, 'Fucking hell ...'

I clocked him checking his watch and guessed that we didn't have much time left. 'So, are you going to talk to Seddon, or what?'

Another sigh. 'This isn't my case, Al. You know that.'

'You're still a copper, though. It's your duty to bring new information to his attention, at least.'

'I don't think there is any new information.' He turned and looked at me, the expression of a doctor about to deliver bad news. 'I just don't think it hangs together.'

'Come on.' I felt like I might lose it at any second and I was clutching on to the edge of that bench for dear life. 'How long have we worked together, Banksy? You knew Johnno, for God's sake . . . you know *me*.'

He couldn't look at me. 'I used to,' he said. 'But, you know . . . *this*?'

By the time he did look up, I was on my feet and away. 'Nice to have a natter and a fag,' I shouted back to him. 'Don't worry, mate, I can see myself back up.'

When I stomped into the lobby, I saw that Lucy's mother and father were standing inside the lift, waiting for it to close. I shouted, 'Hold the doors,' and ran to join them. I pretended not to notice them inching towards the back wall as the doors began to shut.

But it didn't help.

I'm not using the fact that I was angry and looking to lash out as an excuse for what I said. I don't remember the last time I needed an excuse for anything, but it's an explanation, fair enough? Obviously I knew who they were, so I get that it was bad. I knew who they were visiting and I knew exactly why she was there.

As the lift juddered slowly up, I turned round and grinned at them.

I said, 'I've just been shooting up outside.' I moaned a bit and rubbed at my arm. 'Smack is just *fabulous*, don't you reckon?'

171

TWENTY-FIVE

Tuesday morning I was determined to get stuck in, so after breakfast and meds I worked through some old contacts on my phone and made a few calls trying to find the number for Seddon's incident room. The direct line, I mean. I'd wanted to do it the day before once Banksy had left, but I knew that, by then, most of the people I needed to speak to would probably have gone home already. It didn't much matter in the end, because when I got back on to the ward there were too many distractions – George was trying to dissuade Graham from making a fresh dent in the wall with his head and Lauren was shouting at Femi about someone coming into her room and going through her stuff – so I was finding it hard to focus on anything approaching work.

That's been the big problem up to now.

Life in this place, getting in the way . . .

I was never the type to cut corners. Never one to take the easy route, or 'delegate', when most of the time that really means skiving off. No, really, if I was working a case I was like a fucking *laser* . . . I was dead focused. In here, though, it's hard to concentrate on anything for more than five minutes without something kicking off. I can sit in my room and do stuff on my laptop if I have to, but like I tried to explain to Marcus, that's not what being a detective is about.

You need to get out there and engage with people.

Nine times out of ten, engaging with someone on the ward means arguing with them or just keeping them out of your face. Watching them nod off or just amble away while you're talking. Listening to a blow-by-blow account of some sexual encounter that didn't happen or else some half-arsed cobblers about how radio waves are reacting with metal in the vaccinations we were given as kids and turning us into aliens.

Then there's all the other stuff you have to do, the routines that eat into your day. I know, I'm normally the first one to moan about how boring it is in here – at least it was, before bodies started piling up – but there's still the meals and the one-to-ones and the tests and the groups and the community meetings and the washing and the visits and the meds.

Mustn't forget the meds.

Like I said before, I'm still struggling with the best way to manage them as far as making headway in my case goes. It's hard to get anywhere when the drugs are wearing off because I can get a bit jittery, and when they're kicking in I'm every bit as likely to zone out completely. So taking all this shit three times a day means I've only got a small – what do you call it? – window of opportunity, which isn't ideal.

Like I'm going after a suspect with one arm tied behind my back.

It is what it is, though, and anyone who knows me will tell

you I've never backed away from a challenge. They'd definitely say that. Not that I trust many of them now and it's not like they'll even talk to you, but you get what I'm on about.

I got the number I was after in the end, though it took a while and one or two of the conversations were a bit awkward, but I didn't really have a lot of choice.

'Bloody hell, Alice!' DS Trevor Lambert, who I'd worked with a hundred years before. On a team somewhere in south London now. 'Blast from the past or what?'

'Been too long, Trev.'

'What are you up to?'

'Oh, the usual, you know.'

'You still working up west?'

'For my sins, yeah. Listen, there's a murder case and it's kicking everyone's arse, if I'm honest, mate. I wondered if you could do me a favour.'

'What do you need?'

Trevor clearly hadn't heard about my misadventures and I wasn't going to put him straight, was I? It was him that found me the number I needed, as it goes. Called me back with it, good as gold.

'We should have a pint and catch up.'

'Let's do that,' I said.

'Fair warning though, I'm a bit fatter and a bit greyer than the last time I saw you. That's the kids, I reckon.'

'Yeah, we should definitely get together … I'll give you a bell when this thing eases off a bit. Up to my tits at the moment …'

Then, once I'd called the Incident Room: 'DC Seddon isn't available at the moment.'

'I'd like to leave a message, then.'

'What's it concerning?'

'Just tell him it's about the Kevin Connolly murder.'

'Can I take your name, madam?'

'I don't think you understand. I'm actually here. Where the murder happened. I'm on the spot.'

'OK, but I'll still need your details.'

I gave the woman my name then I gave her my rank. She took my mobile number and assured me that a member of the team would call me back.

I stayed in my room for a couple of hours after that, trying to decide the best way forward while I was waiting for Seddon to ring. It was hard, though, because after a while I began to think about Johnno then about Andy and those two-faced psychiatrists at A&E and everyone else who'd betrayed me. I started to wonder if Seddon could even be trusted at all.

I opened my laptop and did some Googling.

How much does a nurse earn?

British nurse average wage.

Steven Seddon Met Police Record.

Just before lunch, L-Plate knocked on my door and strolled in. There was going to be an occupational therapy session in the afternoon, she announced, and was I going to come. I told her that I didn't know they'd found the money to get the OT woman back and Lucy said they hadn't, that one of the staff was going to run the session.

'Probably won't be as good,' she said. 'But it'll be nice to do some drawing again.'

'I've got things to do,' I said.

'Come on, Al, it'll be fun.'

'Will it?'

Lucy giggled and leaned close, whispering, like it wasn't

just the two of us in the room. 'I'm going to imagine her with no clothes on . . . stark bollock naked . . . and draw that. It'll be hysterical. Or repulsive, I don't know yet.'

'Imagine *who* with no clothes on?'

'Debbie. She's the one who's organising it.'

It didn't take me long. 'OK, sounds like a plan,' I said.

TWENTY-SIX

The occupational therapy room had been put back to the way it normally was. The way it had been before Kevin's memorial, I mean. The orange curtains open, a scattering of tables and chairs, the locked materials cupboard at the end of the room.

There were maybe six of us in there.

Me and Lucy sitting together. Ilias, Bob and I think Graham . . . or it might have been Donna. Doesn't matter.

I sat and watched as Debbie opened the cupboard then cheerfully distributed paper and felt-tip pens along with boxes of crayons for the less ambitious and some large pads and watercolours for those who wanted to try something a bit more advanced. She said we could paint or draw anything we wanted to, but lifted one of the ferns on to a table in the centre of the room in case anyone fancied a bash at a still life. One time someone had suggested we should have a life model, but even though Ilias had immediately volunteered the suggestion was quickly given the thumbs-down by the staff. The following week, Ilias had waited until none of the nurses was looking and whipped all his clothes off, which, trust me, is something I cannot ever un-see.

All that hair.

Lucy says that sometimes she still wakes up screaming, though to be fair she does that a lot anyway.

'We've got a couple of hours,' Debbie said. 'So there's no need to rush anything. Let's see what we can come up with.' She took a pad and a few pens for herself and went to sit at a table on her own.

Back when there was still some money so they could do things properly, we used to get up to all sorts in OT sessions. We had a few afternoons messing about with an ancient Wii which was a right laugh. Tennis and *Mario Kart* and stuff. We did drama a couple of times, which I quite enjoyed, but it always ended up a bit lively because Bob tried to turn everything into a sex scene. One week the woman who used to run things even got a friend of hers to bring a potter's wheel in. Again, that didn't go well. Graham immediately used his clay to disable the nearest camera while most of the other blokes just made cocks (their own, all predictably huge), and when the therapist suggested they might want to go in a different direction everyone just started chucking stuff about. I was finding bits of dried clay in all my cracks and creases for days afterwards and there are still a few blobs of it stuck to the ceiling.

Paper and pens was fine for today, though.

I wasn't there because I think I'm Picasso anyway.

'How come you got to go outside yesterday?' Lucy asked.

It was unusually quiet as everyone laboured over their masterpieces, so I took care to keep my voice down, hoping that Lucy would take the hint and do the same. 'It was a police thing,' I said.

'About Kevin?'

'It's not something I can really talk about.'

'Oh, OK then.' She went back to her picture.

'But, yeah.'

Lucy nodded, slashing her pen from side to side on the paper, which she told me later was how you shaded things in 'Are you going to be working on the case, then?'

'I *am* working on it.' I looked down at what I'd managed so far. It was going pretty well. 'I'm working on it *now*.'

I knew I had plenty of time, so I spent as much of it watching our substitute therapist as I did putting my felt-tips to good use. Mostly she kept busy with whatever she was drawing, but she was watching *us* too, because it wasn't like we were art students or anything and a pencil can do a lot of damage in the wrong hands.

In here, almost anything can.

A plastic fork, a broken guitar, a pillow . . .

At the table in front of us, Ilias suddenly screwed up the piece of paper he'd been working on and threw it away angrily. He put his hand up like a schoolboy and waited for Debbie to look up and see him.

'Can I draw a vagina?'

'If that's what you want,' Debbie said.

'Can I have it when you've finished?' Bob asked.

The sun was streaming through the windows and that pissed me off quite a lot, because I'd really enjoyed that half an hour outside with Banksy the day before. The being outside part of it, anyway.

It was hot, so it was hard to concentrate.

I knew that I had to, though; that I needed to make a good job of this. I tried not to spend every second willing the mobile in my pocket to ring and then, when I *did* finally feel it buzzing against my leg, I tried not to kick the table over when it turned out to be fucking Sophie.

Lovely 2 talk to u the other day. Miss u so much.

A sad-faced emoji.

The time went really quickly in the end, and when Debbie announced that we only had a few minutes left I looked across to see what Lucy had come up with. She'd done exactly what she told me she'd do, even if it was a bit cartoonish. I studied the pair of saggy tits with bright red nipples as if I was some expert on *Antiques Roadshow*. I stroked my chin and told her the tits were 'strikingly hideous' and that the curly orange bush that covered most of the subject's bottom half was 'especially disgusting'.

She looked across at Debbie and stroked her own chin and laughed until I thought she might wet herself.

'Right then . . .' Debbie said.

Despite the two hours everyone had put in, they all buggered off fairly sharpish when the time was up – Lucy included – without apparently being bothered about what they'd drawn or painted or daubed and certainly not giving a toss what anyone else might think about it.

I hung around though, obviously, and helped Debbie collect all the work up, except mine which I wanted to keep back until the moment was right. Once the materials had been locked back in the cupboard, she wandered back over to me and rubbed her hands together.

'Shall we have a look at our wee exhibition?'

Mostly it was the predictable scrawls, except for Ilias's vagina, which was remarkably detailed and really quite disturbing. 'Holy fuck,' Debbie said, laughing.

She stopped at Lucy's picture and stared.

'I think it's supposed to be you,' I said.

'Not bad.' She laughed again and pointed at the orange bush. 'Though I don't usually let things get *that* wild downstairs.' Then she held a hand out towards the sheet of paper I was holding. 'Come on, let's have a look at yours then.'

I didn't even try pretending to be reluctant and handed it over.

I'd done much the same thing quite a few times, done it with Johnno and with Banksy. When you've decided it's the right time to casually slide a photograph across an interview room table. A close-up of injuries, a victim's battered face, blood-spattered flesh or clothing. That moment when you show the most shocking picture you can get hold of to the animal you know very well is responsible for it, because you're looking for a reaction or, if you're lucky, an admittance of guilt.

At the very least, you're trying to get a read.

Like I said, I'm not much of an artist, but I reckon I'd managed to get what I was going for. A single bed with guess who lying on it. There was no face, obviously, just the pillow where the face should have been, although I don't think I'd been able to make it look that much like a pillow, so it was more sort of a blurry rectangle. I was pleased with the collection of little bottles, though. Dozens of them scattered about under the bed, with a few of them lying on their side. Best of all was the figure on one side of the picture, shadowy, kind of, like someone was creeping out of the room, with a few tiny dots of red and yellow and blue and green, right at the edge. The flash of a rainbow-coloured lanyard.

I stood and watched Debbie looking at my picture.

I wanted to get that read.

'That's fucking excellent,' she said, pointing. 'Honestly. The way you've done the shadow and everything. You going to keep it?'

I shook my head.

'You could put it up in your room if you want.'

'I don't think so.'

She looked at me. 'You all right, Alice?'

'I saw you at Kevin's memorial.' I waited, just a beat or two. 'You looked upset.'

'Because I was,' she said. 'I still am.'

'I saw you ...' I crossed myself, though after the up and down part I wasn't sure which shoulder you were supposed to touch first.

She nodded and smiled. 'Glasgow Catholic girl,' she said. 'Not a very good one, mind.'

'Confessing your sins and all that?'

'Not for a very long time.'

I gathered all the pictures together in front of her and straightened them. I made sure mine was on the top.

I said, 'Maybe you should think about starting again.'

TWENTY-SEVEN

Wednesday lunchtime, more than twenty-four hours after phoning the incident room and I was climbing the walls – staring at them, bouncing off them – because I was still waiting for Detective *Cunt*stable Seddon to call me back. Actually I'd just about given up waiting, because by then it was blindingly obvious he wasn't going to. I'd half expected to be ignored anyway and you didn't need to be a genius to work out why that might have been.

Who *called? That mad woman who's* in *there, the one who got thrown off the Job? Yeah, well, I think I've got better things to do than waste my time listening to her crackpot theories . . .*

I was damn sure *Steve* had no end of better things to do. Like having a wank or refilling his stapler or sticking needles in his eyes.

Part of me had always suspected I'd end up working this case on my own.

I'm not going to lie, it was a bit scary . . . out of my comfort zone and everything. I'd always worked as part of a team and within that I'd always been partnered up, which was how I liked it. The banter and the piss-takes to kill those endless hours in the car together. Someone always there to celebrate with you when things were going well or help you drown your sorrows at the end of a bad day.

Someone to watch your back as well, let's not forget that.

Even if it didn't work out particularly well for my partner.

Well, if the only way I could get a result on this case was to do it on my own then that was how it would have to be. I'd managed pretty well so far. I wasn't just going to work it, though, I was going to *crack* it … I mean I'd cracked it already, because my crackpot theory wasn't just a theory, but I was going to make damn sure the guilty party got what was coming to her.

I'd do it for Kevin and I'd do it for Johnno.

I'd do it to show Seddon and all those officially involved that they'd been wrong to ignore me and stupid to refuse my help.

I'd do it so all those jumped-up arseholes with pips on their shoulders who decided I should be 'medically retired' would see that I was a copper to my toenails.

I'd do it because it was the right thing to do.

I'd do it for the buzz and the rush of the blood pumping and because for the first time in forever it made me feel like a person again.

I'd do it because so many people had told me not to.

I'd do it because it would be a big fat *fuck you* to everyone who'd conspired to put me in here. To that crackhead with a Stanley knife in his pocket and the pair of Job-pissed pricks who decided I wasn't fit to testify and those doctors who didn't listen when I told them I'd only freaked out because

I'd been awake for forty-eight hours. To Andy ... for sure, and to Sophie and to Mum and Dad and the rest of them. To good Catholic Debbie, obviously, who hadn't got a clue that I'd worked it all out or that I was coming for her and who'd live to regret the day they'd found me a bed on her ward.

I'd do it because I *loved* it.

I'd been keeping a close eye on the time, just so I could be at the meds hatch when it opened. It took some serious self-restraint not to elbow Graham out of the way when it came to it, but in the end I decided that a few more minutes weren't going to kill me. I didn't want to wait much longer than that, though, because I knew I wouldn't be able to do anything – least of all pick up the phone and call in a massive favour – while I was feeling frazzled and fidgety and likely to do something daft. Not a chance. I couldn't do things properly while a whispering voice inside my head was telling me to march straight up to Debbie and pin her against the wall.

The voice nobody but me could hear telling the one that came out of my mouth just what to say.

I know exactly what you did and I know why you did it.

Tempting, course it was, but that was not the way I was planning to go.

Mia opened up the hatch and once Graham had shuffled up and taken his pills I stepped cheerfully forward to collect mine. I smiled and said, 'Thank you,' like a good girl.

A good officer.

Lucky for me that I caught DI David Dinham on his way to work. He was obviously doing a late turn, which was never anyone's favourite, but it had been a while since shift patterns meant anything to me. One day I might get up good and early and the next I won't bother to get up at all. Some days I get dressed and some days I can't be arsed, meaning I'll slob around in the pyjamas I was issued with or, if I feel like making an effort, I might push the boat out and parade around the place in my own trackies and T-shirt, but the point is that it doesn't much matter.

The days are measured out in meals and meds, simple as that.

Lucky, though, because coppers have flappy ears and Dinham wouldn't be free to have the conversation that I was planning while he was sitting in the office. Last thing I'd heard, that office was in Brighton or some other seaside place, which was convenient for me, because him working outside the Met meant there was no reason the Kevin Connolly case would be on his radar. Unlike Trevor Lambert, though, Dinham was aware that I'd been . . . in the wars as far as the Job was concerned, but that was fine.

'Oh . . . hey, Al.' Yeah, he was well aware. 'Listen, I'm in the car, so . . .'

'I do hope you're hands-free,' I said.

'Course I am.'

'Glad to hear it. So, how's tricks, mate?'

'Tricks are . . . good. What about you?'

I don't think he knew the details – where I was and why – but I didn't see any reason he needed to know. 'Well, I've been better, Dave, I'm not going to lie . . . but I've been worse an' all, so no point belly-aching about it, is there?'

'No, I suppose—'

'I need a favour.'

'Right.' I could hear the panic in his voice. 'What sort of favour?'

'I need intel on a suspect.'

'A *suspect*?' He clearly knew enough.

'On an *individual*, all right? Less you know about it the better . . . but I need financials, yeah? What has this woman got in the bank? Savings, mortgage, credit report, all that. Basically I need to know if she's got more money than she should have.'

'Right, and how exactly are you expecting me to find all this out?'

'Oh, come on, Dave.' If I still had access to the Police National Computer I could easily have got the information I needed myself. But that avenue of inquiry had been taken away along with everything else, which is precisely why I was asking Dinham. Why was he making it so difficult? 'Five minutes on the PNC.'

'Are you serious?'

'Five minutes.'

'Look, I don't know how long you've been . . . I mean have you forgotten all this stuff?'

'I haven't forgotten anything,' I said.

'In which case you know that the minute I log on I've left a digital fingerprint. Everything I search for is a matter of record and I'd need to provide a very good reason why I was searching for it. I couldn't even run a number plate for you, and unless this individual gives their consent I'd need a court order to access their bank details.'

I could hear that he was breathing quite heavily. I imagined him sweating a bit, knuckles white around the steering wheel. I almost felt sorry for him. I said, 'I need this.'

'For Christ's sake, Alice, it's a sackable offence.'

'How long have we known each other, Dave?'

'Are you not listening—'

'I *need* this.'

For almost a minute all I could hear was the rasp of his breathing again and the growl of traffic. Finally, *finally*, he said, 'Look, there might be another way.'

I waited.

I ran my finger down the crack in the wall next to my wardrobe.

I pushed a fingernail in and began to dig at it . . .

'There's a bloke I know,' he said. 'Ex-Job, running a private investigation and intelligence firm.'

'Really?' I knew what that meant. Some boozed-up old saddo sitting in a car spying on unfaithful husbands and wives.

'Actually, he's got a decent set-up. I think he can find out pretty much anything. I don't know exactly how he does it and I don't really want to know . . . but I reckon he could get what you're after.'

I scraped harder at the paint around the crack. I picked at it until my fingernail split and rubbed the blood into the dirty yellow paint.

'You'd need to pay him, obviously.'

'That's fine,' I said. 'What's his name?'

'Look . . . give me five minutes. I need to pull over. I'll send you a link to his website.'

'He's got a *website*?'

'Like I said, he does all sorts. Some of it's kosher, but I'm fairly sure that some of it . . . isn't.'

Ten minutes later, he texted me a link and I got straight online.

The Pindown Investigations (stupid name) website was

fairly impressive, no denying it. Some tasty pictures of fast cars and binoculars and computers. All manner of stuff banging on about the wide range of services on offer and the excellent value for money they were able to provide.

Covert surveillance, employee vetting, mystery shopping (whatever that was). These activities were – so they promised – tailored to a client's requirements and 'guaranteed to exceed expectation'. It was handy that I couldn't find the word *ethical* anywhere, but *unorthodox* popped up quite a few times which was nice to see. The fact that it didn't say that they were members of the Association of British Investigators was another good sign, and after a few minutes' digging I found the bit that said they would be more than happy to discuss my particular requirements and provide a bespoke service.

Bespoke was good. I loved the sound of bespoke.

Get in touch, they said. Tell us what you need. We can assure you of absolute confidentiality.

Confidentiality was nice, obviously – like a bonus – but I didn't think it was going to matter much in the end. Once I'd got the intel I needed and you-know-who was being pulled apart in an interview room, all bets would be off anyway, and by the time charges were being pressed nobody would care one way or the other how I'd got the information.

It was all about the result.

I sucked the blood from my finger and fired off an email.

Then I went to get my dinner.

TWENTY-EIGHT

It was one of the best nights ever in the TV room, though for the life of me I couldn't tell you what everyone was watching, because I wasn't really paying attention. Not to the TV, anyway. I'd got in early to bag a VIP seat next to Lady Lauren up the front and sat there, happy as Larry, while she got more and more pissed off because I was wearing my headphones. I wasn't listening to anything, obviously, so I could hear the TV perfectly well, but I just sat nodding my head like I was well into my tunes and really enjoying myself because I knew it was winding her up.

You've got to have a hobby, right?

When Lauren couldn't control herself any more and started waving her arms around and having a go at me, I made out like I couldn't hear. I just shook my head and pointed at my headphones until eventually she started shouting.

'What are you playing at?'

'I can't *hear* you.' I deliberately said it too loudly, you know, like people do when they've got headphones on. I pointed at them again and said, 'I've got *headphones* on.'

'Take them off then.'

It was hard to keep a straight face because by now I could hear other people shouting 'Quiet' and 'Shut the fuck up' from the back. I thought Lauren was going to have a stroke or start frothing at the mouth or something, so in the end I slid the headphones off and looked at her, all innocent. 'What?'

'Why the hell are you watching the telly with those things on?'

'I just like the company,' I said.

The company was no better than it ever was and I was actually there on surveillance, keeping an eye on one particular nurse who was sitting in the corner like butter wouldn't melt. I watched her get up and move between patients, trying to keep a lid on things, because quite a few people were on their feet and shouting by now. That's how it works in here. One patient kicks off a bit and the rest of them tend to join in, like that Russian bloke and his dogs. Chekhov?

I watched her speak calmly to each of them in turn, a hand laid on an arm where it was needed, until some semblance of normality had returned. As normal as it can ever get when a woman is walking from wall to wall and a slightly camp bald bloke keeps pointing at the TV and announcing, 'I've shagged her.'

It was funny, I thought, that the nurse never said anything to Shaun.

I watched her go back to her seat and sit there staring at me. I'm sure anyone else who clocked it thought it was because I was the one who'd started the trouble, but I knew it was because she'd seen me looking at her and that was fine, because I wasn't trying to hide the fact.

I knew she was worried.

I knew she should be.

I stared right back and smiled until she looked away.

Once everything had settled down again, I put my headphones back on, loving how Lauren was still bristling next to me like a fat fucking cat with its fur up. I took out my phone like I was changing the track or whatever, but I was really checking my emails. It wasn't like I was expecting Pindown to get back to me that quickly and certainly not this late, but it couldn't hurt to have a look.

Just spam, and some funny video from my dad which I'd look at later, and a message from Dr Bakshi reminding me that I had my next assessment the day after tomorrow.

I texted a reply to confirm my attendance: Is there a dress code?

Just after half-eleven, Marcus, Malaika and Femi came in. A few extra staff always turned up around this time to make sure the TV got turned off without a row – Lauren once smashed a window when she wasn't allowed to watch the end of QVC – and that everyone was gearing up for bedtime and given extra meds or painkillers where necessary.

I was still watching Debbie, of course, so I was well aware that when I headed out and started drifting towards my room she was following me.

It wasn't obvious, she was far too canny for that, making out like she was gently shepherding several of us towards the women's corridor, just doing her job same as normal, but I could feel her eyes on my back.

So I slowed down, like I was distracted or something.

I let Donna and Lucy go past me, and waited for Debbie to catch up.

She had that concerned face on, the same one I'd seen just before she'd done what she did to Shaun. Someone else who thought they could fool me by wearing a mask.

'Is everything OK?'

'Absolutely,' I said. 'Is everything OK with you?'

'It's not me we're talking about.'

'Maybe it should be.'

She sighed and that mask of concern thickened a little. 'What's the matter, Alice?'

I said, 'Nothing's the matter, everything's great,' and for the first time in a while, I meant it.

'Is there anything you want to talk to me about?'

I knew there would be soon enough, but right then I was happy to enjoy myself. 'I'm fine, Debbie,' I said. 'But thanks for asking.'

'You sure?'

I'd looked on Google, so I knew the right way to cross myself. Forehead, chest, left shoulder, right shoulder. 'I swear to God.'

TWENTY-NINE

I was chatting with one of the janitors who was trying to clean sticky toffee pudding off the camera outside the nurses' station when Lauren came bounding – well, waddling at speed – towards me. Having wound her up so successfully the night before, I was all set for argy-bargy, but I could see immediately that there was nothing to be worried about.

She looked like she'd won the lottery.

She winked at me, rubbing her hands together then pointing towards the closed door of one of the examination rooms at the end of the corridor. She hissed, 'Fresh meat.'

That explained it. 'Serious?'

She nodded and beamed, excited as a kid on Christmas morning. 'Got here a couple of hours ago, Ilias reckons.'

'Yeah?' I was surprised it had taken this long for someone to fill the bed that had been unoccupied since Jamilah had left. It was usually one out, one in, like straight away. I wasn't complaining though. 'Man? Woman?'

'Some woman, apparently . . . fifty-odd, he reckons.'

Donna was passing by on her morning route march and had clearly overheard. 'I've already seen her,' she said. 'Seems nice enough.'

Lauren and I both wheeled round immediately, desperate for more details, but Donna had gone, heading quickly away towards the airlock. It wasn't a big deal because we knew she'd be back again soon enough and there was no way Lauren would let her go next time without pumping her for every bit of info she had.

She'd already begun to sing, throwing her own, horrific idea of twerking into the mix, as she mangled the words of a Bob Marley song.

'New woman, new blood, *new* woman new *blood* . . .'

That should give you some idea of just how giddy the patients in here can turn when a newbie gets brought in. I'm not talking about an Informal because they're rarely worth getting the flags out for. I'm talking about a brand spanking new section-monkey.

Same as I was, a couple of months ago.

It's easy to tell which is which, because it's a whole different process.

The ones being sectioned don't go to the 136 for a kick-off and they usually rock up in an ambulance, fresh from A&E. The Informals are on their own if they're asking to be admitted, or with coppers hanging off them like that poor bastard who'd been dodging traffic. The unfortunates who are likely to be here for at least twenty-eight days tend to arrive with one or two distressed rellies in tow, a doctor or two and maybe a social worker to make an outing of it. They're all over the place most of the time. They're still confused about what had happened to them back at the hospital or why the hell people had turned up at their house with legal documents. They're angry because they think they've been conned and some of them (yours truly, very much included) scratch and spit their way through the admittance procedure like they're being dragged towards a firing squad.

Ah, the procedure . . .

You know when you check in to a nice hotel?

Well it's bugger-all like that.

You know when you check into a shit hotel?

No, not like that either.

There's some basic medical stuff to begin with, which if you ask me is just them going through the motions, really. I mean it *is* a hospital, in case you need reminding. *Oh, your blood pressure's up a bit.* Well, *that's* a real surprise. There's your meds to sort out. The ones you might well be on already – for a dodgy heart, gut problems, diabetes, whatever – and the variety pack of new ones you'll be taking from now on. There's loads more paperwork to be completed and of course you have to be issued with a handful of faded printouts telling you where you are, why you're being detained and who's who on the ward. Your care plan, your daily routine, your right to privacy and dignity . . .

Then, talking of which, you take your clothes off and they dole out the jim-jams.

Then they take your stuff away (remember my potentially lethal bra?).

Then, finally, several hours after stepping into then out of that airlock, you're escorted to your lavish sleeping quarters, where a smiling nurse will show you your bed like you've never seen one before and ask if there's anything else you

196

need. I remember that all I wanted was the Wi-Fi code and for the smiling nurse to fuck the fuck off.

No prizes for guessing who that particular angel was.

So, to take a step back, you can understand why we get so worked up when someone new arrives. Why it's such a big deal. Yeah, it's always nice to see a fresh face, maybe make a new friend, but mostly it's about the pecking order.

A new patient means everyone else moves up one.

Lauren, who already reckoned she was in pole position, was dancing with Graham and Lucy by now. It was like a party. I was all set to stick around, every bit as eager to catch my first glimpse of the gang's latest member as anyone else, but when my phone buzzed and I saw who the email was from, I knew that it would have to wait.

It wasn't like the new girl was going anywhere.

Half an hour later I was back, hanging around near the entrance to the women's corridor with the rest of the welcoming committee – Lauren, Donna, Lucy, Graham, Ilias and Bob – and waiting for the newbie's coming-out parade. Shaun was watching from the doorway of the music room. Tony was sitting by the airlock with his bags packed, but he was watching, too, in case our newest arrival was the Thing.

Everyone was in high spirits, yakking and smiling, so *I* must have looked like I'd just been shagged silly by Tom Hardy or something.

'What *you* so happy about?' Ilias asked.

My grin got even bigger. 'Just ... this, you know. A new face.'

Ilias nodded, peering anxiously towards the examination room. Same as the rest of us, he knew how long the induction

197

process usually took and that, any time now, the latest admission would emerge and be escorted to her bedroom. 'You want to play chess after?'

'Yeah,' I said. 'Sounds good.'

I *was* excited to meet my new wardmate, but the real reason for my good mood was the phone conversation I'd just had with the man from Pindown Investigations, which could not have gone better.

'Howard' was extremely friendly and didn't ask too many questions. He told me how much his 'investigation' would cost and asked if I could transfer half the money straight away. I told him that wasn't a problem (three cheers for that police pension) and asked how long he thought it might take.

'It's all pretty standard stuff,' he said. 'Should have everything you need sometime tomorrow.'

Some deep-seated, law-abiding part of me was gagging to ask *how* he was going to get hold of all this 'pretty standard stuff' but it was just a low, muffled voice, you know? There was something far stronger screaming inside me, desperate to get this information and to *use* it. I didn't want him to know that though. I didn't want anyone to know just yet.

I said, 'Hopefully talk to you tomorrow then.'

When the woman came out of the examination room, me and Lauren and the rest of them surged forward, like groupies outside a stage door. Marcus and George stepped out from the nurses' station to make sure we didn't go any closer and George shook his head, like we were all being a bit sad.

'Come on, give her some room.' He lowered his voice. 'Remember how it was for you.'

I'm damn sure the woman wasn't fifty ... closer to forty if anything ... but I could see why Ilias had told Lauren she

198

was older. I don't think he'd had a proper look. You know how they reckon TV cameras make people look fatter? Well this place can put ten years on you, easy. Sometimes I look in the mirror and see my mum staring back at me.

My mum, if she wasn't well.

The new girl was white and tall and skinny – not *Donna* skinny, but a bit on the scrawny side – with dark hair tied up in a scrunchy. Her head was down, but I saw her glance up at us all, just for a second, and I could see the bruising under one of her eyes. She was moving well enough though, certainly not the usual Fleet Ward shuffle, and I remember thinking that, in spite of everything, she looked ... determined.

'Just make some space and let Clare come through,' Marcus said.

So now we had a name. I nodded at Lucy and Lucy nodded back.

There was a nurse escorting her, of course, a hand on her arm, and it could not have been more perfect. That same mask of concern she'd worn for me the day before. I stared at her, rushing like I'd had a double dose of something, because I knew she was on borrowed time.

As they came alongside us, Lauren reached out a hand and Debbie ushered Clare quickly past. Graham waved and Donna murmured, 'Nice to meet you.'

'I'm Ilias,' shouted Ilias. 'And you're not.'

I watched her being led away towards her bedroom and I had to fight the urge to chase her down and tell her to watch herself. Tell her that this place wasn't safe, whatever it said on her bits of paper. I wanted to point at Debbie and say, 'I hope for your sake that she wasn't the one that examined you.'

'All right,' George said. 'Show's over.'

Lucy and Donna walked away, arms linked, giggling like schoolgirls. Graham took his place at the meds hatch and Lauren wandered over to torment Tony for a while. I stood with Ilias and Bob watching as Debbie opened a bedroom door at the end of the corridor.

'We going to play chess then?' Ilias asked.

I told him to get lost and watched Debbie invite Clare to enter.

Bob sidled up and nodded. 'I did her in a flat in Peckham one time ... the new bird. She went like a bat in a biscuit tin ...'

I was thinking about that mask, about how good it would feel to watch it slip, as I saw Debbie follow the new arrival into the room and close the door behind her.

THIRTY

Dr Bakshi said, 'You look happy, Alice.'

'Because I am,' I said. Because I was.

'That's very nice to hear.' She began slowly turning the pages in front of her. 'And I enjoyed your response to my text message, though I see you haven't dressed up.'

'These are my best trackies,' I said.

It was certainly the most upbeat I'd felt at my Friday-morning assessment session in a dog's age. I could sense something good was coming. Good for me, at any rate. I'd been hoping that Debbie would be sitting there in the circle, like she had been the week before, but they do these things on rotation, so Malaika was keeping Marcus company today. That tight-lipped trainee from last time wasn't anywhere to be seen either. Maybe I'd frightened her off.

So, just the four of us. It was cosy.

Marcus made the official introductions and Malaika did the meds report. I was still 'responding well' to the regime apparently, which was always nice to hear, even though most of the time their idea of *well* and mine were very different.

'By all accounts, you've had a productive week.' Bakshi looked at Marcus, then at me. 'Would you agree?'

'Yeah, I've had a cracking week,' I said.

Malaika nodded, like she was on my side.

'Though I gather there was a minor incident in the television lounge on Wednesday evening.' Bakshi glanced at Marcus. 'Some disagreement with Lauren?'

I laughed and shook my head. 'Just a spot of handbags, that's all. Nothing to get excited about. Lauren didn't think I was giving *Grand Designs*, or whatever the hell she was watching, enough respect. Yeah, it was daft, but I shouldn't have reacted.'

'It's good that you can understand that.' Bakshi turned another page. 'I gather it was an interesting occupational therapy session on Tuesday.'

'You heard that, did you?'

'The nurse who was overseeing the session submitted a written report.'

'Did you see any of the pictures?'

'Unfortunately, I didn't.'

'Oh you should,' I said. 'Lucy's one especially. I swear, she's like the Leonardo da Vinci of pubes.' I stared at Bakshi, straight-faced. I might have been imagining the hint of a smile in return.

'Well, that's all very positive, and I'm delighted that you're making progress. All that said, however, I'm sorry to say that I won't be lifting the section this week.'

'OK,' I said.

I could see that they were all a little taken aback at the calmness of my response, the absence of histrionics, and I have to admit I was pretty surprised myself. No, I probably wouldn't have argued if they'd told me I could trot off home that afternoon, but for the first time in two months I had a reason to be there. A reason to stay, at least until I had the proof I knew was coming, and a chance to act on it.

'Can you guess why that might be, Alice?'

'Why what might be?'

'Why your detention under section three of the Mental Health Act needs to stay in place, for the time being at least.'

'I haven't got a clue,' I said. 'I didn't freak out and show Marcus my tits, did I?'

'No,' Marcus said. 'You did not.'

When I saw Bakshi lift up the sheet of paper, I knew what was coming, but I was genuinely confused.

'At least there was only one late night phone call to Mr Flanagan this week.'

'No way,' I said. 'I never called Andy.' For once I wasn't lying, either, not intentionally.

'Quite a memorable one, though.'

Not for me it wasn't.

'I'm not going to read out what you said, but suffice it to say it was just the one word.' She looked at me, waiting for the penny to drop. 'A very offensive word, repeated over and over again.'

I nodded. Like I'd taken a leaf out of Lauren's book. But I could not remember doing it.

'Oh, right. *That* call.' Malaika shifted in her seat and I swear I saw her trying to stifle a smile. 'Yeah, sorry. I meant to call him again to apologise, but I must have forgotten. It was a moment, that's all, though … of being really angry and doing something stupid. Just one moment, in the whole week.'

Bakshi looked at Marcus. Marcus shrugged.

'Well, I'm taking it as a very good sign that you're not disputing that what you did was wrong.'

'Oh, I know it was.' I wasn't going to tell her that I thought it was piss-funny and I certainly wasn't letting on that I couldn't remember making the call in the first place. 'It was dead wrong.'

Bakshi nodded and began to tidy her papers. 'In which case, on Marcus's recommendation, and in the hope that this progress continues, I'm happy to move you back on to escorted leave.'

That was it. Short and seriously sweet.

I smiled, nice and humble. A day that I already knew would be one to remember had got off to a blinding start.

'Cool,' I said. 'Thank you.'

Clare was sitting with Shaun and Femi at lunch while the rest of us sat together and watched her. Shaun was still keeping up the whole Marcel Marceau thing, but the two women were talking quietly as they ate. I don't think Femi was sitting as close to Clare as she was because of a Within Arm's Length obs stat or anything so I presumed it was part of the normal process of easing the new arrival in gently.

Not wanting to leave her alone with the rabble just yet.

She hadn't shown up for dinner the previous evening and I hadn't been there for breakfast, so for all I knew this might have been her first group mealtime. I asked the others and they all thought it was.

'Has anyone actually spoken to her yet?'

Heads were shaken.

'Not really had a chance,' Ilias said. 'She was with George at the meds hatch first thing and now Femi's stuck to her like shit on a blanket.'

Heads were nodded.

'Femi-Nazi,' Donna said.

'I reckon she's a bit up herself.' Lauren sat back, ready to give her full appraisal of the newcomer, and looked horrified when I stood up. 'Fuck d'you think you're going?'

'Say hello . . .'

I wandered across to their table, told Shaun to budge up and squeezed in between him and Clare. Femi gave me a hard stare, so I smiled to let her know that my intentions were wholly friendly. 'No worries,' I said. 'Just being matey.'

If anything, I was in an even better mood than I had been an hour or so before when I'd sauntered out of the MDR. It wasn't just what they'd said in the assessment meeting, it was what they hadn't said. Not one of them had mentioned the interesting drawing I'd done in the occupational therapy session. Nobody had said a word about any of the conversations I'd had with Debbie over the previous few days.

Like they'd never happened.

That meant that *she* hadn't said anything, and there could only be one reason for that, right?

Guilty as sin and she knew I knew it.

'I'm Alice,' I said. I stuck out a hand. 'Al . . . whatever.' Clare proffered her own, limp hand and I squeezed.

'Clare.'

'With an I or without?'

'Like the county in Ireland.'

'Oh, you Irish, then?' I didn't think I could hear an accent, but she hadn't said much, to be fair.

'My mum is.'

I leaned close to her. Said, 'Listen, why don't we grab a cup of tea and go somewhere a bit quieter for a good old natter?'

'I'm not sure that's a good idea,' Femi said.

'All I'm saying . . .' I looked at the nurse, 'I wish someone had talked to me when I first came in and yeah, I know she's had the official spiel and all that, but she's going to get a much better idea of how things really work in here from someone like me than from one of you lot.' I smiled. 'With all due respect.'

'Sounds OK,' Clare said. A London accent, I decided. Somewhere south of Watford Gap, anyway.

'You make a fair point,' Femi said. 'I should run it past Marcus though.'

'No sweat.' I stood up and reached out a hand towards Clare. 'We'll just be in the music room, so if he's got any problem with it, he knows where we are.'

We'd barely got our arses into chairs in the music room when Ilias came barging in. I asked if he wouldn't mind buggering off and giving us a bit of privacy, but before he'd had a chance to open his mouth Clare burst into tears.

Ilias pointed, looking thrilled. 'What have you done to upset *her*?'

I was searching around for tissues, then saw her pull one from her sleeve and bury her face in it. 'It's not me, you twat, it's *you*.' I walked over to him and whispered, 'I think you just scared her a bit, that's all. Just do me a favour and give us a bit of time on our own?'

Astonishingly, Ilias turned and walked out without saying a word, and by the time I sat down again, Clare had stopped crying.

'You OK?'

She tucked the tissue back into her sleeve. 'I'm fine,' she said.

For the next ten minutes we drank our tea and I gave her the lowdown on Ilias, Lucy and the rest of the gang. I told her their nicknames – well aware that I'd need to come up with one for her – and as many of their strange habits as I could remember. I told her not to let Lauren use her bathroom under any circumstances. I told her about Graham and the waiting, Donna and the constant walking, and when I got to Tony's preoccupation with the Thing, she just stared at me like she'd never heard anything like it.

'I've barely even started, love. Proper madhouse in here.'

She thought that was funny.

I'd just started to dish the dirt on the staff when Clare looked up, noticed Shaun peering in at us through the window and immediately burst into tears again.

'Jesus . . .' I got up to shoo him away and yet again, by the time I'd sat down with her again the crying had stopped and the soggy tissue was being nudged out of sight. 'Is it *blokes*?' I asked. 'You got a problem with blokes?'

She shook her head.

'Thing is, there's quite a few in here, so you might need to have a word with someone about that.'

'I'm fine,' she said.

'You can talk to me,' I said. 'I've had some training—'

'Carry on with what you were saying before.'

I immediately decided that she must have had some kind

of breakdown after being raped. It made perfect sense, and I don't know why I hadn't clocked it earlier. I know they normally try to put patients like her on a single sex ward, but that it isn't always possible. There'd been a woman like that in here when I arrived, and I'd talked to any number of victims who'd been through much the same thing when I was on the Job.

'Tell me about the nurses,' she said.

I moved my chair a little closer to hers. 'Well, I'm not sure if anyone mentioned it to you . . . I mean they almost certainly didn't . . . but we had a murder in here a couple of weeks ago. One of the—'

And just like that, she was blubbing again.

So, not blokes then.

I'll be honest, the on-off waterworks were doing my head in by now, so I got up and opened the door, keen to find someone else to deal with her. I saw Mia outside the 136, so I shouted and waved, and while I was waiting for her to stroll over I decided that – pain in the arse as Clare 'like the county in Ireland' was – I did, at least, have a nickname for her.

Clare, aka Tiny Tears.

It was even funnier, because she was tall, yeah?

While Mia was still on her way across, I felt my mobile buzz in my pocket. I took it out and checked the message.

I think I've got everything you need. Call me for
details. Howard.

Now I *seriously* couldn't care less about the sobbing behind me as I marched quickly past Mia and away towards my bedroom. Funny, isn't it, how the stars align at moments

208

like that – or you think they do – because who do you reckon was the last nurse I saw before I turned on to the women's corridor?

Debbie looked up from the window of the nurses' station as I passed.

'Someone's happy.'

I didn't stop walking. 'Delirious,' I said.

THIRTY-ONE

The man from Pindown Investigations sounded every bit as upbeat about things as I was.

'Like I thought, it was pretty run-of-the-mill stuff. Nothing a bit of know-how and the right computer program couldn't handle. Didn't take me very long if I'm honest, and I'm telling you, Alice, so you know I'm not one of those people who string an investigation out for no good reason except to charge a client more for the job.'

'I appreciate that, Howard.'

'So you'll know where to come if you ever need this kind of service again, right?'

I was running out of patience. About-ready-to-punch-a-hole-in-the-wall running out of it. I needed to *know*. 'What have you got for me then, Howard?'

'So ...' I could hear pages being shuffled. 'The subject lives alone in a two-bedroom flat in Edgware. She runs a small car and, as far as holidays go, last year she managed two weeks in the Scottish Highlands. Went with her sister, I think—'

'What about the money?'

'Well, I'm just giving you the what-do-you-call-it . . . context. But if you want details . . .' More pages being turned. 'She's currently running a small overdraft of £112.75 on an HSBC current account. It's within her agreed limit, but an overdraft none the less. She's missed two mortgage payments on her flat in the last six months . . . there *are* a couple of outstanding credit card debts, but nothing massive and she's got a credit rating of 375 which is about the national average . . . well, a little below if we're being picky.'

'Right.'

'So, whoever she is, your subject isn't exactly minted. I'd say she's just about getting by.'

'What about deposit accounts, savings, whatever?'

'Well, there's a small sum in a deposit account that's tied into her current account, but it's just where any interest gets put. We're talking about a couple of quid, that's all.'

I could feel acid rising up from my stomach, imagined the filthy bubble of it emerging slowly from my mouth and wrapping itself around me. I'd been lying on my bed, but when I tried to sit up, I thought I was going to be sick. 'There must be something else.'

'Not that I could see,' he said.

'What about offshore accounts, overseas banks, trusts or whatever?'

'Sorry, what? You're talking very fast.'

I took a deep breath and said it again.

'Well, I suppose it's a possibility, but that would involve widening the investigation significantly, and—'

'You've missed something. You *must* have done. I mean it's obvious that she's hiding the money, isn't it? Why don't you *get* that?'

He said, 'Do you mind me asking what this individual does for a living? If that's information you're happy to share.'

'She's a mental health nurse.'

He laughed. The useless twat actually chuckled. 'Well, there you go then.'

'What are you on about?'

'Have you any idea how little they get paid? Nurses.'

'She's a *nurse* who's dealing drugs to patients, fair enough?' I knew I was shouting. I could hear my own voice bouncing back off the walls, but sometimes it's the only way to make people see sense. 'She's obviously making a lot of money from selling drugs but for some reason you can't find it. She also happens, *by the way*, to have murdered someone who was threatening to expose her and I know this for a fact, so don't try and tell me I don't know what I'm talking about. Because she's got motive and she had opportunity and I've spoken to witnesses and taken *statements* for God's sake and you were the one who told me that you could get the proof. You *promised* me you'd get the proof and now I don't know what the hell I'm going to do. Do you want her to get away with it? Seriously, is that what you want?'

For a few seconds, all I could hear was the two of us breathing and the noise of Lucy moaning in the room next door. Then Howard said, 'I think I should probably . . . step away from this.'

'Kevin Connolly couldn't step away, could he?'

'I should also remind you that you need to pay the remaining half of my fee—'

'Johnno couldn't fucking step away.'

I was on the floor now, though I still don't remember falling off the bed, and by the time I'd finished swearing at him, my so-called investigator had already hung up.

I remember thinking that the floor was the ceiling and clinging on to the end of my bed for dear life to stop myself falling.

I remember doing a lot of shouting, and even if I can't remember what the words were – I mean there probably weren't any words – I know I *did*, because it felt like I'd swallowed glass for a couple of days afterwards.

I remember someone knocking, asking if I was all right.

I remember ringing Howard back, but he obviously saw it was me calling and didn't answer, so I just did the same thing as when I'd left that message for Andy and said the C-word over and over again for ages. I knew it would be OK, though, because there wasn't any chance Howard would be writing Bakshi a letter.

Mostly, though, I remember my conversation with Johnno, because it was only when he started talking some sense into me that things became clearer and I began to feel they were a bit less hopeless. To see another option.

'It's like with the Evans case,' Johnno said. 'Like with Ralph Cox.'

'Is it?'

'You just need to find a different way, that's all. Something a bit more direct.'

He was sitting next to me on the floor, in that brown suede jacket I always liked. I told him that he should probably be holding on to something if he didn't want to crash into the ceiling, but he told me he could look after himself. He smiled a bit when he said that, like he knew very well how ironic it was.

'I'm sorry, Johnno.'

'About what?'

'About everything, mate. You and Maggie and the baby. Letting you down, I mean.'

'You didn't let me down, you soft sod.'

'You know that when I try to picture your face it's always got blood on it? Just ... spatter. Did I ever tell you that? Sometimes I see it on my fingers, too, and my clothes ... like when you and me were on the Job and they spray stuff with luminol to show up the blood.'

'You didn't let anyone down, Al.'

'I'm a walking fucking crime scene, Johnno.'

'You're not going to let Kevin down, either. I know you're not ...'

And then I was properly calm. Getting there, anyway. I wasn't thinking about the money any more, or gathering evidence; none of it.

I knew exactly what I needed to do.

THIRTY-TWO

I collared her outside the nurses' station after dinner.

'Debbie, can I have a word?'

'Course you can, darlin'.'

'In private, I mean.'

She glanced at her watch then pointed towards one of the examination rooms. 'Let's go in there.'

When I'd sat down, I nodded towards the door she'd left open. 'You might want to shut that,' I said.

She shrugged then pushed the door until it was almost closed. 'I'll leave it open just a little bit,' she said.

Like she thought I was dangerous.

'It's fine,' I said. Because I *was*.

She pulled a chair across and sat down. 'So, what can I do for you, Alice?'

Before I knew what I was doing, I had reached into my pocket for my mobile, pressed a few buttons and was holding it out towards her. 'Look at this,' I said.

She watched, started to smile.

To this day I can't quite explain what I was doing for that minute or so. It wasn't like I'd changed my mind or chickened out or anything, it wasn't any kind of clever delaying tactic. It was a switch that tripped for no good reason. I just forgot myself and . . . went somewhere else.

'That's funny,' she said.

I was showing her the video my dad had sent me a few days earlier. A monkey being shown a magic trick, for fuck's sake. I was smiling *myself*, even though my hand was shaking as I held the screen up. Christ alone knows what happened or where my head was at right then, but looking back now I was like a hitman who pulls out a gun then gets distracted by the colour of the curtains. 'Look at the monkey's face when he sees it . . .'

She laughed at the monkey's double-take. 'Ah . . . that stuff's brilliant,' she said. 'I love all those cat ones.'

Then, just like that, the switch flipped back again. I slipped my phone back in my pocket and looked up to see her staring at me.

'I know what you did,' I said.

'OK, Alice.' She shook her head. 'What did I do?'

'I know that you murdered Kevin and I know you did it because of the drugs.' She looked at me like I was mad and I know that sounds like a strange observation bearing in mind where we were, but trust me, it's a look they try very hard *not* to give anyone in here. They're trained to do precisely the opposite. That's why it made such an impression. 'Kevin didn't want any more to do with the whole thing and he was almost certainly threatening to blackmail you with the drugs you'd already given him and which he'd hidden. The drugs you couldn't find when you went into his room that night.'

'OK,' she said.

It was just pouring out. I couldn't remember the last time I'd felt so confident or in control, so the person I wanted to *be*.

I felt like I was fucking invincible.

'You killed him on your first round of checks . . . or maybe your second, it doesn't really matter. But you'd certainly already done it by the time you went in that third time and "discovered" the body and started screaming the place down. That was pretty clever, I'll give you that much. I'm not sure if you knew Graham had already put the camera out of action or not, but either way he really did you a favour, didn't he? It made everything so much more complicated for the police than it actually needed to be.'

'OK,' she said.

'Then you got scared, because the person who was closest to Kevin knew exactly what you were up to. Maybe Shaun said something to you, told you he knew you'd murdered Kevin, but even if he didn't, you decided it would be best to shut him up anyway. To be on the safe side.'

'You're talking about what happened when Shaun had that episode in the TV room?'

'I'm talking about you silencing a key witness, yeah.'

Debbie nodded, thought for a few seconds. 'So, it was Kevin's room in that picture you did the other day?'

'Right, like you didn't know.'

'And it was me in the room.'

'Who else did you think it was—'

I stopped when I saw George poke his head around the door. I'm not sure if it was the look on my face or Debbie's that he'd clocked. 'Is everything OK in here?'

217

I sat back and pointed a finger. 'You should ask *her.*'

By the time Debbie turned to look at him, she had a very different mask on. Up to then her face had been sort of dry and pinched, but now she was smiling. She said, 'We're fine, thanks, George. It's all good. Alice is just telling me a story.'

THIRTY-THREE

This Is What I Believe.

Believe. Present tense . . .

The Earth is definitely not flat.

5G is not going to turn us all into zombies.

There are people in this world with too much wealth and power who will do anything they have to, including murder where necessary, to mould society into whatever shape suits them, while making sure the rest of us don't know who they are. I'm not talking about spooky shit with robes and candles and human sacrifice. Not secret satanists or people who are really lizards. I just mean rich and powerful people doing bad things to hold on to what they've got and protecting their equally rich and powerful friends. You only have to look at what's going on in the world and that makes perfect sense, doesn't it?

My mum and dad are obviously not part of anything like this and are genuinely good people.

My ex-boyfriend Andy isn't either. He's just a dick.

You have to go slightly mad to become properly sane.

The Beatles obviously existed and they were great, apart from the weird Indian stuff and that stupid song about an octopus.

There were no criminals wearing masks on my television.

Drink and drugs were partly, but not wholly, responsible for everything that led up to me being 'retired', and everything that's happened since.

Johnno died because I was not a good enough copper.

I did not hurt anyone, except when I was trying to protect them and myself, and I would do so again.

Being banged up with mad people is not great for your mental health.

Almost all the people working here do an amazing job, clinging on by their fingernails, and there's rarely a day goes by when I don't think that being a copper was a doddle by comparison.

I was sexually assaulted. I *was*.

If they sent me home tomorrow – to a recovery house for a few weeks probably, then to Mum and Dad's – I would be absolutely fine.

I will meet someone, get married and have a family like everyone else.

At some point, I will work as a police officer again.

Kevin Connolly was murdered just over two weeks ago on this ward by Deborah Anne McClure (FRCN). You already know the hows and whys so I don't need to repeat them. You probably want to know how our conversation in the examination room ended, but there really wasn't much more to it after George interrupted us. All you need to know is that her mask stayed firmly in place until Debbie announced that she needed to be on duty at the meds hatch and left.

She had nothing to say. Nothing.

Yeah, a straight-up confession would have been nice, but that was as close to one as you can get. Her coming clean there and then would certainly have been a good result for me and, bearing in mind what was around the corner, would definitely have done her a major favour.

So, here we are. That's us bang up to date.

Well, aside from the blood-soaked elephant in the room, which is the fact that, two days later – yesterday to be precise – I was the one who found Debbie's body.

PART TWO

FIGHT OR FLIGHT

THIRTY-FOUR

As you can imagine, it's been all fun and games around this place the last twenty-four hours. A right old palaver. The police have packed up and gone, for the time being at least, but everything's still all over the shop.

Everything and everyone.

Right now, we're all gearing up for this afternoon's 'community meeting' which should be interesting to say the least. It's safe to say we won't be talking about how bad the food is, or the need for a private visiting area, or Ilias's constant farting, or any of the other fascinating topics that normally crop up at these things.

Probably just the one item on the agenda this time.

Yesterday . . .

I gave the police an initial statement when they first arrived, an hour or so after I'd found the body, and I reckon I did pretty well, considering I was probably still in shock. This was after they'd bagged up my bloodstained trackies and T-shirt and trainers, and sat me down in an exam room with a mug of tea and a nice friendly DC called Pauline.

Is there anyone you'd like us to call, love?

I hadn't even had a chance to shower, but I know how it works. I told them as much, made sure the officers at the scene knew they were dealing with someone who understood the procedure. Who fully grasped the importance of getting a witness's statement, *my* statement, while everything was still . . . fresh. As I pointed out to Pauline, I hadn't so much as washed my hands yet, so things could hardly have been any fresher.

I think I'll be all right. I've had blood on my hands before.

Pauline and her older male colleague were just the first detectives on the scene, but the MIT that ended up catching the case would probably be a different team from the one that was dealing – or *not* dealing – with Kevin's murder. I guessed the two teams would be putting their heads together at the very least, once the left hand of Homicide and Serious Crime became aware of what the right hand was doing. That's not something you can ever take for granted in the Met, but even allowing for the usual administrative bullshit and basic incompetence, two murders – in the same place in the space of a fortnight – were pretty likely to raise a red flag.

I mean, you would have thought.

'So, you found Miss McClure's body when you visited the women's toilets, is that correct?' Pauline seemed a bit . . . mousy for my liking, then I remembered that she was talking to someone she'd presume was almost certainly traumatised.

I nodded. 'Saw it as soon as I opened the door. Well, you could hardly miss it.'

'What time would this have been? Approximately.'

'It was . . . what, an hour ago? So about half-past three.'

'You could see straight away that it was Miss McClure?'

'Yeah, I saw the ginger hair. I mean I noticed the blood first, obviously. There was a lot of blood.'

'So, what did you do?'

'Well, I had first-aid and life support training when I was on the Job, so I got down on the floor with her to see if there was anything I could do. I mean it was pretty obvious there wasn't . . . I could see how many stab wounds there were . . . but it just kicked in, I suppose. I did CPR for . . . I don't know, half a minute or so? That's why . . .' I held up my hands so she could see the blood dried between my fingers, gathered in the lines on my palm and at the base of my nails.

'What about the knife?'

'That was lying on the floor a few feet away, under one of the sinks.'

'So you didn't touch it?'

I looked at her to make sure she knew what a daft question it was. 'Of course I didn't touch it. Obviously I was aware that me giving first aid might compromise evidence on the body itself. That couldn't be helped, but I certainly know better than to go anywhere near the murder weapon.'

She was writing all this down, ready to pass it on to the full-time investigators, once they were assigned. 'So, when did you shout for help?'

'While I was doing CPR,' I said. 'Then I ran out and I was still shouting and Marcus came in, then Malaika, and they took over. Or maybe Malaika got in there first, I can't remember. It was all a bit panicky.'

'What about before you went in? You didn't see anyone coming out?'

I told her I hadn't.

'You didn't see anyone going in before you?'

I was getting a bit irritated by now and told her that I didn't make a habit of logging activity in and around the women's toilet.

'I have to ask,' she said.

'Course,' I said. 'Sorry for being snappy.'

'It's understandable,' she said. 'This can't be easy for you.'

She asked for my details, so I told her that I was likely to be staying exactly where I was for the foreseeable future, but gave my mum and dad's address as a back-up. When she asked for my phone number, I said, 'Steve Seddon's already got my number.' I could see that she recognised the name. 'Not that you'd know it.'

'It's best that I have it, too,' she said.

Once she'd thanked me for my help and given me a number to call should I be in need of counselling, Pauline wandered out into the corridor to join her colleague, who'd been taking a statement from Marcus.

Marcus came in and sat with me.

'You OK?' He was staring down at the blood that had dried on his own hands. His friend's blood.

'I'm fine.' We said nothing for a while, just stared into space, then I nodded down at his hands. 'You get used to that.'

Marcus took a few deep breaths then looked at me and shook his head. He said, 'What the fu-fu-fuck is going on?'

I'd heard him stammer plenty of times, but it was the first time I'd ever heard him swear.

Now, L-Plate comes running up to me outside the dining room like the world is coming to an end. She looks like she's been crying, though to be fair, she looks like that more often than looking like she hasn't been.

'What's the matter, L?'

'This meeting.'

'I know,' I say. 'Yeah, it's bound to be a bit upsetting, but I think that's what it's for, so—'

'No, not that—'

'So people can let their feelings out a bit—'

'I don't know what to *wear*.'

'*What?*' I watch her shaking her head, clutching at the material of a glittery Dolce & Gabbana sweatshirt like it's some old rag she's pulled on, and I quite fancy punching her in the tits. Instead, I ask, 'Who gives a toss what you wear?'

'*I* do,' she says.

'Are you on the *pull?*' I see a hint of a smile. 'You think Ilias is even going to bother changing his pants? You think Donna won't have the same sweaty tracksuit on she has every bloody day?' Her smile widens. 'Look, I know what's happened is freaking us all out a bit, but this meeting isn't anything to worry about, I swear. It's certainly not something you need to get tarted up for.'

'You promise?' she asks.

I nod, and find myself trying to remember the last time I'd got tarted up for anything.

Mists of bloody time.

It was some stupid office thing I went to with Andy. One of those where they dole out crap awards, and I remember I'd borrowed a dress off Sophie because I didn't have any-thing nice with long sleeves. All night I was letting Andy know, a bit too loudly, that his HR manager was looking at me funny, like he knew something or was trying to send me a bad message. Andy told me to keep it down because I was showing him up, so I just smoked a couple of spliffs in the car park, drank a gallon of prosecco and was sick on the way home.

I never even had Sophie's dress cleaned before I gave it her back.

Now, L-Plate nods and says, 'Sorry, Al . . . having a bad day.' She looks about seven years old, standing there chewing her fat bottom lip like she's trying to be brave, and I feel bad for wanting to punch her.

'No need to be sorry,' I say.

George and Mia wander out of the dining room. They've been setting the chairs up for the meeting. I say, 'All set?' but they just carry on walking towards the nurses' station. They both still look a bit shell-shocked.

I reach out, without thinking, to touch L-Plate's arm, then tell myself off for being an idiot when she flinches. 'Listen, forget what I said. You can dress up if you want. You can wear anything you bloody well fancy.' I nod towards the women's corridor. 'Come on, let's go and get your outfit sorted.'

THIRTY-FIVE

Marcus stands up and says, 'Thank you for all for coming, especially at this very difficult time.' This is no bog-standard community meeting and it's clear he's prepared something when he glances down at what he's written on a small piece of card. 'Obviously, we are all deeply shocked by what's happened. To lose a friend and colleague this way is terrible, but our main concern has to be for all of you. How you are feeling, how we cope with what has happened and how we move on from this, together.'

Graham puts his hand up. When Marcus looks at him and nods, Graham squirms in his seat for a few seconds, like he's embarrassed to find himself in the spotlight.

He asks, 'Has something bad happened?'

Marcus mumbles a few words to Mia who immediately stands up and walks across to where Graham is sitting. She politely asks Donna to move up one, then sits down next to Graham and takes his hand.

I'm thinking that's sweet of her.

I'm thinking that Graham is a bit further gone than I thought he was.

I'm thinking, *deeply shocked* is a bloody understatement and that what happened on Sunday is only the second most shocking thing I can think of. I would have thought the most *holy fuck this is properly bonkers* shocking thing is . . . Marcus standing there, saying all this while he knows damn well that whoever stabbed his 'friend and colleague' to death is sitting right there with him in the same room.

How can he *not* know that?

I can only assume the police have come to the same conclusion. I'm not sure who the Met's hiring these days, but even a bunch of sixteen-year-old work-experience detectives should have figured that much out by now. Yes, there were a couple of visitors on the ward at the time of the murder, but it's hard to imagine that Donna's mum or Ilias's idiot younger brother had much of a motive for killing Debbie. That's if *anyone* had what an ordinary punter might think of as a conventional motive. Rage, revenge, love, sex, money, all the old favourites.

By now you should be well aware it doesn't take much in here.

There were several Informals around at the time as well, of course, but those who were able to provide the police with permanent addresses got the hell out of there as soon as they could. I mean, wouldn't you?

Aside from a couple of voluntary patients of no fixed abode, that just leaves those of us on section plus the members of staff who are still breathing and, like Marcus said, they've all shown up for the meeting.

Looks like it, anyway.

There's maybe twenty people in the dining room.

A big circle of chairs.

Marcus says, 'Before I open the meeting up to the floor, I want to introduce someone who's going to say a few words about the position of the ward moving forward.' He points towards the only person in the room I don't recognise.

Ilias leaps to his feet, looking a bit panicky. 'Where's the ward going?'

'Well, this man will tell you,' Marcus says.

Ilias sits down again, but he still looks worried.

The man – middle-aged with grey hair – stands up and introduces himself as a member of the hospital's Foundation Trust Board. 'I wanted to let you know that there have been ... discussions about closing the ward.' He sounds like someone off the radio. 'At least temporarily, in light of the recent tragic events. It was suggested that it might be better for the mental well-being of all patients if they were moved elsewhere.'

Several members of staff nod. I'm thinking we should probably be more concerned about our *physical* well-being.

'In the end, however, we have decided to keep the ward open and functioning as normal.' He glances at Marcus. 'As normally as we can, at any rate.'

I think that *normal* is not a word he would be using if he'd ever set foot in this place before today.

'Firstly, I must be honest and acknowledge the sad fact that we would simply not be able to find enough alternative beds for everyone, certainly not in London. Secondly, the board was of the opinion that everyone would benefit from as little disruption as possible and that patients would probably be in favour of leaving things as they are.' He looks out at us all. 'That you would prefer to stay together.'

I can see the sense in what the bloke's saying, but I consider asking if maybe we can just get rid of Lauren.

It strikes me that keeping the ward open might be what the police would prefer as well. It's always better if a detective can keep all their suspects in one place. As the posh bloke sits down and Marcus stands up to say a bit more, I'm finding it hard not to imagine the whole thing as some warped, psych-ward version of Cluedo.

Mr or Mrs Mental, in the toilets, with a dagger.

Or an air-locked room mystery. Ha!

Now, various patients have begun standing up and shouting out questions, making observations or just shar-ing random thoughts, while Marcus tries to maintain some semblance of order.

'Can we use the bogs again?' Lauren asks.

'Yes, you can,' Marcus says.

'Good, because the men's bogs stink.'

'*You* stink,' Bob says. 'You stink of fish.'

'Was there a lot of blood?' Ilias asks.

'I don't think it's helpful to talk about that,' Marcus says.

'Where's Debbie?' Graham asks.

Now, it's my turn. I'm sitting next to Shaun and he starts, nervous as a kitten, when I stand up suddenly. 'What about some security?'

Marcus looks at me.

'That's a good idea,' Tony says. 'Stop the Thing coming in.'

'Yeah, but what if the Thing *is* the security?' Lauren asks.

'Oh, Jesus,' Tony says.

Marcus is still looking at me. 'What do you mean, Alice?'

'Well, this place obviously isn't safe, is it?' I look around for some support and I'm pleased to see Lucy and Ilias nodding. 'You have a duty of care and you're supposed to keep us safe. I mean, that's basically why we're here, right? When you're more likely to get killed on a closed national health ward than you are in the arse-end of Hackney on a Friday night, I think something needs to be done about it. I reckon we deserve to have some decent protection.'

Marcus looks at the bloke from the Trust.

The bloke from the Trust seems a little uncomfortable, but says, 'It's certainly something we can discuss.'

'There we are,' Marcus says.

'A couple of big bastards with tasers,' I say. 'Or even better—'

Marcus holds up a hand. He says, 'I think you've had your answer, Alice,' and looks around for another question.

I sit down again and put my earphones in and spend most of the rest of the meeting wondering why Marcus is being so off with me. I also spend a few minutes asking myself why Lauren felt the need to be such a bitch to Tony and thinking how much I'll enjoy telling Ilias *exactly* how much blood there was. The look on the hairy little sod's face.

We all enjoy passing on the details of a proper drama, don't we?

A quarter of an hour later, when the meeting's breaking up, I amble across to Malaika and ask if she fancies escorting me outside for a cigarette. She immediately feels for her own pack and lowers her voice.

'God, I've been desperate for one of you to ask.'

It's drizzling a bit, so we stand close together beneath the overhang at the entrance to the unit. Malaika has crashed me one of her fags to save me the hassle of rolling my own, which is dead nice of her.

Like I said before, she's one of the good ones, and the Brummie accent always cheers me up.

'Police are coming back tomorrow,' she says.

I nod and hiss out a stream of smoke. 'They'll be making an arrest probably.'

'You reckon?'

'Yeah, they'll know who did it by now.'

'I wouldn't bank on it.' She gives me a knowing look.

'You're fucking kidding me,' I say. *'Again?'*

'Graham put three different cameras out of action on Sunday.' She holds up the requisite number of fingers. 'The dining room one, the one outside the 136 and the one in the corridor that covers the women's toilets.'

'Unbelievable.'

'You were talking about making things safer?' she says. 'Back in there? First thing we should do is get Graham moved to another ward.' She hunches her shoulders. It's getting nippy out here. 'The coppers who were here gave Marcus a real bollocking about it. Lecturing him about "serious lapses in security", like it was all his fault.'

'Yeah, well that's because it's made their job a lot harder.'

I stand there saying nothing for a while and thinking about two murder investigations, both with massive spanners in the works thanks to the security cameras covering the scenes being buggered. Yeah, Graham pulls this shit a lot, but even so. Once is seriously unlucky, but for that to happen twice is a hell of a coincidence.

I wonder if the police are thinking the same thing.

'You weren't very fond of Debbie, were you?' Malaika says from nowhere.

'Who told you that?'

'Well, Debbie said something.'

'What?'

'No ... nothing specific. Just that the two of you hadn't really bonded.'

I stare at her. 'What does that even mean? Have you *bonded* with Lauren or with Bob? I'd be amazed if you had. You just hit it off better with some people than you do with others, right?'

'I suppose,' Malaika says.

'To be honest, there's times when I don't know how you stop yourself giving most of the arseholes in here a bloody good slapping.'

She smiles. 'It's a struggle,' she says.

I'm not sure Malaika's being completely upfront about what Debbie said or didn't say to her about me. Still, if she doesn't already know about it, I don't see much point in telling her what *I'd* said to *Debbie* a couple of days before she was killed. What I'd accused her of.

I can't change that, can I?

Even now she's dead, I certainly don't take it back.

We stub our cigarettes out on the wall behind us and Malaika says, 'Come on then ...'

I don't move, because suddenly all I can think about is meeting Billy out here a couple of weeks ago. Those spare joints I stashed inside a pipe, just a few feet away from where we're standing.

A quick hit would be lovely, and there's never any harm in trying, is there? I don't *think* she'd dob me in just for asking.

Truth is, the evil bastards aren't the only ones that can wear masks, and these past few months I've mastered quite a few useful expressions that I can plaster on pretty quick when the situation calls for it.

Shame-faced, aggrieved, dangerous, sad, desperate, untroubled . . .

Now, I do my best to look . . . winsome.

'I don't suppose you fancy taking a walk for five minutes?'

Malaika grins and lays a hand in my arm. She says, 'Don't push your luck.'

THIRTY-SIX

It's quarter-past three in the morning, I'm wide awake and there's blood everywhere.

Or there *was* . . .

I lie in bed and wait for my heart rate to slow a little, then try to regulate my breathing, the way I was taught after this happened the first time. Long breath in through the nose, count to three, then slowly out through pursed lips. It's hard to focus because someone's shouting along the corridor.

I take another long breath in . . .

Early on, I said that I didn't believe the recreational drugs I'd been taking before I got sectioned were the only thing responsible for me ending up here, and I stand by that. Equally, now that I'm clean-and-sober-ish, I don't think the drugs I'm being fed by doctors four times a day – the *good* drugs – are the only reason for what's happening right this minute. What's been happening, on and off, ever since I got here.

Something's messing with my head, though.

Awake or asleep, there's something directing this horror show.

I let the breath slowly out again.

That's one of the problems. Whenever this happens, I'm never sure if it's a dream or not. I mean, I know it's not *real* . . . but when it ends, I don't know if I've woken up or if I was awake the whole time and it's only stopped because my brain's decided it wants to go somewhere a bit less scary for a while. Like a circuit breaker tripping when the current gets unsafe.

Three-two-one . . . you're back in the room.

There was blood, like I said. There's always plenty of blood. Thinking about it rationally – just for a minute – it's all hugely predictable. Wherever I am – and that part's always a bit fuzzy and vague – I can't stop crying and thrashing around in a massive panic, and there's no way I can get the blood off because there's so much of it and when I do manage to wipe just enough of it away to remind myself what my skin actually looks like more comes bubbling up through my pores. Blood that isn't mine, I mean. Like I'm living and breathing and . . . *being* the stuff.

It wasn't my fault. It wasn't my fault. It wasn't my fault . . .

It's Johnno's blood, obviously . . . a fountain of it gushing from the wound in his neck. I don't need Bakshi or anyone else to work that much out.

Or at least, it used to be.

Now, there's even more to wade through, to wash off, to drown in, because Debbie's blood is sloshing about in the mix as well; drenching everything in the dream or the hallucination or whatever the hell it is.

There's a difference, though.

Before, it was all about guilt, of course. When it was over, I would lie awake, breathing like I'm doing now and feel it eating me alive, no matter how many times I told myself that I hadn't been to blame for what happened to Johnno.

I'm not guilty, I'm not guilty.

Not. Guilty.

Now though, I'm feeling something else and it paralyses me far more than guilt has ever done. It's knocking on for half-past three and, if I've had any sleep at all, I know there's no chance of me getting any more.

I stare at the door. I look for a shadow moving beneath it. I listen for the noise of someone outside.

I'm absolutely fucking terrified.

THIRTY-SEVEN

I told you how rubbish I am with names – back when I was on the Job, I had to write them down in my notebook – and, sitting there in the MDR, I forget what the two coppers are called almost as soon as they've introduced themselves. In my head and gone again. So, rather than sit there squinting at their IDs, I decide to go down my normal route and make something up.

It . . . lightens things, which is good. For me at least.

One of the women is shorter than the other and a bit on the dumpy side, while her mate strikes me as slightly posher, so it doesn't take long to give them celebrity alter-egos. A different kind of double act. I just need to get that theme tune out of my head and stop imagining them both with fags on and enormous latex bellies, pretending to be blokes and trying to shag inanimate objects.

Like a pair of fat sleazy Bobs.

DC French looks up and says, 'I understand you were the one who found Miss McClure's body on Sunday afternoon.'

I tell her that she's spot on.

'That can't have been a particularly pleasant experience.'

'I've had worse,' I say.

'Really?'

I look at her, then watch as DC Saunders – who's obviously done a bit more in the way of preparation – leans across and whispers something, then begins turning her colleague's pages for her and pointing something out. I'm assuming it's all there. The flat in Mile End. What happened to Johnno.

'Oh yes.' French looks up and nods sympathetically.

When asked, I tell them exactly what I'd told the detective a couple of days ago. The body and the blood, the CPR until Marcus and Malaika arrived, the knife on the floor underneath the sink. Predictably, they ask me the same daft questions about anyone I might have seen going in or coming out of the toilets before me. I say much the same thing I said on Sunday, though I'm a bit less sarky about it.

'It's a shame you even need to ask,' I say. 'I mean, you'd know exactly who'd been in and out of the toilet if that camera hadn't been buggered about with.'

French's chair squeaks as her arse shifts in it.

'You'd be making an arrest by now, am I right?'

Saunders clears her throat and says, 'No, it's not ideal.'

She looks away, all set to move on. She doesn't change her face, doesn't elaborate, doesn't give any indication that they think a camera being put out of action again could be even the slightest bit suspicious. *Not ideal?* I tell you this for nothing: any faith I might have that this second investigation will be handled any better than the first is already being seriously tested.

'There's something we wanted to clear up,' French says.

'Oh yeah?'

'We've been told by the ward manager that, a short time before Miss McClure was killed, you had accused her of being involved in the murder of a patient here just over a fortnight ago. Kevin Connolly?'

So, that's why Marcus was being weird with me at that meeting yesterday. Debbie had obviously gone running to him as soon as I'd confronted her, probably moaning about unacceptable verbal abuse or some such. Bleating to her boss about me having another one of my delusions or the need for stronger meds to control my fantasies about still being a police officer.

'Well, I'd known she was involved in that murder for a while,' I say. 'I only told her to her face on the Friday. About forty-eight hours before she was killed.'

'I see.'

'And "involved" is putting it mildly, by the way. She was the one doing the murdering.' I sit back and fold my arms. 'I'm relieved that you've finally brought it up, as it goes.'

'Why's that?

'Because it means that you've connected the two murders. I mean, they *are* connected. You know that, right?' I wait. 'Come on, how can they not be?'

French and Saunders look at one another.

'You working with the other lot, then? With Seddon's team?'

'The two investigations have been ... merged,' Saunders says.

'Who's running it?'

They exchange another look. Finally, Saunders says, 'Detective Chief Inspector Brigstocke.'

I recognise the name but I don't know him. 'Is he any

good?' I wait some more, but neither of them seems awfully keen to discuss the capabilities of their SIO. The room's getting seriously warm and I think about asking one of them to open a window.

'You seem tense, Alice,' French says.

'Do I?'

'A bit on edge.'

'Well, of *course* I'm on edge. I'm shitting myself.'

'Why would that be?'

It obviously needs spelling out for them. 'I thought Debbie was running the whole drugs thing on her own, OK . . . but I was obviously wrong. She was clearly working with someone else on the inside and whoever that person is decided that Debbie couldn't be trusted to keep her mouth shut. Look, I didn't make a huge secret of the fact that I thought Debbie was the one who'd killed Kevin, all right? Or that I had my suspicions, at least. So, maybe her accomplice reckoned it wouldn't be too long before Debbie was arrested, and that when she was, she'd spill her guts about exactly who else was involved. So best to get rid of her. I suppose looking at it that way, I'm partly to blame for what happened.'

Saunders is scribbling. 'Right . . .'

'I wasn't the one with the knife though, was I?'

'No,' French says.

'That's something else . . .'

'What?'

'I told Seddon two weeks ago about how easy it would be to get hold of a knife in here and he didn't listen. Wouldn't even return my calls when I had crucial information. If I'd been taken seriously a bit sooner, Debbie might have been nicked long before whoever she was working with had the chance to shut her up for good. That's what I'd call dropping the ball, big time. So yeah, I'm not exactly relaxed right now . . . because chances are whoever carved Debbie up in the bogs knows that I've put the whole thing together. Which means they might decide to come after me next.'

Saunders puts her pen down. 'Are you worried for your safety?'

To be fair to the woman, she looks genuinely concerned. She might not give a monkey's, of course, but it's been a long time since I've been able to tell the difference.

'Always,' I say.

Hang out the flags, Shaun the Silent has begun communicating again.

Notice I don't say 'speaking', because apparently that would be asking a bit much, but he's . . . making himself known.

Something, I suppose.

So, quarter of an hour ago, I sit down next to him to have my lunch and, without looking at me, he scribbles something on a serviette, scrunches it up into a tiny ball and presses it into my hand. A special secret message, just for me. He doesn't seem massively bothered when I open it up there and then, but that's probably because of what it says.

this mince tastes like dog-shit.

No, it's not exactly the Gettysburg Address, but it's a start, right? So I immediately rush off to grab some paper, then come back to see if Shaun has any other words of wisdom to impart. It's got to be worth a try, because if he knew about

246

Debbie killing Kevin, then chances are he knows who her accomplice is.

Who killed Debbie.

So far, bugger all, but let's wait and see?

There's the usual noisy chatter, because by now quite a few others have been interviewed, same as I was, and are mad keen to tell everyone how it went. L-Plate's twittering about her interview like she's just been given the third degree.

'I didn't think those two women were very nice,' she says. 'The ones on Sunday were much nicer. Mind you, they took some of my clothes away with them.'

'Mine too,' Lauren says. 'My best T-shirt and joggers. I'd better get them back or I'll be kicking off big time.'

I pointed out that clothing samples had been taken from everyone, staff included. Without stating the blindingly obvious and telling them it was because they were all suspects, I reassured them that it was standard practice.

'Really though, they were a bit . . . fierce,' L-Plate says.

'Probably lesbians,' Ilias says. The voice of reason as always, spraying the table with gobbets of shepherd's pie.

I didn't think French and Saunders were fierce at all, but I suppose it's daunting if you're not used to it. Or if you haven't been on the other side of the table yourself, like I have. I need to keep reminding myself that this lot are civilians, that they don't know the game. When Donna asks when they'll be taking our fingerprints and DNA, I gently remind her that it's already on record, because the last lot did all that and your DNA doesn't change from week to week, whatever she might have seen on CSI.

Lauren tells me I'm a smartarse.

I tell Lauren she's an idiot.

Big Gay Bob loudly tells *everyone* that DC French could probably do with losing a few pounds, which immediately sends Donna out into the corridor to start walking off the spoonful of peas she's eaten. 'Mind you, I quite like a chubby bird,' Bob says. 'They're always grateful.'

It doesn't look like Shaun has anything else he wants to share, and Tiny Tears has nothing to say for herself either. She just sits there pushing her food around and watching me from the other end of the table, which makes me uncomfortable to say the least. I start to lose interest in the conversation when Tony says he had a feeling that the other copper might have been *you-know-who* and I finally zone out completely when Lauren starts singing 'I Fought the Law'.

Oh, the other big news is that Graham, the Waiter, has gone.

Spirited away while I was being interviewed, just like that. Off to bang his head against a different wall, wait at a new meds hatch and chuck his dinner at the cameras on some other ward. Maybe Malaika said something after the chat we had about security yesterday, or Marcus took the roasting he got off those coppers to heart and decided he had no other option.

Either way, we're a body down.

Three, obviously, if you count Debbie and Kevin.

At least Graham can be thankful he wasn't taken out of here in a bag.

THIRTY-EIGHT

It's been pretty full on since breakfast so, once I've gobbled down the last meds of the day, I decide to retire to my sumptuous boudoir a bit earlier than usual. Getting an extra hour or two of sleep feels like a top idea, plus I fancy some time on my own. Tempting as it might be to veg out in the TV room like I normally do and wind Lauren up if I get bored, I need to chill for a bit, so I sit on my bed working my way through a packet of Hobnobs and dicking around on the internet for a while.

I start to feel more relaxed straight away. Just me, with my finger on a trackpad that can take me anywhere. I laugh out loud when it strikes me that this is the happy place I couldn't get to a couple of weeks back, in that hideous assessment session.

But what is more problematic is yet another email from Andrew Flanagan . . .

I watch a few stupid videos for a laugh and catch up on

some celeb gossip until I've finished the biscuits. Then I spend half an hour cruising some of the newsgroups and private chat rooms where, once upon a time I try not to think about too much, I wasted half my life.

Now, though, it isn't about convincing myself I'm not paranoid. It isn't a question of finding like-minded mentalists, so I don't feel like I'm the only one going through . . . whatever it *was* I was going through. These days, it's just curiosity.

I swear . . .

I watch the vlogs and read the bat-shit comments.

I think, *get a life.*

I only stop when I start to suspect there's someone standing outside my door. Then I'm convinced there is. I know it's not one of the nurses because Mia was round, doing the half-hour checks, ten minutes ago.

I tell myself to calm down, that I've got sod all to be scared of.

I creep to the door and press my ear against it. There's definitely someone there, I can hear them breathing. It's probably the gentlest of knocks, but I step back like someone's let off an air-horn.

'Who is it?'

'It's Clare . . .'

Oh, so now Tiny Tears is talking to me. I open the door and hold out my hands like, *What d'you want?* and watch her standing there looking awkward.

'Were you asleep?'

'Well, if I was, I'm not now, am I?' She looks like she's going to cry and I'm buggered if I'm putting up with any more of that. 'It's fine,' I say. 'I wasn't.'

'Is it OK if I come in?' she asks.

I sigh, and step back to let her in, and she lowers her gangly self down until she's perching on the edge of my bed. She clutches at one hand with the other and shakes her head and says how awful it is, what happened to that nurse. She looks at me and I realise she's waiting for me to agree with her.

'Yeah,' I say.

The look on her face tells me that I haven't quite managed to conjure the pity or sympathy she was expecting and it shocks me a bit, because I was really trying. Debbie is the first murder victim that I've been anywhere near since I left the police. Do I sound uncaring ... do I *feel* uncaring because I didn't much like Debbie and know what she was guilty of? Or is it because the empathy that was there on the Job is something I've lost? Would I be as destroyed as I used to be at the murder of a neglected toddler, or a pensioner who's been battered to death, or *anyone*? I want to know the answer, but at the same time I really don't want to be in a position where I get it.

'So, come on then,' I say. 'How did you end up in here?'

She shakes her head.

'It's OK, you don't have to keep it secret. It's not like prison.' I smile, because I really want to know. 'Well, it's a *bit* like prison.'

'I don't want to talk about it.'

'No probs,' I say.

I reckon her reluctance is a bit strange, though. Most people in here tend to fall into one of two camps. Either they're desperate to tell you everything or they don't believe they should have been sectioned at all and that there's been some horrible mistake. Graham, for all his tricks and tics, was one of the latter, forever waiting for someone to

251

acknowledge their administrative error and tell him he could go home. Kevin and Shaun only ever really confided in each other, but others are a bit more forthcoming about their episodes and misdemeanours.

Ilias kept taking his clothes off in shops.

Bob had a breakdown after his wife left him – what a shocker!

Lucy freaked out after taking too much heroin. Or maybe it was because she hadn't taken enough. Doesn't make much odds.

Actually ... thinking about it, I kind of fall somewhere between the two extremes. Yeah, I'm happy enough to admit that I went a bit bonkers, to talk about the knives and the people on my TV, but I still don't think I should be here. So maybe it isn't quite as clear-cut as I think it is.

Still none the wiser about Tiny Tears, though.

She says, 'I think we could be friends.'

'Do you?'

'Best friends, maybe.'

She looks at me and I shrug like, *Why not?* but something about her is telling me to keep my distance.

'You were so nice, the day I came in.'

'I was being nosy,' I say.

'Nobody else really bothered. I mean obviously they wanted to gawp a bit, but none of them offered to help, like you did.'

'Well, let's see,' I say.

She seems happy enough with that. 'Tell me more about the nurses,' she says. 'You were going to tell me, remember?'

Right. The afternoon she arrived. Before she started blubbing for the umpteenth time in like ten minutes and I lost the will to live. 'What do you want to know?'

252

She shuffles her arse back on my bed a little, makes herself more comfortable. 'Everything,' she says.

There doesn't seem much point in telling her about Debbie, but for the next half an hour or so I give her the skinny on the rest of them. I tell her Malaika's probably the best bet if she needs a fag and that Femi-Nazi's got a temper on her. I tell her that George is a failed copper and that Marcus can be pretty strict sometimes and that she shouldn't hold out too much hope for any deep and meaningful conversation with Mia.

She seems to be enjoying herself. She laughs at my jokes and my daft attempts at some of the accents and looks suitably shocked when she's meant to. I'm actually quite enjoying myself, but then she stands up, just like that, and announces that she's tired. She tells me she wants to go to bed, says it like it's the most important thing I've heard all day.

I say, 'Oh, fair enough,' and watch her walk to the door.

After she's gone, I wait until I'm fairly sure everyone else is in their room and pay a quick visit to all the other women on the corridor. I knock on doors and put my head round. Sorry to disturb you, just a quick question.

I want to know if any of the others have had a visit. If anyone else has been asked if they want to be Clare's best friend.

Nope. Just me.

THIRTY-NINE

Banksy says, 'I'm amazed it took you this long to call.'

'You're happy that I have though, yeah?' I'm trying to be funny, but I'm genuinely chuffed that he's even speaking to me. I think I'd been a bit off with him last time he was here. 'You're happy, I can tell.'

'I'm ecstatic,' he says.

I'm back in my room, watching rain battering at the window and it's almost like I can *hear* the grease from the bacon at breakfast cranking up the cholesterol and turning my arteries to Twiglets. 'You heard the latest news from the Ward of Death, then?'

'Yeah. Like I said, I was expecting you to call Sunday night.'

'I was a bit busy,' I say.

'What the hell's going *on* in that place?'

'You know it was me that found her, right?'

'No.' There's a pause. 'I did not know that.' He sounds concerned and it's lovely. I suppose it's fair enough, because

254

we're close, plus he knows that the last time I was anywhere near a blood-soaked body, things didn't turn out so
well. 'You OK?'

'Yeah.'

'Straight up?'

'Why wouldn't I be?' Stupid question, bearing in mind
what I just said, but Banksy knows better than anyone that,
when I was on the Job, I dealt with far worse things than
a single murder victim on a bathroom floor. I tell him I'm
good, or as good as I'm ever going to be surrounded by nut-
ters, at least one of who's homicidal. I tell him not to worry.
I tell him he's a top mate.

'So, come on then . . . what are you hearing?'

'What am I hearing *where*?' he asks.

'From the MIT. Their plan of action or whatever. It's a
DCI called Brigstocke who's running things, apparently, but
I don't know if—'

'Al . . . we went through all this before. I don't have any
information, because it's not my team.'

'You said you knew.'

'About what happened, yeah. It's not like there's *that* many
murders, is there?'

'I know how many murders there are,' I say.

'That's all, though. Look, if any stuff . . . filters through
or if I happen to hear something, I'll let you know, but right
now you're asking the wrong person.'

'Has someone told you not to say anything?'

'What?'

'Have you been told not to talk to me about the case?'

His sigh rattles a bit. 'I haven't got time for this, Al.'

The rain's getting heavier. Tin tacks falling on a drum.

Above the noise I can hear Lauren singing in the distance, which is definitely the best place for her to be.

'Remember when you were here last time?' I ask. 'When we talked about the drugs gang and how maybe they'd sent someone in pretending to be a patient to kill Kevin?'

'Yeah, and I thought it was stupid,' he says.

'Yeah, and so did I eventually ... and then I *knew* it was because I found out who really killed Kevin, but maybe this time it isn't. A new patient arrived just before Debbie was murdered.'

I let that sink in, then tell him all about Tiny Tears. How she was weird when she came in, and yeah, I know everyone's weird when they come in, but there was definitely something off about this one. I tell him about her coming to my room last night.

'What's wrong with wanting a friend?' he asks. 'Wouldn't you have wanted that when you got there?'

'It was like she had an agenda.'

'Doesn't make her a killer, Al.'

'Like ... commit the murder, then make sure you get matey with the one person on the ward who can solve it, because she's an ex-cop. Same as she solved the last one. Got to be worth thinking about, at least?' I keep at him for a while and I know he's probably not listening, but eventually he promises me that yes, he will think about it.

Then he says, 'Shall I come in to visit next week?'

Before, Tim's always said *I'll be in tomorrow* or *See you on Wednesday* or something, but now he's made it a question, and I suspect that's because he wants me to say no.

I say, 'Only if you've got time.'

*

My dad rocks up in the afternoon. I say *rocks*, but my dad's never actually *rocked* anywhere in his life. He's more of a lolloper, a marcher on a good day, but anyway ... he arrives.

Femi comes to find me and takes me to meet him.

I stretch out a hand for his plastic bag of goodies before I've even said hello.

Of course I'm happy to see him, but I wish he'd let me know he was coming, or at least give me some notice so we could arrange the best time. He still hasn't got his head round the timings of my meds so, depending on where I am in the cycle, he could turn up and find me bouncing off the walls and yapping like an excited dog, or I might be Mogadon Mary. Today, he's drawn the short straw and gets a daughter who's not exactly at her sharpest and talks like she's coming round after an operation. Several times he has to ask me to repeat myself or I just ignore what he's saying completely.

It's not sparkling, all I'm saying.

We're sitting at one end of the music room and Clare's reading a book in the opposite corner. I know she's earwigging and I wonder if she's expecting me to bring her over, maybe introduce her to my dad as my new bestie. After a few minutes she gets up and wanders out, which is a relief, because she's starting to give me the willies.

Once we've got the chit-chat out of the way – *Mum's fine and Jeff and Diane send their best and hope the operation went well* – I catch him up with my news. The latest murder. It takes a while for me to pass on all the grisly details, droning like a recording on half-speed.

It's a few seconds before Dad says anything. He just opens

his mouth and closes it again. Then he says, 'This isn't bloody acceptable.'

He's got a point. I mean, catching MRSA would be bad enough, but nobody expects to be taken into a hospital where patients are getting bumped off every couple of weeks. 'No, it isn't.'

'Do you feel safe?'

'Well, not ... particularly.' It's quite an effort to get such a difficult word out. 'But what can I do?'

'It's ridiculous,' he says. 'Somebody should go to the papers.'

'It's already in the papers, Dad.' They'd run a story in the *Evening Standard* the day before about the murder, though they hadn't named the victim or linked it to Kevin's death. The paper was being passed around the ward like a cheap prostitute.

'To complain, I mean.'

'What's the point of complaining?'

'I can't hear you, love.'

I ask him again. 'You going to go on Tripadvisor? Give it a one-star review?'

He swallows hard and looks upset. 'No need to be nasty,' he says. 'I'm only concerned about you. Alice ...'

I focus a bit and smile at him. 'Yeah, I know. Thanks.'

'So, apart from ... all that. You feeling any better?'

I smile again. Sometimes, straight after a dose of benzos, you can't help smiling even when you've got sweet FA to smile about. 'I feel different,' I say.

'A *good* different?'

I nod. Slowly. 'Most of the time.'

My dad's face lights up. Same way it did when I won the

400 metres in the house athletics or when I played a comedy servant girl in that stupid play in the fourth form. 'That's fantastic,' he says. 'Your mum's going to be really happy when I tell her that.'

'Mum hasn't called me for ages,' I say.

'I know she hasn't, love.' He stares down at his brown brogues for a few seconds. 'Thing is . . .'

'She gets upset,' I say. 'Yeah, I know.'

Twenty treacly minutes later, Dad says he'd best be getting off and I really like having his arm around me as we're walking slowly towards the airlock. He says a cheery hello to Donna, like she's some nice girl he chats to in the post office once in a while, and he even manages a thumbs-up for Ilias who's repeatedly tossing a tennis ball six inches in the air and shouting *Yes!* every time he catches it.

Dad stops when he sees Tony at the airlock with his suitcase. Tony waves and my father raises an arm in return. It's a bit awkward, though, and looks more like a Nazi salute.

'Why does he *do* that?'

I tell him about Tony's non-existent family.

'Well, at least you've got me and Mum,' he says.

'Yeah, but you can't get me out of here any more than Tony's made-up rellies.'

He gets a bit upset again. He's looking at me and, fuzzy-headed as I am, I know he's thinking about that girl who could run really fast and do funny voices in daft plays. He's thinking that he's lost her.

'It isn't your fault,' I say. 'Everything that's happened.'

He blinks slowly and shrugs. 'How can it not be, love?'

'It was Grandad Jim's fault.' I shake my head, sadly. 'Him touching me like that when I was little.'

Dad stares at me.

'Joke,' I say.

Tony is waving again, but now my dad is too stunned to wave back, so I just stand there with him for a bit and I know I'm the worst daughter in the world.

FORTY

I'm mooching around before dinner, bored and not quite sure what to do with myself, when my mobile rings. It's the investigator bloke from Pindown, so I drop the call. I don't really want to speak to him but I'm not going to turn my phone off – I would never do that – so when he calls back again almost immediately, I decide to answer.

It's something to do, isn't it?

He says, 'First off, Miss Armitage, I'm not at all happy about the offensive language on the voicemail you left.'

That makes me smile. A cuntathon I *could* remember. 'It's just a word,' I say. 'Get over yourself.'

'It was abuse, plain and simple.'

I laugh out loud. I'm glad I took the call, now.

'I was in half a mind to report it to the police.'

'Well, we both know you're not going to do *that*.'

That gives him some serious pause for thought. He might be an ex-cop, but he doesn't know *I'm* one or that I'm well aware how dodgy his business practices are. His silence tells me he knows that he's not dealing with an idiot, though.

'Secondly, I'm still waiting for the second half of the payment.'

I'd completely forgotten about it, but I'm not going to tell him that. I'd rather have a bit of fun. 'Well I still haven't decided if I'm going to pay it,' I say. 'I mean I wasn't that pleased with the service. "Guaranteed to exceed expectations", that's what it says on your website, and that would only be the case if I'd had no expectations at all. I had very high hopes, I really did, but frankly, Howard, it was piss-poor.'

There's another pause before he says, 'I'm very sorry to hear that, but I'm still expecting to be paid in full.'

'What if I don't?'

'Then I might have to consider taking legal proceedings.'

It's so tempting to tell him he can whistle for his money. To say, 'So fill your boots', or 'See you in court'. I'm seriously thinking about it.

'So?' he says. 'Are you going to pay, or what?'

I assume that if I was involved in legal proceedings of some kind then they'd have to let me out of here to do whatever's necessary. That would be my right, surely. I mean, what if you get called up for jury service? Do people in places like this ever get called up for jury service? Yeah, I'm thinking it might be fun, taking Howard on, because it's been a long time since I stood up in court, and don't forget, the last occasion when I *should* have been there, I wasn't deemed to be a fit enough witness. I always gave a good account of myself in front of a judge, everyone said that. I prepared well and made sure I did a good job. So if it comes to any kind of legal battle now, I'm damn sure I'll win, and even though I know it won't be the Old Bailey or anything, I decide that I might even be able to get a few other things off my mind while I have the chance.

Bring it on.

Then I see L-Plate walking towards me, and she's usually up for a laugh, and suddenly I can't even be bothered to talk to this bloke any more.

I say, 'Yeah, I'll send it,' and hang up.

L-Plate's about to walk right past me, but I put out a hand. She steps back a bit, obviously. 'Hey, L . . . you want to do something?'

She stares at me and her face looks a bit odd, like she's trying to work something out.

'I'm always up for thrashing you at Jenga if you fancy it.' She doesn't look keen. 'Or we can play cards or something . '

'You are joking, right?' She shakes her head. 'You're un-believable, do you know that?'

'What?'

'After the way you treated me at lunchtime? The way you spoke to me?'

'Eh?'

'I don't even want to talk to you right now.'

'You're going to have to help me out here, L . . .'

I'm sure she's about to storm off, but she's clearly decided to stand her ground and let me have a piece of her mind. Not that she's got an awful lot to spare. 'Well, you certainly didn't need any help at lunchtime,' she says. 'Not when you were calling me a "vacuous posh bitch" or leaning across to steal my food and saying it didn't matter because smackheads don't have a big appetite anyway. Flicking bits of it back in my face, then pissing yourself and telling me to grow up when I started to cry.'

Now she tries to move past me and I put out an arm to stop her.

She screams.

George steps towards us from the nurses' station and I hold up my arms to let him know everything's all right. I keep my voice low and steady. I say, 'Honestly, L, I haven't got a clue what you're on about. Why the hell would I do any of that? We're mates.'

'I have no idea,' she says. 'Because I'm just a pathetic junkie and you're a full-on mental case?'

I close my eyes and try to think. 'I don't believe you,' I say. I'm not sure there's anything else I *can* say.

'Why don't you ask Donna or Bob? They were both there.'

I can't do anything but watch her turn and walk the other way. Then I stand there, with George watching me, and desperately try to recall even a moment of what L-Plate's just described. What I'm supposed to have said to her is bad enough, but I'm way more alarmed by the fact that I can't remember saying anything at all.

I can't even remember having lunch.

When my mobile goes off again, I snatch at it, desperate to let fly at that arsehole Howard with some *properly* abusive language, but it's not him phoning.

There's no caller ID.

I answer and grunt a hello.

There's a few seconds of crackle, half a breath, then the line goes dead.

FORTY-ONE

I try to talk to Lucy while we're queuing up for dinner, but she ignores me and carries her tray across to a table as far away from mine as possible. Ilias wants to chat, but I don't let him. I can't bring myself to eat much anyway so I leave pretty quickly.

I'm all over the place.

I go to be given my final meds of the day, then drift into the music room while everyone else is still eating and grab a paperback. I'm hoping it might distract me a bit. Shaun is the only other person in there but I'm not expecting *him* to disturb me, and he doesn't. I keep an eye on him though, just in case he's got any other messages he wants to send, so with that and the whole Lucy business . . . I find myself reading the same page of the stupid book over and over again.

Lauren saunters in, drops down into the chair next to mine and belches.

'Reading's a waste of time,' she says.

I'm in no mood to rise to her bait. 'You reckon? And here's me with you pegged as a bit of a bookworm yourself. You know, knocking out a few songs then relaxing with a bit of Charles Dickens or whatever.'

She doesn't rise to *my* bait. She just belches again and calmly gives me the finger. Says, 'Twat.'

I make a show of going back to my book, but I only manage half of that same bloody page before she leans across.

'Anyway, I thought you'd be far too busy for reading.'

I put the book down. 'Yeah?'

'Yeah ... you've got another case to crack now, haven't you, Columbo?'

'Have I?'

She leans even closer, heaving her fat tits across the arm of her chair. 'I'm guessing your bedroom wall is like one of those ... boards they always have in the police shows. You know, so the detective can keep track of the murder investigation.' She's on a roll now, enjoying herself. I glance across at Shaun, but he doesn't seem to be paying much attention. 'So there's probably a picture of poor old Debbie taped up right in the middle, with her name underneath, and loads of lines and arrows, all drawn in felt-tip on the wall, leading to the people she knew or whatever. To the suspects.'

'Yeah,' I say. 'It's exactly like that.'

She shows me a few brown or yellow teeth. 'Unless ...'

I look at her. Stupid thing to do, I know, but I can't help myself.

'Well, we all know you thought Debbie was the one who killed Kevin, don't we?'

I don't know about *all*, but I'm not surprised that Lauren knows. Marcus would have discussed it with the other nurses and one of them was bound to let it slip at some point. Or found themselves unable to resist sharing a bit of gossip about one patient with another. George, maybe, or Malaika.

'So?'

'So . . . it must have been doing your head in that she'd got away with it. I mean the police obviously hadn't worked it out or she'd have been arrested, right? I'm not as experienced as you with this stuff, but I think that's how it's supposed to work. So she's just swanning around, free as a bird and all the time you know what she's done. You're the only one who knows that she's guilty.' She shakes her head. 'I'm just saying . . . if that was me I don't think I could have handled it. I don't think I could have coped, seeing that murdering cow every day, laughing and joking after what she'd done to poor old Kevin.'

I glance over at Shaun again. He's hanging on every word.

'Is there a point to any of this?' I ask.

'Only that maybe, seeing as nothing was happening to her and that, you know, justice wasn't being done . . .' She shrugs as if she doesn't really need to say any more.

'Just spit it out,' I say. 'You can sing it, if it helps.'

She slowly brings a finger to her lips like a naughty school-girl, stares at me for a few seconds, then hauls herself up and wanders out. Almost as soon as the door closes behind her I hear scratching and look over to see Shaun scribbling on a scrap of paper. Whatever he's writing doesn't take long and he scrunches the paper into a ball, then steps over to press it into my hand before hurrying from the room.

I open it up and read the message.

thank you

FORTY-TWO

French and Saunders are back for more interviews this morning, and according to Ilias they've brought a friend along, but before I'm called in to see them, I get a chance to say sorry to L-Plate. I know now that all the stuff she accused me of yesterday actually happened, because Marcus made a point of catching up with me before bedtime and asked me about the 'bullying' incident in the dining room at lunchtime. He was not happy. For obvious reasons – like not remembering *any* of it – there wasn't a fat lot I could tell him, but he made it clear we'd need to address my unacceptable behaviour at Friday's assessment meeting.

Looking forward to *that*.

A few of us are in the music room waiting our turn, so I go and sit by L-Plate. She doesn't immediately get up and move, which I take as a good sign. I've had the odd falling-out with her before and I know this is a bit more serious than arguing about a game of snakes and ladders, but she doesn't normally stay angry for very long.

If people bore grudges every time there was a cross word in here, none of us would be talking to anybody.

'Listen . . . about yesterday,' I say.

She says nothing. She's going to make me work for it, which is fair enough.

'I'm really sorry about what I said. The food and everything.'

'OK,' she says.

'I don't think you're posh and vacuous.' Obviously I *do*, but you know, not in a bad way.

'So, why did you do it?' she asks. 'Why did you say all those horrible things?'

'I've got no idea, L. Just a wobble.'

'Then you denied it, which made it much worse.'

'I know.'

L-Plate's still waiting for me to explain, but I don't want to tell her that I simply don't remember. I don't want anyone to know that. It's not like I haven't forgotten stuff in the past, going places and meeting people, whole evenings sometimes, but it's always been booze- or weed-related. Just a woozy blank after a heavy session, where the memories should have been. This is different though, and I don't have any explanation and it's scaring the hell out of me. I have no way of knowing *when* I forgot it or if I was forgetting it even while it was happening. It's not even like it was anything deeply unpleasant or traumatic. I've done far worse things about which I can remember every sordid second.

I should probably talk to Bakshi about it, but if there's something going seriously pear-shaped in my brain, I'm not sure I really want to know.

It's all a bit bloody scary.

269

'I was ashamed,' I say.

L-Plate nods slowly, then beams, then claps to celebrate the moment. Like I said earlier, not a bad bone in her body. Not as many as some of us, anyway.

She starts rattling on about something or other, but before she can get into her stride George comes in and says the detectives are ready for me. I tell L-Plate we'll catch up later and follow him out.

I'm about to knock on the door of the MDR when it opens and a woman steps out. I'm guessing she's the 'friend' that Ilias was talking about and she's certainly a bit more glamorous than French or Saunders. She looks a bit . . . Malaysian, or something? Long dark hair tied back with a red band and a snazzy skirt. I'm still wondering why three police officers have been deemed necessary when the woman holds out a hand and introduces herself.

'I'm Dr Perera,' she says. 'Why don't we talk outside?'

I shake her hand. 'Oh . . .'

'Don't worry, I've already spoken to the ward manager.' She smiles and gently turns me round. 'Come on, it's a nice day.'

We walk up towards the main hospital buildings and find a bench. The weather *is* pretty nice and there's a few more people milling around in this part of the grounds than there are down where the unit is hidden away. We can see the entrance to A&E and, as you'd expect, there's an old dear standing just outside the doors with an oxygen tank and a fag on. I think it's compulsory.

Makes me wish I'd brought some tobacco and Rizlas out with me.

'What kind of doctor are you?' I ask.

'I'm a forensic psychiatrist.' Her voice is quiet, but she's very well spoken. 'I work with the police now and again.'

'Oh, *well*.' I nod back towards the unit. 'This must be tailor-made for you.'

She smiles and she's got perfect teeth. 'You would think, right? Actually this is the first time I've been involved with a case like this. It's normally crimes that are a little more ... outside the normal range, shall we say?'

'What, serial killers, that kind of thing?'

'That kind of thing,' she says.

I'm instantly jealous. 'I *so* wanted to catch a decent serial killer case,' I say. 'Never had a sniff. Oh ... I'm ex-Job.'

'I know,' she says.

I like that she's done her homework and it makes me feel like we're colleagues, so I can't resist asking if she was involved in any of the big cases in London that I can remember. The killer couple from a year or so ago. The case with the cats from before that. I try to make it matter-of-fact so as not to sound like too much of a fan-girl.

'Yes, I advised on both those investigations,' she says.

'Nice,' I say.

'Well, not particularly.'

I look back towards A&E. I'm hoping there might be something exciting to see, someone rushing in with half their face missing maybe, just so I've got some stories to tell when I get back to the ward. The best I can do is a crying child and a woman with her arm in a sling. I watch the old woman stub her fag out and wheel her tank back through the doors.

'I've read your notes, Alice,' Perera says.

'Al,' I say.

She nods. 'But it's always better to hear these things first hand. Can you tell me what happened just before you were sectioned?'

I shrug. 'I smacked my boyfriend over the head with a wine bottle.'

'Right. When you had all the knives.'

'Yeah, to protect him. Have *you* got a boyfriend?'

She says that she has.

'So you'd do whatever you had to if he was in danger, wouldn't you?'

'We haven't been together very long,' she says. 'I met him during one of those cases you mentioned, actually.'

'So he's a serial killer?'

She laughs and her eyes widen, and I think, whoever her boyfriend is, unless he's also a part-time male model, he's definitely punching above his weight. I purse my lips and suck in a noisy breath. 'Going out with a copper is asking for trouble,' I say.

'Well, I know it can be,' she says, 'which is why we don't live together.'

I say, 'Smart,' and yes, I'm well aware she's only giving me snippets of personal information to build up a rapport or whatever. I know how it works. It's fine with me though, because I like hearing it. Bakshi's been treating me for months and I know bugger all about her.

As it is, the softening-up period doesn't last long.

'Would it be fair to say you didn't like Debbie McClure very much?'

I give it some thought, because I think I should. 'We never really got on,' I say. 'Couldn't tell you why.'

'But you thought she was responsible for the death of Mr Connolly?'

'I *know* she was and no, I certainly didn't like her much after that. Just saying, we weren't exactly best mates to begin with.'

She nods. She isn't writing anything down and I wonder if she has some kind of recorder in her bag. 'And you thought you were being ignored by the police who were conducting that investigation, yes?'

'I didn't *think* I was being ignored,' I say. 'I *was* being ignored.'

'So, how did that make you feel?'

'Ignored.'

'Were you irritated? Angry? Were you running out of patience?'

'Yes, with the police. Too effing right I was. I was pissed off at the incompetence of that idiot Seddon and the rest of his team. I mean, it was on a *plate*. It was on a sodding plate.'

She says, 'Right,' then leans her head back like she's just enjoying the sunshine for a moment or two, but I can see the cogs turning. 'After what happened to Detective Constable Johnston, you felt you were denied the chance to give evidence against the man who murdered him. That's right, isn't it?'

'I was a bit all over the place back then,' I say.

'You never got to play your part in getting justice for a murdered colleague.'

'The bloke was put away. That's what counts.'

'How did that make you feel?'

Here we go. Feelings again. 'Look, I know this is what you do, but I've got to tell you that I never worked on a single murder case where how someone *felt* about this, that or the other thing counted for anything. You just have to catch them, right?'

'You're correct, Al,' she says. 'How someone is feeling at a particular time *is* a ... large part of what I do. I believe it can be hugely important, and so do the senior officers who have brought me in to help with this case.' She smiles again, but there aren't quite so many perfect teeth on display this time. 'So I'd be very grateful if you could tell me.'

I sigh and stare across at the entrance to A&E again. Still nothing to get excited about. 'I wasn't very happy about it,' I say.

'OK, good. Thank you, Al. Now, do you think it's possible that you had similar feelings, or that those old feelings resurfaced, when you saw that the investigation into Mr Connolly's murder had stalled? When, despite you putting it on a plate for the police, Miss McClure was getting away with it. Did you perhaps feel ... thwarted?'

There it was, though I'd known it was coming for several minutes. The shrink was laying it all out a bit more politely than Lauren had done last night, but she was saying much the same thing. Asking much the same question.

It makes complete sense, after all. Sitting out here, the pair of us all pally in the sunshine, I don't know if she's going to be talking to Ilias or Bob or the rest of them, but right this minute I'm a suspect. Of course. How could I not be?

When you think about it, I'm the *obvious* suspect.

I understand, but it doesn't mean I have to like it.

'Can we go back inside now?' She's not actually a copper, so I'm guessing she can't really refuse.

'If that's what you want,' she says.

I stand up and start walking back and, once she's managed to catch me up, I say, 'This boyfriend of yours. Is he the kind of copper that gives a stuff about feelings?'

She doesn't answer, so I'm guessing we're about done.

FORTY-THREE

Detectives French and Saunders and their tame trick-cyclist have left and suddenly there's a weird atmosphere on the ward. Weirder than normal, I mean. Usually, at any time of the day or night, there's one or two people plodding around in a bit of a daze, but now it's like *everyone* is ... subdued. Nobody seems very keen to discuss what's been happening, to talk about anything come to that, and I start to wonder if the staff have got together and decided to up the dosage on everyone's sleepy-pills.

If it's something they do whenever it's necessary.

When things get a bit stressful or if they're understaffed.

So make that ... all the time.

I remember reading somewhere that prison officers are quite happy that their prisons are in the grip of a Spice epidemic, because zombified inmates are that much easier to handle. The prisoners are happy being off their tits because it helps them forget they're, you know, *in prison*, and it gives the screws a bit more time to put their feet up and do sudokus. It's a win-win. It's hardly a big leap to imagine Marcus and his team doing whatever it takes to make *their* working lives a bit more peaceful, is it?

I might ask Marcus when I get the chance, but I doubt he'll admit it.

For now, it's just me, Big Gay Bob and Tiny Tears chilling out in the dining room. I'm actually quite glad that there hasn't been a lot of chat about this latest round of interviews, because if it was to start now, I can guess the kind of thing Bob would have to say about the hot psychiatrist.

[*Puts hand on cock*] *I told her to analyse* this!

Instead he says, 'I miss Debbie.'

'Why's that?' I ask.

I'm still thinking he's cueing himself up for a crack about his history of rumpy-pumpy with Scottish women, but he just looks sad. 'Because she was nice.'

'Was she, though?'

'Well, not to everyone, I suppose. Her and Femi didn't like each other very much and she had that big row with George.'

'What big row?' I ask.

'A couple of days before she was killed, in one of the exam rooms. I don't know what they'd fallen out about, but I could hear them shouting.'

I know Debbie and Femi had clashed a few times, but this is the first I've heard about her and George. I should try and ask George about it when I get the chance.

'She was nice to *me*, though,' Bob says.

'Why wouldn't she be? *You're* nice.'

'Thanks, Al,' he says. Then he shakes his head. 'Not nice enough to stop Sandra leaving.'

The wife who walked out on him. Because Bob was constantly shagging other women. Or because he was constantly talking about shagging other women. Or because it wasn't actually women he wanted to shag.

I'm not even sure Bob knows.

The best I can manage right now is, 'Shit happens sometimes, mate.'

'Why would someone kill her?' Clare asks, from nowhere.

Bob looks horrified. 'Someone killed *Sandra*?'

I put my hand on his arm and tell him that nobody's killed his ex-wife and that everything's OK. Then I turn and give Clare a good, hard look. She's been sitting watching me for twenty minutes, keeping shtum even though she looks like she's got plenty to say. Like she's trying to psych me out, you know what I mean?

I can hear Perera's voice: *How does that make you feel?*

Properly uncomfortable, if I'm honest.

What is her fucking game?

'You tell me,' I say.

'I haven't got the foggiest,' she says. 'How could I?'

Why would someone kill her?

All whispery and wide-eyed, she is. Above it all. As if what's happened is just incomprehensible and she's asking the most difficult question in the world. Like it's something *she* can't possibly know anything about, while she's conveniently ignoring the fact that if I'm the obvious suspect – because I thought Debbie killed Kevin *and* I found the body – then the fact that Debbie was murdered five minutes after she arrived on the ward makes Tiny Tears a pretty close second.

'Oh, come on, don't be shy,' I say. 'If you've got a theory

278

then let's hear it. Obviously you'll have shared it with the police by now, but don't keep the rest of us in suspense.'

It probably came out a little more spiteful than I intended and her eyes start to brim with tears as per bloody usual. I don't feel bad, though. I'm perfectly happy to sit here and watch her weeping herself to soggy pieces.

'I was just making conversation,' she says.

'Yeah?'

'I'm interested, that's all.' Her head drops but, by sheer force of will she heroically holds the tears at bay. When she looks up again, there's a hint of mischief, which I do not like one bit. 'You know who killed her though, don't you?'

'Who told you that?'

Even if she intends to tell me, she can't get the words out through the volley of racking sobs that she simply can't fight off a moment longer. She splutters and gulps. She presses her hands to her face to staunch the tsunami of convenient waterworks.

Doesn't much matter. I'm guessing gobby Lauren said something.

George appears in the doorway to see what the matter is. Jesus H Christ . . .

I'm certainly not going to tell Clare why Debbie was murdered. I was very happy to pass on what I knew to the police and alert them to the fact that Debbie had a drug-smuggling accomplice with a very good reason to want her silenced, but I don't see any reason to tell any of these numpties.

'I think it's because she was ginger,' I say. 'Homicidal ginger-phobia.'

Clare's still sobbing, but I know she can hear me and she's got one eye on George approaching with tissues.

'I bloody love ginger girls,' Bob says. 'Minges like copper wire.'

It's great to have him back.

There's half an hour before lunch, so with nothing more exciting on offer, I nip back to my room for a spot of casual Googling. I've just typed in *memory blackout* when my mobile rings. There's no caller ID showing and whoever's calling hangs up after I answer, same as last time. A wrong number probably or scammers of some sort, but still, I'd like to know if someone's pissing me about. Time was, I might have been able to call in a favour from the Forensic Telephone Unit, but those days are long gone. I think about maybe getting Banksy to do it for me, but that would mean asking *him* a favour and I reckon I've used up all my credit.

Back to Google . . .

The first page is full of articles that refer to excessive alcohol consumption and a couple mention Valium and Rohypnol. I don't think anyone's been slipping either of *those* into my dinner, so I try again and add *not drug or alcohol related* into the search. Predictably, this gives me a bunch of pages about memory loss that are specifically about those things but, after scrolling for a while, I find *Other Causes of Memory Blackouts*.

I wish I hadn't bothered.

Low blood pressure seems to be the most common one and there was nothing wrong with my BP when it was checked yesterday, same as it is every bloody day. So . . .

Epilepsy, lack of oxygen, psychogenic seizures. WTF?

I'm fairly sure I'd know if I'd had a psychogenic seizure and, once I've looked it up, I'm positive I haven't. Got to say, though, it sounds exactly like what Shaun had that night in the TV room, and now I'm even more convinced – not that I need to be – that poor dead Debbie would háve known just which buttons to press to bring it on.

She'd managed to shut him up, but imagine how perfect it would have been for her if she'd managed to wipe out Shaun's memory as well.

I'm still thinking about the 'thank you' note he passed me last night.

It seems like *he* thinks I killed Debbie, too.

It only takes a few more minutes' rooting through the search results before I come across pages full of articles about memory loss as a symptom of PTSD. I was expecting as much. I skim-read a few, but I'm not convinced that's what's going on. They're all about memory loss as the brain's coping mechanism, which would mean that, in my case, I would be blanking out the 'traumatic incident' because it's simply too painful to remember. I'm not saying it's a ridiculous idea, but it's been a year and a half since Johnno was killed, so could it really be delayed that much? More important, it's not like that's what being blanked out, is it? I've got no memory at all of flicking bits of fish finger at L-Plate, while I can remember every hideous moment of what happened in that crack-head's flat.

The pattern on that carpet. Blue and green and blood-red.

It doesn't make any sense at all.

I close my laptop and decide that Google is brilliant if you want to know which film you've seen some actor in, or how old someone is, but that using it to try and work out what might be wrong with you never goes well.

I leave my room and prowl around a bit, not sure what to do with myself.

Like a fart in a colander, my mum always says.

They'll have started dishing up lunch by now, but I don't much fancy sitting there chit-chatting with the rest of them. I'm not really up to it. I can usually sweet-talk Eileen into giving me a sandwich or something once the service has finished and they've all buggered off, so I decide to leave it a while.

I walk past George and Femi without saying anything.

I ignore Tony, who's drumming on his suitcase by the airlock.

One of the Informals – who might be called Trevor – is sitting on his own in the music room doing a jigsaw, so I wander in. He's fifty-ish and wears a suit – without a tie, obviously – like he's just arrived from an office somewhere. He's a bit red-faced, like he might be a drinker, but beyond that I've no idea what his story is. I've seen him around the last few days, but we've never really spoken, which is my bad, probably. Normally I prefer to stick with my own crowd, because there are fewer surprises, but right now I'm uneasy about it.

I want to talk to someone I don't know at all.

I sit down and say, 'All right?'

His jigsaw's nearly finished, but he immediately starts breaking it up, not angry or anything, just nice and calm like that's what he has to do because he's been interrupted. He needs to start all over again, simple as that. As soon as he's finished and all the pieces are laid out in front of him again, he looks up and smiles at me.

'All right?'

FORTY-FOUR

'Sorry about your jigsaw,' I say.

'Doesn't matter,' he says.

'Do you always start again? If you're interrupted?'

'Those are the rules.'

'It must happen a lot.'

'Yeah, I've never finished it.'

'Why don't you just take it to your room and do it in there?'

He looks at me like that's just about the stupidest idea he's ever heard, so I decide not to labour the point.

'You got nowhere to live then?' I can only presume, because the police had not allowed him to leave after what happened to Debbie, that his abode is . . . unfixed.

He shakes his head. 'Only for a couple of nights at a time.' He looks around. 'This isn't too bad, though.'

I can't imagine how bad the place where he was staying before must have been. A freezing, rat-infested hovel. Or a Travelodge.

'Don't you think things are a bit strange in here right now?' I ask.

'Well, I'm not sure I've been here long enough to tell.'

'I've been here quite a while,' I say. 'And it feels to me like something bad is coming.'

He laughs. A high-pitched, girlish giggle.

'Why is that funny?'

'I think something bad has already come, don't you?' He laughs again and mimes a frenzied stabbing, like the killer in *Psycho*.

'Something else,' I say. 'Something bad for *me*.'

'Oh, right,' he says. 'Like what?'

I fight the urge to say, *well if I knew what it was I might be able to do something about it*. Instead I just shrug and say, 'Some people in here think I killed Debbie.' I realise that he might not even have been here long enough to know her name. 'The nurse.' Now I'm the one miming the stabbing. 'In the toilets.'

He nods. 'Did you?'

I stare at him and ... *bingo*! All this time I've been banging on to Banksy about killers coming in here and pretending to be patients and it suddenly strikes me that an undercover police officer would make a damn sight more sense. I'm annoyed I didn't think of it before. He comes in a few days after Kevin is killed, because Seddon and his useless team are running out of ideas, then after the second murder there's all the more reason for him to stay where he is. Get to know the suspects a bit better.

Fuck, why not?

It's definitely what *I* would have done, back in the day.

He's holding a hand up now and shaking his head. 'No, don't tell me. I don't want to know.'

If I'm right, he's certainly convincing, but the best UCs are seriously good at this. Problem is, some of them can immerse themselves in their roles a bit *too* much. I knew an officer one time who was undercover for Serious and Organised and, a month after he'd helped bring down one of the biggest gangs in West London, he was done for armed robbery himself.

'I'm not sorry she's dead,' I say.

'Fair enough,' he says.

I move my chair a little closer to his and lower my voice. 'But somebody in here thinks I did it, and the reason *why* I'm supposed to have done it makes me a target.'

'Yeah, you're right,' he says.

'What have you heard?'

'No, I mean you're right . . . that's bad.'

'I don't know what to do,' I say. 'I don't know who to trust.'

'You shouldn't trust anybody.'

'No . . .'

'Or . . . you could trust everybody. That might work as well.'

I watch him smile and give me the thumbs-up. He seems very happy with his plan. He's either a copper who's ridiculously good at his job or he's as mad as a hatter.

'I'm scared,' I say.

'Oh yes, so am I,' he says. 'All the time.'

'I don't like it. I've only ever been really scared once before and I didn't like it then, either.'

'What did you do?'

'I fought back,' I say. 'I got weapons.'

'Right.' That fires him up and he turns his head and starts to look around the room, searching for something suitable. I'm quite excited, so I do the same.

Bongos, the broken guitar, a collection of board games.

Nothing that's going to do anyone a great deal of damage.

He slaps his hand on the table in frustration, then shrugs, as though it was well worth a try. He says, 'Do you want to have dinner?'

It's sweet, like he's asking me on a date, and I find myself grinning.

'Could do,' I say. 'But *just* dinner, yeah? I'm not a slag.'

He giggles again. Mutters, '*Slag.*'

'Then maybe afterwards we can come back here and I'll help you finish your jigsaw.'

His face darkens immediately and he leans forward, wrapping his arms protectively around the scattered pieces. He sniffs and looks sideways at me.

'Oh no you *fucking* won't.'

FORTY-FIVE

Mr Jigsaw – who isn't called Trevor at all, but turns out to be a Colin – is sitting as far away from me as possible without actually being in a different room, and I find myself dining next to Lauren. This is, of course, a major treat. She eats with her mouth open, humming tunelessly through her nose and leaning into me when she reaches for salt and pepper and ketchup. Then ketchup again.

She says, 'That psychiatrist the coppers brought along was nice.'

'Was she?' It's a relief to hear that I wasn't the only patient Perera talked to. But then Lauren spoils it, like she was always intending to. 'Yeah, we had a cracking natter. Talked about all sorts of things.'

I can't help thinking that she means all sorts of people and that what people really means is *me*. Her fat gob twists into that punchable smile, the one she slaps on if she's enjoying herself and whenever she wants me to think she knows something.

What's really annoying is that it works.

'Pretty as well, don't you think?' she says.

'I suppose.'

'Proper lez-bait.' Lauren nods and ladles more stew into her mouth. 'I saw Malaika eyeing her up.'

Talking of which, I'm all too aware that Clare is watching me from the table opposite. She's sitting with Donna and Ilias, but doesn't seem interested in whatever those two are talking about. It wouldn't surprise me if Tiny Tears had cosied up to Lauren as well and is patiently waiting for her to report back on *our* conversation once we've all finished eating.

'She must have had a field day with you,' Lauren says. 'That psychiatrist.'

'Must she?'

'Course. Your thing about who killed Kevin, you thinking it was Debbie and all that.' She leans so close that her greasy hair is like some massive spider on my shoulder and she whispers as if she's making a dramatic announcement in a scary film. 'Murder most *foul.*'

'Oh, fuck off,' I say.

She snorts so some stew comes out, then goes back to her dinner.

I see Tony walk up to the serving hatch and decide it might be nice to join him for a spot of pudding. I tell Lauren to fuck off again for good measure, and when I get up to leave, she picks up one of the plastic knives and jabs it aggressively at nobody in particular.

I can tell that she wants me to notice.

Once we've both collected bowls of runny trifle, I ask Tony if I can have a word. He doesn't look thrilled about it, but I tell him it's all right and guide him gently towards the empty end of one of the long tables. For a big bloke, he's fairly . . . biddable. Mia and Femi are sitting at the far end, but they're gassing away anyway and I know that if I talk quietly enough they won't hear us.

'I think you're right,' I say to Tony.

'What about?'

'*You* know . . .'

Just like that he goes from being wary to proper crapping himself. He starts looking around the dining room frantically, but I reach across and grab hold of his arm. 'It's fine,' I say. 'I swear.'

He looks at me and gradually starts to calm down a little. His chest is still heaving, mind you, and it feels like he could bolt any moment.

'Where is it?' he asks.

'I'm not sure, but you really don't need to worry, because it's not . . . your Thing. It's *mine*.'

His eyes widen. Now he's not going anywhere.

'I reckon I've got a Thing too,' I say. 'But it's different from yours, because I know it's a *person*. I know it's living and breathing and it's walking about in here.'

He looks around again, but more slowly this time and a lot more sneakily, because suddenly we're in this together. He reaches across the table and takes hold of *my* arm. 'I'm so sorry, mate.'

'Thanks.' I shrug. 'At least I know.'

'It *will* kill you, you know that, right? That's the reason it exists. So you need to be careful.'

'Oh, I'm being very careful, and the best part is, I don't think it knows that I'm on to it or that I'm watching out. Does yours?'

'I'm not sure.' Tony screws his eyes up and shakes his head. 'It's so bloody clever, though. Like one step ahead all the time.'

'How did you find out about it?'

He pushes trifle around his dish. 'When I was eleven or twelve. First I thought it was, you know . . . like an imaginary friend? He turned up in my bedroom one night after my dad left, so we'd sit up there and talk about when Dad was coming back and things would be OK again and that was nice.' He smiles, just for a second or two. 'Then, after Mum passed, he came with me to the care home, and once the bad stuff started happening in there he wasn't quite so friendly, you know? One day he just wasn't around, but I always knew he was coming back and that when he did, I wouldn't recognise him. That now it was an *it* and not a *he* any more, yeah? I knew that eventually it was going to hurt me, but the worst thing is, I never understood why.' He lifts up a spoonful of trifle but just stares past me and lets it run off the spoon. 'To this day, I don't know what I did to make the Thing so angry with me.'

We sit there for a while saying nothing.

Over Tony's shoulder I can see people starting to leave. I watch Lauren get up and notice Clare follow her out half a minute later. I glance over at Colin, but any UC worth his salt is way too smart to make surveillance of me obvious.

'Do *you* know, Al?' Tony asks. 'Why *your* Thing wants to hurt you?'

I nod, because I know that telling him will make me feel better. 'Because it thinks I killed someone.'

'OK.'

'And it wants to punish me for it.'

Tony grunts, like that's all perfectly reasonable. He points the V of two fingers towards his eyes. 'Want me to keep an eye out for you?'

I'm not going to walk round the table and hug him, but it's the most I've wanted to hug anyone for quite a while. I thank him, though. 'I'll be fine, Tone,' I say, and I reckon I almost sound convincing. 'You watch out for *yourself* . . .'

For the third night in a row, once I've taken my meds, I decide to duck out of a night in the TV room and head to bed early. Well, to my bedroom at least. I'm not sure I'll be getting a lot of sleep.

As soon as I'm there, though, I wonder if I've made the right decision. I can't settle and it's a constant struggle to hold the scary ideas at bay. With the others around to annoy me or make me laugh or just be their ordinary bizarre selves, at least I'd be distracted and there'd be less time for me to upset myself and dwell on things.

On what people are thinking about me, saying about me.

On what Perera took away from our little natter.

On badness and blood.

On *forgetting* . . .

It's Malaika doing the half-hourly checks on this corridor tonight and, when she knocks on the door which I've taken to locking all the time, I don't want to unlock it. I just stand close to it and tell her that everything's fine.

'Come on, Alice, you know the rules. I have to *see*.'

I open the door a few inches, muster a smile then close it again.

I think I doze off for a while eventually, it's hard to be certain. Asleep or not, it's the usual gory fun-fest, and however much later it is when Clare knocks, I refuse to answer. I just lie here and listen to her knocking until she finally gives up, her mouth close to my door whispering about how she thought we were friends.

It will *kill you, you know that, right?*

FORTY-SIX

I'm like a child that's overtired. I'm fractious and weepy and it's hard to think very straight. Even though I'm physically wiped out and it felt like the walk to the MDR was going to kill me, my brain is still firing off signals so fast that by the time my body chooses to act on one, the instructions have changed. I'm not . . . in sync with myself. It's like I keep deciding to go on a journey, but as soon as I've taken the first few steps, thick fog comes in from nowhere and I get lost straight away.

Does that make any sense? Probably not.

I'm starting to lose track of the days. Easy to do in here at the best of times. It must be Friday because of what I'm doing this morning, so . . . five days since Debbie was killed?

Marcus and Bakshi are both watching me while Marcus makes the pointless introductions then launches into the usual blah-blah-blah about meds and statuses and care plans.

I straighten out my legs and immediately pull them back again.

I fold my arms, then put my hands behind my head, then slide them beneath my thighs.

I hunch my shoulders. I relax them again. Hunch and relax . . .

When Marcus has finished, I can see they're all still looking at me, so I try to concentrate and tell him that I prefer these slightly more intimate Friday-morning get-togethers. It's just Marcus, Bakshi and George today. No trainee-this or Junior-that.

'Every bed on the ward is occupied,' Marcus says. 'And sadly, we are still a nurse down.'

'Nurse down . . . nurse down!' I say it without thinking, like an emergency alert. A tasteless joke. The same way I said *officer down* a year and a half before, in that flat in Mile End, when I was trying to key the radio with those stupid slippery gloves.

'Are you all right, Alice?' Bakshi asks.

Perfectly on cue, I stifle a yawn. 'I'm not sleeping very well.'

She looks at Marcus and says, 'Well, let's see if we can help you with that.'

Marcus scribbles something down, a reminder that I need more pills probably, but I'm thinking that anything short of an elephant tranquilliser isn't going to make a great deal of difference right now.

'The sleeping issue aside,' Bakshi says, 'are things OK generally?'

I nod and say, 'Absolutely.' I'm probably nodding a bit too much.

Things are a long way from OK, but whatever I've said

to other patients, I don't really want to say it to this lot. Nobody here is squeaky-clean all the time, but despite a couple of recent . . . transgressions – the call to Andy and the home-delivery weed affair – they've still been talking about progress, like I'm actually making some. Barring disaster, I'll be out of here in four months anyway, but I certainly don't want to do or say anything to scupper my chances of the section getting lifted sooner.

'Yeah, things are good.'

Bakshi gets down to it. 'I gather Marcus has already told you that we need to discuss the incident with Lucy on Wednesday.'

I'm ready for it. 'Look, I know what I did was totally unacceptable and I've already apologised to Lucy and she's cool about it. It was a blip, that's all.' A smile, a shrug, a *no big deal*. 'Me and L are mates again, so no worries on that score.'

'Well, not on that score perhaps, but my understanding is that you didn't actually remember doing it *at all*.' She gives a little hum, and there's a question mark at the end. 'That has to be a cause for concern.'

Alarm bells are starting to ring a little. I'm sure Lucy wasn't telling tales, but she must have let something slip. 'Well, what I did was a bit . . . vague, that's all. Fuzzy, yeah? It's not like I couldn't remember—'

'OK. That's fine. So, do you remember verbally attacking George yesterday, in the dining room?'

I blink and, just for a few seconds, I consider bluffing it out. I could say 'Yeah, course I do, it was only yesterday', but they'd only ask me to talk about what happened – whatever the hell it was – so I know I'll be found out. All I can do is look at George.

'When you were sitting with Bob and Clare?' he says.

Right, got it. When Bob was talking about how much he misses Debbie and Clare started crying. Yes, I can remember that, but I don't think that's what they're on about.

George is looking at me and I can see he is on my side, willing me to remember. Eventually he sighs and says, 'When I came over to the table, you were verbally abusive, Alice. *Very* abusive.' He's not happy at having to tell the story, that's obvious. 'You kicked a chair, as well.'

Bakshi is waiting.

What the hell can I say? My stomach's jumping and my head is screaming for help and I've got . . . *nothing*. I can only really say sorry to George, so that's what I do.

He nods and sits back. 'No worries, pet.'

'Are you forgetting things a lot, Alice?' Bakshi asks.

Now I'm panic-stricken, fidgeting like I've got fleas and seeing any prospect of early release drifting away up the Swanee. God knows where the idea suddenly came from that I should be honest with them, because, sitting where I am now, I almost never tell the truth.

'It's just those two times,' I say. 'That I know of, anyway. I mean, there might be other things . . . bits of conversation or whatever. It's like . . . the opposite of a flash, you know? Like it's stuff that happens when the lights have suddenly gone off. Just . . . a gap.'

I wonder if they're thinking about transferring me somewhere else, one of the wards downstairs even. If they want to extend the section three and detain me for more than six months, I'm not even sure what number section that is. Then I notice that Bakshi actually looks pleased.

'It's understandable, Alice,' she says. 'These kinds of

blackouts are a well-documented symptom of PTSD. It's just the brain's way of taking care of itself. When it gets ... overloaded, it shuts down for a while.'

'I was reading about that,' I say.

'Well, good. Now ... the PTSD you suffered after the events of eighteen months ago resulted in quite a different set of symptoms, but again this variation is perfectly normal. These things affect people in diverse ways every time. What happened to Detective Constable Johnston led to you having a serious, potentially dangerous breakdown and this time, after the trauma of discovering Nurse McClure's body, the PTSD is taking a different form altogether. The odd ... blip as you call it, and some sporadic episodes of memory loss. It's a rather more benign form, thankfully.'

'Right.' It doesn't feel very benign. It certainly didn't last night when I was lying awake, listening for noises outside and sweating through my sheets, but I see what she's getting at. 'So, what do we do?'

'There is medication that can help,' she says. Marcus scribbles again. 'So we'd like to start you on that straight away. It's actually the same thing used to treat the cognitive symptoms of Alzheimer's.' She smiles at the look on my face. 'Don't worry, you certainly do not have that.'

'That's a relief,' I say. 'Oh, by the way, are you sure I haven't got Alzheimer's?'

George smiles at the stupid joke and I instantly forgive him for ratting me out.

'The tablets won't eradicate these blackouts overnight,' Bakshi says. 'But the symptoms *will* ease and, as you know better than most people, PTSD in whatever form can be resolved with professional help.'

'Thank you,' I say. I'm not sure I've ever said it to her before.

Not meant it, at any rate.

'This is all very positive,' Marcus says.

'Bang on,' George says.

'It's always positive when you can identify a problem early and start dealing with it. If it makes you feel any better, Alice, you should also know that you are far from being the only patient who is ... struggling a little after what happened to Nurse McClure. Some members of staff, too. In many respects, the whole of the ward is suffering with PTSD right now.'

'That's really nice to know,' I say. Things might be looking up, but I still don't think it's a good time to remind him that somebody on his ward is a killer. Or tell him that whoever that is wants to see me dead. 'Safety in numbers, right?'

As soon as I walk out of the MDR, I'm waylaid by Femi who tells me that I have a visitor. Before I have a chance to ask any questions, she's opening the door to one of the small consultation rooms.

'Everywhere else is busy,' she says. 'So I've put your friend in here.'

My visitor is standing up as I step into the room.

'Hey, Al,' Andy says.

FORTY-SEVEN

It only takes a few seconds of me standing there and staring at him, before Andy looks away. I smile, because it's such an unexpected treat to see how nervous he is. He says, 'Oh ...' then reaches down to a paper bag on the table and lifts out the gift he's brought with him.

Now I stare at that instead.

'I didn't really know what to bring,' he says. 'I was thinking maybe a book or something, but I couldn't decide what to get ... and you know, people *always* bring fruit, right? I guessed you wouldn't be short of fruit.'

It's a cactus. A fucking *cactus*.

'I thought it would be nice in your room,' he says.

'Cheers,' I say. 'I'm grateful, obviously, but just saying I can think of a few other things that might have been more useful. I mean ... a vibrator would definitely come in handy.' I sit down then lean forward to study the spiky monstrosity on the table. 'It's the right shape, but I don't think I'm quite that desperate yet.'

There's a dry, perfunctory laugh before he sits down again. Our chairs are uncomfortably close together. 'It's hard enough to know what to bring when it's . . . you know, a *normal* hospital.'

'This *is* a normal hospital. Didn't you see the big sign at the entrance?'

'You know what I mean,' he says.

His hair is a bit longer than it usually is and he hasn't shaved for a few days. I think he's lost a bit of weight, too. He certainly looks different from the last time I saw him; two months ago, when he came in a couple of days after I'd been sectioned. Remember what I said about people going to funerals just to make sure someone was actually dead? He was a bit pale and puffy back then, sweating through his cheap work suit and wearing those shoes I always hated. The ones that look like Cornish pasties. Oh, and he had a huge bandage on his head, mustn't forget that.

Now, I've got to be honest, he looks pretty damn fit.

He's still a massive cunt, though.

'So, how's things going?' he asks. 'I read in the paper about that nurse being killed.'

'Did you?'

He shakes his head. 'Pretty bloody mental.'

'Yeah, it was nice of you to call,' I say. 'You know, to check I was all right.'

'Come on, Al. I knew you were all right. It wasn't like it was a patient, was it?'

'Actually, a patient was killed two weeks before that, but let's not split hairs.'

'You serious?'

'Out of sight, out of mind though, yeah?'

'It's not like that—'

I sit forward suddenly and enjoy the fact that he recoils slightly. 'You *haven't* been calling me, have you? Calling from a different phone then hanging up?'

'Why would I do that?'

'I don't know, why would you do a lot of things? Why would you call the police on me? Why would you put me in here?'

'That's not fair,' he says. 'You know why.'

'Why would you tell the doctors that I've been calling you all the time and leaving messages?'

He blinks. 'Because you *have*, Al.' He sighs and reaches into a pocket for his phone. 'Do you want me to play one of them to you?'

I shake my head and tell him not to bother.

He says, 'No, I really think you should hear this.' He dabs at the screen then holds the phone towards me.

'Hey, fuckface . . . guess who? Yeah, it's Crazy Alice with the word from the ward. Anyway . . . you'll be horrified to know that I'm doing much better, no thanks to you, and that I'll be out of here soon . . . very soon with a bit of luck. I just wanted you to know that. Hope your poorly broken head's a bit better . . . fucking Humpty Dumpty with your broken head . . . but I'm not sorry I did it. I had to, because I knew what you were up to and I still *know, but there's no point you or your friends trying to watch me when I'm around again, because I'll be watching you. OK? Hope you feel big and clever for putting me in here, but all I'm saying, it's going to come back and bite you in the arse . . . because I've had a lot of time to think and now I've decided what I'm going to do and you aren't going to like it one bit. Anyway,*

just wanted to let you know all that. So . . . sleep well and sweet dreams, Humpty.'

'I'm sorry,' I say, once he's turned it off. 'It's the meds.'

Andy doesn't look convinced. I watch him put his phone away and try to scramble my way back up on to my sliver of moral high ground. 'Those emails you've been helpfully sending haven't done me any favours, by the way. But I'm guessing that was the point.'

'I was worried about you,' he says.

'Course you were.'

'I'm still worried about you. That's why I'm sitting here, with a stupid cactus in a bag.'

Through the small window in the door, I see L-Plate walk past, then step back and move to stare in. I presume she doesn't know it's Andy I'm talking to, even though I've told her all about him, but either way she clearly likes the look of what she's seeing. She nods approvingly, then raises her hand to her ear to make a comedy *call me* gesture.

Andy sees me looking, but by the time he does the same, L-Plate's gone.

'So when do you think you'll be getting out?' he asks.

'Depends on how many more of those emails you send to my psychiatrist,' I say. 'How *worried* you are.'

'Come on . . .'

'Four more months, all being well.' *If I survive that long. If I can work out who the enemy is. If my head doesn't get any more messed up than it already is, so I can manage to avoid them or take them on.* 'Why? You worried I might just turn up on the doorstep one day?'

'No.'

'Don't worry, I'll be sure to bring a bottle.'

302

He's probably trying to smile, but his mouth just . . . twists. 'I think it's only fair that I know,' he says. 'That's all. There's still all your stuff in the flat, obviously.'

'You didn't chuck it out? That's really sweet.'

'Seriously, Al—'

'No, it *is*.'

'Where are you going to go?'

'Is that an invitation to move back in?'

For the first time, there's the tiniest twinge of guilt at seeing him look so uncomfortable. My head must be even more messed up than I realise. 'It'll probably be a halfway house kind of place,' I say. 'Just for a bit, then hopefully the council can find space for me somewhere. There's no way I'm going to live with my mum and dad.'

'That all sounds . . . OK,' he says.

'And, you know, I'm still hoping to get my job back. So . . .'

Lucy must be spreading the word, because now Donna is taking time out from pounding the corridor to peer in. It's like a skull looming at the window. I wave her away.

'Listen, Al,' Andy says. So I do, because he says it in such a way that I know it's going to be good. 'When everything happened . . . you said some weird stuff to me, you know? Accusing me of all sorts. Saying I was involved in what was going on or what you *thought* was going on . . . that I was doing things to try and hurt you. Like I was part of some big plot or something. And I wasn't. I promise that all I was ever trying to do was help you.' He leans towards me and he's *actually* wringing his hands. 'You do know that, don't you, Al? I mean . . . you know that now, right?'

I say nothing. I just stare at him until he looks away again.

He really wants an answer. He wants the answer that will

make him happy, at any rate. I'm certainly not going to give him *that*, but I don't particularly feel like telling him what I *do* think, either.

I reckon I've told more than enough truth for one day.

'Trust me, Andy,' I say, eventually. 'I've got far better things to worry about at the moment. Fair enough?' Blimey, I couldn't help myself. I told him the truth anyway.

He seems OK with that, or at least he accepts it's the best he's going to get, so for the next fifteen minutes or so it's just chit-chat. He asks how my mum and dad are, and how Sophie is. What the food's like in here and if I've made any friends. He talks a bit about his job and how he's been finding it hard, but all I can think is *boo-hoo* and it doesn't sound like it's got any less tedious.

I wait until he does a funny shift in his chair and clears his throat. Until he thinks he's done an ex-boyfriend's duty. Until he's about to say, 'Well, I'd best be off' or 'OK, I'll leave you to it'.

'So, you been seeing anyone else?'

'What?'

'Getting any action, now I'm safely out of the way?'

He *ums* and shakes his head. I can't tell if he means *no* or if he's just finding it hard to believe I'm really asking. It doesn't make a lot of difference.

'Don't panic, Andrew,' I say. 'I'm only making conversation.' I'm *not*.

'OK.'

'I don't really give a shit.' I *do*.

There's that shift again. 'Listen, I think I should probably—'

'No,' I say. 'I'm the one who decides when it's time for you to go.' I manage a pretty decent impression of the woman who saw impostors on *EastEnders* and enjoyed slicing up her arms. I roll up the sleeves of my shirt to make the poor sod's predicament even clearer. The woman who fought him over possession of the kitchen knives and smashed his head open with a bottle.

'Yeah, that's ... no problem.' He looks at his watch. 'I'm not in a rush.'

'Great,' I say.

I see him glance at the door, like he's praying a nurse might come in and give him the chance to make a dash for it. They don't, so I sit there and say nothing, watching him squirm and hoping that, if these stupid blackouts do carry on, this doesn't turn out to be a moment I forget.

FORTY-EIGHT

At lunchtime, I eat crisps in my room and think about my conversation with Andy. I can still remember every wonderful moment, thank God. It's obvious that I'm not the only one thinking about it, because by dinner time the Fleet Ward bitches are all a-twitter.

They want details and they want dirt.

It's like we're back at school and they've just found out I was fingered behind the bike sheds by the captain of the football team.

Which I was, obviously . . .

'You didn't tell me he was that good-looking,' L-Plate says.

I try to look offended. 'So what, you think I'd be shacked up with some munter?'

'No, but he's still a bit out of your league,' Donna says.

Big Gay Bob is the token bloke at the table. 'With birds, I always prefer it if I'm the one who's out of *their* league,' he says. 'There's way more chance of getting your leg over.'

Everyone ignores him, though I can't be alone in trying to picture the unfortunate woman who thinks that Bob is a step up. A blind pensioner with low self-esteem, at a push.

'This the ex, is it? The one whose head you smashed in with a wine bottle?' Lauren asks the question nice and casually while she mops up gravy with a slice of bread.

'Yeah, that's him,' Donna says. She helpfully picks up the plastic ketchup bottle to demonstrate. 'She brained the bastard.'

'I hope it wasn't something expensive,' L-Plate says. 'Such a waste.'

I reassure her that the wine in question wasn't one she'd think was expensive, which seems to mollify her. 'Doesn't matter if it's Château Ponce or Château Lidl, does it? The bottle still weighs the same.'

'Why did you hit him?' Clare asks.

Tiny Tears gave me a nod at breakfast, but this is the first time she's actually spoken to me all day. Not a word about her knocking on my door last night and my refusal to let her in. It feels like she's got a game plan of some sort that I can't figure out yet. Same with Colin, aka Jigsaw Man, who's conspicuously ignoring me, which is exactly what I'd expect an undercover officer to do.

'None of your business,' I tell Clare.

Lauren nods slowly. Mutters, 'History of violence.'

'Yeah, and you should probably remember that,' I say.

She laughs. 'I don't care what you've done, love,' she says. 'I'm not *scared* of you.' She says the word like the very idea of it is ridiculous. 'I'm not scared of anybody.'

'What does that mean, anyway?' I turn to stare at her. 'What I've done?'

She shrugs, because she doesn't need to spell it out, then she definitely gives Clare a sly look and I'm pretty sure I see Donna and L-Plate exchange a glance, too. I look across at Colin, who's making out like there's nothing more interesting than his dinner, then over to Mia and Femi who are apparently deep in conversation on a table at the far end of the room. I catch Tony's eye and he winks, as if to let me know he's still watching out for my Thing, that he's still got my back. After our conversation yesterday, I'd decided that he was more or less the only person I could trust. Now I'm not even sure about that.

Lauren's already moved on, they all have, and now there's some aimless chat about people's first pets.

But I'm not really listening.

There was a time not so long ago when I'd strut round this place like I still had handcuffs in my pocket and a taser on my belt. I wasn't looking for trouble, I'm not stupid, but I wouldn't back away from it. Lauren never put the wind up me like she did a lot of people, because I'd dealt with plenty like her on the Job. Women who hate themselves so much that they have to take out their frustrations on other people. On their kids, more often than not. The likes of Lauren in a place like this didn't bother me at all.

I'm not the same person any more.

It's been a long time since I recognised myself. The Alice I was two years ago, I mean. Now I don't even recognise the person I was two weeks ago.

Suddenly, I'm scared of *everybody*.

'Not going in to watch TV?' Marcus asks.

I've taken my meds and now I'm sitting in the main

corridor, my back to the wall outside the nurses' station. It's brightly lit and I've got the widest field of view I can think of anywhere on the ward. I can see people coming from any direction and, if it's someone I don't like the look of, I've got enough time to make myself scarce or get a nurse to sound the alarm. Truth is, I don't much fancy sitting in front of the TV with everyone else, but I don't particularly want to go back to my room, either. Not until I have to, anyway. It's started to feel even smaller than usual, like it's shrinking night by night and if for some reason I let the wrong person through the door, I've got nowhere to go.

'Can't be arsed,' I say.

'There's usually something good on a Friday night, isn't there?'

I don't answer, so Marcus sits down next to me.

'It was a good session this morning,' he says. 'Your assessment.' He waits, but I don't say anything. 'Didn't you think so?'

'I suppose.' I watch Ilias come out of the dining room and start walking in our direction.

'You're actually very lucky, Alice,' Marcus says. 'It might not feel like that now, but it's always so much better when you know what the problem is. These issues you're having are clearly PTSD-related, so now we can deal with them properly. With some patients you never know. *They* never know. Months go by, years even, and there is no explanation for why they're the way they are.'

Ilias walks past without even looking at me and turns on to the men's corridor, presumably heading for his room.

'Is there anything else bothering you?' Marcus asks. 'Aside from the blackouts?'

Malaika comes out of the nurses' station carrying a cardboard box. She takes it into one of the examination rooms. The corridor's empty, so I glance at Marcus.

'Just the not sleeping,' I say.

'OK . . .'

I can tell Marcus isn't quite buying it. He's too good at his job and he can smell bullshit a mile away. I'm wondering how much I can tell him. I mean, normally I'd say sweet FA about what's *actually* going on, because the minute I open my mouth about anything like this they just presume all my craziness from before has dropped in for a visit and I end up rattling with all the extra anti-psych pills. Now, though, *they've* given me an . . . explanation. It's like this new diagnosis they're all so pleased with themselves about has given me a get-out-of-jail-free card.

It can't hurt to test the water a little.

'You quite sure about the PTSD?' I ask. 'What's causing it?'

His grunt is emphatic. 'Your symptoms are very common.'

'I do know about PTSD,' I say. 'It's why I'm in here, remember?'

'Perhaps it isn't as severe as last time, but as Dr Bakshi explained—'

'It's not *enough* though. I found a body. So what?'

'I think for most people that would be traumatic enough. So soon after Kevin's death, too. Let's not forget that.'

'Yeah, but I'm not most people, am I? I saw far worse things than that when I was a copper. Plenty of bodies . . . kids and whatever, and none of that stuff screwed my memory up and all the rest of it. Just saying, it feels a bit . . . convenient.'

Marcus says nothing for maybe half a minute, lets his head drop back like he's happy with a few moments of relative peace and calm. Then he turns to look at me. 'What's . . . *all the rest of it?*'

Malaika comes out of the examination room and walks back into the nurses' station. Ilias emerges from the men's corridor and turns towards the TV room. He gives me a strange look as he passes and I watch him until he disappears.

'I think I'm in danger,' I say.

'What kind of danger?'

In for a penny, right? 'Someone wants to hurt me. Wants to *kill* me.' I see the obvious question on his face. 'The same person who killed Debbie.'

'Why would they want to kill you, Alice?'

I'm not an idiot, so I know that Marcus could be the very person we're now talking about. I don't think it makes much odds. Except for the coppers and that psychiatrist they brought with them, I've thought the same thing, at one time or another, about every person I've spoken to since it happened.

OK, so not *all* of them. Maybe not Lucy.

'Because he or she was working with Debbie,' I say. 'Debbie was using Kevin to smuggle drugs out of here, which was why she killed him and why she was killed. The fact I know that makes me a target.'

It feels a bit odd, saying all this to Marcus, being so upfront and matter-of-fact about what's going on, but it's not like he doesn't know, is it? Debbie had told him exactly what I'd said to her before she was killed. He was the one who passed that information on to French and Saunders.

'I don't feel safe,' I say. 'Locked up in here, I'm a sitting duck.'

I look around. A few more people are coming out of the dining room now and walking in different directions. Patients and staff. Heading to their rooms for a quick lie down before watching telly, outside for a smoke, to the toilets or the meds hatch.

Colin is talking to Tony.

Femi is talking to Donna and Lucy.

Clare is talking to Lauren, the two of them thick as thieves all of a sudden.

'I don't think it's very nice,' Marcus says.

I turn to look at him, thinking that's a strange way of putting it. A massive fucking understatement, considering what I've just told him.

'You talking about Debbie like that.'

'*What?*'

'People I have worked with have died before,' he says. 'You know that. But not like this. Never like this.' He looks at me. 'I went to visit Debbie's sister last night, to pass on my condolences. To see how she was coping. She has been *destroyed* by what has happened . . . the whole family has been destroyed.' He shakes his head. 'So no, what you are saying is not acceptable. Debbie was my colleague, but she was also my friend.'

'Yeah, and Kevin was mine.'

'I'm aware of that, Alice, but the fact remains that it is wrong to attack a person's reputation when they are not here to defend themselves.' He stands up, because he doesn't want to continue the conversation or he's got meds to administer. Either way.

'Well, she's dead so she probably doesn't give a shit!' I shout after him as he walks away. 'Anyway, she's not the one who needs defending.'

FORTY-NINE

Suddenly I'm wide awake and I don't have a clue what time it is, but it's pitch black and I'm tangled in wet sheets and, far more important, I know there's someone in my room.

I know there can't possibly be, because the door is locked.

I know there can't be, because I'd have heard them coming in.

But I know that there is.

The staff all have keys so they can make round-the-clock checks when they need to, and even if it's not a member of the staff, someone might have found a way to get hold of a key. Someone managed to get hold of a knife easily enough, didn't they?

I *told* them. I told almost *everyone*, but they wouldn't listen.

I lie perfectly still and wait for my eyes to adjust to the darkness.

I can't make out a shape and I can't hear anyone breathing but me. I'm not really surprised, though, because whoever's

314

in here with me, they're good at this. I'm struggling to suck up enough spit to swallow, never mind scream, and even if I could, there's always someone screaming about something, so it's not like I could count on anyone rushing down here to help.

Christ, it's going to be so easy, because I've got nothing to fight back with, and now a voice inside my head is telling me, *Who cares? There's not a fat lot worth fighting for anyway, so what's the fucking point?*

I'm not worth fighting for.

So I relax, just a little, because there's not much else I can do, and I think, *This is you, then, you silly, soft cow.* Lying here, giving Tiny Tears a run for her money and waiting for the Thing to do what it's come for.

FIFTY

I'm having breakfast sitting on my own. I say having, I couldn't eat a thing if you paid me, but I'm in here with everyone else because I was desperate to get out of my room first chance I got and now I want to be somewhere I can keep an eye on them all. See who's matey with who all of a sudden and who's giving me evils. Tune in to the chatter. Check out the alliances.

I'm still shaking this morning, but more importantly I'm still *here*.

Obviously . . .

If I was being paranoid, I'd say there *was* someone in my room last night and that it was a warning from a person who's clearly enjoying scaring the crap out of me. Someone there to deliver a simple message: *Best stay on your toes, because I can get to you any time I want.*

If I was being paranoid.

I think it was actually a warning to myself. Early notice that the threat level was being ramped up, the way the government does sometimes with terrorists or whatever. My subconscious mind, having processed all the evidence and read all the signs, laying out a possibility, a probability even, and showing me exactly what could happen if I wasn't careful. Telling me, in no uncertain terms, while I still had a chance to do something about it.

Either way, the message was the same and I received it loud and clear.

Wherever he is, Graham would be proud of me, because the moment the breakfast service is done with and the meds hatch opens, I'm out of the dining room and first in line to get drugged up. I take the three different doses that Femi hands over and signs off on – three, because I'm assuming the new Alzheimer's pills are among them – and go looking for Malaika.

Ten minutes later, I still haven't managed to find her, so I collar George on his way from the nurses' station to the MDR and ask him where she is.

'Malaika's not come in this morning,' he tells me.

'Really?' Malaika was my best bet, same as always. I'll need to find someone else fast.

'Bit bloody short-handed, tell you the truth,' George says. 'I think Marcus is on his way in, and he won't be best pleased having to give up his Saturday—'

'Can you take me outside?'

George rolls his eyes. 'Morning gasper, is it, pet?'

'Yeah, but . . . I just need some air.'

'Well, you'll have to give me ten minutes. Something I have to finish, then I'm all yours. Just one fag, mind.'

'You're a star,' I say.

George carries on towards the MDR and I nip back to my room to grab my tobacco. I'm in and out as quickly as I can, but I still make sure the door's locked while I'm in there. I lock it again when I leave, because the last thing I want when I come back is to find someone in there waiting for me, then hurry out to wait for George at the airlock.

I've only just got there when Tony arrives carrying his suitcase. He sits down next to me.

'They're coming early . . . flown in from Detroit.' He grins and pats his case. 'So I packed as soon as I woke up.'

'I saw the Thing last night,' I say.

'*Where?*'

'In my room. Well, I didn't *see* it exactly, but I saw what it would be like if the Thing was there. The shape and everything.'

'That happens to me all the time.' Tony lifts his case on to his lap, holds it against his chest and whispers, 'What I'm hoping is . . . that when I go, the Thing might stay behind.'

'I thought it always followed you.'

'Yeah, so far. But I was thinking . . . maybe it's getting tired of always changing into different things, or it's stopped being angry with me. I mean it could have killed me by now, if it really wanted to.' He looks at me. 'Yours might give up, too.'

'I'm not going to let it have the chance,' I say.

Why do I keep saying *it*? I know *my* Thing is walking around in here somewhere on two legs. Easier than saying *he or she* all the time, I suppose.

Tony puts out a hand and says, 'Good luck, Al,' like we

won't be seeing each other again. I know he's not going anywhere, but I shake his hand anyway.

'Cheers, Tone.'

Besides which, having seen all those stab wounds in
Debbie McClure, he or she is definitely an *it*.

When George comes ambling round the corner, I jump to
my feet ready to go. He puts on a comical burst of speed and
by the time he gets to me he's pretending to be out of breath.
He's already got the keys in his hand.

'Honestly.' He looks at Tony and shakes his head, then
mimes puffing on a cigarette. 'Bloody addicts, eh?'

I never smoked roll-ups before I came here. Didn't smoke
much of anything come to that. I was one of those annoying
part-time smokers who just scrounged fags off other people
at parties, but now I'm every bit the addict George was talking about, and it's always roll-ups, because it's cheaper and
that's what everyone else in here smokes. These days, I can
roll a fag blindfolded and with one hand, but you wouldn't
know it. Not now, seeing me spill tobacco and tear *two* Rizlas
while I struggle to stop my hands shaking.

'Here,' George says. 'Let me.'

'I didn't think you smoked,' I say.

'I don't, but I reckon I can make a better job of that than
the pig's ear *you're* making . . .'

I hand over the tobacco and the papers and lift my face to
the sun until he hands me back the cigarette.

'Thanks.'

He lights it for me, steps from shade into sunlight himself.
'Those new meds'll kick in pretty quick,' he says. 'Sort these
memory issues out.'

'Hope so,' I say.

'Those *blips*.' George looks at me. 'That's all they are, right, pet?'

I'm trying to decide whether to tell him the truth when I remember what Bob told me on Thursday and decide it would be much more useful to ask George about his row with Debbie instead. I'm just working my way round to it when I spot a bloke walking quickly down the hill from the main entrance towards us.

I stop and stare at him.

'What?' George asks, turning to look.

'Who's that?'

He's not a doctor, because he's already close enough for me to see that there's no lanyard flapping around against his chest, but he's not a visitor, either. Anyone visiting this place is ... tentative. Doesn't matter if it's their first time or if they're old hands, nobody ever sets foot in the Shackleton Unit without a degree of apprehension or, more often than not, plain reluctance. It's never going to be a picnic, is all I'm saying.

You certainly don't walk towards it ... purposefully, like it's something you're looking forward to. Not the way this bloke is bowling down that hill, only a few seconds away now, like there's nowhere else he'd rather be

'Who *is* he?'

'No idea,' George says.

'Can you go and find out?' George looks at me like I'm starting to take the piss and he's done more than enough already. '*Please* ...'

He mutters something under his breath then sighs and starts to trudge up the hill.

I'm still watching the mystery bloke, because there's something far too easy and confident about him. A shape that's familiar. So, as soon as George has taken enough steps towards him, just enough steps *away*, I turn.

And I run.

I'm wearing trainers and I'm fast. George isn't and he's a big bloke, so by the time I turn to look he's already fifty yards behind me.

He's waving and shouting.

I run ... past humming generators and overflowing skips, then across a car park and now it's all downhill towards the side gate. Two people are walking towards me, but they step quickly out of my way. They both look a little alarmed and a glance tells me they're hospital staff who know it's never a good sign when someone comes running hell-for-leather from the direction of the Shackleton.

I run ... and I can see my dad's face light up when I come round that last bend and he's jumping up and down and urging me on and, even though I'm knackered, I find a final burst of speed and sprint towards the finishing line where a couple of the other parents are holding up a tape.

I dip at the last minute, like you're supposed to ...

... out through the gate and then I stop. I'm bent double, panting on a quiet road that I don't recognise, so I look both ways but I've not got the first idea which way I should go. It's been a long time since I've run that fast and it feels like I'm going to be sick, but I know I need to keep running, one way or another, before George catches up to me.

Left or right. Shit ... I need to pick a direction, but I can't, because I haven't got a clue where I'm going.

Just . . . away.

For fuck's sake, Al . . .

Me and Johnno in Greggs, one lunchtime. Pushing the boat out. There's a woman tutting in the queue behind us and Johnno's getting tetchy because I can't decide between a pasty and a sausage roll.

Just pick *one,* Johnno says.

So I do.

FIFTY-ONE

I really don't want anyone to think that I was planning to do this when I talked George into taking me out for a fag. I swear I just wanted to get off the ward for a few minutes and get my head straight. It was only when I saw that suspicious-looking bloke that I knew I needed to get away. It wasn't like I was regretting not having any breakfast and was suddenly desperate for the tea and toast that's sitting in front of me right now.

The café was the first place I came to, that's all. I couldn't run any further, and I wanted to be with people.

With normal people.

There was a reasonable crowd in here when I came in. There still is, but now they're all eating, which I suppose is why the woman behind the counter can take a few minutes off. Anyway, that's what I'm thinking when she waltzes round the counter and walks across to sit down at my table.

She was friendly enough ten minutes ago, when I ordered.

and whatever else has happened to me, I think I've always been a pretty good judge of people. So, when I finally find the courage to look her in the eye, I say, 'I'm really sorry, but I can't pay for this.'

'I guessed that,' she says.

'I mean I *can* . . . but I haven't got any money on me.'

'It's a mug of tea and a slice of toast,' she says. 'I think I'll survive.'

She watches me eat for a while, then turns to wave when one of the other customers leaves. They all seem to know her, so the place has obviously been here a while, and I wonder if she runs it on her own. There's no sign of anyone else, even though there must be someone back there in the kitchen knocking out all the bacon and sausages or whatever. She's wearing a wedding ring . . . so maybe her husband? I'm trying to work out her set-up, trying to work *her* out. I reckon I can still do that. I try to do it with newbies on the ward, same way I did it back before things fell apart, with other coppers, and with suspects, obviously.

I sip my tea and take another bite of soggy toast. I sneak looks at her. I'm not scared any more and I've got my breath back and I'm suddenly enjoying myself, putting flesh on this woman's bones.

She's at least sixty, but she's dyed her hair very blonde like she still gives a shit what people make of her. Or maybe she's done it precisely because she doesn't. Either way, it's good. She sounds local, so I wonder if she's opened a place in the area where she grew up. Or maybe there's been a greasy spoon here for ever, like a family business, and she took it over from her parents. I wonder if that was what she wanted, what she'd imagined for herself when she was younger.

324

I'm making suggestions to myself, trying to guess what her name might be, when she saves me the trouble.

'I'm Sylvia,' she says.

I would never have guessed that. I'd been leaning towards Veronica or Madge. 'Alice . . .'

'So, what's the story, Alice?'

I look at her and she's sitting there like she's just asked me what the time is. She says she knows I've *got* a story, I mean *hasn't everyone*, so the rest of the toast goes uneaten and my tea goes cold while I tell her. Everything. When I've finished, she doesn't look as if she's wishing she'd never asked, but maybe she's just got a naturally kind face.

She nods towards the door. 'That place up the road?'

'Hendon Community Hospital,' I say.

'Yeah.' She gets up and walks across to a tall fridge against the wall, comes back with a can of Coke and sits down again. 'I had a cousin went through the same thing as you. Years ago now. They didn't really call it what it was back then, though. Didn't give it a name. Everyone in the family just said she was *suffering with her nerves*. You know?'

'Is she OK now?'

Sylvia shakes her head. 'She's not with us any more, bless her. Well out of it if you ask me.' She opens her can. 'The suffering bit's right, though.' She looks at me. 'I can *see* it, love.'

I don't know what to say, so I just stare down at the scratched red tabletop.

'I can't even imagine what it's like . . .'

I finally look up and I swear she really wants to know. An old bloke comes in and she asks him if he wants his usual. When he says he does, she tells him to sit down and says she'll be with him in five minutes.

Then she turns back to me.

'Sounds stupid, but a lot of the time you're just ... *irritated*,' I say. 'It's so bloody infuriating when people don't believe you.'

'I know that's how it must feel,' she says. 'But most people just don't know how to react to that kind of thing, do they? I'm not sure *I* do, tell you the truth. You tell someone you're ... I don't know, getting messages from God through the patterns on your wallpaper ... I don't mean *you're* saying anything like that, love ... but what are people supposed to make of it? It's hard to go, "Oh, all right then", because that's only ... reinforcing it, don't you think?'

'Yeah, but it's *also* like me telling someone my name's Alice and them telling me that it's not.'

She nods slowly. 'Oh, righto ... I'm with you.'

'That's how sure you are. You don't just *think* these things, you *know* them.'

She nods again. 'Got it, love.'

'So it's like everyone's basically saying you're stupid or calling you a liar.'

'Or telling you you're mad.'

I laugh, and it's nice. 'Right, but even if you *are* being a bit mad you don't think you are.' Now *I* nod towards the street. 'Nobody over there thinks they're mad. Not properly. Yeah, they might have gone off the rails for whatever reason, but—'

'Everyone goes off the rails now and again,' Sylvia says.

'I know.'

'What use is bleedin' rails, anyway? Just keep you going in the same direction and that's no fun, is it?'

'No ...' She's trying to make me feel better, so I don't tell her that I'd give anything to be back on those boring rails again. Facing the direction of travel. Moving forward . . .

'So, what about you?' she asks.

'What *about* me?'

'Never mind that lot over the road. How are *you* feeling? Now, this minute.'

I look at her and it makes me think about my mum, so I start to cry a bit.

'Come on, now.' She pulls one serviette after another from a metal dispenser and hands them over. I snivel and splutter into them.

'I'm in so much trouble,' I say.

She tells me everything's going to be OK and puts one of her hands on mine. It's warmer and softer than I expect. I don't know if she's forgotten about the old bloke and his 'usual', but after that we just sit there for a while saying nothing, while she glugs her Coke and makes shushing noises.

And for a few minutes, it *is* OK. I forget about Kevin and Debbie and whoever's after me. I forget about Johnno and all the blood that came out of him, because the woman I'm sitting here with is quiet and kind. Because she doesn't make any assumptions. Because she doesn't want anything, or think anything bad, and best of all, I know she isn't judging me.

And then it's over, because I see George jog past the window with a policeman in tow. George glances in and a few seconds later they're both coming through the door.

'Oh,' Sylvia says.

For a moment or two, while everyone in here is turning to see what's happening, I wonder if she's called them. Could she have done it when I wasn't paying attention or when she went to fetch her drink? Maybe she signalled to whoever's in the kitchen.

George walks over to the table, and even though he doesn't look angry, I'm sure he is.

He says, 'Come on, Alice.'

Sylvia stands up, so I do the same.

Then I decide that Sylvia probably didn't call anyone, because when the policeman – who looks about sixteen – puts a hand on my arm, she shakes her head and says, 'There's no need for that, son.'

I promise her that I'll come back to pay for the toast and she shouts after me as they're leading me towards the door. 'You can have a proper fry-up next time. You take care . . . OK, love . . . ?'

FIFTY-TWO

'I'm really sorry you had to come in on a Saturday.'

'I didn't come in just because of you,' Marcus says.

'Oh yeah,' I say. 'Malaika . . .'

'Good job I did, though.'

We're sitting close together in one of the exam rooms. It's warm in here and it stinks of bleach and puke and I remember the two of us sitting in exactly the same place almost a week before. Then, Marcus was the one who needed comforting; stammering out his shock and disbelief at what had happened just across the corridor to a woman whose body was still warm.

Both of us with blood on our hands.

I say comforting, but at a guess – bearing in mind the whole absconding and being brought back by the police thing – that's probably not Marcus's primary concern at this particular moment. Aside from a physical assault, legging it is about as serious as it gets in terms of patient behaviour. I know there's going to be consequences, but I don't have a problem with that and I'm not expecting to get anything you'd describe as a proper bollocking. It's not like I took anyone hostage or went over the wall at Belmarsh or anything.

To be fair to Marcus and the rest of them, even when they're reading you the Riot Act in here, they tend to do it very gently.

'So, why did you run away, Alice?'

'You know why.' He says nothing, like he's forgotten or maybe he doesn't think it's much of an excuse. Either way, it's annoying. 'What I told you yesterday.'

He nods. 'You not feeling safe, you mean?'

'Me not *being* safe,' I say.

'I understand,' he says. 'George says that you saw someone. Outside.'

'Yeah. He looked *well* dodgy, and the way things are right now, I'm not taking any chances.'

'So you ran.'

'I would have come back.' I can see he's got that bullshit detector turned up nice and high. 'OK, so I probably wouldn't. Not straight away.'

'Where would you have gone?'

'I wasn't thinking that far ahead.'

If I'd had the chance to walk out of that café in my own sweet time, I honestly don't know where I would have headed. I'd probably have called Banksy in the end, maybe asked if I could crash at his place. Thinking about it, though, he might well have made the phone call I'd suspected the woman in the café had made, and I probably wouldn't have held that against him.

330

'It was nice,' I say. 'Just being away for a bit.'

'Alice, listen to me.' Marcus puts down his clipboard, the notes for a report he'll have to write on the 'incident'. 'If you continue to take your medication and make an effort to stay calm, so that we can help you ... you can be away for a lot longer than a *bit*. You can go home.'

'Not sure that's going to happen now,' I say.

'What do you mean?'

'I don't know ... things are coming to a head. I'm not saying that's what I want, but I don't think I've got a lot of say in it.' I was thinking about this all the way back from the café and I'm almost certain of it now. The scary stuff's getting really close and I can't stop it because, actually, I'm not sure I'm supposed to. 'After Kevin was killed and I started running round trying to find out who'd done it ...' I see his expression darken. He doesn't want to listen to me bad-mouthing his 'friend and colleague' again. So I don't. 'It's as if I started something, you know? Set a ball rolling. I'm not going anywhere until it hits and even though I'm not thrilled about what's coming, it feels like I need it to happen.'

I take a few seconds then look at him. 'Does that make sense?'

He picks up his clipboard again.

So, clearly not.

'I've spoken to Dr Bakshi,' he says. 'Of course, she was not happy to hear what happened, but she agrees with me that, in all probability, this was just another ... blip. The panic is all part of the same PTSD, and if you continue to take your new medication, we should see some improvement reasonably fast.' He glances down, scribbles a word or two. 'Of course, we can't allow any more time outside, for the time being at least.' He smiles, trying to lighten things. 'George tells me you were really fast . . .'

I smile back. I *was*. I *am* . . .

'And for the next few days we will need to put you back on Within Eyesight Observations.'

WEO is fair enough and it's what I was expecting. I mean, it's a hospital . . . what else were they going to do? Make me wash my own pyjamas? Take away my Scrabble privileges?

'Yeah, so about that,' I say. 'As far as which member of staff is keeping an eye on me all the time, is there any chance I can choose?' Even as I'm asking, I'm trying to decide which of the nurses I trust the most. Or which one I distrust the least.

'I'm afraid that's not possible,' Marcus says. 'It wouldn't even be possible under normal circumstances, and you already know that staffing is a major issue at the moment.'

'So, when's Malaika coming back?' If Marcus had agreed, she would probably have been my first choice.

'I don't know,' he says. 'Unfortunately, she isn't answering her phone at the moment.'

The tiniest of alarm bells rings at the back of my brain, but it's drowned out by the clattering of a trolley outside as Marcus gets to his feet.

'Remember what I said, Alice.'

I walk to the door, and for a few seconds before opening it I just stand there and do the deep-breathing thing. Because I have to and because this is the way it's going to be from now on. I hate it because they're my friends, but I'm scared to death about stepping outside and having to greet whichever member of the crazy gang I run into first.

'You said a lot of things.'

*

332

I curl up in the corner of the music room wearing my head-phones and a *Do Not Disturb* expression and, thankfully, there aren't too many comings and goings. The Jigsaw Man wanders in but just mooches for a few minutes, pretending he's not looking at me, and then wanders out again. L-Plate spots me through the window and comes bursting through the door like we haven't seen each other in weeks. It looks, for a moment, like she might overcome her phobia and actually hug me. Nice as that would be, I tell her I'm a bit down in the dumps and ask if she'd mind sodding off and giving me a bit of space. L-Plate says *no sweat, babe, no sweat*, but makes me promise that we'll see each other later, because, you know, she *really* needs to catch up with me.

I watch her scamper away and think *she's not the only one*.

I stare at my phone for a while, then find myself firing off a text to Sophie: Wassup byatch?

She doesn't reply straight away like she normally does, so I sit there and wonder where she is and what she's doing on a fine Saturday afternoon. In the flat, probably, watching one of those old black and white films she loves, or doing a massive clean which she loves almost as much, or out buying overpriced tat in Camden Market. Sitting in the pub, maybe. *Not* looking at the other drinkers like they're aliens or boring her mates rigid trying to describe the funny music she keeps hearing. Lying in bed with her boyfriend, and not staring out of the window at the lights she can see at the end of the garden. Not telling him she knows he's 'in on it', while he pats the mattress next to him and tells her not to be so daft.

The phone pings.

Sophie Mob: hey you! how's the madhouse?? 🙂

Same as usual.

Sophie Mob: what you up to?

Not much. I've been a bit up and down.

Sophie Mob: 🙁 want me to come and see you?? i can bring chocolate!! 👍 🙂

It's fine, don't worry. I was thinking about you
that's all.

Sophie Mob: thinking about you too. LOTS xx
There's nothing for a minute or so. I think that's probably it, then the phone pings again.

Sophie Mob: just so you know, camilla is WAY cleaner than you but not as much fun 🍾 🖤

She knows all about what had happened with Andy, but I can't decide if the bottle of wine emoji is a joke or not. Nice, either way.

I am Queen of Fun!

Sophie Mob: US when you get out!! 🍾 🍰

I hope it's a bigger cake than that!

Sophie Mob: seriously though. cannot wait. not the same out here without you. 💔

It was stupid, I suppose, to think that Sophie was going to make me feel better. She almost always does, like she's got a gift for it, but all I'm feeling is sad, until the switch goes and suddenly I'm raging. Because none of this is fair and what's happening is not my fault and now I'm scrolling down to the emojis myself and I'm getting busy.

I send the message and immediately feel guilty, so I quickly shoot a smiley face off, but the damage is done.

Sophie Mob: WTF AI??

I sit back, then remember what I forgot, and now I feel terrible because I never got around to saying 'sorry' like I'd meant to. It was why I texted her in the first place, because I should have said it a long time ago. I look up to the camera in the corner of the room and give everyone a big, smiley wave. I've got no idea who's watching, or if they'll appreciate just how *hilarious* I'm being, but it doesn't much matter.

I'm not going anywhere until it hits . . .

The damage is done.

FIFTY-THREE

Forever ago, just after Kevin was killed, but before everything got properly dark, I walked into this room and was greeted like some conquering hero or whatever because I'd scored a bit of weed and been rumbled. Today, though, I don't want to sit and make nice with them all. I don't want to pretend everything's fine and listen to them talking at me, but what I want doesn't seem to count for much any more. I'm not given any choice in the matter. As soon as I set foot in the dining room, Lucy jumps up and I'm all but dragged across to sit down and eat with everyone else, just because I did a bunk and got escorted back a few hours later by a constable with acne.

Jesus, they want to know *everything*. What I did and how it felt. They want me to relive every moment of my great adventure.

You'd think I'd tunnelled out of fucking Colditz.

'Did you put up a fight?' Bob asks.

I tell him that there wouldn't have been much point.

'Didn't you even struggle a *bit*?'

Ilias seems outraged, as though I've somehow let the side down. 'You should have given that copper a good hard kick in the nuts,' he says. 'Got a few decent punches in, at least. They wouldn't do anything because this is a hospital, right?'

'*Special* hospital,' Donna says.

'Because *we're* special,' Bob says.

Ilias is nodding. 'Yeah, of course, so what are they going to do?'

'They could take away my Scrabble privileges,' I say.

Tony laughs, *hurr hurr hurr,* and Ilias laughs, eventually. Even Lauren seems to think it's pretty funny and I wish I was in the frame of mind to enjoy the moment a bit more. Or at all.

'George says you were in some café.' Lauren waits, stabbing at chips.

'Is that right?' I don't much like the idea of George saying anything to anyone. 'What else did he say?'

'You were eating toast.' She senses my unease and pounces on it. 'That a big secret, is it? Another one?'

'What other one?' Lucy asks.

I pretend I didn't hear Lauren's last comment and that it's all a bit of banter. 'Did he tell you what I *had* on my toast?'

'Like I give a toss.' Lauren is furious, suddenly. 'Dogshit?'

You ask me, there's been a bit too much *telling people things* in this place and I should know, because back when I was still trying to solve the first murder, I was the one doing most of it. Now, though, every conversation makes me tense and jumpy. The ones I'm part of, or the ones I overhear, and most especially the ones I'm not around for but know damn well are happening. The whispers and the knowing remarks and the double meanings. *Why did you run?*, Marcus asked. Now I'm asking myself, why I didn't *keep* running. If I had my way, everyone here would be made to shut up right now. Let them pop their pills and do their puzzles and scoff their burgers and chips with their traps firmly shut.

Same as Shaun.

Shaun. Even though he's got more reasons than most to want Debbie dead, he's actually the only one I really trust. Yeah, I considered him as a suspect, but only for like . . . five seconds. Shaun wouldn't hurt a fly.

Lucy says something, but I don't take it in. I'm watching Colin, the Informal, who's sitting on an adjacent table with Clare. I'm wondering what the two of them have suddenly found to talk about.

'Al?'

I'm just a link in the chain of it. This . . . watching. I'm watching them while Mia sits at a different table and watches me and we're all being watched by the camera in the corner. Up to now it's not something I've really thought about too much, but suddenly I understand what poor old Graham used to get so worked up about. Why he chucked mash at the cameras and banged his head against the wall.

I suppose there's a difference because I'm only really worried about one person, while Graham didn't like *anyone* watching. Trouble is, that one person could *be* anyone.

'Alice . . . ?'

I look at Lucy, who stares at me and says, 'You're miles away, babe.'

'She's remembering the sweet taste of freedom,' Tony says.

'It tastes like toast, apparently,' Lauren says.

Bob punches the air and shouts, 'Freedom!' like he's Mel Gibson in *Braveheart*. Donna and Lucy do the same and Lauren starts singing that old George Michael song.

Not freedom, I think. *Safety*. Then it strikes me that, much as a certain person must be chuffed to bits that I've come back – my *anyone*, my *Thing* – they're probably loving the fact that I ran away in the first place. I remember what it felt like in my room the night before. As much as anything, I'm sure that whoever killed Debbie and now wants to kill me is getting off on the fact that I was scared enough to try and escape.

So, I might be back here again, exactly where they want me, but I'll be fucked if I'm going to show them I'm afraid.

'It was good, actually,' I say. 'Getting out for a bit.'

'How was it good?' Donna asks.

She seems desperate to know and I think it's bonkers how quickly people in here have become institutionalized. Most of them are on a 28-day section, which means less time on the ward than me, but they talk like they're lifers. As if going to a café or having a job or even walking about outside in proper clothes is something they can only ever dream about.

'Yeah, *do* tell,' Lauren says.

Then I remember that, for some of them, this is their umpteenth time in this place or another one like it. That they've probably spent more time in those faded pale-blue pyjamas than they have in their own.

Lifers . . .

'Well, just spending a bit of time with normal people.' I nod towards Ilias. 'You know, talking to someone and not thinking they might suddenly take their trousers off.'

Ilias grins and salutes.

'Or just talking to someone who's actually standing still.' Donna blushes.

'Someone who isn't singing all the time or talking about all the women they've shagged.' I look across to the other table. 'Someone who doesn't burst into tears if you say the wrong word and someone who can finish a jigsaw when there's another human being within a hundred bloody yards of him.' I show them all a smile. 'You know, *normal* people.'

Lucy grins and lifts her paper cup like she's toasting us all.

I touch my own cup to hers. 'Don't get me wrong though, I missed you all like mad.'

There are the predictable jeers and groans. Ilias says, 'Balls' and Lauren lobs a chip at me.

'Right, it's ridiculous I know, but I actually did. Look, I would have come back anyway ... I was happy to come back. Happier than I was before I came here, anyway. I know being stuck in this place was never on anyone's to-do list or anything, but it's not that bad, is it?'

'It's awful,' Bob says. 'If you don't think it's awful you probably deserve to be here.'

'OK, sometimes it is ... but the best thing about Fleet Ward is, nine times out of ten, there's something happening. Yeah, it's seriously weird a lot of the time, but you've got to admit, there's always stuff going on. Stuff to look at and talk about and get involved in.' I nod towards the windows. 'We all think everyone out there is living it up, having the time of their lives, but the truth is, most of the time it's pretty dull.' *What use is bleedin' rails, anyway?* 'Well, not in here, it isn't. One thing this place isn't *ever* ... is boring.'

'I'm bored right now,' Lauren says. 'Listening to this.'

'I'm just saying, that's why I'm OK with coming back.

Because there's going to be things happening.' I look at everyone around the table, then up to give that camera lens a good hard stare. 'And whatever happens, I'm ready for it.' I sit back. 'OK, speech over . . .'

Tony smiles at me and winks while Lucy and Donna nod enthusiastically. Ilias actually claps and I want to kiss him for it.

The legs on Lauren's chair scream against the floor as she pushes it back and stands up. 'Right, that's enough shits and giggles for one day. I'm going to get a few pills down my neck, then it's *Pointless Celebrities, Casualty* and *Mrs Brown's Boys.*'

Lauren's announcement of the evening's scheduled viewing, as carefully selected by Lauren, is like a starting gun going off. *If* it was a race that involved standing up and sitting down again, pissing about in the doorway and, in Ilias's case, polishing off everyone's leftovers.

I wander out into the corridor.

Marcus and George are talking outside the nurses' station. Marcus catches my eye and nods.

I smile at him and take my place in the queue for meds.

Once I've swallowed the three different lots of capsules and tablets, I stand around trying to decide what to do and where to go. I'm glad I said my piece back in there. I feel stronger, *readier,* but it certainly doesn't mean I want to spend the evening bunched up with everyone in front of the box.

I can sense someone standing close behind me and I presume it's Mia, taking her WEO duties a bit too seriously. When I feel a hand clutching at mine I turn round and discover it's Shaun.

'All good, mate?'

He starts to pull me towards the TV room.

I say *no* and tell him I'm not up to it, that I'm ready to turn in.

He grunts and keeps on pulling.

Shaun clearly wants company, so in the end I stop fighting him and follow the herd. I'm remembering the safety in numbers thing and asking myself what's the worst that can happen. Then I remember that *Mrs Brown's Boys* is on, and decide that's probably it.

FIFTY-FOUR

I don't recognise any of the celebrities on *Pointless Celebrities*, but to be fair, I'm not paying too much attention to what's happening onscreen. I'm watching the watchers. Tony's gone to bed, but the rest of them are settled in good and proper.

Clare and Colin are still sitting together, just behind Lauren who's in pole position as usual, remote in hand. Donna and Lucy are next to one another, with Bob sunk into an orange beanbag I've never seen before on one side of them, and Ilias sprawled in an armchair on the other. Mia and Femi are keeping an eye on things from opposite corners of the room.

I'm up at the back with Shaun, our chairs so close that you'd struggle to slip a fag-paper between us.

He's still holding my hand.

Twice I've asked him if everything's all right, twice he's nodded and twice I haven't believed him.

There's nothing much to report until Jigsaw Man – who's

clearly never been in the TV room before – speaks up and asks if there's any chance Lauren could change channels. 'Because *Through the Keyhole*'s on in a minute.'

'There's no fucking chance,' Lauren says.

Mia says, 'Come on now, Lauren.'

Lauren turns round and looks at Colin, making it clear that if he pipes up again, she'll stick one of his jigsaws where the sun doesn't shine, piece by piece.

I look at Shaun. 'Why is she always such a bitch?'

Shaun has moved on from the screwed-up scraps of paper routine. These days, he carries a pen and a block of Post-it notes around. Puts what he has to say on paper, then tears off the note and passes it across. Now, he lets go of my hand and does exactly that.

i know why she sings all the time.

'OK,' I say.

do you want to know why?

There doesn't seem much point telling him I don't really care, because he's already writing again. This time, it's several Post-its' worth, so I turn back to the TV until he's finished. On *Casualty*, someone has fallen off a ladder. Shaun taps me on the arm and passes me the torn-off notes one by one.

her dad killed her mum when she was a teenager. not sure how … (more)

I look at Shaun, then I look at Lauren, then I read the next note.

> she's been in and out of hospital ever since. she reckons there's a voice singing in her head all the time. sometimes she sings to drown out the singing in her head ... (more)
>   sometimes she sings along with it if it's a song she knows. now it's just her thing.
>   i think her <u>mum</u> was some kind of singer. in pubs or whatever.

I stare at the back of Lauren's head for a minute or so. I screw up the Post-its and put them in my pocket. 'She's still a bitch, though.'

Shaun shrugs.

'To *you*, especially. Remember that time in here, when she was screaming at you? Just before Debbie came in and ...' I stop because I can see that he's starting to get agitated. It was stupid of me to mention it, but before I can say sorry, Shaun's scribbling again.

> did you like the note i gave you on wednesday?

I'm not sure which note he means, then I see him put a hand over his heart and mouth *thank you*. The message he'd passed to me in the music room, after Lauren had as good as accused me of stabbing Debbie to death.

'It was nice.' I lean so close that my lips brush his ear as I'm whispering into it. 'I know what you think I did ... what lots of people seem to think I did ... but you're wrong.'

345

He leans away and stares at me like I'm talking nonsense, then starts writing again.

serious??

'Serious.'
Shaun thinks about this for a while. Now the man who fell off the ladder has had some kind of heart attack. Bob is asleep on his beanbag and Clare and Colin are talking quietly.
Shaun passes me another note.

i'm glad she's dead anyway.

I nod and squeeze his arm. It's understandable, I think, as Shaun continues to write. Considering that she'd turned the man Shaun loved into a drug smuggler, then suffocated him when he didn't want to play along any more. If I was Shaun, I wouldn't just be glad, I'd be *delighted*.

doesn't matter <u>who</u> killed her.
doesn't matter <u>why</u>.
she was <u>horrible</u>.

I stare down at the pink square of paper and something about what's written starts to nag at me. It's ... the middle bit. Not knowing *who* is fair enough, but how can Shaun not at least have a basic understanding of *why* Debbie McClure was murdered? He knows that she was passing drugs to Kevin to sell. He knows that she killed him.
I point at that underlined *why* and start to ask Shaun what he means, but he shushes me and shakes his head. He's

agitated again. He's poised to write something else, but he seems uncertain. No, he's *scared*, just like he was that night in this same room, right before the am-I-going-to-die business kicked in and he stopped talking.

I watch him write something, then cross it out. He tears off the note and screws it up. He glances at me, then at others in the room – I can't be sure who – then starts again.

He finally tears off the note and passes it to me, low down, like he really doesn't want anyone else to see. It's an odd feeling, being frightened for someone else suddenly, but the look on Shaun's face makes me think that whatever the note says, writing it might be the bravest or the stupidest thing he's ever done.

there's something i need to tell you.

I start to say that we should probably go somewhere else to talk, but then my phone rings, and when I see who's calling I say, 'Later' and stand up fast because I need to answer it. Shaun looks bereft as he watches me leave with the phone still ringing. I'm aware of some sarcastic tutting and catch the look of naked hatred from Lauren at having her peaceful enjoyment of Saturday night TV so rudely interrupted.

It's still ringing as I try to find somewhere quiet to take the call. Or at least somewhere I can't be overheard. I settle for the chair next to the airlock.

'Hey, Banksy . . .'

'I'll have to be quick,' he says. 'I've only got a minute.'

He sounds very serious. 'OK . . .'

'I've just found out. They're going to make an arrest in the morning.'

It's a few seconds before I can say anything or even breathe again. 'Who is? Which—'

'It's only the one team now. An arrest in connection with the McClure murder.'

I stare through the airlock towards the lift. The doors open and I watch a young couple step out and move towards the door of the ward opposite mine. They look nervous. 'Do you know who it is?'

'That's literally all I've heard. The forensic results are in and everything's apparently lined up, so they'll be coming to the hospital first thing tomorrow.'

'Right . . .'

'Just thought you'd want to know. Listen, I've really got to—'

'No worries. Listen, thanks, Banksy . . .' I wait, but he's gone.

I put my phone away, walk back into the main corridor and turn towards my room. This is exactly what I've wanted since the moment Debbie came screaming out of Kevin's room. Since I started coming back to life and feeling like a copper again. This is validation, isn't it?

So I wonder why I barely register that George is talking to me as I pass him, why my heart is dancing so hard that I can see my T-shirt move against my chest and why it feels like I might be sick.

What have I got to be frightened about now?

I open my bedroom door thinking that I don't want to know the answer, but by the time I've locked it behind me, I know full well that I don't have a lot of choice.

FIFTY-FIVE

I haven't slept. I know I haven't. How could I?

It doesn't matter though, because there's still blood.

The bedroom light is on because I didn't want to lie here in the dark and it's about as quiet as it ever gets in here. Just the rise and fall of an indistinct voice which I presume is coming from the nurses' station and the distant hum of those generators I ran past yesterday.

It's almost three in the morning and I've been awake the whole time.

But there's still blood.

'It's not just mine,' Johnno says. 'You know that already though, right?'

I nod. To Johnno, to myself, to the mirror on the wall that's opposite my bed. 'Not even sure you had that much *in* you.'

'It's *hers*.'

'Well, course it is, why wouldn't it be? I was covered in the stuff. Down on that toilet floor.'

Johnno sighs and says, 'Come on, Al . . .'

'Come on *what*?' He says nothing. 'Listen, if you're just trying to put the wind up me, Phil Johnston, you're doing a bloody good job.'

'Look at the evidence,' he says. 'It's what we *do*.'

I'm shaking, but it's all right, because I don't think he can actually see me. Mind you, I was shaking last time he did see me. Last time he saw anything. 'Come on then, smartarse, help me out.'

'You found the body.'

'Nobody's denying that.'

'Just a fact that's worth bearing in mind,' he says. 'A supporting fact.'

'Supporting *what*? Where's this so-called evidence?'

'*They've* got evidence, Al, and that's all that matters.'

'This is getting on my tits now, Johnno.'

'You had a motive,' he says. 'Several motives actually, if we're really going to get into it. You thought she'd killed Kevin who was a friend of yours and you thought she was going to get away with it. You felt ignored, and I mean, why wouldn't you? You felt like your opinion was worth nothing. That *you* were worth nothing. I'm not saying all this just to be horrible . . .'

Fuck it, I'm crying now. 'I know you're not.'

'Oh, and we shouldn't forget that the camera covering the crime scene had been conveniently disabled.' He smiles. 'You and me have got a history with cameras, haven't we, Al?'

'Graham did that,' I say. 'Graham *always* did that.'

'And talking about forgetting . . .'

'Right.' I'm very cold, suddenly. 'I was wondering when we'd get to this.'

'What did Bakshi say, and Marcus? That these blackouts are all perfectly normal. What did Dr Perera say?'

'I know what they all said, but you're going to tell me anyway.'

'It's understandable,' he says. 'When something like this happens. Just because you're not the victim of a crime or even a witness to it, doesn't mean you wouldn't want to wipe it out. Or that the crime wouldn't wipe *itself* out.'

My head aches and my guts are churning and I just want to see that smile again and hear him tell me that everything's going to be all right. I want to *make* him smile. I screw up my eyes and sniff back the snot. 'Isn't this the point where you produce the gruesome photograph?'

'Some things are just too terrible to remember,' he says.

'I remember *you!*' I think I'm probably shouting now. 'I remember every second of what happened that day.'

'Yeah, but that wasn't your fault, was it, Al?'

'It feels like it was.'

'You don't understand,' he says. 'Back then, *you* hadn't done anything . . .'

Johnno's clearly said his piece, because he starts to fade and I know that when he's gone, all I'm going to be left with is his blood. Sloshing around in my head. His blood and hers. I'm crying and shivering and I still can't remember, but whatever's locked up in some part of my brain which I've lost the combination to, there's one thing I've never forgotten.

I lean towards the shadow of him that's still left.

'You were always a better detective than me,' I say.

I don't know long it is – probably just long enough for me to stop being quite so bloody hysterical – before I pick up the phone and dial my parents' number.

'Alice . . . ?'

'Hey, Mum.'

'It's . . .' She's reaching to turn the lamp on and looking at the clock-radio on the bedside table. 'Nearly four o'clock in the morning.'

'I know. Sorry . . .'

I hear my dad mumble something. He'll be heaving himself over in bed about now and asking my mum who's calling, even though at this time of night there really aren't that many candidates. She mouths my name. Now he sits up and mouths something back. Something like *is everything OK?* She shakes her head, *I don't know*, and takes a deep breath.

'So, how are you, love?'

'I'm good,' I say. 'Not sleeping too well, which is why I, you know . . . why it's so late.'

'Only Sophie called us yesterday and she sounded a bit worried.'

'Yeah?'

'Some conversation you'd had with her. I don't know.'

All those knives and coffins and things. 'Oh, she's just being daft,' I say.

'Are you sure?'

'How's Grandma?'

My mum clears her throat. She's probably plumping up the pillow behind her. 'Well, I called her the day before yesterday and she's . . . much the same. She asked how you were doing.'

I doubt that. Last time I saw my grandmother, she hadn't got the foggiest who I was. Probably best, I reckon.

'What did you tell her?'

'I don't remember,' Mum says. 'I think I just said something . . . vague.'

'Well, next time she asks . . .' she won't, '. . . tell her I've been promoted to sergeant, will you? That'll perk her up. Or you could always just rattle out the appendix story, like you did with Jeff and Diane.'

'Yes, sorry, love . . . that just came out.'

'Unlike my appendix.'

'We didn't know what else to say.'

'I'm kidding, Mum . . . it's fine. Just hope they never ask to see the scar.'

My mum laughs. It's a bit nervous, but still, it's not something I've heard for a while. 'We were thinking we might come down again and see you one day next week. Well, *I* was.'

What am I supposed to say? 'You don't have to.'

'I want to.'

'It's fine, honest. I know it's no fun for you.'

'I'm not coming because it's *fun*,' she says. 'I'm coming because that's where . . . you are.'

I don't say anything, because I can't, and I know that Dad is looking at her again, wanting to know what's going on. What I'm talking about. My mum's probably shaking her head at him again or, if she's in the mood, mouthing *shut up, Brian* . . .

'Is there any particular day that's best for you?'

'Not really,' I say.

'What about a time, then? Dad says that when he came in on Wednesday you were a bit . . . I don't know.'

'Yeah, I wasn't at my sharpest. Look, it doesn't make any difference what time you come.' I'm being honest about that much, at least.

'Oh, that's good,' she says. 'Well, I'll call beforehand, anyway. See if there's anything particular you want me to bring ...'

We talk for quite a while after that, twenty minutes, maybe. About if the biscuits my dad brought in last time were the right ones, and the problems he's having with his back, and the day when Jeff and Diane's grandchildren came round for tea.

'I made a Victoria sponge,' she says.

My mum's always had that kind of soft voice. The sort that makes you feel things will get a bit better, even when there's no chance of that happening. I find myself getting sleepy, which is good, because I'll need to be on the ball come the morning.

'Listen, Mum, I'll let you get back to sleep.'

'I'm wide awake now, love. Anyway, you still haven't said why you're ringing at half past stupid?'

That's my mum for you. Always the one to ask the awkward questions.

'I was just ringing for a natter,' I say. 'That's all.'

How can I tell her that I'm calling to say goodbye?

FIFTY-SIX

It's the second day running that I haven't eaten any breakfast, but this time I don't even bother going to the dining
room to not eat, because I want to be ready and I'm guessing
they'll come good and early. It's what I would do. I have a
conversation which I've already forgotten with Femi at the
meds hatch, then another with Donna as I take the bottle of
water and step away to swallow the multicoloured contents
of the paper cup.

The anti-psychotics, the mood-stabilisers and whatever
the new ones are.

Then I wait.

It feels strange around here this morning, though I'm well
aware that could just be me. Projecting, I think it's called.
The members of staff I've run into since I got up definitely
seem a bit tense, though, and I can't help wondering if
they've been pre-warned. It would make perfect sense and
again, it's what me or Banksy or any detective with a bit of

nous would have done. So the arrest team have the ward set up just the way they want, before they come steaming in.

Two, possibly three of them.

An extra person in handcuffs with them when they leave.

Marcus is still around. I've never seen him here on a Saturday *and* a Sunday and although I'm guessing they're still short-handed, because it doesn't look like Malaika's back yet, it might just as easily be because he knows what's going to be happening.

I step in front of him when he emerges from the toilet.

'When are they coming?'

'When's *who* coming?'

It seems convincing, so I decide to give him the benefit of the doubt, and, of course, there's one very good reason why the members of staff might not know anything about it. Why the last thing the police would do is pre-warn them. Because perhaps the person they're coming here to arrest is a member of staff.

Fuck's sake, Al. Keep it together . . .

My voice or Johnno's. It's hard to be sure any more.

It's only fifteen minutes since I took them, but it looks like the drugs are muddying up my thinking already, because I know exactly who the police are coming for.

I take up my position on a chair at the airlock and I'm relieved to see that Tony hasn't decided on an early-morning vigil today. I really don't need any company. I look out through the two doors towards the lift, same as I did yesterday when I was here talking to Banksy, and I think about the couple I saw on their way to the ward opposite this one.

A journey they did *not* want to make.

They were late thirties, tops, so who were they going to

see? It might have been a sibling or maybe a parent, but they looked so bloody nervous that I can't help but imagine they were visiting their own child. A teenager, if I'm right. Even if I don't always behave like an adult, does the fact that I'm so much older make things any easier for my mum and dad? It doesn't take long before I decide it's probably the exact opposite. That teenager might recover, with his whole life still ahead of him, while *my* best years – such as they were – are only visible in a rear-view mirror.

I stare at those lift doors and wait for them to open.

How the hell are my mum and dad going to cope with . . . *this?*

They will, of course, because back when I was having those good years, I saw it too many times to count. Parents standing by their children, no matter what. Bravely, stupidly. I was always kind of . . . impressed, even if I couldn't quite understand it. Some of the things their kids had done that they were happy to overlook. You *can't* understand it, that's what Johnno said, not until you're a parent yourself.

This was back when he was all set to become one . . .

I'm guessing that particular ship has sailed for me now, but there *was* a drunken evening when Andy and I talked about what it might be like and, for about five minutes, I even thought about doing it in here, if you can believe that. Maybe asking one of the ward's many eligible gentlemen to do me a favour, donation-wise, then borrowing a turkey-baster from the kitchen. I think I was well off my tits at the time—

The lift doors open and out they come.

Three of them, I was right. Two uniforms – a man and a woman – and a second bloke I'm guessing is the DI. Fifty-something, with a brown leather jacket over his shirt and tie like he's ten years younger and fitter. As they walk towards the door, I watch him put on a lanyard that's definitely not rainbow-coloured, turn his ID card the right way round and exchange a few words with his colleagues.

Words of caution, probably. A request for those less experienced than him to stay calm, no matter what they might have to deal with.

Bear in mind what this place is . . .

I stand up when the detective rings the bell and our eyes meet through the glass, but then Marcus appears, moving quickly towards the airlock with his keys at the ready. Yeah, he definitely knew to expect visitors.

He asks me if I'd mind moving away from the door a little.

So, I do, but not far.

Once the doors are locked again and the officers are inside, there are handshakes and mumbled introductions. Marcus holds out an arm as if to guide them to a pre-arranged room, which is when I step forward.

'Alice, please—'

I ignore Marcus and step close to the man in the leather jacket. 'Can I have a quick word?'

'That's a bit tricky at the moment,' he says.

He takes half a step past me and I go with him. 'I'm ex-Job,' I say.

Marcus is ready to intervene, but the DI stops and looks at me. 'OK. I know who you are.'

Of course he does.

'It won't take long,' I say. 'It's important.'

The detective nods at his uniformed colleagues to let them know I'm not dangerous – at least not right this minute – then at Marcus. He says, 'It's fine,' and while the two uniforms stay by the door, me and the detective follow Marcus towards the MDR.

It feels like a long walk, suddenly.

Donna is already on the march and stares as she passes. Clare and Colin stand together and watch from the dining room doorway. Bob is gawping outside the nurses' station and, from wherever he's lurking, Ilias gleefully shouts, 'Someone's in trouble.'

For once, he's spot on.

Marcus shows the detective into the MDR, allows me to follow, then before he steps out and closes the door, gives me a look that would normally shit me up for the rest of the day. A warning look, that tells me he's got my number and that I should really think carefully before I do something stupid.

Right now, though, I don't even blink.

The desk is in position, so I'm thinking there must have been a tribunal in here recently, or maybe there's one arranged for later in the day. I stand and watch the DI walk behind the desk, take off his leather jacket and toss it across the chair. He sits down and invites me to do the same.

'I think you spoke to my . . . partner,' he says. 'Dr Perera?'

'Right.' So he's the one. I look at him and I think, yeah, *definitely* punching above his weight.

He introduces himself, but like a few times recently, the name doesn't stick. It's simple enough, but it's . . . gone as soon as it's arrived. It doesn't matter, because I know that by the time this is all over, it'll be a name I'll probably never be able to forget.

'What can I do for you?' he asks.

'Well, I know why you're here,' I say. 'I know how these things work, so I thought I'd save you some time.'

'That's always good.' He waits.

So, here we are, then … and suddenly all those things that once mattered so much seem very far away and utterly unimportant. Like minor bits of mischief and silliness. Masks and the scars on my arm and the clunk of a wine bottle against a skull.

Oh, just bloody say *it, Al* …

My voice or Johnno's. It really doesn't matter. There's no accent, otherwise it could just as easily be a woman bleeding out on a toilet floor.

'My name's Alice Armitage,' I say. 'And I murdered Debbie McClure.'

FIFTY-SEVEN

The detective says nothing.

I stare at him. It's not a hard face, but it looks . . . lived in. There's a thin, straight scar running across the bottom of his chin which, for some reason, makes me trust him a bit more than I might otherwise, and his hair is greyer on one side than the other. I can sense that he's definitely not stupid and, unlike his girlfriend, I'm guessing he's rather more interested in facts than feelings.

When it comes to what he makes of my confession, though, I can't read him at all.

Is he waiting for me to carry on? Surely it's his turn.

I can hear muffled voices whispering outside, then Marcus very much *not* whispering as he tells whoever's eavesdropping to move away from the door. Ilias and Lucy is my guess. I wonder what the two uniforms are doing. If they're clever they'll be drinking tea in the nurses' station or, if they're not, they'll be learning a few lessons I never got taught at the training college just a mile up the road. I almost feel sorry for them, backed into a corner somewhere by a small but well-practised mob, to be mercilessly eyed up, sworn at, sung to . . .

'Why are you telling me that?' the detective asks, eventually.

I'm a bit thrown by the question, you want to know the truth. I've sat where he is now – not the MDR, but you get the idea – and listened to a fair few suspects spill their guts over the years, and *why are you telling me that?* was certainly never *my* first thought. I was always too busy thinking of the work me and everyone else on the team had been saved. My modest shrug at the heartfelt congrats from senior officers, even if the confession was freely offered and I just happened to be the lucky cow in the interview room at the time. The smiles in the office and the pats on the back and all the lovely drinks I wouldn't have to pay for that night.

I'm confused, because I've slapped it on a plate for him, but maybe he's just one of those awkward bastards. Every team's got one.

'Sorry . . . what do you mean, *why*?'

He sighs, like he's just figured out this might take a bit longer than the few minutes I'd promised. 'OK, a different question, then. How about starting with why you murdered Miss McClure?'

This isn't how it's supposed to go. I'm damn sure he knows all of this, but I get it because these days the job is all about ducks in a row, making everything watertight before you take your case to the CPS. A pain in the arse, but you know . . . fine.

So I tell him all those things that his girlfriend had gently suggested as we sat in the sunshine just three days before. Things she would subsequently have passed on to him and that I'd heard from others several times since.

I didn't want Debbie to get away with killing Kevin.

I wanted to see some kind of justice done.

I couldn't stand feeling ignored.

I feel a few warning stabs of panic as I'm running through my motives for murder *again*, so I tell him not to worry if I have to stop for a bit and do some funny breathing. He tells me it's fine and to take as long as I need, but in the end I just about keep it together. Actually, considering where we are and what I'm telling him, I'm amazed that I'm managing to stay as relatively calm as I am about all this. As matter-of-fact.

I suppose because that's what it is.

When I'm done, he asks if I'm all right to carry on.

I tell him that I am.

'So … can you take me through exactly what happened last Sunday? I presume you followed Miss McClure into the toilets … or maybe you were in there waiting for her, I don't know. Tell me what happened once the pair of you were in there together.' He sits back and folds his arms. 'Tell me about killing her.'

For the half a minute or so it takes me to say anything, I'm hoping for some kind of medical miracle, perfectly on cue. For the fog to lift suddenly, like it would if this was a TV thriller, *CSI* or some shit. Obviously, it doesn't.

'I'm not sure I can tell you *exactly*,' I say.

'Well, maybe not every detail then, but … did you come at the victim from behind?'

He waits and I say nothing.

'Did you stab her in the neck first or in the stomach?'

He waits and I say nothing.

'Did you carry on stabbing her once she was on the floor?'

'I can't *remember*.' I hadn't wanted to raise my voice, but it happens anyway. 'Fair enough?'

He nods, like this is exactly what he was suspecting and isn't he just the best detective in the fucking world, but it's ridiculous, because this is surely something else his girlfriend would have told him. Work-related pillow-talk, whatever. Because I was a suspect ... the *obvious* suspect ... Perera would definitely have been in regular touch with Bakshi and Bakshi would have told her all about the memory blips, the PTSD, all of it.

'I've been having these blackouts,' I say. 'You can check because it's all in my notes and it's all perfectly normal. I can't remember exactly *how* I did what I did ... it's like I just woke up suddenly and I was in there and she was on the floor with blood everywhere. But I know I did it, isn't that enough? I *must* have done it, any idiot can see that. *I* discovered the body, *I* knew what she'd done, *I* had a motive.' I'm tired, suddenly. 'I'm not sure how much more you need.'

I don't know what the hell's happening now, because when he looks at me he's calm, like he doesn't need anything.

'Everything you've said may be true,' he says. 'But it doesn't change one very important fact.' He sits forward slowly and rubs a finger along that scar on his chin. 'You didn't kill anyone, Miss Armitage.'

The look on my face is definitely not one I've practised. Christ knows *what* it is, but I see him clock it and suddenly it's like he's my best mate.

'Alice—'

'I don't understand.'

364

'Bearing in mind everything you've told me, I can see why you might—'

'Why are you *here*?'

He sits forward. 'Nobody's disputing that you discovered the body, and because of that, you already know that we were able to recover a knife from the crime scene. Under one of the sinks, just like you said it was. The post-mortem confirmed that this was the murder weapon and forensic tests carried out on the knife since then have provided us with all the fingerprint and DNA evidence we could have asked for.' He waits, to be sure I'm taking it all in. '*That's* why I'm here. Because we have solid evidence pointing us towards an individual on this ward.' Now, he actually smiles. 'It's not *you* though, Alice. OK? It's not you.'

Once the shock has worn off a little, he can obviously see the question on my face, and if he hesitates, it's not for long. I'm probably looking a bit desperate and pathetic by this point, like a dog that doesn't know why it's spent the last week being kicked.

So he does me the favour I'm asking, copper to copper. He tells me who he's come to arrest for the murder of Debbie McClure.

'No way.'

He nods. 'It's their prints on that knife and their DNA. Goes without saying I'd like you to keep this information to yourself . . . for the next twenty minutes or so, at least.'

'Why the hell would they want to kill Debbie?'

'That I can't tell you,' he says. 'Because I haven't got the first idea. I intend to find out though, obviously.'

I'm too stunned to say anything else. Sort of . . . looking down at myself while I'm trying to process what he's told me.

It's not until I see him reaching round for the box of tissues on the shelf behind him that I even realise I'm crying.

'Something else you were wrong about.' He slides the box across the desk. 'Debbie McClure wasn't the one passing drugs to Kevin Connolly, and she wasn't the one who killed him.'

'*What?*'

'They got prints off a few of the bottles that were found in his room. We brought someone in for questioning and arrested them for murder yesterday afternoon. Thought you should probably know.'

I stare at him, struggling to think straight. To think at all.

He stands up and pulls on his jacket. He comes round the table and stands over me, a little awkward. 'Maybe you should give yourself five minutes before you go back out there.'

I can't do much other than nod and blub.

The detective moves towards the door, then stops. He says, 'You've got nothing to feel bad about, you know. You shouldn't blame yourself. I mean, I say that, but you probably will. Because that's what the likes of you and me do, isn't it?'

FIFTY-EIGHT

Obviously I was joking before and I don't really think Marcus and his team ever whack up the dosages to make their lives a bit easier, but you certainly couldn't blame them today. I mean, if ever there was a time that might have called for some creative medication . . .

Everyone does seem strangely subdued, though, and you don't usually get that with all the patients at the same time.

All the patients and all the staff.

Nothing's been arranged, there were no announcements or whatever, but while the arrest is being made the rest of us find ourselves hanging about like statues in the TV room. For once, the telly's just a big dusty box in the corner and nobody seems to care very much. Nobody seems to know what to do or say or why we're here at all.

It's like everyone's just . . . gathered. Cows in a field.

I'm happy enough to sit there and enjoy the stillness and the quiet, and it's lovely to be ignored even if it's only for a few minutes. To vanish. True to form, none of it lasts very long and it's obvious that most of the people I'd stupidly thought were quietly contemplating the morning's events were actually gagging to sound off about them.

As soon as the first one pipes up, the dam well and truly bursts.

'You ask me, it was always on the cards.'

'Yeah, course it was. There was always something very iffy about that one.'

'Not just iffy. *Dangerous* . . .'

'Dangerous, right. I always knew that.'

'No, you did not,' I say. 'None of you knew anything.' Heads turn and, just like that, I'm not invisible any more, but that's all right because I no longer want to be.

It's what always happens, isn't it? As soon as a killer is discovered, they come pouring out of the woodwork: the ordinary gobshites who waste no time in letting everyone know – especially the papers who are usually paying for it – that they always knew there was something 'off' about their neighbour or workmate or acquaintance. I've never been able to abide that sort of cobblers, especially when I was one of those whose job it was to catch the killers in the first place.

To pick up the pieces afterwards.

'If any of you really knew anything, why didn't you tell the people who might have been able to do something about it?' Suddenly, they're all a bit less keen to share their opinions. 'Don't you think that might have been helpful? I mean, if you had, then maybe Debbie might still be alive. If you actually *knew* and you've kept quiet about it until now, then some people might say you're partly to blame for her being killed.'

Now there's some nodding, a few grunts of agreement.

It's nice.

'Yeah, that's fair enough, I suppose.'

'Sorry, Al. Yeah, sounds a bit stupid when you put it like that.'

'Right. I mean, you're the one who understands all this stuff, being a copper and everything . . .'

There are more nods and a couple of them ask me what I think will happen now. I tell them that no two cases are ever the same, then talk them through the basic stages of the process, from arrest to prosecution. I talk and it's the best I've felt in a while, because everyone in that room is hanging on every bloody word . . .

It would be lovely if that was what had *actually* happened after I'd made my big speech about responsibility. It would have been the high point of a very strange day, but life isn't like that, is it? Not on Fleet Ward, anyway.

Instead, there's some cat-calling and a stifled giggle. One of them asks me who the fuck I think I am and someone else tells me to piss off.

They don't even know about who killed Kevin yet – well, the patients certainly don't – and I'm sure that when they do, when they find out how wrong I was, I'll be in for some serious stick.

I can live with that.

I've grown used to being doubted and threatened and scared.

Being laughed at feels like nothing any more.

I'm aware of movement in the corridor outside and someone stands up to announce that the police are leaving. That's the cue for the rest of us to jump to our feet and crowd into the doorway. Nobody says anything, but we crane our heads, elbow and jostle to get a better view.

I briefly catch the detective's eye as he and the uniforms guide their suspect, none too gently, towards the airlock.

We stand and watch as Lauren is led away in handcuffs.

PART THREE

HEADS OR TAILS

FIFTY-NINE

Ilias just called to say Lucy's going to meet us in the pub and he'll be round to pick me up in ten minutes. I told him that was fine. The truth is, though, I'm actually in a bit of a state, because I don't want to keep him waiting, but I'm not ready and I still can't decide which top to wear.

I stand in front of the mirror and hold the two tops I'm trying to choose between up against myself.

Black or red, black or red, black or red?

Why is this so difficult?

I might just toss a coin, like I do a lot these days. I use a heads-or-tails app on my phone and actually it's been working out pretty well. Not just for stupid stuff like which outfit to put on, but for all the important decisions, too. I'm still not finding it very easy to trust my own judgement, but I reckon that's understandable, all things considered.

Just a question of time, really.

I've been out of hospital a couple of months now and I'm

doing all right. To start with, I was transferred to a halfway house type place for a couple of weeks which wasn't brilliant, but then the council came up trumps and found this place. It was here or going back to Huddersfield and even though Mum and Dad said they'd be happy to have me home, I wasn't sure they really meant it. Plus, you know ... *Huddersfield*. This place is handy, because it's just across the bridge from Brent Cross, on the top floor of a house that's been converted into flats. I've got a decent-sized room and access to a small garden. I can't say I've exactly bonded with the other tenants but that's probably no bad thing. The bloke on the ground floor with one ear and a scary dog is definitely dealing crack. For some reason his cooker's out in the hall, so sometimes I come back late and find him frying sausages just inside the front door. There's a woman below me with a baby and I'm not sure which of them wails the loudest, and there's some other bloke I've never seen, but I smell him on the stairs sometimes and I can hear him swearing in the middle of the night.

I think it's best if I keep myself to myself.

That's not to say I don't have a social life, because I get out and about as much as I can. There's no Wi-Fi here, so I walk over the bridge to the shopping centre every day. I sit in Costa for a couple of hours, have a coffee or a sandwich and get online. I try to keep in touch with people. Banksy seems to have gone AWOL, but I talk to Sophie and one or two others.

And I see a fair bit of Ilias and Lucy. They both got out of hospital before me, but we talked on the phone, and as soon as my section was done and dusted and I was finally out of there myself, we started meeting up. If we go out, Lucy tends to pay for most of the meals and drinks, but I think that's fair enough. Even though her parents live in a house that's probably got a gift shop she still gets benefits, if you can believe that, so she can afford to put her hand in her pocket. Lucy's still . . . Lucy, but I don't think she's back on the smack and she actually high-fived me the other day, so she's way better than she was.

Me and Ilias have actually become dead close. We talk all the time and he's got some fantastic stories and even though he's still not great with . . . *boundaries*, I'm not expecting him to whip his cock out at any moment. Like, he told me all about his older brother teaching him to drive and about this horrible car crash just after Ilias had passed his test. He told me how he walked away without a scratch, while his brother's been in a wheelchair ever since. He told me that his brother was the good-looking one and the clever one and, as it turned out, the unlucky one. It was his brother who'd taught Ilias to play chess, too, and he's actually really good.

Well, he thrashes *me* every time we play, but I'm slowly getting better.

Most of the time, when we're together, we end up talking about what happened on the ward. Why wouldn't we? I don't think we'll be sending Christmas cards or anything, but we gossip about what the others are doing and about all the stupid things that happened and we usually end up laughing.

As to what *did* happen on the ward, it would be fair to say I wasn't surprised that Lauren never got charged, or when she came marching back into the TV room on her first night back, every bit as chopsy as always. More so, after being held in a cell for a couple of days. I wasn't surprised when Ilias

375

started pointing and chanting *you're not singing any more* and Lauren slapped him hard enough to knock him off his chair.

If you want to know what I think, the detective's heart had never really been in it. I'd seen it, that moment when I caught his eye as they were leaving with their prime suspect. Of course, he had to arrest Lauren because of the DNA and the prints on the knife. He had evidence. The only problem was the evidence he *should* have had but *didn't*.

Rusty as I was, even I'd worked that much out.

Why hadn't Lauren been covered in blood? I'd seen how much of it there was, I'd seen the stab wounds, so I knew, same as the detective knew, that by rights she'd have been covered in it. They'd taken everyone's clothing away for forensic testing and they hadn't found so much as a drop of Debbie's blood on Lauren's precious T-shirt.

Now, it seems obvious why the detective wasn't particularly worried. He was simply going through the motions by arresting Lauren, when he probably knew all along that he already had Debbie's killer in custody, because it was the same person who'd murdered Kevin.

Poor old Shaun's still in hospital, and so is Donna and Tony got moved to the ward downstairs. Bob's section got extended, although all anybody's been able to find out is that he made 'inappropriate advances' to one of the nurses. I think it was probably Mia, but Lucy says she heard it was Marcus, so who knows? I'm not sure what happened to Tiny Tears or the Jigsaw Man and I don't much care.

We're all doing OK, though, me and Ilias and Lucy. We talk and we share things and we look after each other. Last time we were out, Ilias raised his pint glass and we toasted.

'To the three mental musketeers . . .'

So, this place isn't a palace and I'm not exactly minted and I've all but given up on ever working with the Met again, but I still think I'm doing pretty well. Most important, my head's together for the first time in a long while. I've worked everything out. I know now that what's important when you're dealing with a bastard like PTSD is that you face it head on.

Then, you can *own* it.

If you don't, you're just playing some part you think makes other people comfortable, and that's when you end up with a mask you can't ever take off.

Whatever that Alzheimer's drug was must have done the trick, because the blackouts stopped happening pretty quickly and all those things I'd forgotten started to come back. Just flashes at first, but then longer and longer stretches until there weren't any holes any more.

Now, I can even remember the song that was going through my head just before walking into that toilet and finding Debbie's body. I remember the blood, the shape of it pooling around her like wings and I remember turning and seeing the knife. I can recall every moment of it with perfect clarity. *Too* perfect, sometimes.

I can remember exactly how I felt, too. The desperate need to do something, that instinct to preserve life kicking in, and then the panic and the horror when I realised that I couldn't. The memory of those few desperate minutes in that toilet has returned, complete and terrible.

Only now, of course, I know there was someone in there with me.

SIXTY

I open up the app, press the button and watch the virtual coin spin.

There's a nice, satisfying *clink* as it lands.

I start to put the black top on . . .

Back in the MDR that day, when the detective told me I'd been wrong about who had killed Kevin, I'd felt like a mistreated dog that had been given one final, hard kick for good measure. Sitting there and sobbing, I remembered being with Shaun in the TV room, the night he collapsed and stopped talking. His eyes shifting and fixing on the nurse who was sitting in the corner and me, like the smartarse I am, thinking I knew what he was trying to let me know.

No, not just *a* nurse, you idiot. *That* nurse . . .

I remembered the same terror on his face when he was writing me those messages, when I didn't give him time to explain the very last one.

There's something i need to tell you.

Now I know what that was and I can finally understand what I'd thought was his confusion about why Debbie had been killed. During the course of my so-called investigation into Debbie's death, I'd asked myself a few times if I was being stupid in never suspecting Shaun. Well, I was and I wasn't. The fact is, though he was not unhappy that a woman he hated was dead, Shaun never had a motive for killing Debbie, because he knew she wasn't the one who'd killed Kevin.

He'd known who that was all along.

Malaika.

Now I can't decide which colour lippy to go with, so I quickly reopen the heads-or-tails app and that decides for me.

Electric Orchid, if you're interested.

As to *why* Malaika killed Debbie, the best guess is because Debbie found out about what she'd done and was threatening to expose her. Poor Debbie, who had been trying to do the right thing, but could not have known just what the person she was dealing with was capable of.

The clearer everything becomes in my mind, the worse I feel every day about what happened to Debbie and guiltier about the things I believed she'd done. Not just Kevin's murder, but the whole . . . sexual abuse thing. I *did* believe it, for a while at any rate, but now it seems obvious that it was all about convincing myself (and Banksy) that I was after the right suspect. Maybe I just resented Debbie being a bit . . . offhand when she examined me that first day. Or it could just be that I got what actually went on mixed up with what Lucy told me had happened to her.

To be fair, I was mixing a lot of things up back then.

I say best guess, by the way, because Malaika still hasn't

come clean about a great deal. I only know this because the detective told me a couple of weeks ago, but he didn't tell me too much I hadn't already worked out. The truth is, I put most of it together myself.

I can still do that.

So, here's the thing. You have to walk through *two* doors to get into that toilet. Two doors. There's a pointless little space when you step through the first door before you open another to go into the actual toilet, and those few seconds between the first and second door opening were crucial.

Malaika had stabbed Debbie to death only moments before I went in, and when she heard that outer door opening, it gave her just enough time to duck into one of the cubicles. That's where she was all the time I was on my hands and knees doing CPR and it wasn't until I ran out screaming that she was able to step out of the cubicle and start playing the hero herself. Remember how confused I was about whether it was Marcus or Malaika who'd come in to help first? Well, she'd been in there all the time, and the fact that she'd been covered in blood afterwards, same as me and Marcus, wasn't suspicious because she'd been pumping the dead woman's chest like we had.

Christ, talk about thinking on your feet.

As to whether Debbie's murder was premeditated, they won't really know unless Malaika tells them. When the detective came round, which was nice of him, I was able to help a bit with that, because I remembered Lauren complaining that someone had been going through her room and that was three or four days before Debbie had been killed. The detective told me that was very helpful information, which definitely put a spring in my step. Lauren freely admitted that it was her knife and told the police that before it was stolen it had been hidden in the webbing under her mattress. Just like those DVDs, that day Johnno had been killed. Weird, eh?

There's some suggestion that it might have been Malaika's plan all along to put Lauren in the frame for Debbie's murder, but I'm not sure I buy that. The DNA and prints on the knife alone were never going to be enough to send anyone with a half-decent defence team down. I reckon she just discovered Lauren had a knife, so knew exactly where to get it when the time was right. The detective told me Malaika hadn't said a fat lot, certainly not admitted to anything, but he isn't bothered because they've got enough evidence anyway. The clincher was getting Graham to admit that Malaika had been the one who'd asked him to put the camera out of action that day. Good old Graham. When the case comes to trial, I bet he'll be hanging around by that witness box a good hour before he's due to give evidence.

And when it's my turn?

I swear to tell the truth, the whole truth and nothing but the truth. Well, I'm finally getting my chance, so why wouldn't I?

I jump a little when a handful of grit crackles against my window and, when I stand up to look, I can see Ilias beaming up at me from the pavement. I hold up a finger to say *one minute* and the cheeky bugger holds up a finger that means something entirely different.

I grab my bag, phone, keys . . . check I've got everything.

I hope it's not a stupidly late one, that him and Lucy aren't set on making a big night of it or anything. We've already had several of *them*. Don't get me wrong, I'm bang up for a few drinks and I know we'll have a laugh, same as always, but I don't really fancy being out that long.

These days, I like spending time on my own, too.

I double-lock the door to my flat, then breathe through my mouth as I start down the stairs. I can't hear the woman or the baby or the dog, so a clean getaway looks like it's on the cards.

Ilias has his face pressed against the glass in the front door.

I'm good and ready for a night out, but the truth is I'm already looking forward to getting back. To standing at my bathroom window in the dark and staring out at those milky-white lights, pulsing through the trees at me from the far end of the garden.

EPILOGUE

From: Timothy Banks Banksy1961@hotmail.com

To: Alice Armitage GoAskAlice@btinternet.com

Subject: SORRY

Hey, Al. Sorry it's been so long and that I haven't been to see you in your new place. Sorry I haven't called or returned your messages. I'm sorry if you think I haven't been a good friend, but trust me, I really have. That's what all this is about really and the big SORRY is for what I need to say, what I haven't been brave enough to say until now.

God this is hard to write.

I've been waiting until I was sure that you were doing better and it certainly sounds like you're getting back on track. I couldn't be happier about that, I swear, and I

383

want you to remember that when you get to the end of this. If you're feeling like you never want to see or hear from me again.

The truth is I should never have come to see you in the hospital. I mean, I wanted to see you as a friend, but I shouldn't have helped you. I shouldn't have let myself get involved in it all. I should never have got sucked in.

I need to say straight away that civilian support staff do an important and incredible job for the Met. You did an incredible job and you should be proud of everything you did to help coppers like me. But it's not the same, Al, it's really not and this is the bit I've been most scared about writing, but I just need to say it, nice and simple.

You aren't a police officer. You were never a police officer.

I'm sorry, mate, but there it is. I know that while you were in hospital, a lot of people in there played along with the fantasy. Maybe they didn't know it was a fantasy, I mean you're an adult so why shouldn't they believe what you tell them? Did they ever actually check? The police officers who came to the ward knew the truth, I'm fairly sure of that. The shrink working with them and the DI who made the arrest certainly did, but at any rate nobody ever seemed to contradict you or try to tell you that you were . . . Christ, I don't know how to describe it. I don't really want to say deluded, because that makes it sound like you weren't suffering and I know you were. But it was a delusion and that's all there is to it.

This next bit is difficult, too . . .

It feels like I'm ripping off a sticking plaster or something, but I need to do it.

Johnno was my partner and not yours. My partner, Al. I was the one who went with him to that flat in Mile End and I was the one who watched him bleed to death. I was the one who fucked up.

Yeah, I know Johnno was your friend too, and what happened to him obviously hit you very hard. Every bit as hard as it hit me, harder even, I know that now. I suppose that's when all your problems started, the drink and the drugs, and that's one of the reasons I feel bad telling you all this now, because it could so easily have been me that lost it and ended up the same as you.

Maybe that's why I came to the hospital as often as I did. There but for the grace of God, all that.

I've been talking to the therapist I went to see after what happened to Johnno and she said this was a good idea. Me finally telling you everything, I mean. She told me that it might be painful, but that being honest would be better in the long run. For both of us, she said.

I do feel like I was responsible in some way for what you went through. I should never have told you everything that happened in that flat, because I know now that it's what you came to believe had happened to you. I feel like I planted the idea or something. I know you did believe it, too. I never felt like you were stealing my life, anything like that. I know you couldn't help it, Al. But I also know that I can't carry on pretending it's just this weird thing that happened. We both need to be honest with ourselves.

385

I said something before about being brave enough to finally send this, but I know I'm actually being a coward because I'm just pressing a button and not sitting down and talking this through with you in person. I just couldn't face that, so I'm sorry again. More sorry.

I don't know if this is the right thing to do medically or whatever, but I've looked this stuff up online and nobody seems to know what the right thing is or when the right time might be. It's the right thing for me though, I know that. There have been far too many lies already and my sanity matters every bit as much as yours.

I really hope you've already started coming out the other side of all this. I hope you're better and getting on with a normal life. You deserve to be happy.

I want the best for you, Al, I promise you that.

Take care, mate.

Banksy x

Detective Sergeant Tim Banks read through the email he'd agonised over long into a great many nights and rewritten so often that he'd forgotten what it had said to begin with. He closed the email and dragged it into the drafts folder. He finished what was left in his wineglass, then opened the email again.

He moved the cursor until it was hovering over the send button.

ACKNOWLEDGEMENTS

No reader should be expected to shell out for a book, in whatever format, if its author found the writing of that book too easy. I say that, of course, well aware that you might have been gifted this particular book or found it on a park bench. You might even have nicked it, in which case I hope you feel a *little* bit ashamed. There's always the possibility that you've borrowed *Rabbit Hole* from your local library, which should always be encouraged, but however you acquired it, I think my point holds. Writing a book *shouldn't* be a doddle and it rarely is, but this one, for all manner of reasons, was particularly ... tricky.

I am more than usually grateful for all the help I received.

Thank you, as always, to my amazing agent, Sarah Lutyens, to Wendy Lee, and to Mike Gunn for letting me steal some stories.

Thank you to everyone on the team at Little, Brown/ Sphere which, as I enter my third decade of publishing with them, remains the best in the business, and most particularly to: Charlie King, Catherine Burke, Robert Manser, Gemma Shelley, Callum Kenny, Thalia Proctor, Tom Webster, Sean Garrehy, Sarah Shrubb, Hannah Methuen and Tamsin Kitson. A tip of the hat once more to Nancy Webber for the copy edit. Saved my bacon again . . .

Thank you to my brilliant editor Ed Wood for making everything so much better, and to the best publicist in the game, Laura Sherlock (who is only ever FPN when she needs to be).

Thank you to Sara Vitale, Morgan Entrekin, Justine Batchelor, Deb Seager and all at Grove Atlantic.

I will forever be grateful to SL, a fiercely dedicated mental-health nurse in north London whose time and expertise were invaluable in the writing of this book. I really did forget my wallet. Honestly . . .

And to Claire, most of all – the only other person who understands exactly why this one was so tough.